Glengarth

Alexandra Jones was born in 1943 in India, of British parents in the Colonial Service. Initially she wrote prize-winning short stories, then turned to full-length fiction. She now lives in Kent, and is married with three sons.

Glengarth

Alexandra Jones

Pan Books

First published 1991 by Macdonald & Co. (Publishers) Ltd

This edition published 2001 by Pan Books
an imprint of Pan Macmillan Ltd
Pan Macmillan, 20 New Wharf Road, London N1 9RR
Basingstoke and Oxford
Associated companies throughout the world
www.panmacmillan.com

ISBN 330 39888 1

1 3 5 7 9 8 6 4 2

A CIP catalogue record for this book is available from
the British Library.

Printed by Mackays of Chatham plc, Chatham, Kent

To the memory of my father and his memory of the barque Ayrshire.

'To live in hearts we leave behind, is not to die.'
Campbell.

'Neither of you will breathe a single word of that mad fakir's nonsense to anyone, least of all your mama. You will erase from your minds as though they had never happened, the events of last evening.'

'Glengarth is *mine*! *My* inheritance, *my* pride and *my* curse!'

'WSPU ... it means freedom for all women and a fight to the death.'

'A typical product of the system. Nothing but a handsome, charming, lovable, fickle bloody bastard.'

'Since he can't marry her, he does the next best thing with her. He uses her to humiliate me.'

'There seems to be something wrong with our bloody ships today.'
Vice-Admiral Beatty at the Battle of Jutland.

Preface

Scotland 1917

In the great hall at Glengarth a small, flaxen-haired boy held his mother's hand tightly. 'Mama,' he stared up at the portraits on the wall, 'who are they?'

'Your ancestors, Jamie.'

'What's an ancestor? Tell me about them ... that one there.' He pointed to the dour gentleman in question.

'That's your great-grandfather.' But it was a picture of the laird before she knew him. A young man out hunting the stags over half a century ago, not the irascible landlord she remembered from her childhood.

'And that one next to him in the funny costume? Is he a prince like Bonnie Prince Charlie?'

The woman smiled. 'You could say that, Jamie. He was your grandfather. His name was also James. He spent most of his life in India.'

'Tell me about him, Mama, and India. Is that where they hunt tigers?'

'Yes Jamie, a story of Indian princes just like the fairy tales of kelpies ...' the woman's voice trailed away into silence. How could she tell Jamie about someone they called a Sadhu who was supposed to have put a curse on the lairds of Glengarth? An idle story, which had turned out to contain more than a grain of truth. 'I never knew him, Jamie.'

'Then, is the man next to the Indian prince, Bonnie Prince Charlie?'

'No. That's the Laird Lindsay.'

'He *looks* like Bonnie Prince Charlie.'

'Yes. The Laird Lindsay always looked very fine in his Highland regalia.'

Jamie took up a stance before the portrait of another young man, a mere youth dressed in what appeared to be a sea cadet's uniform. 'I would like to be like *him*!' Jamie's expression was one of pride behind the pointing finger. 'I would like to run away to sea when *I'm* big! Is he my papa? Mama, why isn't *your* picture here with the other ladies of Glengarth?'

His mother hesitated. She looked at the bare patches on the walls where past portraits and tapestries had hung. And even while she knew it did not answer her son's questions, replied, 'Jamie, most of the furniture and paintings were put away when the war started. I expect they forgot about these. We're not supposed to be here, you know. Glengarth belongs to the Admiralty and we're trespassing. Now, unless we hurry we'll miss the steamer to Renfrew as well as the surprise I have for you.'

How could she possibly tell Jamie the truth? Where did she begin?

PART ONE

Baharabad, India: 1898/99

... 'Oh, our manhood's prime vigour!
No spirit feels waste,
No muscle is stopped in its playing
No sinew unbraced.
And the wild joy of living! ...'

Robert Browning
Saul

CHAPTER ONE

Indian night falls swiftly blindly and sometimes savagely.

The road they were travelling was nothing more than a serpentine track through the Terai. An earlier downpour of monsoon rain had filled the ditches, and water overflowed onto their path. A jackal's carcase floated by, trapped in the bare bones of a forked piece of driftwood.

'*Juldi ... juldi hai!*' said James Beauly Roskillen, urging the *rickshaw wallah* forward as though he were a horse. James kept glancing at his fob watch taken from his waistcoat pocket. He was going to be late for the grand *burrakana* to be held in Simla that night. The Viceroy of India, Lord Curzon, would be there, and it would not do to keep the grand man waiting.

But the rickshaw wallah was having difficulty in extricating the rickshaw wheels from the sticky black morass which bogged them down.

Young Rory Duncan, only eight years old at the time, sighed in exasperation tinged with sympathy for the poor Indian coolie who was doing his best. 'Papa, wouldn't it be easier if Lindsay and I got out to lighten the load? We could push while he pulls.' It was a measure of his respect for his parent that Rory, squashed as he was on one side of his father, with Lindsay seated on the other, had not suggested Father should also get out to lessen the weight.

'Stay where you are, boy!' snapped his father, notable for his short temper. 'You'll get your shoes dirty. The fellow is a fool for taking us through the jungle in the first place. Short cut! I'll give him short cut.' He brandished his Malacca cane in the air, once more urging, '*Juldi hai!*'

'*Acha Sahib, acha Sahib!*' The rickshaw wallah redoubled his efforts.

Papa, a red-headed Scotsman, was noted for his hot temper and Rory obeyed the voice of authority. They would not be in this predicament now, he reflected miserably, had not an axle pin on the landau sheered off at a very awkward moment. Papa, Rory and his elder brother Lindsay had been on *shikar*, a hunting expedition. Papa thought it was about time he made 'men of his sons' as he had told Brig, by introducing them to the pleasures of pig-sticking and tiger shooting!

Shikar had taken place at the up-country lodge, Erinmore Lodge, belonging to Brigadier General Sir Dougald MacKincade, or 'Brig' as he was known. 'For God's sake, boy!' his father had yelled earlier in the day, 'stop belly-aching and charge the damn thing! Use the gun if you can't handle the bally hog stick.'

Rory had suspected for a long time that his father would enjoy the sight of his hide adorning the great hall at Glengarth, pinned up beside the ancient tapestries, stag heads and Indian tiger skins which he remembered clearly, despite having been whisked off at the tender age of six from his native Scotland. He had closed his eyes and fired, and for his efforts got himself written up in Brig's Game Book for having bagged an out-of-season quail instead of a jungle hog.

But he wasn't the only one who had got his sights all wrong on that up-country *shikar*. Rory particularly disliked the Collector's wife, a big-breasted woman of hearty appetites, whose sole aim in life appeared to be the total extinction of the Indian population and its wild animals before she returned home to England. 'Ha, got him!' she shrieked in delight before charging off into the brushwood to examine her quarry.

Memsahib appeared none too perturbed to find a perforated native bearer, instead of the usual hog. 'Don't panic,' she bellowed patriotically. 'All in a day's work. If one *will* stray off the beaten track, what else can one expect?'

The poor Indian bearer, who had been beating the scrub for the Collector and Memsahib, was hastily removed from the battle-zone on a *doolie*, a makeshift stretcher, and the *shikaris* pressed on regardless.

Rory observed the pathetic struggles of the native coolie against the laws of gravity and those made by the great white Raj. He heard him groan like a man on the rack, sweat glistening on him just like a horse vainly trying to reach the winning post. At that time of his life, too, Rory Duncan had a fatal preoccupation with death and the macabre. Having seen with his child's eyes the cheapness of life in India, his inquisitive nature was given free rein and full dramatic colour. Would the rickshaw wallah's skull split open with that leather band around his forehead by which he pulled the rickshaw? Would his skinny ribs burst through the thin skin containing his abnormally large heart?

He had overheard a conversation between Brig and Papa once: rickshaw wallah's hearts were supposed to be larger than normal, which allowed them to do the kind of work which would have killed other less well-endowed mortals. Besides, they earned more rupees than the average native servant and, if filthy lucre was the big attraction, then the great white Raj couldn't be blamed if Indian rickshaw wallahs dropped dead at the tender age of sixteen or thereabouts.

Moloch! The beginning of it all, lives that were to become bent grass according to the prophecy of an old Indian Sadhu ...

Rory turned to his brother in the rickshaw, 'Do something!' he hissed behind their father's back.

But Lindsay remained impassive, his face turned to distant toddy trees over which the sun was sinking low, the sky changing from pink, rosy-red and saffron in the west to blue, violet, purple-plum in the east; soon it would be midnight black. Rory himself was unable to look at a sunset again without equating it with the painful bruise on his elbow which went through the same colourful mutations as that Terai sunset.

'It is the bruise of all bruises, Master Rory Sahib,' his ayah remarked when later bathing the battered bone of his young man's ego. 'What you do to yourself, heh?'

'You may well ask, Dharkli,' Rory muttered, even while

keeping the truth to himself as he relived 'the night of the bruising sunset'.

After the landau had broken down halfway home to Tippindee, their own summer lodge in the foothills of Simla, the three of them, plus the two Indian servants attending them, had been stranded. Papa had been angry at 'Indian incompetence' and in picturesque Scottish metaphors had given his servants a thorough dressing down because now he didn't know how they were going to get home before nightfall. Then a lowly rickshaw came along and their father had welcomed the sight with evident relief. The young rickshaw wallah said, 'Take three miles off journey, *Burra-Sahib*, for only seventy rupees.'

Now seventy rupees, Rory knew, would have bought him a good as new second-hand bicycle and so the rickshaw wallah was a crook despite his big white teeth smiling beguilingly at their father.

'Three rupees,' snapped James Beauly Roskillen, which made Rory realize how desperate his father was to get home, as he would normally have offered three annas.

'Five rupees, *Burra-Sahib*. I myself am a poor humble man trying to earn an honest living. I have six babies and a sick wife who is about to give birth to a seventh child.' The rickshaw wallah was nothing if not persuasive.

Rory kept his fears to himself.

With a nonchalant wave of acceptance at the Indian, James left his two servants under the landau, and took his two sons with him.

What the rickshaw wallah forgot to mention to his Scottish master was that the rickshaw was too cramped for three people, too top-heavy, too slow and that the short cut lay through the Terai into which father and sons had no desire to return.

Close proximity to his father always gave Rory breathing trouble. Sitting almost in his father's lap, Rory held his breath and silently suffocated because father hated anyone fidgeting near him. He wasn't even aware that he *had* been fidgeting, he had only been trying to make eye-contact with Lindsay, when his father barked, 'Keep still boy! You'll tip us over if you continue to wriggle around like a worm.'

Rory recoiled from the shockwaves of his father's Celtic temper and caught his elbow on a rusty iron nail fixing the leather weatherproof awning of the rickshaw top to its sides. He could feel the tear even through the sleeve of his thick Norfolk jacket. Having seen others perish in the compound through neglect and disease, he was afraid to die from blood poisoning; besides he hadn't made his will with arrangements for his pet monkey Suzy's adoption. Papa would only give her away to people who would not look after her properly or stick her in a filthy zoo. So, Rory Duncan, like a real true Scotsman, rebelled in the face of injustice. Edging himself off the cramped rickshaw seat, he was ready to jump out in order to lighten the load. But before anyone knew what was happening, the rickshaw did what his father had predicted. It flipped over like a mare foaling, and all three of them ended up in the mire.

Besmirched with the slime of that soggy jungle track, his father's white, tussore tropical suit, which he had recently changed into after the day's *shikar*, now resembled a miner's underwear after a day at the coal face. Rory saw how speechless with fury his father was. His precious *sola topi*, the sun helmet symbolic of the white man's conquest of foreign shores, had come to settle on the grinning skull of a once rabid jackal which had died trapped in the ditch.

A great desire to laugh overtook Rory, but he didn't dare, not when he saw his father's face. Lindsay, too, remained stony faced.

And then the urge for levity died when Rory realized his father's intention. '*No, Papa! Don't do it!*' Rory had already jumped up from the ground and leapt on his father's arm. 'Don't beat him, please, Papa, don't! It was all my fault.'

'Then you, too, will receive a thrashing the moment we get home ... get *out* of my way!'

Neither of the two boys could believe what happened next. Rory could only assume that their father, from loss of his monumental pride and ego, had taken leave of his senses. Silver ferrule catching the last rays of the dying sun,

James began to beat the Indian to an inch of his life. Scrawny arms striving vainly to protect his head and face, the whites of his bloodshot eyes rolling like a stricken animal's, the rickshaw wallah crumpled under the onslaught and lay like a carpet beaten of its dust, face down at his white master's feet.

Lindsay vomited in the ditch.

A horse misused upon the road, cries to heaven for human blood – how often, as a punishment, had his tutor, old boggy Shawmoss forced him to memorize *Auguries of Innocence.* Rory felt sick too. He knew that never again would he be able to recall those words without remembering that barbaric onslaught on the road to Tippindee.

Despite his muddied appearance, with a lordly air James stepped over the bleeding, inert body of the Indian coolie. He retrieved his soggy sun helmet from the ditch, though by now the sun had disappeared and was replaced by the dazzling bright moonlight flooding the Terai. '*Come,* both of you! And keep pace! This has been an *appalling* evening – all on account of native inefficiency!'

'What about him?' Rory asked, pointing to the human horse misused upon the road.

'What about him?' asked the future Laird of Glengarth, and Rory was convinced that his father had inherited the insanity of his inbred ancestors.

'Tigers or jackals might eat him, Papa,' Rory said, willing himself to avoid the ditch over which Lindsay was still retching his heart out.

'That is no concern of mine, nor shall it be yours,' said James. 'The fellow's a rupee shark, that's all. He was probably intending to lead us deep into the jungle and then savagely kill us for whatever convertible money he could make off us.' James fumbled for his gold fob-watch, but it was still safe in his muddy pocket.

'He wasn't much more than ... than Lindsay's age, Papa!' Rory, close to tears himself, realized he was shouting. He didn't care any more. 'And he had children at home, *Father!*'

'You *dare* to use that tone on me, you insolent puppy! Hog-whipping is the least you deserve, and for your damned impudence, you shall have it the moment we reach home.'

Every night and every morn, some to misery are born! Trudging back down that slimy, mosquito-infested path, the short distance they had travelled in the unfortunate rickshaw, Rory was so engrossed in assimilating Mr Blake's intelligent observations regarding the human race, that when his father stopped dead in front of him, Rory bumped right into him. 'Sorry, Papa ...' his apology died in his throat.

An apparition, ghostly and grotesque, an emaciated spectre with blood-filled eyes contrived by a fanatic religious fasting, rose up before them in the moonlight like a spiral of smoke summoned from hell, a corpse from its coffin, a reincarnation of the spirit departed – although reason would have it that the holyman had been squatting on the ground until they had blindly blundered into his moonlight meditations. But right then and there, Rory saw only the unreality and the terror of their predicament.

The Sadhu's pale branched chest, bare and hairless, ribs sticking out like hat hooks, his *dhoti* hanging loosely between his matchstick legs, ten times taller than their father and twenty times more terrifying, almost caused Rory Duncan Roskillen to turn tail and flee, as from the angry jungle hog he had encountered earlier in the day.

Half naked though the holyman was, cloaked only by ragged grey locks in tangled cords reaching to his bulbous knees, not for one moment was the Sadhu devoid of the cloth of human dignity. His majesty was absolute as, in one gnarled and trembling fist, he held fast a bamboo staff like a pestle he'd like to use to grind the white man in the mortar of his misdeeds.

'Today I have witnessed the intolerable pride and barbaric injustice of our conquerors, and, for thy mulct, thou false and hypocritical one, ignoble savage clothed in the garb of thy decadent civilization, division and destruction shall be thy portion. By the holy stars that bear witness this night to the cruelty and evil inflicted upon another, whom thou, whiteman, hast made thy slave, the unquenchable fires of Moloch shall take two and one half of what is thine. In all things henceforth, this curse upon thee and thine shall rest upon *thy* head.'

'Out of my way, fool!' James brushed past the holyman, not the least bit intimidated by the Sadhu's fierce diatribe, for he classified him, along with the rickshaw wallah, as a heathen cow-worshipper and a deranged one at that. He sought to put as much distance as possible between himself and the 'mad fakir'.

It was his brother Lindsay who, years later, broke the spell binding that strange night on the road to Tippindee. By then their grandfather and father were both dead and Lindsay had become the new Laird of Glengarth. Sailing his boat back into Loch Garth, Lindsay had looked up at the brooding castle on the mull – his castle, his forests, his loch and his love: 'Moloch is insatiable!' Lindsay said.

In the dark, the three of them, father and two sons, retraced their steps to Erinmore Lodge.

Later that night, in Sir Dougald's mahogany and aspidistra bathroom of the old Colonial style, James and his sons had another bath. Afterwards, when Rory and Lindsay had been shown to guest bedrooms, their father and Brig reclined on the verandah in planters' chairs, or long-sleevers as they were called. Simla Society forgotten as far as James was concerned, he and Brig relived old hunting exploits and swopped tales of the immortal hills, over the whisky and soda.

The two boys tossed and turned in damp misery under their mosquito nets. The rest of the night progressed slowly for them, like an unpleasant dream recalling the day's strange events, while sleep remained elusive in the insect-ridden hot and humid fist of monsoon India.

The following morning, in the Brigadier General's own official carriage (its back-axle thoroughly inspected beforehand) James and his two sons were taken home to Tippindee.

Their mother stood on the steps of the lodge, anxiously awaiting them, her hand shielding her eyes, golden hair like a halo in the bright Himalayan sun, and Rory's heart leapt in love and joy to see her. But before he could scramble down from the carriage to go and hug her and tell her in his young boy's bubbling way all that had happened to them, his father caught hold of his torn sleeve and held him back.

'Neither of you will breathe a single word of that mad fakir's nonsense to anyone, least of all your mama. You will erase from your minds as though they had never happened, the events of last evening.'

CHAPTER TWO

The heat was a white-hot visible thing assaulting the
senses. Mercury in the thermometer on the verandah
topped the red line at one hundred and ten degrees
fahrenheit. But worse than the heat was the dust. Thick
layers of it clogged the nostrils, irritated the throat and
made eyes and tempers gritty.

Dusky barefooted servants, conditioned by the invincible climate to shake a leg slowly, drew down rattan shades
and wooden jalousies. Coolies watered the tatties which
steamed in the heat, and soon dried out. It was like living
in a Turkish bathhouse; humanity gone into limbo along
with the flaccid green lizards dropping off ceilings, too
weary even to cling to the stucco of their existence.

Lessons over for the morning, Rory Duncan Roskillen
eagerly took himself off to his mother's rooms.

She was preoccupied in writing out garden-party invitations at her little French escritoire placed before one of
the long windows in her boudoir. From here, she could
gaze out upon the dusty palmyra trees looking like tall
forgotten sentinels lined up along the ochre boundary
wall. Or she could watch the *malis*, with their leaky
watering cans, vainly trying to coax the Maharajah of
Baharabad's gardens to resemble something green and
pleasant.

Rory became tired of making faces and hissing stirring
remarks over the wide, stone windowsill at the *punkah
wallahs*. Lazy blighters, snoozing on the verandah, the
strings which ought to keep the fans moving, slack in their
greasy fingers, were his childish thoughts. 'Mama, do you
like India?' he asked, quickly forgetting about the 'lazy
blighters' an expression he had picked up from his father.
He went and stood behind his mother's chair. The back of

her neck fascinated him. It was like a pale stalk bearing a yellow flower. Golden tendrils drifting prettily in the variable breeze of the linen fans – when someone remembered to pull the strings – were as soft and fluffy as dandelion down. He wanted to reach out and caress that soft fair hair swept up in a dignified chignon, or blow on it while making a wish. Instead, he kept his hands and hot breath firmly to himself. Both elbows propped on the back edge of the chair, chin cupped pensively in sweaty palms, his next question emerged crushed between his teeth. 'Mama, do you ever get homesick?'

His mother turned in surprise, pen poised in mid air.

Her eyes reminded Rory of reflections of heaven. They were such lovely eyes, purple-blue like jungle orchids or springtime violets in Glengarth woods.

He wondered how such a sweet and gentle creature could be married to his old and 'bad tempered' father. Rory, being an inquisitive boy and ever mindful of the idle gossip of relatives and servants, allowed very little to escape his attention: Father had been married before, to an Indian princess who was the Maharajah of Baharabad's sister. He had met her in his youth, when he had been attached to the Prince of Wales's entourage during the prince's visit to India in 1875. Papa and the princess had produced a daughter, the Rajkumari Sula, and so Rory felt that allowances had to be made for his father's '*profligate ways*' – no doubt copied from His Royal Highness who, according to adult gossip, had '*liaisons all over the place*'. All this, he had picked up via the grown-ups, even though their conversations sometimes confused him.

Unfortunately, the Indian princess had died in childbed, and James Beauly Roskillen's roving eye had turned next to the Honourable Laura Burrett of Leicestershire. Mama, Rory felt, didn't know what she had let herself in for when agreeing to become Papa's second wife: but he was glad about it, otherwise he wouldn't have been here now.

His mother always managed to look so cool, so calm, so English: Her watered-silk composure in a hot country with his hot-headed father deserved a medal. Pictures of her were etched indelibly on his mind, captured for ever

in sepia reminiscences of mellow summer days: tea from a
silver teapot poured by a lily-white hand; an elegant,
cream lace frock sweeping foreign lawns; large shady hats
adorned with feathers and flowers and artificial birds;
dimples and smiles and the teasing light in her eyes; the
cupid bow of her smile when she found something
amusing – which was quite often, for his mama's sense of
humour could be quite delicious. She reminded him of
cucumber sandwiches, Madeira cake, holly berries and
mistletoe, crisp white snow and laughter, early spring
mornings in Glengarth woods, armfuls of bluebells and all
things nice.

But standing out among those childhood memories
spent between two continents, was her protective love for
him, a love hermetically sealed against the scorching sun,
and which to him at that impressionable stage of his life,
was life itself.

'Sometimes darling, not often. This is my home now,
with your papa. What did you learn this morning with Mr
Shawmoss?'

'Nothing much.'

'Better not tell Papa,' she smiled mischievously.

'Mama, must I go to school in England?'

'Yes, dear, you must. They are your papa's wishes.'

'But why? It's such a long way from Baharabad.'

'Yes, I suppose it is.' She sighed and turned back to her
party invitations.

'Why, Mama?'

'Why is it a long way from here or why must you go to
school in England?'

'Moth-*er*!'

She set aside her pen, her expression guarded when she
offered him her footstool. 'Sit, Rory, where I can get a
better view of you without cricking my neck.' The cupid
bow of her mouth softened into a sweet smile. 'Remember
the gallant six hundred? Their's not to reason why?'

Her smile deepened at his expression of boyish horror.
'Mama, that's positively senseless! If I don't ask *why*, how
will I ever *know* if I'm dying for the right thing?'

'Darling boy, you're hardly going to die because we send

you to school in England.'

'I might. Notorious atrocities are committed in England. Lindsay's best friend, Pilkes Major, who was sent home from St John's College last year, died in a Rugby tackle six weeks after he got to Eton. They broke his neck. It was definitely a case of Sassenachs murdering Scotsmen, just like Culloden.'

She smiled, and ruffled his fair hair. 'Go on with you!'

'It's true! Flunkings, faggings and floggings being the order of the day. I'd rather be thrashed by Papa and old boggy Shawmoss right here in Baharabad, not England. Besides, I can always come and talk to you afterwards.'

She skirted the touchy subject with the dexterity of a diplomat intent upon keeping détente. 'You and Lindsay will be able to spend your school holidays at Glengarth.'

'I don't like grandfather Glengarth – at all!' And he meant it! 'Before we left Scotland to come here, he made it a point of saying, "See you again soon, *Lindsay m'boy*, and purposely ignored me. All he said to me was, get your hair cut! Just because Lindsay will one day inherit Glengarth, not I.'

Rory saw the flicker of a shadow in his mother's violet eyes and then it was gone. She said briskly, 'You, Rory, are in a far more enviable position than your brother. Your life is your own to make what you will of it, whereas Lindsay will have a millstone round his for the rest of *his* life.'

Rory was shocked. 'Is that what you think Glengarth is, Mama, a millstone?'

She turned away, her mood pensive as she took up a silver-framed photograph of a handsome Jacobean house. 'I think I prefer Breedon Hall which is much more conducive to homely living. An ancient Scottish castle perched high on a lonely rock is all very well for those who favour long draughty corridors. But castles and palaces aren't really *home* in the sense that Breedon Hall is ... Breedon-in-the-Wold, how very English it sounds!'

Rory knew then, just how homesick she was. He changed the subject. 'I *much* prefer old Great-Uncle

Neptune. I think I'd rather go and live with him than go to school in England. I know I shall hate them all – the Sassenachs, I mean.' He knew he didn't mean what he was saying, it was just so very unsettling to be moved around all the time as though he were a bit of furniture! After all, Scotland was his birthright and the only place that offered a permanence and stability reaching back hundreds of years. Rory brought his mind back to Great-Uncle Neptune, his grandfather's brother-in-law. Hamish MacDearg was an unforgettable character dedicated to putting the fear of God into the younger generation of Roskillens. Great-Uncle Neptune and grandfather hadn't spoken a word for over half a century. They had quarrelled over a steamship company and that was that, according to family legend. Rory remembered old Neptune very well from family portraits and photographs, and from their last visit to Hamish in Glasgow to bid him their dutiful farewells in case they never saw him again. Hamish couldn't have cared less: And all this India business had only come about because Papa had quarrelled with *his* father, the Laird of Glengarth. It seemed a male family trait, this incessant feuding amongst themselves.

'Darling boy, I don't think Great-Uncle Neptune would know what to do with you. He's very eccentric.'

'So is Grandfather ... and so is Papa.' That, too, must be a family trait, thought Rory, chewing his thumbnail. Maybe they had all inherited an inbred insanity going back to the first mad Beauly whose tomb was in Duncan's Tower, Glengarth, Ross-shire. It wasn't unheard of – look at Macbeth! Lindsay was going to be just the same, stiff-necked, stiff-lipped and dour. He was already showing signs of it. The girls of course were different. Christabel and Kitty were just females who liked pretty frills and dolls and going to fancy-dress parties, and weren't to be taken too seriously.

His mother set aside the photograph of her family home, and picked up a small silver bell on her blotter to summon her maid. She had to dress for luncheon, invariably taken with one of the Maharajah of Baharabad's umpteen wives and female relations.

'Mama, when will I see you again?'

'This evening, dear,' she said in abstraction. 'We'll read together one of Mr Kipling's stories from *Plain Tales of the Hills.*'

'Moth-*er*!' Rory said in exasperation, 'I meant, when will I see you again in *England*!'

'Soon, darling boy, soon.'

'How soon?'

She glanced up at him, then away again, not sure about anything for the moment. 'You must write to me often, Rory. Remind me of the primroses growing in wayside ditches like clusters of sunbeams. Bluebells in Glengarth woods, and the daffodils blowing on the banks of the Breedon. If flowers played music, they'd sound like churchbells rung by the wind. The flowers here never seem quite the same ... and now I am becoming maudlin, which simply won't do!' She rumpled his dusty hair fondly a second time, and then, taking his face between her soft cool hands planted a smacking kiss on his forehead, pink and bumpy with prickly heat rash. She smelled of lavender water, violets and all things nice, and he absorbed her scent as much as her touch.

Mademoiselle Chandelle Beauvier appeared in the adjoining doorway, a pale blue silk afternoon frock draped over her arm. 'Ze *dirze*, m'lady, 'ee 'as let out zee zeams, but he makes for a tcar in ze zilk. I zink it muz be ze vite laze ziz afternoon, non?'

Rory had once heard his papa tell Brigadier General, Sir Dougald MacKincade, whom everyone called Brig, that Chandelle Beauvier had picked up her English in a Cairo bordello. Chandelle's English, however, sounded infinitely better than Shawmoss's French picked up in Bognor Regis Vaudeville.

Rory got up off the footstool and left his mother and her maid engrossed in silk, satin and lace discussion. His mother, he had noticed, was lately becoming increasingly wider around the waist. He knew the reason why, although no one ever spoke about such things. 'And why do grown-ups always imagine children to be blind as well as backward?' he demanded of the empty air before flinging open the schoolroom door much harder than he had intended. I don't know why life is so dashed unfair!

Luncheon with his tutor, Mr Shawmoss, was the worst half-hour in a day filled with all manner of strife. Rory Duncan, even though he lived in a pink marble Elysium with his illustrious parents, two sisters, one half-sister, one brother and a chimpanzee called Suzy, trembled for his life!

'Home' in a foreign land was a grace-and-favour concubine's palace, lent to his father by the Maharajah of Baharabad after the concubine had gone out of favour. It was located at the far end of the substantial royal acres and overlooked a stagnant lake breeding virulent waterborne diseases. Rory was convinced that the lake was responsible for his father's ill-temper, malaria, and a host of other unmentionable maladies besides.

His father trained the Maharajah's string of priceless polo ponies and had the grand native title of *Officer of the Royal Stables* bestowed upon him by the Maharajah in a special ceremony – ceremonies being a way of life in Baharabad. But still Rory Duncan, in a life of material opulence and privilege, was not happy. In fact, he was decidedly miserable as he wallowed in a desert of uncertain affection. The pattern of his days were filled with constant doubt.

'Good afternoon, Roskillen – or is it evening? You are late for luncheon again,' Tutor Shawmoss, bending his thin bamboo punishment stick like a bow, made the boy aware of his tenuous foothold upon an alien land.

'Yes, I know. I was talking to my mother and forgot the time.'

'Punctuality is the prerogative of kings, Roskillen. We are all here to set the heathen native a Christian example. Neither do I care for your tone, young sir!'

Every day apart from Sundays when the whole family lunched and dined together, Rory was forced to take luncheon with his tutor – a rule set up by his father in order to further torture him into submission.

Beside the meal trolley stood an immaculate

Khitmutgar in snowy white uniform and turquoise and jade cummerbund. The Maharajah's livery colours were repeated in the servant's puggaree band. A golden tuft glittered on his head as he stood with arms folded neatly, guardian to this Aladdin's cave of food. In comparison, Tutor Shawmoss, in his pupil's opinion, presented a round-shouldered, lame, scrooge-like apology for a human being.

Shawmoss invariably found fault with not only the food sent from the kitchens, but also the Khitmutgar. With his stick he flicked an imagined fleck of dust from the Khitmutgar's shoulder, lest his hands became contaminated from touching a heathen. Then he ordered the servant straight back to the kitchen quarters, yards away across the compound, because there were no oysters on ice from England. He knew they had arrived at last, delivered by the Maharajah's own train from Bombay. He had just seen and heard that fat slob of the Brigadier General, Sir Dougald MacKincade, enjoying them as he lunched with his alter ego, James Beauly Roskillen of Glengarth.

Many Britishers were in the Maharajah's employ. Mr Shawmoss had been personal tutor to the Maharajah of Baharabad's youngest wife's eldest son. The prince had died at the tender age of twelve (an ominous warning Rory did not think his own father took seriously enough). After that unhappy affair, Mr Shawmoss was made redundant by the Royal Household. Thereafter, he was hired by J.B. Roskillen to turn Rory Duncan into something decent before the boy was sent to Eton.

'Come and get it,' Mr Shawmoss said, the signal for his pupil to jump up with alacrity, eager to wolf down his food just like one of his father's fox-terriers.

And why he doesn't just set down the plate on the floor and be done, I'll never know! Rory thought to himself. He would never forget the first or last sadistic thrashing, nor the early days of the Shawmoss relationship when he had made the fatal error of being too dilatory to the food trolley and had been deprived altogether of his midday meal.

'Not hungry then, uh, uh?' Shawmoss had sniggered.

'Right then, you can memorize Coriolanus' speech to Tullus Aufidious, Act IV, scene V, beginning, "*My name is Caius Marcius*". In Latin if you please, Roskillen.'

Rory had learned his lesson that day and had never again dallied to the food trolley when remembering the gripping hunger pains which had assaulted him all afternoon and evening.

Tutor Shawmoss, greedily swallowing oysters as though they were going out of fashion, mumbled something under his breath. Rory was helping himself to egg custard from the trolley and missed Shawmoss's remark. 'What, sir?'

'*What, what*?' Shawmoss flung aside the oysters and his napkin. He picked up his walking-stick from the desk, also the thin bamboo punishment cane, and limped across the room. Rory heard the cane through the air before he felt it strike the backs of his knees. Bamboo could cut through cloth, even through tartan plus-fours tucked into thick woollen school socks, despite the temperature soaring into the red outside. Rory dropped the dish of egg custard on the floor. The Khitmutgar, rock faced, eyes vacant and downcast, moved forward to clear up the mess of shattered glass and spilt pudding.

Shawmoss took Rory by the ear and drew him away from the food trolley. 'Clumsy wretch! *Repeat*! What are you?'

'A clumsy wretch, sir.'

'Nice boys do not say WHAT, Roskillen. They say pardon.'

'Mama doesn't like me to say pardon. Mama says only shop girls say pardon.'

'*What, what*?' Shawmoss aspirated the words in mimicry. 'I did not quite catch what you said, Roskillen. *WHAT* did you say?'

'Our Father who art in heaven,' Rory muttered, his ear beginning to throb. 'Hallowed be thy name, but *not* yours Mr Shawmoss. God is going to punish you one day because you're so cruel. I'm not surprised he gave you a twisted leg.' Fear and pain made him bold; this was his 'desert of uncertainty' and he was only able to blame his earthly father for it: Papa did not *have* to employ old boggy Shawmoss, were Rory's emotive thoughts concerning his tutor.

'Top marks for courage but not for insolence, or discretion, young sir!'

Thwack went the cane so many times, the humble Khitmutgar standing to attention, unable to interfere, lost count of the strokes. He could only suffer in silence on behalf of the bullied boy.

When Shawmoss had finished wielding the bamboo cane he limped with the aid of his walking-stick back to his desk. '*Stand up and walk, you misbegotten whelp*! Give thanks for being fed at all, Roskillen.'

Rory stood up, put his hands together, closed his eyes and obediently gave thanks even though pain and humiliation brought the tears to his eyes. But, he would *not* give in to old boggy Shawmoss, *ever*! 'I who am a wretched sinner in thy sight, O Lord, do humbly beseech thy forgiveness. I thank thee for my plentiful repast, thy ever bountiful goodness to one such as I, who deserveth not thy grace and favour. I thank thee, I thank thee, I thank thee ...' *ad infinitum, and please God forgive me for hating him with such a burning zeal, but let a deadly cobra creep into his bed tonight*, was his silent postscript.

CHAPTER THREE

The family had not gone to the hills that summer because Sula informed them that their mama was unable to travel on account of her condition.

Mama's actual 'condition' had never been explained, but Rory knew she was going to have another baby.

'Father is an immoral *profligate*' (he had overheard the word used by Sula to describe the British heir to the throne) 'to make Mama suffer so, in this intolerable heat!' he grumbled to his ayah's father one day.

Lunghi was an old Indian retainer, crippled and full of sores. Lunghi haunted the servants' compound. 'All men are disgusting profligates, my son,' replied the old man, calmly sucking on a hookah.

'After all, my youngest sister, Kitty, is nearly six, and Father, at his age, should be past such things by now. He must be at least *fifty*!'

'Men are never past such things, Master Rory-Sahib. They will profligate even unto death.'

Rory, in his own mind, was never quite certain as to the *actual* physical process involved in baby-making apart from kissing. That's why he refused to kiss anyone except Mama, because *she* could only make babies with Papa. Married people were somehow immune from 'baby' scandals. It was all right for them, said Dharkli, his ayah, but not all right for Christabel, Kitty or Sula who were not married as yet.

Neither did he want to be burdened with children before he was old enough. *He* wanted to make a career of horse-betting or peacock rearing – there was money in that, as well as excitement: Maharajahs indulged in both. There was a nice ring to it, *money and excitement*!

Rory's life among the compound servants was an

education in itself; the old man on his *charpoy*, smoking his hookah, was not as squeamish about the facts of life as *the parents* or Sula. He often pumped the old man for details. 'Lunghi,' Rory asked thoughtfully, because he was beginning to get second thoughts about it, 'if I kiss a girl, will she get a baby?'

'Yes, Master Rory-Sahib, if your kisses lead you on to that special place.'

'What special place?'

'That of profound desire, *chota sahib*, which you will soon be approaching if you go on in this way.'

'But what *sort* of place?'

'It is a place desired and sought by every desperate invader, my son.'

'Where?'

'Deep in the well of infinite pleasures, my son, into which one must cast the bucket of desires.'

Rory knew the old man wasn't all there in the head, and made allowances. 'How will I know it's the right well?'

'You will recognize it in time, my son, for you, too, will one day inherit the experience of a million masculine joys.'

'Yes, but *how* will I know it, when I don't know what I'm *actually* looking for? Have you a map, Lunghi?'

'You must follow Victoria and her fellow; they will show you the way.'

'Thanks, Lunghi.'

'Do not mention it, my son. I am at your British service always.'

After that conversation with Lunghi, Rory, still in search of the facts of life, took to secretly reading his father's copy of the *Ramayana* in search of the well of truth. All he managed to glean from it were interesting pictures of Indian ladies with big bosoms.

After Shawmoss's sound thrashing Rory, angry, resentful and light-headed, felt sick. He also had an earache. In fact, he didn't feel very well at all and knew he was in for another one of his bad nightmares that night.

He left the compound and went to his room for his afternoon nap, always taken during the hottest part of the day. On his bed he writhed and twisted in damp misery beneath the mosquito net, unable to get comfortable no matter which way he squirmed.

Suzy, his pet monkey, was one animal his father simply could not abide, for the reason Suzy had once squatted on the ground in front of James Beauly Roskillen to do her monkey-business.

Suzy had been relegated to the servants' compound. If his father ever found the animal on the premises, Shaw-moss had been instructed to take the stick to Suzy's owner.

But Suzy and her owner had ways and means of defying authority and once again Suzy had crept into the palace unnoticed. She patted Rory's head sympathetically.

He patted her head in return. 'You are the only source of affection in my miserable existence, Suzy. I wish I were dead.' That even an animal was kinder to him than the humans around him, made Rory wonder if he would not be better off eloping with Suzy to the jungle.

He must have dozed off in the drowsy afternoon heat. When he woke up he was shivering and sweating and felt as though he were in for another bout of malaria. Malaria was awful; it made one shake and shudder, teeth rattling, head swimming, as though one were going through a snowstorm with a furnace lit inside: and always with the same recurring nightmare that had haunted him for over a year ... a jungle path, and an old Indian Sadhu putting a curse on the family ... he could even describe the holyman in detail, like a skeleton raised from the dead, wild and white and savage, a *dhoti* tucked up between his matchstick legs, red eyes burning fiercely as he barred their way on a lonesome jungle path. Long ragged locks down to his bulbous knees, he held a bamboo staff which he pounded up and down in wrath as he cursed their father. The Indian Sadhu's curse still rang in Rory's ears ... '*on thy head ... on thy head ... on thy head ...*'

Rory shook his head to clear it.

How real was the dream? How real was the curse?

He didn't know, for his life had telescoped together: dreams and reality were interwoven like honeysuckle tendrils over a trellis, so that Scotland and India had merged as one and the same country, while the people in his life were the visionary characters of the *Ramayana*.

After the mosquito net had been pulled down through Suzy's over-exuberant antics, excited at finding herself in her young master's bedroom instead of her usual habitat of Lunghi's dirty little hut, Rory found the best place to lie was stretched out on the floor on his stomach, his left ear pressed to the cool marble tiles to take away the burning ache. Suzy nestled beside him, coy contented. Gentle leathery fingers searched through his hair for nits, disappointed when she could find none to pop into her mouth.

Rory thought of running away. After a while he was forced to admit he had nowhere to go. If he went to Brig, most assuredly, Sir Dougald would send him right back into Father's arms. Then he would be in for another purgatorial week just like the week following his expulsion from St John's College, Simla. Lindsay was still a pupil at St John's; that was why he wasn't at home to be tortured at the hands of a sadistic tutor.

It was all Father's fault. He should never have left Scotland in the first place. If he had wanted to return to India, then he should have come by himself, not drag Mama and the whole family along with him. Papa didn't really want any of them, anyway, only Mama. Papa considered children to be the unnecessary trappings of marriage, there to be punished, not loved; well, he punished Rory Duncan more than the others, that was for sure!

Why did he and Lindsay have to go to school in England in the new year, after having been dragged all the way out to India in the first place? It simply didn't make sense.

But then, nothing that Papa appeared to do, ever made sense.

It was only Mama who made things bearable. She had refused to leave them behind in Scotland when Father had insisted the Scottish weather and the old laird, *his* father, were getting on his nerves. He longed for the sun again, and wanted to return to Baharabad. And Mama had had no choice in the matter. Father's wishes were law.

Rory Duncan retraced the path of his nine-year-old life and came to the conclusion that he was scarred for life. Three years in India had left its mark.

Soon after the family's arrival in India, life had taken a dramatic turn for the worse. He and Lindsay had been unceremoniously bundled off to Prep School in Simla, a rigorous and disciplined establishment run by Presbyterians specifically for the benefit of the chosen few. At the age of eight years, two months and two days he had been expelled, and his academic career appeared to be over before it had properly started. Not that he had minded in the least; but his father had. Father had been informed by St John's pious professors, that Rory Duncan Roskillen was a 'barbarous child with the mentality of a native! His behaviour had been deplorable, his mercenary motives reprehensible and his language! Well, the less said about it, the better!'

And all he had done was climb over the school wall to the local Indian bazaar to barter mutton pies from the school kitchens for an illicit smoke on an Indian hookah. Rory had been at a loss to understand the fuss and nonsense.

But then, *some to misery are born*, Rory told himself.

The silly incident had been blown up out of all proportion – *he was corrupt*! While St John's were prepared to keep Lindsay, the heir to a noble Scottish seat, his dishonourable brother, whose *corrupt* morals at such an early age were truly disgusting, and liable to taint others, would have to go. Expelled! A sin tantamount to seducing the cantonment padre's wife.

But really, he had done nothing! Selling mutton pies in an Indian bazaar while pretending to be a poor orphan boy was hardly a crime worth expulsion, was it? What *really* had made his father angry, was that he had had to postpone *shikar*, a Himalayan hunting expedition with the Maharajah of Baharabad and Brig – an event in itself predisposing to the worst possible beating yet. *Shikar* was a religion to his father, and when he had come up to

Simla, personally, in order to fetch his recalcitrant son without entrusting the task to Rassoul, major-domo and personal servant, Father had been angry!

Papa, on that occasion, Rory remembered all too well, had managed to get through three willow canes, and was only dissuaded from using the hog-whip because of Mama's intervention.

Tearfully, she had asked him, 'Why, darling boy, why? Why did you disobey the rules? Rules are what we are all governed by. They are important for good social development. We *must* set a good example to the Indians, you know, Rory.'

'Well, Mama,' he began, as he lay on his stomach because of a numb bum, though he would not have mentioned it in front of his lady-mother. But because she was as persuasive as his ayah, Dharkli, he told her the full story, 'Fannington Minor bet me ten rupees I wouldn't do it.'

'Do what, darling boy?'

'Sell myself as an orphan in the bazaar, along with St John's rotten mutton pies. I managed to sell all the pies, but nobody wanted me.'

Unbeknown to his mother, Rory Duncan had started on his future career of waging war against the odds. Only much later on in his life could he look back and begin to understand those very 'Victorian attitudes' that had governed the lives of his family, their friends and his tutor. Children, too, had to abide by those 'rules' without questioning, without understanding and without reason. And because he always wanted to know 'why' he had been classified as a 'difficult child'. So he had adopted the attitude, 'might as well be hanged for a sheep as a lamb!' He had rebelled; he had desired to poison off old boggy Shawmoss though he be hanged for it!

But that would be unlikely now, as he was about to be shipped off to England. Perhaps he could murder old Shawmoss on the eve of his departure and then no one would be any the wiser. A fellow couldn't be extradited from England for a crime committed in India, could he? He would miss old Lunghi and his stories, though.

Through his private reverie on the cool marble floor, Rory was suddenly made aware of a lot of noise going on below. He raised his head off the tiles and listened.

The noise increased.

Intrigued, he got up off the floor, took Suzy on his shoulder and crept out onto the gallery. From here he had a bird's eye view over marble banisters into the vast, pillared bowl of the hall below.

Servants were dashing about hither and thither. Chandelle Beauvier was having her usual attack of the vapours and, worst of all, Rassoul, faithful and loving steward of the household, had imprisoned Mama in his servant's brawny brown arms.

Rory was outraged. Perhaps Shawmoss was not altogether a nincompoop, but a far-sighted man who had been perfectly justified in his suspicions concerning Indians! After what had happened at Lucknow and Cawnpore when Britishers were stabbed, shot and fair maidens like his mother (he was a little confused as to the details here) were 'roped' before being thrown down deep, dark wells by angry natives, was this a second Indian Mutiny now breaking out? Was the Maharajah of Baharabad about to murder all the Britishers in his employ? Was the massacre to be spearheaded by the Maharajah's own servants? Were Mother, Father, Christabel, Kitty, he himself, Chandelle Beauvier, the sporting Brigadier and the Protestant Padre about to be stabbed to death and tossed into the lake? Never mind old boggy Shawmoss, it would serve him right! And what a good job Lindsay was in Simla. He'd be able to escape the mutiny and go back to live in Scotland.

In self-defence he grabbed up his father's hog whip left with his other hunting paraphernalia in the game-room, a small ante-chamber leading off from the gallery. It was a last-minute decision, but one of strategy, he felt. Determined to be a 'survivor' in order to go back to Scotland with Lindsay, he would begin by thrashing Rassoul to an inch of his life. Rassoul would release Mama so that she could return to Scotland with them.

Unobserved by servants and other members of the household, Rory, his heart in his mouth, got close enough to his mother and then, with a whoop of terrifying blood-thirstiness he dashed out from behind a marble pillar, brandishing the hog whip. But before he had a chance to lay into Rassoul, someone from behind grabbed hold of his shirt collar and jerked him backwards. 'What do you think you're doing?' Sula demanded.

'What're they doing to my mother? Leave her alone!'

He began to kick and tug and actually bit a bruising chunk out of Rassoul's arm, even while Sula held on to him. '*Leave her alone ... leave her alone, I'll kill you all*...' the hog whip feebly flicked the air. Sula had grabbed his arms.

'Stop it at once, you little fiend!' Sula said angrily.

'Rory, darling, it's all right. Rassoul's not harming me ... he's helping me to get upstairs.' His mother's cool fingers brushed his cheek, a feathery, sweet-scented action bearing the tears away, a touch he would remember to his dying day.

She was taken away from him, and Rory ran after them. But again his step-sister took control and swiftly caught hold of him a second time. 'Stop this childish behaviour at once, Rory ... and give me that hog whip before you hurt someone.' She snatched it from him. 'You're supposed to be in your room at this hour. Get back to your bed before your father catches you.'

He did not hate Sula quite as much as Shawmoss, but came close to it in that moment. 'What's he going to do with Mama? If he murders her, Sula, and throws her down a well, I swear I'll kill all of them ... and you!'

Threats of that nature were like water off a duck's back as far as Sula was concerned – was she part of the conspiracy? After all, she was half Indian herself. Rory glared at her, blue eyes narrowed in suspicion, his scowl enough to make the natives quake.

'For goodness sake, Rory, don't be so emotional! Rassoul's not being disrespectful to your mother. He was asked to carry her upstairs to her rooms because she fainted at the Maharani's luncheon reception, that's all.'

His relief was enormous. But he still did not trust Sula, not fully. She could be as devious as any common coolie.

Besides, he had to be quite certain this wasn't a second
Indian Mutiny. 'Is she going to have her interesting condition now, Sula, is she?' he asked eagerly.

Sula frowned. 'What do you know about such things?'

'I have eyes, haven't I?'

'Don't be impudent!' She boxed his ears and, coming
on top of Mr Shawmoss's torture, Rory yelped like a
puppy whose tail had been trodden on.

Suzy began to dance round them, angrily chattering and
hissing at Sula. Rory hoped that Suzy would do her
monkey-business on the marble hall-floor in front of Sula.
'Anyway,' he added defiantly, trying to ignore the loud
humming in his head, 'I know everything about having
babies. I know how they get here and it's all Papa's fault.
Lunghi told me.'

'You disgust me, you bad boy, associating with such
filthy company!'

'Whether I disgust you or not, makes no difference. My
question was, is Mama . . .'

Sula grabbed a handful of his hair and propelled him to
the nether regions of the pink palace. Outside on the back
verandah overlooking the servants' compound, she leaned
across the coping and shouted, 'Dharkli, come here at
once!'

'No need to shout! Dharkli right here on verandah steps
. . . what you want, Rajkumari Sula?'

Rory's huge fat Indian ayah raised heavy languid eyes at
the princess whom Dharkli took with a pinch of salt, for
the Rajkumari Sula was neither flesh nor fowl nor good
red herring, born as she was with two skins.

'I want you to take this boy back to his room and keep
him there. And make him get rid of that flea-ridden
monkey!' With a disdainful sweep of her jade-green and
silver sari, Sula turned on her heel and marched inside.

Dharkli observed her charge with bulbous jaundiced
eyes before turning her head aside to spit with slow delib-
eration into the compound. A little ball of squidgy pith
and bark landed in the dust. She gnawed off another
chunk from the stick she was using to clean her teeth,
native fashion. When she was satisfied with the feel of the

masticated mess in her mouth, she transferred the wad to one cheek.

She reminded Rory of a chestnut jelly with mastoid trouble. Dharkli burped, 'Aray-barp-ray barp! What you say to her to make her so angry?'

'*Nothing*!' Rory kicked a dusky pink marble baluster that was already flaking badly. Rosy dust sifted upon the verandah floor. Everything, he thought wretchedly, was crumbling around him. He *hated* India and he hated Sula. 'I only asked about Mama's interesting condition.'

'What you want to know about it?'

'Whether her baby's coming today.'

'What you want to know such grown-up things for?'

'That's what Sula said! Everyone around here is so *DUMB*!'

'What you tell to her?'

'That Lunghi told me everything.'

'What that chattering old goat tell to you?'

'Nothing really. Actually, Arjoo told me.'

'Arjoo? That native boy with *chii-chii* habits? He know nothing about anything. Better you learn about *chota babas* in other way.'

'What other way?'

'You go watch Victoria Regina with Naseem, then you know all about making *chota babas*.'

'Thanks for nothing. Lunghi led me up the garden path, too. I've already seen what Victoria and Naseem do together.'

He kicked the baluster again. He knew all about Dharkli's daughter, named Victoria Regina after the Queen of England. Sixteen-year-old Victoria was Kitty's ayah, and Naseem was the sweeper-boy to whom she was promised in marriage. He'd spied upon them illicitly whenever they crept off together to the oleaster bushes, and he didn't care for their grunting noises, just like pigs rolling around in the swill. The expression on Naseem's face as he pounded himself on top of Victoria, made babies seem a most disgusting and painful process altogether, especially when conducted in a place of spiky twigs liable to poke one in all sorts of intimate places.

He asked Dharkli, 'Will they cut Mama's tummy open to get the baby out?'

She thought that very funny indeed, and nearly choked herself on her twig toothbrush. It was some time before Dharkli's cackling died down and she began to chew again. 'You British *baba-log* very funny! And very stupid. Every Indian fellow know baba drop out from between mother's legs, just like cow. White Memsahib no different from sacred white cow.'

It was the manner in which she said it that upset him. Scarlet-faced, he roared, '*You're a liar Dharkli*! You're a nasty fat black witch and I shall tell Papa what you just said about my mama. He'll cut out your *chii-chii* tongue and feed it to the vultures.'

'Aray-barp-ray barp,' she said again, none too perturbed about his threats, 'your name suits you well, Master Rory-Sahib. You *real* English baba with no sense.'

'I am not a *baba* and I am NOT ENGLISH!' He roared like his father, before stalking back to his room with Suzy in tow.

The following morning Rory woke with a sense of impending doom.

Sula stood beside his bed with the mosquito net lifted to one side. She stared down into his sleepy face. Even in his hazy state Rory registered the fact that Sula looked haggard and old this morning.

She was dressed in a fashion he was not accustomed to seeing her wearing. Blue-black hair twisted into a heavy chignon on the nape of her neck, Sula's high cheekbones were gauntly accentuated. Her sultry almond-shaped eyes with their thick black lashes lacked sparkle, and the warm sheen of her golden complexion evinced a sallowness he did not care for. The spirit and colour had faded from his normally gaudy step-sister in all her tinsel Indian finery. This morning, in her black crêpe frock with its long buttoned sleeves and high neck, Rory knew why she had come to him. She looked just like a gloomy painting he had once seen hanging in a crofter's cottage on Inchnadamph.

He remembered the name of the crofter's picture: DEATH!

Sula came straight to the point and for that he could only admire and thank her, 'Rory, child, your mama went to heaven last night.'

Breathing was too painful to utter anything other than a small 'oh!'

While his beleaguered brain tried to come to terms with the facts, she continued in a withdrawn manner, 'A cable has been despatched to Lindsay's boarding school. He will arrive from Simla tomorrow evening. Only then will Papa talk to you children, not before. And I want no trouble from you today, do you understand?'

It was quite unnecessary, *he* would give no trouble.

She dropped the mosquito net and glided like a shadow to the door. He swallowed hard, 'Sula . . .'

Mosquito net encompassed him. He felt trapped like a wounded animal, unable to escape, to run away so that he could lick his wounds in peace and privacy.

'Yes, Rory?' She paused expectantly on the threshold, her delicate fingers, the milky-blue veins of her very small hand wrapped around the heavy brass doorknob, minute details of inessentials honed in on him in those few terrible seconds of his cosy little world being shattered into myriad pieces.

'Sula, when can I talk to Mama?'

'Rory, don't you understand?' she sighed in exasperation. 'I've just *told* you, your mama died in the night.'

'There's just one thing I'd like to say to her, in private, if I may.'

'Rory, dear, dead people cannot hear.'

'Please, Sula, before they put her in the ground.'

Her regal features relaxed. She hesitated: 'Very well. If your father allows it, you may see her when she's decently laid out in her coffin.'

'Thank you.'

She closed the door gently behind her. He sat there numbly, arms clasped around his knees. *Dear Mama, I still love you very much and always will, and I'm sorry for all the worry and trouble I've caused you. I'll try and be very good from now on, if only you'll come back to us. I hope you haven't gone away to heaven, because you're angry with me*: that's what he would tell her.

The door reopened and Mr Shawmoss limped into the room without shutting the door behind him. 'Good morning, young sir, still abed are we? You were supposed to be in the classroom precisely . . .' he took his fob watch from his waistcoat pocket and made a pretence of looking at it, 'precisely six and a half minutes ago.'

'My mother went to heaven in the night.'

'Sincere condolences indeed. However, bereavement is no excuse for disrespect. When addressing me, kindly use the prefix of *sir*!' Shawmoss coughed delicately. 'Ahem . . . your father . . .' he limped to the end of the bed, lifted the mosquito net and smiled one of his reptilian smiles. 'When offering your father my deepest sympathy this morning, we happened to alight upon the subject of your lessons. Your father agrees with me, that on this sad day, you would be better off keeping your mind occupied and off the subject of your maternal loss. Therefore, you will continue with your lessons as usual. I shall expect you in the classroom by, ahhh . . . let me see,' he glanced again at his fob watch, 'by a quarter past seven.'

Less than five minutes to wash, dress, breakfast and get himself to the schoolroom. Shawmoss knew very well he'd be late, and had arranged the schedule accordingly. The punishment for unpunctuality was a sound thrashing with the bamboo cane.

'Very well,' Rory replied, not even hating Mr Shawmoss any more. He just had to accept the fact that life held certain hellish moments nothing, simply nothing, not even the death of a beloved mother, could change.

'Very well, *SIR*!' Shawmoss bellowed in Rory's sore ears.

'Very well, sir.'

He was treated with a little less severity and a lot more respect that day, but that was probably because he was more than a little subdued.

CHAPTER FOUR

Everything had been black: black and unreal and more than a little frightening, even though Rory had tried very hard not to be a 'coward', a species of life-form his father appeared to have no time for. So he contained his fears as best he could. He and Lindsay had worn black serge, Eton suits to Mama's funeral. Sula, Christabel and Kitty wore black crêpe dresses and black veils. The horses pulling the black carriages wore black plumes and the coffin itself behind the glass panels of the hearse was black and ebony and draped with a black tasselled cloth. It rested on a gigantic slab of ice to prevent their mother's body from decomposing too fast in the intolerable heat. Rory had wondered what that could possibly mean – how could mama '*decompose*'?

Sula had no time to explain and so he had asked Lindsay. When Lindsay told him it meant, 'to rot away', Rory had kicked the cemetery gates in frustration, a terrible pain somewhere in his heart. Sula had then hauled him over black coals for showing such disrespect on the day of his mother's funeral. 'Have you so little faith in your Christian God, Rory Duncan, you cannot believe what they teach you? Your mama has gone to heaven and is no doubt looking down on you at this very moment with sorrow in her heart at your disgusting behaviour!'

'Then there's not much point in going to heaven is there, if one has to suffer up there as well!'

Sula boxed his ears.

Such an uncalled for action on the day of his mother's funeral made Rory determined never *ever* to forgive his step-sister. He did not know if Sula was a proper Christian or not. Her religions were manifold. Sometimes she would accompany them to church, and at other times he had caught her on her knees, lighting joss-sticks before some ugly Indian idol adorned with marigold garlands. Besides, Sula always wore a red spot in the centre of her forehead, which *proved* she was a heathen!

In the slanting light of evening their father summoned them into his presence. Now there would be no question of an English public school, were Rory's feelings on the subject of school in England. Papa would keep them all with him in India now that Mama was no longer around to keep him company.

He reviewed the prospect of spending the rest of his life in India with his fierce, red-headed father, with mixed feelings.

Dust motes in the air gathered in kaleidoscopic confusion and made a halo above their father's head. The room was stiflingly hot and smelly, and flies crawled on the net-screens at the windows: great big, bloated blue flies crawling everywhere, making everything *rot*! The rich, exotic and cloying scents of cemetery flowers lingered in his nostrils from earlier in the day, bringing on a headache and making him feel sick. The ebony and ormolu clock on the mantlepiece ticked loudly, reminding him of the happy hours spent with his mother, both of them reading together Mr Kipling's *Plain Tales of the Hills*, *The Phantom Rickshaw* and *The Jungle Book*. Tomorrow the clock would tick again: but never again in the same way. Because, in another ebony box, time would stand still for ever and ever and ever ... and she would never know where that time had gone ...

'If you're going to faint, Rory Duncan, go and do it in the corridor,' his father's voice reached him from a long way off.

Rory pulled himself together and fixed his attention upon his father and what he was saying. His father had luxuriant auburn moustaches, all waxed and wavy. He had hooded grey eyes, very piercing and penetrating, and his coppery hair was sleekly dressed with Oil of Macassar. He was a big, handsome man, very athletic and imposing and Rory Duncan wondered what on earth had possessed his illustrious father to test his strength on a harmless, skinny

young Indian coolie on the road to Tippindee ... 'Why are
you staring at me as though you'd never set eyes on me
before? I find your manner most insolent, young man!'

Again that *voice*! Rory had heard it many times before,
on the Maharajah's polo fields, barking as now, annihilat-
ing the opposition by just one fell *whoop* of the Scottish
tongue. And yet, Rory had heard that voice on other
occasions, when speaking to Mama or the girls, conversing
with Brig, or reciting *Sweet Afton* on Burns' Night, and it
could be as lush as the purple tones of Papa's heather-clad
hills, wooing and gentle and soft like the caressing mists
on Beinn Claidheamh Mor. The trouble was, whenever
Papa spoke to him, he always managed to sound like a
cannon in the valley of death ... he *would* have killed that
poor, helpless young rickshaw wallah on the road to
Tippindee, had not the old Sadhu interfered. And now
Mama was dead. Was this the Indian curse coming true?
Nonsense! There was no possible truth in curses and
witchcraft and things that went bump in the night!

'I asked you a question, young man! Why are you
staring at me as though I were the devil himself?'

'I ... I don't know, Papa. I'm not feeling very well. I'm
sorry, Papa, but I think it's been all too much for me
today.'

'What have I been saying?' asked his father, picking up
a tumbler of water on his desk and passing it across, his
hooded grey eyes above the rim of the glass interrogative
and daunting.

'I ... I ... I ...' helplessly Rory looked at Sula standing
behind their father's chair like his guardian angel. But Sula
preferred to look elsewhere, unwilling to be drawn into
any conflict between father and younger son. Eagerly
Rory drank the water his father had kindly offered him,
and started again as he passed the empty tumbler back to
his father. 'I'm sorry, sir,' he repeated.

James Roskillen sighed wearily and set down the
tumbler with a deliberate carefulness as to its exact place
on his desk. Then, with both elbows poised, he arched his
hands in a pyramid of prayer. 'I sincerely hope,' he said,
with fingers touching, 'you won't be such an infernal

liability to your Uncle Austen and Aunt Ada.'

'I ... I beg your pardon, Papa?' At a complete disadvantage, Rory stared at his father in dismay.

'Let me repeat, for your sole benefit, *I sincerely hope, for your sake, you will amount to something in your future life under the auspices of your English guardians since I have failed,*' he said in one succinct blast.

'England?' Rory croaked. '*LIVE* in England? I thought I was only going to school in England? Scotland is my home, Papa.'

'Well, dear boy, from now on it will be Leicestershire ...'

'Leicestershire? Where on earth is that?' He knew, of course he knew: but he was bent on being perverse. His mother was dead, he wished it were Papa!

'If you take up an Atlas after this interview, you will see where it is in the event of your geography leaving so much to be desired,' said his father with a long-drawn-out sigh.

'Papa,' said Rory Duncan, feeling suddenly very cold and clammy and afraid, 'are we *all* being sent off to Leicestershire?'

'You and Kitty will become wards of your mother's brother and his wife – as I took such pains just now to explain to the others while you chose to close your ears ...'

'Just a moment, Papa,' Rory interrupted breathlessly, 'what about Lindsay and Christabel?'

'They will be going home to Scotland. I have written to your grandfather to advise him of my decision.'

Rory took a deep breath and filled his lungs, 'Why can't Kitty and I go back to Glengarth with them?'

'Because grandfather is almost eighty and doesn't need a kindergarten under his feet all day long.'

'Did *he* say that?'

'No, *I'm* saying it! You, dear boy, would be too much of a burden for him. *Don't argue*! You require a firmer hold than either your Aunt Jean or grandfather Glengarth can give. Aunt Jean has her hands full with her own family and the running of Grandfather's home. She would be quite unable to devote the time required to supervise your activities – especially the leisure side of them which accounts for most of your day according to Mr Shawmoss. You are lazy, insolent, ill-mannered, ignorant and uncouth! Perhaps your Uncle Austen can succeed where I have failed.'

'What about you and Sula?'

'Our affairs are no concern of yours!'

'Papa,' Rory interrupted yet again, throwing caution to the winds, 'if you and Sula are to remain in India, then let me stay with you, *please*?'

'Don't be a fool, boy! India is no place for you. Besides, Sula and I belong here, you don't.'

'But you will be the Laird of Glengarth after Grandpapa dies, and so you have a duty to be in Scotland with us.'

'I will *not* be the Laird of Glengarth after Grandpapa dies,' said James Roskillen, his voice for once subdued, his pebble-cold eyes not upon his family but upon some distant point in his own vision. 'Lindsay has already been made aware of the situation. He will be the next Laird of Glengarth, not I, since I have relinquished my inheritance in Scotland ... *ahhmm*!' James cleared his throat. 'I have been disinherited by your grandfather – much to my delight, I assure you all. It means I do not have to suffer the slings and arrows of his outrageous temperament nor have I to face the prospect of dying of a rheumatic disease in that infernally draughty castle! I like it out here: the climate suits me, the life suits me and I want to stay in this land where your mother ... where both my wives are buried.'

Rory understood his father's reasons. What he could not understand was why his father was splitting up Lindsay, Christabel, he and Kitty as a family.

'Sula's place is here in Baharabad with her uncle, the Maharajah, and the rest of her family,' his father added. 'A suitable Indian marriage has been arranged for her, so there is no question of her going elsewhere. When it is convenient, I hope to repair to Scotland to see you children.'

Rory tried to come to terms with this new, bizarre situation. 'So, you are splitting us all up, Papa, because now

Mama is dead, you no longer want us. I know you prefer
the Maharajah's polo ponies to us, you always have. Just
as you have relinquished the responsibility of Glengarth,
you are ridding yourself of us. You *know* how attached
Christabel and Kitty are to Sula and yet you think nothing
of banishing them to a foreign country without parents
and without anyone to love them ...' Rory's voice began
to tremble treacherously. 'If Mama were alive ... she ...
she w-would n-never for-forgive you ...' he faltered
dismally.

'Be quiet!' Lindsay hissed angrily from the side of his
mouth. '*Grow up!*'

Rory was furious with his brother: Lindsay, normally as
silent and vacant as his pet parrot, MacBeth, would have
jumped off the Taj Mahal if Papa had asked him. He was
afraid of everyone and everything and behaved most of
his time like a stuffed English shirt. 'It's all very well for
you, Lindsay! You're not being palmed off to strange
relations in some godforsaken English county no one's
ever heard of!'

'Don't use language like that in front of me, boy!' his
father cautioned.

Rory said tearfully, 'Papa, I will *not* leave India! If I
can't go back to Glengarth, I would rather live in an
Indian compound than go and live with strangers.' His air
of bravado was deserting him, uncertainty was upon him
yet again. Injustice was being meted out to him, and he
could not accept it.

'*Silence, boy!*'

Lindsay and the girls flinched, even if Rory Duncan did
not.

'You, Rory, have just displayed the very reason why I
cannot send you back to Glengarth. You and your brother
never agree on any account – though it is not Lindsay's
fault, but *yours*!' James jabbed a derogatory finger at his
younger son. 'I am well aware, sir, of your surreptitious
little jaunts into the native compound, and I don't care at
all for your underhand ways. Do not think for one
moment I'm not aware of what kind of little toad you have
picked up in the compound along with your dhobi-itch,

your prickly heat-rashes and your septic boiling earaches! And let me tell you, that not only *Arjoo*, but also that old Bengali-babu of Dharkli's, scratching all day long on his charpoy, would have been turned out a long time ago for corrupting your morals and left to beg in the native bazaar had not your mother's soft-hearted intervention prevented their instant dismissal! However, we shall speak no more about the sordid aspects of your life. You have known from the start you boys would one day be sent back to England to be educated, and that your stay in India was but of a short duration. So I really don't know what all the fuss is about.'

'The fuss is about splitting us up and dividing the family when there's no need. I *don't* understand your reasons for separating Kitty from Christabel when they are so close. It's not so bad for me, I can take the knocks, but what about hurting the girls.'

'The girls are not your problem but mine. All I know is, your grandfather would be unable to cope with your childish tantrums more suited to a toddler of two than a young man of ... how old are you, eight, nine, ten?'

No, you don't even know how old I am, Papa! Rory thought to himself furiously, *which just goes to show how much you care about me*! 'I shall be ten next January, Papa,' he replied stiffly.

'Then it's about time you grew up. You will soon be going off to Breedon Hall to live with your Burrett relatives – in your own best interests, I might add, and that's an end to it!'

'So Kitty and I are the outcasts, just like lepers banished to an outlandish colony?'

'Don't be absurd!'

'Well, I *am* absurd, you're always telling me I'm not from the same mould as Lindsay.'

'And for God's sake, Rory, stop your impertinence! I despair of you.' His father's hand slapped down on his desk and made the water carafe, tumbler, and everyone shudder. 'You are nothing but a wilful, headstrong boy who will come to a very bad end because he has all the makings of a wastrel!'

'Thank you, Papa, now I know exactly what you think of me.' It had been a hellish day for him and he had no desire to break down in front of the girls, in front of Lindsay, and in front of Papa. Rory turned to leave the room but James thundered:

'Come back at once, sir! I have not dismissed you as yet.'

Lindsay, fearful of prolonging the unhappy scene, his back to their father, muttered under his breath so that no one else would be aware of what he was saying: 'Stop it! Don't be a fool *all* your life, Rory! Why do you have to bait him at every turn?'

'Because I *hate* him for what he did to Mama!'

'Oh, grow up!' Lindsay sighed.

Rory shook him off and, taking up a stance on the threshold, turned back to his father. 'Goodbye, Father. I sincerely hope you know what you're doing and don't live to regret such a decision.' He banged the door after him.

Harsh, bitter words spoken in the anguish of the moment, only to be analysed and regretted in after years when time had done its healing work, and he was able to recognize his father's unenviable plight on the day of death.

But he was only a man in the making in that tragic summer of 1899.

PART TWO

'The childhood shows the man,
As morning shows the day.'

John Milton
Paradise Regained

CHAPTER FIVE

Six-foot logs cut from the estate burned in the great fire-place, and still there was a chill in the air. The inner hall was heavily draped in antique Gobelins tapestries to keep out the draughts. But rather than enhance, they served only to add to the aura of decay around Glengarth Castle.

Castles were all very well for kings in ermine robes, thought Lindsay miserably as he huddled closer to the fire, his Indian suntan paled into insignificance after just one week in Scotland. Such austere surroundings were hardly conducive to a family atmosphere and homely living, yet, in a way he was glad to be back.

He thought about the long voyage home and Rory's tedious behaviour. On the night before they had left Baharabad, he had made scenes with their father because Suzy had to be left behind in India. Father had told him the Leicestershire relatives would have a fit if a monkey appeared along with the luggage. Sula had pointed out that Suzy would have to be quarantined because of rabies. In a cage for six months, in a cold English climate, Suzy would surely die of pneumonia. Rory had at last seen sense.

When, on the *SS Britannia* bound for Liverpool, the four of them had been put into the safe-keeping of Sister Agnes and Sister Hilary, two Anglican nuns returning to England, Rory had again played up, displaying his im-maturity through endless practical jokes which had reduced the poor nuns to tears. Having had to spend his tenth birthday on the rock of Gibraltar where the Barbary apes reminded him of Suzy, according to him, his one and only true friend in the world, was truly turning the knife in the wound!

But, in a way, Lindsay felt he was able to sympathize

with his brother: shipboard life had been hellishly boring,
what with all the talk of the Boer War. They had had to
endure the dawn of the new century digesting Kruger for
breakfast, Kitchener for lunch, Buller for dinner, and
drinks in between, served with a dash of Afrikaner!

'You cold, boy?' His grandfather's abrupt question cut
across Lindsay's sombre thoughts.

'Yes, sir.'

The laird and his grandson were having a 'man-to-man'
discussion along with the after dinner Port wine, though
the old laird did all the drinking and talking.

Christabel had been chivvied along to bed by Grandfather, who did not care for too many women around him.
Aunt Jean Hamilton and her two daughters, Moira and
Morag, were in the Solar, where the women of the household were usually banished by the laird. Moira and Morag
were a great deal older than either Christabel or he, and
so was their brother Iain, Grandfather's steward and estate
factor. Iain Hamilton was married, and had two sons,
Aeneas and Bruce. And there again, mused Lindsay, the
age discrepancy was such that the two second cousins
would be no companions for Christabel and himself. Not
that there would be much time to get used to them as he
was off to Eton soon, with a great deal to think about.

'Mollycoddled the lot of you!' said his grandfather out
of the blue. 'Too much mollycoddling ain't good for the
character – makes one lily-livered. Pass the Port, boy.'
The laird helped himself to a liberal dose from the
decanter and shifted his heavily bandaged, gouty leg more
comfortably on the footstool. 'Gives me the very devil,
this leg o' mine, boy. My advice is, lay off the Port,
Lindsay, if you don't care to suffer a life o' misery in y' old
age. Now then, what did you do with yourself today?'

'Nothing much, Grandfather. It's too snowy outside to
do very much.'

'Hrrumph!' The laird snorted derisively, but reserved
opinion until later.

Presently, after a cat-nap of loud snores lasting several
minutes, he jerked upright again in his padded armchair.
His grandson still huddled miserably in front of the fire,

looking as though he wished, in that moment, he were a million miles away from Glengarth. The laird said grumpishly, 'You gone to sleep, boy?'

'Sorry ... I know I'm not much company tonight. I was thinking about other things.'

'Leave the thinking to intellectuals, boy. Far better you saddle a horse and learn to be a laird by popping poachers and rabbits, without *thinking* like a bally professor.'

'Yes, Grandfather.'

'Tomorrow morning, you get out there and learn all about estate management from your cousin Iain Hamilton, and maybe tomorrow night I'll be able to get some decent conversation from you, huh?'

'Yes, Grandfather. Sorry, but I *am* rather tired tonight.'

'Then off t' bed with you, Lindsay m' boy. Can't stand sissy men around me. Pass the Port before you go.'

'The decanter's empty.'

'God's teeth, so it is! Well, send Murray to the cellars to fetch another bottle. Use your initiative, boy! Sha'n't be around for ever, y' know, and then you'll have to start doing for y'self and Glengarth, huh?'

'Yes, Grandfather.'

The following morning, despite the snowy ground, Lindsay rode out on his sturdy Highland-bred horse. Glengarth was an animal sanctuary as much as a forestry estate. As well as the wild animals at Glengarth, pine martens were reared, the dark brown, creamy-throated creatures providing an additional income from their valuable pelts sold to the fur-trade. But the deer were Lindsay's favourite animals, and he hated to see them culled, although he knew it was necessary in order to contain their numbers.

Lindsay, cautiously and without wanting to disturb the wildlife, watched a handsome roebuck scratching the velvet covering off its growing horns. When they sawed themselves against the tree trunks in great numbers, not only did they rub off their own winter protection, but also the bark of the trees, despoiling them and leaving the trees prone to disease.

Lindsay couldn't help noticing too, how the estate seemed to have an air of neglect about it: haphazard felling, a lot of the timber left to rot, and unrepaired fences so that the animals could wander indiscriminately into the plantations. Had the plantations been properly supervised, as well as the animals, this would not happen, thought Lindsay sadly.

But Glengarth was not his as yet, and so he could do nothing for the moment. The roebuck plunged off deeper into the forest at his intrusion, and he lost sight of it. A little while later he witnessed a fight between a wild cat and a golden eagle. The splendidness of two such ferocious creatures, and the cruel beauty of that fight to the death, was both exciting and disturbing.

Without the chattering company of his sister this morning, for Christabel also liked to ride, Lindsay was glad that he had taken his grandfather's advice about not hugging the fireside because he felt cold and miserable, but to get outside and enjoy the freedom and beauty of Glengarth. Lindsay urged his horse down the steep sides of the glen, to the loch shore.

The mail packet, which also brought a small amount of provisions to this part of the West Highlands, had just arrived, belching its last gasp. The *Mary Blythe* was owned by his Great-Uncle Hamish MacDearg from Glasgow, and Lindsay watched Angus MacPhee tie her up at the jetty. The blue and white cross of St Andrew, the Scottish flag, fluttered astern. The last time he'd heard anything about his grandfather's brother-in-law, the old man was on his last legs.

'Morning, boy,' Angus, boatman as well as postman, greeted Lindsay with genuine affection. He remembered the Laird of Glengarth's grandson well enough from four years ago, a youngster who had been carted off to heathen lands by his father, James, because the Laird of Glengarth and the heir apparent had quarrelled.

Wellington boots with a pair of Stewart dress-tartan socks turned down above the boots, a briar pipe stuck in his mouth and belching a little, just like the *Mary Blythe*, Angus took stock of the flaxen-haired lad. 'So, you'er back in the glen, I ken – though the news is from the lowlands and you'er Uncle Hamish. My condolences, boy, on the loss of you'er mother in heathen lands.'

'Thank you, Angus.'

'I'm away to the castle for a wee respite.' He winked meaningly. 'As like as not, the factor'll have a sack o' mail for me to take back to Glasgow.'

Angus stepped off the boat.

'How's my great-uncle?' Lindsay asked hesitantly, knowing full well that he was breaching family loyalties by asking about the health of his grandfather's old enemy.

'Always dying, but bonny nevertheless. Aye, Hamish is bonny and thinking o' modernizing his boatyard in keeping with the new century.'

Angus went on up the glen with the mail to be delivered to Iain Hamilton's estate office.

Lindsay was about to follow Angus, but smoke from the cotter's cottage on the tiny loch-island of Rill attracted his attention. He forgot about returning to Glengarth just then, drawn suddenly by the homely smoke signals – warmth to be found beside a tenant's fireside, and acquaintances that would one day be important to him when he became the laird. It might just prove to be far more interesting, too, rather than listening to Angus's boring gossip. Lindsay urged his horse across the causeway that joined Rill to the mainland.

He did not bargain for the cotter's hostility.

A young girl of about eight squatted on the cottage doorstep, gutting fish. In the bitter weather she wore only a thin homespun dress with a plaid shawl around her skinny shoulders. Her long dark hair whipped into her eyes by the fierce north wind; she scowled at him with such ferocity, for a moment Lindsay thought she would fly at him with the gutting knife.

She looked him up and down as he sat there on his horse, a pale, unsmiling boy resolutely staring back at her.

Lindsay noticed how green the girl's eyes were, and how they flashed him her wild and insolent messages – who did *he* think he was, trespassing on *her* territory! A real little savage, and not a brown one this time, Lindsay thought to himself as he urged his pony nearer. He asked, 'Where are your parents?'

And then the man had come out of the cottage. His jet-black, tangled hair streamed in the wind, his beard was unkempt. Leather jerkin unfastened to expose him in all his grossness, he had a coarse mat of dark hair on his chest. He reminded Lindsay of a huge bear. In the thick leather belt holding up his oilskin trousers, Lindsay saw the dirk.

But what *really* drew his attention, was the roll of bloodstained, fresh animal skins under the man's arm. At once Lindsay recognized them as the highly valued, gold-brown marten furs.

'Och now,' said the man, stooping over the girl gutting fish at his feet, 'didna thy wee black book y' ma's been larnin' ye, no' tell thee o' disrespect, hinny?'

The old family nanny, Miss MacCready, had spoken Gaelic. She had looked after Iain's two young sons, Aeneas and Bruce, for a short time before she died a year ago, while Lindsay and his brother and sisters had been out in India. But now Lindsay recalled Miss MacCready telling him nursery stories in the tongue of the Celts. This was not true Gaelic, only a bastard brogue adopted by those of the south. Lindsay recognized the man for what he was, a n'er do well, a poacher, a 'foreigner.'

The girl scowled at the big dark man in much the same way as she had scowled at Lindsay. Then her tormentor pinched her bare arm. She did not flinch although he must have hurt her.

'Aye,' continued the ruffian, still bent over the girl, his broad back to Lindsay, who wasn't aware that the man was referring to him in that moment. 'And another wee matter o' disrespect about trespassers ridin' for a fall ... *D'ye ken!*' He whirled, his grin broad and wide as he held his dirk in his hand. '*Begone*, fine fellow m' lad, else ye'll end up on the gutting slab along with thy fish!'

Lindsay, foolishly, turned tail and fled across the causeway, the man's deep belly laugh of amusement following him up the glen.

That night at dinner Lindsay asked his grandfather

about the people who lived on the island.

'Fisherfolk,' the laird replied. 'They're all damned fisher folk, crofting folk or thieving folk around here. There's nought else for us in the Highlands except English poverty! Why?'

'Oh nothing, I just wondered, that's all.'

'Come, come!' He had glowered at his grandson and heir. 'Ain't like you, boy, to beat around the bush. Say what's on your mind and be done.'

'I went to the island this morning, and didn't much care for the man living there. He's a bully.'

'Ain't no man living on the island. Donald Gowrie drowned a couple of years ago and there's only his widow and young daughter left on the island. She ain't married again, has she Jeanie?' Snowy white brows lowered across the dinner table, the laird questioned his daughter.

Aunt Jean wore steel-rimmed spectacles and had a thin, angular face. With her grey hair severely drawn back into a bun on the nape of her neck, she looked perpetually harassed. She frowned at her father, and reminded Lindsay of a schoolmistress displeased with her pupil.

Jean was hoping that her father wouldn't say anything truly outrageous in front of the young girls, as he sometimes had a habit of doing. She shrugged her thin shoulders under the tartan stole keeping her warm. Her rather sorry-looking evening gown of black velvet, for she always dressed for dinner, had certainly seen better days, the nap worn smooth and dullish green with age as well as the damp atmosphere of Glengarth. 'Not that I know of, Father.'

'Then she's taken to living with some foreigner, I'll be bound, the shameless hussy. What does the fellow look like, Lindsay?'

Lindsay described the man in detail, but refrained from mentioning the marten pelts. Poachers, he knew well enough, were a menace, a drain on any large estate, and ought to be dealt with severely. So he didn't know why he wanted to keep such information from his grandfather.

'Sounds like that blackguard from Raasay is back. What's he doing here, Jean? You might ask Iain since he's the damned overseer around the place. Now then, if that scoundrel is poaching on my preserves, I'll drill a hole in him *so big* ... the Edinburgh to London Express will get through without *any-ee* trouble! Where Fleddon an Fletcher is, you'll find gin-traps and worse, and you might remember that for some future date, Lindsay. It's rumoured he once killed a man with his bare hands during a drunken brawl at Gairloch. True or not, I *won't* have that scoundrel around Glengarth, no sir! Pass the Port, Jean: and you gels, get yourselves to bed.'

'Father,' said Aunt Jean to the laird, after Christabel, Morag and Moira had dutifully left the table, and very glad about it, as Lindsay saw by their faces, 'Lindsay must leave Glengarth tomorrow.'

'Why? He's only just come *back* to us!'

'He has to go to school, Father. The new term starts in a week's time and he must settle in before then. The train from Achnasheen is unreliable in bad weather, so we must leave him plenty of time for travelling.'

'Where's he going?'

'Now you *know* where he's going, Father! James has had his sons' names down for Eton since birth. Lindsay's *and* Rory's!'

'James? Who's James?' The laird reached for the decanter of Port wine.

'Now, now Father! Stop being naughty! Lindsay is off to Eton – the same as his father, *James*! And the same as his grandfather and great-grandfather before him, and no doubt ...'

'Please hold your chatter, Jean! I'm not a complete and utter nincompoop, though you treat me like one. God's teeth, daughters! They are a father's ruination. Take my advice, Lindsay, m'boy. *Never* have daughters,' he belched. 'And lay off the Port if ye ever wish to reach a sensible old age.'

CHAPTER SIX

Rory had been determined to hate Breedon Hall because Glengarth had been denied him. He did nothing of the sort. He loved the mellow Jacobean house from the moment he set eyes on it. His mother's home, she had told him all about the great Charnwood Forest nearby, of dear old dappled Polly, the nursery rocking-horse, and Nanny Delish, his mother's old nurse, who now ruled the brood of younger Burretts. Even so, his heart still yearned for Scotland, the place he remembered best. After all, he had spent the first six years of his life there. While he was prepared to tolerate his new abode, he was determined to go on disliking his 'Sassenach' relatives – his Aunt Ada especially! He recalled that awful journey a week ago when his Aunt had reduced him to a quivering jelly. She was worse than Sula, Papa and Shawmoss all rolled into one!

The *SS Britannia* had docked at Liverpool on 15th January, a week after his tenth birthday which he had spent in Gibraltar. Lord and Lady Burrett were there to meet the ship. His Uncle Austen was a tall, spare, kindly looking man with rheumy blue eyes and a runny nose brought about by chronic catarrh. In comparison, Aunt Ada was a large, robust woman with a florid face and a wart with dark hairs sprouting from her chin. 'I hope,' she said, 'you two children have not brought a lot of unnecessary luggage with you. The bare essentials, that is all small people like you require.'

'Sula did the packing,' Rory ventured, and received a dirty look from his aunt.

'I hope, Austen,' she said, turning to him, 'you know what you have undertaken!'

Lindsay and Christabel had travelled up to Scotland by

train, in the company of their cousin and grandfather's
factor, Iain Hamilton, and Rory had wished fervently that
he and Kitty could have gone with them. His anxiety had
intensified with every revolution of the Rolls' aristocratic
wheels, punctuated by the funny little chauffeur's Cockney comments. Benjamin Gammon had to sit on a
cushion in order to see over the steering-wheel and had
supplied the only entertainment during that interminable
journey towards an unknown destiny. Deeper and deeper
into the middle heartlands of England swaddled in a thick
blanket of fog, further and further from the golden East,
Rory thought about that other journey from Baharabad to
Bombay with all its exotic nuances of *life* and colour and
excitement. There was nothing much exciting about fog!

'Take note of your surroundings, Rory Duncan,' his
aunt had said. 'The looms of Loughborough gave hosiery
to the world and the Cherry Orchard Foundry, Great Paul
of St Paul's Cathedral. I hope you are paying attention.'

His aunt sat next to him in all her furs and finery.
Several small fox-heads dangled forlornly over her left
shoulder and stared back at him with mournful glass eyes:
they were no doubt mourning their own deadness, thought
Rory Duncan, who at once empathized with those defunct
foxes. The English countryside had nothing on him, so
thickly swaddled in gloom was he. In fact, his fingers and
toes were frozen stiff, despite the warm luxury of the
Rolls.

'What are you dreaming about, Rory Duncan?' Aunt
Ada had asked at the time, peering down at him via her
lorgnette attached to a length of velvet ribbon. 'I've
spoken to you several times, but receive no reply. Most
rude of you! Your father warned me about your difficult
and lazy nature, and advised me to take you in hand
straightaway. I hope he is mistaken as to your character –
or lack of it.'

He couldn't even be bothered to turn his head to *the
voice*! His entire life had been a series of cannons
resounding through the valley of death, and now he didn't
care any more. Let the old dragon breathe fire and brim-
stone over him; he might as well get used to hell.

'Tell me, dear boy, DO YOU SPEAK ENGLISH OR NOT?' She mouthed the words slowly, loudly and distinctly, the way the British Raj, he had noticed, spoke to Indians, fools and foreigners.

Rory filled his lungs to capacity and emulated his papa on Burns' Night. '*Noo, I canna spake Sassenach, Wee, sleekit, cow'rin', tim'rous beastie, O what a panic's in thy breastie! Thou need na start awa sae hasty, Wi' bickering brattle! I wad be laith to rin an' chase thee, Wi' murd'ring pattle!*'

His aunt had almost, but not quite, swooned.

'Heavens above, Austen!' she had gasped in outrage. 'Your sister has a mental defective for a son.'

She had swiftly moved away from him then, as though she assessed his affliction to be contagious. Then she had fanned her florid face with one of her gloves. 'No wonder his father wanted to get rid of him. But he could at least have warned us about this . . . this *pec-u-liar* child! Do you think it could be anything to do with the hot sun on his head, Austen?'

Rory grinned, showing all his teeth, just like a mental defective. 'Och noo, Aunty! Ah alwa' wore ma *sola topi.*'

She had flapped her glove at him, and told him to be quiet before turning away to look out of the window, quite distraught. But she kept her own counsel for the rest of the journey while Kitty slept in the corner of the sumptuous car, and his Uncle Austen tried to suppress a grin behind his handkerchief.

From that moment on, Rory Duncan never forgave his aunt Ada, who was no relative of *his*, though he was quite prepared to put up with his Uncle Austen who was, after all, his dear mama's own flesh and blood.

Rory, during his first week in England, learned that his cousin Rupert, Uncle Austen's eldest son and heir, was away fighting the Boers in South Africa. The only two cousins left at home were soppy *girls*! He'd had enough of Christabel on the voyage to Liverpool, and was glad to see the back of *her*! Girls were a nuisance, and he didn't want to know about them apart from the fact that Jane and Leonora did their lessons with a French governess, who would now be taking Kitty under her wing.

Cousin Humphrey, six months older than he and nearest to him in age, was at his prep school, and the twins, Mordan and Michael, were away at Harrow, so he would not meet *them* until the Easter holidays, as he himself was to be shunted off to prep school in Dorset before he had had a chance to assimilate his Leicestershire surroundings.

All too soon the second half of term at his new school sped by and Rory once again found himself back in Leicestershire. Conversation, as was usual in a household where the eldest son and heir was away fighting for his country, veered to the Boer War and Rupert's great part in it.

'We'll teach those jumped up Bowers a thing or two,' Mordan lisped, shovelling Brussels sprouts into his mouth. 'Who do those puny Afwickaners think they are, declawing war on the greatest nation on earth?'

'Master Mordan, don't talk with your mouth full,' said Nanny Delish, frowning at him over her spectacles while she chalked up the following day's junior menu on the nursery blackboard. Miss Vayer, the girls' governess, had dispensed with its use, as the girls, too, were on holiday.

'You're only supposed to *eat* with your mouth full, Mord,' Humphrey guffawed and earned another frown from Nanny Delish.

'What a *w'awe* inspiwing conversation,' Rory lisped, loath to be outdone.

The three brothers continued to ignore the stranger in their midst.

Nanny Delish wiped Kitty's mouth with a soft white flannel. 'Take Miss Kitty and Miss Leonora downstairs for evening prayers, Sally,' she instructed the nursery maid. 'You boys, hurry up and finish your suppers otherwise you'll be late for prayers. You know how her ladyship hates unpunctuality.'

Oh Lor', thought Rory to himself, clutching his head. Was his aunt going to turn out to be a female Shawmoss? Oh God, please NO!

'I don't like fish,' Humphrey grumbled, and then continued with the Boer saga. 'Anyway, those damned Boers can't last much longer, more's the pity. I wish I could have gone with Rupert.'

'Here, here,' Rory Duncan agreed.

The three brothers exchanged glances. They took advantage of the moment since Nanny Delish had also left the nursery dining-room.

'Thinks himself quite a dawg, don't he?' Mordan said.

'Without a wag, what!' Humphrey again chortled like a faulty tap.

It was Rory's turn to ignore such louts.

Michael, the peacemaker, steered the conversation into calmer waters. 'When he comes home, I suppose old Rupe will marry Charlie.'

'What Charlie?' Mordan spluttered out the sprouts he had assiduously shovelled in.

'You know, Mord! Charlotte the clotted cream cake ... the old Marquis of Frisby's funny-looking daughter.'

'By Jove, Michael! You don't mean the skinny one who looks the same from the front as the back because she has no bosoms! We could grow runner beans up her,' Humphrey added in disgust.

'Now, now, Master Humphrey!' said Nanny Delish breezing back into the nursery dining-room, 'that's no way to talk about Master Rupert's affianced.'

'How did she know we were talking about skinny Charlie?' Mordan hissed behind Nanny's back.

'Nannies know *everything*!' Humphrey replied from behind his hand. 'Nannies are like God, *immortalicsized.*' He raised his voice, 'Nanny, you ought to complain to Cook, this fish is *unspeakable*!'

'It's there to eat, not to talk to, Master Humphrey.'

She went away again on another errand and left them playing with their food.

'I bet old Rupe doesn't have to put up with boiled fish in the mess,' Humphrey grumbled yet again, pushing aside his plate.

'In a mess, or in *the* mess?' Mordan asked.

'Both. I say, Mord, just look at the way cousin Rory

relishes water-soushy. Must be the curry's burnt out his taste buds, eh what?'

'Sassenach swine.'

'*What* did you say, Scotch kipper?'

'You heard.' Rory and Humphrey locked battle glances.

'You said something rude, Scotch kipper. What was it?'

'Mind your own business.' He knew he was laying his life on the line, but he felt he had to assert himself right away, lest the Three Musketeers got away with the idea that he was a moral coward who could be bullied to death.

Humphrey, across the table, grabbed the lapels of his cousin's tweed jacket cut in the Norfolk style. 'I'll make it my business to give you a damn good thrashing, Scotch pancake, unless you mind your manners in front of us.'

'You and whose army, camel hump?'

'*WHAT*?' Humphrey roared, bringing his bunched fist closer to the Scottish nose, itching to flatten it.

'Forget it, Hump,' Michael said. 'He's bragging!'

'Uitlanders and Western Owiental Gentlemen are awl the same,' Mordan drawled. 'Infewior aliens spoiling fower a fight. In my opinion, only an Anglo-Saxon Federwal Empire would bwing such nigger-lovers to heel ...'

'*My God*!' It was Rory's turn to leap up, eye to eye with Humphrey and Mordan across the supper table. He raised his fists in Mordan's face. 'You don't even know what you're talking about, you monkey-mouthed moron! What have *your* ancestors done for the Empire, I should like to know? Mine have spilled guts and blood on every battle-field between Culloden and the Khyber ...'

'Which just goes to prove what miserable fighters they must be,' said Humphrey grinning like a Cheshire cat. 'Told you this one was a barbarian from north of the border, didn't I, chaps?'

'I hope the Boers turn your brother's hide into a water-bottle ... or ... or a tent!' Rory retaliated.

'I say, Hump, this Scotch pancake has just insulted old Rupe.'

'I heard. Didn't know Scotchmen were black, did you, Mord?'

'Oh, ha-ha-ha! Good one, Hump! This Scotch pancake got a bit overdone in the sun, what-ho?'

'Care for a wog poppadom, anyone?' Humphrey grinned even more widely.

'Let's pulverwize him and send him home to his papa like strawbewwy jam on a chapatti, shall we, Hump? After all, we *all* know about the *Raj* wog-lovers and their preference for wog-chapattis, don't we?'

Unfortunately Rory could not see that his cousins were baiting him. Unfortunately, too, Nanny Delish chose the wrong moment to return to the dining-room, just as he shouted across the table, 'Damn your Sassenach eyes!'

'*Master Rory*! I am shocked! That is no way for a young gentleman to talk. You will apologize at once to your cousins.'

'I'm damned if I will!'

Nanny Delish shook her head sadly, her mild blue eyes couched in pockets of wrinkles evincing deep pain. 'Your mama, Master Rory, was the sweetest child I've ever had the privilege of minding. She would turn in her grave if she could hear you now.'

He bunched his fists in his pockets. The reminder of how sweet his mama was, added fuel to fire.

'Apologize at once, Master Rory!'

'I will not!'

'Then I have no choice but to report you to her ladyship. Now then, you boys will all sit down again at the table and finish your meal. If you do not finish in time for prayers, the plates will be put in the sideboard. You will eat cold fish, boiled potatoes, sprouts and cabbage for breakfast. And if you don't eat it then, you will have the same meal dished up to you again and again, until every morsel is eaten. Have I made myself clear?'

'What about food-poisoning, Nanny?'

'Most unpleasant as well as painful, Master Humphrey. So I suggest you do as you're told within the next ten minutes. Do you boys understand?'

'Yes Nanny,' they all dutifully chorused as they made short work of their main course, which was followed by cold tapioca pudding.

Afterwards, it was time for evening prayers.

Leonora was waiting for Rory outside the Shukborough
Room where prayers were held each morning and evening
in the presence of the family and servants. A year younger
than he, Leonora, her prayer-book in one small hand,
caught hold of Rory's sleeve with the other. 'Don't take
any notice of my brothers, Rory. They are bullies, and will
rag you all the time unless you can stick up for yourself.'

'Thanks for nothing!' He shook her off. Leonora had
no doubt been listening at the keyhole to know so accur-
ately what had been happening in the nursery dining-
room after her departure with Kitty. He took his place
beside young and pretty Miss Vayer who was golden like
his mama. But his aunt had other plans for him.

'Rory Duncan, I hear you have been behaving like a
savage by swearing at everyone.' Aunt Ada vanquished
him from behind her lorgnette. 'How dare you display
your barbarous upbringing in MY home! Come out here
in front of everyone and read the text for this evening.
Afterwards, you can copy it out one hundred times. Read
clearly, Luke 15 ...' she jabbed a blunt finger at the open
page of the Bible. 'Likewise I say unto you, there is joy in
the presence of the angels of God over one sinner that
repenteth ...' Go on from there, you're supposed to be
reading, not I. Verse 11, and don't dither or stutter, otherwise I shall double your punishment.'

She loved the sound of her own voice: cannons in the
valley of death! He had jumped from an Indian frying-pan
straight into a Sassenach fire, he couldn't help thinking,
while pain and humiliation, deep and unremitting ate into
his soul.

Rory took a deep breath and tried to control himself.
But he still managed to falter in his nervousness: 'A-a cert-
certain man had-had a son ... two sons ...' Someone
tittered, he guessed it to be Humphrey. Rory coughed and
started again, but received such a look of venom from his
aunt, he pulled himself together and paid attention. '...
and the younger of them said to his father, Father, give me
the portion of goods that falleth to me. And he divided
unto them his living. And not many days after the younger

son gathered all together and took his journey into a far country ...' What a good idea! thought Rory Duncan, and began to make his plans forthwith.

His second mistake was made during the reading of Rupert's letters when prayers and hymns (with Cousin Jane at the piano) were concluded.

Rupert, in his accumulated correspondence from the Cape, vividly described Chronje's forces being driven off into the veldt after the surrender of Paardeberg and the relief of White's garrison at Ladysmith, and Rory Duncan had chosen to yawn!

'*Rory Duncan*!' Aunt Ada's voice had rent the air asunder. 'Your manners are deplorable! Firstly you swear at Nanny Delish and my sons in the nursery, secondly you are late for prayers, thirdly you are a below average reader of the English word, and fourthly you do not hesitate to show your boredom for Rupert's insight into a war to save the Empire! Let me remind you, you young scallywag, that today's commonplace history lesson is tomorrow's example!'

He hadn't a clue what she meant, but then his aunt was like that, her obscure remarks could be calculated to give Nostradamus himself a headache.

'You will go to the schoolroom after prayers,' Aunt Ada continued wrathfully, 'and there you will copy out Proverbs 13 verse 4, one hundred times, followed by this evening's text one hundred times. After that you may take yourself to bed, where you can yawn your head off to your heart's content. Miss Vayer, you will bring me the boy's lines; I shall check his spelling personally!'

He hated her with a burning zeal: more than he had ever hated old boggy Shawmoss.

He hated his aunt Ada even more than that after he had copied out: 'The soul of the sluggard desireth and hath nothing; But the soul of the diligent shall be made fat,' one hundred times followed by the parable of the Prodigal Son, one hundred times.

Vengeance is sweet!

He pretended to be fast asleep when his three cousins came to bed. He shared with them the same bedroom in dormitory-like proximity, without peace or privacy.

When he was quite certain that his three cousins were dead to the world, he crept out of bed and speedily emptied their last-minute, pre-bedtime chamber-pots over their heads. Then he fled to the linen-room where he locked himself in for the night.

Tucking himself among the warm sheets and blankets on one of the wide shelves, he listened to the howls of wrath emanating from the other side of the linen-room door. It was music to his ears.

Grinning to himself, he was only sorry that those three upstart cousins of his weren't Hindus of the caste system who would require three months purification after what he had done to them.

Rory consoled himself with the thought that Cousin Humphrey would also be sleeping with a large, flea-bitten, very stinking dead rat in place of a hot-water bottle. He hoped it had not been discovered as yet, tucked in neatly at the foot of Humphrey's bed.

Rory yawned, free at last to indulge his slothful habits.

He fell instantly into a blissful sleep among the lavender-scented sheets nobody could get their hands on, since he retained the linen-room key.

The following morning Rory was busy saddling up the little grey mare, Misty, Uncle Austen had allocated to him. The stable-yard was glaringly deserted, and he wondered how much his three awful cousins had parted with in the way of bribes, to keep the grooms at bay.

Then they sauntered around the corner, plus-fours, Norfolk jackets and leather boots in great evidence, along with Humphrey's tombstone teeth. Rory pretended he hadn't seen them.

'By Jove, Mord, look at those flaccid girth-straps. One can tell he ain't used to riding horses, only donkeys, eh what!'

'Wrong! Listen, camel hump, I'm used to high-bred polo ponies. Neither did I have to saddle my own horse. We always had servants to wait on us. It's not my fault I have to live with poor relations.'

Mordan came up to him and kicked his ankle. '*Bar-bair-wian!*'

'What a pity you can't speak English, Mord.'

For his Scotch lip, he received another kick on the ankle.

Rory regarded the three brothers steadily: he was not afraid of them; he could stand up to all three, any day! Humphrey's spiky black hair stuck out like an indignant golliwog's coiffure. They all looked as though Nanny Delish had taken the scrubbing brush to them very vigorously indeed. Pale pink English skins positively scintillated in the daylight!

'*Camel-Kaffir!*' Humphrey jeered.

Coming from him, it was *too* much! Rory retaliated. 'It takes one camel to recognize another, eh Hump?'

In the next instant he was felled to the ground with Humphrey's head stuck in his ribs. Winded and hurting badly, for a moment or two Rory didn't know what had hit him. He lay on his back in the recently mucked-out bedding straw and stable manure. Mordan came up and kicked him. 'Take what's coming to you in weturn fower the stinking piss-pots you tipped on us last night, you *bar-bair-wian!*'

Humphrey sat down on top of him. Astride Rory's chest he pummelled his cousin with savage fists. 'And this is for the filthy rat you put in my bed, you filthy rat!' He raised his fist, about to flatten Rory Roskillen's nose but Rory turned his head quickly and Humphrey's fist struck the cobblestones. 'Oww-ouch ...' He sucked his grazed knuckles. Humphrey tried again.

'*Ow's zat!*' He aimed another blow at his cousin's head but Rory managed to dodge the raining blows and pushing Humphrey off his chest, struggled to his feet. He then let fly with his riding boot and caught Humphrey smartly on the shin as he, too, staggered to his feet. '*Bloody wog! Dirty native fighter!*' Humphrey circled his cousin like a prize fighter.

'Listen you chaps,' said Michael hesitantly, not sure whether this business of Cousin Rory coming to live with them deserved baptism by fire. The bullying had all got

rather out of hand. 'He's had enough. Leave him alone.
Three against one ain't really fair, y'know. Can't hit a
fellow once he's down, Humphrey.'

'I'm going to *kill* him, so look away if you can't stand
the blood.'

'*Drop dead, Sassenach*! I'll kill all three of you yet, you
wait and see!' Rory shook the dirty straw and mistiness
out of his eyes and faced Humphrey, the ultimate pugilist.
'Up with them, Sassenach swine!'

Humphrey let fly but Rory Duncan ducked. Coming up
with a fist to Humphrey's big nose, he landed one straight
on it. Humphrey leapt back with blood spurting from his
nostrils.

'*Olé*!' Rory shouted.

'*Come on, Hump*! Slaughter the little toe-wag,' Mordan
cheered his brother on from the sidelines. 'Let's pulverwize the little Scotch poppadom and send him home to his
papa like a mashed stwawbewwy on a chapatti!'

Rory had had enough of Mordan. He turned and kneed
him hard in the groin. Mordan doubled over and
screaming his head off, fell into the manure heap with his
hands clutching his crotch. And in that instant, too, a
voice that could freeze all the fires of hell brought the boys
to attention. '*Rory Duncan of Glengarth, what do you
think you are doing*?'

Rory turned again to see Aunt Ada just like God clad
in female attire striding the cobblestones of the stable
yard. She wore her riding-habit and in her hand she
wielded her riding-crop.

The blood congealed in his veins. She reminded him of
the Princess Mary of Teck, that unsmiling, adopted
German dragon of St George, who would one day rule
England.

'Come here at once, you little hooligan!'

Obediently he went to stand before her, while her three
sons stood in the background, stupidly giggling into their
hands. 'I saw what you did to Mordan. You *are* a
barbarian!'

'He called me names. He and Humphrey started it.'

'I don't care *who* started it. How *dare* you use your feet to fight. How *dare* you insult my sons. How *dare* you presume to be what you are not, you little heathen! Civilized gentlemen do not kick and bite and knee their opponents. Go to your room at once. I'll deal with you later, Rory Dun ...'

He stood his ground. 'Aunt Ada, I have three more names besides the two you already know. They are, Gavin, Will ... ill ... yum ...' The look she subjected him to withered him to a pinhead. He swallowed nervously, his voice fading away into a dismal little silence.

'Go to the nursery at once!' she croaked, finding her own voice at last. 'Tell Nanny that I authorize her to hose you down with cold water, you brat. After which, she may tuck you up in your cot. *GO*! I do not want to see you again for the rest of the day!'

He went.

But he washed his own face and hands. A face that was flaming from Scottish indignation and wrath induced by the hand of the Sassenach. He would never forgive her, never! In the same way that he had never *quite* forgiven Sula for smacking his face on the day of his mother's funeral, he would never forgive Aunt Ada for treating him like a leper.

He didn't call upon Nanny Delish to do any of the things his aunt had instructed. He went to the deserted schoolroom, found a stub of pencil and an exercise book and started drafting a letter to his father and Sula in India.

Dear Papa and Sula,

I can no longer stay in this abominable household. They are persecuting me night and day, just because I was born north of the border. I loved my mama, but I don't love her relatives. They are Sassenachs, every one of them. Uncle Austen isn't so bad, he's more like Mama. But the old dragon he's married to deserves cremating on a ghaut. Sorry to give you something else to think about, but I can't help it. I have decided to run away to sea. I'm going to ask Great-Uncle Neptune in Glasgow for a berth on one of his steamships, otherwise I shall join the Navy. I know you won't approve. I can't go back to Glengarth because Grandfather would send

me straight back here. By the time you receive this letter I
shall be in Scotland ...'

Rory paused and chewed the end of the pencil thoughtfully.

He *couldn't* run away! It would be a very cowardly thing
to do. He tried to analyse his feelings concerning his relatives: no, he did not dislike them exactly. He was just
frustrated in his attempts to get through to them. They
were so very unsympathetic to his plight, treating him like
a baby, a stupid one at that! He just wanted to tell
someone about all his troubles, and there was no one to
listen: no Mama with a sympathetic ear. There was only
young Kitty.

Father had told him on the eve of their departure from
India to always look after his sister as he was her nearest
relative. Kitty depended upon him, he couldn't abandon
her, not his own flesh and blood. He would have to look
after his sister until she was twenty-one, or married,
whichever came first. He would just have to learn to live
with his Leicestershire cousins, and put all thoughts of
Scotland and Glengarth out of his head. He owed it to
Kitty; he owed it to his father.

Rory tore up the letter and dropped the litter over the
schoolroom windowsill. The bits fluttered to the ground
like snowflakes. He saw himself leaning over the ship's
rail, looking down into the tearful face of his step-sister
standing on the quayside. The Rajkumari Sula and her
Indian entourage had wept buckets, so much so that it was
with difficulty he and Lindsay had managed to restrain
their own feelings. Christabel and Kitty had also wept
shamelessly at such a dreadful parting. The warm sea-
breezes had drifted Sula's purdah veil close against her
face as she had raised her handkerchief in one final farewell: and in that moment he had got the closest to ever
loving Sula and his father. He had leaned even more
precariously over the rail and yelled with the full force of
young lungs, 'Sula ... tell Papa I'm sorry for being such a
rotter. But I still love him ... and you ... and Suzy ...'

He remembered staggering back down the gangway to

the cabin he had shared with Lindsay during the voyage, searching frantically for a piece of paper upon which to write a last-minute message to his father. But when he had written it, the words were only paper words and not the words of his heart. He had crumpled the letter into a tight ball and tossed it out of the porthole.

To be abandoned for a second time would cause Kitty untold distress; he simply couldn't do it!

He turned back from the window just as Miss Vayer came into the schoolroom with an armful of bullrushes and wild flowers. 'Goodness! What are you doing here, Rory Duncan? I thought everyone was supposed to be on holiday. You look awful. Have you been fighting?'

'No! I'm going to a fancy dress party!' He stalked out of Miss Vayer's presence. On the way to his bed for the rest of the day, Rory paused outside the bathroom door. Aunt Ada's voice penetrated through the woodwork: 'Gentlemen do not use such words as *wog* or *kaffir*! Never, *never* do they use them! You are a despicable bunch, and deserve Rory Duncan's justifiable scorn. You certainly have *mine*!' *Thwack* was the sound he heard, just like a riding-crop on raw hide.

Rory grabbed a chair, climbed onto it, and peered through the glass panel above the bathroom door. Aunt Ada wielded the whip upon three posteriors in naked, moon-like evidence. He had difficulty in restraining his chortles of glee and covered his mouth with a grimy hand.

'*Ouch*! Steady on, Mother!'

'And don't you *dare* to backchat ME, Humphrey! *Never* again let me catch you three whippersnappers hurling abuse at Rory Duncan whose ancestors gave us an *Empire* to be proud of! *Never* again let me catch you three ganging-up on one lone boy. *Never* use your feet or your knees in a fair fight. Fists, yes! But never any other portion of yourselves, do I make myself clear?'

'*He* kneed *us*, Mama!'

Thwack went the riding-crop three more times in swift succession, and just when Rory was congratulating himself on getting away quite nicely, Nanny Delish found him spying. 'Master Rory! I've been looking for you everywhere!

Her ladyship told me you were to go straight to your bed for the rest of the day, and here you are, gloating upon your cousins!' She cuffed his ear for good measure, though not nearly as hard as he was used to. It had hurt Nanny Delish more than it had hurt him.

'Sorry, Nanny. Just seeing if the bathroom was free so I could wash off all this mess.'

'Then get along to the nursery bathroom, Master Rory!'

'Yes, Nanny! Right away.' She marched him off like a captured trooper from Chronje's forces and he couldn't help feeling very small and insignificant. 'Nanny,' he dared whisper along the way, 'it's only nine o'clock in the morning. Can't I possibly sit in the classroom for the rest of the day and read a book? It's far too early to go to bed, you know, as I've barely got up. I'll be very very good, I promise.'

'Orders are orders, Master Rory, and made for the troopers to obey.'

'Yes, Nanny, I suppose so.'

Neither did he get away without a caning. Uncle Austen, who had obviously had his orders, too, from the General, had to administer six of the best. His aunt hovered, jubilant in the background, while the pained expression on his uncle's mild and harmless face when wielding the cane, made him feel ten times worse than all Aunt Ada's verbal and physical abuse.

After the punishment, Uncle Austen offered him a mint humbug.

Duly chastened, lectured and admonished according to the Parable of the Prodigal Son, Rory, with a huge sigh of relief that the holidays were over, returned to Sherborne, Dorset.

CHAPTER SEVEN

Seated upon his horse, Burrell, Lindsay watched the ruby orb of sun sink low over the Cuillins of Skye. He loved the long summer evenings in Wester-Ross – time that stretched into timelessness. Out on the eel-black Minch, furrowed in red and gold coruscation, herring boats, sails billowing crimson, ploughed the evening tide, heading north to the fishing fields. Below him, at the foot of the cliff, the sea hissed and spumed over the rocks, fountaining silver spray high into the air.

Up on the ros Glengarth brooded indomitably, as it had done for hundreds of years.

In keeping with that sunset hour of reflection, on this day of his grandfather's funeral, Lindsay thought back to that first time he had come up here and watched the land merge with the sea and sky, and how, afterwards, he had ridden through his grandfather's plantations and had watched a fight between a wild cat and golden eagle. Then, emerging suddenly through the trees that were part of the ancient Hebridean forest which once covered the Highlands, he had looked down on the loch, knowing a moment of surprise and pleasure at the beauty of the land he would one day inherit. Loch Garth, he remembered so well, appeared like a silver sea-snake, its eye the tiny island of Rill ringed about by fine white sand.

On that occasion, too, he had first encountered the wild man from Raasay abusing Donald Gowrie's young daughter while she gutted fish on her mother's doorstep. It had *not* been a good encounter, the one thing to spoil his homecoming.

But times had changed. He wasn't thirteen any more but seventeen. The old laird was dead; Glengarth was now his: *his* inheritance, *his* pride and *his* curse!

Lindsay turned away from that summer seascape and
diverted his attention to unsettled business. The man was
still hanging about Rill; he'd seen him again only
yesterday. If Grandfather and Iain Hamilton had been
faint-hearted in evicting the fellow, then it was up to him
now to see to it that no more animals were lost in a brutal
fashion to thieves and poachers.

Loch Garth lay like a brooding purple monster at the
foot of Beinn Claidheamh Mor. Soon the soft night mists
off the great mountain on Inchnadamph would come
seeping into the valley, and he didn't want to lose Fletcher
this time.

Yet again he was too late.

He arrived at the causeway just as Fletcher was pushing
his boat out to sea. The fellow was off to the outer islands
where, doubtless, he would pick up good money for
Glengarth's bounty. Lindsay vowed that he would put a
stop to Fletcher's activities around Glengarth, once and
for all! He was *not* prepared to accept that sort of
poaching, or trespassers on his estate.

Frustrated yet again by the man who was as slippery as
a larded caber, Lindsay was about to turn around and
head back to the castle when something induced him to go
across to the cottage to talk to Donald Gowrie's widow.

She, of all people, might be able to persuade Fletcher to
stop his illegal activities around Glengarth, otherwise,
Lindsay had it in mind to tell her, that she, too, would be
evicted for harbouring a law-breaker on the island.

He wanted his tenants to be aware that a change of
ownership had occurred, that *he* was now the Laird of
Glengarth (even though the estate was held in trust for
him for another four years) and that he was not his old,
sick grandfather who had left the reins of government in
other hands.

Glengarth had been neglected for far too long. He had
seen the state of the forests – compartments gone out of
control; no new planting on any appreciative scale, just
indiscriminate cutting and clearing; fences having all but
disappeared in places; wild animals allowed to wander
everywhere, despoiling the trees. And the tenants had

been allowed to do just as they pleased – poaching the salmon, burning the trees for firewood, and evading the law as well as their rents. Some rents he learned from his cousin Iain, had not been raised in fifty years! Unbelievable!

Grandfather, it seemed, had not wanted to appear like those other landlords: 'Sassenach landlords', as they were referred to in the Highlands. They were the ones who never showed their English faces, but lived grandly in Edinburgh or London whilst their estates were run by corrupt factors who harassed the humble crofters in order to line their own pockets. They had been responsible for mass evictions and migrations from the glens, so that the land could be given over to the more profitable farming of sheep.

But Grandfather had gone the other way – the lines of least resistance, it appeared to Lindsay, who was suddenly looking at things from a completely new angle. Glengarth had gone to rack and ruin, and he wanted to halt the rot right now. So no one, least of all a man like Fletcher, was going to cock a snook at the new owner of Glengarth!

Lindsay knocked several times on the cot door but there was no answer. He assumed Mrs Gowrie and her daughter had taken their fish into Gairloch or further up the coast to Ullapool. He turned aside, ready to ride back across the causeway, when all at once his attention was caught by the tiniest of sounds through the glassless window set high in the wall. It sounded like a kitten in pain.

The pathetic mewing noise was disconcerting.

Lindsay tied his horse to the hitching-ring set into the thick peat walls of the cot and, lifting the latch, entered. The stench inside the cottage made him retch. He recognized it at once as being the high, putrid smell of uncured animal skins, offal and blood.

The cottage was dark and dank, a low peat fire in the open fireplace made his eyes water. In the darkness he stumbled over a low milking stool. As he righted it on its three legs, he slid in some foul mess which had dripped onto the earth and sand floor from an overturned saucepan on the table.

His sixth sense told him he was not alone in that foul cot where a fight had taken place; neither was it a kitten mewling, but something human.

To one side of the tiny living space was another door into what had presumably been an animal byre at one time but was now used as a sleeping area.

'Mrs Gowrie?' he called loudly through the closed door. The mewing stopped at once. 'Mrs Gowrie, are you ill?' Still there was no answer, so he lifted the latch and poked his head over the half door that pulled outwards into the living area.

The byre contained space enough for a hurley-bed on its retractable chains to be opened, or, when not in use, to be closed up against the surprisingly sturdy outer wall of the cot, which had been built up to a depth of several feet by generations of tenants storing their fuel in such a manner. Next to the bed was another low milking stool upon which stood an unlit oil lamp. A broken rocking chair without its runners, was tossed on its side in a dank corner.

Amongst the tattered rags serving as bedclothes, a girl lay curled up on her side, her face to the peat wall.

'Where's your mother?' Lindsay asked, feeling like a horse neighing over a stable door.

There was no response, so he tried again. 'Answer me. Where's your mother?'

'Dead.'

'When did she die?'

'Last Eastertide.'

He was annoyed. Iain might at least have mentioned it. 'Does Mr Hamilton know that your mother's dead and you're living here alone?'

She sniffed loudly, her face still turned away from him. 'I don't know. Mr Hamilton ne'r bothers to visit the island. He leaves us in peace here – as long as the rent's taken up to Glengarth each month.'

'Who looks after you if your mother's dead?'

'Myself.'

'Oh, no! There's a man about this cottage. The boots beside the fireside for a start. So don't lie to me.'

'*He* doesn't look after me!' The young voice was scornful.

'Who are we talking about?'

'My stepfather – they're *his* boots.'

'Who's your stepfather?'

'An animal they call Fletcher.'

That made Lindsay think twice. 'How old are you?'

'Twelve.'

'Why are you crying?'

She didn't answer, but he was persistent. 'Did he beat you?' Lindsay had seen evidence of a scuffle in the main room.

Again there was no answer from the frightened girl, and so he pulled open the bottom half of the door and, ducking his head under the low lintel, entered the byre.

He stood beside her bed, but the windowless darkness was thick and he couldn't see properly. He lit the wick of the smoky oil lamp and held it up to get a better view of her.

She tried to dig deeper into her filthy little nest. Lindsay twitched back her coverings and angrily she snatched them up, her frightened mewings starting up again.

Lindsay took a deep breath, trying to control his sense of disgust.

The reddish marks and the bruises all over her thin little body and newly swelling breasts made him realize that her stepfather did something else to her besides beat her.

Hard dry sobs racked her body, her face in the lamplight puffy and tear-stained.

For the moment, Lindsay ignored the tears. 'Do you know who I am?'

'Yes, m' laird,' she whispered so softly he could hardly catch her answer.

'Don't be frightened of me. I know you're Annie ... I called here once before when you were gutting fish on the doorstep ... four years ago. I'm here to help and protect you. I'd like to start off by getting you to trust me, Annie. Just tell me who did this to you.'

'*I canna!*'

'You must trust me.'

'I trust no one, m' laird.'

'Trust *me*, Annie! I want you to tell me who did this to you!'

'I canna! *HE* made me promise ... so I canna tell ...'

'Well, now,' Lindsay swallowed the lump in his throat. 'How ... how long has your stepfather been mistreating you like this?'

He had expected her to say since the Eastertide of her mother's death, but she surprised him when she said, 'Ever since he came here.'

'Did your mother know?'

'If she did, she never said. Besides, she could have done nothing against him, for he would most likely have used her badly as well.'

'Didn't you ever tell her what he was doing to you?'

'I was afraid ... he made me promise. Besides, I didn't know.'

'Didn't know what?'

'He was doing wrong.'

'But now you do?'

'Yes. He said it was "comforts". I thought ...' her voice faded away into a pathetic little sob.

'Thought what, Annie?'

'It was ... natural. No one told me different.' She sniffled against the wall.

'But now?'

'T'was only when I read it in the Big Black Book I found out it was a sin and mortally wrong.'

'What Big Black Book?'

'The Minister at the Kirk calls it the Bible. I call it by the name my mother and father ... my *real* father, Donald Gowrie ... called it! And it says there about fornicators and adulterers and molesters of children.'

'Go on, Annie, don't be afraid to confide in me. I'm not going to hurt you.'

'When I asked the Minister of the Kirk what was meant by that, he told me, and so I know now 'tis a mortal sin.'

'Did you tell the Minister of the Kirk exactly what he does do?'

'No, m' laird.'

'Why not?'

'I was ... in mortal shame ... I couldna tell him about Fleddon an Fletcher.'

'Do you *like* being beaten and abused by your stepfather when you know now it isn't right for anyone, let alone children, to be abused in this fashion?'

Then she did turn on the hurley-bed, sat up and, tossing her long black hair out of her eyes, glared at him like a fierce little animal. 'I'm not a child! *Begone* from here, m' fine laird! 'Tis Donald Gowrie's daughter ye're insulting, ma fine Sassenach *landlord*, so I'll thank ye to be riding off Rill upon 'y grand horse!'

He had to smile at her Celtic origins as well as her temper. 'Annie,' he sympathized, 'I'm here because I want to help you, not frighten you. I don't want Fletcher on my land again, do you understand?'

'Yes, m' laird,' she muttered.

'I want you to get up, get dressed and go to the big house at the top of the glen and ask for Mrs Hamilton. Tell her I sent you to help out in the kitchens. You must stay at Forest Lodge and not return to the island until I tell you it's safe.'

'I canna leave my home.'

'Why not?'

'I must catch fish to pay my dues, m' laird.'

'What dues?'

'The rent. Fletcher will not pay it. Then I would be evicted from here, with nowhere to go. I canna let that happen, for bad things befall the likes of me without parents and without a home. I see them in Gairloch and Ullapool, waiting for the men on the boats, and I don't want to become like them.'

This girl was only twelve years old, yet she spoke like an old woman with all the worries of the world upon her frail shoulders. And in that moment Lindsay could not help but admire her spirit.

'Listen Annie. This is *my* property, do you understand?'

She nodded. 'Indeed! I speak English, too, m' laird.'

'Then you need not worry about the rent for the moment. I'm not going to evict you. I want you to pay

attention to me, not Fletcher or the estate factor. You
have my word on it. Go to Forest Lodge, and leave me to
deal with the man from Raasay who is doing this to you.
You needn't be frightened any more, Annie.'

'Thank you, m' laird.' She said it proudly and without
subservience.

Lindsay walked out of the cot and down to the water's
edge. The black silhouette of the ros merged with the cold
grey sea. Standing beneath the darkening sky he watched
for signs of Fletcher's return. Loch water lapped smoothly
at his feet, and while he stood on the white sands of Rill
he wondered to himself what kind of beast violates a
helpless and innocent child.

When he saw Annie Gowrie scrambling up the glen in
the direction of Forest Lodge, he untethered his horse and
rode back to the castle for his gun.

In the cold, pale moonlight Lindsay returned to the peat
cot on Rill. He didn't think Fletcher would show himself
until daybreak. He tied up his horse and for the second
time that evening entered the hovel. He took the oil lamp
from the byre. In the open doorway of the cot, he sat
cleaning, trimming and filling the lamp. He could see right
down to the water's edge ... and this time Fletcher would
receive anything but 'comfort'!

After attending to the lamp, Lindsay took in the rest of
his surroundings and shuddered in disgust. There might be
an excuse for poverty, there was none for filth. These
people lived like animals.

He was half-tempted to go back to the castle and get
the stable-boy, Drummond, whom he trusted implicitly, to
come and clean out the cot. But then he thought better of
it. He might miss Fletcher were the man to slip back into
the loch while he went after young Tom Drummond. And
besides, he didn't want to let his retainers know his business – or Annie's. This was a private matter, and so he
decided to deal with it by himself.

Not a person to enjoy inactivity, for he had had it
drummed into his head from an early age that one must
set an industrious example to the Indians, he lit the oil

lamp with his lighter and set about the cleaning himself. He found a bucket, filled it from the loch, and, wonder of wonders, laid his hands on an old bar of lye soap which must have lain on the shelf since Mrs Gowrie herself had last cleaned her home. In his shirtsleeves Lindsay went to work.

The burnt skillet with its revolting concoction of stewed venison he tossed outside – the venison undoubtedly procured from his land illegally, were his grim thoughts. Then he scrubbed the ingrained dirt in the deal table until he almost wore a hole through the wood. He lit a bonfire behind the cot and burned all the rubbish he could lay his hands on, including the rotting, sour skins of slaughtered animals, the odour of which could keep a million moths at bay for miles around.

It took him several hours to set Annie's cottage to rights, for he saw it as Annie Gowrie's cottage now, never Fletcher's, since she had gone to such pains to tell him about who paid the rent.

Afterwards, he leaned on the handle of the birch broom and surveyed his handiwork, with not a little pride. The place was as spotless as a nun's reputation. Embarrassment battled with a sense of humour as he congratulated himself on his night's work. If his grandfather happened to be looking down on him now, Lindsay wondered what he would think of his grandson, the new Laird of Glengarth, who had never in his life had to clean his own shoes, cleaning out a fisherman's pigsty! He put away the broom and bucket, thankful that his cousin, Iain Hamilton, or one of the tenants, hadn't come upon him unexpectedly.

As the grey dawn seeped across western water, Lindsay took his seat at a clean table. Through the open doorway he saw the herring fleet sail out, looking like bloated black flies crawling on the flat grey expanse of the Minch, calm on this summer morning.

Not long after, a solitary fishing boat slipped into the loch and a tingling sensation crept down Lindsay's spine. Fletcher had either spent the night poaching from someone else's estate, or he had brought back an early catch of fish for Annie to sell, no doubt hoping to spend

the day sleeping in the cot after stealing from Glengarth
tonight! Lindsay was well aware of the way villains like
Fletcher operated. He picked up his gun and sighted it as
Fletcher walked up the beach with that rolling gait peculiar to all seafaring men – although this one was more of a
pirate than sailor.

'Annie? Wha's ma wee Annie? Come out o' yon bed an'
kiss thy pa guid morning ...' He stepped over the
threshold and found himself looking down the barrel of a
hunting rifle.

'Stand perfectly still, Mr Fletcher,' Lindsay said, 'and
put your hands out of reach of that dirk you use to carve
up my animals.'

Astonishment had been the man's first reaction and
bravado the next. He swaggered, he smiled, his thick red
lips parting in blubbery amusement, and the teeth of the
bear were terrifying. Very slowly Fletcher raised the back
of his hand to his mouth to wipe away the crusty salt on
his beard.

'*NOW!*' Lindsay cocked the hammer of the rifle, and
Fletcher did as he was told.

'Guid, guid, m' laird! Ye have gumption for an
Englishmon!' Fletcher wagged his giant head in amusement, convincing Lindsay that he was indeed capable of
killing a man, and was no doubt still on the run for it.
'King o' yon castle is dead, long live the King! Ye dinna
lose taime, did ye, ma stripling, in gettin' acquainted with
ye're neighbours? Let mae see, 'twas only yestermorn they
buried yon King o' the castle an' here's the wee cock tha's
hardly crowed, actin' lord muck a'ready!' His tone of
mocking banter changed harshly. 'Tha rent's been paid to
thine vassal, Maister Iain Hamilton, ma Sassenach landlord, so y' canna evict *mae* for no payin' ma dues.'

'I'm not going to evict you,' Lindsay reassured him. 'I'm
going to kill you.'

Fletcher let out a deep belly roar of laughter and once
again his hand sneaked to wipe the salt from his mouth.

'*Keep your hands where I can see them,*' Lindsay said as
he cocked the barrel of the rifle more firmly at the huge
man. 'This gun is trained on your big fat belly, Mr

Fletcher. If you so much as bat an eyelid, I'll blow you apart. But you won't die all at once, I'll make sure of that. And every time you ask for a sip of water because the thirst is burning you up, I'll have the satisfaction of seeing it all ooze out again through the holes I'll make in you if you so much as tempt me. I saw a better savage than you suffer in just the same way in another jungle. It wasn't a pretty sight.'

'My, but they larned ye tae be a bastard guid an' proper fae tha cradle!' he spat contemptuously on the floor.

'Yes, but I was taught to be one. I wasn't born one like you.'

'An' clever with thy fancy words.'

'Which I'm not going to waste any longer on the likes of you. Listen and listen good, Mr Fletcher. I'm not going to kill you here and now because that would be too easy, and there would be no satisfaction in it for me. Neither am I going to hand you over to the law – not yet, anyway. I'm well aware that after a few months of languishing in gaol on a poaching charge, you'll be up to your old tricks all over again. So I'm going to let you go. But I shall watch you and stalk you and hunt you down like the animal you are, and if you so much as dare set foot on my property again, I'll *kill* you!'

The word Fletcher spat in derision was untranslatable. Then he tried wheedling. 'Ye would nac kill a mon fae a wee bit o' poachin' would ye, ma laird?'

'No, I wouldn't kill a man for a wee bit of poaching. But I'd kill you for what you've done to your stepdaughter. The law, Mr Fletcher, doesn't look kindly on a beast like you raping young girls, and neither do decent folk. But nobody is going to find out about Annie Gowrie, for *her* sake, not yours. That's why I'm taking the law into my own hands. I want to teach you a lesson. I want to see you hunted and afraid, just as you've made Annie feel hunted and afraid. I want you to know what a pine marten, a roebuck, one of my stags, and a rabbit on Inchnadamph feels when caught in a gin-trap. *My* animals, Mr Fletcher, frightened, bleeding and suffering an unnecessary, un-dignified death. If I catch you on Glengarth property

again, you'll be strung up – by the law! You've been given
fair warning. Now, turn around and keep your hands UP!'

Lindsay fired a warning blast through the open doorway
which kicked up the sand outside. He had to impress upon
Fletcher he meant business. 'I want your knife and I want
you to walk back to your boat and clear out of my loch ...
and don't tempt me to use this gun because, besides
larnin' me my prayers at my mother's knee, they also
larned me to use a gun *guid* and *proper*! I'll pick you off
like a jack rabbit as easily at three hundred paces as at
three.'

Lindsay moved off the stool to take Fletcher's dirk off
him. He pressed the barrel of the rifle into the man's back,
trigger poised and ready. Then, with the dirk in his own
belt and his boot in the seat of the man's oilskins, he
shoved him out of the cot. 'Get out of here and *never*
come back!'

The man from Raasay made no attempt to hurry back
to his boat, but ambled across the clean white sands of Rill
without looking back once. Yet Lindsay was perfectly
aware of Fletcher's latent ferocity. He was cocky, brash
and disdainful of authority. The killing instinct in him
would never be quenched without a fierce fight.

Lindsay had no doubt in his mind that Fletcher would
be back – his pride would see to it. And in that moment
too, he was half afraid of the trouble he had stirred up for
himself by making such a dangerous enemy.

Fletcher's small boat slid into the loch, and the echoes
of his uncouth laughter reverberated off Beinn Claidheamh Mor.

And if only he could have foreseen the future on that
summer's morning as he stood on the threshold of Annie
Gowrie's home, with the early morning sun gold dusting
the purple waters of Loch Garth, Lindsay would have put
paid to Fleddon an Fletcher then and there.

CHAPTER EIGHT

Rory held in his hand the two letters from India, one from Brigadier General, Sir Dougald MacKincade, and the other from Sula: Papa was dead.

He couldn't help reflecting that over the past few years nothing seemed to have happened apart from a lot of dying and mourning: firstly there had been Mama, then the old Queen of England, Victoria, who had died the year after he had arrived in England. After so long as Monarch of the Realm, let alone Monarch of the Glen, everyone had ceased to remember a time without her on the throne. But she had at last made way for her son, King Edward VII – who seemed none too healthy himself, and now everyone seemed to be looking even further ahead, with a George as King of England before long! Then there had been Grandfather's death six months ago.

Sula had written to say that Papa had been mauled to death by a tiger whilst on *shikar* with the old Maharajah of Baharabad and Brig, that other intrepid Scots hunter who had callously described James Beauly Roskillen as resembling a pair of pink striped pyjamas after they had managed to get him away from the enraged tiger.

Oh! Life was *such* a complication, Rory reflected ruefully. Was this the hand of God moving in a mysterious way, or the curse of Glengarth coming true concerning division and destruction being the portion allotted the lairds of Glengarth? Now it did not matter about their father being disinherited by *his* father: Lindsay would have claimed Glengarth after this tragedy in any case.

Six months ago he had hoped that Lindsay would have put in a good word for him by seeking permission for both of them to be allowed to pay their last respects to their grandfather. But Lindsay had remained aloof, as usual,

and had not stuck up for him at all. Uncle Austen and
Aunt Ada had agreed with the Dean (a foregone conclusion! Rory fumed to himself at the time): Lindsay, Laird
of Glengarth, an adult of seventeen who would be going
up to Oxford in the following year, should be allowed
leave of absence to attend his grandfather's funeral, but
the younger brother, who had barely started his senior
studies, and who was so far behind the rest of the fellows
in his year, must remain where he was for the moment.
Rather than unsettle him by dragging him out of school
just when he had settled in, Rory Duncan must stay put!
And for that kind of gross injustice, Rory felt he would
never forgive The Beak *or* his guardians.

It hadn't been his burning desire to pay his last respects
to an acrimonious old man who had never liked him – an
ancient, decrepit relative whom he could now scarcely
remember or even care about – that had made him want
to accompany Lindsay back to Wester-Ross. If the truth
were known, it was because he had had every intention of
getting old Uncle Neptune on his side. Hamish MacDearg
would never forego the opportunity to gloat over his erst-
while enemy, his brother-in-law, by chucking clods of
earth over the coffin, and Rory had been hoping for an
opportunity to speak to Hamish about enrolling him in his
steamship company, as a boy-stoker if need be! He hated
Eton, he hated learning Latin and Greek and French, and
he hated doing as he was told by his English guardians.
He wanted to learn something *useful*, but adults never
listened! The only thing that made fagging for the toe-
rags of Upper School bearable, was Smyrna and 'The
Bud.'

Rory thought about The Bud and his heart soared.
Until now, his adolescence had manifested itself in smelly
socks, spots and looking at rude postcards of nude ladies
under cover of a dormitory blanket in the Long Chamber
of Eton, or hidden in the lavatory closet. But the moment
The Bud entered his life, all things changed. These days,
he even remembered to wash his comb at least once a
week.

Smyrna, his best friend had effected the introduction.

'I say, Dagger,' Smyrna had said, having christened Rory Duncan with the English word for a Scottish dirk in the endearing way Smyrna had about him, 'the Hag has a rare bud helping her out during the epidemic. She can't be a day over sixteen and is built like second helpings of treacle dumplings. It was awfully jolly having a sore throat with her to administer the gargles. The fellows are dropping all over the place like blow flies with heart failure.'

Fourteen-year-old Rory Duncan had done his best to contract tonsillitis, laryngitis, bronchitis and any other *itis* he could think of, but he had never got within inhaling distance of The Bud. He remained as fit as a fiddle, much to his disgust. Until the day he saw HER in chapel.

'Told you she was a rare eyeful, didn't I, Dagger!' Smyrna, standing beside him in the choir stalls gloated.

The only trouble was, the rest of Lower School were also trying to attract The Bud's attention.

Then Smyrna, who was about as artful at dodging things as Mr Dickens's character of the same inclination, managed to get them out of choir duties the following Sunday morning, informing the choir master that Matron, alias The Hag, wanted them to rest their throats in view of all the laryngitis doing the round of Lower School. Since Rory Roskillen and the Honourable Lloyd Smyrna were the tuneful backbones of the choir, whose voices were in danger of breaking through too much stress, the choir master was easily persuaded: he required their harmonizing vocal chords for the Lenten liturgies.

It worked. Smyrna managed to manoeuvre himself and Rory Duncan into a pew right behind The Bud. Then he accidentally on purpose dropped his hymn book at the feet of The Bud.

'Awfully sorry!' whispered Smyrna down the back of The Bud's neck, 'I hope it didn't drop on your toes. Please let me make amends by taking you to tea at Rosy's teashop, Brocas Street, this afternoon.'

The ice had been broken, though The Bud never even turned her head towards Smyrna who was leering behind her back, because unfortunately, at that very moment,

Matron entered The Bud's pew to take her place next to her protégée.

Matron held on to Smyrna's hymn book and afterwards reported him to The Beak for disrupting the service. Smyrna received six of the best while Rory Duncan was himself suddenly smitten with the pangs of love.

'Gosh, Smyrna, you're right. She's just like a Cox's Orange Pippin,' Rory groaned, his hand on his surpliced heart as he filed into the choir stalls on the Sunday morning after the aborted seduction scene of the week before.

The Bud was in full view, practically opposite him as she sat next to The Hag, as usual. Her magnificent breasts bloomed outward under her overcoat and offered the promise of wonderful things to those who dared approach.

Look, but don't touch, was driving him crazy, and Rory wondered how he could get a message to the divine Bud.

The Lord himself answered his prayer one Sunday morning.

Choir Master had composed a new hymn, complete with words and music which had been transposed on to individual hymn sheets. He wanted the music sheets distributed among the boys and members of staff in chapel, and Rory's hand shot up. He never volunteered for a thing, if he could help it; but now it was beyond his control. He was so nervous, he scrambled off to the back of the school chapel, where, under cover of darkness and his choirboy's surplice, he managed to scrawl with a blunt pencil a hasty message on the back of one hymn sheet in particular; 'Please will you meet me outside Rosy's teashop on Brocas Street, next Saturday afternoon? R.D.R.'

Smyrna had been the other volunteer, but had worked from the front of the chapel to the back when Rory Duncan, his last hymn sheet grasped in a hot and sweaty hand, dumped it in the lap of The Bud.

'I've already got one . . .' she began, but he had already raced back to his place in the choir.

' "*Nunce dimittis servum tuum, Domine*",' he sang more loudly and joyfully than the rest of the choir that morning.

Later that day, he and Smyrna were summoned to The

Beak's office where they received a dozen of the best even though it was Sunday.

'God be in your head, Roskillen, not your pelvis,' said The Beak, or words to that effect. 'What you and Smyrna were doing was lusting after the sins of the flesh. As a punishment for writing nasty little messages on the back of hymn sheets, you will both construe Vergil's first *Bucolic* tomorrow morning – in the original!'

Needless to say, The Bud did not materialize outside Rosy's teashop on Brocas Street on the following Saturday afternoon, nor on any other afternoon. He and Smyrna were grounded for the remainder of that Hilary term. The influenza epidemic over; so was his brief love affair with the Dean's niece who had been helping Matron out in sickbay. She returned to doing whatever Dean's nieces did when they weren't volunteering Nightingales at Eton College. And sad to say, the only reason the Dean himself was involved in Rory Roskillen's affairs was because of the niece, that divine Bud!

Soon after Rory's voice broke and he was no longer required by Choir Master.

He never even knew the name of his first love.

'Never mind, Dagger,' Smyrna consoled him, 'plenty more fish in the sea. Why not join the fellows and me next Saturday in a spot of night life instead?'

'Instead of what?'

'Listen, old chap, upstairs of Rosy's teashop there's a party being held for Garrick's birthday. His older brother is organizing it. Kind of initiation ceremony, comprendo, eh Dagger? There'll be girls, gambling, booze, fags – the smoking kind – the lot. *Sex*, Dagger, and all free! Care to join us?'

'Oh, why not! In view of the fact we're supposed to be grounded, the sooner I get expelled the better, as far as I'm concerned.'

Rory's holidays were always spent at Breedon Hall, a time to dread, as far as he was concerned.

In the long wet summer of 1905 when he was fifteen and a half, Rory knew he had to take control of his own life, if he was ever to be a free man.

The time had come, he felt, to take control – but how? His father had mortgaged him, body and soul, to his English guardians and he could not shake them off. He didn't have any money of his own, only a monthly allowance for necessary personal expenses. His school fees and living expenses were all being taken care of by the unseen hand of his late father's solicitors, Pinnegar, Pedley and Childs of Edinburgh.

Breedon Hall, as usual, was filled to capacity with not only the Burretts but also their house-guests.

With the death of Cecil Rhodes, followed by the Treaty of Vereeniging, the Boer War had ended three years before (though one would never have guessed it to hear Rupert still talking about the best years of his life!) Six months after the Treaty, Rupert married his Charlotte, the 'clotted cream cake', of whom Humphrey, Mordan and Michael still made such fun.

After three years of marriage, the hero of Paardeburg and Ladysmith, when not out hunting with the Quorn or the Belvoir Hunt, was usually to be found in the Shukborough Room of his parents' grand Jacobean mansion instead of in his own drawing-room, even though he and Charlotte had a charming little thatched house with 'eyebrow' windows, in the grounds of the estate. Charlotte was pregnant with their second child. She was usually to be found seated at the card table playing piquet or at the piano playing Bizet. She and Jane were famous for their duets.

That summer, too, the invited house-guests were Tobias Augustus, Viscount Tapstock, a rather lily-livered individual in Rory's opinion, together with his sister, Lady Margaret, known as Daisy, who was Leonora's best friend.

'Question, everyone,' said Rupert from behind *Punch Magazine,* '"For whom do you vote, Curruthers?"'

He waited expectantly for someone to come up with an answer. No one did.

'"Why, women every time, dear fellow!"'

Charlotte looked over the cards at him. She was playing

piquet with Leonora, Daisy and Kitty while Jane occupied the window-seat, reading a book. Humphrey was doodling with one finger on the piano keys, the twins were no where to be seen – thank God, thought Rory to himself as he tried to concentrate upon writing a letter to his great-uncle Hamish MacDearg, who would soon be dead, too, if he, Rory, didn't get a move on back to Scotland.

'By Jove!' said Toby standing before the drawing-room windows with his hands clasped behind his back. 'Never seen so much rain in all m' life! Foxes all drowned in their holes, shouldn't wonder. What-ho?'

'Well, I thought the Suffragette joke was amusing!' Rupert said peevishly when no one took any notice of him.

Charlotte unwrapped another bar of Fry's cream chocolate, and Jane, looking up at that moment from her book, said, 'You'll get horribly fat, Charlie.'

'I'm horribly fat now, Jane.'

Leonora slammed down her hand of cards, just dealt by Charlotte. 'You've made them all *sticky*, Charlie! Rupert, can't you get her to stop eating all that horrid chocolate the whole time!'

'I'm eating for two, Lennie!' Charlotte also sounded peevish.

'You're eating for half-a-dozen!' Leonora snapped.

'Don't be rude to Charlie.' Rupert, just like the good husband he hoped he was, came to his wife's defence. 'Show a little respect, Lennie. Charlie's a lot older than you.'

'Sorry I spoke!'

It was Daisy's turn to be disgruntled. 'Well, I'm tired of playing piquet! I'm *bored*! Isn't there anything else to do in this place?'

Rory groaned to himself; he could feel a family row brewing.

He didn't have long to wait.

Jane tossed aside her book. '*Bored, bored, bored*! Look at you all! You make me sick!'

Toby turned around and gave her an astonished look from under his sandy eyelashes. Rupert's magazine rustled as he sat up and bristled at Jane, who continued undetered:

'If you're so *bored*, Daisy, why don't you go home to mother? Or, better still, why don't you offer your services to a factory in Loughborough making boring hose for the rest of the world to stick their bored little feet into! Why not swop places with some poor little girl of your age living in a back-to-back in Leicester? Or perhaps you'd prefer a night out on the town, forced out onto the streets to earn a dubious living because your father's out of work through sickness and injury and your mother's dying of tuberculosis whilst giving birth to her tenth child – on the floor!'

Daisy's plump pink cheeks turned bright red.

Oh Lor', here we go again! thought Rory. Jane never knew when to keep her mouth shut.

Rupert shifted uncomfortably in his seat while Daisy's brother kept opening and closing his mouth like a codfish face-to-face with a fisherman on dry land. 'I say, Jane, that's a bit rude, isn't it?' Rupert admonished his sister. 'After all, Daisy and Toby are guests in our home.'

'Your home is on the other side of the grounds, Rupert. Why don't you go and drink your own whisky and soda in your own drawing-room instead of getting Hardrace to wait on you, here?'

'I say, old girl, that's *quite* unnecessary!'

'Is it? Just look at you all! You're all so insular and bigoted, you don't even *know* how the other half live! Well, I'm bored, too, just *listening* to all of you. Let's all take a little joyride out into the big wide world, shall we? Let's all cure our boredom by absorbing the *real* sights on our city streets. We can laugh and giggle and thank God we're not like the Irish immigrants sleeping in flooded basements with their pigs. Or we can gaze enviously at a very nice little family – a dozen of them living in one room no larger than the kitchen pantry, half of them rotting away with phthisis while the other half die of starva-tion ...'

'Oh, come on, Jane! That's hardly Daisy's fault!' Humphrey started taunting her further by bashing out *La*

Marseilles on the piano.

'And as for you, you seducer of kitchen maids,' Jane said, rounding on her brother furiously, 'you're no better! In fact, you're worse than the twins, and ... and Rupert smug in his pinks and his drinks and ...'

'I've had *enough*!' Rupert roared, getting to his feet. 'Come on, Charlie, let's go home.'

But Jane, at seventeen, was on her Suffragette soapbox and nothing would shift her now. 'Yes, go on, take Charlie home with you. She ought to be looking after her own child instead of eating Fry's chocolate and playing *games* all day long! Nanny Delish is supposed to be in retirement, yet has to dance attendance on your daughter upstairs in the old nursery. Let Charlie know what it's like to run her *own* household and look after her *own* family, or ... or give birth on some horrible mattress with half a dozen other brats looking on ...'

Charlotte burst into tears, grabbed up the rest of her chocolate bars, and flung them across the room at Jane. Rupert flung open the double doors of the Shukborough Room and Hardrace fell headlong over the threshold.

'Sir, cook would like to know if you and Lady Charlotte will be lunching here today ...'

'No Hardrace, we will be lunching *at home*!'

'Very good, sir.'

'Come, Charlie!' He turned back to Jane. 'And you may be sure, Jane, that as soon as Mama and Papa return from London, they shall hear all about this – this *nasty* campaign of yours!'

Rupert and Charlotte stormed out, and Hardrace was almost bowled over by Jane who followed them out into the hall.

'Neither shall I be staying to lunch, Hardrace! Ask cook to put my share of luncheon into a picnic basket and please inform Mr Gammon that I shall require the Rolls at the door in ten minutes.'

'But, Miss Jane, his lordship gave strict instruction that the Rolls was not to be used in his absence.'

'The Rolls, Hardrace! In ten minutes!' She vanquished him with her icy stare, and Hardrace was lost 'twixt the devil and the deep blue Rolls Royce.

'I say, Jane,' Humphrey, agent provocateur, on his way to the dining-room for lunch, added, 'If you're going to Loughborough to feed the five thousand, it's as well to recognize the fact that Jesus Christ said follow in his foot-steps, not in his tyre tracks.'

'Be quiet, Humphrey!' Jane replied loftily, on her way upstairs to fetch her mackintosh and wellies. 'You're a *worthless* creature, so don't preach to me!'

'God help mankind if women like Jane ever get the vote,' Humphrey, on the way to the dining-room, added with a snort of disgust.

'Hear hear, old boy,' replied Toby, Viscount Tapstock. 'I say, Hump, is your sister a little bit cuckoo?'

'She's *very* cuckoo, Caesar, old chap. Jane adores sitting in other people's nests. The messier the nest, the better she likes it.' He passed Toby the cold platter. 'Do have some of this excellent food to take away the bad taste of this morning.'

'Er ... what is it? Toby asked dubiously as he eyed the dish of cold meats.

'Caesar, old chap, how should I know? I'm not the bally cook. Looks like pickled brain in pork brawn – Irish, I'd imagine.'

'Thanks awfully, but no thanks. I like to know what I'm eating.' He helped himself to some soused herrings.

'Do you think that what Jane said about the Irish living in flooded basements with their pigs was actually true?' Rory said to Humphrey across the dining-table.

'Scotch kipper, you do have a habit of taking things literally! But I suppose there must be a ring of truth in it somewhere, knowing Jane and her good causes. Besides, how else would they have known how to invent the recipe for Irish stew?'

'Amazing what lengths some people will go to,' said Toby, shaking his sandy hair out of his mud-coloured eyes. Then he put down his knife and fork and grinned. 'Oh, ha-ha, Hump, very funny! Flooded basements and pigs – Irish stew, what!'

Rory tossed him a pickled onion. 'Here you are Caesar,

stuff that!' He winked at Humphrey who was tolerable when the twins were not around. 'Or would you prefer a little wild boar in aspic?'

'Good show, Scotch kipper,' Humphrey said, nudging him in the ribs. 'I might learn to live with you yet!'

CHAPTER NINE

With nothing else to do for the rest of the day, Rory took himself off to the old stables adjacent to the new ones, where his uncle's chauffeur spent most of his time polishing the Rolls and fiddling with Rupert's unreliable Tourer – only because Rupert, who didn't know the first thing about mechanical objects, insisted on driving his car like a four-in-hand.

The chauffeur was back after ferrying Jane to Loughborough, and was now busy removing all tell-tale evidence of the muddy and wet journey from his Lordship's prized car. 'Afternoon, Master Rory, sir. You after tinkerin' or chattin'?'

'Good afternoon, Mr Gammon.'

'Gamin – like I tell the others, *Mister* Rory, sir. I ain't one to stand on ceremony like.'

Benjamin Gammon reminded Rory of a pushy little Cockney sparrow.

'Gamin ...' Rory began hesitantly, 'I'd like to learn something about engines. Will you teach me?'

Gammon, standing no more than five feet two, pushed back his greasy cloth cap to the crown of his head and scratched his crinkly black hair whilst subjecting the lad to a grin of wry amusement. 'Blimey! No offence Mister Rory, but I don't reckon your high-class education an' nobby connections 'll put you in line for chauffeuring.'

'I've no intention of taking up chauffeuring: I just want to learn something about engines. You do know *something* about them, don't you?'

Gammon's wizened features cracked open like a dried teasel as he burst forth with wheezy yet raucous good humour. Rory didn't know what he had said to cause Gammon's uncalled for mirth.

'What do I know abart motors, he asks! Cor blimey, guv,' he said pulling his off-duty cap over his eyes. He was not dressed in his smart chauffeur's livery, which sat rather oddly on his diminutive frame, anyway. Gammon, at the wheel of the Rolls Royce, perched on a raised seat and cushion, was a hilarious sight as he peered through the windscreen, and Rory often made jokes about it. 'You name 'em, I know 'em. Panhards, F.I.A.T.s, Mercedes Benz, Renaults, Napier, De Dion, Rolls-Royce – born in a ruddy Rolls, I was.'

'Then you aren't a navy chap as Rupert once mentioned, and a wizard with steam engines?'

Gammon grew sober. 'Not navy like *you* mean, Mister Rory, though I was at sea, once.'

'Why did you give it up?'

'Spot of bother with the old lungs. Also this twisted elbow you see here.' He raised his left elbow which was scarred and locked into only partial mobility.

'What happened?' Rory wanted to know.

'With the elbow? Well, that was a accident with a internal combustion engine on a steamship called the ...'

'I meant, what happened as far as your career at sea was concerned?'

'Well, it was like this, guv, I run off to Deptford to join the Royal Navy when I was knee high to a grasshopper – twelve years old, guv, I was. But the Navy wouldn't 'ave me. Nor would the proper Merchant Fleet. So I signed on as casual labour with coastal-cargo vessels – the Home Trade route, in other words. Stoking ship's boilers fer a living until I got to be chief engineer. But the coal dust settled in me chest and I couldn't breathe when down in the stoke-hold, so I ended up land-lubbing fer a while. Bin 'ere ever since, drivin' motor-cars fer the nobbies.'

'Do you prefer motorcars to steamships?'

Gammon scratched his head again. 'It's a livin', I suppose. Since the gentry don't know the back end of a motor-car from a 'orse, I reckoned I 'ad nuttin' ter lose. So I started learnin' the nitty-gritty ... I didn't want to get the boot, 'cos if the bloomin' motor-car ever broke down on the side of a lonely road in the dead of night, I reckoned

I'd have to be the muggins to fix it. So I learned me my trade, which was bloomin' engines in all sorts of shapes an' sizes, same as I did when I was coasting. Simple as that.' Gammon wiped his greasy hands on an oily cloth.

'That's what I thought. So you must know a fair amount about the trade-routes, eh Gamin?'

'You mean cargo-hauling on steamcoasters, Mister Rory?'

'I mean that precisely.'

Gammon gave the inquisitive boy an odd look from under his dark beetle brows. 'Yeah – I knows abart them, too. What d'you wan' ter know, guv?'

'Everything.'

'Blimey. You serious?'

'You see, Gamin, my great-uncle in Scotland owns a steamship company. If I can go to him with some working knowledge of boats and engines and why the screw steamer often outweighs its advantages, and why they can't berth as quickly or efficiently as paddlers, then he might just take me on to work with him in Glasgow.'

'Blimey, his nibs *is* serious!' said Gammon, whistling through the gap in his front teeth. 'Listen, guv, you take a pew over there, or else get a polishin' cloth and give this 'igh-class lady 'ere a good going over on 'er Royce bumpers, an' I'll tell you about a run I once did from Deptford to Dieppe. We 'ad a cargo of grain in the 'old, see. But not full ter the flamin' brim as it should've bin. Now, as every good sailor knows, grain, like anthracite and chippin's, is unstable cargo – tends to shift in the 'old, see? Now, in a Beaufort eleven, with the winds at fifty-six ter sixty-three velocity – nautical miles speakin' – leaks in the combustion chamber of the *Leviathan* sprung up and the main bilge pump couldn't maintain the water levels … an' that was when I done the old elbow in, so … excuse me, guv, if yer don't mind me askin', 'ow old are yer?'

'Almost sixteen, Gamin.'

'Then take my advice, son. Go back ter school an' stick ter flamin' 'orses. Coastal steamin' ain't fer the gentry like yourself. You 'ave ter be *born* to the sea, with seawater in yer bleedin' veins – if yer get my drift.'

'I'm a Scotsman, Gamin. Born in a room overlooking the Minch.'

'Then say no more, guv.'

Rory's summer holiday constituted time wasted in his opinion. He had spent most of it playing all manner of childish games with the girls, or going on rainy picnics organized by Charlotte, supplemented by rainy nature rambles organized by Miss Vayer. He couldn't bear the thought of such dreary inactivity for years and years to come; he just wanted to *do* something with his life.

When he returned to Eton at the end of September, he formulated a plan to set him free from his guardians.

But he would have to wait until January.

He did not know why it had to be January, except for the fact that he would be sixteen then, and almost a grown man. Boys of fourteen were able to earn their own living, so why not he?

He knew why not, even before he asked himself the question: Aunt Ada would tell him in no uncertain terms that he was a 'gentleman' and ought to behave like one – which meant education first and filthy lucre second.

Besides, up till now, there had always been Kitty to consider. But she was not a little girl any more. At thirteen, Kitty was well integrated with the Burrett cousins and their friends, the Tapstocks of Boxwood Manor, Rutland. Kitty was sensible and mature for her age, with a mind and a will of her own. She didn't really need him any more to 'big brother' her. He was the odd one out, and both he and Kitty knew it.

At the beginning of the Christmas holidays that year, again spent at Breedon Hall, Rory went up to Folly's Point where he always took himself when he wanted to think out his thoughts and his life.

Against the warm brick of the old Jacobean mansion the Virginia creeper, which had made a veritable bonfire of colour against the walls during the autumn, was beginning to fade and die. There had been so much rain, the ground was soggy underfoot, and over the lake in the grounds a diaphanous veil of mist hung like a shroud. He

followed the equestrian path until he reached the woodland beyond the estate boundary, and then carried on to
the drab stone village of Breedon.

Cottage gardens looked straggly and forlorn on this
muggy December morning, the last vestiges of autumnal
flowers such as michaelmas daisies and chrysanthemums
dying off at the approach of winter. He left the village
and, knee-deep in the faded crisp bracken, just like a sea
of fire in the early autumn, he climbed the steep slope to
Folly's Point. By the time he reached the top, he was
perspiring beneath his mackintosh. It wasn't raining, but
the long-distance view of the countryside was obscured by
a thin damp mist.

He took off his mackintosh and placed it on one of the
smooth rocks to provide a dry seat.

Below him lay part of the great Charnwood Forest
where, in Chaucer's time, a man had been able to walk for
days without ever seeing the sky. Outcrops of rock, like
huge triassic teeth, decayed and blackened with age, made
smooth, shiny land marks in the sea of dead bracken.
Often in the past he had sat up here, listening to the wind
when it blew from a certain direction. It made strange
music through the place of the scattered rocks. And in the
eerie silences that would follow the moaning wind, he felt
he had been caught up in ions of time stretching away into
infinity. Past civilizations, unrecorded, were mourned only
by that lamenting wind-music through the iron bulwarks
of another era. Rory took out of his pocket the harmonica
Uncle Austen and Aunt Ada had given him for his
eleventh birthday – the first birthday he had spent with his
Burrett relatives, almost five years ago now.

Where on earth had those five years gone?

He had thought at the time, that he would never survive
his new life for longer than one week! Was it really seven
summers ago that his mother had died?

The trouble was that Rory didn't know what he *really*
wanted. Was independence his sole objective, or was it to
prove to others that he didn't need anyone, least of all his
guardians, or the patronage of his brother Lindsay? Did
he really want to go to sea, or did he want to make his

fortune in some other way? Gammon had fired his imagination, no doubt about it. Yet, all the time underneath, he was fascinated by the power of the modern engine and modern machinery. Was he capable of being an engineer, or was he simply a chap of high-flying ideas who *thought* he could make his mark upon the world? He simply didn't know. He didn't know anything, except that he wanted to return to Scotland.

Rory hardly drew breath while he played the harmonica, his thoughts all the time centred upon what he was going to do!

So absorbed was he in making music, that when he stopped the clapping of hands nearby unnerved him so much he dropped the harmonica into a deep fissure scarring the surface of the rock on which he sat.

'"Universal Pan, knit with the Graces and the hours in dance, led on the eternal spring!"'

Miss Vayer emerged from behind the rock and he could have killed her!

'Sorry, did I scare you?' She smiled as she tossed back the hood of her long, grey cape.

She bore his disgruntled look with grace, and some amusement as she watched him with an arm thrust down the deep crack. 'You didn't drop your mouth-organ down there, did you, Rory?'

'It's not a *mouth-organ*! It's an harmonica!'

'Oh, then I'm truly sorry. Here, let me help you. My arm is thinner than yours, so I might be able to reach it better.'

She climbed up onto the rock, rolled up her sleeve and thrust a pale slender arm into the crevasse. After a while she was forced to withdraw it, covered in scratches and dirt. She had broken her fingernails, too. 'I'm sorry ... I can't seem to reach it, either,' she apologized again.

'It doesn't matter, forget it.' He gathered up his waterproof and put it on.

'No really, I insist. I must buy you a new one as it was all my fault.'

'It doesn't matter. It's not important.'

'Yes it *does* matter! To me. You were playing so

beautifully ... Fingal's Caves, the music of the Hebrides, I recognized it.' She fell into step beside him.

He was head and shoulders taller than the girls' governess. She looked so pretty and demure in that moment with her golden hair caught by a sharp breeze that had suddenly sprung up, he was disturbed by her very feminine presence. He wondered if she had been up here on Folly's Point on other occasions when he had thought he was alone.

Most of the way back to the Hall they were silent – his fault for he did not know what to say to her.

At the door to the conservatory, the way everyone usually let themselves into the house when not wishing Hardrace to answer the front doorbell, she turned to him with a sweet smile. 'Now I know what to give you for a Christmas present.'

'Oh, please don't bother, Miss Vayer.' His voice that had begun as a squeak ended in a growl and he felt ridiculous because his voice broke just when he had thought he had outgrown that silly, adolescent stage.

They hung up their outdoor garments in the conservatory, and changed out of their muddy boots.

Humphrey greeted Rory in the hall as he was about to take himself off to his bedroom. He no longer shared a room with the other three cousins. Humphrey and he had been given separate rooms.

'Mater and Pater want a word with you, Scotch kipper.'

'Why?'

Humphrey had crumbs from a mince pie all round his grinning mouth. 'Far be it from me to spill the beans before you can fart, Scotch kipper.'

'What the hell are you talking about, Hump?'

'Santa Claus does *not* like the pong of your Christmas stocking, Scotch pancake.'

'Grow up, Humphrey!'

Rory was halfway up the staircase when Hardrace emerged from below stairs. 'Oh, Master Rory, her ladyship requests your presence in the morning-room: at once, if you please.'

With a sigh of resignation, Rory retraced his steps, and

banged loudly on the morning-room door.

'*Come*!' The voice through the wood was that of the iron dragon herself.

He opened the door with a certain amount of timidity. 'You wanted to see me, Aun ...'

'Rory Duncan Roskillen, you are a disgrace to this *entire* family!' she came straight to the point without prevarication. 'Austen, speak to the boy, for words fail me!'

'Rory, dear boy ...' Uncle Austen, sunk deep into the leather Chesterfield, surfaced for a moment. He removed his pipe and continued awkwardly, 'it has come to our attention that ...'

But Rory's Aunt Ada, with her customary impatience, took over from her husband who, with his gentlemanly reticence, seldom came to the point: she called it beating around the bush. 'It has come to our attention that you are nothing but a wastrel and a lazy good-for-nothing.'

He had been hoping for too much, obviously. As in the days of Baharabad with his Papa's voice, Shawmoss's voice and Sula's voice making mincemeat of him, Rory shut his mind off.

His aunt brandished a piece of paper under his nose: either his school report or his death warrant: possibly both, he surmised, since the latter was dependent upon the former. 'Do you know what this is?'

'M – m-my school report?' he ventured a guess.

'This is a blackmail letter.'

'Bl-blackmail, Aunt Ada?'

'Yes, *blackmail*! Can you imagine why on earth your Uncle Austen and I should receive such an odious communication?'

'No, Aunt Ada. No possible reason.'

'Then what about this photograph?' She thrust it under his nose. Then she jabbed a finger at it. 'Is that not you in a state of undress, sprawled amongst all the other scally-wags and alley-cats who appear to be in an equal state of undress?'

'Uh-uh-uh ... NO!'

'No? Are you quite certain?'

'No, Aunt ... I mean yes.'

'*What* were you doing amongst those naked women?'

'Nnn ... not naked, Aunt ... tea. We were taking tea at Rosy's teashop ...' he put a finger into his collar to loosen the constriction of his cravat around his throat. 'Well, it was a sort of celebration ...' His voice faded away into a painful silence. She would never understand about Garrick's birthday party on Brocas Street.

'A teaparty? Without your clothes on?'

'It ... it was a warm day.'

'And you were all *drunk*, it appears, on something other than tea! How old are you?'

'Nearly sixteen.'

'Nearly sixteen. I see. Do you wish to see seventeen, young man? Because I don't think so at this rate. You are going to come to a bad end, soon, Rory Duncan, unless you get a hold of yourself. This blackmail letter, together with the photograph, was sent to us by a certain ... certain wastrel who is not brave enough to furnish us with his real name, but resorts to the *nom de plume* of Spendthrift! Does that name ring a bell in your empty mind?'

'No, Aunt Ada.'

'You seem to know very little about your own activities. Simply because I suspect you to be in a perpetual trance! Your last term was a disaster according to your school report. You are a disgrace. You have got yourself into debt through gambling – as this letter purports!' She waved it at him again. 'This Spendthrift fellow demands settlement of your gambling debts forthwith, otherwise he intends to send this ... this obscene photograph to the newspapers. Can you *imagine* what *that* kind of exposure will do to this family's reputation?'

Rory swallowed, but wasn't brave enough to attempt a reply.

'The *shame* of it! Uncle Austen would be disgraced in the House of Lords for having a nephew of such incalculable worthlessness!'

Rory noticed that in her wrath, the insults were getting longer all the time. Even his poor old uncle dared not interrupt in the face of his wife's fierce diatribe. It all served to remind him of the Indian Sadhu cursing his father on the road to Tippindee. He wondered if Suzy was still alive. He wondered if Brig was still alive and spouting Robbie Burns: what a pity India was so far away, otherwise he could have spent the holidays with Brig on *shikar* instead of in Leicestershire with an old buzzard of an aunt.

'*Are you paying attention!*'

'Yes, Aunt Ada.'

'I have not finished as yet!' she said viciously when he made shuffling signs that he was anxious to leave her company. 'As a punishment, your allowance will be cut to a quarter of what it currently is in order to pay off your sordid little school debts. If more debts are accumulated, I will instruct your father's Edinburgh solicitors to take the money from the inheritance that is supposed to come to you when you are twenty-one. When you are penniless and destitute, perhaps you will come to your senses and try and do something with your worthless life, for Uncle Austen and I will no longer bail you out! Your hedonistic lifestyle has got to stop at once, do you understand?'

'Yes, Aunt.'

'The rest of your Christmas holidays will be spent in your room behind locked doors. You will avail yourself of the opportunity to catch up with your studies. You will take your meals alone in your room. You will see no one, you will speak to no one apart from the Rector of Breedon Church who will call upon you daily to instruct you in the ways of a Christian gentleman. The only time you will be allowed to leave your room will be to accompany us to the midnight service on Christmas Eve. Is that understood?'

'Yes, Aunt Ada.'

She could not have devised a worse form of punishment had she received a visit from the Angel Gabriel himself: it was as though the old battle-axe had sensed that he had it in mind to pack his bags and depart the happy home for ever, the moment 'Hark the Herald Angels Sing' had been sung. He would have thought that Aunt Ada would have been delighted to see the back of him: perhaps she was some kind of sadist who enjoyed inflicting pain on adolescent boys – nephews in particular.

Humphrey was lingering in the hall with a smirk and the crumbs of another mince pie around his mouth. Rory took an umbrella from the stand and swiped the grin off Humphrey's face.

The season of goodwill and cheer was not upon him.

On Christmas Eve, while everyone was enjoying themselves, the sounds of laughter and merriment to be heard throughout the house, Rory lay on his bed and wondered who the Scug was who had ratted on him. Could it possibly have been Lloyd Smyrna? Or Garrick himself? Or some other fag from 'The Set' who had it in for him? NO! Impossible! They were all his friends.

But friends were inconsistent. Friends were dispensable. Friends were only friends when they wanted something. Friends were like passing ships in the night, a brief light on the masthead, swaying about and finally disappearing altogether as soon as the passage got rough.

But who could have done such a dastardly deed? For money? Money or love, which was it? Had he pinched someone's girlfriend and not realized it at the time? Not a hope. He was still as virtuous as the day he was born, despite all that the blackmailing photograph had revealed to his aunt. He wouldn't know the first thing about seducing a girl – look what had happened with The Bud! Love gone down the drain for lack of experience.

Then who?

It was a mystery.

But a mystery that had got him into an awful lot of trouble.

To whom did he owe the most money and favours in '*Nonsense*', the common term for the Scugs of Lower School.

He went through a list of names and kept coming up with the same one – that of the Honourable Lloyd Smyrna: if it *was* Smyrna under the *nom de plume* of Spendthrift, then he'd make quite certain that next term Smyrna would receive a near mortal injury that would confine him to a wheelchair for the rest of his life!

On second thoughts that might be a little too drastic: he was not a violent chap. Not unless provoked. Besides, he had formulated a plan that did not include school next term.

Maybe it was some sort of practical joke?

But it wasn't April Fool's Day yet.

Well, whatever! If it was some sort of practical joke by the crumbs who had been with him at Garrick's birthday party, hadn't the look on his aunt's face been well and truly worth it?

But nothing had been worth her verbal abuse. She knew how to insult one better than even old Shawmoss!

Oh well, it wasn't worth getting into a coil about: nothing in life was *that* important. Everything worked out somehow.

To take his mind off the injustices of life, Rory started composing a poem: 'In fever'd dreams her form I see, Clothed in stark reality. Shining stars her eyes anoint, The burial rocks on Folly's Point. O, heavenly body, breath of life, Vanquish this pain ... sharp as a knife ...' He wondered why he had chosen to dedicate it to Miss Charis Vayer as, deep in thought, he sucked the end of his pencil. Why Charis?

He yawned, turned over and fell asleep through sheer boredom.

He heard his name whispered seductively, close to his ear, 'Rory ... Rory, wake up!'

'Ummm?' He turned over, his dreams of fair Charis haunting him as never before.

'Rory ... are you in there?'

He wasn't dreaming. The voices were outside his bedroom door. Rory sat up and yawned again. 'Of course I'm here, Lennie! Where else am I supposed to be? Don't you know I'm the man in the iron mask?'

Again he heard the girls giggling and whispering among themselves, and was annoyed that he couldn't join in the fun – and for once he wouldn't have minded playing their silly games. 'Kitty ... Lennie? What are you two doing outside my door?'

'Releasing the man in the iron mask – hey presto!'
Leonora stood on the threshold, waving the key in her
hand. 'Happy Christmas!'

'Oh Lor', you lovely girls! How did you manage it?'

'Mama and Papa have gone to Boxwood Manor with
Rupert and Charlotte. They won't be back until the
midnight service. A few hours of freedom is all that you
have,' Leonora told him.

'What about the others?'

'The only others left are Jane, Humphrey and the twins
– oh, and Charis. We're all in this together. Come on, we'll
explain on the way downstairs.' Leonora linked her arm in
his. 'But like Cinderella, you must be back in your room
by midnight!' She giggled again, a very girlish sound.

'Go on, then, explain,' Rory urged.

Kitty did the explaining. 'Well, you see, Rory, we were
playing this game Miss Vayer invented. It was called the
twelve tasks of Hercules. We've all had to participate,
including the servants. I had to take possession of the
Queen of the Amazon's girdle. I was *really* stumped until
Miss Vayer suggested I try and get hold of the house-
keeper's belt with the house keys attached. Mrs Braine
was fast asleep in the servant's hall. She'd had a little too
much sherry, you see. But she'd taken off her belt and
cuffs and left them on a table beside her, so it was easy to
get hold of your bedroom key!'

'Goodness, Kitty, you dare-devil!' Rory hugged his little
sister with her rosy cheeks and bright eyes. Then he
turned to Leonora, 'And need I ask what your Herculean
task was, Lennie?'

'Guess?'

'Releasing Cerberus from the infernal regions?'

'Clever boy!'

In the Shukborough Room Humphrey banged him
between the shoulderblades. 'What's your poison, Scotch
kipper?'

'Whisky. Need you ask, Sassenach?'

'Rory, don't you think you'd better not . . .'

'Hush, Kitty, it's Christmas and I've been a prisoner for
eight days!'

'Poor you! I do feel sorry for you, Rory. But you must learn to be a good boy, you know.'

'Yes, I know, Kit, but it's difficult at times.'

Even Mordan and Michael were civilized enough to let him join in their game of poker with Humphrey. But he made sure the betting was within the scope of his pocket, in all, half-a-crown.

He kept looking over his shoulder until Humphrey was forced to say, 'Relax, Scotch kipper. The Mater and Pater aren't due back for a couple of hours yet.'

'Where's Miss Vayer – I thought she was playing games with you lot?'

'She went for a walk up to Folly's Point because she had a headache and wanted a breath of fresh air,' Leonora informed him.

Soon after that piece of interesting information, he lost all his money to Mordan, and so made the excuse that he, too, was in need of a breath of air as he had been cooped up for so long. Humphrey also threw in his hand. Out in the hall he thumped Rory once again on the back, 'You take the high road, Scotchman and I'll take the low.' He winked and shouldered the green baize door.

'Who is it this time, Hump?'

'Flossie.'

'My God, you must have fallen on hard times, Hump.'

'Not a bit of it. Floss is as soft as thistledown.' He touched the side of his bulbous nose meaningfully, and descended to the kitchen quarters.

Rory never did catch up with Miss Vayer. By the time he heaved himself up to Folly's Point, he realized he must have missed her somewhere en route. The place of the scattered rocks was as barren and inhospitable as a graveyard.

He raced back to the house, hoping he would make it before his aunt and uncle returned from Boxwood Manor.

Leonora and Kitty were waiting anxiously for him on the back stairs. 'Where have you been? We've been looking *everywhere* for you! They'll be back soon with Rupert and Charlie and then *we'll* be in trouble for letting you out of your room.'

'D'na fash yourselves, fair maidens. Just lock me in quick and scram.'

He shed himself of his outdoor clothes and dived into his pyjamas.

Fifteen minutes later his aunt appeared at his bedside. 'What's the matter with your breathing?' she demanded.

'It's nothing, Aunt Ada. Just a burning pain in the chest.'

'Have you a temperature?' She put a cold hand on his hot and sweaty forehead. 'I think you have. Are you feeling ill?'

'Very ill, Aunt Ada.'

'How long have you been feeling ill like this?'

'For quite a while now.'

'Why didn't you tell someone?'

'I didn't want to bother anyone. Or give them my germs.'

'I think I'd better send for Dr Clark. You cannot go to church in that state. Heaven knows, you might be sickening for something infectious which you could pass on to others. You really are a foolish boy. You should have let us know you were not feeling well. Stay there and keep warm. I'll send someone in presently with some hot broth for you.'

'Thank you, Aunt Ada.'

She swept regally from his presence and he all but restrained himself from jumping out of bed for sheer joy: Aunt Ada was obviously worried in case she would be had up for manslaughter should he die in custody! She'd even left the door open in her anxiety over his state of health!

After they had all departed for the midnight service at the nearby church, he waited in anticipation for the broth.

As he had so rightly guessed, Charis appeared – in her night attire – bearing a tray of hot steaming soup surrounded by other goodies. Her hair was loose and hung in golden tresses to her waist. She set down the tray on his washstand, locked the bedroom door and picked up the bottle of champagne she had brought with her from his uncle's cellars.

'Happy Christmas, Rory.'

'Happy Christmas, Charis.'

'How is the Nemean lion?'

'Waiting to be slain – I think,' he just about managed to croak.

She smiled. 'You're a *very* naughty boy, you know.'

'I do wish everyone would stop calling me a boy.'

'Shift over then, and we'll see if you're a man or a boy ...' She came into the bed beside him, placed his tooth mug on his palpitating chest, filled it with champagne, and said, 'I'm sorry about the mouth-organ. I couldn't find an adequate substitute for the expensive one you lost.'

'Harmonica,' he croaked again as champagne bubbles rushed up his nose.

She stayed an hour with him, the best Christmas he had ever spent in banishment.

Dr Clark called the following morning to examine the patient. But before climbing the stairs, he first fortified himself on Lord Burrett's Christmas cheer and a good chin-wag with his lordship in his study: well worth the effort of dragging out to visit the sick on Christmas morning – especially when he discovered the ailing bird had flown.

The bed was neatly made, the room tidied, the tooth mug replaced on the washstand, in which a farewell note had been placed.

Rory Duncan Roskillen, much to his poor aunt's chagrin when reading her nephew's note of self-discharge in the presence of the highly amused doctor, was somewhere on the high road to Scotland.

PART THREE

'It is not the crook in modern business that we fear, but the honest man who does not know what he is doing.'

Owen D. Young

CHAPTER TEN

Rory stepped off the Caledonian Railway at Port Glasgow and immediately went in search of his uncle Hamish MacDearg's registered office.

While he had been very young when his mother and father had brought them here to bid old Uncle Neptune adieu on the eve of their departure to India, Rory still remembered the hustle and bustle of Glasgow Harbour. Most of the docks and quays had still been under construction then. He recalled old Neptune pointing out to Lindsay and himself the huge hydraulic machinery sinking concrete monoliths for the quay walls to Cessnock Dock – the name afterwards changed to Prince's Dock in accordance with Royal prerogative.

Expansion of the open docks, for there was no tidal range in the Clyde, was still going on everywhere, and so he wandered around the dry docks, slipways and quays, absorbing the sights and sounds of such fervent activity. This was the very heart of Scotland, and he was in the thick of things – where he wanted to be. This little portion of the British Isles represented life in the raw, and its wealth: the south quay from where coal was handled by huge hydraulic coal-shipping hoists; Queens Dock from where the liners sailed; Plantation Quay where huge locomotives were being shipped to Egypt or India; the coastal trade berths and to the left of Prince's Dock, the mineral quay where the iron ore was loaded. On the south pier he had to dodge the trams, and the huge dray-carts hauling their diverse loads.

The Allan Line passenger steamers he remembered from a time past, and a yearning, deep and strong took possession of him as never before. The smell of it all! Coal and oil and steam, grain and timber, cattle and sheep, rope and tar, salt and fish, and countless other dockside smells, were as potent as the smell of money.

At the Custom House Quay on the north side of the Upper Harbour, Rory looked for the office of the MacDearg Steamship Company. Unlike the other quays, these owner- or agent-allocated berths had no numbers, so it was a question of searching and asking. From here the West Highland steam packets and river passenger steamers of Steel and Bennie Ltd; D. MacBrayne Ltd; and G and J Burns, all the famous names, operated.

He found the office of the MacDearg Steamship Company, eventually. It's grandeur seemed somewhat diminished to Rory, as he viewed the flaking green lettering of the sign on the wall beside the door, with a pointing finger to indicate which was the entrance, though there was only one.

The office was open even though the previous day had been Christmas Day. But Christmas, he remembered, was not a national holiday in Scotland, only Hogmanay. Inside MacDearg's shabby, cramped and dark little premises, a shipping clerk with a green shade over his eyes and faded ink-stains on his fingers, was busily paring his nails, while a huge ledger in front of him remained full of blank spaces.

'I'd like to speak to Mr Hamish MacDearg, please,' Rory began, but the indolent clerk spared him no attention whatsoever.

Rory started again.

'Mr MacDearg, please!'

'Not here, boy.'

'Where can I find him?'

'Who's asking?'

'His great-nephew.'

Then the clerk, who reminded Rory of his uncle Austen's chauffeur, Gammon, did spare him a glance as he pushed his shade further up his forehead with the carpenter's file he had been using on his nails. 'Try the Renfrew Arms'.

'Oh. Oh, I see. Where's that?'

'What?'

'The Renfrew Arms!'

'Renfrew Road – other side of the mineral quay, boy.'

'Thanks.' Rory found his hale and hearty great-uncle at the Renfrew Arms, seated on a bar stool and half in his cups, even though it was only mid-day. 'Uncle Hamish?' Great-Uncle Neptune, with his snowy mutton-chop whiskers, his bleary blue eyes unfocused above the S-bend of his old-fashioned meerschaum pipe, must have been eighty years old if he were a day: and still flirting with the barmaids in exact accordance with snippets of family gossip.

'An' who may you be, boy?' he asked, eyeing the sturdy, golden youth up and down with a great deal of suspicion, as well as apprehension.

'Your great-nephew, Rory Duncan Roskillen of Glengarth, Ross-shire.'

Hamish nearly fell off his stool, not through liquor but through fright. 'Great God in heaven ... you hear that, Elspeth?' he turned to the barmaid before her gantry of drinks, 'This boy's m' Sassenach nephew all the way from Eton in England, no less! What'er you doing here, boy?' He shifted on his stool to get a better view of his great-nephew, whom he glowered at with all the menace he could summon in that put-upon moment.

'Looking for a job.'

'Thought you were still at school?'

'I've left school.'

'Not yet, you haven't ... run away, have you?' Hamish took the pipe from his mouth and spat gustily into a bar-spittoon next to his elbow. 'Egad! The last I heard from Angus MacPhee operating the *Mary Blythe* for me, was that your brother was the new laird and you still with the Sassenachs down south.'

'I've come home, Uncle Neptune.'

'Seems like it. How old are you, boy?'

'Sixteen – in seventeen days time.'

'What're you drinking, then?'

'Whisky, please.'

Hamish roared with laughter and slapped his thigh. 'Elspeth, give the lad a whisky! Be damned, if there's one thing I like, it's sheer Sassenach sauce – and you've more than your fair share, fellow m'lad!' Again Hamish slapped his thigh.

'Have you a job for me?' Rory asked when the whisky was set before him.

'*No siree!*'

'Why not?'

'Because, fellow m'lad, you'll turn tail after you'er glass of whisky, which more than likely you'll throw up in the gutter, before returning to the arms of your Sassenach relatives.'

'I'm not going home. I have no home.'

'Och! Now that's a shame and a tale I'm dying to hear! But not today. Today I'm getting set for Hogmanay and I've a great deal of cupping to do. Listen boy, you an' me got nothing to say to each other. Your grandfather – may he rot in his grave – robbed me of ma kin, ma mony, ma dues an' ma *land*!'

Now why, Rory wondered, had old Neptune become so het up? He had reverted to a thick Lowland accent not hitherto apparent.

'Go back to England, boy. Take it from me, old Hamish ain't got one foot in the grave – yet! As you were no doubt hoping. Hence the reason you've come *hame*! I may not have kin other than you an' Lindsay, but I'd rather leave the *Mary Blythe* and the *Jane Blythe* to a dogs' hame than see the company pass back into the family that once robbed me.'

'I'm sorry. I didn't know you'd been robbed by my grandfather.'

'Och now, there's a great deal you don't know, Rory Duncan Roskillen! So I'll be thanking you to clear off, out o' old Hamish's sight. Go ask your fine brother for a job – or else go an' eat coke with another steamship line.'

'I might just do that.' Rory finished his drink and eyed old Neptune steadily. 'I came here in good faith to offer you my services – for what they're worth. I'm willing to learn. I know all about the diagonal engine and slide valves and air pumps and short-stroke oscillating engines, and one day I'm going to prove to you that I can design a boat better than the ones the German Navy Law is producing! *Turbines*, Uncle! To replace all your old steamships!'

'Egad, you've more lip than a woman's fanny!'

'I thought I'd be able to generate new life into your company by some imaginative *input*! Instead, I get insults. No wonder the MacDearg Steamship Company is on its last legs! I can see it – I saw it in the few short minutes I was in your office! You're unable to compete with those other lines out there, simply because you don't know *how.*'

'*And YOU do, I suppose, you cheeky young varmint?*' Hamish roared.

'Yes! I know exactly how!' Rory said, standing up to Hamish's wrath.

'Egad! Ye're as brazen as your grandfather before you.'

'Maybe. But I'm not as short-sighted as he was – and you still are! I didn't come here to rob you of your steamship company. I wouldn't want it. Not with only two boats in operation – one a mail packet to the Highlands and the other a decrepit old junk plying between Glasgow and Belfast on summer pleasure cruises. What pleasure, I ask myself, in operating a loss-making concern.' Rory headed for the door.

'Come back here, you young hot-head!' bellowed Hamish MacDearg, but his great-nephew with his rucksack, had already stepped out of the door. Hamish struggled off the stool and after Rory Duncan, much to the amusement of the other occupants of the premises, who had been listening avidly to the heated exchange between great-uncle and great-nephew.

Down the length of Renfrew Road Hamish bellowed, 'You show me a pilot's certificate and some navigating experience first, fellow m'lad, before you come barging in here begging to be taken on by this Lowlander who was diddled out of everything by your fine Hi'land grandfather!'

Hamish MacDearg stomped back into the warm and welcoming confines of the Renfrew Arms: 'Egad! Fill the porter to the brim, Elspeth,' he told the barmaid. 'I might just give that Sassenach great-nephew o' mine a headache he'll ne'r forget by leaving him the company after I'm dead and gone. It'll give me the greatest pleasure from the grave to know he's squirming over lack of funds – which his bloody Hi'land grandfather diddled from me when he married my sister!'

Rory, on his long legs, didn't turn back. He went straight to the Centre Pier and berths 21–29 in the South Basin, from where G. Smith and Company operated their ships out of Queen's Dock to India and South Africa. 'Have you got a job for me aboard your boat?' he asked an able seaman swinging from a bo'suns chair along the side of the newly painted merchant ship.

The seaman eyed the stalwart young lad up and down. He didn't look a bad specimen, and might prove to be useful during the trip. 'How old are you?'

'Eighteen.'

'Ain't my business, recruiting. I'm only inspecting the new paintwork to see the barnacles 'ave all been scraped off underneath. Go ask the purser – cabin nine on the fo'c's'le deck.'

'Thanks.'

Rory was taken aboard the *Ailsa Craig* as a fireman for the trip to Cape Town. He had hoped the merchant ship was bound for India, in which case he would have looked up old Brig in Baharabad and tried to persuade the Maharajah of Baharabad to employ him in his father's former job of training polo ponies. But the *Ailsa Craig* was taking timber to South Africa: pit-props for the diamond and gold mines. If that was to be the exchange, then wood for jewels, ivory and gold could not be a bad robbery by English standards, thought Rory as he viewed his sleeping quarters and eighteen-inch locker-space with some trepidation.

Angus MacPhee brought the *Mary Blythe* to a shuddering and rather clumsy halt beside the narrow stone jetty connecting the loch-island of Rill to the mainland. Angus was used to paddlers, the screw steamer taking four times longer to birth than a paddler. But beggars couldn't be choosers, and old Hamish MacDearg was all of that: his boats were so ancient, they beggared description, were Angus's solitary thoughts.

The laird was not on the headland this morning, seated on his fine horse, monarch of all he surveyed – as was usual when Lindsay Roskillen was home: Angus was disappointed. He had much gossip to impart to the laird concerning the recent doings of his younger brother. News had a way of travelling – sometimes the only communication through the glens was through family connections, and the laird certainly had enough of those living in the lowlands!

Maybe the Laird Lindsay was still at his fancy university down south somewhere, mused Angus to himself as he tied up the boat and dragged out the sack of mail for Glengarth's estate office.

The ways of the upper classes baffled him, for how could a man know about the land from books? He had to sink his boots in the soil of his birth, get his hands dirty from it; he had to breathe the air of the glens, and listen to mountain waterfalls tumbling to the lochs to know what it was all about. He had to have the fist of God in his heart as he watched the eagle soar above the valleys of heather, and he had to be humble enough to give thanks for the experience. And so, here was another Sassenach landlord to be sure, in this latest generation of Scottish landowners – despite what others thought about the Laird Lindsay.

It was wonderful Easter weather, as spring in the Highlands often could be. The gorse was in full bloom and the marsh marigolds were bright as sunbeams on Inchnadamph. Beinn Claidheamh Mor this morning, had a halo of whispy white cloud circling its summit. The loch lay like molten silver, the reflection of the blue mountain cast across the water: aye, bonny weather in bonny country, and the two brothers didn't know what they were missing, thought Angus without envy, bred as he was with the detachment of those born to serve.

He shouldered the mailbag and went on up the glen.

Inside Iain Hamilton's estate office, the young laird was in occupancy, seated on the edge of the desk, smoking a cigarette, while his factor, his cousin, occupied the prime seat behind the desk. Angus knew that the estate was still held in trust until the new laird reached his majority, all in accordance with the old laird's will.

'Good morning, Angus.'

'G'morning, m'laird. Thought you'd be in England. G'morning, Mr Hamilton. Nice day.'

'Indeed it is, Angus. And what have you got for us this month?'

'The usual, I daresay. Bills and timber contracts and news of that young rascal, the playboy.'

'Rory? What's he up to now?' asked Lindsay in surprise. 'And how would you be knowing about my brother's activities, Angus?'

'You might well ask, m'laird. But he was in your great-uncle Hamish MacDearg's office on the day after Christmas, fashing himself to take a berth on one of Smithie's ships bound for the Cape.'

'Rory? On a berth to South Africa?'

'Aye. Not as a paying passenger, but as a fireman. He had an altercation with Hamish, m'laird. Asking for a job with the Steamship Company, he was. So then Hamish threw him out of the Renfrew Arms, angered at the young rascal's sauce and the running away from his fancy school down south, so Rory took passage on the *Ailsa Craig*.'

'When was this?'

'Three months ago, m'laird. Christmas day after.'

Lindsay bit his lip.

'You've heard of it, m'laird?'

'Of course ...' Lindsay stood up impatiently. His uncle Austen in Leicestershire had written to him about Rory's disappearance, and so had the Dean of Eton College, but no one had known where Rory had taken himself. While Uncle Austen had assumed Rory had returned to Glengarth, Lindsay himself hadn't really cared at the time, wrapped up as he was in his own life at Oxford. To be told three months later of his brother's whereabouts, jolted a guilty feeling in him. 'Why didn't Hamish tell me this before?'

'Hamish, m'laird, wishes not to interfere in the quarrels of brothers. He expressly bade me, Angus MacPhee,

humble postman that I am, to convey his feelings on the
subject to the Laird of Glengarth, his great-nephew –
which I'm doing. Hamish MacDearg being the boss who
pays me a living wage, d'y ken, m'laird?'

Lindsay and his cousin Iain exchanged glances, which
did not go amiss as far as Angus MacPhee was concerned.
He knew all about Hamish MacDearg's own quarrel with
his brother-in-law, this half-century past. Clan feuds were
nothing new. They usually went on generation after generation, for Scotsmen did not only have a reputation for
itchy feet, but for long memories too!

After Angus's departure, Iain said to Lindsay, 'Great-
Uncle Neptune has never forgiven this family for what he
saw as the fleecing of MacDearg land.'

'What fleecing of MacDearg land?' Lindsay asked,
stubbing out his cigarette in the ashtray on the desk. 'All
the land around here is Roskillen land belonging to the
estate of Glengarth.'

'I'm talking about land in Glasgow.'

'Grandfather had land in Glasgow?' Lindsay asked with
some astonishment.

'Aye! A tidy packet of it too, Lindsay, on both sides of
the Clyde.'

'I didn't know.'

'Nor did I until after his death. He kept that a secret
right enough: or else he'd conveniently forgotten about it,
which is probably nearer the truth. I was sorting out the
land title deeds and other complicated legacies with his
solicitors in Edinburgh, making it all neat before you took
over, when we discovered some papers in Grandfather's
possession appertaining to land between Govan and
Renfrew.'

From the pocket of his worn Harris tweed jacket with
leather patches on the elbows, Lindsay took an embossed
silver-gilt cigarette case, and extracted another Turkish
Latakia. This was news, and infinitely interesting to him.

'I take it you know the fortunes of the MacDearg
family, Lindsay? Although, having said that, Hamish and
his sister Mary-Jane were actually Blythes, not
MacDeargs.'

Lindsay lit his cigarette. 'Yes, I know about them, vaguely. The MacDeargs earned their wealth in the eighteenth century through trading with America: tobacco leaf in exchange for Scottish linen. So, what happened to the family fortune?'

'Well then, these Lowlanders from Glasgow, the MacDeargs, prospered on flax and tobacco until the American War of Independence put paid to that lucrative exchange. The tobacco trade between Scotland and the Americas fell into a dramatic decline. But instead of reinvesting in other up-and-coming trades such as glassmaking or tanning as everyone else was doing at that time, the MacDeargs bought up farmland along the Clyde – mainly at Renfrew and Meadowside. At the time it was thought of as a very foolish investment, the flat land at Renfrew being marshy and prone to flooding. But in view of what has happened in the last fifty years since the Clyde Trustees took over development of the river, the investment was a very shrewd one – though not from our point of view any more.'

'How do our grandparents and Great-Uncle Hamish fit into all this?'

'Mary-Jane Blythe and her brother Hamish were made orphans through the early deaths of their parents from tuberculosis. They were then adopted by their maternal uncle, Grant MacDearg. He and his wife had no children, and so Mary and Hamish were the ready-made family they both wanted. After Grant MacDearg's death, Hamish and Mary-Jane became joint owners of their adopted father's undeveloped lands. Our grandmother held in her own name some poor isolated pockets of ground where the River Kelvin joins the Clyde at Meadowside, as well as an area on the south bank, at Govan.'

'The dowry portion she brought with her when she married our grandfather way back in the 1840s?'

'Exactly.'

'Then where did that leave Hamish?'

'Hamish never married, and therefore has no direct heirs.'

'Yes, I know that! I mean as far as the land went? What

precipitated the ill-feeling between our grandfather and old Uncle Neptune?'

'Grandfather had been leasing his wife's dowry portion to the Glasgow Trustees for lairages. Then, in 1866 Glasgow Corporation slapped a compulsory purchase order on land at Yorkhill and Plantation to provide an extension to Queens Dock, since Port Glasgow was now growing rapidly through increased trade with the rest of the world. This was to be the site of the new Kelvinhaugh wharf. The Trustees then succeeded in getting hold of twenty-five acres of the huge Merklands estate adjoining Meadowside, as well as Meadowside itself. These sites came into the independent Borough of Partick. The whole of this area north of the Clyde was earmarked for development into the twentieth century.'

'So I suppose Grandfather had no choice in the matter, but to sell?'

'Correct. The Clyde Trustees then wanted Govan for the new Cessnock docks – Prince's dock as it now is. For years individual members of the Trust had secretly been buying up the land of the large estate-owners. The whole thing was shrouded in secrecy at the time, in order to keep land prices low. Then, in 1883, the Royal Assent was given for the construction of new docks at Govan. Grandfather, with his interest in his wife's inheritance, had held out against the individuals who required Mary-Jane's dowry portion at Govan. The Trustees again slapped on a compulsory purchase order for land south of Queen's dock – which included Mary-Jane's share at Govan. Grandfather is supposed to have sold off the land for the paltry sum of £1,000 an acre – weighing in the balance what that land was now going to be worth to Glasgow Corporation!'

'Lack of investment foresight – as we can all say in retrospect. Or was he being less than honest with Hamish?'

'I don't know. But Hamish and he quarrelled over the sale of the dowry. It's quite possible that our grandfather also got cash under the table which he didn't declare, in order to avoid paying land taxes and suchlike.'

'Backhanders, you mean, which he kept quiet about at the time? In that case there must be other documents hidden away somewhere.'

'Well, as I said, it's a possibility. Hamish could have found out about the underhand deals, hence the reason for their on-going feud.'

'Don't forget, Iain, we're viewing things from time and distance – a distance of over half a century. We don't know what pressures were put upon landowners at the time, to sell up in the name of trade – which Scotland has always badly needed.'

'Fair enough. But Hamish never ceased to drive the point home to our grandfather of how he had parted with Mary-Jane's dowry for peanuts.'

'What happened to Hamish's share of the land at Renfrew?'

'I'm coming to that. Up till now Grandfather had used Meadowside for the storage of Glengarth timber, as well as his own Highland livestock at the Kelvinhaugh cattle wharf. Way back in the '60s the question of lairages was the all important factor since shipments of North American cattle were being landed regularly at Port Glasgow. Up till then, only Highland cattle had been the problem, brought down on the hoof in cattle-drives from the Highlands. When the question of 'imported diseases' arose, new sites for lairages were always in the mind of the Port authorities. After a government ruling that all foreign cattle had to be rested at the point of disembarkation for a minimum period of twelve hours if they were to be taken beyond the landing area for slaughter, Hamish seized his opportunity by leasing some of his land at Renfrew – Shieldhall, in particular – for lairages.'

'Did Grandfather take him up on his offer?'

'No, not initially – which was stupid of him because he was then leasing lairages at Govan for quite a high rental, according to the old contracts I had to sort through. But pride was the dividing factor in this instance. However, as luck would have it, Govan – as I've already mentioned – was to be developed as a dry dock and the lairages shifted upstream – to Shieldhall!'

'Hamish must have sent up a silent prayer of gratitude,' was Lindsay's cynical remark. But all this was ancient history to him, and of no help to Glengarth – unless flaws could be detected in the old contracts, which no one had yet tumbled to.

'Men make their own destiny by the very nature God sees fit to endow them with, and Hamish was no business man,' said Iain, scratching the side of his neck thoughtfully. The air in the estate office was thick with tobacco smoke from Iain's pipe and Lindsay's strong cigarettes.

'And nor was our grandfather by the look of things.'

'Och, I think he was more wily than Hamish – though not much! Grandfather, as a hereditary landowner, knew the value of real estate. But he made the mistake of assuming that no one could rob him of its rightful value by placing a compulsory purchase order upon it.'

'And meanwhile,' Lindsay concluded sadly, 'poor old Uncle Neptune had to see the gradual decline over the past few years of the rentals on his lairages, with the final closure of Shieldhall.'

'Yes,' Iain said, tapping his pipe against the side of the ashtray. 'The 1896 Diseases of Animals Act which saw the decline of foreign cattle imports must have seemed like the final nail in the old man's coffin – taking into account what also happened to his steamship company.'

'What did happen?' asked Lindsay. 'I never tumbled to the exact reasons for its inability to make money through cargo-haulage – a lucrative business if any, I'd have thought.'

'Indeed. But, as I said, Hamish had no head for business matters. What he got, he spent. With the money from the leased lairages he decided to start a cargo-haulage business as well as running pleasure cruises to the islands. For a while all went well. He had leased off his land at Renfrew to Middow and Strait, shipbuilders and repairers. From here he also operated his own boatyard – but the land was tied up now and all he could get for it was the rental. So Hamish approached Grandfather for ready cash to invest in six steamships. Our grandfather agreed – for the mortgage-value on the Middow and Strait site.'

'Clever of him, and not so unbusinesslike.'

'But our grandfather really had no interest in steam-ships or steam coasting, only Glengarth and the timber it could produce without causing him too much of a head-ache. They overstretched themselves, so that when the lairages at Shieldhall were not bringing in as much as they had envisaged, a couple of steamships had to be sold off. Competition from other companies using more ma-noeuvrable, fast-turning compound engines with twin screw propulsion for sea-going voyages was fierce. And Renfrew is six miles up stream from Port Glasgow, d'ye ken. Then fresh disaster hit Hamish's business when one of his summer-trade coastal steamers to the Summer Isles foundered in a gale with the loss of five lives, which put paid to the pleasure-cruising side of things. He was in massive debt and beholden still to Grandfather, who held the Middow and Strait site as compensation for what he had lost.'

'I see what you mean about bad luck dogging Hamish's footsteps. So he's left now with only two steamers on their last legs because the Middow and Strait land was mort-gaged to Grandfather – the rent for which is still received by us, I take it?'

'Correct. To this day Hamish blames our grandfather for ruining him and his business by making underhand deals behind his back – which is what Hamish swears happened. But our grandfather, too, was in financial trouble at the time, and never fully recovered from the collapse of the MacDearg Steamship Company into which he'd put most of Glengarth's timber money.'

'Hence the lack of reinvestment in our own land,' Lindsay added, now well aware by what Iain was telling him, as to why Glengarth appeared so impoverished: timber revenues had been syphoned off elsewhere, it appeared.

'Way back in the middle of the last century, that land at Renfrew hadn't been worth much, so Hamish and Grand-father couldn't really be blamed for not realizing its potential. Not until the Clyde Trustees started to develop it for the new docks did anyone take any notice of Clydeside. But I think you're possibly right, and that Grandfather did indeed make some underhand deals with individual Trustees to keep Glengarth viable, but without telling Hamish.'

'And without it showing up in the books,' said Lindsay thoughtfully.

'Could be. The old man would try and get away with the smallest penny if he could. It was always a devil of a job to get him to declare his real income to the Revenue Office!' Iain, as the estate factor, knew that better than anyone.

'Iain, have you the contracts of those deals between Grandfather and Hamish?'

'Yes, they're here ... somewhere. Give me a minute to search them out. They're only copies of course. I believe the original contracts are held by Grandfather's bank in Edinburgh.'

Iain eventually found the old contracts for MacDearg land on Clydeside in a box file. He handed them to Lindsay.

After a while, Lindsay looked up with a smile. 'When did you last take a good look at these contracts, Iain?'

'A year ago – after Grandfather's death. Why? What's on your mind, Lindsay?'

'This contract, dated 1857, between Hamish and Grandfather for the Middow and Strait acreage on the Clyde is for a lease of *eighty* years, not fifty! Look ... see for yourself. I grant you, at first sight, the old printing on this copy appears to be fifty, but it's actually eighty! The numeral eight appears to have become smudged, or has been altered somewhere along the line. Two copies of this must have been made from the original, one in Hamish's possession, the other in Grandfather Glengarth's, this one kept here in the estate office for reference, while the original was held by Grandfather's Edinburgh solicitors. We must get a look at that first to make certain of our facts. But I don't think I'm wrong. All we've been subjected to lately in the newspapers, our own Scottish Parliament and the House of Lords over the past five years, is the quarrel between Renfrew Town Council and

the Clyde Trust who want to construct a new dock at
Renfrew. If the Bill does go through this year, then
Hamish's marshy farmlands won't be quite so worthless,
after all. Now then, lady luck being a capricious mistress, I
wonder if Hamish has taken a look at his title-deeds
lately?' Lindsay said with a grin.

'I doubt it,' was Iain's sceptical retort. 'Hamish is so far
gone in his cups, his mind is not capable of handling
contracts, land-deals and making money any more – he's
far too old for that now. All he's concerned about is drink,
nothing else. He'll just sign away that land for £1,000 per
acre in view of what happened over Cessnock.'

'I wouldn't be too sure, Iain. And neither would I put
anything past that young brother of mine. Somewhere in
all this, I cannot help feeling he's lurking in the background for a sinister reason. Rory Duncan has always had
an eye to the main chance.'

'What do you mean, Lindsay?'

'I mean to compare this copy of the forty acre site of
Middow and Strait with the original held, as you say, in
Edinburgh. If, as I believe I am right in thinking, that the
copies are incorrect, and that the contract is indeed for
eighty years *not* fifty as everyone has surmised, then I still
have a holding on Clydeside until the year 1937!'

'And what if you are wrong?'

'Then I am the loser and my brother takes all.'

'*Two* copies cannot surely both be in error, Lindsay?'
Iain protested.

'They can be, especially if they were made by the same
shortsighted hand. But, as I said, we've got to see the
original contract made between Grandfather and Great
Uncle Hamish. And for that I must take a little trip to
Edinburgh.'

'Well, I wish you luck,' said Iain, not at all convinced.
'We can do with the extra rent from that shipyard. Every
little helps in our situation.'

Amen! thought Lindsay to himself.

CHAPTER ELEVEN

Rory spent nine months with G. Smith and Company, three round trips to the Cape and back, and another seven months with Aitken, Lilburn and Company at South Quay, Queen's Dock carrying cargo to Australia. It was called 'big boating'.

The voyages passed uneventfully and somewhat boringly to Rory's mind. Going to sea wasn't all that it was cracked up to be. It was not glamorous, but lengthy, lonesome and lacking in mental stimulus.

He had progressed from junior fireman status, whereby he had to ensure that gangways or hatches were not blocked by luggage or cargo, and that cigarettes were not stubbed out in the sand buckets to be used in fire emergencies, to the engine room, bilge-pumps, and to counteract the perpetual grease and steam.

But in those sixteen months abroad, he managed to save his money, albeit seventeen shillings a week, the amount a single man received on the dole. Rory also managed to earn additional bonuses by volunteering for extra watches during the long voyages.

In the spring of 1907, the *Pride of Midlothian*, on her way back from Sydney, Australia, was being piloted home to the Clyde where the whole of the dockside was festooned in flags and bunting and Union Jacks.

While the other deck hands were crowding the rails to get a glimpse of something special, Rory Roskillen was engrossed in counting out his accumulated wages in the crew's forecastle sleeping quarters.

That was where the First Mate found him. 'Skiving again, Roskillen?'

'No, sir, not intentionally.'

'What're you doing down here then, when everyone else is on deck?'

'Counting out my money, sir.'

'Proper little king, aren't we, fellow m'lad?'

'I beg your pardon, sir?'

'Never mind. Look sharpish and toe the line like the rest, Roskillen.' Then he added as an afterthought, 'You signing on again?'

'No, sir.'

'Why not?'

'I've got other things to do.'

'Such as?'

'Earning more money for a start, sir.'

The First Mate grinned broadly. 'Oh yeah, to buy your own Cunard Line?'

'Something like that, sir.'

'Well lad, as I said, look sharpish, there's Royalty waiting to welcome us home. They're here to open the new Rothesay Dock.'

Rory looked up at the First Mate, whom he did not dislike. He had treated him kindly throughout, and had stuck up for him when the going got rough. 'You're joking, sir! The new docks can't be finished as yet?'

'Why not? Work's been carried out at a spanking pace m'lad, for this is the Clyde, where it's all happening! But you're right. The docks aren't finished – and they won't be for another four or five years, so they say.'

'Then why is Royalty opening them now?'

'Because, nosey-parker, since their Royal Highnesses, the Prince and Princess of Wales, were on a visit to Glasgow, and because work is so far ahead of schedule on the new docks, they're going to lay the final copestone in an opening ceremony. So make sure you don't let down the City Fathers by appearing in scruffy uniform. They might just want you to make them a cup of tea, seeing as how you once told us *your* nobby father went hunting with the Prince of Wales in the Indies,' added the First Mate facetiously.

'But that was with the Prince of Wales's father, who is now King Edward VII. And it wasn't the Indies, it was India.'

'Okay, smart alec. Get your nobby arse up on deck, and

holystoned before you know what's coming to you!'

'Yes, sir!' said Rory, saluting smartly. The First Mate was joking – he hoped!

'Bloody little know-all,' muttered the First Mate under his breath as he watched Mr Roskillen scoot off up the forecastle gangway. But one had to give the lad his due, he was no pansy like some of the casual labour signing on, despite all his nobby connections!

There was plenty of work to be had at Port Glasgow, but to sign on for any length of time with one charter company and their cargo-haulage vessels was a great slice out of one's life: Rory had other plans for himself.

After quitting the great merchant ship of Aitken, Lilburn and Company he signed on for a few more casual trips closer to home. One was on behalf of the Clyde Trustees of Glasgow, who had put in an order with the German firm of Eisenwerke, Nagel and Kaempe, A.G. of Hamburg for an electric hoist to be installed at the new Rothesay Dock.

Electric hoists were already in operation at the ports of Emden and Rotterdam, and the Clyde Trustees had ordered three such hoists for Glasgow. The firm of Sir William Arrol and Company of Glasgow, commissioned for the non-electrical parts of the hoists, were in partnership with Eisenwerke, and the firm was signing on all extra hands on the boats fetching the other hoists for installation. Rory then worked for a brief time with Clyde Navigation on a bucket ladder dredger, *Oyster*, sifting silt from the river. The money was good, and so was the experience he gained of the River Clyde itself.

The next four months he spent on a steam coaster, carrying whatever cargo that was offered on a triangular run between Dublin, Port Glasgow and Liverpool. He enjoyed the friendly atmosphere and likeable Irish crew of the *Tara Belle*, mastered by a Liverpool man, William Lucklace. He did whatever was wanted of him, and those months steam-coasting in and out of Ireland proved to be an invaluable experience in good seamanship.

In the autumn of 1907, under his own steam, Rory applied to train for a pilot's certificate at Darby's Nautical

School in Queen's Road, Everton, Liverpool. Men from all over the United Kingdom went to 'Old Darby' to gain certificates of competency in river navigation and the 'rules of the road'.

But first he had to get himself a sponsor in order to be accepted.

Once again Rory approached his great-uncle Hamish. But Hamish gave him short shrift and sent him packing with the words, 'Get yourself another fool, fellow m'lad, for I'll not sponsor you in anything other than getting yourself stuck up a gum tree. Why the Mersey, for God's sake, and not the Clyde?'

'I have a method in my madness, Uncle!' came back the hot retort. 'But I swear, I'll never bother you again to do *me* any favours!'

'I'm glad to hear it, fellow m'lad, for you'll not be getting any!'

William Lucklace came to Rory's rescue by offering to sponsor him, and in return Rory was affiliated to the company for whom Lucklace mastered, Strangford Brothers of Dublin, who owned the *Tara Belle*.

Pilotage certificates were gained before a committee made up of several local pilots, representatives of shipowners and the Board of Trade. First Rory had to undergo practical seamanship training and examinations at Everton, before he underwent the Board's examination which was mainly oral.

Rory counted out his money carefully. Two pounds, ten shillings for his mate's examination. Three pounds ten shillings for his master's certificate. Four pounds for coaching towards his pilotage certificate. Then there was board and lodging, plus equipment such as exercise books, pens and pencils to buy. Since he aspired towards a master's certificate, he would have to sit all the examinations laid down by the Board of Trade – which didn't leave much over to put towards saving for his own boat. He wondered if he dared approach his English guardians for a slight increase in his monthly allowance – his gambling debts accrued in Eton days were surely paid off by now!

But 'Old' Peter Darby was a kindly and understanding

old salt. He advised his pupils to sign on the dole for seventeen shillings a week, to help towards their tuition, which was personal and friendly.

Models of all kinds of ships were set out before the would-be Masters, Pilots and Mates on the long table in Old Peter Darby's Nautical Academy on the ground floor of a Victorian terraced house. Coloured balls represented the different buoys and sea-markers they would encounter when navigating. Rory began the course in earnest. Sailing under steam and sail, in all kinds of weather, night or day, semaphore, Morse, first-aid examinations, all had to be studied for. 'Young' Peter Darby, the old man's son, helped run the school which was not so much a teaching academy as one big happy family.

Rory also had to attend the Royal Naval Signal School each afternoon in Canning Place, where the Board of Trade had their office. He received tuition in signalling with the International Code of Signals, using flags, semaphore, hand flags and Morse code by lamp and hand flags.

Mersey pilotage embraced a large area, from St Bees Head in Cumberland to the Isle of Man; from the east coast of the Isle of Man to Chickens Rock on the south coast; across the sea to the north coast of the Isle of Anglesey, up the River Mersey to Eastham and Garston. Everything had to be committed to memory. He had already fulfilled his seamanship hours, or sea time – in the voyages he had made on the *Pride of Midlothian* and the *Tara Belle*.

The Clyde was already familiar to him from serving his time on the *Oyster* from Kingston Dock, Glasgow, to Renfrew, taking in Stobcross, Govan, Partick, Whiteinch and Kingsinch, during which he had got to know the shoals, the islands and the approximate levels of the river. In his mind he substituted Mersey for Clyde now, and hoped the general principals of river-navigation and signalling would get him through his approaching examinations.

Rory sat his competency examination at the Board of Trade office in Canning Place where he underwent two hours of gruelling interrogation. Then the last couple of

questions threw him completely, 'Since you served a
certain amount of your time on the Clyde, Mr Roskillen,
what was the dredging depth of the bucket ladder dredger
you were working on?'

He had to think fast, not having expected this sort of
question. 'Er ... forty-eight feet, sir.'

'And what was the nautical power of the *Oyster*?'

'Two hundred NHP.'

'Thank you, that will be all. You will have to await the
outcome of this interview, Mr Roskillen, but we will let
you know as soon as possible whether or not you qualify
for a Merseyside pilot's certificate. Please leave with the
receptionist the address at which you can be contacted.'

And this, thought Rory, was as good a time as any to
make his peace with his Sassenach relatives – the term he
used loosely whenever he wanted to make a point
concerning his Scottish heritage amongst a host of Anglo-
Saxons.

'Breedon Hall, Leicestershire,' he told the pretty, young
receptionist on his way out. 'I can be contacted there
during the Easter period.'

'Thank you, Mr Roskillen.'

'Thank *you*, Miss ... er ...?'

'Brownling. Pearl Brownling – Miss.'

'Miss Brownling ... I wonder. Could you possibly tell
me where a lonely man can have some fun in Liverpool?'

Her smile was engaging. 'Well now, there are the tea-
dances at the Athenaeum, or there's Murray's eel and pie
place down by the harbour where a good crowd gathers
on Saturday nights for a sing-song, or there's ...'

'How about showing me the night spots instead of
telling me?'

Another flighty young man from the Academy, who
would turn out to be no different: here today and gone
tomorrow, a seagull in search of a tasty herring. She hoped
he wouldn't swallow her in one gulp like some of the
others. This time she was prepared to risk it, though her
reply was coy: 'Well now, you're a fast one.' But the
admiring glances she gave him from under her eyelashes
were far from modest. 'And I might just be persuaded –

seeing as how you're a stranger here.'

'Not to the Mersey,' he said, remembering the harrowing questions concerning Mersey navigation from earlier in the day.

'You're still not Scouse, sailor. Not with that plummy accent.'

He smiled, 'So, the world is an oyster.' The look he gave Miss Brownling from his cool blue eyes made her stomach turn over, but in a very exciting way.

'What time do you finish here?' was his next direct question.

Somehow knowing that this was going to be a decision she would always regret, she said, 'Six o'clock sharp.'

'Then I'll be waiting for you outside on the steps at six sharp.'

It was her accent he never quite adjusted to, despite what she thought of his.

Before he left Old Peter Darby's Nautical Academy, the old man said, 'A photograph of the whole class, if you please, young sirs, just for the record!'

This time it was not a simple box camera affair of Smyrna's on Brocas Street, but a perfectly posed and timed exposure of 'Peter Darby's Nautical Academy Class of October 1907 – April 1908.'

The old home hadn't changed a bit.

Rory was welcomed back with a hearty handshake from his uncle Austen, tempered by a cool peck on the cheek from his aunt Ada, followed by the ascerbic comment, 'So the prodigal son has returned! To what do we owe this sudden change of heart – or are you here to borrow money?'

'I've come to say I'm sorry I ran out on you the Christmas before last, but I really didn't like Eton.'

'Eton didn't like you either, you foolish boy. You have turned down a brilliant future as a statesman of stature, an ambassador of your country, or an officer in the Guards, by your foolhardy decision to run away to sea.'

He'd always imagined his aunt saw him only as a suitable candidate for picking oakum in a prison cell. 'I'd

rather make my own future than have it made for me
through the old school-tie network, Aunt Ada.'

'I really do not know from where you get your bizarre
ideas, Rory Duncan.'

'Just put it down to my Celtic origins, Aunt Ada.' He
gave her such a charming smile, her heart melted, but only
for a fraction of a second.

'And the Celts have always proved a headache to the
English, so I must prepare myself to face the fact that this
Easter holiday will be no different. Disaster has a habit of
dogging your footsteps, nephew!'

'Yes indeed, Aunt Ada. But I'm a reformed character
now.'

'I'll believe it when you prove it.' She gave a deprecat-
ing sniff and pulled on her gloves. 'Well, Uncle Austen
and I are off to London. Mr Gammon is driving us to the
railway station. You may occupy the same room that you
had when you were last here.'

'Thank you, Aunt Ada.'

Rory was disappointed. He had been hoping to have a
private chat with Gammon.

After he had tested for strength the same iron cot with
its lumpy mattress where he and Charis Vayer, unbeknown to his aunt, had spent one blissful Christmas Eve,
Rory decided to take himself off to the garage where he
could tinker around for a bit until Gammon put in an
appearance. Much to his annoyance, he encountered
Sutcliffe, the coachman now made redundant since the
advent of the motor-car.

Sutcliffe came upon the wild Scotch boy (as he mentally
referred to the young man) with his head under the
bonnet of the Tourer. 'Af'ernoon, Master Rory, sir. You're
back. Thought it wouldn't be long 'afore you'd come home
suffering from the sea-sickness.'

'Good afternoon, Sutcliffe,' said Rory emerging from
the workings of the Tourer. 'I'm only home for a little
while, and then I'm going back to sea.'

'Young ones these days never know what they're about,'
said Sutcliffe, hoicking in his throat before spitting on the
ground. 'Nasty noisome things what don't drop dung.'

'What are?' asked Rory in alarm, side-stepping Sutcliffe's bronchial activities.

'Need dung for the land. That's what God made 'orses for. Mark me words, Master Rory, sir, five minutes wonder the motor-car, and when it ends up rustin' on the scrap-heap, his Lordship'll come rit back to the landau.'

'If you say so, Sutcliffe.'

'Gel got herself kilt last week. Motor-car ran rit over her ... had to scrape her orf of the road they did, accordin' to the landlord of the Halberd and Scythe in Breedon village.'

'She should have been watching where she was going.'

Sutcliffe threw the wild Scotch boy a sour look before shuffling off with the passing comment, 'Youngsters these days are as bad as them tin things: all gas an' no go ... don't know what the world's comin' to.'

Rory had been working on, or rather, under the car for a few minutes, lying on a piece of sacking on the cold garage floor, when someone else interrupted his concentration. He noticed a pair of shapely ankles standing in a shaft of bright sunlight streaming through the open garage doors. They weren't Charis's ankles, so he wriggled out from under Rupert's car and sat up to see Leonora's elfin face full of hostility.

'So you're back! You might at least have come and told me. I thought you and I were friends.'

'Hello Lennie. My, you've changed!' he added admiringly.

'So have you. You're more eccentric than ever!'

'Oh, why?'

'You know very well why! Not a word! Not a single letter from you, and now you show up here as though we still wanted you back.'

'Don't you, Lennie?'

'That depends.'

'On what?'

'Whether or not you can behave yourself without seducing kitchen maids, like Humphrey ... or ... or governesses!'

'Oh ... oh, I see.'

'No you don't! You're no better than Humphrey, Rory Duncan! So now you're a sailor. Golly. For some time after your disappearance Kitty and I thought you'd been sent to borstal.'

'Where is Kitty?'

'With Daisy at Boxwood Manor. They've become as thick as thieves – though I don't know why. Daisy is *such* a bore! But at least I'll have you all to myself this holiday.'

He sighed. 'I've got work to do, Lennie darling, so kindly buzz off.'

'Working! My word, Rory Duncan, is that what you call it!' She sauntered round him and pulled a face. 'It's Gamin's job to maintain the cars. I really don't know why you enjoy messing around with such dirty, oily things.'

'Machinery,' he informed her, 'is a work of art.'

She raised sceptical eyebrows. He couldn't help noticing that Leonora was looking most fetching. She had grown up. No more the inky-fingered, pig-tailed schoolgirl he remembered from two years ago, but an enchanting young lady in a white dress and gleaming chestnut ringlets beneath her spring hat. She had a nice pair of ankles on her, too. Leonora must be almost seventeen now, and he was amazed at the transformation. For a moment or two he remained tongue-tied, until she said:

'Since Gamin is taking Ma and Pa to the railway station in Leicester, would you mind driving me to Loughborough? Rupert says I may borrow the Tourer if I can find someone to drive it. I know that you must be able to drive a car since you can a ship ... so they tell me.'

'Lennie darling, one doesn't *drive* a ship. One sails it. And cars and ships have nothing in common – apart from engines.'

'And you haven't changed a bit!' She sighed as for a lost cause. 'Well, are you going to take me to Loughborough or not?'

'Why?' Helplessly he raised his blackened hands in the air, exasperated by Leonora's bad timing.

'Typical man, so superior! Why do you think you have a right to know what I do with my life?'

'Because you wish to involve me.' He eyed her with suspicion while he wiped his hands on an oily cloth. 'Have you found a beau in Loughborough?'

'Goodness! Aren't we old-fashioned, a beau indeed!' She twirled around in her white lace dress, the hem trailing on the greasy garage floor on which Sutcliffe had a habit of spitting.

'Careful of your dress,' he warned.

'Blow the dress, what about my heart? You've broken it, Rory Duncan, by running away from me.'

She hunched down in front of him and looked at him with her large cornflower blue eyes. He noticed that her pupils were ringed purple-black, very nice eyes, a very nice face altogether. He cleared his throat awkwardly. 'I'm not going to Loughborough looking like this. You'll have to wait until I wash and change.'

He was back in ten minutes, scrubbed free of oil and dirt and wearing clean clothes over which he had donned a dust-coat for driving. As he adjusted his goggles Leonora giggled. '*My!* Aren't we the intrepid traveller *à la mode*! Will I be safe in your company? You have a certain Bluebeard reputation, you know.'

'Open the yard gate,' he said and she gave him such a withering look, he was vanquished by it.

'Open it yourself, Rory Duncan,' she said climbing into the Tourer. 'It's about time you learned how to treat a lady.' She tossed her head, before tying a white chiffon scarf over her spring hat.

He smiled to himself.

It was a splendid afternoon in April, the air having about it a balmy quality which deceived one into thinking summer had at last arrived. The sky was a deep blue, and huge white clouds sailed over the blueness like Spanish galleons on an infinite ocean. Blackthorn was beginning to blossom, lambs-tail catkins drooped over the lanes and primroses gleamed beneath the hedgerows like clusters of sunbeams. Rory drove the Tourer at a leisurely pace because it was too big to do anything else along narrow country lanes.

Leonora, however, was in no mood to share in his

Eastertide enthusiasm concerning the countryside. She
was bent on business. 'Can't you make this thing go any
faster?' she asked.

'No.'

'Why not?'

'Because I'm enjoying the view – and the company.'

'I have an important appointment at half past three.'

'Why didn't you say so!' He accelerated and she fell
against his shoulder.

'Rory Duncan stop ... stop at once, or we'll end up in
the ditch!' she gasped.

He sighed and slowed down. 'Twenty miles an hour is
hardly fast, Lennie. Why don't women ever know their
own minds!'

'They do,' she retorted, straightening her hat. 'It's the
men who make them change their minds.'

'Lennie dear, would you mind removing that thing
floating around in front of my eyes: it's blinding me, and
that's dangerous while I'm driving.'

'Don't you like living dangerously?' she challenged,
keeping the ends of the chiffon scarf firmly between her
teeth. Then finding she couldn't talk, she removed her hat
altogether and let the breeze take hold of her hair. She
looked prettier than ever unhampered, the fresh air
bringing the colour to her cheeks.

'No, I don't like living dangerously,' he said. 'I like a
certain amount of stability in my life.'

'You've never given *me* that impression, openly flirting
with Charis – who is not from Paris, by the way, as she
likes to tell everyone!' Leonora scoffed.

'You're my cousin, and I'm responsible to your father
for your safety while in Rupert's motor-car,' he said,
ignoring the bait.

'Rory Duncan Roskillen, the Highland Knight
Crusader!'

'What's that supposed to mean?'

Leonora gave him a sidelong glance. 'Charis is a prime
example of your dangerous living.'

'Charis who?'

'Charis as in governess. Miss Smartbloomers would

make Marie Lloyd blush.' Then she changed her tactics and murmured very much like Miss Pearl Brownling with her coy ways – who had turned out to be not so demure in the end – 'And I'm vastly jealous!'

'Why? I'm sure you can think of *some*thing to make Marie Lloyd blush.'

'Is that what you think of me?' Sharply Leonora pinched the back of his hand on the steering-wheel and made him swerve into the ditch. The engine stalled and they stayed there, nose first in old ladies' lace growing by the wayside. 'If Mama found out about you and she romping in public places, Smartbloomers would be sent packing!'

'What public places?' he ventured to ask.

'Folly's Point and your bedroom! You seduced her on the Christmas Eve before you ran away from home. A guilty conscience, I dare say.'

'She seduced *me*!'

'A likely story!'

'Why?'

'Because you're learning to be a philanderer and I don't like it!'

'What has it got to do with you?'

'Because I love you more than ever she could!'

He concentrated on a fly-spot on the celluloid windscreen, and then added more gently, 'I love you, too, Lennie. As much as I love Kitty. You're like a sister to me.'

'Well, I don't love you like a brother but as a lover, so there!'

He turned to look at her, grabbed her by the shoulders and shook her hard to make her talk sense. 'Listen to me, you silly little girl ...' She stared at him with her wide goo-goo eyes, her sweet retroussé nose inches from his.

'I'm listening.'

'Good, then pay attention. It's a good job I understand you, having been brought up with you since we were both knee high to grasshoppers, so I'll forget what you've just said. I only hope you don't go around propositioning every young fellow you happen to take a shine to, because you might just find yourself blushing redder than Marie Lloyd.'

'Are those counselling words from the lips of the *night*-crusader himself – without the K?'

'Pay attention! Men are dangerous animals – so don't encourage them!'

She gave a feline smile. 'Can love between very close first-cousins be called incestuous? Charlotte seems to think so.'

He pushed Leonora away. 'Charlie's right. I don't love you, so get that into your silly head.'

'Fiddlesticks.'

'I beg your pardon?'

'Fiddlesticks, bagpipes and trombones! Why don't you try kissing me?'

'Because I don't want to! You're tiresome and haven't grown up a bit.' He got out of the car with the starter-crank in his hand so that they could get moving again.

Leonora joined him in the ditch, still smiling like Boadicea taunting the Romans. 'You're basically insecure, Rory Duncan. Do you know what Humphrey said about you?'

'I'm not interested.' He jerked the starter handle and the engine did nothing.

'Humphrey said that, because you were deprived at a very early age of mother-love you now require a mother-figure substitute like Miss Smartbloomers with her over-spilling bosom and ...'

Rory lost patience with her. 'Leonora, get back in the car at once, otherwise I'll leave you standing here with your mouth open.'

'I think you're afraid to kiss me. I think you might find I kiss more like a lover than a sister and that my kisses would be infinitely preferable to Miss Smartbloomer's!'

'Lennie,' he advanced on her with the cranking-gear in his hand and she took a hasty step back, right into the passenger seat of the Tourer.

The engine spluttered into life. He wiped his hands on his dust-coat, abandoned goggles, and came and sat beside her. 'Move over. Get into the back if you require so much room.'

'You're such a bore, Rory! Just like all men, who use

women to their own ends. In fact, you're exactly like Mr Asquith!'

'Oh, yes?' He reversed out of the ditch, the noise of the protesting engine hard on the ears. 'Didn't he want to kiss you, either?'

'See what I mean!' She gave a huge sigh designed to annihilate him, her eyes in sheer exasperation seeking the heavens since they had the soft-top of the Tourer folded down. 'I'll tell you what we women will do when we get the vote. We'll use it to stop pompous popinjays like you and my brothers and the rest of your breed from treating us like pet poodles to be powdered, pampered and petted when the mood suits you. Miss Smartbloomers is fair game on your slide-rule of pleasure, so is the overworked factory girl, housemaid, or poor harassed housewife with a baby a year from her careless husband. But one day soon, every woman will be able to tell all you inveterate men to go and get ... get potted!'

'What a lot of p's and aspirations!' he grinned broadly, thinking to himself that Cousin Lennie was pure uncut diamond. 'The word, by the way, is in-vert-e-brate, Lennie darling. Invertebrate men, meaning feeble and spineless.'

'I mean exactly what I said!' She glared at him as they took to the road again. 'I mean *inveterate* men, meaning antiquated custom!'

CHAPTER TWELVE

Leonora asked him to drop her off in the Market Square for her important appointment. When he discovered just how important it was and what she had in mind to do, he wished he hadn't been quite so quick in offering to chauffeur her to her rendezvous. Cousin Leonora was as devious as any other female he knew.

Before he had even brought the car to a standstill by the kerb she had removed a banner and sash from under the back seat, her bottom stuck in the air over the front seat while she retrieved her belongings. He only wished he had been in a position to smack her smart little behind for playing her Suffragette tricks on him. But with two hands parking the car he was only half aware of what she was doing. She opened the nearside door and hopped out quicker than a white bunny from its burrow, to disappear amongst the crowd gathered in the square.

No wonder she had sought him out in the garage! he fumed to himself. Leonora knew full well that he would have to remove himself to get cleaned up before conveying her on her little errand – in which time she had obviously stowed away her Suffragette propaganda! Rory jumped out of the car after her, but Leonora had already vanished in the crowd surrounding her sister.

Jane had taken to her soap-box again and was vociferously expounding her beliefs to a large and motley audience who were there, Rory suspected, more out of curiosity than sympathy. Jane's voice rose above the hecklers and their boos and hisses.

'We are living in the twentieth century, not the dark ages any more – or *are* we? It is about time, in this so-called enlightened age of ours, this year of 1908, that the women of England had the right to vote as their

Australian sisters had a decade ago! Taxation without representation in a country which professes to be the foremost civilized nation in the world, smacks *not* of civilization but of tyranny, dictatorship and injustice! The Womens' Suffragette Movement is born to liberate the women of England ... every single one of you women out there. YOU can help us all achieve freedom, equality and justice. TODAY, NOW!'

While Jane said her piece, the women in white did their canvassing vigorously: 'Please sign your name here ... thank you so much.'

'Excuse me, Madam, you will give us your support, won't you?'

'Here is a tricolour ribbon for you ... and you ... all of you ... the colours symbolize purity, justice and hope.'

'It's them Sufferin' gits, agin,' Rory overheard one man remark to another. 'Balmy in the 'ead, their sort. Me missus wouldn't know a vote from a tote. Nar! Puttin' daft ideas in the 'eads of ordinary folks, them upper-class wimin!' He spat, then shuffled off along the pavement muttering hell-fire and damnation on the Janes of this world.

Rory craned his neck to see what had become of Leonora. He espied her among a group of women, purple and green bands of hope tied across their breasts. They were distributing pamphlets and collecting signatures. He pushed his way towards them and heard Lennie say to a harassed looking woman with several children clinging to her skirts, 'We're organizing a deputation outside the Town Hall tomorrow.'

Rory noticed another kind of deputation heading her way, the blue uniformed officers looking as though they were in no mood for anyone's hanky-panky. Before Leonora could say 'votes for women', he picked her up, put her over his shoulder fire-fighting style, according to the rules learned at sea, and left the Market Square before Leonora got herself arrested. Sister Jane, he decided, would have to fend for herself.

After the initial shock of finding herself airborne, Leonora screamed loudly, pulled his hair and beat a tattoo on his back with her freedom flag. 'Put me down at once, you bully!'

'Shut up!'

'*What?*'

'Shut up, Lennie, for God's sake! Do you want to be carted off to prison with the rest of those silly women?'

'Will you put me down this instant you ... you ... fiend! I shall tell those policemen you're molesting me.'

'I think they're about to do the same to you, so be quiet.'

Jane, catching sight of her sister in the arms of a tall young man she did not recognize at first as their cousin Rory (for she had least expected to see *him* in Loughborough Market Square that afternoon, looking so mature and sun-tanned after such a long absence), stopped speaking, her mouth open in mid-sentence.

But, having inherited her traits of character from her mother, Jane was loathe to let *any* opportunity slip by that would not further her cause. 'LOOK THERE!' She flung out an expansive arm in a truly Thespian gesture and shouted at the crowd who had turned to stare at the young man and young woman engaged in a free for all. 'Look at that man! See how he is ill-treating that woman! That is the way women have always been treated down the centuries, man-handled by the opposite sex, regarded as being no better than a bale of cotton to be tossed over the shoulder. Is it right that a woman should be degraded in such a fashion? Is it right and proper and just that they should be humiliated, their feelings disregarded whenever it suits the purpose of the man? That is precisely what we women are fighting *against*! Witness the white slave in the arms of her cruel master.'

They witnessed, and they began to laugh.

Rory hadn't deliberately set out to humiliate Leonora, only to remove her in the simplest possible way from the crowd and the company of policemen intent on putting her in one of their cells. Besides, he also had his own skin to think of. Uncle Austen and Aunt Ada would not have been at all amused were it discovered that he had used Rupert's car to convey Leonora to a Suffragette rally.

Leonora was becoming vicious. She pulled his hair harder than ever.

'Pipe down, Lennie,' he said angrily, 'before you make a worse spectacle of yourself.'

She spluttered, 'I? *I* make a spectacle of *myself*! How dare you? You are nothing but a monster to treat me like this in a public place.'

'You asked for it.'

A little man came up behind them. He started scribbling down something in a notebook. Rory dumped Leonora on the back seat of the Tourer, pushed her down again when she jumped up to claw out his eyes and then engaged in a hand to hand tussle with her because she wouldn't do as she was told. The little man with glasses wrote it all down at a furious pace. 'Get down and stay down,' Rory warned his cousin, 'otherwise I'll wrap you in your flag and *tie* you down.'

'Just you try!'

He did, binding her to the side of the car with her green and purple sash.

'Untie me at once, you contemptible brute,' she shrieked. 'HELP!'

'Excuse me,' the little man said, '... er ... it is the young Miss Leonora Burrett whose father has a seat in the House of Lords? A friend of Mr Winston Churchill? I'm from the *Leicestershire Morning Chronicle* and wondered if I might bother you with a few questions concerning the Women's Suffra ...'

He wasn't left wondering for long because Rory Duncan picked him up bodily and stopped his questions by rolling him in the travel-rug, with his tie keeping rug and reporter together.

Then he retrieved notebook, pencil and glasses from the pavement and lay them beside the speechless individual from the local press. Only the reporter's owlish eyes and runny nose were visible above the fringes of the rug.

'You've killed him,' Lennie shrieked again. Having freed herself, she leaned over the driver's seat to pull Rory's ear. 'You've smothered him to death ... that ... that poor inoffensive little reporter who did you no harm.

I hope they hang you from the top of the castle ... no, that won't be high enough! I hope they hang you from Folly's Point, you adulterer!'

'Do be quiet,' Rory implored. 'You're giving me an earache, Lennie.'

'You're utterly – utterly despicable! An immoral reprobate and – and seducer of governesses ... at your age, too! You should be ashamed of yourself.'

'If you don't shut up, I'll spank you. Your father has enough to worry about trying to keep Jane out of mischief without having you to contend with as well. Leave all the militancy to Jane. You don't want to be force-fed in some grotty prison cell, do you?'

'Grotty? What's that supposed to mean?'

'Never mind. Be sensible, Lennie. You're much too nice a person to get involved with silly women who are doing more harm than good to their cause.'

'Huh! Who gives you the right to sit in judgement, you interfering poltroon? I *hate* you, Rory Duncan Roskillen, you barbarian!'

'Oh?' He glanced in the driving mirror with a deeply hurt and reproachful expression. 'A short while ago I believe I heard you declaring your undying love for me.'

'Trust you to bring that up, you odious creature! A real gentleman would never have repeated such a confidence in public.' She withered him with her cornflower blue eyes, two bright spots of pink indignation flaming her cheeks.

She looked very pretty in that moment and he couldn't help but be affected by his angry cousin. He only wished she could channel her energies in a more feminine direction – as she had done earlier, while he had chosen to ignore the warning signs.

'I hope they hang you,' she repeated, flopping down on the back seat.

'You've already mentioned your hopes, so can we have some quiet now?'

She relapsed into silence, sulking, but after ten minutes it was too much for her. She leapt up and yelled, 'STOP! Stop the car at once.'

'Why?'

'I think I'm going to be sick. It's all your fault for turning me upside down after my lunch. Hurry.'

He pulled into the grassy verge and stopped the car. Then, before he realized what she was up to, Leonora grabbed her flag and went racing off across the fields, heading for goodness only knew where. He hesitated, undecided as to whether or not he should follow. She was being extremely tiresome; but she was also his responsibility until he got her home. Neither did he want to be hauled up before his aunt as the unwitting instrument of his cousin Leonora's downfall. Leonora could easily get lost, or worse, attempt to sell her votes to some field-hands he spied in the distance, who would be only too willing to liberate her.

He gave chase and caught up with her halfway across a newly sown field of barley. Catching hold of her arm he swung her round. 'I've had enough of your silly games for one day, Lennie! Now I'm going to give you what you've been asking for.' He pulled on one end of her flag-stick while she hung on to the other.

'*Olé!*' She laughed in delight. 'You want to kiss me Rory Duncan – and don't deny it! Hey ... what do you think you're doing?'

'Only this ...' He flung away the flag she had been playing games with and toppled her in the pale green furrow while praying the farmer wasn't around to see them demolishing his new shoots. 'What a pity not all Suffragettes know their place ...' he kept her arms pinned firmly under, and helped himself to all the kisses she wanted.

A little while later she stood up, brushed herself down and gave him one almighty slap across the face that sent him rocking back into the furrow.

'What was *that* for?' he fingered his smarting cheek and stared at her accusingly.

'For taking liberties, you uncouth youth!'

She marched back to the car, her chestnut curls swinging defiantly, her head erect and her pert little nose high in the air. He was left to trail in her wake with her freedom flag.

They did not speak at all until they arrived back at the house, but when once or twice their glances had chanced to meet in the rear-view mirror, Leonora made a great show of shifting her position and her eyes in particular when she caught sight of his amused glances upon her. When he readjusted the mirror so that he could keep her in full view, just in case she decided to do anything else foolish, she uttered deep sighs reminiscent of a martyr whose feet were getting too hot.

Rory brought Rupert's car to a halt at the front door and waited for Leonora to remove herself from the back seat before he dealt with the muffled oaths issuing from under the travel-blanket beside him. The nosey little reporter from the *Leicestershire Morning Chronicle* was not suffering in silence. A veritable barrage of epithets issued forth from him concerning what he was and wasn't going to write about the barbarian who had abducted him from Loughborough Market Square.

But Leonora made no attempt to move. 'Now what's the matter?' Rory asked. 'I thought you couldn't wait to be shot of my company.'

'To be shot is what you deserve! But that would be too good for you. They ought to hang you. And if those kisses you gave me were the kind you and Miss Smartbloomers indulged in, then you ought to be ashamed of yourselves.'

Rory opened the driver's door and scurried round to Leonora's side. Opening her door he bowed, one hand tugging his forelock in an act of deep humility. 'Forgive me, m'lady, for not opening the door for you. I clean forgot your equality was still only verbal.'

She scooped him up like a piece of dirt in her disdainful blue glances. 'What a pity your character doesn't match your twenty-four carat looks, you uncouth youth.' She twitched aside the hem of her white lace dress as she swept past him. Leonora rang the front doorbell with great showmanship.

Hardrace opened the door.

'Hardrace,' Leonora said curtly, 'there's a body on the front seat of the Tourer. If it's not already dead, would you kindly show it to the morning-room and give it some brandy. *The Morning Chronicle* shall be made fully cognizant with the facts, and will be informed of how badly I've been treated by a certain individual of dockside speech and habits.' Chin in the air, she marched into the Hall.

To give him his due, old Hardrace never batted an eyelid as he unravelled the mummified body from the travel-rug, nor did he bat an eyelid as he guided the tubby little reporter, blinking owlishly without his specs, into the morning-room; Rory could only admire the sang-froid of the Sassenachs.

'Extraordinary race the English,' he told the little man from the newspaper world when he handed him back his belongings. 'Such Spartans! Enjoy your brandy, I'm just going to put away Cousin Rupert's car – he's my Sassenach cousin. I don't often resort to name-dropping, as I like to avoid the limelight. But if there's anything else I can do for you concerning the Women's Suffragette Movement when I get back, I'd be delighted to oblige.' He bowed on his way out, chuckling to himself because of the dirty looks the reporter gave him – as though he'd like to garrotte Rory Duncan Roskillen rather than ask him any more questions concerning his involvement with the Women's Suffragette Movement.

Rory took the Tourer back to the garage where Gammon was awaiting him like a monkey on hot bricks. 'Blimey, Mister Rory – they said you was back. I hope you ain't done his nibs's car a injury, otherwise I'll be up for the chop meself.'

'Relax Gamin. All ship-shape and Bristol fashion. I'm glad I found you. I was wondering if you'd do me a favour.'

'What favour, guv?'

'Like breathing the hot air of a steamship's engine room when putting to sea on my behalf this time?'

'Come again, guv?'

'Well, it's like this, Gamin. There's a nice little boat for sale in an Irish boatyard, which'll only cost us £49.'

'Only £49, Mister Rory? Excuse me, guv, what is it, a bleedin' canoe?'

'Better than that. Though it does need a little work on it. That's why I wondered if you'd care to oblige. I need a First Mate-cum-Chief Engineer to help me coast her along with cargo.'

'Blimey! His nibs *is* serious!' Gammon's monkey-eyes lit up with enthusiasm. 'Well, seeing as how I'm a honourable man meself, I'd have to give notice to his Lordship in the proper fashion, like. One month, he'd expect from me, Mister Rory. But I dare say, in that time I could teach that old coach and horses man, Sutcliffe, to steer the Rolls.'

'Well good luck, Gamin, because we'll be sailing for Dublin a month from today.'

'You got a partner, guv!' Gammon winked, pushed up his peaked cap to the crown of his head and proceeded to scratch his crispy gipsy curls in delight. 'It's bin a long time since I smelled coal dust and charcoal, so I reckons I can do with a change of scenery.'

'What about the gammy elbow and the breathing problems?'

'No problem, guv.' Gammon flexed his bad arm. 'I reckons if I can drive a Rolls I can drive a engine, and the old breathing tubes've had a chance to get back into the pink, all things considered.'

A few days later a letter arrived from Liverpool, handed to Rory by his Aunt Ada. 'I hope it's not another blackmail letter, Rory Duncan.'

He opened it in her presence – just to prove to her that he was a reformed man. Then he took her completely by surprise by his smacking kisses on each of her florid cheeks. 'Aunty, dearest. I have just received my Merseyside pilot's certificate. I've passed, I've passed!' He hugged her again.

'Well then,' she said, trying to maintain her equilibrium. 'I suppose this calls for a celebration. I shall ask your uncle Austen to bring out the champagne to toast your success – I'm glad to say you're not as stupid as I had once supposed.'

A compliment indeed, coming from the old buzzard herself, thought Rory happily as he set his sights next on a pilot's certificate from the Port of Glasgow. He also handed her the photograph, a decent one this time, unlike Smyrna's cheap tricks when they had both been at Eton together. 'Aunt Ada, no blackmail photography this time ... do you like it?'

She put her pince-nez to her eyes and smiled. 'Yes indeed! You look most *distingué*! I think your father would have been relieved to know that his younger son has managed to pull himself up by his own boot-straps suitably well, despite all his fears to the contrary.'

'Thank you, Aunt Ada.'

' "Peter Darby's Nautical Academy Class of October 1907 to April 1908 ..." ' she squinted. My word! Hardly the end of April and we have the photograph already! Whatever next? I think, Rory Duncan, your *volte-face* is deserved of a family portrait to be painted from this photograph, though somehow I can never quite reconcile the newly acquired subject of photography to the art of the genuine portrait painter. But, mayhap, we will find a suitable portrait painter who will one day get you hung in your ancestral home.'

'Thank you, Aunt Ada.' He had never realized the old girl was possessed of such a subtle sense of humour; or maybe it was old age catching up with *him*!

She dipped her head, the signal to make himself scarce while she took herself off in a rustle of taffeta petticoats to peruse her menus of the day.

PART FOUR

'Twas but a dream. But had I been
There really alone,
My desperate fears, in love, had seen
Mine execution.'

Robert Herrick

CHAPTER THIRTEEN

Lindsay spent his twenty-first birthday quietly at Balliol College, Oxford, and his last Commemoration Ball not so quietly. On that occasion he met Lady Iona Cowall Lennox from Edinburgh. Iona was the sister of a friend of his from Eton days. Lord Robert Cowall Lennox, descendant of the Lamont Chiefs of Toward, persecuted and dispossessed by Calvinist-backed Campbells in 1646.

'Iona, I'd like you to meet my friend, Lindsay Beauly Roskillen, Laird of Glengarth. Lindsay, this is my sister, Iona,' Robert introduced them.

'Now that's an ancient fiefdom in Wester-Ross, isn't it?' she asked.

He was glad she had decided to talk about Glengarth and not himself.

'One of certain antiquity, yes,' said Lindsay, trying to smile less stiffly than usual. He had forgotten the art of smiling, which, up till now, he had regarded merely as a courtesy effort. Not any more. Iona Cowall Lennox, in the first few moments of their meeting, created a deep impression on him. In her summery picture hat and flowery chiffon dress, with her red-gold hair and dark blue eyes, Iona reminded him of a Renoir painting. She was the loveliest creature he had ever met, and he felt tongue-tied and rustic in her presence.

'Awfully remote, isn't it, stuck out there in the back-woods of Ross-shire?' She pulled a face, though it could never be anything but a pretty one to Lindsay in that moment of awareness.

'I like the solitude,' he replied, trying not to sound too defensive. But he had never been good at small talk, and found it difficult now, even though he was trying hard to create a good impression.

'But of course you live most of the time in Edinburgh or London?'

'As a matter of fact, I spend a great deal of time at Glengarth.'

'Oh, oh I see.'

'Iona, Lindsay is *not* an absentee landlord,' Robert said with a smile. 'He takes his lairdship very seriously.'

'Indeed!' Iona replied. She changed the subject. 'How's the batting going these days, Lindsay? I remember watching you in the Eton versus Harrow match at Lords one year.' Her sapphire eyes sparkled up at him beneath the brim of her picture hat. 'Robert had a broken leg, I recall, and was out of the running that summer, so he couldn't join you in *the* most memorable match of the season.'

'I'm flattered you should remember,' he said, and because he was embarrassed, hastily offered her something to eat from a plate of canapés on the buffet table beside them.

'An honourable innings,' Robert added. 'My broken leg was all Iona's fault.'

'It was not!' she hotly denied.

'Oh, yes it was! You see, Lindsay, one of her wretched high-bred horses sat on me. Otherwise, I might have shared in your glory, instead of being lashed to a hospital bed.'

'Big head!' said Iona laughing, as she pushed her brother playfully on the shoulder. 'He's no good with horses: accident prone in the saddle and unseated at the first fence.' Nibbling a canapé while she held a glass of champagne in her other hand, she gave a throaty little laugh that made Lindsay want to hear her laugh many many more times.

Later that day he had an opportunity to get to know Iona Cowall Lennox better. More beautiful than ever in her ball gown, Iona captured his heart and attention completely.

'Excuse me,' said Robert, sensing the strained atmosphere between his sister and his best friend, 'I think Rosemary has been dancing with that ruffian, Carlyle

Edenbridge, long enough.' Robert disappeared into the throng of dancers gathered on the improvised wooden dance floor under the marquee. Iona immediately picked up the threads of their conversation from that afternoon, as though they had never parted company over the canapés.

'Are you a good horseman as well as a good cricketer, Lindsay?' Iona turned her full attention upon him now that her brother had left them in search of his fiancée.

'Oh, I don't know about that,' Lindsay smiled to himself at her earnestness. 'But I do ride a lot when I'm home. It's our sole means of transport through the remoter parts of the Highlands.'

'Haven't you a motor-car?'

'No. I don't like cars. Besides, they're totally unsuitable in the mountains and glens.'

'No trains, either?'

'A new line has recently opened to Achnasheen which connects us with Inverness. Otherwise it's the old pony and trap to Gairloch or Ullapool, and the coastal steamer.'

'Primitive!' She made wide eyes at him.

'Yes, I suppose so.'

'Don't you ever visit London?'

'Sometimes. We have a town house in Park Lane, shared by all the family. It came as part of my mother's dowry from the English side of the family.'

'Isn't your family also connected in some way with people from Glasgow?'

Lindsay was secretly amused. Robert had obviously briefed his sister on Roskillen family history prior to this meeting. 'Yes. My grandmother was from Glasgow. She was one of the Blythe-MacDeargs before she married my grandfather.'

'Yes, I think I've heard the name. They operate a steamship line, don't they?' she added with the utmost diplomacy.

'Well, that's rather a grand way of putting it. My great-uncle Hamish MacDearg owns two ancient steam coasters, and that's about the sum total of it, I'm afraid.'

'Well, I usually travel to Ireland by the Burns-Laird line

whenever I attend the Irish races.'

'Don't ever mention Burns-Laird to Hamish MacDearg! Or the names of any of the other more illustrious lines.'

'Why?'

'Sour grapes, I think. He aspired to be in the same league but could never quite manage it. But it's a long story best kept for some other time. Would you care to dance, Iona?'

'I'd be delighted.'

He had never held a woman in his arms before. Lindsay didn't even know that he *could* dance! He had only ever watched from the sidelines, but now, with Iona in his arms, dancing seemed the most natural thing in the world.

Afterwards, together with Robert's fiancée, Rosemary Stewart, the four of them took out a punt and had a moonlight picnic on the river. It was a wonderful night, an idyllic interlude, for it was a moment which comes but once in a lifetime, unforgettable, unrepeatable, and Lindsay realized it all too poignantly.

Robert and he deposited the girls back at a friend's house with their chaperones and lady's maids, as the girls had come to Oxford especially for the week of celebrations preceding the Commemoration Ball. Lindsay stood alone on Folly's Bridge. The night sky had paled to mother-of-pearl and the last lingering stars were vanishing above the boathouses. Lovers, arm in arm, meandered along the towpaths, bleary-eyed and dewy-eyed. Lindsay dropped his cigarette butt into the river and watched it swirl away on the strong current. The resolution that he made to himself in the dawn light, was that one day he would marry Iona Cowall Lennox, who would be the perfect mistress for Glengarth.

Soon after going down from Oxford he went North to claim what had become his legal inheritance since his twenty-first birthday. Glengarth would, from now on, be administered the way he wanted, without trustees and guardian-managers like Cousin Iain Hamilton to tell him what he should or should not do with the forests.

His grandfather and great-grandfather had built up the flagging family fortune on the three Ts – timber, tar and turpentine. Resin had been tapped from the fir and pine plantations for generations. The advent of the paraffin lamp way back in the '70s, had increased revenues from wood-tar. But now the civilized world had electricity. Paraffin lamps would soon be as obsolete as candles. An increase of crude petroleum from America was also robbing Glengarth of its income. The only way to keep the estate viable from now on, would be to explore other options open to them.

Neither had Lloyd George's recent budget helped the grave economic situation facing the Highlands. The political implication in the Scottish Parliament brought home to Lindsay that times and attitudes were fast changing concerning those who 'grew rich while they slept'. He wished that were so in his case, for there wasn't a night he did not lay his head on the pillow without seeing Glengarth either falling into the sea through neglect, or becoming a hotel for rich grouse-shooters and American playboys – a thought which made him shudder. Higher death duties, increased taxation and super-tax, and those most iniquitous of all taxes, those on site values, leaseholds and undeveloped land, affected his inheritance every way he turned.

The minute that he was back in Scotland, Lindsay tackled Iain about the need for reafforestation on a major scale, attention to be transferred from the ancient blackwood plantations to concentrate on other newer varieties of trees, softwoods in particular.

'God in heaven, are you mad?' Iain asked, eyeing the Laird of Glengarth over the desk with horror. 'We've been growing hardwood trees here for donkey's years, and ...'

'And that's the trouble, Iain,' Lindsay interrupted swiftly. 'We've always done everything at Glengarth in the same old-fashioned way, generation after generation. Glengarth has never kept pace with the outside world, so that now we're a million light years away from civilization! Just take a look around the place – there isn't going to *be* a Glengarth in another ten years, not unless we stop the rot right now!'

'What are you trying to say, Lindsay?'

'I've been looking at these figures ...' Lindsay thrust a column of figures for projected yields under his cousin's nose. '*Profit Margins* – take a good look for yourself, Iain. Not even a projected yield of thirty tons of new wood a day. Glengarth can do better! I'm not letting fifteen hundred acres of valuable land go to rack and ruin through bad management ...'

'Are you saying I've been a bad manager all these years?' Iain, red-faced, demanded.

'All I'm saying is that Grandfather was quite content to go on as his ancestors before him. You told me yourself that he was no businessman – as was proven by his selling off valuable tracts of Clyde farmland for peanuts to the first bidder. But I'm not blaming you for anything. I know how perverse and set in his ways Grandfather was. I just think it's time we made a few changes around here.'

'I'll thank you to know, Lindsay, that I was running things around here when you were in nappies!'

'Fair enough. But I've outgrown them now. While I don't want to denude the estate and destroy the last vestiges of Hebridean forest, I think there is room for improvement. Firstly to make Glengarth viable, and that means recultivating where we fell and not to waste what we've got. Secondly to grow what is in demand. I know that the market for hardwood has dropped dramatically since our shipyards are building steel-hulled ships and don't require our kind of timber anymore; but no new markets have been sought, whatsoever! The whole estate is on a downward trend.'

'Don't say another word, Lindsay!' Iain held up his hand. 'What you're actually saying is, I've not been doing my job around here.'

'Look, Iain, I know how difficult the situation is, what with the shortage of funds, of foresters and skilled estate-hands because we can't afford to pay them better wages. But you've got to admit that something has got to be done to reverse the grave situation facing us. The demands of the industrial revolution decimated these ancient forests of ours, yet Grandfather undertook no long-term reafforest-ation. It seems to me that he was content to be a privileged landowner and nothing more.'

'Go on,' said Iain quietly, prepared to listen and then to argue. 'I know you're questioning my methods, too!'

'Landowners' privileges are diminishing all the time. Some of us have now got to start earning a living – not a bad thing from the majority viewpoint I suspect. But tough on the likes of us who have to pick up the remnants of a way of life our ancestors once took for granted. Some of our plantations are way beyond their prime. A sheer waste of resources. Our seeding and germination programme is way behind schedule, not to mention non-planting when some of the trees have blown down in the winter gales – and that is only because sphagnum moss has been allowed to take hold and weaken the roots. Then there is wide-scale destruction caused by the wild animals allowed to wander willy-nilly into the compartments that *are* under cultivation – which don't amount to much on the scale of things. Neither is there a single "Keep Out" notice visible on our land ...'

'The old laird did not care for signs.'

'Well the new laird is saying put them up! The tenants just take what they can lay their hands on for firewood. We've simply *got* to generate new life-blood into Glengarth. We've got to search for new outlets, plant new trees and altogether step up the proficiency and productivity of the plantations.'

'And what new markets have you in mind, Lindsay?'

'The furniture and house-building trades, for a start, where softwoods are in great demand.'

'So you're suggesting digging out what's been growing here for generations and starting all over again? It'll take years to get those plantations going again on a profit-making scheme, and right now we need every penny we can get from what *is* already there and what *can* be sold.'

'That's my point precisely! You and I both know forestry isn't an overnight money-spinner. But we've simply *got* to set our sights on the future. The way things stand we're going to be left with a lot of dead wood on our hands, no new markets, and no Glengarth! I've been taking a close look at what we're doing on the plantations, and what struck me most was the sheer wastage. I want to embark on a felling and clearing operation to get rid of what is not required since most of the trees are past their prime anyway. Right now the felling in some of the compartments has been delayed long enough, and ...'

'Then find me the foresters willing to work for the wages we pay them!' Iain said, getting very annoyed with Lindsay. 'I know it takes a new broom to sweep clean, but what you're suggesting won't simply sweep clean, it will scour us of everything we've got!'

'The most precious thing we've got is land, and the remainder of the old Caledonian forests. Let's just protect what we *have* got for our future and the future of Glengarth's heirs. Your sons also have rights in this land.'

'I'm not blaming you, Lindsay. I know what a vicious circle it is. But it will require effort and money we haven't got.'

'If I can go to the Investment Banks with a feasibility study of what *can* be done here, I can raise money to invest in our future schemes. I know that what I have in mind to do is the only way to get ourselves out of the mess we're in – and don't tell me we're keeping our heads above water like you used to tell Grandfather in order to keep him happy, because I'm not my grandfather.' Lindsay lit a cigarette and inhaled deeply.

His cousin's blue eyes were accusing. But Iain only lived from day to day, and lacked imagination in all things, were Lindsay's thoughts in that moment.

'Where do you propose to carry out your new programme of reafforestation?' Iain asked as he tapped out his cold pipe in the ashtray on his desk.

'Inchnadamph.'

Iain looked up in astonishment. 'Inchnadamph? The soil is impoverished up there what with all that heather and gorse. It'll cost a pretty penny to rejuvenate the land – that's if you can ever get the top soil up there.'

'We'll do it.'

'And what kind of trees are you thinking of planting?'

'Larch.'

Again Iain looked bemused. 'Lindsay, you know damn

well larches won't survive here! Larch forests were wiped out in the Hebrides thirty years ago.'

'The European larch, yes, but I'm thinking of planting a new species of Japanese larch found to be resilient to the kind of disease that killed off the European larch on this coast. And not only larch, but spruce as well. I also want Corsican pine to replace the old Scots pine because it doesn't take so long to mature. You know yourself that the rest of Europe is way ahead of us in timber production. We're twenty-five per cent down compared to our competitors on the Continent, simply because we have not set aside new areas for reafforestation.'

Iain pulled a dour face, 'Won't be worth the money and effort involved. We'll have to employ a regular army to cart good top soil up to Inchnadamph.'

'Then employ an army, Iain, but I want it done. There are at least two hundred and fifty acres of wasted land on Inchnadamph that can be put to good use. Softwood trees are infinitely suitable to wet and exposed upland sites like Inchnadamph. We've nothing to lose and everything to gain. Once Inchnadamph is cleared of heather and everything else sapping the soil, we'll be able to get a good return on our investment.'

Iain shook his head in disagreement. 'I just don't understand you, Lindsay. Here you are saying you want to replant with soft woods, clear out all the old blackwood plantations that have been providing a good income in the way of railway sleepers, pit-props and telegraph poles for donkey's years, not to mention *unprofitable* turpentine and such spin-offs as wood-wool and paper, and yet you're wanting to plant larches up on Stag's Meadow which can only yield tanning-bark and *turpentine*!'

'Not in the new furniture industry! And not for the twentieth century – it's called setting one's sights on the future, Iain!'

Lindsay could see that Iain thought he was truly crazy. He blew a smoke ring to the ceiling and started again. 'But we mustn't put all our eggs in one basket, Iain. That *would* be foolish. Of course we'll continue supplying the railways, telegraph services and coal-mines with their sleepers, telegraph poles and pit-props, but we'll *also* plan new softwood plantations. As we both know, the main business of the forestry industry is to grow trees to provide timber – but the maintenance of employment, plus providing new or alternative employment in rural areas like Glengarth, must be a major consideration, too. I've got to show the banks I mean business for the future by presenting them with a set of figures they *know* means business. Mixed forestry providing alternative markets, what's so intimidating about that?'

'Nothing. Nothing at all. You've ambition and drive and imagination, and that's to be admired when so many around here are content to see the Highlands as a backwater where nothing can flourish. But you're hoping for too much, Lindsay. Business gets taken to the valleys and the Lowlands – not brought up here. There are *no* new markets for the likes of us stuck up here in the remoter parts of the Highlands, and certainly no overnight fortunes to be made. Transport costs are too expensive, for a start.'

'That's where you're wrong, Iain. I *know* there's a future for Wester-Ross, a better one than we've ever had. New pulping-mills and wood-processing industries; not to mention Hydro-electric power stations and if, in the likelihood of a war at some future date, when one bears in mind Germany's fervent activity with her new Navy Law, timber is going to be in greater demand than ever. Wood is what we depend upon, so let's make it pay!'

'If you say so. You're better travelled and more worldly than I, Lindsay. But I'm warning you, don't run before you can walk.'

Lindsay smiled again and stubbed out his cigarette. 'I can't let that young brother of mine beat me in the art of business, now can I, Iain?'

'Rory? Rory's nothing but a turncoat who went to sea to spite the family by joining forces – or at least trying hard to – with that old rogue, Hamish.'

'Rory's clever – cleverer than you and I put together. Just wait and see. Now then, getting back to the programme I have in mind, I want to guarantee timber supplies to the Government in any capacity wood comes. Inchnadamph is going to waste. Waste land costs money – as the Chancellor of the Exchequer has made painfully clear to the likes of me: productive land yields profits. Development of one's resources is what it's all about, Iain, so take it or leave it, but I'll do it my way. Now, if you don't mind, I'd like to take the books with me so that I can go over them again.'

Iain rummaged through a drawer, and while he was searching for the account books said with his head down, 'There are tenant properties on Inchnadamph – crofters who have had the tenure of the land for generations. What do you propose to do with them, make them homeless?'

'I will do as I like with them, Iain.' The laird's voice was tautly controlled. 'Glengarth is *mine*! *My* inheritance, *my* pride, and *my* curse!'

Lindsay took a deep breath, and resorted to another Turkish Latakia. 'Shift them elsewhere, anywhere. Compensate them if you have to but clear Inchnadamph ready for planting. Employ a regular army, employ who you like, but do it.'

Iain, his head just above the desk, continued to stare at his cousin. In the end he said, 'Very well, if that's your wish. But let me tell you this, Lindsay, that what you intend to do puts me in mind of the evictions in times not so long past, when *our* people were turned off their land by landlords such as yourself. Think about it, my laird, and then make your decision. If you want Inchnadamph, then *you* go and evict your tenants, for I'll not do it!'

Lindsay saw that it was no use trying to reason with Iain. He was as stubborn as their grandfather had been. He opened the office door and on the threshold ground out his newly lit cigarette under his heel. 'It shouldn't be too great a hardship, Iain.' Lindsay replied coldly. 'Since the soil on Inchnadamph is impoverished, I'm sure the tenants up there will be only too glad to take themselves and their animals where there's better grazing ground.'

'And where might that be?'

'Why, Iain, I'm surprised you haven't noticed! All around Forest Lodge – must be at least sixty acres on which to rehouse tenants: the land grandfather gave you donkey's years ago, but still happens to be in *my* name … I took a look at the deeds of property, and land-titles, just to make perfectly certain of what I own and what I don't.'

'Lindsay, I've no wish to quarrel with you. You're the laird so you're entitled to do things your way. But while we're on the subject of evictions for those who happen to pay their rents, what's happening about the tenancy of Rill? The rent's not been paid on the cottage for nigh on five years now, and it's falling into disrepair. It seems a total waste of resources since Annie's living with us and Fletcher's done a bunk. Can't you rent it to some other family?'

'I can but I won't. Leave Fletcher to me. And if the cottage is on a fully repairing lease, see that it doesn't fall into any more disrepair.' Lindsay closed the door of the estate office behind him.

Outside in the courtyard, he drew a deep breath. That kind of head-on collision with his cousin, who was, after all, still the overseer and estate factor, made him realize that Iain and he would never see eye to eye when it came to running Glengarth.

CHAPTER FOURTEEN

In Strangford's boatyard, Dublin, Benjamin Gammon thoughtfully scratched his head, his expression one of utter dismay. Inspection of the *Drogheda* over, he voiced his opinion. 'Blimey, guv, you're flamin' nuts you are!'

'Why?' Rory demanded.

'This ain't a steam-coaster, it's a bleedin' Mayday call! Just look at 'er guv! Blimey, it'll take months makin' this old tub fit fer the sea again. No wonder she was only forty-nine quid. Me, I wouldn't give forty-nine farthings!'

'No one's asking you, Gamin.' Rory hesitated. 'But it can be done, can't it? I mean, she's sound engine-wise, so what's a little bit of joinery and suchlike?'

'A *li'le* bit of joinery an' suchlike, 'ark at 'is nibs!' Gammon did a little rotation on his heels and almost fell through the rotten floorboards of the forecastle deck. 'Nar guv, you've got your 'rithmetic scuppered. It'll cost a arm an' leg ter put this ole crate ter sea again. She's only fit fer the scrap yard.'

Suddenly Rory was having second thoughts about the *Drogheda* now that Gammon had aired his professional opinion. He felt decidedly put out. The same feeling he had experienced one Christmas when Lindsay had a new hunting-rifle and he had been given a pair of leather boots with steel toecaps. He felt in some way deprived. For the past month he had dreamed of nothing else except the *Drogheda* and what he was going to do with her to earn himself a little extra cash.

Gammon, seeing Rory's crestfallen look, said, 'Watcha aimin' ter carry in 'er?'

'Anything that's offered: timber, coal, grain ... that sort of thing.'

'Yeah, includin' flamin' wild animals! Listen guv, yer

goin' ter need rigged derricks, an' they're bloomin'
expensive.'

'I know!'

'On what route?'

'Glasgow to the West Highlands to Belfast and then
Garston. Four-square, Gamin, on a most profitable
steam-coasting route. I've worked it all out.'

'How many men you aimin' ter employ?'

'Five or six – including ourselves.'

'Who'er you tryin' ter impress, guv?'

'Cut it out, Gamin!' Rory said angrily.

'I ain't a flamin' charity, guv, so whatcha aimin' ter pay
me as yer First Mate as well as Chief bleedin' Engineer?'

'Thirty bob a week.'

'Blimey! I *am* a bleedin' charity!'

'Well, do you want the job or not? Or would you rather
return to Leicester in the boring role of my uncle's chauffeur?'

'Ambition guv, is me second name.' Gammon grinned.
'You still aimin' ter buy the old tub despite what it's going
to cost you ter make her sea-worthy again?'

'Yes.'

'Where's all the dough comin' from?'

'None of your business! I've managed to save up – a bit.
Besides, in the not too distant future I shall receive an
inheritance from my late father's will – I hope.'

'It'll take more'n two an' a arf years to get this old
bucket sea-worthy again. Ten more like,' said Gammon
sceptically. 'I'm going below ter take another good squint
around, guv, before I make up me mind.' Gammon item-
ized details as he inspected the shell of the *Drogheda* for
the umpteenth time: 'Garboard strakes *definitely* need
replacin' with new timber. Well, I suppose there's an
engine room what ain't bad ... an' two more sleepin'
spaces for the first and second engineers, meaning me an'
me. Forecastle quarters for crew; saloon an' sleeping
accommodation with ablutions chamber for his nibs orf of
the main saloon; galley aft an' a good old-fashioned coal-
burning bogey which might work again once it's de-rusted
– nothing like a good old bogey fer a pan fry-up, when the

frost is thick as barnacles on the eyebrows. Boiler room, engine room ... accommodation ain't bad, I suppose.' Gammon scrambled up to the bridge again. 'Cost a bleedin' fortune, but I reckons *anything's* possible, if yer've got the ready. Offer Strangford thirty quid, guv, and not a penny more.'

Rory grinned broadly. 'Then you'll come in on this with me?'

'Can't very well refuse now, can I? I gorn an' given notice ter his nibships an' his Rolls – no offence ter your uncle, Mister Rory, sir. So, challenge is me third name. Where're we going ter repair this old tub, that's what I'd like ter know?'

'Right here. Since I'm affiliated to Strangford Brothers and their boats for another few months, I don't see why they won't let me keep her here while she's undergoing repairs – for nothing.'

'I get it. Charmed our way inter the boss's heart already, have we? Well Mister Rory, sir, I got to admire your spunk. But it ain't going ter be an overnight job – not if yer contemplatin' coasting along with the company.'

'I have to obtain my Glasgow Pilotage certificate next, Gamin. The only way I'll obtain my sponsorship is to stick with William Lucklace for the moment. So hire help to get the boat fixed up, as I shall be away for most of the time earning *your* wages! I want the *Drogheda* ready as soon as she can be. Time means *money* to me!'

'Yeah. An' Rome wasn't built in a bleedin' week, either, so what about me, guv?'

'What about you?'

'Like I said, I ain't a charity and thirty bob a week ain't going ter pay fer a decent board an' lodgin' in Dublin.'

'What's wrong with the *Drogheda*? After all, you *said* her accommodation wasn't bad,' Rory reminded him.

Gammon scratched his head beneath his greasy cloth cap and once again convinced Rory that the Cockney sparrow who had run away to Deptford to work his way up from deck-hand to Chief Engineer, was host to head lice. 'There's none like the flamin' upper classes ter pull rank! Right you are, guv, I'll do what you want, if you do what *I* want! Termorrer I'll have a list a mile long for the ship's chandler, the timber merchant, the cordwainer, the ...'

'Butcher, baker and candlestick-maker. All right, Gamin, a list!'

'Let's 'ope you own the ready fer all this little lot. Bloomin' 'eck, 'ow I wish I'd kept me bad chest an' gammy elbow ter meself an' stayed with his lordship, where I was comfortable with a decent living wage.'

Rory grinned and left Gammon to his grumbling assessment of the *Drogheda.*

Firmly on the ground again, he looked up at Gammon on the bridge where he was about to reinspect the rotten wood of the wheelhouse, and said, 'Hey, Gamin, since I'm now your new boss, when the crew *do* start arriving, *don't* call me his nibs or nibships. Just show a little respect, huh? Otherwise we might have a mutiny on our hands.'

Gammon sauntered to the rusty taffrail of the boat, uncomfortably keeling over on the repair-ramp in dry dock, to portside. Sticking his thumbs into the lapels of his loud-checked Newmarket jacket, he looked down into the smooth and untroubled face of 'his nibships' with admiration: here was a young fellow who knew *exactly* where he was going, Gammon was glad to say. A steady head, a cool nerve, and above all, a monumental cheek, set him head and shoulders above other young fellows of his age as well as class. This one was a real sport! *Mister Rory* had Gammon's fullest admiration and, in that moment too, he was prepared to give of his very best to his saucy young Scots boss, born with a silver spoon in his mouth. 'Right you are – *Mate!*' He put his thumb up.

Rory went on his way, knowing full well that Gammon was a law unto himself.

Suddenly he had cold feet: what on earth, he asked himself, had made him embark on such a venture? He didn't know the first thing about mastering a boat on the high seas. He didn't even have enough money of his own to finance the operation, but had had to borrow a goodly portion of it from his cousin Humphrey – who, surprising enough, had been most amenable, and more than generous as far as a gentlemen's agreement stood.

Oh, well – Rory set his shoulders – he was committed now and there was no turning back without losing face. He didn't think he could bear it if old Hamish, Lindsay, his Sassenach relatives, and everyone else were to turn round should he fail in what he had set out to do, and say, we told you so!

But he was *not* going to fail! he told himself sternly as he went to the Strangford office to find out what boat he was supposed to join, and what cargo she would be carrying.

He spent six weeks coasting with china clay from Cornwall to the Pool of London, thence to the Channel Islands with Ramsgate coal in return for Guernsey and Jersey tomatoes and cream, potatoes and fresh flowers for the West Country hotel trade. When he returned to Dublin in June, Gammon had made a start in repairing the *Drogheda*: he had also found a helper:

'This 'ere is my man Ackker from Limerick, guv. He was valet to a Naval Commander from Limerick what first served on Nelson's flagship as an Able Seaman. But his decrepit old nibships kicked the bucket a few months ago and Ackker was left sellin' lifeboat lotteries on Dublin's fair streets. I picked him up in a certain public house, an' signed him on. He's a dab hand with the tar brush, guv, an' you owe us six week's wages.'

Rory gave them a fiver each.

'Beggin' your pardon, Mister Rory, sir,' Gammon paused with the parts of a bilge-pump in his greasy hands, 'we're a bit short – like. Me three nicker – him one.'

'Then put it on tick, Gamin! We've got other things to buy for the boat.'

Gammon didn't argue, and nor did the new man who seemed willing enough to turn his hand to anything. Limerick valet indeed! Pull the other leg, thought Rory. Ackker was going to be another liability, Rory could see.

He spent a week in the Strangford boatyard helping to renovate her, and then signed on again for another trip, this time carrying Welsh slate to the Pool of London, then back to Belfast with coal. He needed every penny he could earn.

In the autumn Rory was due to start his Pilotage examinations with the Port of Glasgow – but first he had his cousin Humphrey's twenty-first birthday ball to attend. He was also looking forward to seeing Leonora again.

Even as Lindsay watched, the afternoon light on the hillsides changed subtly to draw out the variegated greens of the forests. In the distance the great shoulders of Beinn Claidheamh Mor rose out of the swirling mists which had begun the day, but were now swiftly dispersing as sunlight bespattered the valley.

A day of natural comparisons, of rare human discernment – not morbid introspection as lately he had resorted to. Untrammelled by the diversions offered by the bright city lights or the wealthy socialites of Edinburgh and London, he had been quite satisfied with his own company – until now.

But now, in the harmony of nature, that serene setting, restlessness tormented him yet again. He was suddenly discontented with it all, when hitherto he had been at one with Glengarth.

The ling was in flower. The sea-breeze ruffled his fair hair. It rustled through the leaves of the trees, the heather, and rippled the surface of the loch. He saw the obtuse line of his own isolated horizon set against the mountains, the sea, the forests and Glengarth: man in his infinite ego still wanted to set himself above God. Possession of the earth and all its creatures, its beauty and its life-giving substance, that's what man wanted. Dynastic parallels, man following in the footsteps of the creator, that was what it was all about – that is what one hoped it would always be about.

Lindsay turned when his name was called.

Aeneas and Bruce, Iain's two young sons, scrambled up the slope with their puppy, Bonnie Prince Charlie, yapping excitedly behind them.

'Hello, Cousin Lindsay,' Aeneas said breathlessly as he fell at Lindsay's feet, his freckled urchin face squinting up at the laird who, with the sunlight at his back just then, towered above the youngster like a golden god. But Aeneas now a sturdy lad of thirteen, was not afraid of the laird even though he had heard Gilbert Lucas tell how a lot of them were in the glen. 'We've been to see the salmon leaping up near the waterfall. Gilbert Lucas says they're spawning.'

His younger brother Bruce, and the dog, poured another avalanche of loose scree at Lindsay's feet. 'They're early, aren't they, Aeneas?' Lindsay smiled down on the red head of his eager young cousin. 'It's only July and the salmon don't usually come upstream till August. Are you quite sure you saw them – or is it not all a figment of your imagination?' Lindsay teased as he rumpled Aeneas's bright hair affectionately.

'Sure I'm sure, Cousin Lindsay. Gilbert Lucas is burring the waters tonight.'

Gilbert Lucas was Iain's deputy – a man Lindsay detested.

But Aeneas was not to know the factions that existed at Glengarth. He paused, and gave another thoughtful squint up at the man they called 'the laird'! The name sounded very grand to Aemeas. 'What's figment?'

'Concoction, invention.'

'Like the flying machine?'

'No, not like the flying machine at all. Airplanes are real enough. A figment is something unreal, something that has no existence outside one's own imagination, Don Quixote.'

'What donkey?'

'Aeneas,' Lindsay said hastily before they got carried away in lengthy explanations, 'how would you like to come fishing with me tomorrow morning?'

'Gosh thanks, Cousin Lindsay!' Then his freckled face dropped a mile. 'I haven't got a real fishing-line because Bruce broke it.'

'You can borrow one of my rods,' Lindsay reassured Aeneas.

'Gosh, thanks, Cousin Lindsay,' Aeneas breathed joyfully.

'Is Christabel with your mother?'

'Yes, Cousin Lindsay.'

Christabel often took tea at Forest Lodge with Shiona, or Iain's sisters, Morag and Moira, who also preferred the company at Forest Lodge rather than the dour constraints of the castle. Lindsay had been on his way there when the boys had come racing out of the trees in hot pursuit of him. 'By the way, Aeneas,' Lindsay said, 'I don't want you and Bruce playing on the timber chutes. It's highly dangerous. If the men send down logs to the loch while you're sliding on one of the chutes, you'll both be killed.'

'Sorry, Cousin Lindsay, but it's fun.'

'It might be fun, but you're not to do it. I don't suppose your father knows what you and Bruce have been getting up to, otherwise I'm sure he'd tan you both very thoroughly.'

Enough said: Lindsay could tell by their faces the two boys had heeded the warning – he hoped it would last!

At Forest Lodge, he handed them into Annie's care and she bundled them off to get washed and changed before tea. Christabel and Shiona were taking afternoon tea on the smooth green lawn surrounding the house in the forest. The view to the south had been cleared of trees to open up a panorama of the loch and the opposite side of the glen.

'The new roof looks grand, doesn't it, Lindsay?' Shiona searched for his approval. 'The thatcher and his assistant weren't long at all doing it, considering the amount of thatching that had to be done. I hated those drab slate tiles which let in the rain every five minutes.'

'It could have been reslated,' Lindsay said, helping himself to a slice of chocolate fudge cake. Mrs MacNee, the Hamilton cook, always baked a fine cake, and chocolate fudge cake was his favourite.

Shiona smiled over the teapot. 'Don't look so worried Lindsay! The repairs will be coming out of our pocket, not yours.'

He covered his confusion by saying, 'I'm not worried about that. I'm just not sure that thatch is the right thing to have as roofing material with so many trees around.'

'Don't worry! It's not only weatherproof, but also fire-proof – a special coating into which the thatch is first dipped, so there's no need to fear.'

Christabel screamed and dropped her cup in horror. 'The little beasts! I'm going to *throttle* them!'

She ran over the lawn to where Annie was sitting sewing under the trees while the two boys in her charge pretended all innocence as they scattered sponge crumbs to the birds.

'What's the matter with her?' Lindsay asked Shiona who was grimly picking up pieces of broken china, while Christabel had eleven year old Bruce pinned over a garden bench, giving him a thorough good walloping on the seat of his clean dungarees.

Shiona showed Lindsay the cause of Christabel's anger and disgust. In the bottom of her cup wriggled hordes of little beige baiting-worms. 'They're always doing it to unsuspecting guests, the rascals!'

Lindsay hurriedly set down his cup. He had already drunk half. He poured the rest on the grass and saw the baiting worms in the bottom of *his* cup, too!

He stepped over the grass to join his sister.

Christabel was giving the boys a piece of her mind. 'If ever I catch you two doing anything so disgusting again, I'm going to take the stick to you myself!' She turned to Lindsay in exasperation. 'I don't find their pranks at all amusing, but cruel. Yesterday they tied Bonnie Prince Charlie's tail to the bell-rope in the sitting-room. The day before, at the castle, Murray discovered them *and* the dog, suffocating in three suits of armour! They remind me *too* much of brother Rory and the evil pranks that he used to get up to.' Christabel turned to their nurse. 'Annie, kindly control these brats better. Otherwise we'll have to replace you with someone who has more experience in handling boys. We don't want them to grow up into uncontrollable delinquents – do we?' She turned to her brother. 'Lindsay, these two boys need the firm hand of a tutor at their age, not the feeble administrations of a nursemaid!'

Lindsay saw the colour suffuse Annie's cheeks; the barbed look in her flashing green eyes reminding him of a time past. But this time Annie held her tongue and looked away when she saw him staring at her. Lindsay didn't think Christabel should have blamed Annie for lacking control over her high-spirited protégés. One needed eyes in the back of one's head to keep up with the antics of the two brothers. But Christabel was right. It was time they were taken in hand. He must speak to Iain and Shiona concerning a proper education for their sons, not the lackadaisical environment of the village school at Gairloch or the soft touch of a young nursemaid, even though he knew Shiona would hate the idea of her beloved sons having to be sent away to a boarding school. Christabel marched off, back to the tea table, her palms no doubt smarting after warming the seat of Bruce's pants.

Aeneas turned to Lindsay who was still intent upon the fishergirl from Rill. 'Cousin Lindsay, will you still take me fishing tomorrow morning?'

'Not unless you go and retrieve your worms – we might have need of them.'

Annie, a glimmer of a smile illuminating her gaunt features, closed her sewing basket and got up off the picnic-rug. She began to fold it neatly.

He was glad he had made Annie smile. Lindsay retraced his steps across the lawn. 'Christabel,' he said, taking his place at the tea-table again, fresh cups and a new pot of tea brought out to them by one of the maids, while Shiona and Annie took the boys back to the house, 'I'm going to Edinburgh the day after tomorrow. Care to join me?'

'Can't. I'm off to London in the morning.'

'Not one of your Suffragette rallies again?'

'And why not? The Women's Movement is gaining momentum all the time. I have nothing else to do. I'm meeting Christabel Pankhurst in London. We're off to Paris after the London meeting. Cousin Jane Burrett will be joining us. As our Midlands organizer, she is also very involved.'

'I see. I suppose you'll be staying at the Town House?'

'Don't make it sound like a watering place for commercial travellers! Pankhurst and I require a temporary base.

Does that pose a problem?'

'Not at all. It's for the use of family members when in London.'

'Though it's actually in your name. I know, men inherit the earth, and we women inherit the dirt.'

He refrained from comment. He knew how dear to his sister's heart was the campaign for women's rights, and he wouldn't have dared voice his opinion on the subject. He just hoped that she and her more militant friends, Cousin Jane Burrett from Leicester included, wouldn't chain themselves to the front railings of the house in Park Lane, as they had on a previous occasion. It had provoked a great deal of publicity, which had turned out to be not so much concerned with the question of equality for women, but with the illustrious connections of some of the young women who had joined the Pankhurst Movement.

'I don't mind what you do with your life, Kiss,' he said, using his affectionate name for her, 'but please don't stick your banners and posters everywhere. Last time, the drawing-room had to be redecorated because the silk wallcovering came away with Mrs Pankhurst's face. I can't afford any unnecessary expense at the moment. The money has to be spent on Glengarth.'

'Yes, I've heard from Iain about your new project concerning the wasted land on Inchnadamph. Dearest brother, I promise! Pankhurst Junior and I have a lot of organizing of the Womens' Movement between London and Edinburgh, as well as with our counterparts in Paris. We have to rally all the support we can get. Equality for women is going to be Parliament's big issue in the next sitting.'

'And their big headache,' Lindsay cynically added.

Christabel tapped him on the arm with her well-buffed fingernails. 'Tell me why you're off to Edinburgh so suddenly? You hate the city.'

'I'm going to buy Cousin Aeneas a brand new fishing-rod in Edinburgh.'

Lindsay, to himself, smiled serenely. His blurred horizon had at last come into perspective: he was going to ask his Renoir girl to marry him. The question was, would

Iona be willing to marry *him* after such a short court-
ship!

Rory was in Liverpool when he received an urgent
message via the Lloyds Signalling Station to contact Lord
Burrett at Breedon Hall. When he telephoned his uncle,
there was no mistaking the anxiety in Uncle Austen's tone.
'Rory, I wonder if you can meet me in Birmingham as
soon as possible?'

'Why, what's the matter? Is someone ill?'

'Not ill, dear boy. Kitty's in prison.'

'*Prison?*' Rory croaked. 'Kitty in *prison*?' What on
earth could mild and gentle Kitty have done that was so
awful that she had been taken to prison? Rory wondered
in that disorientated moment, believing that his uncle had
got his female relatives mixed up. 'Kitty wouldn't hurt a
fly.'

'The Prime Minister is not a fly, Rory. She and my
wretched daughters have got themselves into trouble by
associating with a wild bunch of young women who
decided to stone Asquith when he was making a speech
regarding the Conciliation Bill at the Bingley Hall last
April. Sentencing was postponed at the time pending
social enquiry reports. But now the verdict is, that the
Suffragettes involved in that unfortunate episode are to be
committed to prison for a minimum term of two months. I
myself have only just returned from business abroad. Aunt
Ada gave me the astounding news that the girls have been
in prison for the past five days. She is quite happy to leave
them there, but I am not. Dear boy, I would like you to
bring yourself to the Winson Green Prison, Birmingham,
as soon as possible.'

'Yes ... yes, of course.'

Rory took the train from Liverpool to Birmingham, and
three hours later, was admitted into Winson Green Prison
where he was shown into the Prison Governor's office. His
uncle was speaking to someone on the Governor's telephone, while the Governor himself was tapping the top of
his blotter in a little finger-dance of annoyance.

Rory was surprised to see Toby, Viscount Tapstock.

'Hello, Toby,' he whispered, 'don't tell me Daisy's in prison, too!'

''Fraid so, old chap. This Suffragette thing has really got out of hand. Mama is going to use the birch on Daisy the moment she arrives home. The gals, y'know, were staying with us when they suddenly disappeared from the house last April, to take the train from Oakham to Birmingham for the express purpose of harming Mr Asquith. Now they have received their comeuppance. Premeditated murder ain't a little offence, y'know.'

Rory felt light-headed. He hadn't eaten a decent meal all day and could have done with a sandwich just then. His uncle appeared to be arguing quite vociferously with Mr Churchill at the Home Office, and seemed likely to continue thus, until he got his way. In the end, Lord Burrett, tall, spare and rheumy-eyed, banged down the telephone with a satisfied smirk on his aquiline features and turned to the Prison Governor. 'Mr Churchill has given me his solemn word that within the next few hours a document of release will arrive on your desk, signed by him and sent from London via special courier. Now I should like to see the young women in question.'

With a sigh of resignation – and relief, Rory felt – the Prison Governor handed them over to a wardress who took them across to the Women's Section of the prison. They were again kept waiting, this time for long hours in the wardress's office, while endless cups of strong sweet tea were brought them. In the early hours of the morning Jane and Leonora Burrett, Margaret Tapstock and Katherine Roskillen were set free, their release personally secured by Mr Winston Churchill at the Home Office.

Rory was dismayed at the state of the girls. They had been in prison for five days and seemed to have accepted the fact that they were to be kept indefinitely at His Majesty's pleasure. But Lord Burrett had decided enough was enough and had used his elevated status to secure their release. Jane showed her chagrin at having been released sooner than most of her fellow Suffragettes, simply because she was who she was. 'Papa, you should *not* have interfered. We are fighting a just cause and you have no right to deprive us of our dignity!'

'No more, please, Jane. We'll discuss this matter at home,' her father said.

In the custody of three masculine-looking wardresses in uniform, the girls were grubby, unkempt, their clothes torn, fingernails broken. Leonora sported a huge bruise on her cheek as well as a black eye.

Dawn was breaking over the city when Lord Burrett ushered the Suffragettes into the Rolls, he himself having personally driven the Silver Ghost from Leicester as he wanted no gossip from chauffeurs and suchlike about the upper classes getting themselves sent to prison!

'Rory, dear boy, I wonder if you would drive us home, please? I'm rather tired,' Lord Burrett said, and added unnecessarily, 'I'd deem it a favour.'

'Of course, Uncle.' Toby was pushed into the back seat along with the girls, while Lord Burrett sat with Kitty in the front. Rory was infinitely glad he was driving, otherwise he might just have wrung Jane's neck for having got Kitty and Lennie involved in her militant Women's Movement.

Ten miles from home, trouble flared when Lord Burrett asked his daughter Jane what had made her decide to join the brigade that had stoned Prime Minister Asquith. 'Don't ask me why, Papa,' she said, 'you'll never understand.'

'You're right, my dear. I *don't* understand!'

'But I shall continue to fight beside the Pankhursts and all the others like them, Papa. We shall yet win suffrage for women, or die in the attempt.'

'Then please, Jane, do not involve Leonora, Kitty or Daisy. They are none of them of age as yet. To abduct Daisy from her own home, from under the nose of her mother, was totally irresponsible of you while you, Leonora and Kitty were guests under the Countess's roof. Your behaviour is inexcusable. Your own mother is up in arms about the whole affair and has threatened to banish you from the house altogether.'

'If that is her wish, so be it. I have places, and friends in London to go to. And Daisy is not a child. She is old enough to make up her own mind. She was fully aware of what was going to happen, and I exerted *no* pressure on her whatsoever! She joined us of her own free will.'

'I am sad, Jane. Deeply sad and troubled that you have become involved with a band of militant young women. A woman's place is in the home, not on the public highway, throwing stones at Prime Ministers and other well known figures in Parliament.'

'I'm sorry, Papa, that you are opposed to the liberation of women. I would have thought better of you. Progress cannot be stopped, and every woman has a right to be free. Universal suffrage is what we are striving for, and we will win it! Only when there is equality of the sexes can women hope to gain a fair deal from life.'

Leonora, who had been staring glassy-eyed at nothing, opened her bloodless lips to say, 'It was horrid, truly horrid! Far, far worse than I had imagined. Papa, when one reads in the press about the ill-treatment of Suffragettes in prison, it's nothing to what *really* happens! We weren't given any of the rights given to political prisoners. We were treated with open hostility, mockery and brutality. We were subjected to worse degradations than the lowest of the low – it was *unbelievable*!'

'Lennie, please don't talk about it any more,' Kitty whispered from the front seat, her teeth starting to chatter badly. Her uncle tucked the travel rug around her. Kitty rested her golden head against her brother's shoulder, and Rory could have beaten hell out of Jane in that moment.

'Kitty, I've *got* to talk to Papa about it!' Leonora said fiercely behind Rory. 'He'll be able to tell Mr Churchill what *truly* goes on in the third ward! Papa, listen to me. Mr Asquith doesn't want to listen to us, and nor do any of the other men in Government. We women are fighting very hard for ourselves in a man's world. But because we're the wrong shape for the Houses of Parliament no one takes us seriously. Men think that they can patronize us, tell us we've been naughty little girls, go home to mother. But we're not going! In prison, if you don't co-operate, they thrust a horrid tube up your nose and into your stomach – it's called forced feeding. You're tied to a chair or onto a stretcher. The wardresses sit on you to keep you still – even the doctor, who is usually a man! If you struggle, they hit you and punch you until you're quiet or unconscious. Then they force the most revolting mixture into your body until you're sick.'

'Is that what happened to you, Lennie? Is that how you got the bruise on your face and the black eye?'

'I don't wish to talk about me ... I don't want sympathy, only justice. I want you, Papa, to tell Mr Churchill to put an end to the awful things the Suffragettes have to endure in the name of liberty! We've committed no crime, and yet we were given only a daily crust of bread and a filthy wooden bowl of cocoa to live on ...'

'Don't say I didn't warn you ... I told you, I *told* you, what it might be like!' said Jane to her sister through gritted teeth. 'This isn't a parlour game, Lennie, it's a question of life and death! If you didn't have the guts for it, you shouldn't have agreed to accompany me to Birmingham ...'

'Jane, please let me finish,' Leonora insisted.

'Girls, girls! *Please!*' Uncle Austen beseeched.

'Papa, I *will* speak! We were stripped and searched and de-loused, just as though we were ... we were common prostitutes. Then there's a ghastly device they call a stomach pump ... it's never washed, but goes from one patient to another. The stomach tubes lie in unwashed bowls on the floor, amidst all the vomit and blood and ... oh, God!' Leonora suddenly covered her face with her hands and began to sob.

'*Stop it, stop it!*' Jane cried. Leaning across Toby, she struck her sister a resounding slap across the cheek. Leonora crumpled against Viscount Tapstock who was unsure of what to do in that crucial moment when feminine issues took precedence over all else.

Rory stopped the car. He told Kitty and Daisy to stop howling, and getting out of the car, opened the rear, near-side door. He hauled Jane out onto the wet and slippery road and shook her till her teeth rattled. 'I've had enough of you. Leave my sister and Lennie out of all this, do you hear? If you fill their heads with any more Suffragette nonsense, I'll break the gentleman's code of never striking a woman.'

'And I'd believe it of you, you ... you *Chauvin*!' Jane said savagely. 'Lennie's right. How dare you assume to know what is right for *my* sister or *your* sister, or even Daisy Tapstock!'

'I dare because I am a man! I dare because you are nothing but a militant female who *enjoys* making other, innocent people suffer.'

'In what way do the Suffragettes make other people suffer?' Jane demanded.

'Oh, no? What about incendiary bombs designed to start fires in pillar boxes and public places. What about *stoning* people? What about influencing innocent young girls into *your* militant way of thinking, so that they themselves have to suffer in a vile prison? You, and women like you, are a menace to women's suffrage, not a help. Jane Burrett, you make me *sick*!'

'How can someone like you – a man, and a privileged one at that – possibly understand, Rory Roskillen?' Jane asked in despair, as she pushed a limp strand of hair out of her eyes. It was still raining and they were both getting very wet.

'I understand Jane. I understand a lot better than you give me credit for. Your so-called acts of faith, hope and charity, with women's votes thrown in as an extra bonus, are ways of drawing attention to yourself. I know your motives – I've resorted to them often enough when I, too, wanted to 'get noticed'. You see, you and I are awfully alike in some ways, Jane. We're both basically unsure of ourselves, lost as we are among more illustrious members of the family, way down low in the great scheme of things. We *want* to gain attention sometimes.'

'That,' said Jane, shaking her head sadly, 'is a typical *man*-thought!'

'Very well, but that's my opinion. You go to prison if that's what you want, but leave Kitty out. She means a lot to me. And so does Lennie. Please don't get them involved in any more of your foolish pranks!'

For an answer Jane struck him across the face, just as

she had done with Leonora a moment ago. And Rory, so inflamed, struck her in return.

More a spontaneous protest gesture rather than an out and out assault, and not nearly as hard as Jane's stinging slap had been, but Rory himself was stricken.

By the side of the rain-washed road, they stared at one another for a long moment. Then Jane said in a small voice, 'Don't call this a foolish *prank*, Rory. It's not a game, it's deadly serious. I will die for what I believe in. I will *never* give in!'

'I believe it.' He rubbed his cheek ruefully, and re-membered the slap Leonora had given him in the middle of a barley field. It appeared that a man's face and pride had become a target all round for the Women's Suffragette Movement. 'I'm sorry I hit you back,' he said stiffly, trying to salvage a little dignity from this whole, sordid episode, and sorry that he had lost his temper with her.

Jane smiled rather forlornly. 'I'm glad that you did! At least *now*, Rory Duncan, we're equals in a man's world. Blow for blow! Let's get back into the car, shall we, before we die of pneumonia?'

CHAPTER FIFTEEN

The whole world beyond Rory's bedroom windows was wonderful. The sun was shining, the sky was blue, the grass was green and the birds sang lustily in the branches of the chestnut trees. He washed, dressed, slicked down his hair with damped hairbrushes before whistling his way downstairs.

'Sign, please.'

He turned.

Behind him Leonora dogged his footsteps to the Shukborough Room. She thrust a dance-programme with a pencil tied to it with a pink ribbon into his hand. 'I never sign anything unless I know what it's for,' he said.

'Sir Roger de Coverley. I'm trying to make up the numbers.'

He signed his name with a flourish against two waltzes as an excuse to hold her tight. 'Where's your little ink-blot from the *Chronic Times?*' he asked.

'Working for a living, which is more than can be said of a certain individual of gutter habits.'

'Truce, Lennie, you know how much I love you, dearest, so when shall we elope?'

'Charlotte said you're not as bad as you try and make out. I disagree. I think you're heartless, chauvinistic and unpolished.'

'And your well-polished, silver-pated little reporter is everything your heart desires, I suppose?'

'Not quite. But he's useful to the WSPU by reporting our intentions with the *utmost* accuracy and attention to *truth.* Unlike other men, he is fighting on our behalf. However, I'd still prefer you, had you not descended from a long line of lunatics.'

'But a very illustrious line, nevertheless.'

'Nevertheless, nothing. The deranged spirit of a Scottish grandmother assuming to be the reincarnation of Beauly the First's mistress still lurks in your makeup, Rory Duncan Roskillen.'

'I resort not to cosmetics, my angel. What you see is all God gave me.' He gave her what he hoped was a disarming smile, but Leonora refused to be compromised. 'I know that you haven't forgiven me for kissing you so ruthlessly in a barley field, but you asked for it. However, I apologize. I should have known better than to kiss you.'

'I refuse to mention the subject. You are still nothing but an uncouth youth.'

'Thanks, Lennie. Still, I couldn't help *but* be fascinated by Mr Llewellyn's article on Dalton's grandly painted water-closet. Quite flushed with excitement he was the other morning. I wondered what he was doing in the new bathroom, peering into ablution bowls and chamber pots, and could only assume he was tossing up whether or not to wash his face in our toilet water as he had none of his own.'

'You're incorrigible!' But she did smile. 'Rory, be nice to David this evening.'

'I'll try, but I don't promise to dance with him. I'm jealous of the attention you pay him, and would ask you to marry me if I wasn't so afraid you'd turn me down.'

'You wouldn't be wrong either – I'd never be sure what kind of foreign body I'd find in your bed!' She skipped off towards the Shukborough Room and slammed the doors in his face without knowing what he really felt for her.

He stood there ruefully contemplating the oak panelling and why Leonora had to be his first cousin instead of an unrelated female he could flirt with to his heart's delight. But it would be wrong of him to encourage anything romantic; it just wouldn't be right or proper.

Humphrey thumped him between the shoulder blades. 'Don't do that, Hump!' Rory spluttered, 'I'm extremely fragile this morning.'

'You look it, Scotch kipper. What happened to your face – the new footman mistake it for your shoes? Or is it all that coal-hauling you've been doing recently?'

'*Ho-ho*-Hump! Does your mother honestly want me to sing you a paean of praise today?'

'God forbid! It's too early to stomach your accent. It's bad enough listening to it in church or over the scrambled eggs and kedgeree.'

They entered the Shukborough Room together.

As Jane was in London, busy with her Suffragette propaganda, Leonora had taken her sister's place as chief resident pianist. She struck up, *Happy Birthday to You*. Humphrey was duly buried beneath a stack of birthday presents from family and household staff, among them a chocolate cake from cook and a multicoloured scarf three miles long knitted by the housekeeper in between bouts of sherry-swigging, which, in Rory's opinion, accounted for its aereated appearance.

Good wishes and wrapping-paper out of the way, the ritual of morning prayers was said, taking him back to the first time he had experienced the family's traditions. How insidious, Rory realized in that heartfelt moment, had been his integration with his Leicestershire relatives – who weren't such a bad bunch after all was said and done.

Rory, who had no wish to give Humphrey his birthday present in a room full of people, left it until the crowd had dispersed. Humphrey, too, had lingered over a hearty breakfast, and so they were alone when Rory took from his pocket a small box and passed it across the table.

'If it's another set of cuff-links, Scotch kipper, I'll throw them back at you.'

'There's gratitude for you! Open it, Sassenach, then pass comment.'

'Wind, more likely,' said Humphrey, who had retained his caveman instincts. He undid the pink bow and opened the box. His grin was wide, all his tombstone teeth displayed in genuine appreciation of the joke. 'You have a sense of humour about as twisted as Quasimodo's back,' he said.

'Why, Hump?' Rory asked innocently.

'You bastard – but it's acceptable.'

Rory, too, grinned. 'Casanova tied his with pink ribbons, Hump, so don't dispose of the trimmings. It was the most useful and affordable thing I could think of – for you.' He broke off the conversation when Leonora poked her nose into the breakfast-room.

'Still eating! You'll get fat, you two. Is that Rory's birthday present to you Humphrey? Oh, do let me see! I wondered if he'd forgotten.'

'Buzz off, Lennie,' Humphrey growled, and stuffed the gift-box quickly into his pocket.

'What did you give him?' Lennie demanded.

'A Marie Stopes tie, Lennie darling,' Rory said as he took her arm and led her away with a sly wink over his shoulder at his cousin Humphrey. 'Lennie darling, I bet you can't say, Able was I Ere I Saw Elba, backwards, before we reach Folly's Point.'

'Why Folly's Point? Are you going for a walk up there in the hope of encountering Miss Smartbloomers again?'

'Not if you accompany me.'

'Well, I suppose a walk with you is preferable to playing piquet with Charlotte, although I've promised to help her supervise the flower arrangements later on, for tonight's grand ball.' They encountered Tobias on his tardy way to partake of breakfast.

'Hello, Toby,' Rory greeted him. 'I didn't know you'd become part of the family.'

'Rory, there's something I wish to ask you.'

'Then shoot, old man, I'm all ears.'

'It's about Kitty.'

Leonora took her leave of them rather hastily. 'Excuse me, if we're going up to Charnwood, Rory, I'd better fetch walking shoes.'

Rory noticed the flush that had suffused Toby's speckled face. 'What about Kitty?' he asked.

'As her nearest and dearest relative, I wish to ask you for Kitty's hand in marriage at some future date ... er, not so future,' he waffled in his maddening fashion.

'Good God, Toby!' Rory stared at Viscount Tapstock in some confusion, as well as acute dismay.

Tobias seemed equally taken aback by Rory's outburst. '*Naturally,* I have already approached Kitty's guardians in the matter, and have *also* written to her elder brother, the

Laird of Glengarth. However, I'm also asking for your approval, Rory, because I know how very close you and Kitty are.'

'And for that reason, Toby, I cannot give you an answer – yet. After all, Kitty is my dearest possession and I must be absolutely certain of her future happiness. Do you promise to love, honour and obey her?'

'I say, old chap, have you been at the champagne already?' Tobias asked, with a certain degree of disapproval in his mud-coloured eyes.

'Don't change the subject, Toby!' Rory answered sternly. 'Answer, yea or nay? Do you love Kitty?'

'Of course!'

'No "of course" about it! Do you promise to look after her for a whole lot better and not a lot worse?'

'I cannot seriously believe you are resorting to this kind of facile behaviour over a perfectly serious matter.'

'Don't be pompous, Toby. Does Kitty love you?'

'Naturally.'

'No "naturally" about it. Love is the least natural thing in the world. At best it's an illusion and at worst it's a terrible let-down. But yes, if Kitty loves you and you love her, I suppose there's nothing I can say or do in the matter ... but I do wish you hadn't sprung all this on me quite so early in the morning. Ask me again tonight, and I might say nix again.'

'I really do not need your consent, Rory. I shall wait for that of the Laird of Glengarth, in view of the fact that he is Kitty's elder brother. I merely approached you in the matter since Kitty has a high regard for you and wished me to seek your blessing in the first instance.'

'And what about you, Toby?'

'I never know how to take you, Rory. Even after all these years as your friend.'

'Then that's probably because you still don't understand the Celts, Toby.'

'The Celts are a conquered race, Rory, endorsed by the Union of England and Scotland – 16th January, 1707, if my memory serves me correctly. So what is there to understand?'

'Then I suggest you'd better start swotting up on them again, Caesar, old chap, since this is one *Celt* who has never been conquered – treaty or no treaty! Since Kitty is of the same breed, if you ever try and conquer her, you'll have a barbarian from north of the border to deal with, understood?'

Toby smiled in his superior fashion. 'Good Lord, Rory! What are you implying?'

'Hands off my sister! She's far too young and innocent for you.'

'Kitty's becoming my wife one day soon, will make me the happiest man alive, Rory.'

'I sincerely hope so. She wouldn't want a dead husband.'

'I know she feels for me as much as I feel for her. I am prepared to wait for her hand in marriage.'

'As long as her hand is all you want.' Rory scratched his ear thoughtfully. He had no wish to jeopardize his sister's future happiness should old Tobias Augustus have second thoughts about saddling himself with an eccentric, seafaring barbarian for a brother-in-law. 'What do our guardians think of the arrangement?'

'Pending the Laird of Glengarth's approval to an early engagement, they have given us their blessing.'

Rory realized that all Kitty's little trips to Boxwood Manor as Tobias's sister's best friend, had not been in vain. Romance had blossomed while he had been away at sea. But Kitty had not been brought out into society as yet, and would be unable to judge for herself whether or not Tobias would make her a suitable husband. As far as he was concerned, he didn't dislike fusty old Tobias; it was just that Kitty had met no other suitor as yet – his aunt's responsibility! He had never envisaged Kitty as someone's wife, just as his young sister who required his protection. But, there again, Kitty was Leonora's age, and yet he had already made advances towards Leonora – hadn't he? All this matrimonial business was rather sudden, and was giving him a headache.

'Look Toby, if you and Kitty love each other and want to marry, then all I can say is, *sant'i' fa*!'

'Meaning?'

'Meaning, if you ever make her unhappy, I'll turn you inside out.'

'I understand your feelings, Rory. No man is ever good enough for a father's beloved daughter or a brother's beloved sister. I realize you've been cast in both roles since Kitty and you were left together at a very early age without parents.'

'I'm glad you're so understanding, Caesar, old chap, so let's just wait and see what Lindsay says, eh? You've obviously been dreaming of Kitty all night, hence this early confession. So, I should go and wolf down what's left of the cold scrambled eggs before the euphoria of love goes further to your head.'

The rest of the day was spent in a semi-comatose state as far as Rory was concerned – mainly because he had hit the champagne soon after that breakfast conversation with Viscount Tapstock.

Rory was glad to see that he had been placed next to Leonora at Humphrey's birthday dinner that evening, prior to the real celebration in the marquee erected in the garden while the ballroom was being refurbished.

'Don't forget,' she whispered as they shook out the table napkins, 'that the first dance is ours.'

'If your Bible says so, Lennie, then it must be gospel ... and if it's saddle of lamb next, will you be a lamb and share my saddle as I'm vegetarian?'

'If you're behaving so outrageously tonight when it's not even your birthday,' she murmured, trying to keep a straight face while soup was being served, 'what on earth are you going to be like at *your* twenty-first birthday party?'

'Between now and January I hope to have sobered up a little. I'm also hoping for some money. Lennie, my sweet, will you promise to *faire une promenade avec moi, dans les rhododendrons après la premier danse*?'

She giggled into her soup, 'Is that all the French you managed to acquire during your Eton days?'

'Not quite.' He avoided looking at Aunt Ada.

'Tell me more! I'm all agog,' Leonora said.

'I don't think your mother'd approve.'

'Nor do I, Rory Duncan! What a pity you're my cousin. It would have been rather fun to elope with you.'

After dinner the ladies adjourned to the drawing-room for coffee, and the port, brandy and cigars were brought to the table. The appropriate toasts were drunk to Humphrey's manhood. Rory was almost asleep when Humphrey's voice brought him up with a jolt.

'And here's to Rory, the Scotch kipper I'm going to flatten before the night is through.'

'Ha-ha-Hump. Why?'

'For old time's sake.'

Afterwards, Rory walked out on the terrace for a breath of fresh air. The night was warm and dry, perfect party weather. Strains of music drifted across the lawns as the orchestra warmed up in the huge marquee erected down by the lakeside. It looked like an ocean liner decked out with coloured lights, bunting and balloons.

Rory danced with Leonora, while Toby never let go of Kitty. Then, much to Rory's annoyance, David Llewellyn from the *Leicestershire Morning Chronicle* barged his way in and broke the spell. Over her shoulder, as David was about to whirl her away, Leonora said with a subtle little smile, 'Welshmen, unlike Scotsmen, are so considerate, so articulate and so . . .'

'Electro-pated?' Rory offered as he viewed the reporter's premature bald patch with a huge amount of dislike.

'Un-Scottish!' was Leonora's parting shot.

'Aunt Ada,' Rory said, boldly approaching her for a dance, 'may I have the pleasure of this foxtrot?'

'How kind, dear boy,' she murmured with a flushed, glazed look on her florid face, 'but I've promised the next dance to your uncle . . . Austen dear, doesn't this bring back memories of Amalfi and that foreign Count's villa in which we spent part of our honeymoon?'

Rory got the distinct feeling that he was being cold-shouldered. Even Charlotte, his perennial champion, was dancing with someone else. So, what does a male gilli-flower do, pray tell me? Rory asked himself despondently.

He goes in search of the female of the species! he reminded himself, and unearthed the loneliest and most flat-chested little wallflower imaginable, sipping lemonade amongst the potted ferns, aspidistras and chaperones. She told him her name was Susan Jenny, which Rory took to be her given names. She was from Texas in the United States of America. Unfortunately, she was also only four-teen years of age. Afterwards, he relieved a footman of his tray, a bottle of champagne and two glasses – just what he required!

Picking his way carefully through clutching bodies everywhere, especially on the back stairs, Rory headed for Charis's room. Although Kitty and Leonora had grown up and did not require the supervision of a governess any more, Charis had stayed on at Breedon Hall as governess to Charlotte's young daughters. Rory gave a quick light tap on her bedroom door, and, because it was unlocked, walked straight in. Charis Vayer was in bed, with someone else.

They hadn't even bothered to switch off the light as they rocked together in sweet abandonment. He stood on the threshold and gaped like a startled guppy at Humphrey, astride Charis as though he were riding with the Quorn.

To back his way out now with the champagne would truly put the finishing touch on the evening, and Rory felt he couldn't afford to lose further face now. So he brazened it out. He closed the door carefully, and as Humphrey and Charis hurriedly pulled up the bedclothes, made his way unsteadily towards the washstand where he set down the tray, tempted as he was, to toss the lot into bed with them. But that, he decided, would have been an utter waste, so he carefully poured out two glasses and one dented tin tooth-mug of champagne.

He handed Humphrey one glass, Charis the other and, taking up the tooth-mug, sat down on the end of her single cot that accommodated two people perfectly. 'You lowdown, fornicating bastard,' Rory said as levelly as he could to Humphrey. 'You stinking, rotten, filthy, double-crossing, son-of-a-bitch, accusing me of things you've been doing yourself.'

'Mater,' Humphrey said, maintaining his composure even though he was as naked as an ape, 'would be mortified to hear you use such bad language in the presence of a lady.' He reached across Charis's ample bosom for a mint humbug on the bedside table, even though champagne had been poured for him.

'Charis, what the hell are you playing at?'

'It's none of your business, Rory.'

'If this is the kind of flattening you promised me, Humphrey, I don't think it's very funny!' Rory jerked the lip of the mug towards Humphrey who was smirking like an imbecile. 'I never want to speak to you again!' Rory gulped down the mugful of champagne and helped himself to more. 'What's your little game, Humphrey?'

Humphrey grinned. 'All's fair in love and war, Scotch kipper.'

'What are you talking about?'

'I got married today – well, it was this morning, actually.'

'Christ! Does the bride know?'

'Tell him, sweetheart.'

'Humphrey and I are married, Rory.'

His jaw fell open and he almost lost the champagne. He slid to the floor and stayed there. 'You've married Charis? Why?' he managed to croak at last. 'No, don't tell me – you've got her into trouble, the same as Flossie Newton from a time before, eh Hump?'

'Well, that's about it, I suppose.' Humphrey continued to suck nonchalantly, the mint humbug pushing out his flabby cheeks.

'And did you marry Flossie as well? Be careful, Hump, bigamy is a prisonable offence.'

'Flossie lost the baby in the end, so it wasn't necessary.'

'Bad luck, Hump. Congratulations, Charis. What else can I say except that I wouldn't be in your shoes for the world, you two, when my aunt gets to hear of this shotgun wedding. Do you do this sort of thing often, Charis?'

'Seducing young men, you mean, Rory?' she asked, tossing her golden tresses out of her eyes, her smile secretive.

'Schoolboys, I meant.'

'Only when they themselves are willing.'

'You're a nyphomaniac, Charis.'

'But we had a good time, didn't we, Rory? Even though it was short and sweet.'

'Hump this ... this woman is nothing but a *nympho*! Besides, she's ten years older than you!'

'You're talking about my *wife* now, Rory. So I'll thank you to keep a civil tongue.'

Rory almost choked. 'You're letting your emotions carry you away – as I almost let mine, once! What a good job I ran away to sea, that's all I can say. Otherwise I might have been in the same boat as you. Listen Hump, I hate to see you do this to yourself. If you've been held at gunpoint, or you're being blackmailed by this ... wife of yours, I know a way you can get the marriage made null and void by tomorrow morning.'

'Oh, yes?'

'*Oh, yes!* You see, Charis is an imposter. Lennie told me all about her. Mademoiselle Charis Vayer from Paris, is not a legitimate French governess at all. Her real name is Cynthia – Cynthia Smith, can you believe that?'

'I know. She has told me all about her past life.'

'She has?'

'Oh, yes. The marriage certificate is quite legitimate, I assure you. And thank you, Scotch kipper, for being so concerned on my behalf. But I can take care of myself.'

'Oh, God!'

In the silence a moth fluttered against the window pane, trying to get out. Rory stood up, opened the window and let it fly away. Turning back to them, Rory asked Humphrey, 'Do your ma and pa know about this?'

'Nope.'

'Why did you do it? Why did you let her blackmail you in this fashion?'

'I didn't. It's nothing to do with blackmail, Rory. We love each other ... don't we, sweetheart?' He leaned over her again and planted a smacking kiss on her voluptuous white shoulder. 'It makes no difference to me, Scotch kipper, what you and she did together. She's been honest

with me all along. She has told me all about her former
marriage, her son, her mother who looks after her son and
about you. You were a temporary diversion that's all –
sorry old man, but there it is. We came together when we
both realized nothing else mattered in the world ... that
must have been shortly after she'd admitted to slaying the
Nemean lion,' he said with a smirk which made Rory
Duncan feel even more humiliated. 'You see, Scotch
kipper, she was trying to find herself again after years of
unhappiness and hardship. Of course she has admitted to
me of other relationships with men, but none of them
brought her lasting happiness – until she found me.'

'Oh, God!' Rory said again, wishing he was not quite so
drunk.

'Charis is my middle name, Vayer was my maiden
name, Rory. I've always been called Charis instead of
Cynthia because I prefer it. My father was French, and
Vayer sounded more professional than Smith when I was
looking for a governess's post requiring good French.
That's why I reverted to my maiden name. So you see,
Rory, there's nothing sinister at all about me.'

Oh, God! Rory felt nauseated. Was the man so incred-
ibly naïve? He couldn't believe it of Humphrey. But then,
Rory realized old Hump had always worn his hearts on his
sleeve – Flossie Newton was only one of a number, so
Charis, alias Cynthia Smith, and Humphrey made a good
pair. 'Who was the lunatic clergyman who married you two?'

'An Anglican priest from Leicester – for a substantial
donation to his church roof fund.'

'Before or after you realized she was pregnant?'

'After. I've known as long as she has about her ... er,
condition.'

'A defrocked priest to all accounts – then you still have
a chance to get the marriage annulled before your parents
find out, Humphrey.'

'But I don't want to get it annulled.'

'Enough said, then. I'd better be off and leave you two
nymphs fornicating to your hearts' delight.' Rory put down
the tin mug on the washstand and went to the door.

'By the way, old chap, any chance of getting back some

of that money you borrowed off me for your boat?'
Humphrey asked.

Rory regarded him steadily, and then smiled. 'Sure,
Hump. I'm putting to sea again shortly, and will repay you
every last penny, 'ere long.'

'Not too long, Scotch kipper. Need every penny I can
lay my hands on, what with the expenses of the new baby
and all that,' Humphrey added somewhat sheepishly. 'You
see, I think the trust coming my way today, might not
stretch very far now that I'm a married man.'

Rory leaned against the door. Then he started to laugh
as the funny side struck him. But he laughed with relief
more than rancour. It was wonderful to be a free man
while Humphrey had saddled himself with responsibilities
he couldn't even begin to imagine: Humphrey as father
then husband, must surely be the biggest joke of the year!
He had gained the last laugh on his old sparring partner,
after all!

'I'll be damned!' Rory picked up the champagne bottle
by the neck. 'Women! I'll never trust them again as long as
I live,' he said, and meant it. 'As for you, Humphrey,
you're the cretin I always thought you were and more
immature than I'd ever imagined. Still, he who laughs last,
laughs longest. As for you, Charis – sorry, I mean Cynth, I
knew you were clever at playing games, but never realized
just how clever. At least you managed to catch *one* of us
to furnish you with an honourable title. And since the
better man has won, *sant' i' fa*!' Rory stripped off the
bedsheet and tipped the remaining champagne over their
naked bodies.

'Go away, you vulgar schoolboy!' said Charis laughing
good-naturedly. 'All right, truce, no more hard feelings.'

'You're so damn right, Marm! You see, my chitterlings
have never let me down – as *his* obviously did with you
and Flossie Newton. A pity my birthday present came too
late, eh Hump? But thanks for the good times, both of
you, and congratulations. As the Norman lord said to the
Saxon wench, *droit de seigneur* might be gauche, but I'm
right glad I did!'

He ducked as their champagne glasses were hurled at

him. He avoided the splinters and opened the door. 'You know, you two ought really to turn the key in the lock if you don't want midnight intruders.'

Rory went downstairs again. The first sight that greeted his jaded eye inside the marquee was David Llewellyn dancing with Charlotte. He went up to them and tapped David smartly on the shoulder because he was sick and tired of the sneaky little reporter elbowing him out the running every time his back was turned. 'Excuse me, your editor's on the line. He says, if you don't get back to Leicester for the story that's about to break, you're fired.'

'What story?' David blinked owlishly, his glasses steamed up in the humid atmosphere under canvas.

'How should I know? I don't write for the *Chronic Times*.'

'Rory,' Charlotte said when David had gone in search of the telephone, 'you really are a glutton for punishment!' She shook her head in dismay over his juvenile mentality and aptitude for practical jokes.

'The story of my life, Charlie, one constant battle after another. It's called survival.'

'Will you ever grow up?'

'Only if you promise to divorce Rupert on grounds of desertion and marry me instead. By the way, does he know he'll only unearth mummified Egyptians in the Valley of Kings and not foxes?'

She smiled. 'He and Lord Carnarvon are still digging.'

'What on earth made him want to join the Theban expedition?'

'The lure of buried treasure of the pharoahs, I suppose.'

'Well, I can't be accused of being the *only* eccentric one in this family.'

'I never thought you were ever eccentric. I think you have all your wits about you. It's just that you're a little immature for your age.'

'Thank you Charlie. I truly love you. You were always my one true champion among the Sassenachs.'

'When are you off to sea again?'

'Tomorrow – today, I mean. By the way, where is Lennie?'

'She wasn't feeling very well and went to bed about an hour ago.' Charlotte became serious. 'Rory, I hope you don't mind my saying this, but I know how much Lennie thinks of you, so please don't play around with her feelings as you do with all the others.'

'What others? And who's playing around?' He was deeply offended because Charlotte thought so badly of him – without reason. 'I'm deadly serious where it concerns Lennie. She means a lot to me.'

'Then I'm glad to hear it. But neither you nor Lennie are ready to commit yourselves to each other. It's not wise, either, for first cousins to marry.'

'What's that supposed to mean, Charlie? I've never asked Leonora to marry me – we're just close cousins, that's all.'

'Then as long as that *is* all, we'll say no more upon the subject.'

He was glad about that. But he wished to set the record straight. 'You're right, Charlie, both Lennie and I have a great deal of growing up to do before we commit ourselves in any way to *any* one in particular ...' Rory was suddenly aware that someone was sending off-shore signals in his direction.

He looked over his shoulder again and caught the glint in her eye, her luscious red lips curving a little roguishly when she knew she had gained his attention. He was intrigued. 'Charlie, my darling, who's the gorgeous creature sitting among the hot-house ferns? She wasn't here earlier this evening.'

Charlotte turned her head and said, 'Heavens! You don't mean that child sipping lemonade, do you? That's Susan Jenny, better known as Spinning Jenny for the little wallflower she always is at these functions.'

'No, not Susan Jenny, I've already had the pleasure of *her* company. I mean the lady she's talking to, the one in the tight silver dress, feathers in her hair and diamonds all over her.'

Charlotte looked again, the potted shrubs and the bandstand obscuring her vision. Rory did a neat little shuffle-about with her so that she could get a better view of the lovely lady. 'Now I see ... goodness, Rory, you don't want to tangle with that woman. She's a veritable man-eater and ...'

'Who is she, Charlie?'

'Susan Jenny's elder sister. The family are distantly related to Lady Glover through marriage. They're staying at Boxwood Manor as Toby's guests, since Lady Glover is his aunt. They are extremely wealthy Americans, and somewhat vulgar in my opinion.'

'Tell me more about Susan Jenny's big sister – her name for a start.'

'Elizabeth. *Mrs* Elizabeth Roebling Chanin!'

He was truly downcast then; every interesting woman he happened to meet was already spoken for – until Charlie said, 'She's divorced, and widowed. Several times. And all before the age of twenty-six. I believe she got married at a young age and within an equally short space of time rid herself of husbands one, two and three. They were all very much older than Lizzie. She sticks to her maiden name, *Daddy's* of course, as it has the ring of money about it – too much of it. Her father's an oil-tycoon and Lizzie stands to inherit his millions as there are no male heirs in the family. They call it black gold in America.'

'Introduce me, Charlie,' he said, his interest in Mrs Roebling Chanin having just increased a millionfold.

'No!' Charlotte pretended to be shocked by his mercenary intent.

'Please?'

'Not until you know what you're letting yourself in for. She's a very eccentric person, *very*! They say she wears knickerbockers, and a diamond in her navel. She also smokes like a factory chimney, terrible Turkish cheroots – you can smell them from here. I must say I don't care a great deal for her, too brash. But then, I suppose she can afford to be since her husbands all left her money and fast cars, and her father is reputed to sink oil-wells at the rate of one per day – they all seem to strike what they're looking for, too.'

'Don't do this to me, Charlie,' he groaned. 'I promise I

won't flirt with anyone but you if you will just introduce me to her. I only want to ask her what the weather is doing on her side of the bank-vault.'

Charlotte laughed. 'Very well, you have been warned. It's a brave man who wants to tangle with Lizzie Roebling Chanin!'

She was quite the most peerless creature he had ever met and Rory wondered why he hadn't noticed her before. She had of course been screened by a bevy of red-faced young gentlemen dancing attendance on her behind the potted aspidistras. He decided to join her admirers.

She stood in the centre of that jungle of flora, and fauna – all of them hungry beasts on two legs – a sylvan goddess holding court to lesser mortals of the earth. But when their eyes met the second, and then the third time, Rory Roskillen felt he had struck lucky at last.

'*Doggone it!*' Susan Jenny pouted, 'I saw him first, Lizzie!'

Rory patted her teenage head. 'Your turn next,' he promised. After all, the way to an heiress's heart must surely be through the ugly sister. So, if Rory Duncan Roskillen played his cards right tonight, he decided he couldn't lose.

'I, er, didn't quite catch your title,' Lizzie Roebling Chanin said to him while they danced. Her head was thrown back a little so that her white throat arched towards him in a way that made him want to gulp for air. Realizing that he must be behaving like a rustic, he took his eyes off her gorgeous breasts, partially revealed by the *décolleté* gown, and looked instead deep into purple eyes.

'Neither did I ... catch a title, I mean. You see, it's like this, Mrs Roebling Cha ...'

'Oh, do call me Lizzie! Names are so boring when they're doubled up. The only double barrels I care for are the liquid ones from Devanna Prairie, Texas.'

'How right you are ... er, Lizzie!' Then he tried to explain to her that his blue-blood was in no way diluted despite the fact that he was title-less. 'My brother, Lindsay Beauly Roskillen inherited the title of Laird of Glengarth. Scottish titles aren't quite the same as English ones, you see, because the English stripped the Scots of everything after Culloden. I'm the younger son – so I got left out. I've had to make my own way in life. It's as simple as that, Lizzie.'

'You don't say! But I like your cute accent, hon.'

He smiled. 'I had Viking ancestors, Lizzie.'

'That accounts for it, then. But aren't you just the tiniest winiest bit an Honourable?' She sounded disappointed in him.

'Oh, yes, I'm quite honourable,' he reassured her.

'Your brother, the Laird Lindsay, does he live in a Scottish castle?'

'Good lord, yes! Where else?' he managed to put her mind at rest.

She smiled at him in a way that made him eager to impress her in all manner of ways. So he went overboard in telling her all about his ancestry, about Glengarth Castle, the family coat-of-arms, and the suits of armour his brother had inherited. She was impressed, he could tell. He refrained from mentioning the fact that rusty suits of armour were just about all Lindsay *had* inherited, apart from a monumental headache in keeping Glengarth solvent.

'But do tell me a little about yourself,' she said. 'What is a Viking doing so far south?'

'The Vikings, Lizzie, fraternized with the Gaels to produce Scotsmen with itchy feet running in their blood. But it's a long, steamy story reserved especially for long, cold nights.'

She gave him a searching look from beneath her silky black lashes. Mrs Roebling Chanin was quite the most intriguing brunette he had ever met, right down to the very last diamond clasp securing the egret plumes in her priceless coiffure.

She whispered confidentially, 'Are you interested in fast cars, Rory?'

'I'm interested in anything fast, Lizzie.'

Her scarlet fingernails bit into his arm a little harder and her red mouth came closer still. He could feel her hot breath on his chin. 'I think you're a very lovely man,' she said, and he liked her sincerity. She tilted her head back to get a better view of him. 'Yes, you really are a Viking-man. But you'd look even more the part with a beard. Tell me, does your brother have Viking-gold hair and such nice, mischievous blue eyes?'

He knew she was parodying him, but did not mind a bit. They had all imbibed a little too much champagne and the euphoria of the evening lingered. 'No, Lindsay has always been an old-looking, silvery-blond man. His hair, his eyes, his nature, everything about him is exceedingly grey and unmischievous. You wouldn't like him at all, Lizzie.'

'I'd still like to meet him sometime,' she replied with a smile.

This woman was just another Charis Vayer, Rory came to the conclusion. Out for a title, that's all. And American women were especially to be wary of – not that he *had* a title to offer her!

'However,' she continued, apparently liking the sound of her own voice, 'appearance means nothing. I had three lovely men once. They were *all* descended from Mount Olympus – or so I thought at the time. They're all dead now. I swear I shall never marry again, as I simply cannot abide wearing widow's weeds.'

'How ...' he cleared the frog in his throat. 'How did they die?'

'In various tragic ways.' She then proceeded to tell him her entire life story. He managed to bring his mind back to what she was saying when she was only half way through: 'Husband number one was dear Jay-Jay, Count Jean-Jacques Bonn-Aberville. He was a French wine baron. Jay-Jay was mad about racing cars and it was he who introduced me to the racing circuit. But, tragically, one day Jay-Jay just disintegrated in front of my very eyes. His voiturette was incapable of the high speed he was travelling at, and blew up. Poor Jay-Jay ended up as dead meat on the Dieppe run. He was doing eighty miles per hour ...'

'Eighty! Whew! That *is* fast!' Rory said.

'Yes, Eighty! All I had left after that was his French

château and vineyards. I could have stayed a French
Countess but I kindda got lonely. So I married Horace
Dillinger next, and *what* a gopher he turned out to be!'

'But he was rich?'

'Oh yes!'

'How did *he* die?'

'Burst appendix.'

At least it wasn't a burst tyre. He endeavoured to
appear sympathetic, 'How very tragic,' he murmured.

'Well, Rory, hon, ever since I've been looking for a man
to fulfil my needs like Jay-Jay. I thought I'd found him
when I met Clayton Cooper in Indianapolis. But that man
didn't know what the hell was going on between a front
and a back axle so I had to ditch him fast before I lost my
sanity.'

'He was your mechanic?'

'He was my last husband, sugar, and what a gopher! He
knew nothing about a split-path hydro-mechanical drive
and I need someone who knows all about a split-path
hydro-mechanical drive.'

'You do?' he said in astonishment.

'Sure, hon.'

He cleared his throat, 'I do.'

'You do?'

'Sure ... I mean, yes, I do.' Thank God for Gammon
and the informative hours he had spent on the cold floor
of the garage during his school holidays, learning all about
engines and motor-cars and everything else mechanical,
Rory thought to himself in that moment when he was
trying to impress as never before. 'I know all about the
outer wheels having to rotate faster than the inner wheels,
especially at high speeds and around corners. A differen-
tial gear-system, able to drive two shafts: typically the
right-and left-hand shafts of a back-axle, should, not only
in theory, but in practice, be able to ...'

'Slow down, slow down! You're a dream come true,
dare I say it ... Listen, hon, we're going to build us a
motor-car that's going places ...'

'*Oh, no we're not!*' he said firmly. 'I'm a steamship man
myself. At present, one of my fleet is undergoing repairs

in Ireland. I'm off to Dublin tomorrow – I mean today – to inspect the progress being made on her. One has to keep the workers on their toes y'know, Lizzie!'

He noticed the dawning respect in her eyes, and knew he had scored another point in his favour. She was impressed, he could tell. 'Listen sugar, why don't we sit this one out and talk about it?' She dug down into her glittering evening bag and extracted a cheroot which she fitted into an ebony and diamond cigarette-holder. 'I hope you're not one of these lily-livered English guys who object to women smoking, Rory hon?'

'No indeed,' he said as he tried to contain his choking fit when she enveloped him in a cloud of Turkish smoke. 'I'm Scottish – I don't mind at all.'

'Now then, sugar, tell li'le ole Lizzie here all about steamships, will you? I'm a woman of appetites as you've no doubt gathered by now. They don't call me the Gorgon for nothing! If I'm impressed and interested enough in this steamship company of yours, I might even think about doing a deal with you. A partnership, so to speak, whereby I put up the black gold for your li'le ole expertise. I knew you were different from all these other gophers the moment I clapped eyes on you.' She winked at him, blew smoke at him, and made Lady Glover sneeze in disgust.

The night hadn't turned out to be totally unproductive, after all, Rory reflected happily as they both sat down together in the dining-room to consume bacon, eggs, sausages and kidneys in company with other hung over guests. He felt singularly pleased with himself, but much more so with the gorgeous Lizzie Roebling Chanin from the United States of America, God bless Charlie!

CHAPTER SIXTEEN

Rory stood alone in the Shukborough Room, and for the first time ever, felt at peace with himself and his surroundings. He had come to recognize what the word 'home' truly meant. He smiled ruefully, remembering the *badinage* and backchat between him and his cousins, the term 'Sassenach' he had heard his Scottish father once use, and how he, the son, had become a Sassenach himself!

Breedon Hall was at peace with itself too, after the night's rowdy party that had not finished until six o'clock that morning. He looked at the deserted gardens and parkland. Wisteria like swollen bunches of mauve grapes festooned garden walls. Roses spilled over in colourful profusion and a heavy somnolency filled the afternoon. One of the gardeners was tidying the grounds, using a pointed stick to pick up and shove into his sack the strewn paper, bunting and burst balloons littering the lawns.

Sunlight through the French doors dappled the Persian carpet on which he stood and a peculiar nostalgia filled his soul. Here was a family room, hugging to itself the remnants of the past, absorbing them into plump cushions and armchairs, filing them away amongst the miscellaneous music sheets still scattered on top of the grand piano. His aunt Ada's voice came back to him over the years, chiding him for being late for prayers during that first school holiday of his, spent right here in this room of memories. How far away India seemed now, the pink palace at Baharabad, the up-country lodge at Tippindee, his father's polo ponies and fox terriers, old Brig with his whisky, nautch-girls and Robbie Burns' poems, his mother's loving, tender smiles, her touch, her grace ... and her death that had changed the world for him.

The years coalesced. He heard again Rupert's vibrant

laugh, Leonora's clear, sweet voice singing Strawberry Fair, Jane and Humphrey playing a duet at the piano, Mordan lisping out his crackpot jokes, Michael's never-failing diplomacy, and he wondered what life held in store for them all.

Happy, sad, good, bad, all of them memorable times. But now he realized the party was over, the 'desert of uncertainty' spanning his childhood and youth – that had turned out to be not quite so bad after all – fled away for ever on that short hot summer amid 'memories vague of half forgotten things, not true nor false but sweet to think upon'. He couldn't remember who had written those lines, but they underlined completely his feelings of nostalgia and anti-climax.

In danger of becoming sentimental, Rory helped himself to a drink. The double doors just then burst open and Humphrey and Charis stood on the threshold, both looking as though they were about to meet their Waterloo.

'Say a few paternosters for us, Rory. We're about to face my makers.' Humphrey gave a sickly grin and put out his hand for the glass. 'My God, let's have that drink first, Scotch kipper.'

'It's only soda water.'

'Anything, just *anything* to stave off the final moment. I think this must be the feeling one gets when facing death on a battlefield ... wish us luck. Come along, old girl, let's get it over with.'

Rory suddenly felt sorry for them, although he didn't know why he should.

A little while later, just as he was crossing the front hall on his way upstairs, the morning-room door was flung wide open and Aunt Ada loomed large on the threshold. She looked like God in female attire as she directed Adam and Eve out of the garden of Eden. Rory managed to dodge behind the roodscreen in the hall, lest her eye and her wrath fall upon him also.

'*GO!*' she said in the hoarse-tempered voice he had learned to dread. He trembled for Humphrey and his new wife. 'Go!' And, like Jane with her Suffragette rubbish, never darken those doors again. How *dare* you both! How dare you do this to us, Humphrey? How could you have behaved with such abandonment under this roof with this ... this *creature*? How can you betray your father and me in this wicked fashion after all we've done for you? How dare you enter into this ... this *mésalliance* without our knowledge, without our blessing and without our consent! You are nothing but the black sheep of the family and you, Miss, are a ... are a *strumpet*!'

'Mama, she is my wife ...'

'She is *not* your *wife*! She will never be recognized as your wife as long as I live! Miss Vayer, you should be ashamed of yourself. You were brought into this household in a position of trust, which you have abused! You have used your elevated position as governess to my girls in order to get your claws into one of my sons, and that I find inexcusable. You are an unworthy woman, a disgrace to your profession, a cheap fortune-hunter and name-seeker. I will see to it that you never get hold of a respectable post as a governess to anyone's girls again! I never want to set eyes on either of you again. And when you are disillusioned and destitute, Humphrey, *don't* come bleating home to your father and me.'

'No, Mama ... but I am of age now and know what I'm doing.'

'Do you, Humphrey? Do you know what you have done?' Her eyebrows arched. 'I think not. Do you think the King will want you in the Guards after this ... this *mésalliance?* I doubt it very much. So what do you propose to do with your worthless life?'

'I'll ... I shall ... look around for ... for something.'

'Haven't you done that already? Haven't you "looked around" and found *something*! Don't tell me that this ... this *woman* is going to support you until you go down from Oxford, on whatever pittance a third-rate governess can bring!' She flicked her hand in the general direction of Charis's abdomen, 'Especially when she starts to produce children.'

'Mama, that is our business now. Charis ... well, actually, her name is Cynthia ... we are both of age and ...'

'Both of age perhaps, but with very little sense between

you. You are nothing but a deceitful boy. And why is she suddenly Cynthia? Her name has always been Charis Vayer, or was that another one of your lies, Miss Vayer?'

'No, your ladyship. My married name is Smith. Vayer was my maiden name. I have always been called Charis although I was christened Cynthia. The only thing I lied about was my married status.'

'You have another husband?'

'He's dead. Killed at the battle for Spion Kop during the South African war. As a widow, I had to earn my own living.'

'You are not from a respectable French family, then?'

'My father was a French chef, my mother an English chambermaid. They both worked in the same hotel in Maida Vale.'

'*Maida Vale?*'

'Maida Vale, London.'

'Is that so! Humphrey, you did this thing yesterday morning, with this ... this *imposter* who submitted lies to us on her curriculum vitae. You knew full well that your father and I could do nothing to annul your marriage. A *person* we would not have approved of! She is a fortune-hunter, nothing more, and the sooner you realize it, the better! Now go. Your father is too distressed to discuss this matter any further. I shall *never* forgive you for marrying in this hasty and disgusting fashion. Are you expecting? Is that the reason for this disastrous liaison?' Lady Burrett turned her attention back to the unfortunate former governess.

'Yes, your Ladyship,' said Charis, her face as waxen as cerecloth, and Rory had to admire her pluck in sticking to the truth.

'I thought as much. Well, there's nothing further to say in the matter. I always knew you would get into hot water one day, Humphrey. You know, Miss Vayer, you are not the first woman this wretched boy has got into trouble?'

'Your Ladyship, I know all about Flossie Newton and how she was bought off to prevent a family scandal.'

'Oh, do you? Then accept my congratulations, Miss Vayer. At least you've come to a better end than the housemaid. I don't want to talk to either you or my son any more, so please leave at once.'

Rory had never seen two people disappear so fast. Before his aunt closed the morning-room doors fully, he heard her say to his uncle hiding discreetly in the background, 'Bad blood runs in this family, Austen! Your nephew, Rory Duncan, is no better than Humphrey. The Roskillen name will no doubt come to a sticky end, too. Mark my words ...' The doors slammed and Rory heaved a sigh of relief before sneaking out of his hiding place; the old dragon must have known he was there, hence her disparaging parting shot!

'Where's Leonora?' he whispered to one of the housemaids sorting linen on the upstairs landing.

'Gone for a walk, Master Rory.'

'Do you know where?'

'Charnwood, I think.'

'Thanks.'

Vivid recollections were his, but only in after years when the tumult and the shouting had died down. Rory remembered quite clearly the picture of Leonora that day, seated in the place of the scattered rocks. The brightness and the blackness was all around her, part of the achromatic shadows that would envelope so much of their lives, swiftly following that sweet brief interlude.

She sat on a smooth black rock, her long black skirt tucked around her ankles. She wore a white lace blouse which reflected the brilliance of the afternoon sunshine soaking into the bracken-bound earth. She seemed to him in that moment to be a creature of vaporized sunlight, insubstantial as gossamer webs lacing bracken to the rock that supported her. Upon her chestnut curls a small straw hat perched at a rakish angle, banded by a black-and-white checked ribbon. The long ends of the ribbon drifted behind her, caught by the summer-light breeze that always lingered with the ghosts haunting Charnwood's ancient burial ground. Leonora held a book in her lap, though her attention was caught by a hawk hovering high in the sky.

He knew that she had been crying the moment he came

beside her, panting with exertion.

'I've been watching you,' she said, closing the book. 'Running through the bracken like a slug on a racecourse.'

'How complimentary!'

'So, now you've come to tell me that you, too, are off to faraway places, just like all the others.'

'Lennie . . . I have to go. I can't stay here all my life.'

'I know that, dearest Rory.' She ran her fingers through his hair as he leant beside her against the smooth rock. 'I'm just sad, that's all.'

'Why, my darling girl?'

'Because, last night seemed to be the end of everything as we know it, and the prelude to something we neither of us want. I can't explain it, Rory, but things have changed. *We* have changed, and the world will change with us.'

'It's a sign, I suppose, of growing up.'

'I suppose so.' After a while she asked, 'Did Mama and Papa take the Charis business well?'

'No.'

'I didn't think so. First Jane because of her involvement with the WSPU and now Humphrey and Charis.'

'That's not the only reason why you're upset today.'

She smiled the Mona Lisa smile. 'Rory, darling, men want to change the world, but women aren't allowed to change their *lives*!'

'Why do you want to change your life, Lennie? You have everything to make you happy, so why are you sad?'

'It's not as simple as that, Rory. I'm born into a position of privilege, yes, and I'm grateful. But I'm in the minority. So many millions of women out there are born to nothing! They have no voice, no status, no privileges. They're just owned like slaves, simply because they're poor and un-educated and . . . and afraid!'

'Afraid? Of what?'

'Men. The man has always been seen as the bread-winner who deserves every consideration. It's simply not fair! Women have a right to do something with their lives other than to produce babies! So, it's up to women like my sister, your sister – Christabel in this instance, not Kitty – the Pankhurst women, and . . . and *me!* to close ranks, simply because we are better equipped to face the world of men on an equal footing. Don't you see, Rory! Education makes us independent. A career for a woman, other than being lumped under that derogatory heading of housewife and mother, is *so* important for *all* women! We can never be free otherwise.'

He swallowed, his throat feeling very dry. The tangled elements of this conversation with Leonora made him nervous. 'Then you're really serious about the Women's Suffragette Movement? Is that what you're trying to tell me, Lennie?'

'Yes.'

He took a deep breath. 'Perhaps it's just as well Kitty wants to marry Tobias. I can't help feeling that this is all your fanatical sister Jane's fault!'

'And yours!'

'Mine? What has *my* sister to do with it?'

'Christabel at Glengarth, not Kitty. She and Jane met each other in London during some rally or other. They're both very dedicated to the Movement. Jane sometimes stays at your brother's Town House in Park Lane, which he allows Christabel to use as her London headquarters. Your Christabel, that is, not Chrissy Pankhurst.'

Oh God, they were all in this together! He had had no idea. He had thought that Winson Green Prison had cured them of all such Suffragette nonsense.

'Rory, if Kitty wishes to get married and have babies, that's up to her. I want to fight alongside Jane and the other Suffragettes for better conditions for *all* women. Is that so very different from you, who wants to do something which everyone sees as utterly crazy, too?'

'Is getting married and having babies so very terrible for a woman?'

'You're not a woman, so you'll never know.' Leonora slid off the rock and with her book under her arm, started off downhill. 'It's the situation now that we are *subordinate* to men, nothing to do with the actual process of *having* babies!'

He ran after her. 'I'm sorry Lennie. I just don't understand, that's all.'

'No. Men never do.'

'Please don't be upset. It's hard enough trying to battle with the rest of the world, let alone you.'

She stopped and turned and waited for him. Then she dropped her book in the bracken of the fox covets and put her arms around his neck. 'I love you like a brother, Rory Duncan!'

'But I don't love you like a sister any more, so what do I do?'

'Just be careful of Mrs Roebling Chanin, that's all.'

'Meaning?'

'Be careful, Rory, she'll swallow you whole, if you let her.'

'And you be careful, too, Lennie. Because the Women's Movement might do the same to you.'

Looking back, he wished he'd never uttered those words – just words, nothing more. Yet they turned out to be so prophetic, caught up for ever in a struck chord in his heart.

But on that lovely day they just linked arms and walked back in a companionable silence to the mellow Jacobean house browsing in the late afternoon heat haze.

CHAPTER SEVENTEEN

Lindsay met Iona Cowall Lennox again in the house of a fashionable dowager during one of that lady's claustrophobic soirées. Iona, of course, would not have expected to see him there.

Lindsay was flattered, as well as gratified, by Iona's reception of him.

'Why, the Laird of Glengarth, of all people! How nice to see you again, Lindsay. I thought you never attended these functions, being somewhat of a recluse tucked away amongst your heather hills.'

'Don't believe a word of society gossip,' he said light-heartedly. 'I'm delighted that *you* are here this evening, Iona.'

She made a face. 'Lady Conningbide invites *the* most obnoxious people to her *loathsome* soirées. It's as though she does it deliberately to see what pleasure *can* be had by collecting together the worst of Edinburgh's tedious intellectuals! I only accepted her invitation because I happen to be in Edinburgh and not Henley! And she is my godmother!' she added, laughing.

He had known it, for Lady Conningbide had arranged the meeting on his behalf – but that was *their* secret!

'Edinburgh at this time of year is awfully unfashionable as everyone is off to their hunting-lodges in the glens,' Iona continued. 'And because Robert, Rosemary and I are rather tired of the same old circuit down South, we decided to do other things this year. So tell me, Lindsay, what have you been doing with yourself these days?'

'Nothing much.'

'Oh, come now! I know you're a man of few words, but I can't believe you do nothing all day long! And as I'd much rather listen to you than the ex-Turkish Ambassador waffling away about Isvolsky's bargain with Aehrenthal regarding the annexation of Bosnia and Herzegovina, let's go and sit over here quietly while we pick holes in everyone's character.'

Chuckling to herself, Iona drew him away to a secluded corner behind some tall indoor palms where they could talk together quietly. The sweetheart chair she had located helped considerably.

Lindsay could hardly take his eyes off Iona. She presented another image altogether, compared to the innocent picture of the Renoir girl in her flowery organza frock and summery hat one afternoon during Commemoration week. Tonight she was both sophisticated and elegant. She wore a black velvet, tight-waisted frock in the Pompadour style popularized by the 'Gibson Girl'. Lalique jewellery and an osprey feather in Iona's high-piled coiffure of red-gold hair, added the distinctive touch.

In that moment, too, he would have given anything for a cigarette, for he never knew what to do with his hands when he had to sit still and make witty conversation. But it would have been impolite in front of Iona, and so he tried to contain himself.

Iona, noticing Lindsay's fidgety manner, one hand in his pocket as he endeavoured to relax beside her, came to his rescue in a charmingly thoughtful gesture. 'I know you smoke like a chimney, Lindsay, so please go ahead. It doesn't bother me – unless they're those awful cigars the Turkish Ambassador smokes, while making everyone else suffer over the problems of his country.'

'Are you sure, Iona?'

'Of course, Lindsay. I never say something I don't mean, so feel free to smoke if you wish.'

He relaxed, and took out his cigarette case. They spent the next hour in delightful harmony, discussing all sorts of unrelated subjects, though never politics. He told her his dreams for Glengarth and how acres of new trees had recently been planted as part of a long-term forestry plan, and she told him about her horses and her dreams of winning the Edinburgh stakes that year.

At length, Lindsay plucked up courage to say what had

been on his mind all evening. 'Iona, I'm spending the next few days in Edinburgh. Couldn't we meet for dinner and the theatre? Perhaps tomorrow evening?'

'Oh, Lindsay, I'm so sorry! As you know Robert and Rosemary were married a few months ago. They're now back from their honeymoon, but Robert's father-in-law has invited us all to join him at his villa on one of the Greek islands during July and August. We're catching the boat-train from Victoria tomorrow evening, so I have to leave Edinburgh in the morning.'

He tried to mask his disappointment. 'Well, the moment you get back from your Greek holiday, you must let me know.'

'Oh, indeed I will! You may be sure of that. What a pity you couldn't join us in cruising the Aegean.'

'As delightful as it sounds, I'm afraid I couldn't spare the time at the moment.'

They listened, then, to an operatic rendering of Donizetti's *Don Pasquale*, with Ernesto declaring his love for Norina despite the Don's objections, and shortly afterwards, Lindsay took his leave. He felt that Lady Conningbide had arranged the evening's entertainment specifically on his behalf, but to know that Iona had other plans for the next two months had unsettled him. He realized he was behaving rather boorishly by leaving so early, but he really felt unable to endure any longer so many stuffy people with their pointless conversations. As he took his coat and white silk scarf from the footman, he was aware that Iona stood at the open salon doors, watching him with a perplexed look in her eye.

'Lindsay, must you go so soon?' she asked, stepping out into the vestibule.

'Iona,' he said without thinking, 'I came here tonight to ask you to marry me. Since cruising among the Greek Islands seems to be of more importance to you than what I feel for you, I'd better go now before I make a worse fool of myself.'

He did not stop long enough to see her flounce back into the salon, her blue eyes angry and hard, a set line to her mouth. Lindsay was only aware of the pain he had seen flicker in her eyes, before she had turned away from him.

He decided to walk the Royal Mile, his desire for fresh air all at once overwhelming. Aware that he had lost Iona for ever in those few foolish moments of pride getting the better of disappointment, he stopped to light a cigarette under one of the gas-lamps, when a voice at his elbow said, 'All alone tonight, luvvy?'

He was about to tell the street-woman to lose herself when he raised his head from the flame of his lighter and saw that she was wearing a tight black dress, her white bosom pushed up above the low cut of the bodice. Her jewellery was cheap, her hair bleached a brassy yellow, but she had an imitation osprey feather in her hair and her bright red smile was comforting. The Gibson Girl was everywhere it seemed.

'Want some company on your lonely walk, sir?'

He felt that he did; and she was humble enough not to require any mental effort from him. She accompanied him back to his hotel. 'Five quid the front door, ten the tradesmen's entrance, but whichever way you choose, luvvy, make it snappy.'

Only afterwards, when her cheap perfume still lingered nauseatingly in the room, when sitting alone on the side of the bed, when he realized he had smoked a dozen cigarettes one after another, and that he had not enough money left to buy Aeneas his fishing-rod, did Lindsay go into the bathroom and vomit. The prostitute was the first woman he had ever had.

Rory had had to use all his charm and powers of persuasion to dissuade Lizzie Roebling Chanin from accompanying him to Dublin. She wanted to see his 'fleet' of steamships! As one look at the shell of the *Drogheda* would have been enough to scotch any hope of a long-term business transaction with her, Rory had had to do some quick thinking. The euphoria of the night of Humphrey's ball dispersed in the cold light of day: he remembered his wild conversation about his steamship business, his ambitions and his financially sound status.

Lizzie would soon realize what a tissue of lies he had spun her and never trust him again. He couldn't jeopardize his whole future career on account of the *Drogheda*.

'I don't think so, Lizzie,' he had told her very frankly over the telephone when she spoke to him from Boxwood Manor where she had been staying, 'not this time. I'm a very busy man and have too much to do between Dublin and Liverpool to spare any time right now. Perhaps we could arrange something at a later date?'

Using the tactics women had often used on him in the past, Rory felt Lizzie Roebling Chanin would take the bait the moment he played hard to get. He was disappointed when she did not. She made no alternative date with him.

'If that's your wish, hon. You know what you're doing. I only made the suggestion because I'm a li'le old business-woman myself and hate to pass up any deal which might make me richer than I already am. See you anon, hon.'

A woman after his own heart, Rory had reflected the moment he ruefully hung up the receiver.

He was absolutely amazed at the transformation to the *Drogheda*: he simply could not believe his eyes when he arrived in Dublin two days after Humphrey's birthday ball. Gammon and Ackker had certainly shifted their backsides in getting her seaworthy again, and Rory felt that he owed them more than just their wages.

'How did you manage to get it all done so quickly?' he wanted to know. 'The last time I saw her she was nothing but a derelict hulk needing months of repair work.'

'Glad you recognize it, guv, but its like this. Ackker and me done a deal with Strangford, and they got their own boatyard men to do the tricky jobs on 'er. Eight of us, working round the clock to make 'er ready, quicker than what Rome was built.'

'What deals have you been doing behind my back, Gamin?' Rory asked with a certain amount of alarm. 'I hope you haven't been signing away my boat to Strangford after I bought it off him for thirty quid – as you recommended.'

'Nah, guv, nothin' like that.' Gammon pushed back his cap and scratched his head. 'It's like this, see. Soon as she's equipped and ready for sailing, 'er maiden voyage will be to Garston an' back for his Strangford nibs, the cargo we carry for him transported buckshee, like.'

'*For nothing?*' Rory said, shaken by what Gammon was saying. 'You *know* we can't afford to do that kind of deal. We need every penny we earn on that first haulage run of hers.'

'Yeah, yeah, boss. But you got to be wise in this lark. The longer she takes to get repaired, the more money we lose. An' you said yourself, guv, that time was money to you. So I reckoned that if we could get the professionals workin' 'er over, the quicker you'd put 'er to good use.'

'And what cargo have you arranged to carry buckshee for Strangford?'

'Black oats an' Irish spuds outwards, coal an' timber back.'

'Timber? But she has no derricks. And her hold isn't big enough for coal and timber!'

'Me and Ackker got it all fixed up, guv, so don't yer worry. We're getting the derricks fitted termorrer. The coal will be bunged into the hold, then atop of the hatch an' up on deck we got plenty space ter stash the timber.'

'All that for nothing? I just hope she won't go down on her maiden voyage with a loaded cargo when a gale hits us in the middle of the Irish Sea.'

'Trust me guv.'

'I am trusting you, Gamin! And that's what worries me.'

'Beggin' your pardon, Mister Rory, sir, I didn't spend eighteen years sea-coasting in worse crates than this one, not to know what I'm doing!' said Gammon, for the first time getting angry about the whole thing. 'You asked for me 'elp, an' that's what I'm givin' you. Though why I bleedin' well goes to all the trouble puttin' me back out for someone what don't appreciate the trouble I bin to gettin' his flamin' boat fixed beats me. If you don't like me methods, guv, I quit. I ain't a bleedin' charity, y'know.'

'All right, Gamin, don't get shirty with me. I know I owe you a great deal, but you're going to have to wait for it in view of the fact that you've just signed away my first cargo-run for nothing!'

And Cousin Humphrey would also have to wait for repayment, too, thought Rory, who had been counting on making a 'little' money on the *Drogheda's* first trip to Liverpool.

Ackker appeared in the yard carrying something in a sack slung across his back. 'G'morning, sir. Faith marlin', 'tis busy everywhere today, an' warm for the summer.' He set down his load, took out his handkerchief and wiped his streaming brow.

'Good morning, Ackker. What have you got there?'

'To be sure, 'tis a little bargain I picked up in the flea market early this mornin', sir. Wait till you see her.' He opened the sack and brought out a rusty old bell. 'Solid brass she be, sir.'

'Looks like solid rust to me.'

'Oh, no, sir! Fit for His Majesty's ship, this one. From a grand liner, if my name is not Reginald Ackker, sir. She'll make a darlin' sound once I get her rigged up appropriately upon the wheelhouse. Wake the dead, she will, sir, an' the crew at watch.'

'If you say so, Ackker.' Rory turned back to Gammon. 'When will she be ready to put to sea?'

'Ten days, give or take a week or two,' said Gammon sulkily, still smarting from his young Scots boss's distrust of him.

'Just let me know when, Gamin, and I'll try and get back for her launching. I'm going to be very busy in the next few weeks, as I'm off to Liverpool to drum up business for us, then to Glasgow to obtain my Clyde Pilotage certificate and secure us a berth there. Glasgow is where we'll be based – I hope.'

'No need to fret yerself, Mister Rory, sir. Benjamin Gammon's got yer best interests at 'eart.'

'I've been saving-up a bottle of champagne especially for the day we cast off from here.' It was a vintage bottle from his uncle Austen's cellar, which he had managed to get hold of without Hardrace knowing. Gammon appeared less than impressed. 'By the way, Gamin, I've decided to change her name.'

'Change 'er name, guv?' Gammon looked anxious. 'We just gorn an' painted it all new!'

'Well, you'll just have to get Strangford's painters to repaint it then, won't you.'

'What you changing it to?'

'*Lady Leonora.*'

Gammon grinned. 'Then I don't reckons I mind a bit. Her nibships always was a spry young lass. An' we need a bit of good fortune across the Irish Sea.'

Rory next had business to attend to in Liverpool and took the ferry back to Holyhead. He had to make business contacts now, signing up a cargo haulage run which would provide him with a firm foundation to his business.

The small village of Garston lay five miles up the River Mersey with a population of just over one thousand people. But Garston was also the hub of fervent industrial activity. Iron and steel works, saw-mills, foundries, engineering works, salt and copper works, sail-makers, tin and copper smiths, bobbin factories and tanneries. It also boasted a dry dock and ship-building yard. Business boomed at Garston, and now that he had his Mersey Pilotage certificate safely under his belt, people would be more willing to trust him with their cargoes.

But Rory went first to Canning Place, Liverpool, to look up his little friend, Pearl Brownling. She was not there. The new office secretary told him that she had resigned from her job.

'Do you know her address?' Rory asked the new girl.

She gave him a funny look. 'What's it to you?'

'I'm a friend of hers! I want to know how I can contact her.'

'She might not like that.'

'Do you know where she can be found?'

The girl shrugged non-committally. 'She used to lodge in Robin Close. That's all I know about her.'

'What number?'

'How should I know! I only work here.'

He sighed in exasperation. 'Thanks a lot for your help!'

Looking for Miss Pearl Brownling in Robin Close, Liverpool, would not be an easy task. His main reason for recontacting Pearl, was because she had once mentioned to him during one of his evenings in her company, that her father owned a bobbin factory. Whether in Garston or Liverpool, he wanted to find out, simply because this was his first business 'contact'. Bobbin and spool makers required wood; wood meant timber; factories required coal to fuel steam-engines and boilers. Besides, it was 'who' one knew that could open up doors that would otherwise be closed in one's face. One local businessman with a name, could lead to others.

At the entrance to the Board of Trade's offices, he turned back and retraced his steps to the hostile receptionist hunched over the typewriter on her desk. 'What now?' she sighed.

'Do you know anything about Brownling Bobbins and where their factory is?'

'Never heard of them.' She examined the letter she was supposed to be copying and reached for the eraser because she had made a mistake.

He hesitated. Then he addressed the top of her head. 'You know, Miss, you shouldn't really be doing this job. You're so bloody miserable, you're enough to put even the typewriter off.'

'I only do it for the money.'

'Don't we all,' he muttered to himself on the way out.

Rory went to the main post office and managed to gain the exact location of Robin Close. He took the tram, and wished he'd never bothered. Robin Close was in the seediest, most run-down part of Liverpool, beneath the railway arches of the North Western Railway, in an area known as the Limehouse.

Outside a block of tenement slums he started asking his questions. He supposed it would have been much easier in the first place to try to locate Brownling's Bobbin factory – if it existed! But he had had reservations upon that score. It would have been far simpler, from his point of view, for Pearl to make the introductions on his behalf where her father's business was concerned. Right now he doubted the story she had given him. At the time of dating her, he had imagined Pearl Brownling to be from a stalwart middle-class family. He had never dreamt that she had lied about her background.

In the middle of the cobblestone street that ended in a cul-de-sac backing onto the railway, several women and children were washing clothes at a standpipe. He brazened it out, and asked if anyone knew of a Miss Pearl Brownling who had lodged in the Close. The women stared blankly at him.

So much for Mr Balfour's Beer and Bible Act, thought Rory to himself, as he viewed a couple of drunks lolling in the gutter. Stories of Jane's back-to-backs in Loughborough and the Irish sleeping with their pigs in flooded basement cellars came back to him with uncomfortable reality when he confronted the inhabitants of Robin Close, all of them terribly poor, unkempt and ignorant. The women and children eyed him up and down with a great deal of suspicion, and silence.

He was about to give up his search when a young girl in a grubby pinafore over a ragged dress, clogs on her bare feet, tugged his sleeve. 'She used to lodge with me mam, mister. But she ain't here any more.'

'May I talk to your mother?'

The small girl giggled and wiped her nose on her pinny. 'You got a sweet for me?'

He gave her a ha'penny, and in delight she ran ahead of him. 'This way, mister.'

'What's your name?' he asked the girl as he followed her up a set of dingy wooden stairs in the tenement building.

'Maisie Marsh. What you want Pearl for?'

'I'd like to speak to her.'

'Ask me mam then. Mam ... Mam!' she shouted, barging through an open door into an upstairs flat. 'There's a man here what's asking for Pearl.'

A harassed looking woman with a basket of clothes set before her on the kitchen table, stopped sorting the dirty linen she was forced to wash and iron on behalf of people better off than herself. They were the folk who did not live in this low-class area of Robin Close, but occupied the better housing areas – like this young man intent upon bothering her. By the cut of his jib and the clothes he wore, he was certainly not the kind of visitor they were used to seeing in Robin Close.

A line of wet washing dangled above her head, and under the table a group of small children with dirty faces were playing with two mangy kittens looking equally starved as they. The woman blew a strand of lank hair out of her eyes and subjected him to the same hostile stare he had received outside by the standpipe.

'What you want from us, Mister?'

'Mrs Marsh?'

'That's me. You ain't the rent collector, are you?'

'I'm enquiring about Miss Pearl Brownling who used to lodge with you.'

'What d'you want to know about her?'

'Her new address – if you have it'

She sniffed. 'Pearl ain't from these parts. She's from Garston. She was only here for temporary lodgings till the baby was due.'

'Baby?' he found his voice drying up.

'That's right. She didn't want her folks finding out, so she came here to hide herself away till it was all over. Nice gal, too. Shame. You the father?'

Rory swallowed. He didn't know what to say. He felt extremely ill all of a sudden, and wished he'd never embarked on this kind of sleuthing – for mercenary gain, he had to tell himself in that awful moment when the truth at last dawned on him.

But he had to get this over and done with as soon as possible, if he didn't want to throw up in this woman's presence. 'Where is Pearl now?'

'In the Workhouse Infirmary. Things went wrong. She's still there.'

'Where is the workhouse?'

'Two streets away. You'll find it easy enough from the smell of it.'

'Thank you.'

She sniffed again and watched him run down the stairs.

Outside in the street Rory took several long deep breaths. His hands were shaking like a palsied old man's.

He tried to get a grip on himself. What did he do now? Did he run a mile, or did he go to the Workhouse?

For some reason, inexplicable even to himself, he went to the Workhouse. He was taken to the Infirmary and there he found Pearl, quite unrecognizable as the pretty young receptionist who had flirted with him for a few happy days when he was at the Nautical Academy at Everton. She was in bed, the rough blanket drawn up to her chin. A thin, pale, ugly creature who was all burning eyes and hollowed cheeks, she looked closer to being a corpse than anything else. He was appalled.

'Blood-poisoning,' had been the nursing-sister's comment after his brief shocked glimpse at the sick girl, before he had turned tail and fled the ward. He had demanded to know what was wrong with Pearl; in turn she demanded to know his identity. 'Are you the young man responsible for Pearl trying to do away with herself and her child?' The question had been to the point and brutal.

'No,' said Rory curtly, feeling it was nothing to do with this woman anyway.

'Then what is the purpose of this visit? You'll only cause her more grief. She doesn't want any visitors.'

'Is there nothing that can be done for her?'

'No. The wages of sin, young man!'

'Has she no relatives?'

'She doesn't want her parents to find out about her self-inflicted ailment. I'll also thank you, young man, to respect the wishes of the dying.'

'Self-inflicted? Dying?'

'I know I shouldn't be saying this, but it's a criminal act to try and bring about an abortion. But who's to blame some of these poor souls when the man deserts them? I do my duty and say nothing because I like to think I'm a charitable woman. Pearl tried to get rid of the child she was expecting before she came here. Knitting needles – they all try it. Mrs Marsh, the woman she was lodging with, brought her to us when the haemorrhage was too bad to stop at home. Pearl got an infection, you see, which caused widespread damage to her insides. The poison has now entered her bloodstream and weakened her heart. She's dying of the fever women are prone to when this sort of thing is done.'

'And the baby?'

'Stillborn.'

He could not help feeling that it was for the best.

'Don't tire her needlessly,' had been the further warning.

He had crept back to her bedside, while longing to run away from that sordid public ward where other women screamed and spat and writhed, and the smell of urine and excreta was worse than anything he had ever inhaled in his life.

Pearl did not recognize him at first. She didn't even look at him. She kept her face turned to the wall while he bombarded her with questions. 'Pearl, for God's sake, what have you been doing to yourself? Look, if you don't want your parents to know anything about this, how can *I* help?'

'Go away,' she whispered, silent tears coursing down her gaunt cheeks. 'Go away, please.'

'All right. But I'll be back tomorrow – and the day after, and the day after. Every day until you're better! You're going to get out of here, Pearl. You're going to get better!'

She didn't have the strength to answer.

He left two guineas with the nursing-sister. 'That's for a decent doctor to attend her – one who knows how to save her life!'

A few days later when he called to see Pearl, he brought with him a bunch of flowers as well as fresh eggs, a jar of brawn and a bottle of brandy – on the nursing-sister's recommendation when he had asked what food might pep up the ailing girl. But Pearl was not in the ward, and her bed had been stripped of its linen.

'She went into a coma and was removed from here,' the Infirmary sister informed him.

Rory swallowed. He couldn't ask the question.

'No, she didn't die in here, though she might be dead now for all I know,' said the Infirmary sister, realizing that this young man was no doubt feeling very guilty indeed over *his* part in the Pearl Brownling affair, hence his confusion.' The police got in touch with her folks. It was best. She was using up too much of our time nursing her when this is supposed to be a place for poor folk who can't afford better when they're taken sick.'

Relieved that Pearl hadn't died in the night, he was still perturbed. 'In a coma, you said. Then, was she well enough to have been moved so suddenly?'

'As well as she will ever be.'

'What made you get in touch with her parents?'

'She was unconscious and didn't know anything. Her father, you see, had the police looking for his daughter when she went missing after resigning her job at Canning Place two months ago. They all thought she'd been murdered by some Jack-the-Ripper character. When I notified the police to get in touch with Pearl's parents, they got Mr Brownling right over here without delay. He is not an easy man to have to deal with and accused the Infirmary staff of negligence, maintaining that it was our duty to have told him about his daughter when she was first admitted. But she's of age, and one had to respect her dying wishes. When it became obvious she was near the end, it seemed right to tell her family – they're of the Bobbin works at Garston, so they've plenty of money to do right by Pearl. It's better she dies at home rather than in a Workhouse Infirmary, with only a pauper's grave to go to.'

'Do her parents know the real reason for ... for her condition?'

'They were not told about the child she tried to rid herself of. They were merely told that she was suffering from a heart condition and was brought to us after she collapsed in the street.'

And that, Rory supposed, was that! But at least Pearl Brownling had returned to her own home to die in comfort. And since there was no sense in stirring up another hornet's nest by visiting her at her parents' home out at Garston, he felt it best to leave well alone. Pearl's father might have been less than welcoming if he discovered that he had known his daughter who had been bedding with strange men in Liverpool!

Well, it now appeared that his first attempt to do business with a leading Garston figure had ended in utter disaster.

Rory just hoped it wasn't a bad omen for the future.

Lindsay woke in the middle of the night from the throes of a dream that had become a nightmare.

He had been dreaming of a beautiful mermaid with flowing black hair and green eyes. She had lifted her arms, seeking to entice him into the depths of the ocean. And because he *wanted* to be enticed, he had willingly succumbed to the mermaid's charms. But the moment he held her in his arms, she swam away from him and the woman he was left holding was Iona. She had fallen overboard during her Aegean cruise. Iona wore a tight, black Gibson Girl dress, with egret feathers in her hair. He looked closer then, and saw that they were not egret feathers at all, but Medusa snakes coiled in her rich red-gold hair. They began to crawl out of her hair, over her face, smothering her, and the black dress had wrapped itself tightly around her like a shroud. Horrible, slimy monsters in the Aegean Sea were trying to tear her limb from limb, and he could not battle with the sea-monsters that began to devour him, too. The empty black sockets of Iona's eyes accused him of betraying her, her red mouth distorted in abuse ... *On thy head ... on thy head ... on thy head* ... A man was laughing, a ghastly, skeletal apparition in a white dhoti dragged up between his matchstick legs, a stave of wood in his knarled old hand which he was using to pierce a woman's heart. And because she wore black, he had assumed the tortured woman to be Iona – until he looked again and saw that it was the mermaid with the face of Annie Gowrie from Rill ...

'NO! Oh, God ... *NO!*' He sat up in the bed, bathed in perspiration. He was trembling all over, feeling sick, feeling terrible, the stomach cramps he often suffered from returning with a vengeance. He lay still, feeling the dampness of the mattress at his back, trying to combat the pain in his body, but seeing only the flickering shadows of those dark sea-monsters staining his bedroom ceiling.

He reached for the cigarettes on his bedside table.

The orange glow of gas-lamps outside the hotel window cast an eerie light in the room. He could never bear to feel closed in, and always slept with the curtains drawn back, and the windows wide open.

Slowly reality began to dawn on him as he reoriented to the world about him. He was not in that awful hotel room in Edinburgh where he had coupled with a common whore just for the experience of sex. He had been back at Glengarth for a week.

But the gas-lamps? Where was that lurid light coming from?

Then he leapt out of bed and to the window.

His bedroom had a view of the glen, the loch, the forests, and with slowly diminishing incredulity he saw what was happening, could *smell* what was happening! Trees, whole compartments of them, all his newly transplanted saplings, thousands of them, blazing, crashing, terrifyingly dying in a holocaust of destruction.

He couldn't remember getting dressed. Halfway up the glen, he was still fastening his clothes.

The smell of resin and pine carried on the dense black, acrid smoke which poured through the valley, confounded his reason.

Then, all too soon he realized the direction of the wind: Forest Lodge, with its newly thatched roof, was right in the path of destruction.

Long before Lindsay reached the house, he saw it glowing through its glassless windows, timber and thatch burning like a haystack.

Everyone from the glen was there, panicked out of their beds, desperate to put out the fire, all of them hopelessly and helplessly inadequate against the ferocity of those flames.

The main fire-fighting services arrived on the scene at the same time as he himself got there. The sudden hissing spurt of hose-water directed at the already half-gutted shell of the main house was only a gesture. Like a madman Lindsay flung himself at one of the forest wardens, 'The family ... are they out?'

'We're doing our best ... there are two already out on stretchers ... can't be sure who they are, servants or family. But they're on their way to the hospital ...'

'The boys?'

'No, m'laird,' someone else approached, ''twas Maister Hamilton and his lady wife.'

'The boys, where are the boys, for God's sake? Annie ... Annie Gowrie? Let me go, *let me GO!*'

'For Chrissakes, m'laird, ye canna go in there! It's an inferno.'

'Lindsay, don't be a fool! It's impossible. You'll only risk your own life.'

He thought he saw Christabel in Gilbert Lucas's mackintosh, a headscarf, gum-boots, thought he heard her say, 'Annie didn't stay the night at Forest Lodge. She's safe, Lindsay, on Rill.'

'But the boys, Aeneas ... Bruce?' he sobbed, not believing this was happening to him.

'We're doing what we can for the poor fellows, m'laird, but they were sleeping in the box-room at the top of the house, till the new wing was completed ...'

They held on to him while another igniting spar exploded in the air, '*Don't hold me!*' He tried to wrench his arms free, but was dragged back from rushing headlong into the blaze. He wanted to scream and shout and blaspheme and tear away from every damn person holding him back, but he could do nothing.

He stood there, a man outside the shell of himself.

He saw again an Indian ghaut by a railway track. He heard again the voices, of Rassoul who had accompanied them along with Sula, Dharkli, two other servants, all of them taking him and Christabel, Rory and Kitty to join the *SS Britannia* at Bombay for the journey home: Christabel, a small girl, asking Rassoul, 'What is that horrid smell?' And Rassoul's reply: '*It is flesh, Missy-Sahib, human flesh. The ghaut is a place where bodies are burned so that the ashes may be borne away on the river. All Hindus wish to find that sacred river which flows from the toe of Vishnu. They will become purified of their sins,*

restored to happiness and will joyfully return to the gods ...'
For Lindsay Beauly Roskillen, Laird of Glengarth, God was nowhere to be found that night, only Moloch.

PART FIVE

'The heights by great men reached and kept,
Were not attained without exertion,
But they, while their companions worked,
Were contacting the proper person.'

Spectator

CHAPTER EIGHTEEN

Hamish MacDearg lingered in a horse-drawn cab near the headquarters of the Clyde Trustees' meeting chamber on Robertson Street. From this vantage point he could also keep an eye on the comings and goings of the different departments of the Harbour Master's office.

Not feeling at all well, the old man resorted to the 'water of life' from the silver flask he kept in his pocket for moments of stress. It was his own special remedy for *la grippe.*

His patience rewarded at last, Hamish spied the young fellow he had been seeking, stepping out smartly from the Harbour Master's office. Hamish gave a grunt of satisfaction. He repocketed the flask and sticking his grizzled head out of the cab window, bellowed with the full impetus of a sore throat, 'Rory Duncan of Glengarth, com'ee here this minute!'

Under the fizzing gaslights illuminating the wintry streets of Glasgow, Rory turned around, and the cabby in his box, frozen stiff from inertia, let out a huge sigh of relief. He had been anxious to avoid bits of masonry and the scaffolding which might fall on his horse and cab, standing as they were so close to the work going on for the new extension of the Clyde Navigation Trust building in the Broomielaw.

'Uncle Hamish! What a surprise! What are you doing in town?' Rory said, going up to the cab, and smiling into the grizzled face of his great-uncle.

'I'm searching for a moment's peace from bad conscience, that's what I'm doing!'

'Oh! Why?'

'Come inside an' I'll tell you why. I'm dying, an' wish to make my peace with God.'

Rory looked over his shoulder. 'Sorry Uncle, it's only me.'

'Enough sauce, young fellow m'lad. Climb aboard.'

Rory did so.

Hamish banged the knob of his Malacca cane on the roof of the cab: 'Take me *hame*!' he bellowed to the cabby seated atop.

'So!' Hamish said, while the horse's hooves beat out a steady rhythm on the cobblestones of old Glasgow, 'You've won a Clyde Pilotage licence, I hear.'

'Gosh, Uncle! I didn't *win* it, I *earned* it.'

'Glad to hear it, boy. Whose heart have you been worming your way into *now* to get such manly recommendation?'

'Lord Inverclyde and Sir Thomas Mason.'

'Huh! Damn knowalls! Mason's only a builder, d'ye ken?'

'Queen's Dock and the Forth Railway Bridge can't be bad contracts for a builder, Uncle.'

'An' now he's Chairman of the Trust – I'm a Glaswegian born an' bred an' ne'er had such honour. But I'm not prying into your fancy business, mind! I just wanted to see how you were faring after the last brush off I gave you. So what were you doing in the Harbour Master's office just now?'

Rory smiled to himself, and leaning back against the upholstered seat spoke to the cab roof. 'Lodging the names of my crew and their places of residence. I don't want a penalty of £2 per man for contravening any Port Authority regulations, Uncle.'

'Glad to hear it.'

'I couldn't afford it. But I was also enquiring about dredgers.'

'*Dredgers*?'

'And hoppers.'

'An' hoppers, well now! Dead end job, dredgers. I tried it once. Filthy polluted job, what with all the sewage they pump into the Clyde.'

'They've cleaned up the river since your day. And maybe you didn't go about it the right way – the dredging side of things, I mean.'

'Egad! No, maybe I didn't! But you won't get promotion on dredgers an' hopper barges. To become an Able Seaman, one has to serve time on a proper ship.'

'I'm not looking for promotion. I've no desire to be an Able Seaman, and I've been on *proper* ships.'

'Then what are you looking for, Rory Duncan of Glengarth?'

'To own the world. To have it at my fingertips.'

'How so?'

'*Trade,* Uncle Hamish! From the comfort of a plush office in the new Clyde Trust building. That's why I took my Merscy and my Glasgow Pilotage examinations – not because I envisage spending my life piloting other people's ships, but because my own cargo-boats will be exempt from Pilotage dues when coming into port.'

'Egad!' Hamish gave a roar of laughter, and ended up spluttering. He brought out his flask of whisky, unscrewed the cap and took another hefty swig. Above the flask he eyed his great-nephew with renewed approbation. 'Oh, merciful God, to be young again an' to entertain such *dreams*! You have the monumental sauce of the devil himself, Rory Duncan! Ye're no Hi'lander like thy fine grandfather an' thy brother, the laird. Ye're a Lowlander, a Blythe, born an' bred!'

'But not a MacDearg?'

'Aye, a MacDearg, though they're not of your kith an' kin. But ye have the MacDearg's drive for pow'r an' mony!'

'What's wrong with that?'

'*Nothing, nothing*! I'm an old man. It's my privilege to linger in the past, a relic of the past, before the thees and thys, the ye's an' ayes were done away with in this modern age that has come upon the world so suddenly, when a stripling can teach his great-uncle to suck eggs! The graces of the past, in speech an' writing, d'ye ken, the esteem of old age, long gone, makes me dwell now on the moments of a misspent youth.'

Rory could see that Hamish was well into the 'ubesque', his meanderings of the mind disconcerting. 'As a matter of fact, Uncle, I was also trying to find a berth for the *Drog* ... the *Lady Leonora,* my new boat. I'm operating out of Glasgow now. Port Glasgow is so overcrowded, I have to push in whenever a berth becomes temporarily unoccupied.'

'Och aye! With what cargo are you operating?'

'General cargo at present.'

'Which means bugger all. You want proper contracts, laddie.'

'Yes, but it's only the second trip and ...'

'And the first trip?'

'Black oats and potatoes out of Dublin, bound for the Highlands, then back with coal and timber from Garston.'

'Make much?'

'Well ... er, not exactly.' Rory scratched his ear. 'It was done for nothing, as part exchange for repairs to the *Lady Leonora* by Strangford Bros, Dublin,' he added quickly.

Hamish tittered. 'So! The future occupier of the Chairman's seat at the Robertson Street headquarters of The Trust, is well set to becoming rich – for nothing!'

'Well, it wasn't quite like that. You see ...'

'An' you pay your crew with a tot o' rum a piece an' the cat-o'-nine-tails. Egad! You're a caution, Rory Duncan. But never mind, you'll learn. How did she serve you, this *Lady Leonora*?'

'As near as perfect.'

'Describe her.'

'There's nothing to describe ...'

'She's a relic, then. Just like you'er old great-uncle Neptune and his steamships, eh boy? Or else you can't tell the back-end of a dredger from the bows of the *Aquitania* when they're both jostling for position in the Clyde. Come now! Describe you'er grand steam-coaster.'

'She's very small, a hundred and eight feet in length by twenty-one. Very old – forty-five years. Built of bog-oak with wood decks, not atop iron or steel. Short counter stern, fore staysail, main and mizzen tri-sails. Two hatches to one hold with an overall capacity of twelve thousand cubic feet. Side bunkers of thirty tons and water ballast thirty tons. Two masts and two winches – but with new derricks recently fitted for timber hauling.'

'Sounds as though she'll put water on her in the first gale.'

'She's low when fully loaded, but she didn't drag water when bad weather hit us off Amlwch.'

'You got your Master's certificate yet?'

'Not yet. But I'm working on it.'

'Who mastered her then?'

'I did ... well, sort of. I had a more experienced crew aboard, but because I own the boat, I was her master for the short trip.'

'An' there's another mistake boy. You can't be the peanut an' the monkey at the same time.'

'I've no intention of doing any such thing. I just feel that, for the moment, I ought to gain all my sea-going qualifications and be able to master a boat as well as pilot one, so that when things go wrong I know what I'm shouting about to the crew. On the *Lady Leonora's* first trial run after her repairs, I wanted to see how things went, that's all.'

'If you ever need a good master, there's Big Sandy Fergus from Greenoch requiring a steam-coaster. He's done with the Merchant Navy and wants to stay closer to home and family. You'll find him in the Pointhouse Inn most evenings – though I prefer the Renfrew Arms, m'self.' Then old Hamish repeated himself. 'Yc'rc no' Hi'lander like Lindsay, who'd ne'r concern himself with "trade" nor shift his noble arse in a million years. Lindsay is your grandfather all over again!'

Back at his house in Pointhouse Street, Govan, Hamish stepped down from the cab, leaving his great-nephew to pay the cabby. With his foot barely in the door, his house-keeper rushed forward to scold him. '*Mr MacDearg*! Where have you been? The doctor called upon you this afternoon and found you gone from you'er bed. You'er *very* naughty, you know.'

'D'na fash you'er self, woman!' he growled, stamping his way upstairs after having thrown his great-cape in her face.

'Now you know, sir, he gave strict instructions that you

were to stay there for at least a week! You have a very bad
chest, and pneumonia will finish you off. I've had the
warming-pan in you'er bed since I found you missing from
it, so up to you'er room at once!'

'Egad, woman! I'm not your grandson! I had business
to attend in the city. Send that great-nephew o' mine up
once I'm in bed. An' bring us both some supper!'

Mrs Fleming pursed her lips and said no more as she set
about preparing supper for her irascible employer and a
relative with whom she was only just acquainted. And it
was funny, she thought to herself, how distant relatives
always managed to turn up at the bedside of an aged and
ailing relative in the hopes of being left *something*!

After a good old-fashioned supper of herrings fried in
oatmeal, then a dessert of mouthwatering petticoat tails,
followed by rich plum cake and cocoa, Rory knew why
old Hamish had lived to such a ripe old age. He could
have done with a Mrs Fleming aboard the *Lady Leonora*
instead of Gammon's perpetual bogey pan-fries.

While Rory sat in an armchair beside his great-uncle's
four-poster bed, eating his supper from a tray poised
precariously on his knees, Hamish sat up against the
stacked pillows like a king. An old-fashioned nightcap
covered his grizzled locks; butter and herring juice stained
the front of his bleached linen nightshirt. He wiped his
mouth on a pristine white linen napkin and reached for his
tobacco-pouch. 'I know the old gal doesn't like me
smoking in bed for the holes that appear in the bedsheets
by morning, an' that whingeing doctor attending me,
doesn't like me smoking at all. But if I'm to die, then I'll
do it the way I want – happily. Fetch us a tot of ubesque
from the tea-caddy over there, boy, and pour two – one
for you an' one for me.'

Old Hamish started to cough and splutter again and
Rory turned hesitantly, wondering whether or not to
encourage him in drinking and smoking when he was
suffering from influenza, bronchitis or whatever.

'As a reward for being so danged perverse in getting
you'er Pilot's licence, I'll let you have a free run of m'boatyard, an' the *Jane Blythe's* place at the coastal trade berths

in Glasgow Harbour for the *Lady Leonora*. Berthing fees
are all paid up for the year. I'm not a man who likes to
cheat an' rob people of their dues,' he added pointedly.

Rory almost dropped the half-bottle of whisky kept in
the old man's tea-caddy on top of the chest-of-drawers.
'That's very kind of you, Uncle,' he said after he'd got over
his initial surprise.

'Kindness be damned! Both my boats are bound for the
salvage yard. But I'd prefer to part with the *Jane* than the
Mary. The *Jane* doesn't carry summer passengers any
more. She doesn't conform to these danged new seafaring
regulations the Maritime Board are always imposing on
me, so she's laid up in m'boatyard at Renfrew. The *Mary*
will keep for another few years. Besides, she does a good
little run with the mail as well as general provisions to the
West Highland fishing-ports. There now, that's off
m'chest, I can die with a peaceful conscience.'

'What's the catch, Uncle?' Rory blurted out, feeling
sure there was one.

'The catch, fellow m'lad, is I'd prefer to die in ma own
bed an' not in the poorhouse. I'm under-capitalized –
always have been since your fine Hi'land grandfather
robbed me of ma dues. It's too late for me to start
rebuilding the business. You can do that now. Sixty-one
per cent share in all your profits until the day of ma death
an' then it's all you'ers.'

'Twenty.'

'*Done*! Egad, you drive a hard bargain lad. How's that
fine brother of yours since the firing of his property?'

'I've no idea. I never enquire into Lindsay's affairs and
he never enquires into mine.'

'I see. Well, then, ma will is in the bottom of the caddy
along with the whisky. I've set aside a small yearly sum for
Mrs Fleming who has served me well all these years. See
that she gets it.'

'Of course.'

'An' since this bloddy house – which is all paid for,
mark you – will also be coming to you, make sure you
don't kick her out if she wishes to stay. Now clear off. I've
said ma piece, an' if I die in ma sleep tonight, it's only

because you lead a charmed life, Rory Duncan of Glengarth!'

Rory took his coat from Mrs Fleming and let himself out of the house. He did not know how to take Hamish. As likely as not, the moment old Neptune felt well enough to get back on his bar-stool at The Renfrew Arms he would change his mind about leaving anybody anything! But he was pleased about the paid-up berth for the *Lady Leonora* in Glasgow Harbour. And, if the *Jane Blythe* was worth salvaging, he might just make Hamish an offer. But it would have to wait another six months when he would receive his coming-of-age legacy provided by his father's estate. Only then could he think of expanding the business. He only hoped that an accumulation of debts over the last few years, wouldn't swallow up the whole of his inheritance. Wages and operational costs of his boat ate up borrowed money at a most alarming rate.

Meanwhile, Rory felt that he would lose nothing by going to talk to Big Sandy Fergus at the Pointhouse Inn.

A few days later Rory, who had taken rooms at the Broomielaw, was surprised to receive a letter from Mr Brownling of the Brownling Bobbin Works, Garston, handed to him by his landlady:

Dear Sir,
   It has recently come to my knowledge that you are the young gentleman responsible for having saved by daughter's life when she collapsed of a heart-condition on a Liverpool street. I wish to extend to you, dear sir, a loving father's heart-felt gratitude, and so, too, does Pearl's mother, for having had our daughter admitted into hospital for prompt attention, while appreciating the fact that the Workhouse Infirmary, being the nearest place of charity, left you with little choice in the matter. However, since Pearl was brought home to be nursed by caring people, her condition is somewhat improved, though she will always remain, according to the doctor attending her, a sickly woman who is unable to resume her former independent way of life. But the fact that Pearl's life was spared by Almighty God is all that matters to us. I therefore take this opportunity (since Pearl tells me you are

the proprietor of a small cargo-haulage business) that if ever I can be of service to you, in any way whatsoever, please do not hesitate to call upon me when you are next in Garston. Pearl too, extends her personal message of gratitude for what you did for her.

I remain, yours faithfully,

Edward G. Brownling.

The address was given as 'Harcourt Hall, Garston, Liverpool'.

And if truth could be fabricated, then Pearl had certainly done that, and Rory wondered why. But he was not going to argue the fact that he was hero and not villain in Mr Brownling's eyes. With a smile to himself, he pocketed Mr Brownling's letter.

The *Lady Leonora* was due back in Glasgow, bringing a consignment of granite chippings from the Caernarvon Bay quarries. When she failed to arrive on time Rory became anxious. Speed was of the essence in this business, the swifter the delivery and unloading of the cargo, the sooner the vessel could be assigned to another run. Coastal steamship owners were all in competition with one another. The bigger and faster the boat and the more efficient her master and crew, the more money in the pocket of the owner.

The man mastering the *Lady Leonora* this time, was a Captain Thomas, who had signed on for temporary 'Home Trade' trips while awaiting command of a Merchant ship to the Far East.

When he signalled ahead from Ramsey to Port Glasgow via the Lloyd Signal Stations that the *Lady Leonora* would be delayed for at least five days as they had run into a 'spot of bother' off the Mull of Galloway with a fractured steam pipe, and had been forced to seek shelter in Ramsey Bay, Rory, reading between the lines, wondered just how bad was the 'spot of bother'. He remained on tenterhooks. He could ill afford to have his one and only steamship inoperative for any length of time. He knew from previous experience that off the Mull of Galloway there was a vicious tidal race, and that on the

East side of the Point of Ayre was a gravel bank, known as
the Whitestone Bank. Between this narrow channel, less
than a mile wide, the tides were extremely strong. With an
unstable cargo like granite chippings, the *Lady Leonora*
could sustain untold damage – if she didn't go down with
all hands on deck.

To take his mind off his problems, he went to have
another look at a dredging plant he had had his eye on for
some time. It was laid up in the Middow and Strait boatyard at Renfrew, adjacent to his great-uncle Hamish's own
small boatyard, which was how it had caught his attention
in the first place.

The dredger had capsized and was being sold off as
salvage, but the asking price was still £3,520, a fortune to
him at the present time. Could she be put back into operation? Rory wondered. Could Gammon, with his inventive
talent and wizardry when it came to machinery, be able to
repair the dredger? Or was it beyond recall? Was he not
being over ambitious in trying to compete with the Navigational Trust's own fleet of modern, self-propelled
machinery, and more than a little naïve when it came to
setting himself up for contractual dredging, taking into
consideration that the new floating plant stock owned by
the Trust cost in the region of £34,000 apiece, while he
didn't have a penny to his name?

But Rory knew that opportunities to make big money
through contract dredging were exceptionally good. The
river was always silting up. Local shipbuilders had to
contract-out for the removal of silt building up at the ends
of the launching ramps, floating bays and fitting-out
quays, and while the Trust held the monopoly of dredgers,
punts and tugs working the river, the actual maintenance
of private shipyards was not their responsibility.

A deep new channel with a minimum depth of thirty
feet had been requested by the shipbuilders, which would
mean a greater dredging fleet to be operational at all
times. Competition was fierce for dredging contracts, as
the price of seven shillings per punt was the going rate. He
was also aware, from his time serving as a deckhand
earning three shillings and twopence a day on the Trust's

number seven dredger, that contractors, eager to make quick profits, in most instances carried out the dredging work in a very slipshod fashion. They tended to concentrate on firm soil nearest to the deposit grounds, for time meant money when on piece-work. There was no check on measured quantities of silt brought up from the river bed, as only the volume deposited was in any way assessed. Until a ship ran aground and drew attention to the sludge and soft silt building up from lack of attention in the more difficult reaches of the river, no one was willing to do anything about clearing it. So there was plenty of opportunity, and profit, in this dredging business – provided he had the right kind of floating plant.

In the end he said, 'I don't think so, Mr Middow. She's a much older machine than I thought, and far too expensive for the condition she's in.'

'She's just been lifted from the silt and sludge where she's been lying on her side since she capsized. But she's still not bad for her age. Hull hasn't worn thin at all – in fact, she's only seen thirty years active service and these things have a working life of fifty years or more.'

'Yes, but I'd also have to have a hopper barge to carry away the silt, and I can't afford that as well – not just at present. The salvage-work that is going to be required to get the dredger into service again, is not going to be easy or cheap.'

'£2,500, and that's my last offer,' said Alistair Middow of the Middow and Strait boatyard. 'Look, Mr Roskillen, I'll be perfectly honest with you. I'm selling the business as well as my boats because I can no longer afford to compete with the big boys like Simons, Fleming and Ferguson, or Lobnitz. Since the death of my partner, Basil Strait, two years ago I've been carrying on here practically single-handed. When we first started out in boatbuilding and repair work it was in the early days of steam and sail. But things are different now, when one sees the giant monsters plying the Clyde these days. I'm too old to change my ways or my ideas. And besides, my lease has expired on this site, and the new rent increase introduced by your great-uncle Hamish MacDearg, since the freehold of this site has reverted back to him, makes me feel that the time has come for me to sell up and retire gracefully.'

Rory's ears pricked up. 'Hamish MacDearg owns the freehold of this site?'

'Aye, he does. Though it's not as simple as that. There was some dispute over ownership of the site between your grandfather, the Laird of Glengarth, and Mr MacDearg who mortgaged it to him. For the past fifty years I've been leasing the yard from your grandfather's estate, and that's where my rent's been paid.'

'I see ... well, thank you, Mr Middow. I'll think about the dredger and give you my definite answer in three weeks time. Rory shook hands with the old man and left the boatyard, his thoughts centred upon old Neptune's stake in the Middow and Strait yard.

But before he could tackle Hamish upon the subject, the *Lady Leonora*, without steam-power and with damage to her engines, forecastle quarters and her bows, was tug-towed back into the Clyde, her master and first engineer intent upon murdering one another.

In the *Lady Leonora's* mess room saloon, Rory listened to each individual member of the crew separately as to why her cargo had to be jettisoned overboard, and how damage to the boat had been sustained. There were six members of crew, Captain Thomas, the first mate, the first and second engineers, a fireman, and Ackker who was both cook and deckhand. 'The fact remains, Mr Roskillen,' said Captain Thomas, 'your crew are an unruly bunch and only wished to see me get the sack.'

'Too flamin' true guv!' was Gammon's rendering later. Rory had finished questioning Captain Thomas, the first mate, and everyone else, as well as reading over the log of the voyage in order to gain a clearer picture of what had happened. 'He never should've ignored coastguard storm warnings and put into the teeth of a West-Nor'-West. It hit us right off the Point of Ayre. Now you knows yourself, guv, how anthracite, granite and grain can shift like cascara in a dowager's bowels, an' that's exactly what happened'.

'I see.'

'So his nibships says jettison it.'

'The right course of action to have taken when it meant lives were in the balance, Gamin, surely?'

'Beggin' your pardon, Mister Rory, sir, we wouldn't have been in the predicament we was, if he'd listened to the storm warnin's in the first bleedin' place! Then, instead of ridin' the waves with the bluff on our bow while holdin' just enough steam-pressure to maintain steerage, his nibships wants full throttle while he decides ter flamin' well turn her around in a Beaufort ten! Now then guv, twelve-foot-high waves pooping into the galley an' engine-room, to my mind, ain't a nice way to drown.'

'What happened then?'

'Then, with two of 'em holding down the wheel, it was like ridin' through the throat of a bleedin' shark after the chippin's went overboard, what with the wind an' waves tossing 'em back at us.'

'Why did Captain Thomas decide to turn her around, instead of carrying on towards the Solway or even Wigtown or Luce where he could have taken shelter?'

'Because he thought he was bleedin' nearer to Ramsey, an' besides, we hadn't seen a bunkering station fer a 'undred miles.'

'Stop exaggerating Gamin, and get to the point. You mean you ran out of coal?'

'Too true, guv! Eight tons per twenny-four hours steaming, the *Lady* needs, an' 'er bunkers were low when the storm hit us. At the Ramsey anchorage, we just bunkered enough to get us back into the Firth of Clyde. Then, when he decides to go *back* to Ramsey, it took us forty-eight hours with us making heavy weather all the way. The coal what was left was near useless as dammit, wet as his nibships hisself!'

'What did you mean about Captain Thomas "*thought*" he was nearer to Ramsey than the other sheltering ports?'

'Well, I wasn't going ter say this, guv, as a man's personal life is his personal life, like. But he's a flamin' nutter! He brought us rock-dodging through the Skerries, so close to shore we 'ad to 'old our breath 'case we rubbed

shoulders with the bleedin' lighthouse an' the 'arry
Furlong reef both at the same time. Then right up through
Banana Bank and Ramsey Sound he did the same, with a
flamin' Bible in one 'and, and a map in the other instead
of plottin' our course proper-like on the bleedin' chart an'
log. Then, 'arf way round the Point of Ayre, his nibships
decides ter port 'er helm, while there's water rollin' over
the stoke-hold plates so that ash an' coal was shoved into
the bilges. Then main engine starts racing, so that one of
us 'ad ter stand by to ease off pressure to prevent engine
damage, an' *he* starts singin' "Rule Britannia" an' "Eternal
Father Strong Ter Save"!'

'What did the rest of the crew do?'

'We bleedin' didn't sing, that's for sure. Tryin' ter maintain steerage pressure, an' hopin' the condenser wouldn't
get wet, we tried injecting sea-water ter clear the bilges!
But we managed, guv, an' kept the *Lady* limpin' into
Ramsey at two knots an' hour until 'er engines packed up
altogether. Mercifully the storm and winds had abated by
then, so we managed ter go under sail though it was hard-
going with the steerin'. That's when we slammed the
Nelson Buoy, while I'm thinkin' that *someone's* goin' ter
be collectin' his Lloyd's insurance, pretty soon! But,
beggin' your pardon, Mister Rory, sir, I tells yer one thing,
Ackker an' me ain't puttin' ter sea again with Cap'ain
bleedin' Thomas!'

'You don't like Captain Thomas?'

'You *could* say that, guv.'

'And the rest of the crew?'

'Likewise.'

'Why don't you like him?'

'He's orf his bloomin' rocker, that's why!'

'He's a very good captain and comes highly recommended.'

'Not with granite chippin's, he's not. An' cistificates are
all very well, guv, but in the end, I don't like ter see me
bloomin' life tossed between anyone's Cap'ain an' Gawd
Almighty. He's a religious nutter, that one.'

'Point taken, Gamin.' Rory hesitated and then decided
to be honest with Gammon, 'Captain Thomas doesn't

want to master with us again as he doesn't consider the *Lady Leonora* or her crew to be quite his type of "vessel".'

'Thank Gawd fer that.'

'Big Sandy Fergus will be mastering for us as soon as she's repaired.'

'Blimey, guv, you ain't 'arf takin' it well.'

'Well,' said Rory thoughtfully, weighing up loyalty and friendship against everything else – he had decided to pay off the rest of the crew apart from Gammon and Ackker – 'it hasn't been very profitable for us lately, has it? It's not your fault this voyage was a disaster, and there's always next time to recoup our losses – I hope. Meanwhile, we've got plenty of work to do getting her repaired and ready for the next run.'

'Sorry about the damage to the *Lady*, guv, but I did me best in the circumstances. An' since his nibships was in charge, I couldn't very well tell him 'er old engines couldn't take the strain of full steam ahead into them Atlantic rollers.'

'Yes, well, it was only cargo I lost this time, not the crew, so let's just be thankful for that. We've now got ourselves a nice little boatyard of our own to work from. It's actually my great-uncle Hamish's but he's letting us use it. I also want you to give me your opinion on a dredger that's going pretty cheaply.'

'Blimey, guv, you're running quicker than what I can walk!'

Rory slapped Gammon between the shoulderblades. 'Are you sure you aren't an Irish tinker, Gamin?'

In January, Rory received a letter from the firm of Pinnegar, Pedley and Childs, the firm of Edinburgh solicitors who administered the estate of Glengarth. He opened the letter eagerly, but received such a shock he had to sit down to finish reading it:

Dear Sir,

As a matter of courtesy we feel sure you would wish to be advised that the balance of your account on the capital sum of £1,000 per annum plus interest earned, invested by your late father in the year 1900, and held in trust until this year of your majority, 1911, is overdrawn. We tender a statement of account to show how and where the monies on your behalf have been spent.

While taking into consideration that your attendance at Eton College was curtailed by two and a half years, thereby making a substantial saving of £630 per annum, as well as the three years envisaged for your stay at Oxford, for which the sum of £3,000 had been set aside (part of the original inheritance of £1,000 per annum with interest accrued), of late your expenditure has altogether eroded the monies intended for your gentleman's education and the interest earned on that original sum invested by your father.

To the purchase of one steamship, crew's wages, and the setting up of the cargo-handling side of your business venture, involving insurance cover, etcetera., have been added our own legal and administrative fees in handling your personal as well as business affairs. As you will see, this leaves you with an outstanding amount of £1,785-10s-4d to settle.

Perhaps you would be good enough to call upon us at our Edinburgh office to discuss this matter. Furthermore, we would be glad to advise you in any future financial undertaking, i.e., as in stocks and shares rather than in steamboats entailing a great amount of capital outlay, which, at present, is not at your disposal.

Assuring you of our prompt, professional and personal service at all times, we are,

Yours faithfully
Cranston Pedley.

'Damn!' said Rory, a huge disappointment settling upon him, for he had been counting on at least £5,000 of his inheritance to set him up in the dredging business. Instead, there was nothing, absolutely nothing. What was more, he was in so much debt, it was frightening.

CHAPTER NINETEEN

Harcourt Hall, Garston, was five miles up the River Mersey from Liverpool. It was a robust Victorian Gothic mansion overlooking the harbour, with Brownling's Bobbin Factory adjacent. Rory was duly impressed by the trappings of trade.

He had not given it much thought before, but now he wondered what Pearl Brownling was doing as a humble receptionist at the Board of Trade offices in Liverpool. Surely, a girl from a background like hers did not have to earn her own living? Even more important, how come her parents had allowed their daughter to go out into the big wide world of temptation to work for herself? Most strange! But then, who am I, he asked himself, to pry into the affairs of others. People did all sorts of things, for all sorts of reasons, which might seem out of character and inconsistent to those of a more rigid imagination, so whatever Pearl had chosen to do with her life was between herself, her God, and her parents.

Rory was shown into the vestibule by the butler, and then a trimly uniformed maid appeared to take his coat. She dropped him a curtsy.

'Mr Brownling is expecting you in the Ivory Room, sir. Please come this way,' said the butler after the maid had relieved him of his coat and scarf.

He followed the butler's stiff back along an impressive length of carpeted corridor flanked by good pieces of furniture, paintings and impressive-looking Ming vases, which might or might not have been genuine.

Someone was playing the piano in a distant part of the house. He wondered if it might be Pearl. A nice girl who had somehow got herself into trouble. But then, some nice girls do, and some don't. He tried not to think of *his* part in her past affairs.

Mr Brownling greeted him effusively, shaking hands with gusto, as though he were meeting a long lost friend. 'It is indeed an honour for me to welcome you, Mr Roskillen, to my humble home. My wife and daughter are looking forward to having you stay to dinner with us this evening, as indeed am I. We trust you will not disappoint us.'

Cigars and whisky were brought by the butler.

Mr Brownling was a big bluff man with heavy dewlaps, who reminded Rory of a well-nourished bloodhound. His host's hospitality and friendliness, however, went unsurpassed.

Rory also sensed that Brownling was not a man to be easily trifled with – or indeed, one easily fooled. Ushered into a deep leather armchair, Rory and his host conversed man-to-man, while waiting for dinner to be served.

The Ivory Room was all that it purported to be. A number of large glass cases contained exquisitely carved pieces of ivory in different colours and textures, obviously worth a fortune, even though Rory knew nothing about ivory. He took in his surroundings with a great deal of interest, which did not go unnoticed by his host. 'What you see is the collection of a lifetime. Gathered here in my "museum" are ivory pieces from all over the world, Mr Roskillen, although the insurance for this personal indulgence of mine, beggars me!'

'I can quite believe it, Mr Brownling.'

Rory was then plied with questions by Mr Brownling concerning his 'steamship business', which he tried to answer without giving too much away.

'The *Lady Leonora* was unfortunately laid up for a little while at my boatyard in Renfrew following storm damage when returning on a home-run with a cargo of chippings. The damage has now been repaired, so I took the opportunity to travel to Garston aboard her, while her master takes her on to the London River.'

'With what cargo, Mr Roskillen?'

The question was put as subtly as any of His Majesty's Customs and Excise officials, and Rory was well aware of it.

'Bulk cargo for Pwllheli, then Welsh slate to the London River. From there she will go to the Channel Islands with cement, picking up "deck cargo" of fresh farm produce from Jersey and another stop for Cornish kaolin, bound for Dublin and Belfast. From Ireland, home again with Irish oats, potatoes and wheat.'

'You sound as though you have a substantial Home Trade route, Mr Roskillen; have you?'

'Yes. Even though I haven't been in the business very long, I've discovered that opportunities are always there for those willing to recognize them.'

'Pearl tells me that you yourself are the brother of a Laird of Scotland, no less, Mr Roskillen?' Edward G. Brownling went on to add, from behind his stout cigar and glass of whisky.

Rory regarded the tip of his cigar (never having smoked one before, but desiring to keep up an affluent image) before taking up his glass of whisky to stop the choking sensation rising in his throat. Not wishing to be brash about his family connections, he replied quietly: 'Yes, Mr Brownling, my brother, Lindsay Beauly Roskillen is the Laird of Glengarth.'

'Indeed, indeed! And what makes a member of the upper-classes want to lower himself through association with the "trading classes", Mr. Roskillen?'

'An accident of birth, Mr Brownling. I am the younger son of my father, and I have to make my own way in life. My brother and I are separate entities. We have nothing in common except blood, which, when analysed, comprises ninty-nine parts water. The solid part is what I have to put in myself. I don't *have* to do it, and no one is forcing me. But it's something I feel I must do: a compulsion, an inner drive which propels me towards contributing something to this world instead of always taking from it. Trade is what made this nation great, sir, and I'm interested enough to be seduced by the profits that can be had from fair trading.'

'I *like* that, I like that!' Mr Brownling thrust his cigar towards Rory. 'That smacks of a down-to-earth honesty, young man. I don't care too much for pretentious young

men who're all blue-blooded bluff. So! You have to earn
your own way in life as the younger brother of a Scottish
Laird, and you do it without side. That goes a long way
with me, Mr Roskillen. I worked myself up by my boot-
straps, too, working in my father's bobbin factory from the
age of eight. But now I own salt works, a match factory,
prosperous bobbin works in Garston as well as
Manchester, plus a lot of other business interests along the
way. Not to mention a priceless ivory collection and a
well-respected place in Liverpool's Chamber of Commerce.'

'Well done, Mr Brownling,' Rory could think of nothing
else *to* say.

'Indeed, young man, it was! Sheer hard grit never hurt
anyone. It's the layabouts of this world I have no time for.
But now, the Scots are canny traders and I like doing business with them. As you know, timber is the basis of my
prosperity. We make looms, bobbins, shuttles, pegs and
anything else wooden required by the Lancashire cotton
industry – the goose that lays the golden egg. Lancashire
cotton and our "Satanic" mills, Mr Roskillen, close them
down and I go down the drain, too, along with Britain's
prosperity.'

'From where do you buy your timber?'

'Beechwood from south-east England chiefly, and the
rest from abroad – Scandinavia.'

'The Hebrides?'

'A little, not much. Scottish timber was mostly felled
during the last century to fuel England's so-called industrial revolution. What remains is expensive because it's
protected. Added to production costs is the cost of transportation by sea, which made me turn to other more
competitive markets.'

'My brother owns extensive tracts of Caledonian forest.
Timber is the basis of *his* prosperity,' Rory said, hoping
that *all* Lindsay's forests hadn't been destroyed by the fire
that had consumed so much of his holding. 'Perhaps, Mr
Brownling, we could strike a bargain? I could bring you as
much timber as you wanted from Glengarth aboard my
cargo-coasters fitted with derricks for just that purpose,
once you and I and Lindsay could agree to a price?'

'I will give it my utmost consideration, Mr Roskillen, for it sounds a good enough proposition to me.'

'Thank you, Mr Brownling.'

'I'll tell you something else, young man.'

'Yes, sir?'

'Recognizing your golden opportunities is the first step towards making your way in this world. The second rule in my book is that nobody gives anything away – without a catch. So it's down to brass tacks in the end, which means your *own* industry and expertise – good solid hard work counting for most in the end, for nothing else brings satisfaction like it. This is not my ivory tower, Mr Roskillen, though some might think it: I *earnt* my rewards!'

And upon that 'canny' word of advice, Mrs Brownling appeared on the threshold with her daughter whom she wheeled in an invalid chair. Pearl looked very blue and breathless, but Rory was glad to see that she was a little more like the pretty girl he had dated when he was at Darby's Nautical Academy, Everton, and less like the corpse he had steeled himself to visit in the Lime Street Infirmary. She greeted him shyly and with reserve.

Her parents were obviously still ignorant of what she had tried to do to herself. All through a very stiff and formal dinner in a vast, icy-cold dining-room, waited upon by a bevy of efficient maids and footmen, Rory suffered from inward pangs of guilt and disquietude. Pearl, seated opposite him, he sensed to be equally ill at ease.

Later that evening, just before he announced his attention to leave, Mr and Mrs Brownling slipped away with such ill-concealed haste, that the two young people thrown suddenly into each other's company, did not know what to say to one another.

Pearl broke the ice first. 'Thank you for coming to call upon us, Rory. I do appreciate your visit. I know you could have chosen to ignore my father's letter, and me, which would have been so much easier for you.'

'I'm glad I came.'

She blushed. 'Always the perfect gentleman!' Pearl was trying hard to put him at ease. 'I wish I could believe you, Rory.'

'It was much harder for me to visit you in that awful Infirmary place on Lime Street,' he told her frankly.

'I know. And don't think I don't appreciate what you did for me while I was ... while I was ...' she was unable to finish the sentence.

'Dying?'

'Yes, Rory, *dying*! And we both know it.'

He cleared his throat awkwardly. 'Is that why ... I mean ... in Liverpool, when we went out together a few times, and at first you led me to believe you'd be quite willing to sleep with me, yet we always ended up only holding hands in the back row of the music hall, it was because you knew all the time, about the ... the baby, I mean?'

'Yes, Rory, I was already six weeks pregnant when I met you in April last. I was hoping to make up to you, you see ...' She clutched his hand in her own thin, frail little hand which, despite all the care and attention showered upon her by a loving and caring family, refused to lay flesh upon its bones. 'But I couldn't do it. I couldn't pass another man's baby off as yours, because, just in those few short afternoons or evenings we met, I really got to like you and respect you and ...' her voice faded away into a pathetic little silence.

'And what, Pearl?' Rory prompted.

'And I wish it could have been different.'

'Is that why you left this lovely home of yours to become a receptionist at the Board of Trade offices?' he asked, 'because you didn't want your parents finding out?'

'Yes. They accepted the fact that I just wanted to do a little bit of secretarial work – father likes to see women taking a stand for themselves sometimes; he's very fair like that. But he would never have accepted the fact of my being an unmarried mother. The shame and disgrace for both of them, Mother too, would have been more than *I* could have borne. You see, Rory, the man whose child I was carrying, and whom I had always assumed was as much in love with me as I with him, was the assistant manager at my father's bobbin works. Father promoted him because he said he was a bright, up-and-coming man, with a good future on the managerial side of the business, and also because he was a single man. Father would not have given him the promotion so soon, otherwise.'

'So what went wrong?'

'He turned out to be married, with a wife and family living elsewhere.'

'And your father still does not know?'

'No. *I* only found out *afterwards*. He who had promised me the sun, moon and stars, wedding bells, everything, *after* we became lovers ... I was truly besotted with him, you see, Rory ... turned out to be an out-and-out rotter and rascal. He refused to take responsibility for my child. I didn't know what to do then, and that's why I did what I did. At first my parents weren't worried about where I was staying, because it was with friends of the family. And then, when I left these people, I never contacted them or my family. I was going to after it was all over, but I didn't know trying to abort a baby of eighteen to twenty weeks could be so dangerous. That was during the July, when you came to see me in the Infirmary.'

Rory took a deep breath. 'You ought to have told your father about the scoundrel he was nurturing, Pearl. The man *used* you!'

'I couldn't do that; he had a wife and family to support.'

'God, girl! You almost died because of him! Your whole life has been ruined, not just your health.'

'Rory, dearest Rory, you restored my faith in men. When you came to see me in that Infirmary, and did such sweet things on my behalf, knowing that my circumstances could not have had anything to do with you as we never ever made love, then yes, I could have willingly died from shame and misery, not just blood-poisoning!'

'What price love, eh, Pearl?'

She smiled. 'You're just saying that. I know you don't love me.'

'How do you know I don't?'

'A woman can tell. But don't worry, the feeling is mutual. I want you as a very dear friend, not as a lover. In Liverpool it was very hard for me not to *use you*, Rory Roskillen – and you yourself were willing enough, too, I remember!'

'Oh yes. I *never* turn down a pretty face or can resist a genuine offer,' he said with a bright smile he was far from feeling after Pearl's sad confession.

'And in that respect, you are like all the rest, Rory Roskillen – though perhaps not nearly as bad as some!'

'How do you mean, Pearl?'

'A typical product of the system. Nothing but a handsome, charming, loveable, fickle bloody bastard.'

'Thank you Pearl, for your high regard for me.'

She smiled. 'Oh, you know what I mean. Now that my life's been given back to me, I don't want to marry anyone. But if I do, he would have to be Scouse, and one who doesn't mind a woman with a bad heart and ailing condition, who, if she ever became "indiscreet" again, *would* surely die.'

After that there was nothing more to be said. He squeezed her hand tightly and made her wince. 'I'll be back,' he promised.

'To break my heart, I daresay. But I know it's for my father's sake, not mine, and for that I cannot condemn you. He thinks very highly of you, and would no doubt try and get you into the Liverpool Chamber of Commerce if you wanted to do business here.'

Rory pulled a face. 'No thanks. I'm a Scotsman, born and bred.' Then he added thoughtfully, 'This ... this man from your father's bobbin works, whom you must still see quite often as the place is right next door, if he ever revised his decision and was able to marry you, would you still want to marry him, Pearl?'

'Yes. Tomorrow.'

'Then, perhaps, one day he might do right by you,' said Rory, who had never yet been able to fathom out a woman's mind, let alone her heart!

'Perhaps. But, for the moment, I've got everything that I want right here with my own kith and kin. I can't ask for more, Rory. I'm really *so* lucky to have a family that's close and considerate – after what I've done behind their backs.'

'I'm glad, Pearl, that everything has turned out for the better. Glad for your sake.'

He took his leave soon after, but with an extremely heavy heart. He felt sorry for Pearl, but he could do nothing more to help her. He could only hope that Pearl Brownling would one day meet and marry the genuine article, quite unlike the base creature she now thought *every* man to be.

Hamish MacDearg accepted his great-nephew's offer to take the *Jane Blythe* off his hands for a nominal sum of money – which he had not received to date. But he was willing to waive payment for the time being, as the *Lady Leonora* was now making a tidy little profit in which he had a twenty-per-cent share. In Hamish's opinion the *Jane Blythe* was only fit for the scrapyard but Rory had other ideas. He hoped to salvage and repair the *Jane*, as he had done with the *Drogheda*, renamed in her born-again status as the *Lady Leonora*. Alistair Middow also made him an offer he could not refuse, by selling him the salvaged dredger for £1,000 as he was desirous of winding up his Renfrew boatyard business as soon as possible now that he had made up his mind to take himself off into a graceful retirement.

With all this salvage work going on on his doorstep, Rory accepted Gammon's offer of help in the boatyard, rather than putting to sea again as the *Lady Leonora's* first engineer.

'I reckons you need me here more'n Big Sandy, guv. 'Sides, first engineers lookin' fer Home Trade routes are two a penny, so's you can easy get yourself a new crew.'

'I'm the boss, Gamin, not you. I'll think about it. I might not want your Cockney nits plaguing me in my boatyard.'

Gammon grinned.

'What do you know about diesel engines and turbines?'

'Not a sausage, guv. Why? You thinkin' of converting the dredger ter turbine power?' added Gammon facetiously.

'I've just been reading about Germany's new submarine boats, Gamin, and I've come up with some very interesting facts – which I'm not going to tell you about now as we've work to do. Two steamcoasters making double the profits – which I'm now glad to say the *Lady* is making since being mastered by Big Sandy Fergus – means I'll be able to retire that much earlier.'

'Go on with you, Mister Rory, sir, *you'll* never quit. You got diesel power runnin' in yer blood. What use you goin' ter put the *Jane* to, provided she can be salvaged an' refitted?'

'Home trade coasting, what else?'

'My man Ackker, guv, wants ter know if he can stay.'

'Stay where?'

'In the boatyard.'

'You mean he's fed-up with coasting, too?'

'Not fed-up, guv; he rather depends on me, like, since I picked him up in Dublin when he was down an' out.'

Rory looked startled. 'You two haven't got some sort of illicit relationship going, have you, Gamin!'

'Do me a favour, guv! Nothin' like that. But Reginald Ackker is gettin' on a bit – especially in the 'ead – an' would take ter the bottle again if I lets him out of me sight with Big Sandy Fergus on shore leave. Them dockside brothels, guv, ain't no place for Ackker. There's no knowin' what he might pick up an' bring aboard the *Lady* if I wasn't there ter supervise his career, like.'

'God forbid! All right, he can stay – as long as he does a good job with the tarbrush and caulking, fifteen hours a day, seven days a week.'

'You got my word on it, guv.'

A few weeks later, with the *Lady Leonora* under the command of Big Sandy Fergus and a new crew kept busy between the various Home ports, Rory himself was occupied with supervising the repairs to the *Jane Blythe* in Hamish's boatyard, as well as work being carried out on the salvaged dredger still in the Middow and Strait boatyard next door.

Gammon and he were in the boatyard office, pouring over the blueprints of the *Jane Blythe* together with her scale measurements. They also had the original drawings of the floating-plant made by the now defunct Glasgow firm of Girdwood, and were hoping to work from these in order to put the dredger back in service. A loud honking of a klaxon on the apron in front of the office and dry dock area, drew their attention away from boats.

'Blimey it sounds like a motor-car, guv! What's a motor-car doin' here at this flamin' time of day?'

'It's one o'clock, Gamin!'

'Yeah, an' bleedin' Sarrerday lunchtime an' all! I needs a pint an' a sandwich, guv, even if you don't!'

'I do Gamin, I do! But Sarrerday lunchtime or not, answer the doorbell and find out who's outside.'

'No peace fer the wicked! Now I'm the bleedin' butler!'

Nevertheless Gammon stomped outside to find out who was disturbing the peace of 'doon the watter' in a motor-car, much less how it had got there!

A few moments later he reappeared in the office. 'Blimey, guv! There's a Delaunay-Belleville parked outside with a dame what looks like King George in drawers. Blimey, she's a beaut!'

Rory looked up from the clutter on his desk – or rather, his uncle Hamish's desk. 'The Delaunay or King George in drawers?' he asked.

'The car, guv, the car! Dames are all the same under the chemise, but a engine under the bonnet purrs different every time.'

'And that,' said Rory Duncan, standing up and throwing a pencil at Gammon, 'is *some* analogy! Did you find out her name?'

'Says she's Lizard Rolling Shannon – sounds foreign, she does, but not Irish.'

'Oh, go back to sleep, Gamin!' Rory hastened outside onto the launching quay, his heart giving a little lurch of surprise. 'Lizzie!' he greeted her in astonishment, 'What on earth are *you* doing here?'

'Gee whiz, hon! They told me I'd find you here, but I never believed it for a moment. What do they call this place, the End of the World?'

'Scotland, Lizzie, Scotland! This is actually Renfrew – six miles from Glasgow.'

'Feels like it, hon.' She yawned. 'Forgive the sighs, honeybunch, but it's a long way from the city lights.'

'How did you get here, Lizzie?'

She patted the leather upholstery of her peerless car, and peered at him from the driving seat before reaching for a pair of dark glasses beside her. Wrapped in silver fox furs she looked like a million dollars and his heart somersaulted yet again. 'Then they hustled me onto this thing they call a ferry, and *pulled* me across all that water! God! It was awful!'

He grinned. '*That* was the Renfrew ferry!' Rory suspected that no one at Renfrew had ever seen a car like Mrs Roebling Chanin's in their entire lives! 'Don't tell me you drove up here all by yourself from Boxwood Manor, Lizzie?'

'Sure, sugar, why not. Texas is five times bigger than your British Isles, y'know. But I didn't come from Leicestershire.'

She pronounced it as Li-cester-shire. Rory had to smile to himself.

'Then where?'

'This cute li'le old palace they call Soho.'

'Buckingham Palace, Lizzie! Soho is a place in London inhabited by half of China.'

'Same difference to li'le ole Lizzie here. But I'm only kidding.'

'Kidding?'

'Joking, hon, joking! Where's your sense of humour since the birthday ball?'

'Oh, oh, I see!' She must be, he thought to himself, if she could equate the acreage of the British Isles to that of the State of Texas!

'Your King Georgie Porgie isn't going to invite the likes of Lizzie Roebling Chanin to Buckingham Palace, now is he, hon?'

'No. No, I suppose not. Anyway, Lizzie, what're you doing here so far from the bright lights of London?'

'Well, as sure as hell you're better company than some of those English gophers with white ties, black tails and plums stuck in their gullets. Besides, I'm mighty lonely for a *real* man after Jay-Jay disintegrated along with his Grand Prix racing car. Châteaux and vineyards don't give a woman sexual satisfaction, hon.' While Rory took a deep breath, Lizzie took out a solid gold cigarette holder at least six inches long, into which she inserted a Turkish cigarette not much shorter than the holder itself. After blowing smoke in his face, she smiled up at him. 'You're as good-looking as ever, honeybunch – more, if I dare say it, since greasepaint suits you! Why haven't I seen you around the Stately Home circuit lately?'

'I'm very busy, Lizzie.'

'That's what I like about you, Dirk, a classy guy who gives me the brush-off with such style.'

'I'm not brushing you off, Lizzie, I'm tied up at the moment. And the name's Rory.'

'Doing what, Rory?'

'Steamships.'

'Oh, yeah – the lil'le ole company you were telling me about at Humphrey's birthday ball. Well, now that I'm here to offer you a partnership, how about showing me around?'

'With pleasure,' he smiled as he opened the driver's door, Lizzie perfectly matchless as far as any other female he had ever encountered, was concerned. 'What would you like to see first, my fourteen Pacific and Orient world-class liners, or my Transatlantic fleet?'

'No kidding!'

'Yes, I'm joking, Lizzie. I must be perfectly honest with you. All you are about to see is one old steamcoaster called the *Lady Jane* and one old dredger without a name that has just been brought up from the bottom of the Clyde. The *Lady Leonora*, my own "sea-worthy" steamship, at the moment, is carrying cargo, on her way to the Scilly Isles – I hope.'

'What's a dredger, hon?'

'Do you really want to know?'

'Not really.'

'Good. We'll talk about it back at my place.'

'Where's that?'

'The Broomielaw – in Glasgow. I've taken rooms there ... er, apartment in your jargon, Lizzie,' he added quickly, when she appeared flummoxed. 'You *can* stay, can't you?'

'As long as you like, Dirk. You see, hon, I have a twenty-first birthday proposal to put to you, which I'll tell you about later as it's somewhat of a surprise.'

'You have?' the question stuck in his throat. 'How did you know about my twenty-first birthday?'

'That Lennie child – your cousin – told me. She was hoping to see you for another grand party, I guess.'

'When?'

'At Lady Glover's country house weekend party – you English are always partying!'

'I'm Scottish,' he reminded her with a smile.

'Yeah, I guess. Sorry, hon. I know how some people hate it when others get their nationalities mixed up. Lennie also told me she was a Suffragette – whatever *they* are!' She dragged on her cigarette with extreme elegance, and again gave him one of her dazzling smiles. 'You see, Dirk, how people are still thinking and talking about you even though you're on the other side of the world.'

'No wonder my ears were burning!'

He drove her exquisite car back to his lodging house in the Broomielaw for the sheer thrill of being at the wheel of such a fabulous piece of machinery. Then Lizzie decided upon a 'crate' of champagne to be delivered to the flat – Röederer, Cristal Brut, and he admired the way she placed her order at the local vintner. Her car, parked near the scaffolding scarring the new premises of the Clyde Navigation Trust building close to the Broomielaw Bridge, also attracted a flurry of excitement and attention. The Delaunay-Belleville seemed to sit well outside such a prestigious establishment, and he only wished he were the proud possessor of such a car: and then he warned himself, don't run before you can walk, *Dirk*!, wishing Lizzie would get his name right.

She decided to 'change into something more comfortable,' and spoke to him over the threshold of the open bathroom door while he popped the cork of the vintage Röederer. 'I'm kind of celebrating, too, hon! I just signed a contract for me and my li'le ole daddy. He trusts me implicitly with this money-making business. Enough to fill the Suez Canal with crude for a couple of years! It's a deal which'll make Standard Oil look real sick.'

'Congratulations, Lizzie.'

He knew that Elizabeth Roebling Chanin had more dollars than it would have taken to purchase the United Kingdom from their Majesties, her fortune drilled from the bottomless pit of Devanna Prairie, Texas, and comparable only to that vast wealth of the Rockefellers and Vanderbilts, and Rory was fully aware that he himself was nothing more than a small bubble of crude in her barrel. Money that couldn't even be counted made *him* feel sick and dizzy! How could he possibly compete in such company?

And then he told himself that there was no need to compete with the likes of Lizzie Roebling Chanin – he just had to be himself.

Lizzie appeared from the bathroom, clad in 'something more comfortable', which happened to be her bare skin. The electric light behind her made a silhouette of her magnificent body against the darkness of his shabby little bedroom so that she appeared like Aphrodite rising from the foam. Standing there, stark naked apart from a garland of diamonds in all their matchless perfection right down to her navel, her showy gold cigarette-holder held like some kind of phallic symbol, she made him catch his breath.

Lizzie drawled in her Texan accent, 'Since you've now taken off your diapers, Viking-man, you match your performance to mine, and the diamonds are yours.'

His answer got stuck in his throat.

They never quite made it to his saggy single cot. On the threadbare carpet, he took her down in the first act of an animal passion that was to last him for a long time to come.

A month later Rory received a letter from Lizzie:

Darling Rory,

Just a little something to show you my appreciation. Ever since my last husband's death I have remained unserviced – a nun in all respects. My energies have been concentrated on business, nothing else until I met you at your cousin

Humphrey's birthday ball. My life has never been the same since. I have thought of no one but you, sweet Viking-man, that is why I had to come to Scotland after you. It was well worth the effort. Never have I been serviced so well or for so long! You were *mag-nif-i-cent*, Rory Duncan of Glengarth, dare I say it! Here's to a long and happy relationship – we even made the champagne last for four days, didn't we, sugar? – which shows how much time we spent doing other things! But now to business. With the money, buy that little old boatyard you had your eye on – and don't deny it! You talked enough about Mr Middow Strait to last me a lifetime! It's a twenty-first birthday present along with a new dredger I ordered for you. Gammon has the details – he was sworn to secrecy when I was at the boatyard. I want to go into business with you, hon, and fast! That's my surprise. Lizzie loves you, sugar, and can't wait to see you again. I'll be coming up to Glasgow very, very shortly, just as soon as I've clinched my new oil deal down south. And I can't wait to feel what else you can do for me, honeybunch.

All this, for services rendered,

Your little old Lizzie who loves you madly, sweet Viking-man!

Hundreds of crosses embellished her letter.

He looked at the cheque again and again, and not only felt sick and dizzy but faint with ecstasy: Lizzie had sent him thirty thousand American dollars! It was to be drawn against the Devanna Oil Company, Texas. In translated terms, that meant approximately, oh bliss, *ten thousand pounds sterling*! He had never held so much money in his life: he never knew such money *existed*! One small bubble of crude in her barrel of fun, perhaps, but a millionaire's legacy to him. And if this is what a millionairess's gigolo could earn himself in four days, what price pleasure!

'Which just goes to prove, Dirk, old chap,' he said to the tom-cat from downstairs, 'that it's not *what* you know, but *what women* you know! God bless you, Lizzie, darling.' He kissed her cheque in the absence of the peerless creature herself. Then, before she could change her mind and redraw the cheque, he went out to deposit it in his bank and on the way home stopped to buy his landlady a bunch of red roses and a pound of kippers for her cat.

CHAPTER TWENTY

Lindsay had rented a modest villa on the shores of Lake Garda. Mountains and water: the scenery reminded him so much of Scotland, the ache within him was unassuagable.

He stood by the window of his studio overlooking the smooth, untrammelled surface of the lake and his thoughts were of Glengarth. He longed to return. But memories, like snowflakes turned to ash, kept him away.

Oh, God! This was not life; it was merely existence!

Riva or Trenta for the essentials. Neighbours with whom to pass the time of day, but that was all. Letters from home. And memories, always those haunting memories that chewed up the edges of the mind, gnawed into the soul, and left a torrent of hatred in their wake. Was this to be the sum total of his life? he asked himself.

The nightmare was ever with him: snowflakes that drifted aimlessly on the wind and dressed the great mountain, Beinn Claidheamh Mor, in a white veil that covered Inchnadamph. Snowflakes lay on the surface of the loch like unmelted tears, frozen in the ice-cold drifts of despair.

He dreamt that he heard a voice saying, *Tread carefully through the snow, my laird, for it will burn you, and scar you, and eat you away like a raging sore festering beneath the deceiving white linen.*

He dreamt that the snow turned to ash: ash that made the bracken curl, the heather die. Charred and dead, the purple heather was swept away on the Western winds, and pine cones, black and shrivelled, lay abandoned on the shrouded earth.

He dreamt that the desolate forest mourned for Iain and Shiona Hamilton and Bruce. It mourned for his Aunt Jean, left to carry the burden of her family destroyed by one moment's act of madness. Burning inside with remorse and the unspoken accusations in the eyes of Moira and Morag, the bewilderment in young Aeneas's eyes, without parents and without his ever-present companion, his brother, Lindsay mourned for himself.

He could hear the screams, his own among many, and he put his hands over his ears to shut out that condemning voice. 'On *thy* head, on *thy* head, on *thy* head ...'

He dreamt of an Indian Sadhu driving a stake through the heart of everything he loved and cared for.

Fists clenched, he raised them to his eyes, and saw again the thick white bandages covering his hands. He had sworn vengeance on Fletcher for what he had done. There was no doubt in his mind that the man from Raasay had deliberately set out to destroy the forests upon whose revenues the estate of Glengarth depended. He knew all about it from Annie Gowrie, for he had almost choked the truth from her. She had been hiding herself away on Rill, with the full knowledge that Fletcher had returned to Glengarth. But Annie, in her own fear and misery, had not realized Fletcher's intention until it was too late and she had seen the flames of the forest mirrored in the waters of Loch Garth. The mad man of Raasay had returned to the island that night, bent on revenging himself upon the Laird of Glengarth and his property, without realizing that he would also destroy the lives of innocent people dwelling in the path of those vicious winds driving the fire before them.

But that was only Annie's story.

And afterwards, after his superficial burns had healed, to leave behind for all time the scars of that terrible night, Lindsay had taken his boat out, in search of Fletcher. He had combed the ports, the fishing-villages, every loch, every glen, every yard of the coastline from the Mull of Kintyre to Cape Wrath. He had searched for Fletcher in the Western Isles and the Summer Isles, and then he had gone to Stornoway after him. He had spent long weeks brooding alone on the islands of Lewis and Raasay, watching, waiting, willing him to appear so that he could make Fletcher pay for what he had done ...

But the cost had been too high, and would *never* be fully paid.

Lindsay's final decision to leave Scotland had been on account of his cousin Iain Hamilton. Iain recovered from the second-degree burns he had sustained in the fire, only to be told that his wife had died in hospital of first-degree burns and that his younger son had been suffocated by the smoke before the fire-fighters could reach him. The shock was too great. He lost his mind and his reasoning. While Aeneas was being taken care of by his grandmother and aunts Moira and Morag, Iain had taken himself off to Ullapool where he steadily began drinking himself to death. When, some weeks after the Glengarth tragedy, the police had called upon Lindsay, they had a further shock in store for him. The body of his cousin, his factor, had been washed up in Grunard Bay. Suicide had been the verdict.

In that moment Lindsay knew that he would probably have done the same had he been Iain Hamilton.

Leaving the management of the estate to Gilbert Lucas, and the running of the castle to Christabel and their old retainer, Murray, he left for Brussels without giving a damn: Glengarth could fall into the sea, for all he cared.

But it had not been as easy as that: he had thought of nothing *but* Glengarth while he had been away.

He wanted to *kill* Fletcher! After nearly two years he wanted more than ever to find Fletcher and tear him apart. Fletcher now had a price on his head, arson and murder, on account of what had taken place at Glengarth. Annie Gowrie's own testimony concerning the activities of her poaching step-father was enough to hang him. But Lindsay wanted to get to Fletcher first, *before* the police!

Yet, out of the nothingness that had descended upon him after the fire at Glengarth, he had discovered an aptitude for painting.

He threw himself wholeheartedly into artistic creativity. He read endlessly from the classics, biographies, and huge historical tomes, *The Decline and Fall Of The Roman Empire*, Homer's *Odyssey*, Lord Macaulay's *History of*

England. (He thought of his grandfather's library at Glengarth, where nearly all the books had, at one time, belonged to a lending library in Dunbartonshire and wondered how the old man had got away with it all those years – a fine of tuppence a week on all those books would have ruined him.) And for light relief Lindsay read the forbidden version of Giovanni Boccaccio's *The Decameron.*

Now, with his sister Kitty's letter clutched desperately in his hand, he was faced with a dilemma he had never expected. The year was 1911, he was twenty-four years old and going nowhere fast. Kitty, oh, Kitty, he reproached her silently and tormentedly, after reading her letter: why are you drawing me back against my will?

He hadn't set eyes on his youngest sister since the day they had parted company in Liverpool, eleven years ago. Of course he yearned to see his sister after all these years; he wanted to know that she was happily married and settled; yet he wanted, above all, to remain where he was.

And while he, Christabel, Kitty and Rory had corresponded off and on with each other down the years, a house divided cannot stand – a sorry state of affairs augmented by their father. And yet he had yearned to get closer to them, his sisters and his brother whom he did not know. He had tried, yes he had tried. Allowing them use of the Town House, allowing Christabel free rein, even when she went so far as to imbue Kitty and their cousins in her Suffragette ideals. So now, with Kitty's wedding invitation in his hand, here was the ideal opportunity to bring the family together again. Blood after all, must be thicker than water.

'How lucky Toby is!' he said to Kitty, when finally he capitulated and went to England to attend her wedding. Kitty reminded him so much of their mother.

'I don't like your moustache, Lindsay!' Kitty stood on tip-toe to kiss him. 'You've only grown it so that it hides that beauty spot on your top lip.'

'A mole, Kitty, not beauty spot!' he said, somewhat bashfully.

'Then, I liked your distinctive *mole*, Lindsay, so take off all that hair, it doesn't suit you! You remind me of Papa.'

'Is that a bad thing?'

'Not at all! It's just that a moustache makes you look so *old*!' she said laughingly. Kitty's blue eyes widened in delight when she unpacked the straw surrounding her wedding present from him. 'Lindsay, they're *beautiful*! Thank you so much. Tobias will be as delighted as I am.' Very carefully she brought out one of the pink Murano glass chandeliers and planted another kiss on her brother's cheek, despite the offending moustache. 'Tobias is a dear.'

'Surely not, Kitty!' Lindsay pretended to be startled.

'Oh, no! Not the roebuck kind! Now you're teasing me, as Rory used to. You'll meet Tobias at the altar tomorrow,' she promised, delighted that Lindsay had consented to give her away – even though she retained a tiny guilty feeling that Uncle Austen had renounced that place of honour to the elder brother, despite the years Uncle Austen had been her careful and dutiful guardian.

Kitty was married the following day from her uncle and aunt's home, the wedding ceremony taking place at the little village church of Breedon in the Wold.

After the reception when Kitty and her new husband set off on their honeymoon to the Holy Land, Lindsay, once more, felt lost and disembodied.

Should he return to Italy, or should he return to Scotland?

Having made the effort to cross the English Channel, did he now have the courage to cross Hadrian's Wall?

He stayed at the Town House in Park Lane, London, while making up his mind what to do. And then fate turned the thumbscrews on him, and he was left with little choice. The *Titanic* disaster brought Iona back into his life.

Robert and Rosemary Cowall Lennox had been aboard the luxury liner when it had plunged into an iceberg off Cape Race. Neither survived the tragedy. Iona was at the Memorial Service in London, held a month after the disaster.

Dressed in black, just as he remembered her in the role of the Gibson Girl, Iona said to him after the service, 'I'm simply devastated, Lindsay. I cannot believe this has happened.'

'It's terrible, simply unbelievable,' he replied sorrowfully, unable to fully express his feelings concerning the loss of a deeply respected, personal friend as Robert Cowall Lennox had been. He felt a need of Iona as never before, when remembering that other tragedy he had managed to live through. He wanted to tell Iona that, in time, the terrible pain of loss would become just a dull ache of acceptance, and she would come through it all right, though the memories lingered on. That even those ghostly memories were acceptable in the end, for they kept alive the spirit of those that were gone for ever, lest we forget.

'Who would have thought that a ship like that could have disappeared without trace in just a few minutes, taking with it all those people! I thought they said it was unsinkable,' Iona lifted her veil to mop her eyes.

'Iona, if there's anything I can do, please don't hesitate to ask for my help,' Lindsay told her.

'I'm going back to Scotland tonight, will you travel up with me?' she asked him outright.

Destiny, it appeared, had decided to pick up the threads of his past to entwine them once more with the future. And since she had made the first move, he took his cue from her. 'Iona, I haven't stopped thinking about you for the past three years. Marry me before I do anything else foolish,' was his heartfelt plea in their private first-class compartment on the train to Edinburgh.

'Lindsay, when I first saw you at Lords all those years ago, I promised myself I'd marry you one day. We won't talk about what happened at Lady Conningbide's, but I've been trying to analyse your reasons for your abrupt dismissal of me that night. I know now that it was partly my fault. I should have postponed my trip to Greece.'

'But will you say yes *now*!'

'*Yes*!' This time she kept her veil off her face to smile at him, a pale and tremulous smile which touched him deeply.

'Oh, Iona!' He embraced her like a drowning man finding at last a spar to cling to.

And after he had kissed her and she had returned those kisses wholeheartedly behind the drawn blinds of the *Flying Scotsman*, she said, 'So now, tell me, Lindsay Roskillen, what have you been doing with yourself in Italy apart from avoiding me?'

'Painting. I was quite good at it. One day I might get some of the pictures framed and hang them in the great baronial hall at Glengarth,' he said, carefree for the first time in three years. 'They tell the full story from my black mood to my blue mood, while I made the in-depth discovery that mountains and lakes – be they ever so Scottish or ever so Italian – have that same enduring quality sought by the Women's Suffragette Movement.'

Her beautiful head resting contentedly against his shoulder, the sorrow Iona had felt by the death of her beloved brother, as well as a charming sister-in-law, was all at once diminished by sharing the loss with this man, little more than a stranger, who had asked her to marry him – a laird whom she had admired for a long time, though always from a distance. She wondered if anyone had come *really* close to Lindsay Roskillen, for he was a man not easily approachable.

But he still fascinated her, and she was determined to get to the core of him. Now that the distance had closed, she was prepared to forgive the Laird of Glengarth all his odd little quirks. 'And what might that be, pray?' she asked, playfully blowing out the flame of his cigarette lighter. 'This all-important quest sought by the Women's Suffragette Movement?'

Lindsay, the unlit cigarette in his mouth and one arm around Iona's shoulders, flicked his lighter again, and this time managed to light his cigarette before Iona blew out the flame. 'Perpetual possession of a man's soul. It was an interesting discovery.'

Lindsay Beauly Roskillen, Laird of Glengarth and Lady Iona Cowall Lennox of Edinburgh, were married in a special civil ceremony in July 1912.

On his return to Scotland, Lindsay was more than appalled by the state of things at Glengarth. He told himself that no one was to blame except himself. He accepted total responsibility. But it was hard.

Fences on the estate had been torn down, most had fallen into disrepair. Sheep, cattle and deer had been left to wander indiscriminately through the plantations – wild now since no new planting had been done after the forest fire. The earth was impacted, saplings weak and wilfully destroyed, timber stocks diminished because people had been pilfering the logs for fire-wood. Rents had been raised without justification when the mood suited Lucas. The foresters – those remaining – were up in arms against Gilbert Lucas's high-handed and domineering ways since he had run things at Glengarth to suit himself and no one else. As soon as Lindsay reappeared on the scene he was met by a deputation of plaintiffs barging into the estate office, demanding to talk to the laird, demanding to be paid wages in arrears, demanding all sorts of things Lindsay was quite incapable of dealing with without knowing the full facts.

After he had them laid before him, the first thing he did was to sack Gilbert Lucas who had been factor since Iain Hamilton's death.

The maintenance of the castle itself had been another problem. Aunt Jean Hamilton had left Glengarth, and was now living in Aberdeen with Moira and her husband, a rich businessman who owned the thriving 'Fortrose Malt Whisky Company'. They had adopted Aeneas, and Lindsay was glad to know that the lad was at last happily settled far enough away from Glengarth for his peace of mind, with his favourite aunt. Moira and John Fortrose would see to it that Aeneas was given a good home and education.

Morag still lived at Gairloch with her husband, the Minister of the Kirk. Christabel, caught up with the Women's Movement, spent much of her time between London and Paris, and so Glengarth had been left without a chatelaine. Murray himself, Lord Roskillen's old retainer, was too infirm as well as partially blind, to be of any use at all. So it was with some surprise that Lindsay had listened to Murray telling him what a treasure the 'young lassie' had been around the place, taking it upon her 'frail, wee shoulders, to dust and polish and wield the broomstick upon those who didn't pull their weight around the place during the laird's absence'.

'What wee lassie?' Lindsay, confused, had asked Murray.

'Why, m'laird, Annie Gowrie from Rill! Since the Lodge was burned to the ground, she's taken to living here in the castle. Promoted herself, aye, to cook and house-keeper, and a right proper bossy-boots is Annie Gowrie from Rill.'

Murray had shuffled off then with the silver-polish in one hand and a candlestick in the other, leaving Lindsay smiling to himself.

Iona threw herself into the daunting task of redecorat-ing and refurbishing Glengarth Castle while he concen-trated on the outside. Soon the catalogues and samples arrived along with the builders, decorators, electricians and plumbers, Iona not one to do anything by half measures. The whole place was going to get a face lift – at Iona's expense, she told her husband, since she had come into a substantial legacy upon her brother's death.

Lindsay found a new steward to take the place of Gilbert Lucas. A quiet, middle-aged, unmarried man, Mr Mitchell had worked among the forests of Canada and Borneo and knew a great deal about tree-management. Together, he and Lindsay embarked on an intensive programme of reafforestation previously attempted in only a half-hearted fashion, until the firing of the Forest Lodge Plantation had altogether destroyed Lindsay's will to con-tinue the programme first outlined by himself to Iain.

At last, it seemed, he was sailing into calmer waters. He was married to beautiful Iona, the Renoir girl of his dreams; he had found good and reliable retainers to take the place of the old; Iona's inheritance would keep Glen-garth on its feet until he could restart the forestry side of things; and once more he held the reins of Glengarth firmly in his hands. The only other thing he desired most in the world would be to know that Iona was having his child so that the future of Glengarth would be secured into the next generation.

According to the doctor attending Hamish MacDearg, the old man was breathing his last.

'Aye, he's always been breathing his last, Mr Roskillen, as Mrs Fleming and myself will testify to the fact. This time, however, the Bailiff has come for him surely, surely! He is demanding interest upon a mon's life. Three score years and ten, that is all a mon's entitled to, so Hamish owes interest on his overdue stay in God's Hotel.' Dr Grimble stepped over to the chest of drawers and opening Hamish MacDearg's tea-caddy, helped himself to a tot of malt before he departed the house. 'I'll be back tomorrow, if he doesn't die tonight.'

As soon as the doctor had gone, Hamish opened one eye and gasped. 'For, 'tis as Luke says, the things which are impossible with men, are possible with God! Fetch us a wee drap, there's a good fellow.'

Rory complied with his great-uncle's wishes, not sure he was doing the right thing by giving old Hamish malt whisky when he was supposed to be dying.

'How many steamships d'you now own, nephew?' Hamish croaked, his nightcap askew on his grizzled locks.

'Four, Uncle Hamish.'

'Four, egad! Are they in good working order?'

'They're earning me my living, Uncle Hamish – plus the dredger and hopper which Lizzie bought me.'

'Lizzie, egad! Strange lady, a bit flighty. Marry her an' you'll rue the day. Bed her to you'er heart's content, but never marry her, for she'll break you'er heart by stepping all over it the moment you slip the ring on.'

'Yes, Uncle Hamish.'

Lizzie Roebling Chanin had sent more fruit and flowers that day, and Hamish was touched by the thoughtful gesture (though he would never admit it) from a foreign woman, the likes of whom he had never encountered in his long life.

Hamish had met the American lady on one occasion only, and that was when she and he had argued over the contract and land value of the Middow and Strait site. Meanwhile, a man called Lucas – Gilbert Lucas – had rushed down from Glengarth, Ross-shire, saying that *he* had the Laird of Glengarth's interests at heart, and the site could not be sold without the new Laird of Glengarth's knowledge and consent, since it had been leased to Lord Roskillen in the year 1857 in return for monetary favours. These dues had not as yet been fully recovered, and the Middow and Strait rent-money was to be continued to be paid as a retainer fee. Since the Laird Lindsay was in Italy, this monthly sum of money, plus interest on overdue rent (as was frequently the case, since Mr Middow had a bad cash-flow problem) would still have to be paid to the estate of Glengarth, until the Laird Lindsay decided to return to Scotland.

Lucas was a little bit crazy, Hamish MacDearg had thought at the time, for the contract clearly stated that the freehold of the Middow and Strait site reverted to *him*, Hamish Blythe-MacDearg, after fifty years, and it was fifty-*five* years since those signatures of 1857. Lucas was a villain! Thank goodness, thought Hamish in that moment, he had had the sharper wits and keener eyes of his nephew, who had looked into the legalities of that rather confusing contract which Hamish had forgotten all about. If it hadn't been for Middow wanting to sell his boatyard, Hamish would have gone to his grave without ever having reclaimed his lawful dues!

Mrs Roebling Chanin had wanted to buy out Middow and Strait lock, stock and barrel, with Rory Duncan in overall control. But she put her own price on the boat-yard, way below that of its current market value. In other words, she was trying to do what the old Laird of Glengarth had once done to Hamish MacDearg! But Hamish MacDearg was a wiser man – or, at least, hoped he was! He didn't care about the tangible assets in the way of a few old steamboats and hopper-barges in need of urgent attention. That side of things was down the drain anyway, since Middow was unable to manage his business affairs adequately without his lifelong partner, Basil Strait – God rest his soul!

Hamish and Mr Middow had almost come to blows
over the final price of the boatyard – taking into consideration fifty years of goodwill and business. Glengarth's
administrator had wanted to sue them both for negotiating
terms of business on an estate neither had legal claims
upon. In the end Gilbert Lucas had settled for a month's
rental, pending word from the Laird of Glengarth. Dues
he had no doubt put into his own pocket in the absence of
the Laird himself, had been Hamish's thoughts at the time.
Lizzie had then threatened to buy out the ill-fated White
Star Line unless Mr Middow and Hamish agreed to agree
upon everything, including *who* retained chairmanship
and overall control in the management of the two
adjoining boatyards at Renfrew.

Agreement had been reached at last. Upon the amal-
gamation of the old MacDearg-Blythe Steamship Company and the Middow-Strait ship-building yard, a new
company would be formed without the previous mid-
Victorian image.

The Chanin-Beauly Line, Renfrew, Scotland, was registered in that year 1912. The name suited Lizzie Roebling
Chanin and her partner: it did not suit Mr Middow or
Hamish who found themselves being pushed out of the
lime-light. But as minor entities on the Board of Chanin-
Beauly directors, they had little say in the matter, especially since the American woman was putting in all the
money to launch the new company and its steamships.

Rory Roskillen was appointed Managing Director of
the Scottish side of the business, Lizzie herself being bent
on opening a transatlantic office, in New York.

'Gee hon,' she told Rory, 'this is a whole new game for
me. Steamships are something I never thought of until you
came along with your li'le ole expertise. But it makes
sense. Hell, what good is it being rich if you can't have fun
getting richer still!'

He found himself entirely in agreement; she was paying
his salary plus his 'perks' so how could he possibly
disagree?

A reputable firm of Glasgow solicitors handled the legal
side. Hamish's agreement with the Laird of Glengarth in

the year 1857, to run for a period of fifty years on the Middow and Strait site, *had* reverted to him, therefore the Chanin-Beauly Line had no legal obligation to the Laird of Glengarth, and could use the site. Rory and Lizzie celebrated by adopting a House Flag and their own special steamship colours.

In his heart of hearts Hamish was proud of his nephew.

Rory Duncan Roskillen was not like his grandfather a bit – not a bad hat at all! He had made a good start, even though he had a long way to go if he ever wanted to occupy that favoured seat at the Clyde Trust offices on Robertson Street.

Since White Star had gone out of favour through the *Titanic* disaster, Rory Duncan, with his steamship colours of bold white herringbone arrows in double bands to depict strength, ringing the tall dark-blue smokestacks of his two newest and most modern of steamships, was an up-and-coming entrepreneur to be reckoned with. Such were Hamish MacDearg's thoughts as he drew towards his end, even though he knew he would never quite forgive *any* Roskillen! He had come full circle with the Highlanders, and was glad to leave them to it, at last. 'Rory Duncan, just make sure, fellow m'lad, ye give y'old uncle Hamish a sailor's funeral. I want to be buried at sea. In ma hey-day, I mastered the fastest tea-clipper to India, d'ye ken?'

'I didn't know that.'

'There's a lot the younger generation ne'r cares to know about the older, simply because they ne'r care t'listen! But m' stories of India fired you'er father's imagination, and that was why James always had a hankering after the Far East. As a wee small boy, he was all ears when I sometimes took maself up to Glengarth on one o' m' rare visits hame t' see Mary Jane after her marriage to the Laird o' Glengarth. Your father cut his eye teeth on adventure stories to the China Seas, the Indian Ocean, to the Javas and the Spice Islands. In his nursery, with Nurse MacCready alwa' ready tae listen too, mony a happy hour was spent tale-telling. And surely as God forged Scotland in the wrought-iron works of his mountain factory, the

Welsh are not the only bards! Celts have it in the blood, d'y'ken, of which ye are part, Rory Duncan! Thirst for adventure, story-telling, exploring way beyond anything a mon knows to what God *wants* us to know!'

Old Neptune drew fresh breath, the bard truly in his soul right now, Rory couldn't help feeling.

'As soon as James was out of petticoats, he was a-raring to go far beyond Scotland's boundaries in search of adventures furnished by old Uncle Hamish MacDearg from Glasgow, his mother's seafaring brother! Aye, and that was the reason why I never married! Unfair to the woman t' have tae live without her mon, years on end. But they were good old days, and I never missed a woman in ma life.'

'I thought it was because you and Grandfather had quarrelled over certain land-contracts and your steamship company in which he claimed joint-stock interests?'

'The quarrel was a simple one. The greatest issues in life have a benign root, so remember that m'boy. Your grandfather wanted a responsible son and heir to take the management of Glengarth upon his ain shoulders. But James was never responsible – in fact, he was downright *irresponsible*! Your noble father craved the exotic life. After he ran away from Glengarth and its responsibilities to marry some Indian princess, your grandfather blamed *me* for filling James's head with nonsense. The quarrel was on account o' that, nothing more, nothing less. James, married to a black woman, his first Maharanee wife or whatever, was more than your fine Hi'land grandfather could stomach!' Hamish went off into an orgy of laughter that ended on a gasp of fright. Blue in the face, he asked Rory to open the window.

'Leave me now, Rory Duncan, and send Mrs Fleming to me. Come back and see me tomorrow ... if I'm still here ...' Hamish drifted off against the stacked pillows, and Rory crept away with a sigh of relief. The old codger was made of strong stuff and wasn't about to give up the ghost just yet!

When Rory returned the following evening to visit Hamish, his uncle had deteriorated. Mrs Fleming had been sitting with the old man, but left the room the moment Rory appeared, her whispered comment on the way out, 'He's much weaker, Mr Rory, but tries bravely to rally every now and then. Don't tire him unnecessarily.'

'I won't.'

Hamish, sensing his presence, presently murmured, 'In the wardrobe ... top shelf, is ma strongbox. It contains ma last will and testament, boy. Fetch it here. Ye'll find the key in the bottom of the tea-caddy.'

Rory got up and went to the wardrobe, found the box Hamish wanted, and the key. He turned the key in the strongbox containing his uncle's last will and testament. Hamish's breathing was shallow and laboured, but he struggled to speak:

'Paper, only *paper*!' Hamish had tears running down his cheeks. 'I *wanted golden sovereigns* which he wouldna part with, even though *gold* was what he got in exchange for his *timber*!' He was weeping openly now, salty bachelor tears for a time misspent and a youth long gone, as well as the opportunities lost, and Rory's own heart was wrenched in those final moments with old Neptune.

But, Rory told himself unsentimentally, Hamish was, and always had been, an emotional man, swinging from highs to lows, and always at a loss to cope with life the moment adversity came.

'Your fine Hi'land grandfather left me with useless *paper*-mony for the rest of ma days! Aye – worthless bonds in Greenock's James Watt Dock that went bust so that the Harbour Trust couldn't even pay back loan interest, let alone redeem any of it's blasted bonds! But now, old Neptune will have the last laugh on him, for the grandson will *pay* for a right royal funeral, from his ain pocket, out o' *paper* mony!'

'Please don't upset yourself, Uncle,' Rory urged, anxious in that moment to take his leave of Hamish, for Lizzie was waiting for him back at the Broomielaw flat. They were both off to London for a few days, as Lizzie had oil-business and banking interests to attend to in the City. Rory had decided to go with her, leaving the management of the shipyard to the real experts. With efficient and reliable office staff supervising passenger and merchandise shipping operations from new offices in the Broomielaw, and the dredging and excavating side from Hamish's old Port Glasgow offices (since modernized and redecorated) Rory felt he could, at last, safely take a much needed break. So Hamish dying at this very inconvenient moment was most thoughtless of him!

'I want a flag o'er ma coffin, Rory Duncan – the Cross o' Saint Andrew, *not* you'er Union Jack rubbish. I want a gun salute as they toss ma body to the waves. I want you an' thy fine Hi'land brother to rot in you'er graves for the sins o' your thieving grandfather. Hamish Blythe-MacDearg, robbed of his dues, his kinfolk, and his boat-yard, by scheming noble Roskillens of Glengarth – pillaging Vikings, no less! Hamish MacDearg will ne'r dwell in a pauper's grave, for the great-nephew, on borrowed mony from that grand American lady he beds, will bury him in style ...'

Rory took up the piece of parchment paper from the bottom of the box, signed by his great-uncle: 'I, Hamish Blythe-MacDearg, bequeath to my nephew, Rory Duncan Roskillen of Glengarth, Ross-shire, all that his noble grandfather bequeathed to me – bugger-all! He may have this useless paper money his grandfather repaid me with, and may he print his arse upon it. Signed by me, Hamish Blythe-MacDearg, on this first day of January, 1906, following a visit from the great-nephew himself. This will supersedes all others I may have unwittingly made at odd times', had been the hasty postscript. The two signatures bearing witness to the will were those of Big Sandy Fergus from Pointhouse, and Elspeth of the Renfrew Arms – a very odd will indeed, Rory couldn't help feeling, until he examined the 'paper-mony'.

Would such a will hold up in a court of law?

Rory didn't know the first thing about Scottish or English law, but he did know that what Hamish had fool-ishly thought of as worthless 'paper money' was not quite as worthless as he had imagined; in fact, their intrinsic value was greater for Hamish would only have gone out and promptly spent his gold sovereigns in the Renfrew Arms!

True enough there were bonds issued by the Greenock Harbour Trust for the ill-fated James Watt Dock that ran into financial disaster a year after its elaborate opening in 1886, but there were other bonds, too. Hamish had lumped them altogether with the useless Greenock issues.

When he sorted through the bonds Hamish had stockpiled for half a century, Rory realized that, somewhere along the line, whether in his dubious dealings over the Middow and Strait site, or for strips of land sold off at random, or for payment of steamship cargoes conveyed on his boats during the early part of the last century, Hamish had managed to acquire gilt-edged securities issued by the Clyde Trust in the opening years of the Trust's foundation.

Oh my God, thought Rory in that wild moment of reckoning, these Clyde Navigation Trust Bonds are worth a *fortune* by today's standards: Hamish has been sitting on a gold-mine all these years, and never knew it!

'Uncle Hamish,' Rory began, and then stopped. He looked to his great-uncle to answer a few more questions. But Hamish, gurgling horribly, had his eyes closed. He couldn't ask the old man any more questions, for it appeared that Dr Grimble was telling the truth after all. The final death rattle was in the old man's throat.

CHAPTER TWENTY-ONE

Annie Gowrie was deeply perturbed. Through the adjoining door between bathroom and master bedroom, while she was drawing the Lady Iona's morning bath, she could hear them quarrelling again.

The laird and his wife had been married two months, and yet the rot had already set in.

Why was it that those who had everything still managed to be so discontented and selfish? Annie asked herself in that turbulent moment.

She came to the conclusion that between God, the Devil and Mankind itself, a situation of contrariness had been deliberately contrived to keep everyone miserable.

But then she herself was guilty of those sins; she, too, was discontented and contrary and wanted more all the time – especially the Laird!

Not true! she told herself, more in the way of knowledge, expression, education and understanding, for *they* were the essential keys to unlock the doors of her humble fishergirl existence to something better. Not that she craved the world of Lady Iona, or wanted to live her totally self-absorbed lifestyle: she would simply hate that! *Liar*! she told herself in the next breath.

Annie was only thankful for all the lessons learned in her meagre existence. First from her own father and mother, then from Minister MacIntyre of the Kirk at Gairloch, who was married to Moira, the laird's cousin. Then from Iain and Shiona Hamilton who had been like second parents to her, teaching her good English, teaching her the ways of a lady, teaching her reading, writing and arithmetic, teaching her anything she wanted to know, until their savage, evil deaths had left her a second time bereft of human comfort, logic, and faith, without anchor, without purpose, yet with so many questions seeking a plausible answer. And, above all, lessons from the laird himself, the young boy who had come riding into her life from a time past, and who continued to haunt her even though he had grown to manhood and she to womanhood.

Irreconcilable lives, Annie told herself often and often enough, and yet she could not help thinking about him constantly. He was part of her wanting, leaving her taut with the knowledge of better things.

She knew, yes she *knew* how much of a lost soul was the Laird Lindsay, just like herself.

But why?

Annie didn't *know* why, she couldn't begin to imagine why or why not: she merely accepted, even while she had a feeling within herself that although he loved his wife, all was still not right with him. She hated to see him made so unhappy by the Lady Iona and her stubborn, selfish ways.

Take the flower and the bee, dependent upon each other for survival yet separate in a dignified relationship with neither bee nor flower *owning* each other – why couldn't marriage be like that? Annie mused to herself. That's what she would want from her marriage – that is, if anyone ever wanted to marry her! Innocence destroyed, a wilderness of dark pain and evil still surrounding her, it was hard to forget all that had been done to her at the hands of man she likened to the Devil himself.

The aching gap in her life could only be filled by one person, yet that, too, was an impossible dream.

Annie couldn't really blame *him*, the laird! She maintained her partisan loyalty. She couldn't blame him, because, in her heart of hearts, she knew that she loved him as she loved no other person in the world. He *was* her world, and the two years he had spent abroad recently, had been like a living hell for her. The Laird Lindsay encompassed her future as he had encompassed her past, ever since she had been an eight-year-old girl gutting fish on the doorstep of her parents' humble cot shortly after her mother, still suffering from a broken heart and not right in the head after her husband, Donald Gowrie, had perished in a storm at sea, had taken up with the monster from Raasay.

And even though the Laird Lindsay was now married to the beautiful Lady Iona from Edinburgh, Annie could bear it, for at least she was able to see him every day, and know that once more Glengarth held him fast.

But he, unused to living in close proximity with a woman of capricious ways, didn't know how to handle his rich, indulged wife.

Amid all the feverish activity going on everywhere, she had decided to go to Paris to view the Worth Autumn Collection. 'But you *can't* Iona!'

Annie could hear the laird's deep rich accents from the other side of the door, while, afraid to intrude upon their quarrel, she lingered in the sweet-scented steamy atmosphere of the Lady Iona's bathroom.

'You simply *can't* leave me in this turmoil with all the builders and decorators and upholsterers everywhere. It simply isn't fair when I'm up to my ears trying to put the estate back on its feet.'

'Please don't be so *possessive*, Lindsay! I'm not used to being owned by anyone.'

'I'm not *anyone*, Iona, I'm your husband!'

'You're my *gaoler*!'

Women were unpredictable creatures; Annie had heard it said often. Did the laird know how unpredictable his wife could be before he had married her? Theirs had been a stormy relationship right from the word go; everyone at Glengarth had been aware of it the moment the Lady Iona had stepped over the threshold. Was the laird so blinded by her beauty he couldn't see, didn't *want* to see what he had married in such haste?

Annie listened to their quarrel and wasn't one bit ashamed of herself.

There was a short sharp silence. And then the laird's clipped tones again. 'Very well, if that's your wish, *go* to Paris. After all, it's *your* inheritance propping up Glengarth. I can't begrudge you a holiday in Paris on your own money.'

'I don't begrudge the money, Lindsay. It's *you* who feels

the pinch in your pride, not I!'

Annie heard the bedroom door slam behind him as he left his wife's presence.

Annie ventured out of the bathroom. 'The bath is ready, m'lady.'

'Thank you, Annie.'

But Iona made no attempt to get out of bed. Her breakfast tray discarded on the quilted counterpane, she indolently flicked over the pages of the fashion magazine, *Bon Ton*, temper evident in the heightened colour of her cheeks.

The Lady Iona's lack of consideration regarding everyone and everything, made Annie inwardly boil. Well! Let her bath get cold, Annie thought furiously to herself, and serve her right! She had no intention of carrying up any more buckets of hot water from the kitchen, a back-breaking task to say the least! Annie grabbed up the breakfast tray, and made her way to the door, heading down to the kitchen quarters, without another glance at the lady still abed, though it was eleven o'clock in the morning!

The disharmony between the laird and his wife was soon forgottèn when word reached Annie that her stepfather, Fletcher, had been seen on Eriskay.

Tom Drummond, the laird's groom, brought her the news. It gave Annie a nasty jolt. After so many years, the last few spent in the conviction that the wild man of Raasay had perished in the fire he had started, which had consumed so much of her life as well as the Laird of Glengarth's, brought back to Annie all the anguish, the pain, and the recriminations she had borne on that dreadful night.

Annie wondered if she ought to tell the laird about Fletcher's return.

Then she thought better of it. The Laird Lindsay had enough to think about at the moment. Annie cautioned Tom Drummond to say nothing to the laird, either.

A few days later, while Annie was brushing out her mistress's glorious hair, the laird arrived on the threshold

of his wife's bedroom. Tomorrow, the Lady Iona intended
leaving for Paris, so Annie knew very well why the Laird
Lindsay had presented himself on his wife's doorstep this
night.

She put down the hairbrush and, bobbing a token
curtsy, made haste to leave the room.

'Don't go, Annie!' Iona grabbed Annie's wrist, forcing
her to stay.

'Please leave us, Annie,' the laird said, in that cold,
detached voice Annie and everyone else took as a warning
sign that the laird was displeased and angry.

'I want her to stay,' Iona insisted. 'She hasn't finished
attending to me.'

Annie looked from one to the other in bewilderment.
She was upset and embarrassed by their behaviour – just
like a couple of spoilt children. 'Excuse me, m'lady,
m'laird,' she said hurriedly as she brushed past the laird
standing in his dressing-gown in the doorway. She left
them both to fight it out without her standing there as
umpire.

'I thought you loved me,' Lindsay said to Iona, the
bedroom door wide open.

'Lindsay, of course I do!'

'Then your notions of love aren't mine. I want to know
your reasons for repugnance concerning our marriage
vows.'

'Oh, don't start that all over again, Lindsay! I *told* you
why! You must give me time.'

'How much time? We've been married *seven weeks*! Yet
you still avoid me as though I had the plague.'

She shrugged, her manner as brittle and cold as the
Arctic winds from the north, communicating itself to him
in a horrible way. 'Your obsession with siring an heir for
Glengarth is indecent, Lindsay. I told you, I *don't want*
any children just yet.'

'I understand that, and respect your wishes. What I
can't understand is your coldness towards me every time I
approach you. Not even five minutes in bed do I get with
you! A few chaste kisses, and then Goodnight Lindsay!
Our disastrous honeymoon I was prepared to accept

because it was a great transition for both of us so soon after your brother's death and the tragedy of Glengarth. What I'm not prepared to accept is your shirking of your marriage vows two months later!'

'I'm shirking nothing, Lindsay! I've thrown myself wholeheartedly into your schemes concerning Glengarth – out of my own pocket, incidentally. Do I complain of your impoverished circumstances? No! I help you where I am able financially. So I'll thank you not to harass me until I'm *ready* to bear your heirs!'

He looked at her sadly. 'Iona, you don't *really* love me, do you?'

'I do, Lindsay, very much. I respect you, and hope you respect me, too. I think we have a very stable and compatible marriage – which is only spoilt by your hasty desire concerning that undignified business of ... of having babies! I don't like children. I've never had anything to do with them, and I don't get on at all well with them. I just *know* that a baby right now would be the worst possible thing for me.'

'Isn't that what marriage is all about, having children? There's nothing undignified about it at all, only your attitude.'

'At the moment I'm not ready to cope with a family – I can hardly cope with *you* if the truth were known. I'm sorry, Lindsay, but at times you're more like a child than a grown man in the wanting of your own way all the time. I'm not used to that. Besides, having a baby would ruin my figure. I would be quite unable to wear any of Monsieur Worth's wonderful and excruciatingly expensive clothes for the new season.'

At a loss for a suitable answer, he endeavoured to keep a cool head. Lindsay took out his cigarette case from his dressing-gown pocket.

'Please don't smoke in my bedroom, Lindsay, it upsets me.'

'You had no objection to my smoking the night we met at Lady Conningbide's.'

Until that moment he had been unaware that Iona was possessed of a fiendish temper. With one irate sweep of her arms she cleared all the scent bottles and silver trinkets off her dressing-table. Crystal splinters and expensive liquids stained the bedroom carpet. '*Annie*!' She screamed, '*Annie Gowrie*! Come here at once and clear up this mess!'

Lindsay stared at Iona, as shattered by her behaviour as her scent bottles smashed to smithereens on the floor. Iona swivelled on her stool and regarded him contemptuously. 'Get out of here, Lindsay. Go beget your heirs somewhere else if you wish to act like an animal, but leave me *alone*!'

He turned his back on her and without another word walked out of her presence.

Annie, who had been going through the pretence of sorting linen in the airing cupboard along the corridor, was suddenly ashamed of herself for eavesdropping so blatantly.

Hurriedly tossing aside the sheets and pillow cases she had been putting into the airing cupboard after ironing, Annie went in to the bedroom to clear up the mess of broken glass and spilt scent, her hands itching instead to slap the Lady Iona in order to bring her to her senses.

To Lindsay's everlasting astonishment, the following morning Iona was breakfasting in the dining-hall even before he had a chance to come to terms with the evening before.

Iona usually breakfasted in bed and eventually managed to see the light of day round about lunch-time. His habit was to breakfast alone in the solitude and peace of six in the morning, then ride through the plantations before facing the day, head on, in the estate office – round about eight o'clock.

He was therefore surprised and delighted to see Iona in a black velvet riding habit piped in green, a smart little emerald toque with a feather perched on her Titian hair, sipping coffee at the long table the morning after the night before.

'Hello,' he greeted her warily, 'this *is* a pleasant surprise.'

'Good morning, Lindsay. I'm sorry about last night.'

He almost dropped the coffee-pot as he turned to face her. 'No need to apologize. My fault entirely.' He concentrated on not spilling any more coffee on the sideboard and took his place at the long refectory table, with the distinct feeling that this was what it must be like to be placed end to end with Iona in the family tomb.

'May I accompany you this morning, Lindsay?' Iona asked, not looking at him at all, but at the portraits of his ancestors lining the walls of the baronial hall where they ate and lived and entertained, and were overshadowed by a feudal past. Iona hated Glengarth, and only Annie Gowrie knew how much!

'Of course.' His answer was a hollow, echoey reminder of the uncharted distance between them.

'The horses are saddled and ready.'

'Good Lord! Don't tell me you managed to wake lazy Tom from his bed at this ungodly hour of the morning?' Lindsay did not know why it was such hard going between Iona and himself, but the atmosphere could be cut with a knife.

'I saddled them myself. Even a good hearty kick in the rump couldn't move the Drummond wretch.'

'That's my Tom!' Lindsay smiled at Iona over the rim of his coffee cup. 'You look nice this morning. I like the hat.'

'Thank you, Lindsay.' She scraped back her chair, picked up her riding-gloves beside her plate, and tugged them on. 'Well, come on, husband, *if* you're coming.'

He gulped down coffee dregs and followed Iona outside to the courtyard.

A thin, misty drizzle obscured the glen. They clattered across the wooden drawbridge and under the moathouse. Lindsay only hoped that Mr Mitchell in residence, presumably still asleep above them, would not be awakened by such early perambulations on horseback.

He and Iona took the stony path up to the rocky promontory overlooking the formidable Minch. By the time they reached the headland, the sun was creeping into the heavens. Over the Western sea, mist and water parted in golden rays to reveal a flotilla of ships creeping almost furtively northwards, hugging the coastline. It was like an incomplete stage-set, stage-curtains drawn away before time to give the audience a feeling of insecurity and restlessness; Lindsay felt as though he were peeking at something forbidden.

'That's not the fishing-fleet, surely?' Iona asked.

Something about the camouflaged convoy was sinister and perturbing.

Lindsay said thoughtfully, 'Battleships of the dreadnought type'.

'Dreadnoughts?' Iona hunched her shoulders against the coldness that suddenly enveloped her.

'Yes. I expect they're on their way back to Scapa Flow after practice manoeuvres in the North Sea: All show, to scare off the Kaiser.'

'Dreadnoughts! What a terrible-sounding word. Then you don't think Germany *will* actually declare war on us, Lindsay?'

'I don't know ... you're shivering,' Lindsay said, wheeling away from the sombre spectacle of warships. 'Come on, let's warm up, I'll race you down the glen.'

Iona was gone, a challenge like that irresistible.

Watching Iona galloping down to the loch shore in a superb display of horsemanship, Lindsay thought he had never seen anyone ride as Iona could ride.

'Lindsay,' Iona laughingly called back over her shoulder, the bitter sweet air, so chilling it made ice-cream of her breath, 'let's go across to the cottage and get Annie to cook us a real Highland breakfast. Murray's coffee always gives me dyspepsia. I want to try, for a change, real oatmeal porridge, Aberdeen toast, Scotch marmalade, all washed down with real Highland bitters.'

'Iona, don't insult Annie. You'll find none of that in her cot.'

'Oh, you've been there before, have you?'

'Yes. Yes, I have. I'm her landlord, remember?'

'Then don't sound so defensive every time the name of Annie Gowrie is mentioned! If I had a nasty turn of mind, I'd almost think you and she had something going between you. You haven't have you?'

'Don't be ridiculous!'

'All right, subject changed. Why is it called Rill?'

'I don't know ... maybe it's short for rillet meaning something sliced off, chopped up, potted meat, that sort of thing.'

'Rillets of potted or minced ham!' She laughed merrily again, the colour in her cheeks enhancing the sparkle in her sapphire eyes, the feather in her toque waving defiantly as she tried to wheel away from him. 'An educated guess, Lindsay, but not quite right,' she told him. 'A rill is Gaelic for a stream or trench. I've done my homework, you see, via Julian Mitchell who mentioned it in the first place.'

'That's what I said – Gaelic as well as English for stream or trench, from the German word "*rille*" if my memory serves me correctly' He stopped teasing and came abreast of her and reaching over grabbed the reins of her horse. '*Stop*! I haven't time to waste, Madam, and I certainly have no wish to breakfast with Annie Gowrie and her porridge. I have to be in the estate office by eight o'clock sharp!'

'I've never been inside a crofter's or fisherman's cot, Lindsay, so don't spoil my fun! I want to see how the other half lives – and dies. They're so small to look at, just like doll's houses. Can human beings really dwell inside such insufferable places?'

'Iona, please don't insult Annie! She's very proud of her cottage.'

'Why *Lindsay*! What makes you think that I'm insulting Annie?' In the saddle, perfectly poised, Iona turned to him with some amusement.

'Iona, I've been inside one of those places,' he said abruptly, 'and I assure you, it's nothing to lose sleep over. And neither do I want to breakfast there, thank you very much. Come on,' he jerked his head to indicate the path he wished her to take. 'Let's ride over to the Lower Compartment to see how my new trees are faring. Mr Mitchell is a wizard where forestry and tree-management is concerned – not to mention Gaelic stories!'

'The new saplings can't be more than a foot high! You

only planted them a month ago. You're obsessed with regrowth Lindsay, not only in the wood but also in the womb! I think I know why you don't want to go across to Rill. It's all to do with Annie Gowrie's step-father, isn't it? He was the one who set fire to Forest Lodge, isn't he?'

'Iona, I have no wish to talk about it, please.' They rode in silence for a little while and up near Stag's Meadow Lindsay asked her more cheerily, 'So tell me, what kind of outfit are you thinking of buying from Mr Worth?'

'None. I've changed my mind. I'm not going to Paris now.'

He looked at her in surprise. 'Oh? Bad dreams last night concerning his styles and prices?'

'Something like that. If there's going to be a war, Lindsay, I'd rather be safe at home, not stuck in Paris which is too close to the Kaiser for my liking. Last year, while I was travelling through Europe with Robert and Rosemary, we saw the way Germany was forging ahead with her railway systems. What with their new German Navy Law, Robert said then, that it looked very much as though Germany was mobilizing for a war.'

Lindsay didn't know how to answer. He, too, in the two years he had spent abroad, had seen, heard and read about Germany's programme of mobilization, her tentacles reaching out as far as the Baltic coast. 'It's possible,' he said, 'but not very likely. Haldane's off to Berlin on a Peace Mission, so I think it's safe to say for the moment that the Kaiser's only breathing hot air over everyone.'

'Let's hope so.'

They changed the subject and dashed off up the glen, taking the long way back to the castle. As they clattered once more beneath the gatehouse and Mr Mitchell's bachelor residence, Iona turned to Lindsay and said, 'Mr Mitchell tells me that Major Pemberton-Fookes over at Inverdune has a superb stallion for sale.'

'Have you seen it?'

'Yes, as a matter of fact I have. I want it, Lindsay.'

The short sharp pain in his breast was nothing to do with Iona and her wants he told himself. 'When did you go over to Pemberton-Fookes's place?'

'Last week.'

'Without telling me?'

'You were too busy on the estate.'

'I'd have found time to ride over with you.'

'Oh, it wasn't necessary for you to come. Julian accompanied me. He knows all about racing stock.'

'Julian?'

'Mr Mitchell.'

He didn't know why, but the way Iona had said it, as though she were covering up more besides, made Lindsay tighten his grip on the reins, at the same time trying to keep a grip on his emotions. Deceit in any shape and form he loathed, and to know that his own wife had gone behind his back to make underhand deals with lecherous old Pemberton-Fookes whom he utterly detested, made Lindsay feel somehow betrayed by Iona. 'Whose idea was all this, going over to Inverdune to inspect a racehorse?'

'Mine of course.'

'Why didn't you come and ask me for my opinion?'

'I told you – you were busy.'

'And Mitchell wasn't? I pay him to run my estate for me, not run after my wife!'

'Lindsay! For heaven's sake,' she said half-laughing, half-annoyed, 'there was nothing in it. We simply rode over to Inverdune together to look at a superb horse I wish to buy.'

'Get down!'

'What?'

He dismounted and went to her side. 'Get down! Upstairs, Iona, *now!*' He dragged her off her horse, Karneval – a perfectly good animal; he could see no need of another one – and hustled her unceremoniously towards the castle entrance.

'For heaven's sake, Lindsay,' Iona said through gritted teeth, as smiling, she tried to keep control of her own temper. 'There are servants watching us.'

'I don't care. Upstairs, Iona, I want to ask you a few questions – about Julian!'

'Lindsay, I . . .'

'And don't "Lindsay" me any more!' he said curtly,

something inside him snapping as he shoved her inside the master bedroom. Nights spent sleeping apart from her were beginning to catch up with him. He wanted her as never before, her persistent denial of sexual relations with him, destroying him through sheer frustration, loss of ego and loss of patience. She had no right to do this to him!

After slamming and bolting the bedroom door, he took her by the shoulders and shook her so hard, her teeth rattled in her pretty head, not to mention the feather atop. 'Don't you *ever* try those underhand tricks on me again, Iona. Anything you want from me, you come out with it straight, do you understand? *Do you?*' He shook her again, harder than ever.

Iona gave a frightened little jerk of the head.

'I want no more of your sly ways and I won't have you wheedling favours from me or anyone else – and that includes *Julian!* I simply don't understand you. Before our marriage you gave me the impression of being a sensuous, hot-blooded woman, yet, as soon as the wedding ring was on your finger, you turned as frigid as a leg of lamb in a cold store! Neither do I want your second-hand attention any more ...'

'Lindsay, I ...'

'Shut up!' He pushed her down on the bed.

'What are you going to do?' she asked nervously when he started to unbutton her damp riding jacket.

'Just this ...' One hand on her breast, he drew her head to his lips and crushed her in a kiss that left her gasping. 'I'm making you an offer, Iona ... I don't want a beautiful live-in companion any more, to admire from her distance but never to touch. So if you co-operate with me, I'll treat you like a lady, if not, I shan't spare your finer feelings, my dear. Now, either way, I mean to have you as my wife. I believe your price is one thoroughbred Arab Stallion.'

He never stopped to think whether or not a husband could be accused of raping his own wife. And the ludicrous thing about it all was that Lindsay got the distinct impression Iona had been building up to this rough kind of treatment all along. For some reason she wanted to fight him in the retention of her virginity, but was not at all dismayed to lose it the moment he got passionately angry with her. Had her denial of him been her way of punishing him for having snubbed her at Lady Conningbide's, a woman scorned?

Their long overdue love-making and the consummation of their marriage at last concluded, Lindsay smoked a cigarette in satisfaction and without her objection. 'Iona, promise me one thing.'

'What?'

'You won't ever wear black again. Any colour, please, except black. I won't even mind you wearing bright red.'

'Bright red with my colouring? You're crazy, m'laird!'

When he'd smoked his cigarette, he took her again, but this time at a more leisurely pace. When she kissed the mole at the corner of his top lip, which was hidden beneath his manly moustache, Iona, a sparkle in her eyes as she continued to massage his chest, murmured, 'What a strange, *strange* man you are, Lindsay Roskillen, and what a fool I've been, m'laird! I'm, oh, so glad I changed my mind about Paris,' she sighed in contentment. '... If you want to come back tonight to keep me company, I shall raise no objection.'

The marriage bargain had been struck in the market place, was his rueful conclusion.

CHAPTER TWENTY-TWO

Welshmen by the name of David seemed to haunt him at every turn: David *ap Leicestershire Morning Chronicle* still hounded Leonora, and David Lloyd George had just presented his budget to the nation. He had driven out opposition ministers Balfour and Lansdown to side with the Lord's rejection of the budget as a whole. The tricky problem of the Irish Home Rule question had been the deciding factor, so that the Prime Minister had been forced to go to Sandringham to inform the King of the unresolved Commons versus Lords crisis: Parliament was expected to be dissolved in the very near future.

Rory sighed, and reached for the glass of malt on the table beside him. Smug in his new-found security, at last he was free to indulge his hedonistic habits to his heart's delight! And all under my 'ane steam' Aunt Ada! Rory smiled to himself.

He turned the page and read that the Metropolitan Police had been sent to enforce law and order at Welsh pit-heads. Germany had embarked on a formidable armaments programme, the Kaiser kicking his cousin George in the teeth since his uncle, Edward the Peacemaker, had been laid to rest. The New German Navy Law had panicked everyone to retaliate, with cries loud and vociferous from the front benches to get British shipyards busy again. It looked as though war with Germany was imminent. Bad news abounded everywhere on this day of November 18th, he reflected morosely.

The question of National Military Service he regarded with scepticism. Acts of violence perpetrated by the Womens' Suffragette Movement made him not exactly angry, but uneasy. He sighed again, glanced at his watch and despaired that it was only mid-afternoon. Time crawled by in Park Lane. In his shipyard at Renfrew, time flew by on silver wings, more so since he had received an order for two submarines to meet the German threat looming on Britain's Naval horizon.

To break up the monotony of his London interlude, he had arranged to take Lizzie to the opera that night. Afterwards, they were going to Pagani's with some of her rich American friends.

Rory finished his drink, took a long leisurely bath and it was while he was dressing to go out, that his sister Christabel, who was also staying at the Town House, knocked on his bedroom door and shattered his entire evening.

'Rory, there's a woman downstairs asking for you. She wouldn't tell me anything other than that it was important.'

Wondering what was afoot, he ran downstairs, half-dressed. A very dishevelled young woman, her face bruised and dirty, her clothes torn and dusty, nervously fingered a green and white badge pinned to her lapel. Rory had never seen her before, but she knew his name.

'Mr Rory Roskillen?'

'Yes.' He felt uneasy. 'What can I do for you, Miss ... er?'

'Florence ... Florence Terry.'

'Miss Terry.'

'I'm sorry to trouble you, Mr Roskillen, but a friend of mine asked me to get in touch with you. You see, there was a lot of fighting today and ...'

'What fighting?'

'Between the Suffragettes and the Police.'

'What has this got to do with me?'

'A great many poor women have been badly hurt. That's why you must come at once. Miss Burrett needs you.'

'Miss Burrett?' He knew he was sounding like a caveman's echo, but all at once he was unable to cope with a situation that had become one of feminine issues beyond his comprehension.

'Jane Burrett – your cousin.'

'Oh yes ... she is my cousin. What of her?'

'Well, Jane was with us. She had to leave us because she's helping to organize a deputation to the House of

Commons after what happened today. But it's really to do with Leonora ... she's in a cab parked around the corner. She's hurt I'm afraid ...'

Rory stared at the young woman, a funny feeling settling around his heart.

He did not recall, until a long time afterwards, that he had dashed out of the house, his shirt-cuffs dangling ludicrously around his wrists. Fresh from his bath, his hair damp, the whisky slowing down all his reactions, he couldn't help wondering why he had come to London in the first place and not stayed put in Scotland where he felt infinitely safer.

'I hope you don't mind, but Jane told me to bring her sister here where Leonora would receive private medical attention, rather than take her to the local charity hospital ... the cab-driver hasn't been too helpful as he knows we're Suffragettes. The road is chocker-block as everyone is rallying in Hyde Park, so he stopped around the corner.'

'Everyone?' He wasn't really listening to Miss Florence Terry.

'Suffragettes.'

The shock of seeing Leonora bloodied, beaten, torn and trampled upon, filled him with a terrible anger against the Womens' Suffragette Movement.

Yet anger destroys; he had learned that much. He gathered her up in his arms, and then instructed the cabman to drive to Lindsay's house, never mind the mass of people in the street, or the blood staining his white shirt as it stained Leonora's white dress.

He held her close. He held her like a lover. Her hair had become unpinned during the fight on the streets. He demanded of her, 'Why, oh, *why*, did you start this all over again? I thought you'd learned your lesson in Winson Green Prison, Lennie!' But Lennie was unconscious. He knew he would not have been able to meet the challenge had she been able to respond.

The doctor was sent for as soon as Leonora was placed in bed in one of the guest rooms in the Town House. Rory telephoned Uncle Austen and Aunt Ada at Breedon Hall. They said they would drive down at once. Afterwards, while the doctor was upstairs with Leonora, he and Christabel listened to Miss Terry's story.

'Jane and I share lodgings in Camberwell. We both work full time for the WSPU. Last evening, Leonora turned up on our doorstep saying she wanted to join the Suffragette Movement as a full-time active member. She had been staying with Lady Daisy Tapstock in Sloane Square, and was due to return home to Breedon Hall. Then she told us she had postponed her departure for a few more days as she wanted to see Jane. Jane was going to inform her parents of her sister's whereabouts first thing this morning. But before she could get in touch with them, we were instructed to try and get a petition through to Parliament – it was important, you see. Leonora accompanied us ... and then it all started to happen. We had no idea that our peaceful deputation would have such a horrendous outcome. They said that the violence started with men from the East End who were against the Women's Movement, and who had been bribed to start a fight with us. Then the Police were drawn in and everything got out of hand. We were kicked and pushed and hit with staves, and Leonora was thrown to the ground and trampled on by those horrible men in their hob-nail boots ... Jane and I managed to pull her away and into a shop-doorway. Then we got a cab and Jane told me to bring her sister here. She said you'd know what to do. She said it was best Leonora wasn't taken back to our flat in Camberwell because of Lord and Lady Burrett's views regarding the WSPU.'

Rory didn't know what to say.

Christabel, at length said, 'How I wish I'd let Uncle Austen and Aunt Ada know of their daughter's intention. Her involvement in all this might have been averted. She's not strong enough to withstand physical violence at the hands of those East End brutes!'

Rory looked at his sister in alarm, 'What do you mean?'

'Leonora telephoned me the night before last, about ... about going to Jane's flat. Jane didn't want to lodge here any more. She regarded this Town House as another "family trap". She decided to live out – in Camberwell lodgings, if you must know. She takes women's suffrage very seriously – as we all do. I told Cousin Leonora to think carefully about what she was doing, but she insisted she wanted to join the rank and file . . .'

'Join the rank and file? Christabel, what are you talking about?'

'WSPU . . . it means freedom for all women and a fight to the death. Leonora has pledged herself to the cause. She went with her sister Jane on the East End march, and got hurt as a result. The working classes know no bounds, Rory. They saw us as a threat – we, the privileged few against poverty, against discrimination, against white women's slavery! East End men saw it as a threat to their male supremacy, their manhood, their masculine survival! They wanted to retain their hold upon their wives, their daughters, their mothers, their aunts – *all* womanhood. They want to hurt *us*, The Suffragette Movement, for threatening *them*!'

He found it difficult to maintain a level tone. 'I see. Does your Women's Movement stop at murder? I don't think so. I think you and the rest of your mob are totally irresponsible! Go on! Go chain yourselves to park railings, hurl stones through shop windows and at Prime Ministers. Set alight to post-boxes or fight with the police. *Damn* you, Christabel!'

Rory slammed out of her sight just as the doctor and Mrs Roberts, the housekeeper acting as chaperone, descended the stairs.

'She'll be all right! Scratches, bruises, concussion and a couple of broken ribs, nothing too terrible. I've given her a sedative. She'll be as right as rain tomorrow. Call me if you're at all worried about her. Good night.'

Dr Swinburne took his coat and hat and was away in his evening dress, more intent upon his dinner-party or wherever else he was despatching himself that evening. In that moment, Rory could have hauled Giles Swinburne back, for his total disregard of Leonora's condition.

As soon as the front door had shut behind the rapidly receding figure of the doctor, Rory turned to Christabel. 'The moment Uncle Austen and Aunt Ada get here. I'm

off! You're nothing but a two-faced bitch, Christabel!
Pretending you have at heart Lennie's welfare, or that of
Kitty, Daisy or Jane, when all along you've been indoctrin-
ating them with your evil propaganda. Women like you
and Christabel Pankhurst don't need the vote, you need
locking up! I'm going upstairs to sit with Lennie until her
parents arrive to take her home. I wish to God I hadn't
invited myself to stay, then *you* might have been in *her*
shoes in Parliament Square instead of turning your Janus
face to me by offering me tea and sympathy! You always
were two-faced, and I pity Lindsay for having had to put
up with you all these years!'

He ran upstairs, away from her, but she pursued him
relentlessly.

'Rory, none of us knew this would happen!'

'For God's sake, Christabel, do people have to get
injured or *die* before this madness stops?'

'Yes, Rory, it's a fight to the death.'

He didn't bother to reply.

Sitting beside Leonora's bed, Rory scribbled a hasty
note to Lizzie Roebling Chanin, apologizing for his non-
appearance at Stravinsky's, *Le Sacre du Printemps* that
evening at Covent Garden Opera House. He gave it to a
messenger boy to deliver to Lizzie's Mayfair residence,
with the rebellious feeling in him that fate was always at
his throat no matter how hard he struggled against the odds.

A few days later Lizzie found time to travel back with him
to Scotland.

'Hon,' she said, when they let themselves into their
mansion on Buchanan Street, the grand house being their
latest acquisition, 'I'm sure as hell getting precious little
work done these days. Never mind ...' she kicked off her
shoes and ran laughing up the stairs without caring if the
housekeeper in the attic heard her, '*encore, encore, pronto,
pronto* ... I can't wait: oh, and bring the champagne with
you, Rory hon!'

The lifestyle he and Lizzie were living was exhausting to
say the least. Indulging in more play than work, he had a
lot of catching up to do as far as the business side of things

was concerned. He found it hard to concentrate when Lizzie offered so many other diversions.

When the telephone by the bedside rang late one afternoon, he was once more in bed with Lizzie, the champagne in free flow. Rory picked up the receiver.

'Kitty,' Rory said, sounding as though he had a sore throat, feeling as though his eyes were stuck to the ceiling. 'Where are you?'

'Have you been drinking?' were her first critical words.

'No, I have *not* been drinking!' he replied dishonestly. 'I've been working!'

'Rory, I'm at Breedon Hall ...'

'Breedon Hall? Why? Have you left Tobias? Have you and he quarrelled? Is that why you've returned to Breedon Hall?'

'I rang your office in the Broomielaw, then Christabel at the Town House, then your Club. One of your old cronies ... Smyrna, I think he said his name was, gave me this number. I didn't know you had moved from your lodging rooms in the Broomielaw, Rory. You could at least have tol ...'

'Kitty, darling, can we have this conversation tomorrow?' he pleaded.

'Rory, this is serious. I think you ought to come at once. Lennie is asking for you.'

'Ask ... *Lennie*? Kitty, talk sense, will you!'

'Leonora is *dying*! She wants to see you.'

'She's dying to see me?'

'Rory,' Kitty sounded as though she was having difficulty holding back the tears. Leonora, *our beloved cousin*, is dying of a lung disease. These are her last moments on earth. She didn't want you to know that she had a terminal illness. But now she is asking for you. Rory, for once in your life *do* something will you, that isn't completely selfish!' Kitty had started to cry.

He stared into the mouthpiece of the receiver. Then he hung up.

He could not wake Lizzie who had had too much champagne, so he left a note on the pillow, explaining his hasty departure.

There was no car to meet him at Leicester. He hitched a lift on the early morning milk-cart, among the shining aluminium churns. Hardrace took his coat and scarf and his hastily packed travel-bag. The first two people he saw lurking behind the rood-screen in the hall were Humphrey and Charis. 'What's wrong with Lennie? What's going on, Hump?' Rory, bewildered asked his cousin.

Humphrey was unable to speak. Charis gave him the answer. 'Leonora died half an hour ago, Rory.'

A fist to the jaw, straight to the point and brutal: a kind of dying deep within himself, Rory left the house.

He went up to Folly's Point to be alone. Folly's Point, a lonely rich eccentric's stone monolith pointing the way to the stars with the honest-to-God inscription, 'There but for the grace of God go I.' Folly's Point represented his adolescent years, his growing up, his re-participation with the human race after his mother's death when he was adopted by his dear old Uncle Austen into his family. Folly's Point rising out of the great Charnwood Forest, had been his 'running away' place, to play his harmonica in peace and privacy ...

Among the ghosts of Charnwood, hours later, someone disturbed him, just like a time before: 'Rory, don't sit here any more, you're frozen!' Charis put her cape around his shoulders.

'Why did she die, Charis, *why*?' he demanded to know. 'Nobody told me she was going to die ... nobody told me ...' He sobbed into his hands, 'I loved her – more than cousins *should* love, I suppose.'

'I know that.'

'What else, Charis, what else should I know?'

'Rory, Lennie had tuberculosis. Something not you, nor I, nor God himself can cure. There was nothing anyone could do to save her life. She was a very sick young woman ...'

'Don't say that! Don't say it! Don't say that she's dead ... please don't say it ... God! Why did she rejoin the Women's Movement, why?' He raised his tear-stained face to the stars, demanding the answers.

'It was nothing to do with Black Friday, or the

Suffragettes you seek to blame, or anyone else, Rory. Don't apportion blame. Leonora would have died in any case.'

'Don't say it, Charis!' He shook his head, eyes closed, the breath in him painful to breathe. He was unable to accept God's decree. 'I loved her – more than a sister. Beyond myself even.'

'Rory, you'll come to love someone else beyond yourself, one day soon. Love changes as we ourselves grow.'

'NO! Love is *constant*!'

'The trouble with you is you won't accept! You won't accept that life is here today and gone tomorrow. You won't accept that it is a fleeting thing, like mist on water. You always want to make it so hard and tangible and there to be imprisoned! Don't do it, Rory! Love changes. The terrible thing about love is that it changes everything – our attitudes, our wants, our innermost selves the longer we live and the older in experience we grow. Life changed for me at Spion Kop. It will change for you. One day you will find another girl in your life: not another Leonora perhaps, but a woman who will take you a step forward in finding yourself again.'

They stayed there, holding hands like little children, while the bleak morning set its resolute face towards another day.

CHAPTER TWENTY-THREE

Lindsay was disappointed when, on a specially arranged trip to Glasgow, he arrived at the offices of the Chanin-Beauly Steamship Company in the Broomielaw, only to be told that Rory was in America.

He took in his surroundings. The thickly carpeted, mahogany-panelled, spacious premises in which he found himself, radiated that quiet efficiency, and plush ambience of a prosperous business. Rory had indeed done well for himself, was Lindsay's jealous thought just then. But Brother Rory always did have an eye to the main chance. He had heard from Angus MacPhee as to his brother's movements: first from humble fireman; then to gaining his Pilot's licence for Mersey and Clyde navigation; then the purchase of an old steamboat; followed by more steamships. How? A picture on the wall was of a luxury transatlantic liner, the *Devanna* painted in the Chanin-Beauly colours, their flag a wheatsheaf in a double circle of herringbone-stitch, depicting strength, resolution and prosperity. Now he had heard he was building submarines! How could he have got so far so quickly?

'Do you know when he will be back?' Lindsay asked the efficient-looking, middle-aged secretary behind her pince-nez and stenographer's notebook.

'He didn't specify, sir. But if it's important, Mr John will see you. He's General Manager. Your name, sir?' The pencil hovered over the pad.

'Oh, er ... it doesn't matter. I wanted to speak to Mr Roskillen personally. Good day, Miss ... er ...'

'Crawford.'

'Good day, Miss Crawford.'

Lindsay left the Broomielaw in rather more haste than he had entered, leaving behind a perplexed Miss

Crawford. 'Who was that?' Mr John asked, creeping out of his office as soon as the visitor had departed. Mr John liked to keep a low profile: an Office Manager must maintain his dignity in order that the office staff respect him at all times; especially when the MD and Chairman were overseas.

Mr John would never have admitted, even to himself, that he was afraid of confrontations and that's why he left Miss Crawford to do the dirty work.

Shrugging her shoulders she said, 'He didn't leave his card. But I'll stake my reputation, that it was Mr Rory's brother, for they're alike as two peas in a pod!'

'Wonder what he wanted,' said Mr John thoughtfully, 'unless he's come here personally to dispute the Renfrew site and boatyard which Mr Rory was left by an uncle of his. Shady dealings there, somewhere along the line, for there's no clear contract on *who* owns that site according to rumour.'

'Hurumph!' Miss Crawford cleared her throat and said briskly, 'Well, that's none of our business, Mr John, it's for the Company's solicitors to sort out. Now, about those stabilizing bilge keels and triple-expansion engines to be fitted in Mr Rory's new ship, can you sort out a date of delivery with the manufacturers who dither about between us and our rivals? We cannot let the Allan Line beat us in the launching of *their* new ship!'

'No indeed, Miss Crawford,' replied Mr John, who was as hen-pecked at work as he was at home. But he never was any good at sticking up for himself where bossy women were concerned. Begrudgingly he recognized the fact that the office would not function so smoothly were it not for Maud Crawford who flew the flag during the boss's absence overseas.

'Oh, by the way, Miss Crawford,' said Mr John, suddenly remembering the telegram in his pocket. 'This wire arrived shortly before the brother's intrusion into these premises. A few days ago, Mr Roskillen and Mrs Roebling Chanin were united in New York City.'

'*United*?' Miss Crawford took off her pince-nez. It dangled over her bosom on the end of its black velvet ribbon. 'You mean they are married?'

'In a manner of speaking, Miss Crawford. Mr Rory and Mrs Roebling Chanin are setting up a Transatlantic office.'

'Then somewhere we have a bottle of Fortrose Malt Whisky still in its Christmas wrapping, Mr John. A wee drap is in order, I feel, to toast the success of the new, amalgamated steamship line.'

'Indeed, Miss Crawford. We will pass it around the office so that everyone might drink to the health of the happy liaison.'

Christabel was once more in residence at Glengarth, having spent several months roaming between Paris and London on behalf of the Women's Suffragette Movement.

Lindsay was happy to see Iona occupied in 'vamping-up' the castle to suit herself without any more talk of deserting him for Mr Worth or Madame Cheruit, famous dress designers of Paris.

Iona threw out all the old suits of armour which had taken pride of place in the grand baronial hall. Moth-eaten stags' heads, antler coat-hooks, old guns and anything else that conflicted with her idea of Oriental Art were placed in dank and dark storage.

The Great Hall at Glengarth Castle began to resemble an Eastern potentate's harem, but Lindsay kept quiet about it, and let Iona have her head. If Iona was happy, then he was happy. He couldn't bear to row with his wife.

He did draw the line, however, at having his sober dressing-room turned into something resembling a Japanese garden-cum-bathhouse, with flowered and flocked wallpaper and bamboo furniture. He compromised on a Whistler picture instead, but lost the battle over the decoration of the master bedroom. With glass mosaic patterns everywhere, he was made aware of what the Blue Mosque in Constantinople must be like. Since he and Iona now shared the same bed, he forbore to argue with her on what adorned the walls, as long as she continued to adorn his nights.

He gave thanks that the Solar had not as yet been touched; it was the brightest and most pleasing room in the castle with extensive views across the Minch. Christabel and he invariably scurried away to the Solar for some peace and quiet and sanity, while the rest of the castle vibrated to workmen's hammers, saws and untuneful whistles.

'Iona wanted me to tell you that Her Friend hasn't paid her a visit recently,' Christabel began the conversation one afternoon with her nose stuck in Walter Scott's *The Bride of Lammermoor*. 'Not since the middle of September, in fact.'

'Her friend?' Lindsay regarded his sister blankly above the newspaper he had been reading.

She didn't look at him, but continued to nibble a ginger biscuit, depositing crumbs between the pages of her book. 'Oh, Lindsay! Must I really explain to a grown man? It's now the middle of November! Iona's monthly cycle has gone haywire.'

Comprehension dawned at length. 'Oh ... oh, I see what you mean. Is she sure?'

'I suppose so. Robby Robinson says it'll arrive about the middle of next June.'

Lindsay rustled the newspaper and cleared his throat.

Christabel looked up then. 'Aren't you going to say something – like how proud you are to be perpetuating the line?'

'Yes, yes of course.' He folded the newspaper and, smiling at Christabel's tone, put the paper to one side. 'Of course I'm happy, very! But why couldn't Iona have told me herself?'

'Oh, you know Iona. She's a bit of a prude. Her Scottish grandmother's fault of course. She was the one who gave Iona her staunch Presbyterian upbringing and peculiar old-fashioned ideas, abandoned as she and Robert were by their filthy-rich, divorced parents. Too much money and lack of a stable family life, has never compensated for Iona's innate prudery.'

'And you're one of the *avant-garde, outré*, new women, calling themselves Suffragettes, I suppose,' he teased.

'Yes. I'm fighting for freedom from prudery that inhibits wives from telling their husbands anything about their bodily functions. Women have as much right to be outspoken as men.'

'Is that why you're reading *The Bride of Lammermoor*?'

She tossed the book at him and chuckling, Lindsay threw it back. 'Let's hope it's only another book Grandfather "acquired" from a Dunbartonshire library and not a priceless first edition!' Then he added slyly, 'When *are* you getting married, Kiss?'

'When I meet a Statesman on his way to becoming a Prime Minister sympathetic enough to give women the vote.'

'Enough said. Truce, sister, dear.' He stood up and went to the door. 'Where's Iona?'

'Out riding.'

He frowned. 'Should she be? Now that she's having a child, I mean?'

'Don't ask *me*, Lindsay. She's *your* wife.'

He hesitated, his hand on the doorknob, and then decided to say it, after all, 'Kiss, I know you're useless around here and are only a decorative spinster-appendage at Glengarth, but it's nice to have you around. I'm glad you're back.'

'*Aunty* Christabel!' she pulled a face at him. 'Thank *you*, m'laird!'

Lindsay had managed to secure a valuable Government contract to supply timber to Clydeside, a programme of thirty-five ships of the dreadnought type being required before the year 1920. He had enough reserve stocks left at Glengarth to meet the extra demand.

His little trip to Glasgow in order to see Rory, was to try and make a business deal with his brother, one in Glengarth's favour. He had wanted to ask Rory to transport the timber to Clydeside aboard his own coasters fitted with steel derricks which speeded up the loading and unloading of the logs. Until now the transportation of timber had been done by 'rafting' down to Glasgow, or else accomplished manually onto hopelessly inadequate steamers. It was a very unsatisfactory, inefficient way to handle the logging, but Lindsay saw a way now to make the operation far more cost productive.

He was sorry that he had been unable to talk things over with his brother – the only one able to give the go-ahead to an undertaking which would benefit the Laird of Glengarth as well as the Chanin-Beauly entrepreneur!

In order that Glengarth could survive into the future, Lindsay, with Mr Mitchell's expertise, had begun to re-define the old forestry compartments and outline new plantations. Thinning, selecting, discarding, planting and regenerating were all stepped up, and extra men were employed on the estate as timber orders continued to flood in. If there was going to be a war, then Lindsay could only view it from a selfish angle, the salvation of Glengarth, for timber would be at a premium.

Julian Mitchell and he were working together on a project to widen and make safer the access roads through the forests in order to minimize the danger of fire sweeping from one compartment to another. The narrow weed-infested paths on the old plantations had done nothing to prevent the Forest Lodge fire getting out of control, and all that had to be changed.

'I also want two new look-out towers placed here and here ...' Lindsay told Mitchell as they studied the map pinned on the office wall. He ringed the sites with a red pen.

Julian Mitchell drawled in his Canadian accent, 'Are all the trees to be felled in the Lower Valley compartment by the end of this month?' He puffed a cloud of smoke into the room and regarded the laird over the bowl of his briar pipe, reminding Lindsay uncomfortably of his cousin Iain Hamilton in that moment.

'Yes, they're about ready. We've got to meet two-thirds of our quota by the end of the month, so we might as well take them from Lower Valley. Leave the High Hills plant-ation for now.'

'And what about Inchnadamph? Are you proposing to start on that project yet? There's a mighty lot of waste ground there, though most of it's poor.'

'No, forget Inchnadamph for the moment. We're running to the limit of budget-expenditure and I want us to get back on our feet after the Forest Lodge fire that took such a toll of our stocks. I can't afford to do anything with Inchnadamph right now.'

The truth was, Lindsay wanted Inchnadamph to stay wild in memory of his cousin who had been dead-set against turning crofters off their land. Inchnadamph had become the burial ground for sad memories.

'If war does come, Lindsay – very likely now since Haldane's Mission to Berlin went up the creek with all his hopes for peace – you realize timber prices are going to drop, don't you? The Government will step in and impose a ceiling on the price of timber.'

Lindsay pulled a rueful face. 'Yes, I realize that's a possibility. However, there might not be a war if Haldane can do something better next time he meets with the German Kaiser – in which case all this pre-war activity can only do us good. We're busier than we've ever been, and as long as we can meet our targets for the coming months, Iona can have her electric lights and new bathrooms up at the castle – not to mention a gold-plated nursery!'

He was content: life for him was beginning to look up at long last.

But plain sailing and peace of mind were rudely shattered one snowy January morning. Lindsay told himself much later, he ought to have known his joy could never last.

He had been away in Edinburgh on essential estate business. The pony and trap had met him at Achnasheen railway station. Tom Drummond had been in attendance, and his first words were, 'Thank Gawd, ye're back, m'laird.'

'Why? What's up, Tom?' he had asked in alarm.

'Miss Christabel will tell you, sir,' Tom muttered, and got the pony and trap moving at a sharp pace, even though the road was treacherous.

Christabel was always the soul of decorum; to see her so agitated was even more disconcerting. She was there to meet him in the courtyard as soon as he arrived home. 'It's Iona, Lindsay. She was thrown from her horse. Robby and the midwife are with her now.'

'Midwife?' he said stupidly, as he and Christabel made a dash for it across the slippery courtyard. 'The baby isn't due for another five months! Oh, God, Kiss, she didn't take that wretched horse out this morning when I told her not to ...' They bumped into Annie Gowrie on the stairs, upsetting the boiling water in the jug she was carrying and scalding Annie's hand. She didn't murmur as she quickly side-stepped out of their way.

Doctor Robinson was coming out of Iona's bedroom when Lindsay and Christabel panted along the corridor. Robby Robinson was about to shrug himself back into his tweed jacket. He reached out and grabbed hold of Lindsay's arm, preventing him from entering Iona's bedroom. 'Don't go in there yet, Lindsay. 'Tis no place for you at the moment. Come ... let's go and have a whisky while we talk.'

'I don't want to talk, I want to see my wife.'

'Christabel, make this brother of yours do as he's told. Now then, let's go to your study, m'laird, for I've a few wee words to say to you before you see Iona.' Firmly he drew Lindsay downstairs again.

Robby Robinson knew that the laird never touched drink, but he still shoved a glass of whisky into his hand. 'No good in beating around the bush and making things more painful, Lindsay, so I'll get straight to the point – she's lost the baby through a miscarriage ... *Sit down,* will ye?' He forced Lindsay back into the chair. 'Drink the whisky, it'll steady you for what I'm about to say ... There were complications, bad ones, rupture of the womb – in medical jargon, an aborted foetus with a resulting uterine rupture. But it's no good blaming the wee lassie, it was an accident. Iona doesn't know, and she'll *not* know until she's fully recovered. I've staunched the bleeding by packing her, but she needs to get to the cottage hospital fast. I can stitch her up there, and she'll get the proper necessary after-care. Annie and Craigie are preparing her for the short journey to Gairloch. I've telephoned the postmistress, and she's seeing to it that the ambulance is sent out at once. Iona's life is in the balance, Lindsay.

She'll die unless the bleeding can be stopped within the next two hours.'

The room began to swim around Lindsay. 'Complications ... rupture, is she going to be able to survive the journey to the hospital as well as the operation?'

'I hope so – I shall do my best. She's heavily sedated at the moment, but we'll soon have her all sewn up and back as new ... well, er ...' he rubbed his chin thoughtfully and stared down into the laird's pale, drawn face. 'Not quite good as new, so it's no use pretending otherwise. She'll ne'r be able to carry another child. Iona will be barren after the operation.'

'Oh, God ... I told her ... I told her about that infernal horse ... oh, *God*!'

'Now, now Lindsay, it's no good blaming Iona – the deed is done. She is a very sick lassie at the moment. Pray for a miracle she doesn't die, that's my advice. Now I'm away to the hospital to get myself prepared for the operation. The ambulance will have qualified attendants and a nurse, and with Craigie doing the necessary Iona will be in good hands. It's no use your coming, too. You'll only get in everyone's way. I'll ring you from Gairloch when the operation is over Don't bother to see me out. I know the way by now.'

Lindsay wasn't even aware that the doctor had gone. He sat there like a man turned to stone, and it was only when the whisky glass in his hand shattered, cutting him badly, was he aware of how hard he had been gripping it. Blood and alcohol spattered his trousers, and hastily he bound his hand with his handkerchief before getting up, and going to Iona's room.

Like a man going through the necessary functions of life without feeling or knowing what he was doing, Lindsay flung open the door to Iona's bedroom and stood on the threshold.

Iona, her eyes closed, her brilliant hair spread out against the stark whiteness behind her, represented an image so ugly to him in that moment that he could not bear to look at her. He did not know whether Iona was conscious or unconscious. He did not care.

Nurse Craig stood on one side of the great bed, Annie Gowrie on the other. 'Get out,' he said to them. They looked at him as though he'd taken leave of his senses, which he, in that awful moment, had. 'Get out!' Lindsay repeated.

Annie moved towards the door, but Nurse Craig stalled her.

'Stay where ye are, Annie Gowrie!' She turned her wrath upon the laird. 'How *dare* ye, m'laird, how dare ye come in her disturbing your poor wee wife when she's needing all the rest and quiet she can get? Don't you know she'll die if she starts another bleed? Annie and I are attending upon her in order to give her the most comfortable journey to the hospital, so I'll thank ye, m'laird, to leave this room at once!'

Lindsay ignored the nurse. 'Iona,' he said to her, 'Iona, listen to me. I told you never to take that brute of a horse out in your condition. I should never have bought it for you, but by God, you'll ride it no more. Saladin will be disposed of as you've disposed of Glengarth's heir, even if I have to shoot it myself!'

Nurse Craig flew at him. '*Out*! Out of here, m'laird, before I telephone Dr Robinson and Annie fetches Mr Mitchell to drag you away and to you'er senses!'

Lindsay shook off Nurse Craig's imperious hand on the sleeve of his jacket, and turned to Annie. 'Was the baby a boy or a girl?'

Annie hesitated and stared helplessly at Nurse Craig, who shook her head.

'Answer me, Annie Gowrie, otherwise I shall give you back, personally, to your step-father and he can do what he likes with you.'

Annie swallowed. 'A ... a boy, m'laird.'

'Fetch him to me at once. *Fetch me my son.*' Annie made a sound in her throat like an animal trapped. She turned to Nurse Craig. 'My son, Annie! Bring him to me at once.'

'M'laird, the wee bairn is dead.'

'I know, but I wish to see his body.'

'Ye canna m'laird,' said Nurse Craig. ''Twas a premature foetus miscarried in a bad way and ye'd not like to be seeing what ye've lost.'

Lindsay willed himself not to take hold of the old woman and strangle her with her own bonnet-strings. 'I want my son,' he said through gritted teeth. 'So you will bring the baby to me, in his cradle, dressed in his christening robes. Do you understand, Nurse Craig?'

She stared at him in horror, so, too, did Annie Gowrie. Nurse Craig drew herself up fully and regarded him in disbelief, in bewilderment and in contempt. '*Nay*! I'll do no such thing, m'laird! What ye're asking me to do, is an affront to common decency, to my profession and to your wife! I'll not do it.'

'You will, because I order it.'

'You not only insult yourself and your poor wee wife, m'laird, but Annie Gowrie and me – a practising midwife for nigh on thirty years and never once asked to do what ye're asking me to do! That wee object is damaged and would never have been born a normal human being ...'

'What are you saying? What are you trying to tell me, old woman!'

'M'laird, the baby was deformed. It is an incomplete foetus born before its time, and would never have been carried to full term. It was rejected from the womb, and therefore is not to be considered as a viable bairn requiring Christian burial.'

'*God dammit*! Spare me your professional tongue, woman! What have you done with *my* son?' he asked, the blood pounding in his temples.

'The foetus is awaiting disposal in the bathroom ...'

He took a step towards her, ready to toss her out of the room. 'By God, I'll see to it that you're struck off the register of practising midwives ...' Annie hastily stepped between the laird and Nurse Craig.

'M'laird, I'll fetch the wee bairn in his christening robes for you. I'll bring the bassinet to your study.'

Nurse Craig stared dumbfounded at Annie Gowrie. About to say something to the girl, she thought better of it, snapped her mouth tight, and turned back to her patient. Let Annie Gowrie sort out the laird and his ghastly request, she thought furiously to herself as she prepared the Lady Iona for the horse-drawn ambulance that was to take her to the cottage hospital in Gairloch.

When Annie had done his bidding, Lindsay, before shutting himself away with the remains of his dead child, gave instructions to Julian Mitchell to have Saladin destroyed.

PART SIX

'Again deep groves wave in the wind
And flowers gleam in the dark fens
Of the tangled woods;
And many a bird and many an insect keeps
Its dwelling in the shade and man doth bend
His lonely steps to meet the angels there.'

Percy Bysshe Shelley

CHAPTER TWENTY-FOUR

Lindsay soon realized Bonnie Charlie would never make a gun dog, and abandoned all hope of ever training him towards a responsible attitude. Bonnie Charlie was born to romp and he did it with gusto. But he was an amusing companion whose company he preferred to that of most human beings.

The dog had been with Annie Gowrie on the night of the Forest Lodge fire, otherwise Bonnie Charlie might have alerted the family to the danger they were in when the wind blew hot ashes and sparks onto the newly thatched roof. Lindsay blamed himself, memories of that terrible night still haunting him years afterwards. He should have *insisted* that Iain and Shiona replaced the slate tiles with which the house had been originally built. But Shiona had wanted a thatched roof because it was picturesque!

Annie's reason for having taken the dog with her to Rill on the night of the fire was because Bonnie Charlie had a septic paw and had kept the whole family awake with his whining restlessness which had caused them sleepless nights for a week. The way things had worked out, they'd have been alive now had Bonnie Charlie stayed at home with his septic paw ... and so his thoughts continued on that never ending spiral of self-recrimination he found hard to live with. Long walks by himself, or with Bonnie Charlie by his side, riding through the glens on his horse, were the only activities that brought him some measure of inner peace, exorcising his soul of the devils plaguing him.

'Good dog, *fetch*!' Lindsay threw the stick once more, but the silly animal flopped down and looked up at him with tongue lolling wetly, tail thumping the warm heather.

Lindsay tried again. This time a loud whirring from low scrub close by produced a capercaillie, its black summer plumage and fan-shaped tail silhouetted against the bright sunlight on Inchnadamph.

Bonnie Charlie bounded after the bird, yapping excitedly.

'*Leave*!' Lindsay shouted. The season was too early for shooting grouse. They had been after rabbits, not Highland birds. But Bonnie Charlie had picked up an interesting scent and went dashing after it, away ahead of his new master.

Descending into a rough hollow at the foot of the mountain, Lindsay came across Annie making a fuss of the dog. 'Hello,' he said in surprise, 'so that's why Bonnie Charlie's noo aw'a!'

Annie wore her best tartan skirt, and a white bodice low and laced in front. They were all part of his wife's wardrobe discarded and given to servant girls such as herself; but he was not to know that. She had nothing on her feet. Her long black hair stirred in the wind, drifting freely to her waist.

Looking at her, the spirit of freedom and youthful energy, Lindsay was tormented by all that he had lost as far as Iona was concerned.

Annie herself, with his eyes upon her, felt that inner yearning for him reassert itself. His loneliness and misery of the past five months, ever since the Lady Iona's tragic accident, made her long to reach out and hold him tight to her, with all the reassurances she could give him to make him a happier man.

She continued fondling the dog and ignored him.

'Annie?'

She looked up, her eyes like glittering green glass. She was not shy, afraid or subservient as he thought she might be. 'Yes, m'laird?'

The look in her saucy eyes reminded him of the time he had first seen her, a little girl gutting fish on her mother's doorstep when he had ridden his pony to the fisherman's cottage on Rill. She looked at him now much as she had looked at him then, curiously, proudly, almost insolently.

Lindsay turned away, confused and angry with himself, as well as with her. He never knew what she was thinking, only what she made him feel whenever they ran into each other at odd moments around the estate or in the castle. Lindsay whistled for the dog to follow him, but Bonnie Charlie preferred Annie's company and didn't come when he was called. To keep up appearances Lindsay went on his way without the dog, the whistle on his lips cheery and bright, '*Coming through the rye*'.

He found himself ascending the steep side of the glen, to where Forest Lodge had once stood. He hadn't ventured here in years; had avoided it since the night of the fire. The gutted building reared out of the green grass growing over the downstairs floor. Blackened timbers stuck out like the charred ribs of a cremated body, and he made a mental note to have the rest of whatever was left standing, completely razed to the ground. He wanted it cleared for the spring planting of a new spruce compartment. He wanted the blistering memory of Forest Lodge and of his cousins erased from his mind for ever. The site would be given back to the forest, and no one would ever know where a home had once stood.

Lindsay set down his game bag and propped his gun against part of an interior wall. Here and there pieces of wallpaper fluttered like mournful handkerchiefs sopping up the tears of that never-to-be-forgotten night. Bits of rain-soaked plaster disintegrated at his touch.

In the ruins he picked up a relic from Aeneas' and Bruce's nursery days. The paint had been burned off the clockwork train but the key was still in the engine. He turned it and surprisingly the clockwork mechanism whirred into action, unaffected by heat, rust or time. Lindsay put the toy in his pocket and took out his cigarette case: Tantalus for ever attempting to drink the receding waters of hell, were his melancholy thoughts in that lost moment. He closed his eyes and leaned against the wall, the cigarette his poisonous companion.

When he opened his eyes Annie Gowrie was standing before him.

She was tall for a girl, slender as a willow wand, hardly

the fashionable figure at all. Annie was not beautiful, not
when each feature was examined separately. Her hair was
too straight, nose hardly *retroussé* but long and thin,
almost witchlike, cheekbones not classically defined, but
gaunt and sharp, like rocks protruding above white water.
Her mouth was not soft and vulnerable but wide and hard
and unyielding, her chin not prettily rounded, but strong
and determined and daunting. But her eyes … yes, the
eyes! Annie's eyes were beautiful: they were the windows
of her soul, beguiling, transforming her, making one forget
the rest of her while they drew one deep into her hungry
depths, reminding him of the spirit of the sea, the mountains, the eternal forest.

Nature reverting to nature the moment man's
restraining hand was removed, Annie, the fishergirl from
Rill, was part of that untamed spirit of Glengarth, with a
wildness about her no man could tame no matter how
many years she had been forced to grow in the private
garden of a laird's castle …

He looked at her for a long time. He rediscovered her.
And in those first few moments of a new awakening,
Lindsay challenged her free spirit; he wanted to know her
reasons for disobeying him to return to her island home. 'I
told you never to go back to Rill until I gave my permission.'

'I know, m'laird, but there's things that must be done
there,' she said in her soft lilting Gaelic way.

'What things?'

'The maintaining of the property for a start.'

'That's my responsibility.'

She dug her bare toes into the soft loam of Forest
Lodge. 'It's the only way for me.'

'What do you mean?'

'I must live with it and face the truth; it's the only way
for me,' she repeated.

'It wasn't *your* shame, Annie, you were only a little girl
at the time.'

'I'm a child no longer but a grown woman, and Fleddon
an Fletcher knew it the night he came back for me, the
night of the fire. I must live with that, too.'

'Don't Annie, don't talk about it.'

'But I must ... and so must you. I want to help you, m'laird, the way you once helped me.'

'How can you possibly help me, Annie Gowrie?' he asked with a deep sadness as he stared away to the top of the pine trees.

'By sharing your grief. You are lonely and alone. I see you eaten up every day by your life of loneliness ...'

'I like my solitude.'

'Solitude, m'laird, is not the same as loneliness. Loneliness eats into the soul when there's no one to turn to for help and comfort. I look at you, I watch you, and I've seen the way you sometimes look at me up at Glengarth.'

Startled, he regarded her in astonishment. '*How* do I look at you?'

'The way you did just now, and the way you're looking now. The hunger and the wanting.'

'What else do you know about me?'

'That you're a very unhappy man who wants to be made happy.'

'Can you give me back Iain and Shiona Hamilton and their son, Bruce? Can you give them back to Aeneas made an orphan through a madman's lust for revenge? Can you make Iona a wife to me again? Can you give me back my dead son or all the sons Glengarth will never have?'

'No. But I can give you back yourself. Here, where you stand among the ghosts which haunt you.' She began to unlace her bodice. Her actions graceful, unselfconscious, natural as an autumn tree shedding its unwanted leaves. She slipped the garment onto the grass at his feet.

He turned away from her angrily. 'Annie, I don't need you to be my scapegoat!'

'Why won't you look at me? Is it because you're afraid? *Look!* See for yourself, no more bruises or blemishes or any other marks of the flesh mauled by an animal. A clean slate to write on – for both our sakes, m'laird.'

He turned and looked at her then, at the golden silkiness of arms and legs and breasts and he knew he wanted her as he had always wanted her, despite everything.

Slowly he stubbed out his cigarette before reaching for her. He drew her to him, clasping the slender column of her throat, her mouth close to his. Against her lips he spoke softly and possessively. 'Then know this, Annie Gowrie, I'll break you in half if you ever mess me around as your stepfather and my wife have done.'

Loving her on the wild grass was sweet and fierce, her body beneath his soft and pliant, responsive in an act of giving as well as receiving. And in that final moment when he crushed Annie Gowrie to himself, and the aching desire had become the spasm of completeness, echoes of themselves reached far back into the shadows of the past and made that cinderbed of revenge a wholesome place again.

They stayed there all night, sheltered by broken walls, until the full June moon had risen above Inchnadamph and Beinn Claidheamh Mor was bathed in silver. Her long hair was damp, clinging to her face and body and to him, and he went on loving her until the mountain emerged once more through the morning mists presaging another fine day. And only then did Lindsay take Annie back to her cottage on Rill.

That short warm summer, loving Annie in the heather, or in her homestead, wherever and whenever they found a moment to be alone together, rolled away as the storm clouds rolled in from all sides to overshadow the best days of his life.

Summer gave way to autumn, and autumn to winter once more.

Europe had become the chessboard of nations, a Teuton versus Slav game of incalculable foolishness. Austria and Germany, Russia and Serbia, Turkey and Bulgaria, Greece and Rumania; while Britain watched and waited on the sidelines.

But Lindsay didn't care what went on around him; he was happy, truly happy for the first time in his life.

Busy all afternoon in the gun room, Lindsay whiled away the tedious hours checking over an odd assortment of armoury until he could be together again with Annie who now encompassed his life. But Annie had disappeared for the past week, and he was anxious to know why and where. He didn't like it when she went off fishing among the outer islands without telling him.

His fingers had become stiff and shiftless, the atmosphere icy in Duncan's Tower, which dated back to the days of Duncan Beauly, the first feudal lord of Glengarth, descendant of Vikings. Glengarth had been added to, pulled apart, destroyed and rebuilt over the succeeding centuries, the old castle guarding the Minch as patched as a homemade quilt! Until Iona's latest folly, that of turning it into an Oriental hotch-potch. But now Iona had even lost interest in her renovation and refurbishing plans for Glengarth, and Lindsay couldn't help wondering what kind of mischief its next owner would do since Iona certainly couldn't continue the line.

He didn't want to think about it, and took his mind off his insoluble problems to pat his faithful hound's head. 'Come on, Charlie boy, time for tea.'

Bonnie Charlie didn't move, but he did deign to open one sleepy eye to give his master an old-fashioned look, as though he were half aware of the thoughts whirling inside Lindsay's head.

'All right then, stay there and freeze to death,' Lindsay told the dog and opened the heavy iron-studded door. Bonnie Charlie soon bounded up and shot ahead of him.

Lindsay bumped into Christabel climbing the steep spiral staircase, and said in surprise. 'What're you doing up here? It's out of bounds, Christabel.'

Duncan's Tower was crumbling and badly in need of repair, and because it was so dangerous he had given orders for everyone to keep out, he himself being the only one to come here to attend to what required to be done from time to time in the armoury.

'Iona and I were beginning to wonder if you'd died in your sleep and Murray hadn't mentioned it. Are you going to take tea with us today or have you some other excuse to keep you away from your wife's side?'

'What's that supposed to mean?'

There was no one to hear them in this lonely part of the castle, but Christabel lowered her voice to hiss belligerently, 'Lindsay, you're behaving in a disgusting fashion by flaunting Annie Gowrie in front of us all.'

'Christabel, don't use that tone of voice on me.'

'Oh, come off your high horse, Lindsay! Don't act the grand laird with me. I'm your sister, and no one else is going to tell you what a fool you're making of yourself. Had you been discreet, everyone could have forgiven you. But you're behaving shamelessly. You're making Iona *very* miserable by the way you're carrying on with Annie. I feel very sorry for your wife. The atmosphere here is intolerable. It has gone from bad to worse, so much so, my nerves are suffering. Iona weeps all day long and practically drowns everyone with her orgies of self-indulgent misery, while all you can do is chase after a common fishergirl and housemaid! You don't care, do you, *who* knows you spend more time in *her* cottage and bed, than your wife's?'

'No, I don't!' he snapped, his manner reverting to icy composure when he wanted a cloak to defend himself. 'What I choose to do with my life, Christabel, is *my* business.'

'*Not* when it affects the whole family. Everything is falling to rack and ruin, while you don't seem to give a damn. It's your responsibility, Lindsay, to do something about law and order and a certain amount of respectability around this place!'

'You just leave me to *my* business. You do as you wish, Christabel. Go to London, Paris or wherever, with your Suffragette propaganda, but leave me to run Glengarth my way. And leave Annie Gowrie out of it, do you understand?' He lit a cigarette, and repocketed his gold cigarette case. 'I'll not have you interfering in my life. I'm tired of your spinsterish rule in *my* household. I'm tired of Iona's histrionics all day long, and I'm tired of Glengarth.'

Tea with the two of them, his weepy wife and nagging sister, suddenly more than he could stomach, Lindsay brushed past his sister, almost unbalancing Christabel as he descended the steep winding stairs from the armoury.

He slammed the outer door of Duncan's Tower. Christabel wrenched open the heavy wooden door in his wake. 'Don't slam doors in *my* face, Lindsay Roskillen! You're a moral coward, you know that? What you can't face up to, you choose to ignore.'

'Leave me alone, Christabel.' He strode across the castle courtyard and she had a job to keep up with his long stride.

'Lindsay, where are you going?' Christabel demanded.

'None of your business.'

'Rill, I suppose?'

'Maybe.'

'Lindsay, listen to me! Why can't you spare your wife at least one hour of your week?'

'Because I prefer eating bread and cheese in a fisherman's cottage, Christabel, rather than having my afternoon tea or my dinner wine soured by Iona's damn tears all the time!'

'Lord, but I'd have believed it of Rory, never you!' She went into the castle proper and slammed the heavy door so loudly, Bonnie Charlie started barking hysterically outside it.

Lindsay didn't take tea with his sister and wife in the Solar. Nor did he go to Rill. He went instead, that evening, to Gairloch, to take supper with his cousin Morag and her husband, the Minister of the Kirk.

Iona was all by herself in the Solar when he went to her the following morning. She had a tartan rug around her legs, and was looking tearfully out of the windows to the sea. She had thrown her tapestry work on the floor in a fit of temper and now nervously twisted a damp handkerchief in her hands. She looked up at him, the stranger who was her husband, with dark-ringed bloodshot eyes, not the sparkling sapphire eyes of his Renoir girl who had captivated him a lifetime ago. That slim and lovely Iona had vanished on Saladin her infernal horse from Inverdune, and had been replaced by a puffy, unkempt shadow of her former self. Iona had even hacked off her glorious hair to spite him.

'Go away, Lindsay, I don't want you here.' Stubbornly she set her face and turned away from him.

'I've brought you a present,' he said.

'I don't want it.'

'You will when you look at her properly.' He placed the bitch puppy in Iona's lap.

Iona hesitated. Two pink spots burned brightly on her cheeks. 'Is this another cruel joke of yours?'

'What on earth do you mean?'

'A bitch for a bitch?'

He seemed astonished by her reasoning and almost smiled. 'Good Lord, Iona. It never crossed my mind.'

'Give it to Annie Gowrie.'

'I bought it for *you!* Take it as a peace offering from me. I'm sorry you always think so badly of me, but my motives this time were genuine, Iona.'

She had been about to toss the dog off her knees when it licked her face and hand before settling comfortably into the tartan rug to sleep.

'I got her in Gairloch. I thought she'd be company for you,' Lindsay went on to add.

'Don't add insult to injury,' she retorted bitingly.

Lindsay pulled up a chair and sat down in front of her so that she would look him in the eye properly. He took Iona's hands in his, determined she would not pull away this time. The spidery little toy dog remained quite still, snoring gently while her owners indulged in a tug of war above her ears.

'Iona, I will try very hard to spend more time with you if you will do something for me. Halfway, Iona, halfway, and we might just be able to resolve this awful situation between us. Listen to me, please. The puppy is from a litter Morag did not know what to do with ... that's where I was last evening, taking supper with her family at Gairloch. Now I want to talk about you. There's nothing wrong with you any more. Doctor Robinson, as well as all those Harley Street specialists you've been to see, tell me there's no reason why you cannot walk. You're suffering from hysterical paralysis, that's all.'

'That's *all*! My God, you're brutal!' .

'I didn't mean it quite like that, forgive me. What I'm trying to say is, the reason why you're stuck in that wheelchair is because you've made up your mind never to walk again. There's no physical cause for your paralysis, only an attitude of the mind.'

'Are you calling me insane now?'

He sighed. 'Iona, don't be perverse. I know what you've been through since your fall, but your spine was not injured in any way apart from a temporary numbness of the spinal nerves. Robby Robinson told me you damaged yourself internally when thrown by Saladin because you were carrying a child at the time, a uterine rupture, is what he said. But there's no other damage to you apart from ... from being unable to conceive any more children. But it's not the end of the world. We'll adopt children. We'll ... we'll do all the things you want to do again.'

She broke down and wept all over the dog. 'I don't want other people's children! I want *ours*! I wasn't ready to have that baby when we were first married, and now it's too late. You forced that child on me, Lindsay, for the sake of your precious hereditary line and ... and ...'

'Iona, that's untrue and you know it!'

'It's true! You didn't want me for any other reason. You wanted an heir for Glengarth and that was all. The speed with which we were married was positively indecent and ...'

'You listen to me, Iona. You were the one who couldn't wait to get married after your brother's death. We could have postponed the date of our marriage for as long as you wished, but you didn't want to. You said that my absence in Italy had not altered what you felt for me, and how nice if we could get married straightaway without anyone knowing. Neither did I want all the fuss and nonsense of a grand wedding, and that was why we got married so soon after we met again. Nor did I want to lose you a second time around, so please don't make such harsh accusations. I waited for you for seven weeks after we were married to come to my bed, allowing you time to adjust to me and your new role as Glengarth's mistress. I'm not the one, I think, who has been unreasonable in all

this, but you. You have been monumentally selfish at
times, spoilt and as petulant as a child. Perhaps that was
your doting grandmother's fault, I don't know.'

'There are a lot of things, Lindsay, you still don't know!
And that's how to make a woman happy!'

'Marriage is a partnership, Iona, and the rough goes
with the smooth. You were willing enough at the time to
consent to be my wife. You knew the responsibilities
Glengarth would entail. You knew how lonely and remote
it was up here in the Highlands, far away from your
parties and soirées in Edinburgh and London, and you
didn't mind then about giving it all up. Don't change your
tune now. I think all would have gone very well during the
pregnancy had you not wilfully disobeyed Robby
Robinson and me about not going riding until after the
baby's birth. To take out that highly strung horse in the ice
and snow was just asking for trouble. But now that we've
got trouble, we've got to try to get out of it. I'm willing to
start again and do my part if you'll only meet me halfway.'

'That's easy for you to say. You've still got two legs.
You're still able to function as a man, whereas I'm now
nothing but a useless, barren, ugly old woman! I've
become overweight and unsightly just sitting here day
after day in this chair, and I've got you to thank for ruining
my life! Go away, please, before I end it all by jumping
out of this window – and then you can have your low-bred
whore!'

'Iona, please don't say that about Annie. *Never* say it!'

'*Get out*!' she screamed.

A few days after Christmas and now eleven months since
Iona's accident, Lindsay decided to try again. Iona had
kept the dog with her and was spoiling it horribly
according to Christabel. When he went into the Solar to
take tea with them, Iona was feeding it a chocolate biscuit.
She had had her hair done and wore a very becoming
afternoon frock. The tartan blanket was neatly folded on
the window seat.

Iona looked up at him, and smiled, shades of the Renoir
girl still there. 'This disgusting creature has no manners,

Lindsay. It wets where it sleeps, all over my rug!'

He took the bitch puppy away from her and noticed the pink bow on its head. 'Isn't Kiss having tea with us this afternoon?' he asked, even feeling in the mood to call his sister by her childhood name.

'She's gone to look for Kirsty to take the dog for a walk since I can't.'

Kirsty was Iona's new maid, a crusty spinster of fifty in Harris tweeds and fur boots. 'Iona, I want you to do something for me,' Lindsay began.

'Not wash the blanket, I hope.'

He smiled and put out his hands. 'Hang on to me and try to stand.'

'I can't. Don't ask me to even try.'

'Come on. It's almost one year since the accident. You've *got* to try and get about again. Just try, that's all I'm asking.'

'You're always asking me to do the impossible.' But Iona did give him her hands, making an effort to rise out of the wheelchair. She managed to get herself up, her bottom hovering two inches above the cushions. She took a deep breath and slowly raised herself further still with his support until she was standing upright. Then nerves got the better of her and she fell against him with a gasp.

He held her close for the first time in months, and felt her trembling response. 'I can't, Lindsay, don't ask me to any more,' she whispered. 'I've a terrible pain in my back. It's as though I've been cut in two.'

'Poor Iona ... but at least we've made a start, my dear.'

He lowered her down again into the wheelchair and she began to sob. Lindsay looked upon Iona's downbent head, knowing deep in his heart that Iona's state of depression was centred around Annie Gowrie and the place she now occupied in his life. But he couldn't give up Annie, even if it meant an overnight cure where his wife was concerned. 'Iona, please don't cry,' he said helplessly. 'It upsets me terribly to see you like this. But at least we know you can stand, and you wouldn't be able to do that at all if you had no feeling in your legs ...' The door opened and Christabel entered.

'I can't find Kirsty ... oh, but now Lindsay's here, perhaps *he'd* like to walk the dog as he bought it in the first place, Iona. I hope, Lindsay, you've locked up Bonnie Charlie, as the two just don't get on. He almost had her for a breakfast romp the other morning ... didn't he, my poppet?' She picked up Iona's dog and made a fuss of it and Lindsay could see that they were going to have trouble with Bonnie Charlie and this lady 'toy-dog' when she was a little older, something he'd never thought about until Christabel mentioned it.

Christabel went on to say, 'we have one week to finalize arrangements for Hogmanay. I've sent out the invitations ...'

'I don't want any Hogmanay celebrations this year,' Iona interrupted.

'Well, my dear, we can't let down our tenants and workers for the sake of private grievances. You needn't fret about it, Iona, I'm attending to everything ...' she turned to her brother with a change of subject: 'Lindsay, we can't think of a name for her, what do you suggest?' Christabel asked, her attention centred once more upon Iona's new pet.

He looked at the pink bow and the toy dog's silly expression as Christabel tickled its stomach, 'Bon Ton?' he suggested.

'Now why didn't I think of that? Oh, listen, that must be Murray with the tea,' Christabel added, when someone banged on the door. 'Lindsay, open the door before he drops the tray on the threshold.'

But it wasn't Murray, it was Julian Mitchell. Lindsay closed the door behind him as Mitchell looked as though he had serious business to discuss.

'Sorry to disturb you, m'laird, but can I have a word with you in the estate office?'

Lindsay looked over his shoulder at Iona and Christabel's expectant expressions, both of them seeming glad that he was going to spend the afternoon with them. 'Can't it wait?' he asked Mitchell.

'No, m'laird.'

'Oh, very well!' He turned back to his wife and his

sister, still in playfool mood with Bon Ton. He was glad to see Iona had perked up again and was smiling, so it hurt him to have to make the apology: 'I'm sorry. I have to go. More estate business I'm afraid.'

'The story of my life, Lindsay,' Iona said, the dullness back in her eyes as she turned away to the window and the stormy Minch.

Lindsay followed Mitchell across the courtyard into the office, and watched in fascination when the factor began to unroll what looked like a curly black sheep skin, fresh and bloodied.

But it wasn't a sheep skin: it was Bonnie Charlie's hide turned by a poacher's cunning knife into a hearth rug.

CHAPTER TWENTY-FIVE

Lindsay waited for Annie on the dark wet shore. He had been waiting for several hours, time spent between the cottage and walking the shores of Rill.

He shivered in the icy Celtic night, a combination of nerves, forboding and everything else that tormented him. When her fishing boat sailed into the loch, he let out a sigh of relief, hating it when Annie went fishing alone in stormy weather. Wraiths of mist swept down from the glen, seeping in under sweaters, burrowing into one's very bone marrow.

By the light of the hurricane lantern he had set down on the causeway, Lindsay helped Annie to tie up her boat.

Even though he was numb with cold and anxiety, Annie, in her thin, wet, homespun clothes was oblivious of the weather or any discomfort. 'Where have you been these last few days?' Lindsay demanded of her, quite unable to control the sharp criticism in his voice.

'On Errin.'

'Doing what?'

'Visiting my ain kinsfolk. I've no' seen for nigh on a year.'

'I've been out of my mind worrying about you.'

'You need not, m'laird. I can take care of myself.'

'Oh, Annie!' Lindsay put his arms around her and held her tight. Her hair, her clothes, wringing wet, she smelled of the tangy sea. 'Annie, you're not to take out that wretched little boat of yours, any more, do you hear? You're like a block of ice, and if you don't drown first, you'll surely die of pneumonia.'

'I hear ye, m'laird, but the attention's lacking. If I don't catch fish to sell fish, who'll pay the rent owing on my cottage now I've lost my job up at the castle?'

She made him angrier still, and unhappy. 'If that's your only reason to go fishing, then don't! I don't *need* your wretched rent.'

'I'm thinking differently, m'fine landlord. Besides, I feel better paying m'dues – in my own way.' She pushed him away. Getting into her boat again, she began tossing the heavy fishing-nets onto the causeway. Lindsay helped her spread them out flat, even though he could hardly see what he was doing.

Afterwards, they retrieved the precious hurricane-lamp, and on the way back to her cot, Lindsay said, 'Your step-father's back and poaching on my preserves again.'

Annie remained silent.

'Did you hear what I said, Annie?'

'I heard, m'laird.'

She lifted the latch and entered, waiting for him to step inside before she dropped the heavy safety bar into position. While he lit the oil-lamp with his lighter Annie stirred the peat into life. Still they did not speak. Annie clattered bowls and plates from a shelf and began to lay the table.

'Annie,' Lindsay said, 'get out of your wet things first before you start attending to supper ... and really, I'm not hungry right now, so if you're doing it only for me, forget it.'

She left the living-room and went into her bedroom to change. Presently she re-emerged with her wet garments which she slung across the line above the fire to dry. The cottage was neat, clean, homely and welcoming since Annie had been dismissed from Glengarth by the Lady Iona, for now she had more time for herself. At the laird's expense, improvements had been made to the property. A scullery had been added, and the tiny cow-byre converted to a decent bedroom so that Annie was comfortably accommodated in a dignified fashion. Annie had promised to pay him back, her independence something he was unable to reconcile.

Lindsay accepted Annie's depression: she was so much a part of him. He sat down at the table and took out his cigarette case while she towelled her long hair beside the

fire. Then, tossing back the straight, raven-black swathe of
silk in which he breathed the scent of mermaids, the
eternal sea, the pine forests, the essence of Glengarth, and
all things dear to him, Annie looked at him long and hard.
'Well, now,' she said, 'let him come and if *you* don't kill
him, *I shall*!'

She sat down in the rocking-chair that had belonged to
her mother, the chair since mended by Tom Drummond
to whom Lindsay gave all the odd jobs around Rill, for
Tom was guaranteed not to chatter aimlessly to other
hands on the estate.

Lindsay flung his half-smoked cigarette into the fire.
His elbows propped on the table, in a weary gesture he
swept his face with his hands. 'Oh, Annie ... *am* I cursed?
Is Glengarth my curse?'

'What are you talking about, Lindsay?' Annie asked,
getting up again and going to him. Running her fingers
through his fair hair, she murmured softly, 'what sort of
talk is this, m'laird?'

'First my own family ... my mother, my father, my
cousins, then my wife's accident. And now this ... this
savage, mindless killing of a dumb animal to sever my
final link with everything I've held dear from the past.
Bonnie Charlie should have gone with Aeneas when the
lad was sent to Aberdeen to live with my cousin Moira.'

'You canna reproach yourself for that, Lindsay! What
has brought this on? Aeneas has probably forgotten all
about Bonnie Charlie by now.'

Lindsay buried himself in Annie's loving warmth, and
Annie, wrapping her arms around him, drew his head
against her breast. 'Your infernal stepfather, just this
morning, took it into his warped head to skin the dog
alive. Bonnie Charlie's hide was delivered to the estate
office this morning.'

'Oh, no!' She crushed him closer still. 'Oh, no! Oh,
Lindsay ... what is he trying to do to us?'

They held each other tightly. 'To *me*!' Lindsay said
against her. 'To me, Annie, not you. He's trying to undermine me, and my will to resist him. In numerous ways he's
trying to hit back at me for what happened all those years

ago. He's never forgiven me for whisking you out of his clutches to go to live at Forest Lodge.'

She said sadly, 'There are some people born into this world who are so wicked, Lindsay, they get pleasure from doing terrible things time after time, with no feeling and no thought to their victims. They are lost souls, and worse than animals. There's nothing anyone can do to change them.'

'Oh, yes, there is ... there's one thing to be done with the likes of Fletcher, and this time, Annie, he's not getting away with it. It'll be him or me, I swear it.'

'Don't do anything foolish, Lindsay. He's a devious man. If anything happened to you, I don't know what I'd do.'

'Nothing's going to happen to me, Annie,' he reassured her. 'Now then, let's change the subject shall we? What have you got to eat?'

She smiled and went to the cupboard. 'For someone who's not hungry there's biscuits ... and ...' she rummaged around looking for something else to tempt him with from her meagre larder. She turned back to him and shrugged. 'Sorry, m'laird. Had I known you'd be staying to supper I'd have stopped at Gairloch to buy my fine landlord caviare and truffles.'

'What do you know about caviare and truffles, fisher-girl?'

'Oh, I'm not altogether uneducated, m' fine laird: I hear tell your grand brother with all his steamships and ocean liners berthed at Clydebank sits in a gilded bath all day eating caviare and truffles and sipping champagne with his mistress who's a millionairess!'

'And I suppose you heard that fine tale from Angus MacPhee,' Lindsay grinned, 'who gets everything wrong!'

'Never mind from where, is it true?'

'Why, what's it to you, sweet Annie, if it *does* happen to be true?'

'I *like* hearing how a body lives when not from Glengarth, Gairloch, Ullapool or Applecross.'

'You've a lot of finding out to do, then, Annie Gowrie, since the news we get up here in the Highlands is always several months stale. And if you must know, I don't like caviar, I've never tasted truffles and I only drink champagne once in a blue moon. So, is there a piece of cheese I might have with these rock-solid ship's biscuits sitting here since your great-grandfather went fishing a century ago?'

'Only with green bits growing.'

'It'll do.' He sighed. 'No wonder you're as skinny as a lathe, Annie. You exist on the smell of fish-scales! I'll send someone along tomorrow to stock your cupboard.'

She pulled a face. 'Clothes from my lady's chamber and food from my lord's table; the humble fishergirl is surely going up in the world! But no thanks, m'laird: I'll do my own shopping if you don't mind.' She slammed down in front of him the platter of cheese and ship's biscuits bought a month ago in Gairloch.

Using his dirk, Lindsay began peeling off the mouldy rind from the cheese, but Annie got cross. 'Put away that iniquitous looking knife, m'laird! There's proper cutlery to be eating with.'

'I'm getting into practice for what I'm going to do to your stepfather.'

'Aye, I'm aware o' that, but dinna fash, y'self, *bodach*, at *this* table!'

His grin broadened, for Annie's strange mixture of Gaelic and English when aroused, was entertaining! Her early transference to Forest Lodge and Glengarth had obviously confused her, to say the least.

'Och! Put away the dirk, Lindsay. 'Tis like shoes placed on a meal table, disrespectful and full o' bad luck. You can keep you'er bad luck up at the castle, I'm thinking.' She thrust a table knife, instead, into his hand.

But he, too, was stubborn, and didn't always like to be bullied by Annie who could be extremely forceful when she chose. 'Thank you, but your kitchen knife is blunt. I'll use the dirk, *Uisga Caillich*, if you don't mind!'

'Ach! So ma fine Hi'land landlord is familiar with witches, is he?' said Annie, her hands spread wide on her hips, 'Then *here*!' She fetched down a jar from the shelf and tipped the money on the table. 'Here's the rent-money for this week.' She leaned across the table, her elbows firmly planted among the biscuits and cheese, her slanting green eyes mocking. 'Will there be anything else, m' grand English landlord?' The words rolled off her tongue, rich and wonderful and all-Annie!

Lindsay swallowed a piece of sweaty cheese and moved the coins around with the point of his dirk. 'Why, Annie Gowrie, you've short-changed me! Your rent's just been raised.'

'If you weren't o' noble birth, m'laird, ye'd be a rascal!'

Laughing, he put the point of the dirk to her softly swelling cleavage, Annie's bodice not quite fully fastened, he suspected, in order to gain his fullest attention and admiration. 'I've a wee bone to pick with you, *Uisga Caillich*.'

'And what might that wee bone be, m'laird?'

'Saladin. I never mentioned the subject before, but I will now, simply because gossip is rife in the glens.'

'Saladin?' Her green eyes were wide and remarkably vacant.

'A matter of principle, Annie Gowrie. I believe you took it into your sweet head to contradict my orders concerning Saladin.'

'Saladin, m'laird?'

'Iona's horse, Annie, so let's become serious for a moment, shall we? You sold Saladin to a horse-thief in Gairloch when I told Mr Mitchell to get Tom Drummond to shoot the beast.'

'Beast is no word to use on a helpless and frightened animal like Saladin, Lindsay, for there are many more *real* beasts around Glengarth, and two-footed ones at that!'

'I *ordered* Saladin to be destroyed. It's not for you to contradict those orders.'

'Ach!' She waved her hands airily, 'Mr Mitchell agreed with me, 'Twas bad business shooting an innocent creature and a valuable one at that, m'laird, for when you came to your senses, you'd ha'e hated yourself. So we agreed to sell Saladin for a good profit.'

'Ach! did ye noo? So what became of the good profit, ma lassie?'

'I gave it to the Miss Christabel.'

Lindsay, astonished, looked up then from the mouldy cheese he was dissecting with his knife. '*Christabel?* What on earth for?'

'For her charity work.'

'What charity work?'

'Women's charities in Edinburgh and London.'

Lindsay started to laugh. He went on laughing.

At length he caught his breath to say, 'Annie Gowrie, you're priceless! My sister's only charity is the Women's Suffragette Movement. Do you know what that is?'

'Of course!' She drew herself up proudly. ''Tis for all the poor women who have to suffer at the hands of their men in this world. 'Tis for the likes of me destroyed by an animal called Fletcher.'

He looked at her a long time. 'Yes,' he said in a more subdued manner, 'I suppose you're right.'

'Mr Mitchell, Tom and I did no harm. We conspired, yes, to save the life of a poor dumb animal – a very valuable one too! So don't be angry, Lindsay.'

'I'm not angry, I'm amazed. Amazed at the loyalty of all my faithful retainers who know how to save me from hating myself the morning after the night before.'

Lindsay put away his hunting knife, sheathing it into the leather belt of his faded cords tucked into riding boots. He scraped back the stool. 'Well now, since your debt to me has increased, I'll take the rest in kind ... this kind.' He lifted her out of the rocking chair.

She raised no objection. He carried her over the threshold to the bed in the byre.

A steady drumbeat roused Lindsay early the following morning. Unable to get back to sleep, he decided to investigate. It sounded as though the logs sent down the timber-chutes from the forests to the loch had come adrift.

Annie continued to sleep on in her dreams. Lindsay lifted the bar securing the cot door and let himself out into the wintry morning. The north wind ruffled the waters of the loch. Out on the Minch the waves flung themselves at the rocks, churning up a boiling, white-crested froth. Today was no day to put to sea; he was only thankful

Annie had returned safely home from her trip to Errin.

Lindsay felt in his jacket pockets for his cigarettes but couldn't find the case. He remembered then: he had left it on the table from last night.

Rather than go back for it and disturb Annie who was tired after her sea-faring expedition to Errin, he decided to take a walk round the island without the pleasure of his pre-breakfast indulgence of a cigarette.

To the north-east of the island, timber was scattered everywhere, the logs bumping into each other and making the drumming noise that had awakened him, some piling themselves up on the island while others floated seaward. Somebody, Lindsay couldn't help feeling, had been very negligent when securing the log-rafts awaiting despatch to Argyll and Glasgow. He wished now he had pursued his earlier intention of asking Rory to convey Glengarth's timber to Glasgow on his modern coasters fitted with the proper derricks. In the end pride had got the better of good sense, and he had abandoned the idea of such a deal with his brother.

The wild cat and golden eagle, each born of the same environment, yet constantly at war with one another: sometimes he felt like that with Rory.

With a view to hurrying back to the estate office to get Julian Mitchell to send some men to resecure the timber, Lindsay turned away from the log barrier and the next moment was felled to the shore by a savage blow between the shoulder-blades.

The breath knocked out of him, he lay on the white sand of Rill, gasping with pain and shock and anger.

He looked up and beheld the grinning, bearded face of Fletcher.

'Gude mornin' m'laird!' Fletcher's loud belly-laugh unnerved Lindsay. The man hadn't changed a bit. If anything, he had grown wilder, dirtier, uglier.

Fletcher flung aside the pit-prop and in the instant he unsheathed his dirk Lindsay reached for his. 'Ach noo, ma laird,' Fletcher sneered. 'D'y'ken who's for the skinning?'

'You Fletcher, *you*!' Lindsay said.

'Ach!' Fletcher shook his bear-like head. 'Annie

Gowrie's grown, I ken, an' got womanly parts since laist we met. So the grand laird is no' so high-minded any more, about whose doing the laying of her, eh, ma fucking Sassenach landlord!'

White rage churned inside Lindsay. But the anger he kept from spilling over into his actions. Wild cat, or golden eagle, which was he?

He must keep a cool head and not let Fletcher's crude jibes precipitate him into losing his grip on the situation, for Annie's sake.

Lindsay faced Fleddon an Fletcher, the dirk he had used to pare Annie Gowrie's sweaty cheese, clutched tightly in his hand.

Fletcher jabbed his dirk at Lindsay, toying with him. 'Come, fight like a mon, ma laird! Show thy noble spirit an' prove thy spunk ain't milk-juice!'

Jabbing and darting his dirk in Lindsay's face, he had been edging him all the while towards the barrier of logs at the water's edge.

Knee-deep in the loch, Lindsay was forced further and further backwards, all the time carefully watchful of Fletcher's knife hand. Fletcher came on relentlessly, snorting with effort, lunging savagely through the drifting logs, aiming for Lindsay's throat. He flung himself sideways, out of Fletcher's reach, and went under.

Breathlessly Lindsay surfaced, shocked by the icy water into near numbness. The tide was strong. But despite his ungainly size, Fletcher was agile and nimble on his feet. Thrusting his whole weight forward, his head down like a charging bull, Lindsay felt the blade of Fletcher's knife tearing through cloth and muscle. There was no pain, only a burning sensation in his right arm while lochwater turned red. He lost his knife.

Lindsay stumbled, the freely floating logs getting in his way. He lashed out at Fletcher with his feet and left arm, the right one hanging useless.

Then Fletcher himself stumbled, half-turned and over-balanced as a log, swept in by the waves, caught him unawares behind the knees. Panic was written on Fletcher's face before he plunged under the water. In the moment that Fletcher surfaced, gasping and choking, Lindsay realized the man couldn't swim.

He seized the opportunity to entice Fletcher deeper into the loch. 'Come on, what are you afraid of?' he challenged.

Fletcher, up to his neck in water, his dirk held high, stabbed uselessly, Lindsay just out of reach of the point of his dirk.

He was unprepared for Fletcher's next attack. Grabbing hold of a log, Fletcher used it as a caber. It struck Lindsay full in the chest.

Knocked off balance, Lindsay went under. Fletcher seized the moment and his chance to grab Lindsay's legs, dragging him towards the shallow edge of the shore. Then he took hold of Lindsay's hair, pulling his head out of the water: 'Ach ... bleed now like a pig while I cut thy throat ma fine landlord ...' but Fletcher had not made allowances for the loch shore shelving deeply, nor the soft sucking movement of the sand beneath his water-logged boots. He felt himself sinking. Terrified of ending up under the water a second time, he stumbled backwards and Lindsay, beneath the water-line, his lungs bursting, made a grab for Fletcher's knees.

Brought down, Fletcher parried hopelessly with the dirk. Lindsay let go of the man's legs and concentrated on holding Fletcher's bearded face in the water keeping it there with the whole weight of his body clamped down athwart Fletcher's burly shoulders.

Unable to breathe, water in his nose, throat and lungs, Fletcher's nervously flexing fingers under the water, let go the dirk. It sank out of sight into the silt tossed up by the two fighting men.

Yet still he was not beaten.

Muscular, strong and powerful, Fletcher's neck and shoulders had an animal strength far superior to that of Lindsay. He jerked his head up, catching Lindsay on the jaw, then jabbed both elbows back at the same time to Lindsay's midriff.

The thump on the jaw from Fletcher's mighty head knocked him almost senseless and even while the world swam before Lindsay's eyes, Fletcher came up out of the water, gasping, snorting, swearing in fury as he launched himself on top of the man *this* time he was surely going to kill with his bare hands. It would not be the first time he had killed a man with his bare hands! At last, to put an end to this fine laird, this proud Sassenach landlord, this Roskillen upstart, would be *all* pleasure. He grabbed hold of Lindsay's injured arm. Wrenching and twisting, like a shark shaking and renting its prey; a wolf destroying the rabbit; the wild cat overpowering the golden eagle ...

Every agonizing contortion increasing the distance between his body and mind, Lindsay's shout of pain smothered by Fletcher's bulk, was lost to the stormy morning. Then the wild man of Raasay dragged the Laird of Glengarth by the collar to the sandy white beach surrounding Rill.

On firm land Fletcher felt safer, more in control. His strong hands clamped around Lindsay's throat, choking the life out of him. He squeezed and squeezed with no mean strength, seeing the laird turning blue and bulge-eyed in his last struggle, and Fletcher's smile was that of the killer shark.

The mad face in front of Lindsay's eyes was that of an Indian Sadhu crying vengefully, '*On thy head, on thy head, on thy head ...*'

The waters around him blood-red, Lindsay lost his grip on reality. His last conscious thought was that this time he really couldn't do anything more to protect Annie Gowrie from her stepfather: Fletcher had won.

Annie Gowrie stood nerveless, the piece of driftwood still in her shaking hand.

The Laird of Glengarth lay curled up on the shore, white sands stained with fresh blood.

Her stepfather, Fleddon an Fletcher, lay on his back after the blow she had struck him with the piece of drift-wood. His head lay at a strange angle, his eyes staring at the grey sky. Harsh, gurgling sounds came from his throat. Frothy blood-flecked spit dribbled into his tangled wet beard. His slack, rubbery lips pushed out with each noisy exhalation. Annie was aware of nothing and everything in that terrifying moment when she saw herself with the sin of murder, the ultimate sin, added to all her other sins.

She dropped the stave of wood, and with a whimper of fright, fell to her knees beside the bleeding, deathly still form of Lindsay, her laird.

'Lindsay, oh, Lindsay. I think I've killed him ...'

She lifted him to her as best she could, unable to bear the thought that the person she held dearest in her life, was also dead.

Moving him brought a positive response. He began to cough and splutter, his breath catching in his throat: 'An ... Annie, don't hold me so tight ...'

Tears streaming down her face, half laughing, half crying, hysterical with relief, Annie hugged him tighter still. 'Oh, m'laird! Thank God ... oh, praise be to God on high!'

He opened his eyes, blinked and smiled up at her. Lindsay struggled to sit up but Annie held him close, cradling his head in her arms, crooning and crying until he had to find the wherewithal to recapture his dignity. 'Annie Gowrie, *let go*! You're suffocating me.' Lindsay put a hand to his head, weakness destroying his will to resist Annie's ministrations.

'You're hurt ... oh, don't die on me now, m'laird ... is the pain bad? Let me see ...' She eased off his torn, wet jacket and examined his injured arm. ''Tis a nasty gash through the shoulder, and muscle of the upper arm. I think you'll be needing stitches in that wound ... we'd best get you to Dr Robinson at once to get you mended.'

'Annie Gowrie, you're a witch,' said Lindsay, feeling as though he could sleep for a week. 'How do you know I'll mend?'

'Well, m'laird, you're certainly not going to die on me now! Not after I've just lost my soul to the Devil by killing Fletcher for you. You'll mend. Nurse Craigie and Dr Robbie Robinson are my good friends, just like your cousin Morag and her Minister husband at the Kirk in Gairloch. I learn things from my friends – amongst the teachings, how to take care of the sick and needy.'

While Annie spoke in breathless bursts of nervous energy, she tore the hem of her nightdress to make a staunching bandage for his arm.

Lindsay said, 'You're a saint as well as a witch, Annie Gowrie. So tell me what happened just now?'

'Oh, Lindsay, I hit him. He was strangling you to death, so I hit him hard on the back of his head with the piece of wood I picked up while he was kneeling over you. I think I *must* have killed him.'

'I hope so. You'll have put paid to all my worries.'

'It's no jesting matter, m'laird. I didn't intend to kill him. 'Tis a mortal sin to take life, no matter how evil that life may be ... they'll hang me if he dies,' Annie gibbered, suddenly overcome by nerves.

'Annie, don't be silly, Don't worry about it. You saved my life – would you rather he had killed me?'

'No! Don't even think such a thing, Lindsay!' She hugged him again, too tightly, and Lindsay winced with the agony of love inflicted on his torn arm, not to mention the rest of his battered, bleeding body. But he loved her too much to grumble about his plight.

'I *had* to hit him, Lindsay,' Annie explained. 'Oh Lindsay ... you are the whole world to me, I *couldn't* let him kill you. Then he would have come after me again. I heard you leave the cot, so I came after you with this ... knowing how you always have a craving for these special cigarettes of yours.' She handed him the gold-plated cigarette case he was loathe to do without.

'Annie,' Lindsay said, looking at the remaining cigarette ruefully, 'you're a darling girl. But the matches in my pocket are wet, so how am I going to light my last cigarette? I don't suppose you've brought my lighter with you as well?'

She shook her head. 'I just grabbed the cigarette-case, not thinking that you'd left your lighter by the lamp after you'd lit it when we got home last night.'

Lindsay put the cigarette-case back in his pocket and held her close instead. He glanced across at Annie's stepfather. 'He doesn't look very dead to me. Are you sure you hit him hard enough?'

'Please don't make light of it, Lindsay. I hit him ... very hard.'

'A cracked skull ... broken neck perhaps: his head seems at a funny angle. Don't worry Annie, you haven't killed him. He's unconscious, that's all.'

'What are we going to do, Lindsay?'

Lindsay thought about it: at least his little fishergirl wouldn't have the monster's death on her conscience since it appeared Fletcher was still breathing. Lindsay didn't care one way or the other. He would gladly have stuck a dirk in Fletcher right there and then, finishing him off altogether and for ever, had not Annie been present.

'Annie,' he said thoughtfully, 'find his fishing-boat and bring it round to this side of the island.'

'I'll try ... what are you thinking of doing with him, Lindsay?'

'We're taking your stepfather for a little joy-ride, *Uisga Caillich.* We'll put him in his own boat and tow him out to sea. It won't be our fault if a storm overtakes him off Cape Wrath.'

Lindsay placed a reassuring hand on Annie's shoulder.

And then he started to shiver as the chill wind, combined with the delayed reaction of shock, struck him. Annie put his jacket back over his shoulders before she left him to find Fletcher's boat. 'Oh, Annie!' Lindsay shouted after her, 'bring my lighter with you.'

Lindsay contemplated dousing Fletcher's body with fuel-oil, and then setting alight to it, just to make quite sure he wouldn't return from the dead. But he rejected the idea in the end: it was far too barbaric, far too theatrical, far too Viking! The police would be down on him in no time! Far better to dispose of Fletcher in the simplest possible way, so that no finger of suspicion could be pointed at himself or Annie Gowrie from Rill.

Lost in a limbo-land, his shoulder and head throbbing painfully, Lindsay sat down on a log. Not knowing what to do with his hands without a cigarette to hold, he clasped them tightly between his knees. It helped to lessen the pain, the strain, and the blood seeping through the flimsy makeshift bandage.

Beinn Claidheamh Mor was all but invisible through the murky mist and low cloud. As he stared into the distance, he heard Annie's voice: 'Lindsay, I can't bring the boat any nearer. The logs are all over the place ...'

Lindsay willed himself to get up off the log and take hold of the body of Annie Gowrie's stepfather.

His boots sank into the soft white sand: millions and millions of shellfish, crushed through the ages, these were the sands of Rill. He did not know why he had thought of such a thing at that moment, as he dragged Fletcher's inert body over the sands of Rill, but everything had suddenly assumed a larger than life dimension, with the contours of his own perceptions more sharply defined. He shook his head to clear it, blood and sweat mingling.

Perspiration froze under his wet clothes. Lindsay did not know how he did it, but as he sweated and strained with only one arm to drag Fletcher over the beach, he knew he was chancing his life.

It was a lengthy, gory business, leaving tracks behind him which he did not even care about nor consider in his haste to get rid of Fletcher's half-dead body. He had a piercing pain over his right eye and his right arm had started to bleed profusely, the bindings on his arm having become quite useless.

He willed himself not to give in.

He grit his teeth while he alternatively dragged, then rolled Fletcher's gross body to the cove where Annie was able to bring his fishing-boat close to the shore. She helped toss the body of her stepfather into the bottom of the boat. When they reached Lindsay's larger steam-powered boat, they attached a line from the stern of his boat to the bows of Fletcher's sailing-smack. Then they towed Fletcher's body to the open sea.

The storm hit them off Cape Wrath, just as Lindsay had predicted.

It was a risk he had been prepared to take.

Cutting loose Fleddon an Fletcher's sailing-smack, Lindsay and Annie abandoned the wildman of Raasay to

the elements and the murderous rocks that had long ago
been the cause of the sinking of the last of the mighty
Spanish Armada.

Well now, thought Lindsay without an ounce of
remorse, let Fletcher join the ghosts of the sea.

Afterwards, they headed for Lewis, where the *Flower of
the Glen*, his grandfather's steamboat, rode out the worst
of the storm in Stornoway harbour.

Forty-eight hours later they sailed the *Flower of the
Glen* back into the loch. Silver-grey and strangely peaceful
under a luminescent sky, everything was washed clean
again by the storm that had left no trace of the bloody
fight between Fletcher and himself on the white sands of
Rill.

Several timber rafts passed by, transporting the re-
gathered and securely lashed logs to the shipyards and pit-
heads of Glasgow.

Up on the rocky mull, Glengarth stood solemn and
imposing against its woven tapestry of the variegated
forest. Lindsay breathed once more the familiar scent of
pine mingling with the salty sea-breezes. He listened to the
call of the herring gulls wheeling and diving over the black
rocks, and he put his uninjured arm around Annie's
slender waist.

She was at the helm, her green eyes reflecting the pine
forest. Her hair was part of the refreshing breeze, her
voice and laughter, echoes of the sea. 'Home and dry at
last, Annie,' Lindsay said. 'And home, my dear, is where
the hearth is ... or is it heart? I can never remember.' He
smiled down at her, looking so serious while she concentrated in bringing the big steamboat into a safe berth. 'As
there's plenty of timber lying around your island, please
can we have a log fire tonight instead of that wretched
peat which gets in my throat and eyes?' Lindsay implored.

'No m'laird. Peat is what humble folk like myself burn.
Logs are only for the grand ones up at the castle.'

'And Annie ...' Lindsay ruefully contemplated his
useless arm in its sling.

'Yes, m'laird?'

'Once upon a time there was a land called Baharabad

belonging to a rich Maharajah – that's an Indian Emperor in case you didn't know. Inside the Maharajah's pink palace there dwelt two little boys and two little girls who dreamt of snow-covered glens and mountains in the blinding heat of this Maharajah's exotically flat country. And one of the little boys had a parrot called Macbeth. Macbeth never learned a darned thing. You remind me very much of my uneducated green parrot.'

Her silky black hair caught by the wind, brushed his unshaven cheek. She tossed her head disdainfully. 'You're an education to me, my fine landlord. I know that if ever I'm to hang for Fletcher it will be in worthy company.'

Lindsay squinted up at the lonely, grey castle, battle-scarred by time and tide. He recalled his grandfather's words ... *An eye for an eye, Lindsay and make no mistake. It's as the good book says. And remember, too, m'boy, everything in life has its price ...*

'Annie,' Lindsay said solemnly. 'I love you more than I've loved anyone in my life. I love you more than Iona. Don't ever fling that love back in my face.'

'I could never do that, Lindsay, my laird. For I, in return, love you more than life itself.'

Together, they brought the *Flower of the Glen* safely home to her moorings.

CHAPTER TWENTY-SIX

Hogmanay, and a fine banquet was to be held in Glengarth's baronial hall to which everyone who was anyone in Edinburgh, Aberdeen, Glasgow and even as far away as London, had been invited. The household servants, tenants, foresters, estate workers and their families, had had their party separately the previous day, leaving them free to help out at the castle on *the* night.

Christabel sent a message to Rill, requesting Annie's assistance at Glengarth, as they required all the helping hands that could be mustered. Annie had not returned to the castle since the Lady Iona had found out about her relationship with the laird, and had dismissed her.

Iona had been very fond of Annie whom she had befriended and made her confidante. For Annie to betray her in such a low fashion was the last straw as far as Iona was concerned. Annie herself understood Lady Iona's reasons entirely. But Annie eased her conscience by telling herself that she loved Lindsay, her laird, more than the Lady Iona had *ever* loved him. She loved the laird more than herself, more than life itself, more than the decrees of society, and so she could endure the humiliation, the gossip, and the isolation. At least now she had her cottage and Lindsay all to herself. So when the message from his sister arrived, asking her to come to Glengarth, Annie had been both surprised and suspicious.

Annie had sent back a stiff little reply, informing the laird's sister that 'Annie Gowrie would be unavailable on Hogmanay night'.

But Christabel was nothing if not persuasive. She sent another message conveying the fact that the old retainer, Murray, would otherwise be left on his own to wash and polish the mounds of silver, which would be unfair to an old man of his age and infirmities. So Annie went back to Glengarth: but only for one evening she promised herself, fully aware of how ruthless and vindictive Christabel Roskillen could be.

Annie was glad that the great hall resembled its baronial status this night, rather than a Japanese flower garden. Lady Iona having lost interest in 'Art Nouveau' and everything else, the suits of armour had been restored to their rightful place; so had the family portraits, lairds' hunting trophies, bagpipes and swords, much more in keeping with a medieval castle!

Annie, ruefully contemplating her lowly status in the laird's grand life, blew a limp strand of hair out of her eyes, and then dashed her soapy hand across her forehead. Why was life so unfair?

'What ails thee, Annie Gowrie?' Murray asked, rheumy old eyes in their semi-blindness frowning at her above the silver salver he was carefully wiping. As was the custom on special occasions, and according to old Scottish tradition, when it came to washing the family silver, the servants were tucked away behind some screens at the far end of the hall where guests couldn't see them. The old retainer and Annie Gowrie had been given the more menial task of washing the used cutlery, polishing and rewashing the silver in the presence of the owner of that silver, the laird.

Annie closed her eyes tight, hoping to shut out the image of the laird and his wife seated on the dais in their finery, surrounded by all the lordly rich from other grand houses. Their lives were a million light years from hers. Annie wondered what it would be like to have everything in the world without having to snatch it, fight for it, ask for it, or work for it.

Annie held her red chapped hands under the hot, soapy water, with the steam in her face, and the soreness was not in her hands but her heart. In her mind's eye she could see Lindsay in his old tweed jacket with the leather patches on the elbows, and faded cords tucked into high riding boots. His 'working gear' he called it, for his boots were usually dusty with the sands of Rill, or caked with Glengarth soil when 'heeling' his new saplings, or working in the glass-houses where the seedlings and saplings were nurtured for the first two years before planting out. These were the times she loved him best of all, for he seemed more human, a man like any other, not a noble being far above her station in life!

She thought about how his fair hair turned silver in the sunlight: just like his eyes. He had strange, chameleon eyes; one minute they could be a warm, laughing grey, the next like a frosty morning in the glen, icy, hooded and sinister. There was almost an albino look about him when he was angry, upset or displeased with something: it was as though the colour had been wrung from him. His moods were so unpredictable! He could be warm and loving, thoughtful and generous, as when he had saved her from Fleddon an Fletcher. But he could also turn swiftly to a monster, an aggressive, arrogant, hurtful, distrustful and destructive monster! He had destroyed the Lady Iona, that was for sure! Annie was afraid of that secret side to Lindsay's nature, the core of which she herself was unable to penetrate.

And Annie would feel lost: lost and alone and infinitely vulnerable. Yet she loved him so much. She had loved him from the very first moment he had ridden his horse across the causeway, only a boy and she just a snippet of a girl gutting fish on her mother's doorstep. She had loved him even more when he had come riding back to remove her out of reach of the man who had taken possession of her, body and soul, with his vile appetites.

Yes, she loved the Laird Lindsay very much. She loved him every moment of the day and night. She loved him when he rode his horse along the white shores surrounding her island home, the water and the sands over Burrell's hooves as they both waited for her to sail her fishing boat back into the loch. She loved him with all her heart in the firelight when they were alone together in the cottage after a day on the sea. And she loved him when she saw him outside her cottage, romping with the dog, tugging a lobster creel out of Bonnie Charlie's jaws and paws – until

Fletcher had gone and killed the dog, too, skinning it like a rabbit and turning the laird into a killer himself.

So why did she hate the sight of him tonight? Annie tortured herself further. Why did she hate the sight of the laird seated there in all his fine Highland regalia, next to his beautiful, wealthy, barren wife who was learning to walk again with his help and encouragement? She looked so angelic tonight, in her white satin frock and plaid sash adorned with a lucky rabbit's foot set in sparkling diamonds – not the tartar with the spiteful tongue, she usually was.

On the other side of him sat his frosty, unemotional sister who could be as ruthless and self-seeking as the rest of her ilk. Christabel Roskillen had a silken tongue more devious than a serpent's, were Annie's resentful thoughts. Suddenly she hated them all so much, she wanted to destroy their world – a world that had placed him up there on a pedestal while she was left to pick out the bits of food stuck on the prongs of his silver forks ...

'Have thee gone to sleep in the tub, Annie Gowrie?' Murray's querulous old voice intruded yet again upon her jumbled thoughts, everything coming together on this night to make her discontented for the first time in her simple, uncomplicated life.

Annie opened her eyes. She took her hands out of the basin, wiping them hurriedly on the cloth for polishing the silver. She knew she would never again be contented with the portion allotted her, not after tonight. She fished in her pocket and drew out a piece of folded paper. 'Give this to the laird, but make sure no one sees.'

The old man in his dotage never questioned anything, trained all his life to obey commands like a dog unto its master. He put his right hand behind his ear, 'What's that ye say, lassie?'

'The laird!' she mouthed, pointing to herself. Then she put her finger to her lips and shook her head as she thrust the piece of paper into Murray's leathery palm.

Slowly comprehension dawned. 'Aye,' he said, pocketing the note. 'Foolish, foolish! Ye're both playing with fire,

Annie Gowrie, an' I'm a foolish body, too. But 'tis no place o' mine to judge thee and he.'

She knew her message would be delivered safely, for Murray was loyal to the laird to his last drop of blood.

Annie finished her chores before returning to her cottage to wait for Lindsay to come to her. She would not normally have bothered the laird on this important night of the year, but Annie was distraught. Besides, the laird had become part of her being, and she needed him as much as anybody.

Annie waited over two hours for Lindsay, hoping Murray had delivered her note without the laird's wife or sister finding out. Annie sat in her rocking chair, in her lap the Bible her father and mother had taught her to read from the moment she could walk and talk.

The 'Big Black Book' had taught her many things: it had taught her geography, history and social customs; about paradise, and Adam and Eve; about love and hate, good and evil; it taught her about God, and about heaven and hell, about the Devil and his wicked angels; about Jesus, his parables and his disciples, among whom were counted two fishermen. The 'Big Black Book' had opened up new vistas for her, lands across the seas she would never visit, and foreign people she would never meet; and it spoke of mortal sins such as envy, jealousy and resentment. It had taught her to think for herself.

She liked reading, and one day up at the castle, while she had been dusting the shelves and shelves of books in Glengarth's library, wondering to herself how so many books could have been written and brought together in one place, the laird had discovered her spending more time reading than dusting. He had given her *The Heart of Midlothian* by Sir Walter Scott. And she had loved him more than ever for his being aware of her as a person and not just as an object around his castle. She had treasured that book, and kept it for a long time reading it over and over again, before she had at last reluctantly returned it, carefully and exactly as it had been lent to her.

But tonight she didn't read. Tonight she waited for him

to come to her while she held the Bible in her lap and
relived the night of the Forest Lodge fire when Fletcher
had come back for her. She heard again those childish
voices of Aeneas and little Bruce, discussing the 'bug-a-
boo' and the 'bogey-man' their spinster-cousin Christabel
frightened them with in order that they should behave
themselves.

Annie had loved those children as though they were her
own. Their fanciful innocence was beguiling and so
amusing to listen to while they told each other disjointed
tales of the kelpies discovered through the story books.

Fleddon an Fletcher had only meant to fire the plantations in order to hit back at the laird, never dreaming that
the sparks and hot ashes driven before the wind would be
blown onto the newly thatched roof of Forest Lodge....
Annie tried not to think about it.

The fire ran away with them all that night, including
Fletcher, she thought miserably. Annie put her head in her
hands. Her mother, poor soul had been out of her head,
grief stricken over her husband's death – Annie's own dear
father, like a guiding light himself, whose flame had been
cruelly extinguished one stormy night at sea. Mother had
taken up with Fleddon an Fletcher in return for his
support, for a widow with a young child to bring up alone,
was not an enviable position to be in.

But the ruffian from Raasay had come to the island to
torment them, his kindness and charm in the beginning
soon disappearing, to be replaced by his true, barbarian
self. Mercifully, Annie's mother had been spared much
more of Fletcher and his evil ways, for she had perished
from a chill of the lungs after being caught, just like her
husband, in a storm at sea. She had died within the week,
her frail, undernourished, and hard-worked body unable
to fight the fever. Annie was left to her stepfather.

And sea-storms were God's judgement upon fisherfolk
who defied the elements, thought Annie restlessly. She got
up and put away the Bible on the shelf above her bed, too
much melancholy thinking by herself not good. She took
her plaid shawl and walked slowly back to Glengarth
Castle.

As she approached the gatehouse and crossed the wooden bridge spanning the grassy moat, she saw the laird standing in the shadows under Mr Mitchell's flat. The feeble glow from the ancient horn-lantern hanging high above his head reflected off his fair hair and illuminated his dear and familiar face. A feather tracing her heart, she clutched her shawl tightly across her breast, and ran to meet him.

He *had* been true to her, after all! He *had* been on his way to Rill to spend the rest of the night in *her* company, not with the grand ones from far away, were Annie's joyful thoughts in that moment. '*Lindsay, oh, Lindsay*! I thought Murray had forgotten to give you my message … I thought you were never coming … Oh!'

It wasn't the laird.

Annie felt a fool, her joy giving way to a terrible embarrassment as, in confusion, she stared into a face that was like Lindsay's but not Lindsay's. The stranger into whose arms she had flung herself seemed as astonished as she, but his hearty laugh as he reluctantly released her was reassuring. 'Well, if that ain't the best danged New Year's greeting I've received in a long time!'

Now that Annie could see him more closely, there was much about this stranger that was quite different to the Laird Lindsay. For a start, he spoke with an unfamiliar accent. The line of his jaw was squarer, determined-looking. He had a cleft in his chin, with a special attractiveness about the way he smiled. He was more broad-shouldered and half a head taller. His hair was not as fair, but held rich, reddish lights, a wonderful colour. The eyes, too, told them apart. This man's were bluer, more open, his manner more spontaneous and charming, whereas the laird was always so reserved, cool and detached. Annie knew that Lindsay's smiles often came from a paper pattern, not his heart. Lindsay, as much as he loved her and she loved him, would never have extended a passionate greeting quite so openly, with arms welcoming her warmly and blatantly.

So this must be the brother who had done great things with Hamish MacDearg's old steamship company, were

Annie's thoughts. She had heard the family talk a lot
about 'Rory Duncan', and his ambitious ways. And now,
after all these years, he had come home to Glengarth,
even though he had dwelt in Glasgow – which wasn't that
far away to have paid the occasional visit to his relatives!
Annie wondered what had made him stay away until now.

'I'm sorry ... I ... I thought you were the laird ...' She
broke off, even more confused and feeling out of place.

His eyes dancing, he said, 'Just my luck! And I thought
a bonnie Hi'land lass like you was after me for my ... self
...' Hesitating, he turned around, a shaft of light falling
over the worn cobblestones of the courtyard as the doors
of the great hall opened, letting out a babble of sound and
laughter.

A man stood illuminated in the light, dressed in clan
tartan, impressive in his green and gold and scarlet kilt,
stark white shirt with front frills and dark green, velvet
jacket, bonnet and plume. This time there was no
mistaking the laird. He said something over his shoulder
to someone at the door before it was closed and the light
vanished just as if someone had flicked off a switch. He
descended the steps lightly to the courtyard, dark again
after that brief illumination from inside the castle.

'Please,' Annie whispered to Rory, standing in the
gloom of his ancestral home, 'don't let him know I came
here ...'

'But I thought ...?'

'*Hssht*! He comes ...' She darted back into the shadows
and Rory was left at a loss, wondering who this sprite of
the night happened to be. She was tall, lithesome and
green-eyed. With her long, black hair drifting freely to her
waist, she was like a sea-nymph, a Lamia, casting a magic
spell over him. In her thin, plaid shawl, homespun grey
skirt, and bare feet defying pneumonia on this freezing
night, she intrigued him and he wanted to know more
about her. Why she was seeking out his brother in such a
surreptitious fashion.

Lindsay crossed the courtyard to the moathouse. 'Who's
there?' he called out sharply, aware of the fleeting
shadows and the figure of a man captured beneath the

horn lantern, who seemed to be talking to himself.

''Tis I, you blind Scotchman! Don't you recognize your own brother?'

'Rory?'

'The only one. It's a brau brek moonlech necht to say auld lang syne and all that other old Scottish twaddle. The limit of my Gaelic exhausted, I'm glad to say, how are you Lindsay, old fellow?'

Annie heard Lindsay's attractive laugh, a rare sound but always a joyous one. 'Good Lord! So the prodigal son has returned at last. I wondered if you'd ever show up again ... Happy New Year, Rory!'

'The same to you, Lindsay. Sorry I'm not a black man to bring you luck on this bonny night, but lead me to the fatted calf and ubesque and I'll die a happy one.' They greeted one another with hearty backslaps and good humoured chuckles. 'My, it's good to be home, brother!'

'It's good to have you back, Rory. Why didn't you let us know you were coming?'

'Because, dear fellow, telephones and telegraph in this outlandish place appear not to function as quickly as my two legs ... even the pony and cart from Achnasheen station was moribund. So I decided to trek the distance along the old grassy military track haunted by headless Clan Chieftains. Well, aren't you going to ask me to come inside your mouldering relic, or must I stand out here all night freezing to death?'

They went inside the castle, hall doors opening again to let the light and warmth and happiness inside momentarily escape into the deserted courtyard.

Annie walked back slowly and thoughtfully down the hill, the grass stiff and icy between her bare toes. Not used to shoes, except when the weather was snowy or wet, she had forgotten to put them on in her impatience to see the laird again. She had wanted to talk to him so badly, tell him her secret, and now it was not to be: she would have to contain herself until another, more suitable time. Her breath in freezing clouds drifted in front of her face, she and the winter's night united in empty cold exclusion.

Annie took out her fishing-boat that night and stayed

away among the outer islands. She wanted Lindsay, her
laird, to know what it felt like to be shut out of a person's
affections. She wanted to allow him time to miss her. She
wanted him to know what it felt like when *he* went away
without explanation. She wanted him to realize just how
much he would miss her and how much he needed her!

Lindsay was not to know that Annie had left the island,
for he himself had been making arrangements to go to
Ayrshire, and then Glasgow, on a business trip. Rory's
reappearance in his life, saved him the immediate prospect
of Glasgow, for business could now be discussed at Glengarth. The main issue at stake was the dispute over exact
ownership of the Renfrew site where Rory now had a
thriving dredging business.

'What do you mean?' Rory demanded of his brother.
'You know damn well Hamish left his boatyard at
Renfrew to me – it was all settled at the time of his death.
Lizzie bought the adjoining yard off Alistair Middow. So
you can't get away with doing a Grandfather Glengarth
act on me, Lindsay!'

Lindsay smiled smoothly. 'The contract is in dispute,
I'm afraid, like it or not.'

'Then what was that piece of paper our solicitors
accepted regarding the land-contract reverting back to
Hamish after fifty years? Your own factor, Gilbert Lucas,
saw it and accepted the agreement.'

'Then our solicitors and my factor were at fault. But
they were not to know that the original document *does*
exist, appertaining to Hamish's Renfrew interests.'

'Oh, damnit, Lindsay! Don't keep patronizing me in
that tone of voice.'

'Very well. Just let me say this ... here is the *real
contract* for the Renfrew site.' Lindsay went to his desk
and took from the drawer a piece of yellowed parchment
bound with a red ribbon. 'What Hamish had in his possession was a copy – a very mangled, blurred copy as far as I
can gather. I took a little trip to your Glasgow offices last
winter to discuss the matter with you. Unfortunately, I
didn't know you had taken yourself off to America with

your millionairess, or that you would remain illusive for so long. Every time I tried to catch you on this side of the Atlantic, they told me you'd just skipped back to your New York office. But now you're here permanently, compare this contract with Hamish's. I went to see your solicitor before I left Glasgow, so at the time it wasn't altogether an abortive trip; he showed me the copy of the Renfrew agreement between Hamish and Grandfather, who had put up the money for Hamish's steamships in 1857.'

'What is the point of all this, Lindsay?'

'The point is, you owe me six years substantial rent on the leased site out at Renfrew, from where you and your ex-partner operated ... and I can't say I'm at all sorry about your split with your rich ladyfriend as American women are only out for themselves.'

'What the hell are you talking about, Lindsay?'

'Two erroneous copies of the Middow and Strait contract were made,' Lindsay said. 'The original contract is for a period of eighty years, not fifty as seems to have been mistakenly identified on the copy kept in our estate office as well as the one in Hamish's possession, the one subsequently handed on to you. Falsification or genuine mistake, take it as you will, Rory, but the fact remains, Grandfather Glengarth held an option on the Middow and Strait yard for *eighty* years, not fifty. The dog-eared copies look as though they were supposed to run for fifty years, but a five and an eight are digits that can easily be mistaken, or interchanged if the writing gets worn. Hamish misread his copy-contract, as I nearly did with Grandfather's.'

At this juncture Lindsay refrained from advertising cousin Iain Hamilton's own oversight, for he too, ought to have taken a more diligent look at such an old and valuable contract without 'assuming' it to be in order. He added, 'And solicitors themselves aren't above making errors of judgement, especially if they employ half-blind and senile copyists in their legal department, as was probably the case way back in 1857!'

'What rubbish!' Rory challenged. 'Numeric "50" was

also written down as "*fifty*", as is usual with all formal contracts.'

'Granted. But since Hamish's version too, became smudged somewhere along the line, he could easily have himself erased the lettering following the number of years the contract was supposed to run. But *eighty*, not *fifty*, Rory! Take another look at *your* copy when you return to Glasgow, and you'll see for yourself. The copies simply do not tally with the original, which was not in Edinburgh after all, but right here at Glengarth all the time.'

'Explain yourself, Lindsay,' said Rory in exasperation, getting more and more confused by this Middow and Strait boatyard contract out at Renfrew.

'Oh, suffice it to say that I spent a wasted two days in the Edinburgh offices of Grandfather's solicitors hunting down that original version of the contract, when it was here all the time. Grandfather Glengarth, who seemed to be of an eccentric disposition all his life, not just towards the end of it, had a habit of hiding valuable documents in his library – namely as bookmarkers. He had a morbid distrust of all banks, solicitors and trustees as far as I can gather.'

'Here, let me look at that piece of parchment for myself,' Rory said, and Lindsay happily handed it over.

Much to Rory's chagrin, the original document in his brother's possession clearly stated a period of eighty (80) years running from the year 1857. It was in a much more 'readable' condition, too, than the copy he had placed with his own solicitors in Glasgow. Hamish *could* have 'doctored' his own copy of the contract; or the wording had indeed worn out over the years – especially if Hamish had kept it in his old tea-caddy, which he used as a repository for all sorts of strange things. But *two* 'doctored' copies somehow stretched credibility, and so Lindsay's argument that the two copies had been wrongly made by a legal copyist of the time, the fives and eights being mistaken, seemed to be the most plausible.

Rory gave his brother the benefit of the doubt, reluctant as he was to admit defeat over the valuable Renfrew site.

Without his own copy of the contract in front of him,

he was unable to judge. Rory refolded the parchment and handed it back to Lindsay. 'Where did you find that? I thought your factor said that Grandfather Glengarth's contract had either been destroyed, or there wasn't one.'

Lindsay's lips twisted in a wry smile. 'I discovered it in *The Heart of Midlothian.* Someone had been desirous of reading it after she came across it whilst dusting the library. So I let her have it. I think she must have read it many times, because, when it was eventually returned to me, I tossed it on my desk without a second thought, where it lay buried for a few more months. Annie never mentioned the book contained anything other than Walter Scott's written word. She must have thought that the parchment had been left in as a bookmark, returned it, *per se* one missing land contract for a very valuable site. I must ask her sometime why she never mentioned it.'

Rory, with a grin, got up and helped himself to a glass of malt. 'For a man who doesn't drink, I wonder why you keep the stuff so readily available in your study?' he mused, replacing the stopper on the decanter. 'But I'm dashed glad you do!'

'It's there for Robbie Robinson's regular visits. I don't touch whisky.'

'Well, *sant' i' fa,* anyway. I know you're leading up to something else, so fire away, m'laird! But really, Lindsay, are you so hard up you're quibbling over six years rent?'

'It's not as simple. You know it takes a fortune to keep a pile the size of Glengarth viable. I scrimp and save wherever I can. Death duties owed after Grandfather died have been bankrupting! I'm doing the best I can to bring the forestry side of things into line, and I am succeeding slowly. But it's *too* slow and I always have a cash-flow problem. Therefore, in return for six years rent-free accommodation at Renfrew, I want a third share in the dredging business you operate out of that boatyard.'

Rory burst out laughing. Genuinely amused by Lindsay's audacity, he went on laughing. Lindsay did not share in his brother's hilarity. 'Why don't you wait until Lizzie and I go public? Then you can *buy* your way in legally!' Rory added.

'*Are* you going public?' Lindsay asked with considerable interest.

'I don't know,' said Rory more soberly. 'Lizzie and I had discussed it at one time. Although, in the end, a division of assets was amicably agreed upon, it has somewhat soured our business relationship over the past year. I hasten to add, she was fed up with me, and not the other way around. We didn't always see eye-to-eye in the way the steamship company should be run. However,' Rory paused, and went to the window. He was not desirous of spilling out his heart and soul to his brother. He was only glad he had heeded Hamish's advice and never married Lizzie. The last two years had been bad as far as his personal affairs were concerned. 'I wanted to go public as a means of limiting personal liability, but Lizzie decided to keep the Chanin-Beauly Line as a private enterprise. We're still bashing out the legal side of things since the split in our partnership. It remains to be seen how much I get out of it in the end. She put up most of the money – in fact, almost all.' Rory half-turned from his view of the Minch, and said over his shoulder in a deliberately light-hearted manner, 'Limited liability would have meant you'd have had to go to the shareholders for your six year's rent, dear brother!'

'I also want you to take Glengarth timber to Glasgow for the loading and transportation fee of three shillings and sixpence per ton.'

'Good God, Lindsay!' Rory's jaw dropped. 'We're supposed to be talking business, not highway robbery! My timber-coasters are the very best operating out of Glasgow, built with the strongest, most efficient and most modern of winching derricks and machinery. Please don't insult me.'

'Then, pending your acceptance of the Renfrew situation, and that the land was certainly not Hamish's to part with until the year 1937, you are beholden to me for allowing you to operate out of Renfrew for the last six years, without paying a penny! The interest, too, must have been mounting steadily since 1907 when Hamish mistakenly stopped paying *his* dues!'

'Lindsay, I'm solvent enough to remove my dredging-business, with its reputation for giving value for money, to another location. I daresay the Clyde Navigation Trust will lease me one of their sites, in view of the work R.D. Roskillen has already efficiently undertaken on their behalf.'

Lindsay smiled. '*Touché*, brother! You're a rogue and always have been, so we'll talk business on the way to the coalfields. I've managed to outwit the Norwegians on a most lucrative Government contract for pit-props. Until now, the bulk order for pit-props has been to the Baltic. I passed on my concern as to this sorry state of affairs to the Scottish Minister of State. In the event of a war with Germany and a German blockade of Northern waters being imposed, our coalfields would be in danger of shutting down altogether from a lack of necessary material such as pit-props. There is one thing to be said of this German Navy Law threat, and that is, it has done Glengarth the world of good!'

'I'll drink to the Kaiser, then,' said Rory, helping himself to more Scotch, 'since he has done me a favour, too. According to Fisher and other Lords of the Admiralty, Rosyth is to be the location of a new Naval dockyard and battle-base, with the main Mediterranean fleet absorbed into the Atlantic and Channel fleets ... by the way, I hope you haven't any spies listening at the keyhole,' said Rory, lowering his voice.

'Glengarth Castle, Rory is absolutely sound and spy proof, I assure you!'

'And draughty with it. Well, as I was saying, the second reason why, like you, I am crowing, is that an order for a fleet of *Dreadnought* and *Invincible* prototypes, with the first ever big gun on a non-fixed range, is to be built in Scotland. British warships will now be able to outrange even torpedo attack. However,' Rory sighed, 'protection for merchant shipping, I feel, is going to be our major headache. German U-boat attacks on our merchant fleet will leave us starving in these islands unless someone can think up a way to outwit the Boche. Gamin and I are trying out our own experiment – a sonar tracking and attacking device.'

'How do you know how to do all these things?' Lindsay asked in amazement. 'I mean, you've had no naval or mechanical training, or even business training, come to that. Yet you've got your finger in every pie, as far as I can tell.'

'All bluff, Lindsay. I'm really just a little fish swimming along with the bigger ones – in other words, a shark parasite. Benjamin Gammon, my first mate, as I still like to call him, might not be a shark but he's certainly a wizard with engines and inventions – bogus stories included. His repertoire is formidable! I have learned everything I know from him about boats and steam-engines and merchant-shipping. And he is a man also sorely lacking in formal education. So you see, one can do without experts and their phony advice. A chap without Pliny, Homer or Virgil, can still get to the top if he has three vital qualities: common sense, a nose to sniff out the best deals, and the guts to implement them.'

'Ah! Come on, tell the truth!' Lindsay interrupted. 'Other people always furnished you with a leg up the ladder. You didn't do it all by yourself even with your first mate's help.'

'Fair enough. And that's what I mean about bluff. Great-Uncle Neptune was the second person in my life to have a great influence. His lack of faith in me, while treating me like one huge joker in the pack, kept me going even when the ride got very rough indeed. But in the end, God bless him, the old codger coughed up! Lizzie Roebling Chanin was the third person to give me my big break into the stuff of dreams – money, and plenty of it. It got me started from humble beginnings, to what I have today. And fourthly, there is a very good business friend of mine in Garston, who sponsors me in all sorts of things with the Chamber of Commerce – including that of a patent for my own particular invention of a sonar navigation and tracking device.'

Lindsay stubbed out his cigarette in the ashtray on the table beside him. He got up out of the leather armchair in which he had been ensconced during this first-ever, heart-to-heart conversation with his brother. He glanced at his watch, his desire to see Annie making him impatient to get on his way. 'Well, tomorrow I'm off to Ayrshire if you want to accompany me. We'll go in my boat – my one and only! Unlike you, with a whole fleet at your disposal.'

Rory smiled. 'Fair enough. And afterwards we'll go to Glasgow where I'll give you a grand tour of my ship-building yards ... I say mine, but my ex-business partner could just as easily claim them for herself. I am only a paper-millionaire, if the truth be known.'

'And so am I if they use my trees for wood-pulp,' Lindsay quipped.

'We'll see. And I'll certainly think about carrying your timber and pit-props. But not for three shillings and six-pence.'

'No. I didn't think you'd take up that offer. See you in the morning, Rory. I'm setting off as soon as it gets light.'

'I'll be on the jetty,' Rory promised. Then, remembering the revelries of last night, and that today was the first day of the New Year, 1914, he held out his hand. 'Happy New Year, Lindsay.'

Lindsay grasped his brother's hand. 'The same to you, Rory.'

CHAPTER TWENTY-SEVEN

Being Annie, she was too proud to beg, so she played the game of love her way.

Annie returned to Rill ten days later and found out that the laird had gone with his brother in the *Flower of the Glen* to Ayrshire, hopefully to obtain further timber contracts. After that, Murray informed her, the two brothers were off to Glasgow.

Murray didn't know when the laird would be back, and no, he hadn't left Annie any personal message, although he had gone looking for her on New Year's Day.

She left Murray to his loud snoring beside the kitchen range at Glengarth.

Lindsay, she knew, had never mentioned the subject of his injured arm to anyone except Dr Robinson. His wife and sister had been given no real explanation of his absence or his injuries. The laird did not have to make excuses to anyone as to what he did with his private life. And in this last respect, Annie realized how disparate their lives were.

Then she made up her mind to end the relationship once and for all, because his station in life and hers were at the opposite ends of the pole; he was only using her while it suited him! She resolved to try to forget him, that he didn't matter to her any more, so why should she lose sleep over him? If he cared anything at all about her – as he declared so often that he did – why hadn't he left some sort of message of reassurance regarding Hogmanay night when she had asked him to come to her cottage? Why had he ignored her plea? He surely could have sneaked out at some time during the celebrations, even though his brother had arrived unexpectedly. And if Lindsay had been unable to get away from his guests and his host's duties, then he could have sent a message via Murray or Tom Drummond – just a simple note of love from him, wishing her a Happy New Year, that's all she had wanted.

Annie again set off fishing by herself, even though the weather and the white water was dangerous.

Then, one day, while Lindsay and Rory were in Glasgow, Christabel appeared on the threshold of Annie's cottage in all her fine furs. Annie couldn't help thinking how bonny the sister looked and how out of place in this humble cot. And Annie was wary. She didn't trust the laird's sister an inch, for if she required assistance up at the castle, she usually sent a message and it was Annie who went to her. Never had she lowered her grand self to come to Rill.

'Good morning, Annie, I want to talk to you,' was Christabel's self-assured greeting as she marched straight into the cottage without being invited.

Annie at once resented that condescending and patronizing air inbred in women like Christabel Roskillen. This was still *her* cottage and *her* ground. 'Good morning, m'lady. What brings you here at this hour?' was Annie's chilly greeting towards her visitor. She closed the door. She knew exactly why *m'lady* was here, and was prepared to throw her out at the first opportunity.

Christabel smiled. 'What a sweet little house you have, Annie.' Her blue eyes swept her surroundings, never missing a thing. She could not have been blind, even through she pretended to be, to Lindsay's gun propped in the corner and, staring her in the face, an old jacket of his hanging behind the door. 'So warm and homely,' she added, with that vacant lip service Annie knew was as shallow as unleavened bread; for the likes of Christabel Roskillen never went out of their way to scatter pearls before swine. 'Every last detail tended with a loving hand. No wonder you didn't want to stay at Glengarth, Annie, with its long, draughty corridors and chilly rooms which poor Iona and I have to put up with.'

Coercive flattery out of the way, she indicated the stool her brother usually occupied. 'May I?' Christabel sat down. 'The reason why I've come here, Annie, is to try

and persuade you to return to Glengarth to look after the
Lady Iona.'

Annie looked at her in surprise, unable to mask her
dismay. 'I cannot.'

'And, pray, why not?' Christabel's cool blue eyes were
vaguely hostile.

'The Lady Iona has a new maid now; she doesn't need
me.'

'Yes, she does. In fact, the Lady Iona herself asked me
to call upon you in person. She wants you to come back to
Glengarth, Annie.'

'After she dismissed me, m'lady?'

'Yes, Annie.'

They eyed one another steadily, both knowing that Iona
had been hurt badly as the innocent party in all this. The
Lady Iona had had no choice but to dismiss Annie
Gowrie from her employ. It had led to the disparaging and
humiliating talk going on around the estate concerning the
wanton young woman the laird had taken into his bed
because his crippled wife was unable to give him what he
wanted, and Annie Gowrie had been only too obliging.
Oh, Annie knew how the gossip circulated, but she was
not ashamed of her affair with the laird, and wanted the
sister to know it.

'Why does she want me back now?' Annie asked curiously.

'The Lady Iona is willing to forgive you, if you and
Lindsay part company.'

It was an order, not a statement. Annie turned her back
on the laird's sister.

'She cannot get along with Kirsty,' Christabel continued
regardless. Annie could be very difficult and stubborn,
Christabel thought. She didn't particularly like the girl, for
Annie always seemed so surly and secretive. 'You know
how they fight like cat and dog all day long. Kirsty has no
patience with the Lady Iona and her moods. We all know
how Iona requires a great deal of attention as well as toler-
ance – which Kirsty isn't prepared to give willingly or
cheerfully. If you're at all worried about your role at Glengarth, don't be.'

Christabel hesitated, then tried again in the face of Annie's rigid silence. 'Iona is well aware of my brother's past relationship with you. She is prepared to forgive and forget, only because she knows that Lindsay will never divorce her to marry you.'

Still Annie stayed calm and quiet.

'Men in the laird's position take mistresses only as a passing attraction – we all know that.' Christabel, in a derisive little gesture flicked a gloved hand in the air, as though she were brushing away an irritating fly. 'My dear Annie, the Lady Iona and I are well aware that it's an acceptable practice – as long as everything is conducted discreetly and with dignity.'

'Say what you've got to say, m'lady, then please go,' said Annie, trying hard to keep her temper.

'Why, even Kings of England take mistresses behind the backs of their Queens. *Pink tickets,* my dear – as such adulterous liaisons were called in India. Something, of course, I wouldn't expect one who has not travelled abroad to know about.' Christabel paused, moistened her lips. 'You, my dear Annie, are my brother's pink ticket. But my sister-in-law and I are both prepared to accept you back into the fold as long as you do not make a nuisance of yourself any more, or embarrass us as you have done.'

Annie felt her face flame. She wanted to smack the laird's sister's fine face and she wanted to do the same to the laird's wife. But she controlled her urges and listened to what else *m'lady* had to say in her refined, authoritative and condescending manner.

'I'm the only one at Glengarth at the moment who appears to be able to deal with Iona's truculent moods. But I have to go to London. Kirsty is less than useless. I need you ... we all need you to attend to the Lady Iona's welfare.'

'No, m'lady. Never!'

Christabel frowned, and then lowered her head to fidget with the fingers of her sleek, white kid gloves. 'Do you know the secret of Duncan's Tower, Annie?'

The blood that had rushed to Annie's face during Christabel's insulting invocation drained away just as suddenly, and Annie swayed dizzily. She held on to the edge of the table to steady herself, and then the familiar sickness was back in her stomach and she had to seek the privacy of her bedroom.

Annie felt much better after the nausea and sickness had passed. How she hated that woman, the laird's sister! She lingered in her bedroom as long as she could. She washed her face and hands again and again, pouring cold water over her skin and scrubbing it dry – anything to prolong the time. With luck Christabel Roskillen might get tired of waiting, and return to Glengarth.

But when Annie re-entered the living-room Christabel was still sitting patiently on the stool, and Christabel's eyes were like chips of blue glass. She had removed her gloves. They lay neatly before her on the table. 'Morning sickness, Annie? How very tiresome for you. Come and sit down.'

'I prefer to stand, m'lady.'

'Does my brother know about this?'

'About what, m'lady?'

'Don't be tiresome, Annie Gowrie!' She flicked a derisive hand in the general direction of Annie's abdomen. 'About this . . . this new development.'

'If you're talking about the child I'm expecting, no, he doesn't know.'

'And he must *never* know!' Christabel got up off the stool and began to walk round the room. Then she took up a stance by the fire, and turned to stare into Annie Gowrie's pale, thin face. What on earth did Lindsay see in the creature? she asked herself. The girl was nothing to look at, and had a figure to match her face, plain, straight and wooden! She was hardly what one could describe as attractive, or even appealing. Simply a humble, ill-educated, wanton woman who thought she could better herself by becoming another Lily Langtry! 'You must get rid of the baby at once,' Christabel almost snapped.

Annie made a choking sound, willing herself not to strike the laird's sister.

Christabel Roskillen, as sterile as the Lady Iona herself, had come here with one intention only, and that was to destroy Annie Gowrie's happy and contented little world which encompassed the Laird of Glengarth: and she did it beautifully.

'I asked you a question just now, Annie, about the secret of Duncan's Tower ... yes, of course you know what is contained in there,' Christabel added softly. 'After all, you helped set it up, didn't you? And so I think you owe us all a great deal, my dear, hmm?'

Annie was unable to speak. She was too afraid.

'While I live at Glengarth, my brother's secrets are safe. But if the Lady Iona provokes Lindsay too much, there's no knowing what he might do to further torment her. Now that brother Rory has arrived on the scene, it's going to be even more difficult to keep the truth to ourselves. You're the only other one, apart from myself, in a position to protect Lindsay and his wife from gossip-mongers as well as Lindsay's own black moods. You can help to prevent a tragedy, or you can be the cause of one. It's as simple as that, Annie.'

'What do you mean?' Annie looked at Christabel challengingly.

'You *must* see a doctor who will get rid of that baby you are expecting.'

'With all due respect, m'lady, it's none of your business!'

'It *is* my business, and I'm going to tell you why. You *cannot* have the Laird Lindsay's child! The reason why the Lady Iona gave birth to her baby prematurely was Lindsay's fault, not the Lady Iona's ...'

'Forgive me, m'lady Christabel, but the Lady Iona lost her baby before time, because her womb was ruptured. I know, I was there when they attended to her after the riding accident ...'

'That is according to Dr Robinson and Nurse Craig who have also been protecting my brother. The truth is, had not the accident occurred at a very convenient time, the baby would still have died. Iona *willed* that accident upon herself for reasons I'm now going to make very clear to you. Iona's children would all have been born with defects, with gross deformities just like the poor, twisted creature

embalmed in that foul shrine you know all about since
you ...'

'No! *Stop it! Stop it*!' Annie covered her ears, begging
her to be silent, but Christabel pursued the matter as
though she were gloating:

'The Laird Lindsay's life, Annie, was ruined from a very
early age. Ever since his days in a *very* sick and sadistic
school out East. Every pupil at St John's had an illustrious
title and inheritance to look forward to. But there was also
a vile corruption in that school – the only way the boys
could get through their day. Like so many of them who
came back with more than just sunshine in their bones,
vice was also injected into their blood. My brother's vice,
Annie, cultivated out of a boyhood and a future he was
unable to face, killed the Lady Iona's baby, and it will kill
yours. The sins of the fathers are visited upon the children,
isn't that what your 'Big Black Book' taught you? *Opium!
My fine, upstanding brother can't do without it*!'

In the terrible silence that followed Annie fell down on
the stool Christabel had just vacated.

'Oh, yes, you may well look at me like that, my dear.
Lindsay's life is wasted – he will die without the substance
that keeps him relatively sane.' She turned away from the
look on the fishergirl's face.

'Why is there so much hatred in you?' Annie asked,
shaking her head from side to side. 'Why are you doing
this? Are you mad?'

'Tainted blood runs in our family, Annie. Dr Robinson,
Nurse Craig, Iona, and now you, know it. When Iona
found out that her child would be a monster through
tainted blood, she deliberately rid herself of the child she
was carrying by causing Saladin to throw her from the
saddle ...'

'You are a *liar*!'

'No, Annie, I am telling you the truth ...'

'The truth like you told her! To deliberately unsettle
her? *You ... you* are the monster, no one else ...' Annie
was weeping now, unable to control herself any longer.

Christabel ignored her. She continued on her own vein
of thought, spoken it seemed, to further torment Annie.

'Whether Rory knew about opium or not at St John's, I don't know. But he at least had the guts to get himself expelled before he, too, was corrupted. Far better *he* had inherited the title, not Lindsay, who was always of a very sensitive, caring and gentle disposition. But it was not to be, and Lindsay's life has been wasted as a result. Your life will also be ruined, Annie, unless you rid yourself of the diseased child you are carrying.'

Christabel's face, Madonna-like in its beauty, was composed beneath the silver-fox fur hat. Annie pitied her in that moment, pitied and hated her for destroying her world, for tearing it into ugly little pieces just because *hers* had been torn into ugly little pieces, scattering those pieces all around, destroying every last vestige of faith Annie had left in human nature.

'Why is there so much hatred in you?' she repeated, recognizing it for what it was, deep and strong and repelling, like an evil odour permeating out of every pore of this dreadful woman's skin. 'Why are you so dead inside? Why does hatred and jealousy and … and, I don't know what else, eat you away, so that you want to destroy everyone around you when you have so much more than anyone else?'

'Hatred, Annie? I hate no one, least of all you. I want to try and help you. I don't want to see you go through what Iona has been through – or myself. I know you still do not believe me about the laird, but have you ever asked yourself why he never passes around his gold cigarette case when he offers cigarettes to his guests. He keeps the contents of the gold case strictly for himself: *opium* cigarettes, Annie! And when he doesn't smoke the drug, he snuffs it, or injects himself with it!'

'Please … I don't want to hear any more,' Annie begged, the sickness from her stomach rising once more into her throat.

'You've *got* to know. You're owed that much since it now affects you and the child he has fathered on you. But it will never be born normal, Annie, believe me. Lindsay is the last of a long line of noble Roskillens to inherit Glengarth.'

'Don't ... don't destroy him like this please ...' Annie's plea was a whimper of distress, a seeking of mercy at least, for the sake of the child she was carrying.

'My dear girl, the Laird Lindsay was destroyed a long time ago. There is nothing left to destroy. My father, the schools he attended, his friends, and the Indians themselves, perfected the job on him. Lindsay is not your glamorous idol, the noble lord of Wester-Ross, as you and everyone else imagines him to be. He's a weak, hollow, frightened man, afraid to death of the world, but most of all afraid of himself.'

Christabel circled the tiny living-room, her agitation increasing. 'Let me tell you something else, Annie: I only discovered the extent of my brother's addiction and dependency on drugs the day of our grandfather's funeral. On that day, I discovered him as sick as a dog, in pain, and terrified of his new responsibilities. He showed all the symptoms of a moral coward, which he is! As sick as any coward could be. They were withdrawal symptoms, for the drug he cra ...'

Annie made a move to get up and get away, but Christabel, with a hand on Annie's shoulder, forced her down again on the stool. 'Listen to me first, then run away if you must. In the past, Lindsay had been supplied with opium through his influential friends and contacts. But when he had to rush back to Glengarth to take up his title and his new responsibilities, he *had* no Windsor supplier to stem his craving. He was in a dreadful state on the day of the old laird's funeral. When I found out the reason for his terrible condition, I made certain he never again suffered in such a way, nor gave us cause to be humiliated in front of Glengarth's retainers. I had a governess who went home in the holidays. When I was fifteen she took me to London on that first holiday of mine away from Glengarth. In due course, she also got me caught up with the Women's Movement. Among other things, I managed to get hold of a supplier of opium for my brother's needs. The pattern was established, London, Edinburgh, Aberdeen, Paris, Berlin, any big city where the drug could be easily obtained: I was my lonely, sick and frightened brother's new lifeline, Annie, no one else.'

On the day of his grandfather's funeral Annie remembered that Lindsay had called at the cottage, hoping to find Donald Gowrie's widow, but had found only the daughter. She had been twelve years old, Lindsay seventeen, the new laird. He had found her, and she too had been sick and in pain, raped by her stepfather. Lindsay's own sickness and the state he was in on that day of his grandfather's funeral, was probably for that reason alone, not the reasons the sister mentioned.

But Annie kept her thoughts to herself while she listened to the full story. 'The Suffragette Movement provides me with a good cover, an excuse to haunt the big cities for my brother's sake, even though I detest city life and much prefer it here in the isolation of Glengarth. I gave up my own life and happiness to be beside him always, to shield and protect him. I am the *real* mistress of Glengarth, Annie, simply because I am the *only* one who props up it's grand laird and his noble house!'

'Better you gave him a more valuable kind of support,' Annie said bitterly. 'Better that you should have sent him away to a proper place to cure him. Not continue to tear him apart by feeding him with more destruction.'

Christabel turned aside, as though she hadn't heard Annie's heartfelt accusation, and she spoke in a faraway voice to the dull glow of the peat fire. 'I did it for him. I gave up my own love – a love you'd never understand about, Annie – and my own life for him. Lindsay means a lot to me, much more than Rory or Kitty, because we understand each other. We're more than just brother and sister, Annie ... we're the closest of friends. So you see, my dear, he needs me more than his beautiful, barren wife or his low-born mistress.'

'Are you going away again in order to obtain *more* drugs for the laird on your *Suffragette* visit to London?'

'Yes, Annie. And while I'm gone you must get rid of that child you're carrying. I will pay the doctor's fee and whatever else you ...'

'I'll not murder my baby for *your* sake or anybody else's sake, m'lady! So get out of here.' Annie stood up.

'Pink ticket, rail ticket or opium ticket, get out of here, please!'

Christabel went to the table, took up her kid gloves and began putting them on. She concentrated intently upon fitting them neatly and very precisely to her hands as she pressed down between each finger. 'Make no mistake, Annie. When you present my brother with a dead or badly deformed child, an idiot unable to function without those same drugs that keep the father going, Lindsay will destroy you as wilfully as he has destroyed himself and others – his own wife included. He will blame you for his own shortcomings, and the moment he becomes disenchanted with you, beware. He will break your spirit as cruelly as he has broken the Lady Iona's.'

'Get out!' Annie said, pointing to the door '*Get out!*' she screamed. 'You're as twisted as the rest of your noble family with their skeletons rotting away in worm-eaten mausoleums. You came here with your vile stories and your *lies* for no other reason than to destroy me! You and Lady Iona have done this thing between you because you know that *he* loves *me* more than either of you! I don't care what you or she thinks of a laird's bastard gotten out of a *low-born fishergirl*! I only care about him and I'm happy with him the way he is. And I know something you don't, my fine lady. Your brother is contented and happy with *me*, no matter what you think. And whether he takes opium or not, I'll have his child, and if it's born with three heads and six legs or none at all, I'll still love it the way the father loves me! *Now get OUT!*'

Annie thrust Christabel out of her cottage and slammed the door in her face. Then she threw herself down on the bed she had shared so often with Lindsay. She stayed there until he returned from Glasgow, and put her life to rights again.

But somehow, things could never be quite the same again; somehow the spark had gone from the relationship and she was left shivering beside brutal truth, her unwelcome companion. Wondering, every time he took out his gold cigarette case, if it contained drugged cigarettes, she would eye him across the table while he was busy with his paperwork. Suspicion and dread accompanied those account books, estate ledgers and forest yield tables, over which he would pour for hours, even after a long day outside on the plantations.

She knew fear could be read on her face, in the light of the oil-lamp, for every snappish reply of his, every sarcastic curl of his lips, every change in *his* expression, every swing of his mood, every puff of nervous energy behind his cigarette, destroyed her, bit by bit.

Or was it all to do with the seeds of doubt being sown in her mind by his evil sister, and this was merely her imagination playing tricks on her? Had Christabel been telling the truth?

Across the heather and the sea, across the fireside, across the book that lay in her lap, the days and nights presented a long drawn-out fight with herself, her spirit undermined by that burning question gnawing away at the edges of her mind: should she tell him about the baby? Or would it be better not to?

'Why are you staring at me like that, *Uisga Caillich*?' He made her jump.

'Was I? I'm sorry.' She bent her head to her needle-work.

He lit his cigarette and pocketed the lighter. If he could have leaned backwards on the three-legged stool, he would have done so. Lazily, he blew a smoke ring to the heather-thatched roof. 'You're keeping something from me, Annie. What's on your mind?'

'Nothing, m'laird.'

'So, it's back to the laird business now? A sure sign that you're annoyed with me. Speak, woman!'

'What did you do in Glasgow?'

'I went aboard a luxury transatlantic liner where I was treated to caviar and champagne. And then I went aboard a battlecruiser where I was treated to the shock of several big guns being tested close to my ears. I met a funny little Cockney with a bent elbow and lots to say for himself – my brother's pigmy shadow and first mate! I learned about steamships, steel-hulled ships, cetane turbines and a man called Rudolf Diesel. Is there anything else you'd care to know about my trip to Glasgow, my little witch?'

'Is there going to be a war, after all?'

'No, Annie, there's not. Everyone is just ... being prepared, that's all.'

'I'm glad. I should like to see Glasgow one day.'

'Then you *shall* see Glasgow. We shall go there together. I'll get my brother to wine and dine us aboard one of his great big luxury ships. You'll like that, Annie.'

'I doubt it ... a princess's life is not mine, m'laird.'

'Why now, Annie! Don't be sour.'

'I'm not sour, Lindsay ... just tired. That's all.'

'Then come here.' He reached for her as she went past him to put away her needlework box in the corner. 'Let's kiss and make up. Preferably in bed.'

'No, not tonight. Your sister has gone to London, and I promised I'd go up each evening to help Kirsty attend the Lady Iona.'

He gave her a strange look. 'Then you've left it rather late, haven't you? Iona goes to bed at nine o'clock every night. And why her sudden change of heart? I thought she'd ordered you out of her sight.'

'Well, things have changed since your sister went to London. I can't go back on my word – though I wish now I'd never said yes.'

'Why did you, Annie?' He looked her steadily in the eye.

She shrugged. 'Kirsty and your wife don't get on at all. Lady Iona asked me to come back.'

They said no more, but walked in comparative silence all the way to Glengarth, the laird carrying his heavy ledgers under his left arm as the muscles of his right arm were still weak.

CHAPTER TWENTY-EIGHT

One afternoon Annie was on her way to the Solar where the family liked to take afternoon tea. Iona occupied the room most of the day, sitting in her wheelchair while doing her tapestry work by the big window overlooking the Minch. Annie knew that Iona could walk perfectly well, but that she preferred to be in her wheelchair when the laird came in. Sitting there, meek and mild, as though butter wouldn't melt in her mouth, underneath it all, Annie couldn't help feeling, Iona was playing upon her make-believe symptoms as a kind of vicious reprisal to remind him of what she had to suffer on *his* account – she was no more paralysed than the man in the moon!

Annie asked herself again and again whether or not she was being a martyr to herself by coming back to Glengarth in the afternoons and evenings to attend upon the woman who hated her for having stolen the laird's affection, and who despised her for it. Iona went out of her way to pass cutting remarks, to demean her whenever Lindsay was present, to scold her for the smallest thing, so Annie wondered why she had let herself in for humiliation on this scale.

And then she knew why – for the money. She had been offered good wages by the laird's sister who ran his household since Iona had lost interest. Annie welcomed the money, which she put aside for a rainy day. Thank goodness, she couldn't help reflecting, that even at nearly four months gone, she hardly showed at all. The way she tucked her shawl over bodice and top half of her skirt, helped disguise her figure, and she made a pretence at being hungry so that she was given extra portions of food when working at the castle. Cook's only comment was, 'Thank goodness you're eating better now than in days past, lass! You're looking much bonnier, aye, than you ever did when fishing for a living. So ye'd best stay here as housemaid.'

Thank goodness, too, that no one suspected her condition. Mrs MacBaine's innocent comment put Annie at ease, and morning-sickness only troubled her on Rill. But soon, soon, Annie thought, a month or two at the most, she would have to disappear for a while, until after the child was born. She planned to go to Errin, where she had a married cousin on her mother's side living. She would have the baby in Goldie MacGarron's household. Afterwards, she would have to make arrangements for someone to foster the baby until a time that she would be able to care for it herself. She just prayed it wouldn't be badly deformed or so ugly that no one would want to foster it.

The laden tea-tray in her hands, Annie saw the laird's brother ahead of her, he too heading for the Solar. He came to Glengarth more often these days, Annie had noticed. He and the laird were apparently doing business together.

Annie slowed down and let him enter the Solar ahead of her.

Rory stood on the threshold, 'Hello, Iona.' Annie, keeping her distance, heard him say, 'All alone?'

Her mirthless laugh reached Annie. 'I'm always alone, Rory. Leave the door open, if you please. If Murray's bringing us tea this afternoon, he'll drop everything if he has to open the door as well.'

'Where's Lindsay?' Rory asked cheerfully as he went inside the room. 'Hunting, fishing or hounding Mr Mitchell?'

'All three probably. Lindsay's capacity for every type of sport is quite remarkable.'

Annie hesitated, unsure of whether to enter with the tea-tray or quietly go away again while they were having this conversation.

'But more likely, my dear Rory,' Iona's voice was clear and penetrating, 'Daddy's gone across the water to see a fisherman's daughter. She thinks I, as well as everyone else at Glengarth, is blind and stupid! She is beneath contempt!'

'I'm sorry, I didn't mean to pry.' Rory cleared his throat awkwardly.

'Oh, don't apologize. It's common knowledge, and *you* might as well be made aware of the facts. Since he can't marry her, he does the next best thing with her. He uses her to humiliate me! To beget a bastard.'

Annie put the tray on the floor outside the door, about to flee back to the kitchen quarters. She would never, never come here again! she promised herself. And as she turned round, she saw *him* standing behind her!

Lindsay must have heard every word, too.

Annie made to brush past him, but the look in his eye and the way he grabbed hold of her arm, prevented her from escape. 'Where are you scampering off to in such a hurry, *Uisga Caillich?* Aren't you going to be mother, and pour tea for us?'

'No, let me go, please ...' She tried jerking out of his grasp but his fingers on her arm tightened painfully as he forced her over the threshold with him.

Rory and Iona's surprise was displaced by dismay. Then Rory smiled brightly, his usual friendly manner trying to make light of the tension prevailing.

'Ah, the man himself! Iona and I were just talking about you, wondering where you'd got to, Lindsay. Glad to see you've collared Annie with the tea. I'm parched, Annie so get pouring. And are these delicious-looking griddle scones ones you've made with your own fair hands?'

Lindsay ignored his brother. His steel-grey eyes upon his wife, he said in clipped tones. 'Annie, I don't believe I've introduced you to my brother ... Rory, this is my mistress, Annie Gowrie ...'

'Lindsay, for God's sake ...'

'Shut up, Rory. Iona tell my brother the reason why I took this little slut of a fishergirl into my bed. Go on, tell him.'

'Lindsay, for heaven's sake let Annie go, and leave Iona alone. I'm really not interested in what you do with your life ...'

'But I want you to know. I want you to be under no delusion whatsoever concerning Annie's function in this household. You'll know everything there is to know and then perhaps you might not be so ready to pay attention to Iona's snide remarks the moment my back is turned. Come on, Iona, speak. Tell him why I sleep with Annie, and not only sleep with her but . . .'

Annie twisted out of his grip. '*Stop it! Stop it!* Please, stop it!' she said.

But as she turned tail to leave them to their own quarrels, Lindsay, in two strides had gone over to Iona, and lifted her out of her wheelchair, and only Iona's sharp scream made Annie stop in her tracks.

'Better still,' Lindsay said, his mood grim and defiant, 'let's show him shall we, Iona? Come on Rory . . . follow us. Iona will show you the reason why I "use" Annie Gowrie in order to beget bastards.'

Iona screamed and struggled, a trapped animal sound shredding the nerves. '*No Lindsay, please . . . Don't do this to me! Please, I beg of you . . . Rory! Don't let him do this to me . . . Lindsay, NO!*'

All the way down the length of the corridor and up the stairs they could hear Iona screaming in Lindsay's arms. But Rory did not follow them. Instead, he turned desperately to Annie, his blue eyes clouded with anxiety. 'What is going on here, Annie? Can you please explain?'

The familiar sickness rising in her, she said weakly from where she leaned against the door jamb, 'You've got to stop him.'

'Stop him from doing what? Look, I make it a rule of mine never to interfere in other people's squabbles, especially between husband and wife.'

'But you don't know what he does . . . I don't want her to be hurt and humiliated in this fashion. Neither will you when you find out how he punishes her for disobeying his orders concerning the horse he didn't want her to ride while she was carrying a baby. He won't forgive her, and he'll never forget. He just goes on and on tormenting her in this cruel fashion. You must stop him from doing it any more.'

'I don't live here. It's none of my business. *You* tell him.'

'I can't, I've tried. You're his brother. He might listen to you.'

'I doubt it. Lindsay's never listened to me in his life. Anyway, I don't know what all this is about, and I don't think I wish to know.'

Her hand against her heart to stop the racing palpitations making her speech incoherent, Annie took a deep breath. There was only one way, and that was for him to find out for himself. 'Come with me. I'll show you what I mean.' It was useless trying to explain. She didn't have the words to describe what she wanted him to know. He must see for himself.

Reluctantly he followed her. Annie took him to another part of the castle, the old round tower, ancient, dangerous and dark Duncan's Tower. On the first floor the armoury was housed; the trophy room was above the armoury. The laird had forbidden anyone to go to the tower, and had placed a notice to this effect at the bottom of the stairwell.

They could hear Iona's muffled cries from somewhere below, and Rory turned to Annie, his own face mirroring disquietude. 'For God's sake, tell me what this mystery tour is all about, Annie ...' Rory began, but fell silent when she made signs to him to be quiet.

Lindsay was coming *up* the narrow winding stairs from the tower basement, not descending them from the armoury or the trophy room. Annie drew Rory back into one of the deep, fissured window-alcoves from where, in times past, archers had fired their arrows upon invaders from the sea.

Iona appeared to have fainted. Her head, the brilliant hair cut short to spite her husband, lolled against the shoulder Fletcher had knifed during his fight with Lindsay on the shores of Rill. Annie knew that the torn muscle in Lindsay's right arm and shoulder, stitched by Dr Robinson who had believed Lindsay had injured himself with one of the timber-saws when felling, still had not healed properly and gave him considerable discomfort.

Lindsay paused near them, adjusting Iona's position in his arms, and even while Annie held her breath, Rory made a slight movement to waylay his brother. Annie jerked Rory's sleeve, making him hold still until Lindsay had left the tower.

Lindsay, even if he sensed their presence, went on his way with Iona. The moment they had gone, and the studded outer door had crashed shut behind him, Rory demanded, 'What *is* this all about, Annie! What's going on here? Haunted castles, blood-letting in dungeons, screams in the dark, they're all for the fairy stories, not real life. What's he been doing to Iona down there with only Beauly's bones for company?'

'Come,' she said, leading the way down to the ancient burial place of the first Beauly who had come across the seas from the north, to set his seal upon Ross-shire. 'See for yourself what kind of fairy story this is. The room is never locked,' Annie explained, 'nor is the outer door of the tower because he uses this place as ... as an *aumbry*, ever since he lost any hope of an heir for Glengarth. It's a shrine to punish his wife and himself.' Annie held the door open for Rory to enter.

He walked into the stone cold, circular room, smelling of death and decay, of countless generations of Clan Chieftains hiding their secrets in the self-same manner as Lindsay was now doing, secreting them away behind dungeon walls.

Rory took in his surroundings without knowing what to expect. He realized with a shock that this was *not* a nice place to be in. 'Why, Annie, the wretched place is done out like some funeral parlour for devil worshippers!'

'Yes,' she said bitterly, 'and here's your fine brother's sacrifice on the high altar of his madness and rage. This is what he makes her kneel before and worship ... this *thing* they created together, the sacrificial offering!'

Annie swept off the black silk cloth with the gold edging that covered the glass casket lying on top of the high stone tomb in the centre of the room. And because she couldn't bear to look at Rory's face, she turned away.

'Oh, my Christ!' Rory sank to his knees, his forehead resting against that revolting altar. 'Oh, my Christ, he's mad!'

Annie gave a deep sob, unable to control herself. 'No, he's not mad. He's perfectly aware of what he's doing. He's been badly hurt, and he wants to hurt everyone else, but he's *not* mad.'

Rory took a deep breath and gathered his wits together. 'He's insane, Annie, believe it! Only a very sick man or a pervert would do this to his wife.' He looked up at the fishergirl keeping her face hidden in the shadows beneath the incense burner which cast a feeble glow above the tomb where the remains of the first and the last Roskillen were left to decay. His handsome face ravaged in that moment of truth concerning his brother, Rory said condemningly, 'And you let him touch you? How *could* you!'

It twisted her up inside to hear him talk like that. 'No,' she said, not looking at him as he knelt there, knuckles white as he gripped the black altar cloth. Rory was furious with Lindsay for subjecting Iona to this kind of mental torture. The 'thing' lying in the glass casket, was enough to give anyone the creeps, its dried-out, shrivelled and twisted black body and grotesque head complete with membraneous cowl, an affront to any Christian.

He did not know why Annie continued to defend him. 'Lindsay felt betrayed by the Lady Iona. He would have loved her totally, had she only gone halfway to meeting him by being a loving and caring wife. But she never did because she never knew how ...' Annie's voice faded away into the gloomy shadows.

She bit her lower lip, not knowing whether to say any more, or just keep quiet: there was very little she *could* say in Lindsay's defence after this.

'Go on, Annie,' Rory said gently. 'I want to hear the rest, now that you've opened my eyes to the magnitude of Lindsay's warped character.'

'Lady Iona only thinks about herself and what *she* wants. It wasn't her fault entirely. Part of it was her rigid upbringing by an Episcopalian grandmother ... that's according to rumour. Anyway, the Laird Lindsay cannot bear failure in any form ... least of all a form like that.' Again she hesitated, trying hard to swallow down the saliva gathering in her mouth, and the nauseous feeling in her stomach. 'Because the Lady Iona lost any chance of giving Glengarth an heir, he had that poor, misshapen, ugly creature embalmed and left there for ever to look at, the only son and heir he'll ever have. It's for them to worship together, he and his lady wife. That's what I can't bear, the mockery of it all.'

Rory rose to his feet heavily. He passed a shaking hand over his clammy forehead. 'Cover it up, please, Annie. I can't bear to look at it ... it's far too horrible. No wonder you couldn't find words to describe it. Poor bloody Iona!' He made for the door and hastened away up to level ground again. He gulped down the fresh air! It was nice to smell the sea again.

Annie covered the glass casket and followed him outside. He was waiting for her, and turned at her approach. The stiff breeze ruffled his hair, and his expression was sorrowful as he searched her out: 'You must love my brother very much, Annie Gowrie, to put up with all his lunatic ways.'

'Yes, I do.' She couldn't tell him that she also owed Lindsay a great deal. He would never understand after what he'd just seen. She faced Rory resolutely. 'You *must* help him, and the Lady Iona.'

'How?'

'Ask him to have it buried properly so she can never see it again. Ask him to put the remains of that dead baby in the family plot up on Inchnadamph. Ask him, please.'

'I'll do my best.'

Annie hesitated, meaning to ask him something else, but not sure how.

'Yes, Annie?'

'Why does he call it the Altar of Moloch?'

Rory searched his own mind for the answers as he squinted at the scudding clouds above Beinn Claidheamh Mor. He thought back to the dim past, for memories misted over by time and tide.

He thought back to a night on a lonely jungle path and his father's brutality upon a helpless Indian coolie doing his best to get them home safely. He thought about the merciless flogging the rickshaw-wallah had received at the hands of James Beauly Roskillen. *A horse misused upon the road, cries to Heaven for human blood: Auguries of Innocence!* How often had he been forced by his tutor, old boggy Shawmoss, to learn those words by heart, for some imagined, or boyish, misdemeanor. He thought about how callously his father had left that injured, bleeding, rickshaw-wallah in the ditch, to be further mauled by wild animals of the jungle. And he thought back to the Indian Sadhu on the road to Tippindee and the curse that had been put upon the heirs of Glengarth unto the third and fourth generation of them that hated.

Rory recalled Lindsay's strange words to him not so long ago, when they were both sailing home in the *Flower of the Glen* after their business trip to Ayrshire. He had been at the helm, and Lindsay, standing next to him, had stared up at Glengarth dominating the wild and beautiful mull: his castle, his land, his forests, his glen, his loch and his love. And even in the moment that Rory had felt a wild pang of jealousy stab his heart for the place he, too, loved best in the world, and for that very reason had stayed away until the lust in his heart had been exorcized, Lindsay had said: '*Moloch is insatiable!*'

He had not understood his brother *then*. But he did now.

And then he shrugged off such superstitious nonsense. Life was shaped, not by fools and curses, but by one's own resilience and endeavour.

He said to Annie Gowrie, 'Biblical symbolism, Annie. Moloch was the god of the Ammonites. Children were made to pass through fire to him. It means the sacrifice of anything we hold dear.'

Annie knew about the heathen Ammonites. What she couldn't understand was why Lindsay had chosen the awful name of Moloch for his dead heir. Perhaps she didn't really care to know, after all. She bit her lip and remained silent.

Watching the nuances of expression on Annie's face as she warred with her own thoughts and feelings, Rory laid a reassuring hand on her shoulder. 'Look, Annie, all this business has come about in a very silly fashion. When we were boys in India, a dotty old native soothsayer prophesied something to do with Moloch – you know the kind of jibberish these fellows spout. Lindsay's obviously taken the whole thing a bit too seriously. Moloch got stuck in his mind, and he thought it a good name for ... for, well yes, doesn't matter. But it's nothing to lose sleep over, I assure you. Please don't fret over it. Life is full of odd bodkins and boathooks imagining that life has cursed them for some reason.'

Rory suddenly smiled at her, and to Annie, it was like seeing the sun bursting through rain clouds.

They parted company in the courtyard. But afterwards, back in her cottage on Rill, Annie reread the story of Moloch and the Ammonites.

CHAPTER TWENTY-NINE

April, and the sharp winds blowing across the sea. Spring, when the earth re-emerged through winter's melting snow and the sun gilded the mountain. The deer through the heather of Inchnadamph, the white sands of Rill, a fishing boat on the loch, here lay Annie's treasures. The Western Isles, the setting sun on the Cuillins of Skye, the soughing breeze through pine trees, a world moulded by the elements, water, wind, sun and soil. This was her world, a quiet backwater of Wester-Ross, placid, tranquil and familiar. A girl who knew nothing about the rest of the world, its politics, its wars, nothing at all beyond the fringes of a heather and peat cot, yet she had the love of a laird to keep her warm: '*A bonny, bonny laird*', was the song in her heart as she roamed barefoot through the glen.

With the beginning of a new life inside her, in that spring of 1914 Annie Gowrie was as happy as she had ever been.

But how far was she to wander from all that was dear to her. How much was she to learn, and, beyond the fringes of her home shores, how irrevocably was Annie to change!

She climbed up to Inchnadamph, to the mossy hollow at the foot of the mountain where she often went when she wanted to be alone.

The sight of the laird's brother invaded her privacy. He was reading a newspaper, the breeze trying to tug it from his hands. He folded the paper untidily when he saw her, and sat up with a big smile. 'My!' Rory said, boldly sweeping Annie in his admiring glance. 'The girl who walks so beautifully barefoot. Come sit beside me and tell me the story of your life, coral-shell Annie. I don't bite so stop looking at me as if I might.'

Annie stood mute and awkward, and a little irritated by

his manner, which took all things for granted.

'No? What a shame!' Rory continued regardless. 'It's not often I wax lyrical about a woman's toenails.' He went back to his newspaper, and pulled a face. 'Talk of war, talk of Suffragettes and what price fish in Fishmonger's Hall, uh, Annie Gowrie?' He peered over the pages, ignored the seriousness of her expression and grinned charmingly at her. 'Are you a Suffragette, too, coral-shell Annie?'

'No, m'lord.'

He was amused. 'Listen, Annie Gowrie, Rory Duncan's no lord even if his brother is. So keep the title for the laird; he's welcome to it.'

Annie shifted from one foot to the other, and was about to turn tail and leave him to his newspaper when he said, 'He'll never marry you, Annie. He's only using you. Why do you let him treat you the way he does?'

Then she did turn to run away through the heather.

Rory jumped up and ran after her, and the newspaper was whisked away by the breeze. 'Don't be angry, fisher-girl ... I'm sorry for sticking my nose in when it's none of my business. It's just that you're worth more than Lindsay offers, so don't do this to yourself Annie ...'

She whirled to face him. 'You're right, Mr Rory Duncan, it's none of your business. The laird doesn't *use* me, he happens to love me! So don't insult either of us!'

Annie fled, but Rory soon caught her up again. 'Sweet fishergirl, I didn't mean to make you angry. Or insult you or Lindsay. I have this dreadful habit of sticking both feet and elbows into everything. Change that look on your face, Annie Gowrie, because if the wind veers, you'll be stuck with that scowl – and you don't want to look like a witch on a broomstick, do you?'

Once more she stopped dead in her tracks to put him in his place, a sharp retort on her tongue, but he gave her such a contrite look that she bit back her temper. Annie returned the smile, a weak one of forgiveness.

'That's better,' he said, and fell into step beside her. 'Where are you rushing off to, Annie Gowrie?'

'Fishing.'

'I thought so. I've watched you with my heart in my

mouth from the causeway, taking that leaky little boat of yours out in stormy weather, and I wonder that Lindsay lets you risk your life like that.'

'It's my boat,' she said, walking faster, 'and my life. I live it the way I want.'

'I can see that,' he said, glancing meaningly at her bare toes. 'Doesn't the heather tickle them and make you laugh. Never for one moment did I imagine a pearl of a girl with eyes like emeralds, hair like a mermaid's and toes like coral-shells hiding away at Glengarth.' Skipping along sideways, he continued to fool about, his hand over his heart and a tragic look on his face. 'Oh, if only I were a handsome knight on a dashing white charger! I'd fight the kelpies and whisk you away to a land where we could live happily ever after! How say you, Annie Gowrie? Would you be willing to ride with me into the sunset?'

Annie made up her mind that Rory Duncan was nothing but a smooth-talking flirt, glib of tongue and manner. She concentrated on gathering up the dry nets laid out on the causeway, and putting them neatly into her boat. Rory helped. Then he said, 'Let me come fishing with you, Annie. There's nothing much for me to do today since the business can take care of itself. Besides, I've lost interest in making money. I'd much rather sail away into the sunset with a pretty mermaid for company.'

Of course she knew he didn't mean it. Annie wondered why he now spent so much time at Glengarth when his real business was down in Glasgow. She hesitated, and then said firmly, 'No. I prefer to fish alone. My boat isn't big enough for two.'

'Of course it is!' he scoffed. 'Come on, Annie, be a sport! I'd give my right arm for a wee boat-trip with my favourite mermaid.'

'That won't be necessary,' Annie replied, trying hard not to smile, and encourage his boldness. 'Keep your right arm; you might have need of it.'

'Then it's yes?' he asked eagerly.

She shook her head.

'Then we'll go in my boat? How about that?'

Again she shook her head.

'Please Annie, it's such a lovely day. And two of us will catch more fish than just one. Say yes, otherwise I'll be miserable for the rest of the day.'

Annie hesitated a second time. It was indeed a lovely day, the sunlight sparking off the loch and the mountain, the air sharp and bright and filled with the salty tang of the open sea. His cheerful company and zest for life would certainly make the time go faster, too. 'No,' she repeated firmly, and began to cast off.

Rory jumped in despite her protests. 'Annie,' he wasn't joking this time, 'the Minch is an evil stretch of water, and the weather is capricious today. It could easily blow up into a squall, and I'd be left standing on the shore worrying about you.'

'There's no need to worry on my behalf. I can take care of myself.'

'I'm a good swimmer and can save you from drowning,' he added slyly.

'Mermaids can't drown,' she reminded him.

'There! I knew you'd be happy to have me along.' He beamed in delight.

Annie pretended indifference. 'There's an art to throwing the nets. It isn't easy; it takes skill. Often I come home with nothing.'

'Believe me, I know the feeling,' he said, taking the tiller, his blue eyes twinkling. 'Do you like to sing while you're fishing, Annie Gowrie? Let us sing together and be happy today.'

They also laughed a lot that day, until Annie had to admit to herself she was glad he had kept her company after all.

At the end of the day they brought a good catch home to Gairloch where Annie soon sold it, with just enough herring over for supper. 'You're rich, coral-shell Annie,' Rory laughed when he counted out the money in the bottom of the boat.

'It'll pay my rent and that's all,' Annie replied cautiously.

'And I'd have thought that brother of mine would have let you live rent-free ...' Rory could have bitten out his tongue, his light-hearted, yet thoughtless remark striking deeply. He could see the look of pain that suddenly darkened her green eyes before she turned away from him. 'Sorry, Annie, I didn't mean to be offensive.'

'No offence taken.'

They set sail for home, and then the sickness started. What with the rising swell of the sea and the smell of the fish clinging to the nets, Annie was unable to control herself. Hanging wretchedly over the side of the boat, she felt terrible, and wished the sea would swallow her up in that moment.

'Annie,' he said kindly, coming to her rescue. Standing behind her with one comforting hand over her clammy forehead, the other around her middle, Rory held on to Annie's heaving body to prevent her falling overboard. 'I invariably do it after too much champagne, so don't mind me.'

She was grateful to him for trying to put her at ease, but it didn't help. If anything, she felt worse.

Afterwards she huddled in the bottom of the boat with her wet shawl wrapped around her shivering shoulders. Rory took the shawl away and made her put on his thick fisherman's jersey. 'Look here, fishergirl, just stop arguing with me and do as you're told,' he said firmly. 'I don't want you giving my nephew – or niece – pneumonia.'

Annie burst into tears.

Somehow he wasn't doing very well today, he told himself, and didn't know why he was putting his foot in it the whole time. Shut up, he warned himself.

The boat was listing too far, choppy seas slopping over gunwales. Rory concentrated on righting her.

'Tack with the wind,' Annie mumbled wretchedly, her hands over her face.

'Annie Gowrie, I do know how to sail a boat,' he said with a bright smile when she looked up at him, her face tear-streaked and woebegone.

'Well, you might be fine with sailing ocean-liners, m'lord, but you're not much good with fishing-smacks,' was her prompt retort. 'Here ... let me. I feel much better now.'

Annie's fiercely independent spirit and sheer grit made him admire her from the bottom of his heart. 'Does my brother know?' he asked in the moment she took the tiller into her own hands.

'Know what?'

'Oh, come on, Annie! I'm not an untried youth still wet behind the ears. A fishergirl who depends on a living by fishing, isn't going to get much of a living fishing every time she's sick taking her boat out, now is she? What's going to happen when you can't sail this tub any longer?'

'That's my business.'

'And after the baby is born?'

'That's my business, too.'

He was exasperated. 'I know it's none of my business. But Lindsay is my brother, and that *is* my business! Neither is he the caring sort, take it from me, Annie.'

'Yes, he is. He'll take the responsibility of his child.'

'By putting it in a casket next to the other one?'

She stared at him, her knuckles white as she gripped the tiller. 'You're cruel, too ... just ... just like the rest of your family ...'

He dropped to his haunches in front of her, 'Oh God, Annie,' he apologized, 'I'm sorry ... I didn't mean that. I just want you to be happy, and I can see you're not.' He took her hands in his but she pulled away.

'Don't,' Annie said stiffly, the boat keeling over, sails and steering forgotten. He had voiced all the terrible fears she herself entertained.

'Annie,' he said gently, 'don't cry. I didn't mean what I said. I'm just concerned about you, that's all.'

'I know all about the opium,' she raised her head and faced him fully. 'Your fine, upstanding sister made sure that I knew all about the laird being a drug addict from his boyhood spent in India. She left nothing to the imagination. She told me my baby would be as deformed and as brainless as the one the Lady Iona lost!'

'Annie, Annie, calm down!' Rory tried to reassure her. 'Look, my sister Christabel was just scaring the hell out of you without really knowing what she was talking about. She and Iona are obviously jealous of you, for the attention

Lindsay is paying you when they *have* no man in their lives! Iona lost Lindsay's love, but that is not my business. Listen to me, fishergirl, if it's any consolation, opium might be addictive but it's relatively harmless stuff. Out East, in China and India, they give it to women after childbirth, and in depressive states. Men who have taken it all their lives, and still go on living into their extreme old age, are proof that the stuff doesn't kill or make one deformed. My brother isn't a monster through opium smoking, though he can sometimes be a devil when he's under extreme stress – as we all can be, with or without an addiction to drugs.'

She wanted to believe him. Oh, so badly she wanted to believe him! 'Well, the only truth I know is that I love him. He is my whole world.'

Annie noticed the way he looked at her then. A strange, haunted distraction about him, with the light gone from his clear blue eyes. 'Shall we go home?' he said, returning to the halyard tackle.

Lustily, he began to sing, then. His voice was good and true and she liked listening to it. He was still singing when they brought the boat into Loch Garth.

> 'Jockie lo'ed Madgie for Madgie had money,
> And Sandy lo'ed Mary for Mary was bonny,
> Ane wedded for love, Ane wedded for treasure,
> So Jockie had siller and Sandy had pleasure ...'

Lindsay was waiting on the causeway, his face a white mask of fury.

'Why were you singing that song?' Lindsay stared down into the upturned face of his brother and Annie as they brought the boat alongside. Rory threw him the mooring rope, but Lindsay stood on the end of it without bothering to tie it to the bollard.

Annie tossed out the wet nets, recognizing Lindsay's mood for what it was, but attempting to ignore it.

'I want to know why you were singing that song!' Lindsay repeated.

'Because we felt like it, man,' his brother replied care-lessly as he jumped onto the jetty and secured the boat himself. He reached down and extended his hand to help Annie out of the boat, but Lindsay pushed his brother aside.

'Leave her alone, Rory, just leave her alone if you know what's good for you.' Lindsay, taut as a coiled panther ready to spring, hauled Annie onto the jetty.

'I know what's good for me, Lindsay, so dinna fash yourself, man. Now get off the nets will you. I'm trying to lay them out neatly without your great galumphing feet all over them.' Rory began to whistle cheerfully, but Lindsay cut him short.

'What were you and Annie doing together all day?'

'Singing and fishing and talking. What the hell do you think we were doing? You know, Lindsay, *you* should try singing more often instead of being so tense the whole time ... there you are, coral-shell Annie, all done and safely home. You're right mermaids don't drown, provided they have a knight in shining armour keeping them company.' Rory deliberately linked his little finger in that of Annie's, a trysting gesture designed to invoke his brother to further anger. 'Thanks for a lovely day, coral-shell Annie. Perhaps we can do it agai ...'

'I told you not to touch her!' Lindsay pulled Annie away roughly, and in that moment Rory had difficulty in keeping his hands off his brother. He would have knocked some sense into Lindsay, had it not meant upsetting Annie.

Rory shrugged his shoulders and shoved his hands in his pockets for safe-keeping. He strolled off down the causeway, back to the mainland, singing as he went.

'Jocky was laird both of hills and of valleys,
But Sandy was nought but King o' gude fellows ...'

Lindsay turned to Annie. 'What were you two doing together?' he snapped.

'Fishing, singing and talking – like he said.' Annie turned to walk off but Lindsay grabbed her arm and almost tossed her back to his side.

'Don't you *ever* go near him again,' he said savagely.

Only once before had she seen him so out of control and that was on the day he had stormed into his sick wife's bedroom demanding to see his dead son. Annie felt her own temper rise beyond the bounds of reason: 'And don't *you* tell me what to do!' she flared, jerking out of his grasp. 'I'm not your slave!'

Quickly she walked away, hating herself for having caused him even a moment's jealousy, but still not prepared to be put upon by him in such an unwarranted attack.

'*Annie, don't walk away from me like that*!' Lindsay shouted after her.

'Then don't treat me as if you couldn't care less about my feelings,' she called back.

But she did stop and allow him to catch up with her. 'We were doing nothing, just sailing and fishing together – and singing.'

'So you prefer his company to mine, is that it?' Lindsay demanded.

'At the moment, yes! He's good company. He's kind and considerate and cheerful! He makes me feel happy. He makes me want to laugh and sing.'

'And I don't?'

'No, not when you're in this mood. You don't own me, my laird, though you might own everything else around me.'

He looked at her hard and long, his eyes like two pieces of flint cutting her soul.

Then he relaxed and took out his gold cigarette case. Shielding the flame of his lighter, he lit his cigarette and inhaled deeply. Repocketing the lighter, Lindsay smiled down at Annie. 'So! The fishergirl has grown tired of the laird and now she's casting her net about elsewhere. I see!'

'No, you *don't* see!' Annie faced him challengingly, her fists clenched in exasperation. 'You don't see how your insane jealousy can destroy us, Lindsay! You don't see how possessive you are and how cruel you can be. Your brother means nothing to me. I don't even *know* him. I love *you*, not him!'

'Do you mean that, Annie?'

She sighed, and shook her head at his silliness. 'Lindsay, my laird, if you don't know that by now, then *you* are the one who cannot love me. And that makes me unhappy.'

He put out his left hand, the cigarette held in the other. 'Annie, my Annie, come here to me.'

She went to him and he tossed his cigarette on the sands before he put his arms tightly around her. His kiss was prolonged, fierce and passionate, the ferocity of his embrace designed to show her where she belonged. Gasping for breath, Annie laughed and said, 'There's herring for supper, m'laird, and fresh cheese from Gairloch.'

'Thank you, Annie, but I can't stay for supper tonight. I only came to say goodbye as I'm on my way to Achnasheen.' He glanced at his watch ruefully. 'I hope the station master can delay the train for me. He knows I intend catching it.'

'Why don't you go back to Glasgow with your brother, who has his own boat?'

'I don't want to go to Glasgow, but Edinburgh. I have some business to attend to there.'

Annie then hugged *him* tightly. 'Oh, Lindsay, must you leave tonight? Why can't you go tomorrow instead?'

Tonight she had been intending to tell him about the baby. He had never reapproached the subject, so she wondered if he really believed what his wife had said to his brother on the afternoon he had lost his temper with Iona after her ill-chosen remark about a fisherman's daughter and a bastard. Perhaps Lindsay was waiting to hear the news about the baby from her own lips, rather than listen to a secondhand source, and she at least owed him the truth – how she dreaded having this child in case it turned out to be like the 'thing' in the glass casket on the altar of Moloch!

But now that he intended to go to Edinburgh, this was obviously not the right moment to seek his reassurances. Annie supposed a few more days would make no difference.

'Annie, I *must* leave tonight. I have an important

meeting with the Scottish Secretary of State first thing tomorrow morning, which I cannot postpone.'

'I understand. Take care then, and return safely.'

All at once a great weariness seemed to drag at her, the long day's fishing taking its toll. It would be good to have an early night after all. And Annie knew, too, that it would always be like this. There would be times when Lindsay had this depleting effect upon her. These were the lost moments of her life, ephemeral as the butterfly's hold on the world. And that, despite her love for him, she could not hold him at all – as she had once so foolishly supposed. No one could, not even his lady wife, for Lindsay Beauly Roskillen was his own man.

Annie watched him as he strode off along the causeway, back to his castle, with the sea wind ruffling his fair hair. Slowly and thoughtfully she went on up the beach to the warmth and safety of her humble cottage where she would have to take supper on her own. All of a sudden she longed for Rory Duncan's cheerful company across the platters of fried herrings and fresh cheese.

CHAPTER THIRTY

The sun was high and bright, although a keen sea-breeze tempered any warmth the sun might have. Flurries of sand were tossed across the beach, and over the cottage doorstep where Annie was busily gutting fish.

She looked up when a shadow fell across her. Brushing away the stinging strands of hair that flicked into her eyes, she was surprised to see the laird's brother, who was supposed to be on his way back to Glasgow.

'Hello Annie,' he said, standing over her, his hands in his pockets and a real lady-killer smile on his face.

She did not know why, but suddenly she felt shy and gauche in his presence, and very unsure of herself. 'Good morning, m'lord.'

'I told you before, I'm no lord nor master. How about just calling me Rory, uh?' He dropped to his haunches beside her and took the knife from her hands. Skilfully he began to gut the fish lying in a basket beside her.

Immediately she felt at ease, his company charming as well as disarming, and she was glad, after all, he had sought her out. 'Where did you learn to do that?' Annie asked him, not a little amazed at his versatility: 'A fine man like yourself?' she added laughingly.

'Aha! Before I became the big boss of the Chanin-Beauly Steamship Line, Annie, I learned my trade by sailing the seven seas as well as a lot of little estuaries. I handled all sorts of cargo and commodities, and learned to skin a fish so that I could eat it without a lot of scales and bones filling my mouth. Such knowledge is required in the event of being cast away on a desert island with a beautiful mermaid, d'ye ken.'

'I thought you were off to Glasgow this morning,' she said.

'Oh, Glasgow can wait. I have more important things on my mind at the moment than signing papers.'

'But can they get along without you?'

'Oh, yes. My staff are well trained. I'm only required as a figurehead who has to raise the money for an important merger, a new steamship or shipyard, and to wheedle his way into securing Government contracts for battleships – that sort of thing. Nothing very important, or exciting.'

'I don't believe you,' she retorted, listening to him with avid interest, yet without knowing half of what he actually meant – his kind of business far above *her* head! 'I think you must be a very clever and important man to have made such a big company out of nothing. I have heard tell how your ships are bigger and better than even the Allan steamships.'

His eyes twinkled merrily. '*Luck*, Annie! Without it a man can still be talented, but with it, he holds the world in the palm of his hand and makes talent work for him. I'm not talented, or clever, or even very important. But Lady Luck has been my obliging companion all along the way. I met the right people at the right time. Yes, I fell in with an heiress who happened to take a shine to me. She didn't know where else to invest her vast wealth. So I persuaded her to put it where my mouth is, and surprisingly we made a success of our partnership – business, I'm talking about here, not marriage.'

'Yes,' Annie agreed, 'that must be what they call luck. Although I think it would be much easier for someone like yourself to meet a very rich woman and marry her, because you mix in that sort of worldly company all the time.'

'Not so, Annie. Millionairesses don't grow on trees y'know. I had to work very hard on Lizzie ... er, in a manner of speaking.' Rory scratched his ear, and thought about the diamond necklace Lizzie Roebling Chanin had given him for services rendered, which he'd promptly converted to hard cash. He'd been able to buy his *own* shipyard at Govan with the money, and Lizzie had never forgiven him for dispersing of her jewels which she had sworn blind were Marie Antoinette's. 'Relax, Lizzie,' he remembered telling her at the time. 'The fellow at Hatton Garden said they were flawed.' Lizzie had threatened to sue both the jeweller and him, until he'd reminded her that diamonds locked up in a bank vault were a slow investment, whereas a shipyard undertaking a Government war-programme order for Dreadnoughts and 'KIL' class ships was likely to bring her lasting glory when her name was whispered in the gilded corridors of power. Lizzie had had the intelligence to recognize the validity of his argument, and with a sense of relief on his part, the subject of the diamond necklace had been dropped.

'Now I just sign on the dotted line when my ladyfriend wants me to, and the money keeps on rolling in,' he told Annie. 'Mind you, she does get hopping mad if I'm not at my office desk in the Broomielaw when she wires me from New York. But I've learned to live with her abuse, so it's no hardship.'

'Didn't you love her?' Annie asked boldly.

He seemed to hesitate. 'I thought I did – but I think I loved the idea of being courted by a millionairess even more.' He chuckled and, like a tortoise from its shell, stretched his neck from the roll collar of his thick fisherman's pullover Kirsty had knitted him – the laird's brother, Annie knew, being the only person fusty old Kirsty, who was still the Lady Iona's maid despite their arguments, seemed to have taken a fancy to.

'Do you always treat them so ... so casually?' Annie asked.

'Who?'

'Women.'

'Lor', what questions this mermaid asks! No Annie Gowrie, I don't! I take women very seriously – very seriously indeed! I adore women. The prettier they are, the more I adore 'em.'

'And your ladyfriend?'

'She booted me out the moment her eyes alighted on an English Peer of the Realm suffering from rigor mortis – his father's. His Lordship couldn't pay the thirteenth earl's death duties, and wept about selling off his millions of inherited acres, along with the stately home the size of

Blenheim Palace. So Lizzie willingly stepped into the breach and I was relegated to the past tense.'

'I'm sorry,' Annie murmured sympathetically, not knowing what else to say, while marvelling at the way the other half of the world lived their lives.

'Don't be, Annie. It was a relief to tell the truth. Lizzie was not at all my type of woman, being far too bossy and unfeminine for my liking. She soon got started on her newly inherited Countess-ship by attempting to restore the fourteenth earl's flagging ego, as well as his stately home, in which was housed a genuine, unchipped, Marie Antoinette, eight-hundred piece dinner service – one of many. He also gave her a distinguished coat of arms. It was all Lizzie was ever after. Lizzie had everything in the world, you see, Annie, except a noble title and a cultural heritage. So she bought them, and got a step nearer to the English throne. Now that she *does* have everything in the world, I wonder how long it will last. So you see, Annie, one doesn't *love* American ladies, only their eccentricities.'

'Did she take back the steamships to give to her new husband?' Annie asked.

The simplicity of her direct questioning made him smile.

'Good question, Annie. And no, she did not! No Scottish Steamship Company for his fourteenth Lordship to get his grasping English hands on. Lizzie, however, does have a say in the Company's affairs, since she is still my business partner. But she rules the roost from New York, where she has persuaded her English earl to live for a while, not Glasgow. I managed to come off quite well in the end – her settlement to get rid of me in order that she might become a *real* English Countess, was worth three years of sleepless nights.'

Annie changed the subject from the present Countess to the late cousin: 'Were you in love with your cousin from England – the one who died?'

Again he seemed taken aback by her direct questioning. The knife he was using slipped on the stone slab and set her teeth on edge. 'Leonora? How on earth do you know about her?'

'There was talk up at the castle about how you ran off
with the American lady after your cousin's death. Your
sister Christabel said you were angry with the Suffragettes
and blamed them for her death.'

'Christabel always assumed she knew more than anyone
else – Little Madam Knowall, I used to call her when we
were children in India. He tossed the gutting knife in the
air in a juggling act and deftly caught it again before
resuming his task of helping with the fish.

'Did you love your cousin then, more than your American lady?' Annie was more than ever curious, but hoped
he wouldn't be offended by her inquisitiveness.

She need not have feared. He was very honest about his
feelings, even though she had blatantly prompted him to
reveal them. 'Annie Gowrie, love is a diamond. Each facet
of a diamond reflects its own nuances of colour and light,
bringing to the whole jewel a flawless unity. But if one of
the facets reveals the slightest of imperfections, then the
whole diamond is marred ... Hmm!' He cleared his throat
loudly: 'My relationship with Mrs Roebling Chanin was
founded on sex and business. We would have been quite
incompatible as husband and wife. Neither of us wanted
marriage to hamper our style ... well, so *she* said. As far
as Leonora was concerned, she was pure uncut diamond.
We were drawn together by our environment, our home-
life which created an atmosphere of warmth, companion-
ship, friendship and security – good soil in which to
nurture young love. And that's all it was, puppy-love,
untried by the cutting-tool of real life. Lennie was twenty
when she died. After her death the cutting-tool suddenly
began to work on this rough diamond. That was when I
decided to stop fooling around and start taking life a little
more seriously. It hasn't worked.' He raised his head and
smiled at her. 'I'm still on the look-out for a flawless
diamond, though I rather feel I could settle for an emerald
instead.'

Annie stood up and wiped her hands on her pinny. She
pressed her hands to her back, trying to ease the tired ache
and the stiffness in her body. 'I must collect peat from
Inchnadamph, otherwise I'll have no fire tonight. I've run

out of fuel because I've been too lazy all week to gather it.'

'Then let me cut it for you.' He threw the last fish back into the basket and took the catch inside. In the tiny kitchen that had been added to the back of the cot, there was ice in which to pack the fish. It was sent down from Glengarth to keep the day's catch as fresh as possible for as long as possible. Annie had Lindsay to thank for that, his thoughtfulness in such matters quite touching at times.

She wondered how long he would be away in Edinburgh. He had made no mention of when he would be returning. She took her shawl, and a spade to cut the peat.

Rory picked up the empty creel beside the dying fire, and on the doorstep squinted at the grey clouds scudding across the sky, the weather soon changing on this fickle west coast of Scotland. 'Looks like rain,' he said.

But the rain held off until the peat was cut, and the creel full. On the way back, they stopped to put flowers on one tiny grave in particular, beneath the pine trees.

Annie had gathered marsh marigolds while Rory had been cutting the peat for her. The marigolds gleamed like a bunch of sunbeams in that dark and lonely place in a corner of Stag's Meadow. Rory took one of the flowers and laced it into Annie's knitted shawl. 'For you: I give you all my heart, Annie, not just a part of it.'

'Listen to the forest whispering,' she said, a lump in her throat because he was so thoughtful and kind, and because she was beginning to like him more than she should.

The wind keening through the trees sent shivers down her spine. She hated this place, more so when she thought of the deformed infant beneath her feet, at last buried in the ground away from the Lady Iona's sight. 'Quick, let's run!'

He picked up the heavy creel of peat and carried it on his shoulder. Laughing together, they hastened down the glen, Annie casting away the gloomy forebodings that had assailed her in that sad little family cemetery on Inchnadamph. Before they reached the cottage, the rain came down in a solid sheet of water, soaking them both.

Rory set down the peat creel beside the fire and then

left the cottage. She would have asked him to dry himself first, and then have a bite to eat, but he seemed in rather a hurry to get away: neither did she feel it was the right thing to do, inviting him in during Lindsay's absence.

From the doorstep, Annie watched him kicking up the sand which the rain pock-marked in its lancing ferocity. His hands in his pockets, oblivious of the downpour, he sang at the top of his lungs:

'Jocky was laird both of hills and of valleys,
But Sandy was nought but King o' gude fellows . . .'

Annie sat before the glowing fire banked high with peat. In her lap she held the 'Big Black Book', though her concentration was taken by the wind rattling the door. Westerly gales were frightening in their intensity. She hated them when she was all on her own. The roar of the angry sea lashing the rocks at the foot of the ros filled her ears, and she was only thankful she hadn't been caught in her fishing-boat in such a storm.

Then a louder rattle at the door, a decidedly human one this time, made her jump almost out of her skin. Hoping that it was Lindsay returned from Edinburgh, her heart soared, and she leapt up to answer the door.

Annie lifted the heavy wooden bar securing the door, and bracing herself against the howling wind that whipped through the cottage, saw Rory standing there in the rain-lashed night.

He held out her shawl to her. 'Wet, I'm afraid. You dropped it this afternoon during our mad dash down the glen. I thought you might have need of it, so here it is. You'll have to dry it before you wear it, though.' He paused awkwardly.

'Thank you.' She took it from him, unsure of what to say or do next as she struggled to keep the door from slamming in his face. 'You shouldn't have come all this way on such a night . . .'

She had intended saying goodnight and shutting the door, but he had his foot in the way. 'Dash it all, Annie, that was just an excuse. May I come in? I've something important I want to say to you.'

She opened the door wider. He stooped beneath the low lintel, as Lindsay also had need to do, in order to avoid bumping his head. Annie took Rory's mackintosh cape and shook it out before hanging it on a peg behind the door. She handed him a towel to dry his hair after he had removed his gumboots, which he left by the door. He padded over to the fire in his thick woollen socks. Still they didn't speak, Annie only conscious of the drawn thread of heightened awareness between them.

She sat down again in the rocking chair beside the fire, and looked up at him enquiringly. Rory had removed his Aran jersey, tossing it over the clothes-line above the fire, before perching himself on the edge of the table. His shirt-cuffs damp, he gripped the edge of the table with both hands.

'Annie,' he began awkwardly, 'I know I've no right to say this in view of my current record, but I swear to you on that Bible you hold, that what I'm about to say is the truth, the whole truth and nothing but the truth ... I think I've fallen in love with you.'

She stared at him, her jaw dropping.

The words wouldn't come, no matter how hard she tried.

Through his cotton shirt, she could see his rapid heart-beat – could almost *feel* it – like a trapped bird furiously beating its wings against the bars of a cage. She realized then what an effort it must have been for him to admit such a thing, when he knew exactly the place she occupied in his brother's life.

Annie didn't look at him; she tried to avoid looking into his hopeful eyes. She said slowly, 'You *think* you've fallen in love with me ...'

'No ... I put it badly. I *know* I've fallen in love with you, Annie.'

'How can you know? You don't know me at all. You've only been here on a few occasions, and so you cannot know anything at all about me.'

'I know my feelings for you. Feelings that won't go away, though I've tried so hard to forget about you. But I can't. I think about you all the time – every day and every night. Why do you think I come to Glengarth so often? For Lindsay's sake? Or to do timber business? No, Annie. I come here because of you, and for no other reason. I can't stop thinking about you. The moment I'm in Glasgow I'm planning on when next I can return to Glengarth to see you ...'

'Don't say things like that when they're not true! It's a cruel thing to do, playing around with my feelings just because you think I'm *fair game!*'

'Oh, *no*, Annie! That's not true at all! Please don't think so badly of me. You're wrong. I love you. I ... I didn't return to Glasgow this morning, when I knew I ought to have done, simply because I'd rather be here with you. I came here tonight to ask you to consider marrying me ...'

She put her hands over her ears. 'Go away! Don't do this ...'

He took a step towards her, but she waved him back. 'Don't come any nearer.' She took her hands away from her face and raised her head to look him fully in the eye. Two fierce spots of colour burned her cheeks and her green eyes flashed him angry signals. 'How dare you think you can come here like this, knowing your brother's away, yet hoping to entice me during his absence. What do you take me to be, Rory? You know I belong to Lindsay, and yet you think you can treat me like a ... like some sort of common woman who is willing to sell herself to the highest bidder ... Go away!'

'I think of you with love and respect Annie ... please, believe me. I'm offering you marriage. I'm offering you better things in life than ...'

'Go away, Rory. Leave me alone. Don't insult me any more, please.'

'Listen to me first, Annie, and then I'll leave you in peace. Don't refuse me before hearing me out, and don't condemn me. I love you. I love you more than I've ever loved any woman in my life. I want to marry you more than anything I've ever wanted in my life, so please ...'

'Then you're mad!' she said, cutting him short. 'Your only reason for coming here tonight to ask me this thing, is because you think I'm without a husband for myself and a father for my child, and so you *think* you'll take pity on me, and that I'm stupid enough to believe your cruel story about love and ... and ... and ...'

'Why would I want to do that?'

'Yes, why would you, when you can have any girl you want? Someone pure and pretty, wholesome and fresh, rich and well-connected. So why would you want to marry me? I'll tell you why! You think you can outsmart your brother by taking me away from him ...'

'Oh, God, Annie! Don't be ridiculous! Don't say such things. Don't even *think* them ...'

'You can't love me! You know nothing at all about me. What I am, what I'm like – nothing! I've known your brother all my life. He's the one I want.'

'I know what you must be thinking, Annie, and I can't blame you. But I promise you, I'm not the fickle gigolo you imagine I am – a charlatan, a n'er do well who sponges off rich women. I'm not offering to marry you out of gallantry, pity or anything else – I'm not that gallant or noble. Only selfish, selfish for love, *your* love.'

'While I carry another man's child? Did your fine sister send you here to offer the fishergirl marriage in order to preserve the reputation and the noble face of your family? Did she?'

'Now you insult *me.*'

'Then it's about time you realized what it felt like to be hurt badly, insulted and ... and laughed at! I wouldn't put anything past that sister of yours, and I'd like you to know it.'

'This is nothing to do with my sister, Annie. This is between you and me, no one else, even though you are carrying my brother's child. But we both know he'll never divorce Iona to marry you. I know Lindsay better than you, Annie Gowrie, and my brother's pride is also his downfall. His pride supersedes everything else in his life, including love. Iona is his shield, his coat-of-arms, if you like. She still has something to give him which you cannot provide him with – forgive me, but I have to say it – status and prestige. Not to mention money and influential contacts provided by name and ancient family ties.

Lindsay *needs* Iona, whether he chooses to believe it or not. How long are you prepared to go on being second best in his life?'

'I am not second best in his life – I am the *first* one in his life!'

'Fool yourself if you must, Annie, but don't ruin the life of your child because you cannot face up to the truth. How many more children has he to father upon you before you wake up and realize you'll never be anything to him except a *mistress*? Someone he'll keep hidden away for ever in her island cot because he doesn't consider her worthy enough to grace the high-table at Glengarth? Why are you denying yourself, and your child, the chance of a better life?'

'There *is* no better life than the one I have here.'

'For now, perhaps. But you're worth far more than my brother is prepared to give you. So don't waste yourself on him, that's all I'm saying.'

Annie couldn't stop the violent trembling of her body as anger and fear and a whole host of other strong emotions swept over her. Knowing that he spoke the truth made her even less sure of herself. But she didn't need his pity or his smug, self-assured conceit. 'Go away, Rory, before I really lose my temper with you. Don't come here pitying me and insulting me. Leave me alone to live my life the way I want. I shall have my baby without outside interference – especially from you.'

'No, Annie, I won't go. Not until I know your real reason for denying yourself. You're doing yourself a disfavour by clinging to idle dreams centred around my brother. Dreams are all they are, all they ever will be. Dreams that will never come true. But together, you and I can make a fresh start that has nothing to do with dreams, but with *reality*!'

'I don't love you! Will you understand *that*!' she interrupted angrily.

'I understand. I wouldn't presume that you could love me as you love Lindsay, and I'm prepared to accept that. But love has many facets, Annie, just like a diamond. And love can grow if it's properly nurtured. I know it can.

Together, we can make a new life for ourselves. You and I *together*, Annie, can give the baby a decent home, provide for it, educate it, give it love and the proper guidance ... We can be *real* parents; whereas, as Lindsay's mistress, you will only ever be a third-class citizen while your child is termed a bastard.'

'Yes, and that's a name your fine sister and the Lady Iona have both bandied around in front of me. Sticks and stones may break my bones, Rory, but hard words I couldn't care less about. *I'll* give my child a proper home, and the proper care, and the proper love, without being too afraid of what others might call it. I'll *never* leave Rill because I'm happy here, no matter what you might think or feel, my fine business gentleman with his *English* upbringing!'

He had to smile at that, despite the passion behind Annie's outburst.

'Annie, Annie, just listen, please.' He dropped on his heels in front of her. Taking her icy hands in his firm, warm, strong grip, Rory chafed them between his palms. 'I know you feel like this now. But after the baby's born you might think differently. I'm prepared to wait, allow you time to think about what I've said. I'll go away, back to Glasgow, or America, if you want me far away from you. But please think about it, Annie. Don't deny three people – yourself, myself, and the coming baby – the right to happiness, just because you think you owe my brother something.'

She shook her head emphatically. Close to tears, she just wanted him to go away and leave her alone. Annie took a deep breath. 'I can't marry you, not now, not ever, because I don't love you. When I went to Lindsay, we both knew there could be no question of marriage. We both understood that the only place I could ever occupy in his grand life was the hide-and-seek one of mistress, never wife. You're asking me to marry you for all the wrong reasons. I'm not stupid. Pity is a poor foundation for any marriage. I'm only a fisherman's daughter with no background, nothing, while you're the laird's brother. A man with chances galore to marry a woman with wealth and prestige, with all the glittering trappings of a life that isn't mine.'

'Annie, you've not been listening to a word I've said. I *could* have married for all those worldly reasons, but I did not! I've had every opportunity and more to meet other women – heiresses in their own right, titled women, beautiful women, sexually attractive women, witty women, amusing women, red, brunette and blonde, and without sounding conceited, I could have had a damn good fling with most of them.'

'Then why didn't you!' she said savagely.

'I did sometimes. Not any more though. None of it, not money, fame, beauty, wit and wonder, make for happiness. I know that now.'

'Then what does?'

'These past few weeks with you have been the happiest of my life. You've shown me that there are so many more things to life other than the glamour, the wealth, the privileges and the status that have always been so much a part of my own existence – *existence*, Annie, not life! You've taught me that there are good, solid, basic values to be considered above all else, and that a simple marsh marigold is of far greater value than all the diamond necklaces in the world. When I saw your face light up yesterday afternoon over a simple moorland flower, there was sunshine from that marsh marigold reflected in your face. Suddenly I knew where I belonged. All that may sound very arch, and very trite, but it's the truth. I love you. Marry me tomorrow and make us both happy.'

He still retained her hands in his, caressing each finger in turn while he opened his heart to her. She shook her head. 'I can't Rory,' she whispered, 'so please don't ask me again. Wherever we go, whatever we do, I'll have no place in your fancy world. Rill is where I belong. I shall have Lindsay's baby when it's time, and afterwards I shall go on living here as I've always done. You don't want to marry a woman who bears another man's child, even if that man is your own brother.'

'If you haven't told Lindsay about it, and he suspects nothing, why tell him? It would be our secret.'

'A secret that's bound to come out sooner or later. Your sister knows whose child it is, and if she hasn't already told him, he'll find out.'

'Christabel hasn't told Lindsay. I know that for a fact. She mentioned it to me, surely, but I told her it wasn't her place to say anything to Lindsay before you had spoken to him – as she was going to do. I know my sister can be very interfering, but she has great pride in Glengarth and the reputation of its noble laird. I think she was rather hoping that you might lose the child prematurely as Iona lost her baby, and then you'd realize she wasn't being intentionally unkind in telling you about Lindsay's addiction, but that she was merely warning you for your own sake.'

'You told me opium wasn't harmful, and the laird needed it because sometimes he couldn't take the stress he was under.' Annie looked at Rory, and there *was* pity in *her* glance. 'How can I prevent that kind of love happening again and again, if I love the laird and he loves me?'

'How can I answer that, Annie Gowrie?' he replied. 'You make me jealous, you make me frustrated and you make me sad. All I can say is, how envious I am of the love you give my brother who offers you nothing, while I would lay down my life and all my steamships at your feet.'

'And now you are being dramatic. Come on, get up off your knees,' she urged, trying to make light of his earnestness.

'Annie, will you think about what I've said,' he pleaded, grasping her hands tighter still.

'No. No, I won't even think about it Rory. Just supposing I did consent to marry you, and just supposing the child born – your brother's child – was like that twisted, black and blue creature caught up in the membrane cobweb of its own cowl, would you be prepared to accept it then? And supposing it lived? Supposing it lived to be a helpless, dependent, deformed imbecile, unable to function without the supportive efforts of others, what then? Would you be ashamed of it? Would you lock it up in an asylum? Would you look after it for the rest of your life, and worry about what would happen to it when you were dead? Supposing I died in childbed, and you, because you had married me out of pity, or concern, or ... or for some other silly reason, were left to bring up your brother's monster without Annie Gowrie, what then?'

'I would honour our marriage pledge, Annie.'

'Noble words, Rory Duncan! You're daft as a brush, you know ...' She smoothed the damp hair back from his forehead, his face on a level with hers, while he knelt in front of her, clasping her hands tightly between his own.

Annie searched deep into his candid blue eyes, and thought about all the things she was rejecting for reasons unclear, even to herself. And she was half-tempted to say *yes, yes, yes*! Let's do it! Let's run away together and start life anew. Take me away from here! Take me away from the tragic memories and the sorrow that invades my life and let Lindsay face his own destruction through drugs ... Instead, Annie's reply was, 'You're a nice man, Rory. Thank you for making me the offer of marriage, but the answer is No!'

'I don't care. I love you more than he. I want to make you happy ... I want to give you, and the child, a new start in life ... please, Annie, why won't you even consider me as a husband?'

And even in that moment when he went delving into her innermost soul, the wind whipped into the cottage and Lindsay stood on the threshold, his hunting rifle over his arm.

CHAPTER THIRTY-ONE

Lindsay's mackintosh dripped water at his feet. Annie stared transfixed at the deepening puddles on the earthen floor over which she had placed freshly woven, heather mats only that morning.

Rory was on his feet now, and the 'Big Black Book' lay forgotten in Annie's lap, while the wind through the door rustled the pages, rattled the pewter mugs on their hooks and threatened to wreak all sorts of havoc in her cottage unless Lindsay shut the door quickly.

'Annie, tell us why you can't take my brother up on his noble offer of marriage?' Very carefully, too carefully, Lindsay closed and barred the door. Then he stepped over to the table and put his rifle down on its scrubbed surface.

'Lindsay ...' Annie swallowed, her voice feeling cracked and hollow in her throat. She gripped the arms of the rocking chair, her whole body suddenly weighing her down like a sack of coals. 'It's good to see you, Lindsay. When did you get back from Edinburgh?'

'I never went to Edinburgh, Annie.' Lindsay took off his mackintosh and hung it over his brother's mackintosh cape behind the door. He turned, a smile on his face as he ran his fingers through his fair hair to displace the raindrops, before reaching into his pocket for his cigarette case. His smile was not reflected in his eyes.

Lindsay's eyes were cold and grey and dead. That depleted look in him Annie had learned to dread. His eyes never once wavered from her pale, stricken face.

She noticed that he had on his old, worn, Harris tweed jacket with leather patches on the sleeves, the jacket he always wore when out hunting on the estate.

Why had Lindsay lied to her about going to Edinburgh? In finding her own answer, Annie was terribly afraid.

Lindsay was in one of his strange moods, and there was no knowing what might happen.

Rory turned to his brother and said, 'You're a bastard, Lindsay. Tell us why you've been spying on us!'

'Oh-oh!' said Lindsay, a sudden glint in his eye. 'Guilty conscience, brother?'

'Grow up, Lindsay!'

A short sharp silence followed. Then Lindsay said, 'I recall that same remark being uttered by myself, to you, on the day of our mother's funeral. You were being a thorough little blackguard to our father, and everyone else, including Sula. I'm so glad you followed my advice, and can now turn around and say to me, your host, grow up Lindsay!'

And, all the time, a horrible cynical smile played around the corners of his mouth – a mouth whose attractiveness Annie had thought enhanced by the beauty-mole which he had covered by a moustache because he regarded it as an effeminate attribute detracting from his masculinity. But not now, not any more was he her idol. In that moment Lindsay seemed almost ugly to her. Annie stared at him without really seeing him. He was a total stranger to her this night. There was no hint of gentleness and nothing attractive about him at all. The grim, hard line of his mouth and cruel light in his grey eyes, the cold, hard, brutal brittleness in every word he uttered, every action of his, every calculated remark designed to sting, hurt and destroy, made her aware of him as a man hollowed out by a terrible deprivation that had nothing to do with money or success, but with something black and sinister leaking through the surface of his whole being. What had happened in his life to make him so empty and hollow? Was it something outside himself, or something inside, something inherent in his nature to create the profound depression he so often experienced? Annie couldn't begin to understand.

He had been playing with his unlit cigarette, but now he turned up the flame of the oil-lamp, and lit it. Then, in a casual attitude, he leaned against the peat wall of the cot, to regard his brother and Annie with wry amusement.

'Please don't let me intrude further upon the heart-rending scene I witnessed just now. Rory, get back on your knees. Annie, let's see again the look on your face when he begged you to marry him and you refused. By GOD! This is the stuff of Hollywood Iona is mad to see in Edinburgh! Silent movies they call them, though she made it sound like a dashed thoroughbred horse!'

He was not making any sense. Rory wondered how much opium Lindsay had been taking.

'Let's pretend I'm the director of a silent movie, shall we?' Lindsay continued. 'Annie, give me your tragic face. I'm the man not invited to join the party, and I *beg* of you, tell brother Rory why you can't take him up on his offer?'

'Leave her alone, Lindsay,' Rory said. 'Leave us both alone, damn you.'

Lindsay blew a smoke ring to the ceiling, and looked at his brother through narrowed silver eyes. 'I will. Once I've established the facts. I don't like being made to look a fool by you or this wanton wench I once rescued from the gutter. I should have saved myself the bother, eh, Annie?'

'No one is making you look a fool, Lindsay, only yourself.' Rory's manner was calm, despite the provocativeness of Lindsay's jibes.

Annie was conscious once more of that invisible cord of enmity between the two brothers: each of them pulling a little this way and then that, in a vicious tug-of-war. She wanted no part of their private feud. She got up to hang the kettle over the fire to make cups of tea to soothe everyone's nerves, when Lindsay crashed his fist onto the kitchen table and frightened her to death. Annie dropped the kettle, and the water on the fire made the peat hiss and smoulder unpleasantly.

'Rory, you make the place look untidy. Annie can't bear untidiness or dirtiness in any form, can you, my dear?'

'*Jesus*, Lindsay! What's got into you?' Rory asked despairingly.

'*Opium*! Isn't that what Kiss told you? Isn't that what she poisoned *your* mind with, Annie Gowrie? Kiss knows I'm addicted to opium and to certain moods, certain

displays of fantasy, certain flights of imagination, certain
pains of withdrawal when the body remains unsatisfied.
All drug induced. Isn't that what my sister told you? Isn't
it, Annie? Did she tell you, Rory, that our father had the
same problem, and that is why Grandfather Glengarth cut
him out of his inheritance? Did she? The curse of Glengarth,
Rory, is our legacy of the East! So now you know.'

Annie sat down. Into the darkness of her hands
covering her face, she prayed Lindsay's own darkness
would go away.

'Annie,' Lindsay said evenly. 'I asked you a question. I
want an answer. Why won't you take Rory up on his offer
of marriage?'

'Because I don't want to marry him. I want to marry
you, but I know that is not possible.'

Lindsay brought the three-legged milking-stool beside
her. 'Why is it impossible?'

'You're already married to the Lady Iona.'

'To the *LADY* Iona.' He nodded his head like a
marionette and sat down on the stool. 'You have your
answer, Rory,' Lindsay said, looking up at his brother.
'What a treasure you're losing yourself. Annie wants no
other man except me. See how those copper pans gleam
on the shelf behind you? Annie's work of art. She's an
utterly dedicated housewife. A treasure! Her caring little
touches have turned a dirty old man's pig-sty into a home
for a laird! Isn't that right, Annie?' He clamped his hand
around her wrist, fingers gripping like a vice.

'For God's sake, Lindsay,' Rory interrupted, 'control
yourself. Living out here in the wilds for so long, have you
forgotten how to behave decently?'

'Yes!' Lindsay's eyes were wide and staring. 'My mother
was a lady, that I'll admit. But my father was less than a
gentleman, and I have been made to suffer for his sins.'

'Forget all about Moloch, for Christ's sake ...'

'Christ and God!' Lindsay mocked. 'Don't blaspheme,
Rory. Annie doesn't like it. What were you saying about
Moloch?'

'I said forget it! Forget about that crazy Sadhu on the
road to Tippindee. You've let outside forces influence you

for too long. Destiny isn't *written*. Destiny is handled by *ourselves*.'

'How can I forget? India destroyed me! You know that. You knew about Chindwin of the compound didn't you?'

'Yes. But you destroyed yourself, Lindsay. You didn't *have* to take the stuff. Each of us has it within our power to defeat the enemy lurking within us. The *pleasure* of temptation is what you craved, Lindsay, and you gave in!'

'Oh, *Brother Morality*! Save me your preaching! I get enough of it around here what with my wife, my sister and my mistress!' Then Lindsay sneeringly asked: 'And what about the temptation of theft? What about the *barbarian* enemy lurking within us? You returned to Glengarth to steal from me. You came here to steal *my woman*!'

'Lindsay, I swear to you I did not. Annie has a right to life, too!'

Lindsay exhaled loudly, and the pain in his eyes was contagious. Annie felt it; his own brother felt it. And they were both at a loss as to how best to help the Laird of Glengarth.

'Annie has a horror of dirt, Rory,' Lindsay repeated himself. 'Anything unclean gives her a guilty conscience – what one might call a Lady Macbeth syndrome. Cleanliness and Godliness, that's what Annie wants in her life.' Lindsay picked up the Bible that had dropped on the floor beside the rocking-chair.

Flicking through the pages with his cigarette in his mouth, his eyes narrowed above the haze of blue smoke, Lindsay mumbled tightly, 'What is it tonight, Annie Gowrie? The Song of Solomon, eulogizing Sheba's navel like a goblet? What about her breasts like twin roes? ... Annie's aren't bad either, Rory.'

'Lindsay,' Annie began, 'don't do this to us.' But he ignored her.

'However, by now you've probably uncovered Annie's secrets for yourself, uh, brother of mine? What about her thighs? The work of the hands of a cunning workman? Come on, Rory! Let's have your opinion. You were quite ready to give it just now.'

'Lindsay, I think you'd better go.'

'No! *You'd* better go! This is *my* cot, *my* land and *my* woman! *You* get out of here!'

'I'm not leaving Annie alone with you while you're in this vile mood.'

'Oh, she's used to it. You've got yourself quite a knight in shining armour now, haven't you, Annie, darling? Let's see … I have a feeling you were reading all about the Marriage Feast at Cana. Most appropriate!' Lindsay tossed the Bible back into Annie's lap 'I should read the lesson of the woman taken in adultery, Annie. I fear Mary of Magdala has lost her little tongue to the cat tonight. You didn't invite me to supper, Annie? Or is three considered one too many on this occasion? You really are not to be trusted, my dear. You didn't lose much time in playing fast and loose the moment my back was turned – but then, I suppose it's to be expected from someone used to bedding with an animal.'

'Cut it out?' Lindsay's eyebrows arched cynically. 'From throbbed in his temple.

'Cut it out?' Lindsay's eyebrow arched cynically. 'From where I wonder did you glean *that* piece of vocabulary? Ah yes, it must be from the American dockside you've recently been inhabiting. How's the timber haulage business going, brother?'

Rory gave a deep sigh. 'Hell's bells. You really are a screwed-up bastard – as they *also* say in the States!'

Annie bit her lip and studied the plaid pattern of her skirt. She wished that both of them would go away and leave the cottage to her. Lindsay again took hold of her wrist, forcing her to look up. 'Why did you invite him here tonight, Annie?'

'She didn't. I invited myself,' Rory said, bracing himself against the edge of the table.

Then in another burst of temper, Lindsay dashed his cigarette into the grate before striking the stool away from under him. With a sharp pull on both Annie's wrists he forced her to her feet. 'I want to look at you, Annie. I want to admire the clothes you're wearing. Why are you dressed up so prettily in your best bib and tucker? Is it because you knew I was coming home tonight? Or because of brother Rory?'

'Don't Lindsay ...' Annie begged. 'Please let me go ... I'm only wearing my best because my other clothes got wet in the rain.'

He turned her around to face his brother. Standing behind her, Lindsay wrapped his arms tightly across Annie's breast. His eyes fixed upon Rory's stern, set features, he *wanted* to make his brother jealous, as he had been made to feel jealous just now. 'She's mine, all mine! Body and soul, I *own* her. I *paid* for her with my own life ... eh Annie? You may not have her.'

'Annie,' Rory said, making a move to the door, and reaching for his mackintosh. He put his boots on. 'We're getting out of here. Leave her alone, Lindsay. She's coming back with me to Glengarth.'

'Iona doesn't want her at Glengarth ... which is a great pity. I can do with Annie in the big bed tonight ...' Lindsay began to caress Annie's shoulders. 'All this provocative bareness, Annie! Is it for me, or him?' Then he began to unlace the front of her blouse and Annie tried to stop his hands, but he ripped the laces. His lips against her neck, he murmured as he cupped her breasts in his hands, 'She revealed herself to me one day, Rory, just like this ... no, perhaps I won't let *him* see your beautiful naked breasts, after all, Annie, since they belong to me.'

Annie closed her eyes, even as Rory turned away and lifted the heavy bar off the door. She knew that if she said one word in her own defence, Lindsay would humiliate her even further. She only hoped that Rory would hurry and go before he had cause to regret his decision in coming to the cottage tonight.

'"Thy belly is like an heap of wheat set about with lilies ..."' Lindsay began smoothing down the front of her skirt, his actions calculated. 'Why didn't you tell me, Annie? You thought I didn't know about the child, didn't you? You thought I was too stupid to find out about it: too blind to be aware of the fact you were soon to be a mother. By not saying anything to me, were you trying to deceive me as Iona did? Were you hoping to marry my brother and pass this baby off as his?'

'For God's sake, Lindsay! What's the matter with you?
Calm down, will you? You're just not making sense ...'
Rory hesitated by the door, loathe to leave Annie in
Lindsay's mad embrace, yet he knew it would probably be
best for him to go. Lindsay might calm down then.

Lindsay ignored his brother, and continued to taunt
Annie. 'I'm not that naïve, my skinny little fishergirl. I
know it's not due to all the good food I've been sending
down from Glengarth that you've fattened up so nicely.
Christabel and Iona have very long tongues, fishergirl, and
gossip is rife up at Glengarth. But I wanted *you* to tell me,
not my wife or my sister!'

'Leave Annie alone, will you!' Rory's voice had an edge
to it.

'So that you can have her? *Never!*' Lindsay rent the
blouse in two, shocking Annie out of her docility. Up to
now she had not struggled against his gross behaviour
because she did not want to provoke him further. But this
time Lindsay had gone too far and she kicked out with her
heels against his shins. Lindsay, his laughter devoid of
humour, struggled to keep hold of her hands, twisting
them up behind her back. 'Aren't her breasts the sweetest
things you've ever seen, brother? Go on, take a good look,
Rory for *looking* is all you'll ever get from Annie. She's
mine!'

Rory didn't say or do anything. He just stood there like
a mute, while Lindsay continued to behave like a
barbarian. Annie couldn't believe it.

'Come on, Rory ... I'm sure you've seen it all before,
and done it all before, so don't be shy. Annie certainly
won't be, for this is how she revealed herself to me one
day in the charred ruins of Forest Lodge. Lovely, isn't she,
dear brother? And all mine. Mine! Mine to have and to
hold and to do any damn thing with. Mine, like every hill
and valley, every tree and flower, every inch of loch and
forest. I own her as much as I own Glengarth, Loch
Garth, the *Flower of Glengarth*, Rill and this cottage with
the fire that warms you both while you make a mockery of
me by laughing behind my back!'

'Goddammit, Lindsay! Nobody's laughing at you. It's

all in your mind. What the hell is there to laugh about?'
Rory was angry now, his fists bunched as he stepped away
from the door to face Lindsay across the table. He leaned
on his outstretched arms as if forcing himself not to use
them on his brother. 'I haven't touched, Annie, if that's
what you're worried about.'

'But you'd like to. The eyes, Rory, the eyes are the
windows of the soul. Your eyes gave you away just now!
Star-gazing into Annie's while you knelt so chivalrously
before her when you proposed. And she, caressing and
fondling you like a lover? Oh, yes, I've had my eyes on
you two – from the High Hills plantation where one can
get a good view of this island and cottage. I've had my
spy-glasses trained on you two for quite some time now –
every time you come to Glengarth to see her, in fact. I
know your real reason for coming here so often, brother,
when in the past you never came nigh or near the place. It
isn't anything to do with timber or lumberjacks, is it?'
Lindsay took a deep breath.

'I've watched you two together, laughing and singing
and making a damned undignified exhibition of yourselves in front of all the servants and tenants. And I don't
like to be made a laughing stock before my estate-hands.
You betrayed me, Annie, betrayed me with my own
brother, sold yourself to him ...'

'No, Lindsay, I did not!'

'Don't lie to me, fishergirl! Don't be a liar as well as a
slut.'

'I've never lied to you, never ... please let go of me ...'

'The truth, Annie. I want the truth. You and he have
become lovers, haven't you?'

'No!'

'*The truth*! I want the truth, Annie!'

She could hear him grinding his teeth close to her ear,
Lindsay forcing her head back by pulling on her hair.
Annie gasped with fear and pain. And not once did his
fine brother step forward to prevent Lindsay from hurting
her. Annie began to sob. 'Lindsay ... I've told you the
truth ... you're hurting me, please let go.'

'Annie, I warned you once before, at Forest Lodge,

don't trifle with my feelings. I shall break you in half ...
now, the *truth*! You and he have become lovers, haven't
you?'

'No, m'laird ... don't do this to me. I love only you ...'

'The truth, fishergirl.'

'No ...'

'Annie, the truth! I'm waiting ...'

'Damn you to hell, Lindsay, leave her alone!'

'You keep out of this, Rory, or it will be the worse for
Annie. Annie, I'm warning you. Have you made love to
my brother?'

'*No!*'

'He loves you ... he said so himself. And you love him
too, don't you? Now that you know the truth about the
Laird of Glengarth and his addiction to opium, you've
turned to the laird's brother for your "comforts" eh,
Annie Gowrie! Do you love him?'

'Please, my laird, don't do this ...'

'Do you love him more than me, Annie?'

'*No!*'

'The truth, Annie. *Yes or no!*'

Annie could feel her spine breaking in two as Lindsay
forced her down to her knees by pulling back on her long
hair. She couldn't take his cruelty a moment longer and
cried, ' *Yes, Yes, Yes! I love him ...*'

Only the sound of her dry sobs rent the stillness.

Only then did Lindsay stop bending Annie backwards,
breaking her in two as he had once threatened. Breaking
her spirit and her heart.

Only afterwards did that night on Rill come back to her
in all its sordidness, and only then did she have the
courage to let go of Lindsay, her laird.

Annie stumbled away from him. She snatched her
damp shawl from the clothes-line on which she had
thrown it when Rory brought it back to the cottage.
Suddenly, within her, flared a deep black hatred against
the two brothers. Rory had not lifted a finger to help her
in the face of Lindsay's treacherous behaviour. She hated
as she had never hated before. Not even that stepfather of
hers who had destroyed her as a child did she hate as

much as these two grand brothers who saw themselves as gentlemen ... Annie clawed blindly for the door, tears running down her cheeks.

Rory stood in front of the door, refusing to let Annie go out into the dark night alone, but with every intention of escorting her away from Rill and back to Glasgow if necessary. He said with the utmost control, while Annie, her shawl clutched tightly, leaned against the door, crying silently. 'You forced that confession from her, you fool. You know damn well she only loves you. For God's sake, Lindsay, she's carrying your child ...'

'Mine or yours?' the laird asked.

He took out another cigarette from the gold case lying on the table and turned to light it from a taper taken from the mantlepiece, but the fire had gone out. Lindsay held the taper to the flame in the glass funnel of the oil-lamp, his brows interrogative as he met his brother's eyes across the table.

'Hells bells, man,' Rory replied, 'I've crawled through some gutters in my time, but never one as filthy as your mind.'

Lindsay laughed scornfully. 'Well, then, Rory, since I believe you're hell bent upon marrying Annie Gowrie, my common-law wife, I think I ought to describe to you the state in which I found her. Then you'll be under no illusion *whatsoever*, as to what you're picking up.'

'*Lindsay, No!*' Annie turned her tearful face to him while the pain twisted in ugly coils inside her. 'Please don't tell him.'

Lindsay stared at her for a long moment, his eyes narrowed above the glare of the oil-lamp. 'No, Annie, my sweet! Even though you betrayed me to my own brother by spurning the love I had for you, I shan't do the same to you. I haven't spent my time providing you with an education of sorts, clothes, food and a roof over your head, to throw it all away on him. So I'll keep you until death do us part!' He came across to her and kissed her gently on the forehead. 'I love you, Annie. Never again throw that love back in my face.'

Still smiling down at her stricken expression, Lindsay

said in a cultured English accent only he knew how to use with deadly intent, 'After all, the King of the Castle still has need of a dirty rascal's little whore, eh, Annie Gowrie?'

'You *bastard*!' Rory sprang at him in the second that Lindsay reached for the gun lying on the table. 'I've taken just about as much as I can stand from you for one night ...'

Lindsay cocked the rifle at his brother. 'Stay where you are, Rory. Murder, they tell me, is easier the second time, and even easier the third ... ask Annie. She'll tell you what became of her stepfather. I did it for her sake and I'll do it again – even against my own brother. And then I will put a bullet through *her* head. A lover's tiff, a crime of passion, the triple tragedy at Glengarth ... I can see the headlines already ...'

Annie didn't wait to find out what would happen next. She wrenched open the cot door and fled into the stormy night.

She ran and ran, not stopping to think where her feet were taking her.

Everything, all her senses had been paralysed, her heart and soul trampled on by Lindsay, so that all she wanted to do was lose herself and never ever see Lindsay again ...

Up on the mull the high winds pulled her to the edge of the cliff. Poised above the ink-black rocks, darker than the harsh night, Annie saw the white water, and was tempted by those darting, licking, moist white tongues of destructive spume. Fascinated, she stared down at the empty blackness lit only by those teasing tongues of the kelpies of the sea. Annie, the mermaid, she wanted to ride out the night on those sea-horse spirits. The salty, cleansing, all-abrasive sea that would wash away her sin and her shame and a love betrayed ...

'*Annie*! *Don't do it*! For God's sake, he's not worth it. *I love you ...*'

The wind took Rory's voice and tossed it over the cliff edge. Annie heard Lindsay's voice in reply. 'Leave her alone! *She's mine, all mine ...*'

Too late, Lindsay, m'laird, Annie thought grimly, too late!

She turned to them, her back to the angry sea: two golden brothers by day, mere shadows of themselves this night as they stood poised on the black mull. Standing against the backdrop of wind-lashed, stormy forests which made a mockery of their thin, precarious, fanciful lives, Annie knew the choice was hers.

She stepped back, even as they came cautiously forward fearing for her safety. Well, let them! Annie laughed in their fine faces. 'There's things in this world, my lords, that can never be owned by the Roskillens. Annie Gowrie is one of them ...' Annie felt the turf sag beneath her feet. Soggy and dangerous after all the rain, even the cliff wanted to carry her down to the sea which would wash away all her sins – murdcrous, adulterous sins, the worse kind to be found in the 'Big Black Book'. Then all at once the cliff began to crumble away from under her, and in that moment when a precarious freedom was offered her, she didn't want it.

She screamed, reaching out for both of them. Oh God, she didn't want to die ... not yet ... not yet ... her life, the new life inside her, were far too precious to throw away for the sake of two selfish men ... '*Rory ... Rory!*' Annie screamed, scrabbling at the grassy edges of the mull, '*Rory ... save me ...*' Everything was light and space and air around her. Clean, pure, sweet-smelling freedom, the very breath of death ...

And as he reached out his arms for her, Annie knew she wanted the captivity of life more than anything else in the world.

PART SEVEN

'... A "Trafalgar" on May 31st, 1916, would have re-established British naval supremacy for a long time to come. Such ascendancy depends as much upon moral as upon material factors ...'

Commander H.H. Frost (USN)
(Battle of Jutland)

CHAPTER THIRTY-TWO

In September Annie went to Gairloch. Struggling up the steep cobblestones to Nurse Craig's house, the terrible pains started again, and she had to lean against the seawall until she felt better.

Annie dared not think about what would become of her if the old nurse was no longer living at Gairloch. She closed her eyes and prayed hard. Shivering more with fear than with the brisk wind skeeting off the sea, she closed her eyes and prayed long and hard. It helped to take her mind off herself and what was happening to her.

Her clothes felt stiff and sticky with sea-water, chafing her skin and causing the wind to feel even more barbed as it whipped through her. Annie moved off slowly. Only another hundred yards to go, she told herself. She couldn't remember the exact time her waters had broken, only that it had happened while she had been sailing her fishing-boat back into the loch.

She managed the distance before the next contraction made her bite her lips and cling for support to the porch wall of the tiny house overlooking the harbour, where Nurse Craig had lived all her life.

Annie banged and banged on the door, and because the nurse was so long in coming to answer it, Annie sank down on the doorstep with the sweat breaking out on her forehead. If Craigie didn't hurry herself, the baby would be born right here on her doorstop, thought Annie as she tried not to cry out against the waves of pain tearing her apart.

She remained there, hunched against assault – Nurse Craig was not living here any more. Perhaps she had died and the news of it had passed her by. She hadn't visited Gairloch in months, so would be none the wiser. Now what did she do? Now she wished she had stayed with her relatives on Errin and not undertaken this journey by sea so that Nurse Craig could attend her. But she had been determined upon it, and no one had been able to dissuade her from her intention to give birth to the laird's child on the soil of Ross-shire.

She took off her shoe and banged the heel on the wood. Craigie had always been hard of hearing.

Still, no one appeared, not even a neighbour. It was as though the country's recent mobilization for a war against Germany had made everyone hide themselves away in terror of their lives, afraid to death that the enemy had already invaded the British Isles. Nursing her miseries, Annie knew she would have to seek help elsewhere. She did not want to go to Dr Robinson, who had no idea of her condition. Besides, it did not seem politic in the circumstances.

Annie got up off the doorstep, wondering if she could make it to the cottage hospital, when she saw Nurse Craig struggling along the road with a laden shopping basket. Annie sank down again, weak with relief.

'Annie Gowrie, what's been happening to you, lass?' Nurse Craig almost dropped her basket of groceries, for she had been determined to 'stock-up' before the inevitable shortages came. She, for one, did not believe the story put about, that the war would be over by Christmas. 'Lord preserve us, lass, I've not seen you in these parts for months and months ...' and then she noticed Annie's swollen shape. 'Well now, ye'd best come inside, lass, before the bairn is dropped on m'doorstep!'

Nurse Craig put Annie into her own bed.

Hours and hours, years and years later it seemed to Annie, the frail voice of the midwife reached her down the length of a long dark tunnel. 'Go ahead, lass ... the bairn is almost born. Scream as much as y' care to, for I'm deaf to most things these days, and will n'er be telling thee to shut you'er mouth in the manner o' ma practising days.'

And then Annie didn't see her or hear her any more, for Craigie faded away and other presences filled the room.

' 'Tis a son he wants,' Annie shouted as she slipped down the cliff face. 'An heir for Glengarth . . .'

But even this one was not to be, for she was taking him with her: together they would be dashed to pieces by the kelpies of the night riding the rocks . . . Annie screamed and screamed, terrified of falling into that dark abyss. The wind was howling, the sea a fearful roar in her ears. She remembered the man, a gentle, golden man soothing her, telling her to hold on, his distorted face preyed upon by shadows of storm clouds mocking the paleness of the moon as he searched her out from above. And she, with an agonized tearing in her heart, her mind, her soul, her body, each part of her separated from the rest of the world, had felt like a broken vase.

And even while thoughts of death had flitted through a mind clouded by sorrow and betrayal, still Rory had clung to her, refusing to let go, coaxing her back to life, refusing to give her up to the kelpies of the night, reaching down in a lover's embrace, wooing her into strong arms, telling her that mermaids couldn't drown.

Then, just when the sea was about to swallow her up, he had given her back her rationality, so that a new realization was born in her. Life was too precious to waste for any reason whatsoever — even a noble one, the sacrifice of her own self for that of the Laird Lindsay of Glengarth!

Yet, the pieces of the broken vase were all there – the agonizing weeks following that terrible night had proved to her that they were still all there; they just required gluing back together again to make, not a perfect vase, perhaps, waterproof and flawless any more, but something reshaped to serve another purpose.

Annie saw again the faces gathered around the graves . . . she was back in the pine-grove on Inchnadamph. Servants, tenants, foresters, estate-hands, and all the high-and-mighty ones from as far away as Edinburgh, Aberdeen, Glasgow and London, wept as they looked down on the freshly turned earth on Inchnadamph, nodding sadly and saying, 'What a terrible thing to happen! It was all the mermaid's fault. She came between them, you know, the whole family, like an evil sprite, a

Uisga Caillich, bewitching both the brothers.'

And while the Minister from the kirk, the Lady Morag's husband, read the 'Big Black Book', she had hidden herself among the pine trees, hoping to remain with her own sorrow, unseen. And yet it was as though, from across that distance of peat and heather, her guilty soul had been revealed. And it was as though she heard God himself above his Ministerial white collar, speaking to her in fierce and fiery words while looking her straight in the eye. *'The sins of the flesh have found ye out, Annie Gowrie. The price paid is high, for he was a gude mon in caring about the simple folks around here ...'* But it had only been imagination and a great sense of guilt speaking to her, for she had not been there other than as an outsider, too grief-stricken and too torn apart to stand with the other retainers of Glengarth by the laird's coffin, preferring to keep her distance, preferring to creep back unseen after they had all dispersed, preferring to mourn alone. Only the three people who had mattered most in the world to the Laird Lindsay were missing from the mourning gathering: his capricious wife who had left her wheelchair to go and live in Edinburgh now that *he* was dead and gone; his handsome brother who had returned to Glasgow even though he was the new Laird of Glengarth, unable to reconcile that tragic inheritance and how he had acquired it; and the humble mistress with her own part to play in such a tragedy.

Then the nightmare became the reality; they started to hack down his forests; they started to take his home apart. They stole his loch and his boat, his island and his people, and they put up signs on Rill, *Property of the Admiralty.* And one morning she had looked out of the cot, to see battleships coming stealthily into the wide, deep loch like pale grey crocodiles, killing ships that were designed to destroy. And there were men on her doorstep, men in uniform, who told her she must leave the island while the war was on.

She had stood on the shores of Rill before her exile, and she had let the white grains pour through her hands. She remembered his words, an echo of happiness when her life had encompassed a humble cot and a handsome laird. *'Shellfish, Annie. Myriads and myriads of shellfish crushed out of existence by time and tide.'*

And she went on screaming because the crushing hurt so much; because she too, was being compressed into something unrecognizable; because now she would be just like one of those shellfish, nothing more than a microscopic part of time and tide that no one would even remember! And, crushed out of existence, out of mind and out of time, crushed by the events that had destroyed her meagre existence surrounding a monumental love on Rill, she knew that her life had changed for ever ...

She had taken herself up to the lonely grove amidst the pine trees on Inchnadamph. She had culled the marsh marigolds off Inchnadamph and divided them between him and his wee son, that tragic product of what? The curse of Glengarth? She didn't know, she didn't *care* any more!

Locked into the secrets of men beyond the fringes of her own shores, important men already making preparations to fight a war, she had gone away to Errin, to relatives who were strangers. It was the hardest thing she had ever done in her life, for now there would be no one left to put fresh flowers every day on the two graves ... *no more flowers* ...

''Tis a boy, Annie Gowrie!' Nurse Craig proudly placed the first delivery she had made in a very long time, into the hands of the mother. 'The bonniest wee laddie I've brought forth since ... since ma practising days!' She beamed just like a marsh marigold.

Afterwards, smiling down at the red-faced, wrinkled creature that was her very own son, Annie asked fearfully, 'Is he as he should be, Craigie?'

'Ach! An' why shouldn't he be, Annie Gowrie?' she answered crossly. Then she tickled the tiny infant wrapped in a shawl she herself had knitted for another baby a long time ago. 'Aye, lass, he's perfect. Just perfect! With all the right number o' fingers an' toes, an' the correct working part needed for a bonny wee lad. Just let's be praying, lass, he'll no' be growing up as crusty as the laird.'

Annie looked at Craigie in dismay. 'Who has been telling such tales?'

'Y'self, lassie! No one but y'self! There's no' much a midwife canna glean from the delivery room. But ma lips are sealed, for there's mony a secret locked inside *this* old body! An' when the Lord's scribe unlocks the door to me, Annie Gowrie, he'll suffer a fit o' the writer's cramp. Now get thee some rest, while I mind the bairn.'

He was indeed the bonniest baby in the world, and no trouble at all. All those months spent worrying and working herself up into a rare dither over what sort of monster would be born to her, faded into nothingness now that she held her son in her arms. Annie wondered what the laird's sister, with her wicked tongue, would say now, to the Laird Lindsay's son born not only perfect, but handsome and intelligent, too!

Annie did a lot of thinking in the days following her confinement at Nurse Craig's tiny house in Gairloch. Those evenings, sitting in the cosy parlour, Craigie's knitting needles clacking away nineteen to the dozen while she made Jamie a blue matinée coat – with bootees to match – were full of warm memories for Annie, even though they sometimes sat before an unlit fire. Everyone had been told to economize on timber and coal.

Neither did Craigie light the lamps on this particular evening, a nippy one in late September, with the threat of early snow on the mountains of Torridon and Slioch.

She and Annie sat in the companionable glow of the peat fire, the front-room curtains open and the moon and the stars doing the lighting for them. There was a world of peace and security in this tiny room away from the war in Europe. And after so many months of her own private anguish Annie never wanted to leave this house. But she knew that she must, very soon.

The old nurse sensed Annie's inner turmoil: Annie Gowrie was fretting over her baby's future. Craigie was loathe to raise the subject of adoption, for such a recourse, she knew, would break Annie Gowrie's heart; and yet it seemed the only solution to the problems facing the lass.

Unable to take her fishing-boat out to sea because she had the baby to think of, how was she going to make a living to support both herself and her child? These questions, Craigie knew, were gnawing away at Annie's very vitals. She had noticed the signs of strain in the deep little crease of anxiety between Annie's green eyes, permanently clouded with troubled thoughts, and the dark shadows that hollowed out her cheeks.

Craigie decided to prompt Annie towards some sort of decision, rather than have her pine away and sour her milk, which would do herself and her wee baby no good. Jamie was going on four weeks now, and Annie's fretfulness was increasing. 'It's time ye were away from here, Annie Gowrie,' Craigie said, her concentration absolute upon her knitting needles.

'I know,' Annie answered miserably, realizing that she must have out-stayed her welcome by now. Neither had the old nurse accepted a penny towards food and expenses, not that Annie had much money left anyway. What she had managed to save from her fish-money would have to be eked out during the next few months while she nursed Jamie.

Annie's answer contained a core of desperateness about it. 'Craigie, I've been wracking my brains on what best to do for Jamie. I'll have to give him away ... for others to look after. Living with me will not provide the kind of life a laird's son ought to have. Will you help me look around for a suitable family who will treat him well?'

'I'll do no such thing, Annie Gowrie. Selling you'er baby for money is a sin!'

'It's not the money I want. I want Jamie. But how am I to keep him when I have nothing to give him?'

'I would have thought that the Laird Lindsay, or his grand relatives, would have made provision for the child,' was Craigie's pithy opinion.

Annie bit her lip. 'I'll not beg from them, Craigie. The Roskillens may have come from a line line of Scottish nobility, but I'll not ask them to support the laird's *bastard* – which is what the laird's fine sister called *my* son!'

'Lassie, don't get me wrong,' Craigie said briskly as she

turned a row and started again. ' 'Tis not for m'self I'm wanting you out o' here. But for *you'er* sake, you've got to start elsewhere. The Lord knows, I'm thankful o' the company, an' ye're no trouble, Annie, neither is the bairn. But ye ought to be getting right awa' from here. You'er eating ye're heart out o'er what happened to t' laird – who was naught but a mon for all his lordly airs and graces.'

Craigie sniffed deprecatingly, remembering the awful scene in the Lady Iona's bedroom between herself and the Laird Lindsay. She had never forgiven him for the dreadful thing he had made Annie do with that poor, wee, distorted creature miscarried by the Lady Iona. 'Ye've made you'er self ill o'er him, I ken. Hiding you'er self away on remote islands, starving you'er self among strangers. 'Tis a miracle to me how ye haven't drowned, plying that boat o' yours up an' down the coast. But now the bairn's arrived, ye'll ha' to think again, Annie.'

'Fish is all I know about, Craigie,' Annie said while the sky and the sea merged together in the dark shadows of night, and water reflections played upon the front-room ceiling. Annie rubbed the window-pane, misted with her breathing. 'What else am I fit for?'

'Ye ne'er were well-padded, but ye're thin as a caber now, what with worry an' pining, an' everything else! If ye go back to you'er fishing, Annie Gowrie, ye'll fall ill, as surely as I sit here now. Then who'll look after Jamie?'

'Don't tell me what I already know!' Annie said, turning on her fiercely. 'Life is terrible enough for someone like me, without making it worse! I'll take care o' Jamie, my way ... I'm still thinking about it, believe me, Craigie. Every day and every night I think about what's best to do for Jamie, and I go round and round in circles because I don't *know* what's best!'

'Then, if, as ye've been telling me, the new laird has written to you with fresh proposals of marriage, ye'd best be taking him up on his offer!'

'Never!' said Annie fiercely. 'He asks me out of a sense of duty, nothing more. And I feel ... affection for him, nothing more, for it was the Laird Lindsay who was, and will ever be the only one for me.' Annie wrung her hands desperately: 'Oh, how I wish Rory Roskillen had looked to saving his brother that night on the mull, not me! How I wish he had saved the Laird Lindsay's life, not mine!'

Nurse Craig looked over her spectacles at Annie, her pale blue eyes full of pain on Annie's behalf. 'That's no way to be talking, Annie Gowrie, when ye've a noble bairn to think about! We can all regret the past. The ros crumbling awa' with the laird, while he an' his brother were trying to save *you'er* life, was in God's hands that night. No amount o' recriminating will change things. Nor bring back you'er fine laird! And what ye three young people were doing out on the ros in a terrible storm that night, beats me!' She turned another row. 'Annie Gowrie, I ha'e ma ane suggestion for stopping this discontent eating you'er heart an' soul awa'. Ye're needing t' be thinking o' other things ... things right awa' from here.'

'I belong here ... Glengarth, Rill, they are my home,' Annie said dully, tracing patterns on the steamy window-pane with her finger.

'After the bairn is weaned, Annie, why don't you ta'e you'er self o'er to Edinburgh to become a nurse? They're needing good, caring gals like you'er self as nurses. You can be trained to gude use while there's a war on.'

'Like a dog? Go away, Craigie!' Annie said angrily. 'An' who'll be paying for my fine training to become a nurse? Besides, the war's not going to last. They say it'll be over by Christmas.'

'But you'er training'll ne'r be in vain, Annie Gowrie! It'll serve ye after the war, too, an' provide ye with a safer living. Nurses are always in demand, peace or war.'

'Me? A nurse?' Annie scoffed at Craigie's fanciful ideas. 'I'll be no good as a nurse. Fish is my business. What do I know about nursing anyone?'

'Ye didn'a fair too bad wi' the Lady Iona,' Craigie said craftily, stopping her knitting to look over her needles at Annie. 'I ken gude material when I see it. Ye can also read and write. You talk as a lady should talk when the mood suits ye. The training ye've received at Forest Lodge an' Glengarth all these years, Annie Gowrie, can be put to a gude purpose now, for there's women in this war doing all

sorts o' things once only the men were allowed to do. It'll
be a war to change everything, mark m' words, Annie.
An' if ye don't want to be a nurse, there's the munitions
factories cryin' out for women workers. Besides, a full-
time job awa' from here will take you'er mind off you'er
ane sorrow and pining, for there's nothing like hard work
t' drive awa' personal grief.'

'And what about my baby? You've forgotten about
Jamie. Who'll be taking care o' him while I'm forgetting
my miseries in Edinburgh or Glasgow or Applecross?'

'Ma' self. I'll take care o' the wee body for thee.'

'You?' Annie looked at the old nurse in utter disbelief.
'I couldn't let you do that!'

'Why not, indeed?' Nurse Craig chuckled at Annie's
amazed, as well as hopeful expression. 'Bless ye, Annie
Gowrie! There's no need to sit there with you'er mouth
hanging open! Craigie's managed more bairns in her ane
lifetime, than ye've ha' hot dinners! Jamie'll give this old
body a new lease o' life. I'll mind him like ma ane bairn,
ne'r ye fear, lass. Then, when you'er training's finished, ye
can come hame t' take old Craigie's place as practising
midwife from Applecross to Kinlochwe!'

Annie didn't know what to say. Overwhelmed by the
flood of fresh possibilities Nurse Craig had opened up for
her, she saw an entire new future blossom, even while
destroying all that had been dear to her – if only she had
the courage.

'As a nurse, Annie Gowrie, ye'd n'er want for work, for
there's always someone in child-bed, sick-bed o' death-
bed. An', after the war's o'er, ye'll be able to give Jamie a
gude, secure hame – just as the Laird Lindsay would ha'
wished for his ane son.' Her dim eyes unable to see fine
work, she worked by instinct and touch to every last stitch
of the garment. And that was the way with most folk,
Craigie reasoned: instinct and touch made one aware of
the real person beneath. She focused on Annie Gowrie
above her knitting needles and she said, 'Think on it,
Annie Gowrie. An' dinna fash you'er self o'er the wee
bairn. I've handled enough in ma time to ken what I'm
about! An' dinna fear, either, I'll be dropping dead, for

this body's got plenty o' spark in her yet!'

And so the seed was sown in Annie's mind.

In the quiet moments when she nursed her baby at her breast, or when she lay awake at night, unable to sleep, but watched, instead, the play of the water shadows on the bedroom ceiling, she told herself that life had to change. It had to go forward, it had to be recaptured, relived, striven for all over again, for the sake of her son. She thought about what dear Craigie had said about becoming a nurse. And the more she thought about it, the more the idea appealed to her. She thought about it all night, and in the morning she said to Nurse Craig, 'Craigie I can sell my fishing boat to raise the money for my nurse's training at the Royal Edinburgh Infirmary where you qualified under the Nightingale régime.'

Nurse Craig shook her head sadly, and dashed Annie's hopes straightaway. 'Ye'd need to be selling half a dozen fishing boats, lassie, to keep you in training for nigh on three years!' She lifted her hands out of the basin of soap suds, for she had been helping Annie to wash Jamie's baby clothes in the scullery. She dried her hands and went into her tiny living-room where she began rummaging through a stack of magazines and newspapers. She found what she had been searching for in a recent newspaper advertisement. 'I've a much better idea, Annie Gowrie. Why don't you take yourself where they will pay *you*! "The Queen Alexandra's Royal Naval Nursing Service (QARNNS) NEED YOU! PAY YOU!" Take it away with you and think on it, lassie.'

Why not? Annie told herself. The sea was in her blood, wasn't it?

Founded in 1902, the Queen Alexandra Royal Navy Nursing Service wanted single women for the war effort. The pay was one shilling and four pence for a trainee probationer, plus overseas allowance and extra annual emoluments for experience. 'Apply now to your Regional Hospital for details of QARNNS recruitment.'

Her nearest QARNNS recruitment hospital was in Aberdeen.

It wasn't an easy decision to make, for Annie knew that

she'd be away for a great deal of time. Her son would have to grow up without her. But he had a good substitute in Craigie – a foster grandmother able to give him the start in life he needed. And if she herself was earning money as a Queen Alexandra Nurse, she would be able to afford to give Jamie all the little extras.

Following those first random seeds craftily sown in Annie's mind by the shrewd and discerning old nurse, Annie wrote away to the QARNNS hospital in Aberdeen. She was duly accepted for training on the two references she sent back with her application form, one from Nurse Craig and the other from Dr Robinson – in whose ear Craigie had whispered the secrets of Glengarth!

'I knew it all along, Craigie,' had been his artful comment. 'There's nought that escapes me between Applecross an' Kinlochwe! You an' Annie Gowrie between you, are a couple o' crafty spinsters! An' the sooner that gal's away from Glengarth, the better for her! Let's hope she'll be liking bedpans better than fishing for lairds!'

'*Hrumph!*' had been Craigie's retort when she snatched the signed reference for Annie Gowrie from Robbie Robinson, who had given her a very old-fashioned look as he tucked his reading glasses back into his pocket.

Annie, however, still sold her beloved fishing boat, one that had belonged to her father and, therefore, was of special value to her. When Jamie was weaned six weeks later, she gave the money to Craigie for Jamie's keep – with the solemn oath extracted from the nurse, that should Jamie become sick or was pining for her, she was to be sent for immediately. Nurse Craig solemnly promised.

With the money she got for a valuable brooch Lindsay had given her, Annie bought a few decent underclothes. Shoes, stockings and uniform would, of course, be supplied by the hospital. The rest of the money she put into a savings account, to provide for a rainy day.

Having settled her personal affairs, Annie set off on the train from Achnasheen to Aberdeen, over the Grampians. To go so far by herself across Scotland filled her with trepidation, although she had never given a thought to sailing her flimsy boat, in all kinds of weather, from the Summer Isles to the Outer Hebrides.

At the QARNNS hospital, her feet were crammed into thick black stockings and laced black shoes, her body into terrible, strange clothes with a high starched collar as sharp as a razor to cut her throat. Then she was draped in a voluminous cardboard-stiff apron; a complicated, frilly headdress to hide her hair, like a nun, and a scarlet cape, completed her new image.

At the end of the day, not only had the starch gone out of her clothes, but out of Annie Gowrie, too! Feeling as limp as a rag, she told herself that she had been mad to listen to old Craigie telling her to exchange fish for forceps!

As a probationer she had to learn First Aid, Medical Instruments, Stretcher Drill, Dispensing, Operating Theatre Techniques, Pathology, Cooking and a host of other subjects besides. She had to undergo monthly progress reports before the fierce QARNN Matron, and three stages of examinations. The first was after three months probationary service, the next at six months and her final examination after twelve months. Then she had to undergo a further year's training, six months on a surgical ward and six months on a medical ward. The grades she could achieve were Very Good, Good, Fair or Indifferent. She would also be expected to undertake some sort of specialized training, as in the X-Ray Department or Operating Theatre.

A year after leaving Gairloch and Jamie in Nurse Craig's capable hands, Annie received her distinguishing badge which all Sick Berth Attendants, Qualified Sick Berth Ratings and Queen Alexandra's Nursing Sisters could gain – a Red Cross set within a small circle, worn on the right uniform sleeve just above the elbow. She was proud of her achievement, Very Good, on her certificate, but prouder still of the Geneva Red Cross she was now qualified to wear along with other members of the Naval Nursing Community. A year left to go!

After her qualifying examinations, Annie was entitled to a few days off. She used them to visit Jamie. At sixteen months, he was a bright and beautiful child. He seemed to enjoy stringing together long, complicated words for such a small boy, and Annie was terribly proud of him. She took him to Glengarth, and together they placed flowers on the graves at Inchnadamph. In the castle itself, the furniture and family portraits were being removed for storage; the war had not ended at Christmas 1914, nor Christmas 1915, and now it seemed as though it would *never* end. January 1916, Hogmanay: her first pilgrimage in what was to become an annual one to Lindsay's grave with their son.

After her few days leave, she returned to the main QARNN hospital in Aberdeen, and from there was posted to the Royal Naval Auxiliary Hospital at Kingseat, fourteen miles from Aberdeen. The hospital, a mental asylum in peace time had been converted to receive injured Naval Service personnel from the Home Fleet based at Scapa Flow, but not their families; family members were nursed at Aberdeen.

Annie was nursing here at Kingseat when, at the end of May 1916, the biggest naval conflict since Trafalgar took place between the British Grand Fleet and the German High Seas Fleet, off the coast of Norway to the Heligoland Bight. It was known as the Battle of Jutland.

CHAPTER THIRTY-THREE

After Lindsay's accident in April 1914, Rory, haunted by the memories of his brother and Annie Gowrie, felt he was partially responsible for Lindsay's untimely death. Unable to settle down to anything, least of all his new role as the next Laird of Glengarth, he had returned to Glasgow on the day of his brother's lying in state in the great hall at Glengarth. He could not even bring himself to attend Lindsay's funeral.

He had hoped to pick up the threads of his steamship business and forget all that had taken place at Glengarth after his unfortunate re-entry into his brother's life. A brief time at Eton when he was first there, with Lindsay in Upper School and shortly to go up to Oxford, and a sporadic correspondence thereafter, had been the sum total of their relationship since India, and yet, in certain ways, he had felt very close to Lindsay. Could it have been anything to do with that bond between them, made all those years ago when their father had sworn them both to secrecy after that bizarre affair to do with the old Indian Sadhu on the road to Tippindee? He didn't really know; so many things in life had no cut and dried answer, were just a part of life's unfinished pattern. But, above all, he had desired that he, Lindsay, Christabel and Kitty should be reunited as a family after their divided upbringing, and it had ended up disastrously.

Then, after Annie's refusal, yet again, to marry him, his sense of rejection was total. She had written very forthrightly on the subject of marriage to him from the island of Errin, following his letter which had been forwarded from Glasgow to Glengarth and then to relatives with whom Annie was staying during the months preceding the birth of her child. After that short sharp refusal in June, he had

heard no more from her. He was only glad that she had
relations to turn to in her hour of need, even though they
might be of distant connection.

He had left the steamship company in the capable
hands of Mr John and Miss Crawford, Mr John being
given the authority to sign company cheques. Elizabeth
Roebling Chanin, now Countess Albion, had taken him to
task: 'Rory, hon, what are you playing at? I'm too busy
rushing between the li'le ole Stately Home in vintage
England, and keeping my end up in New York. I'm in
transworld ocean liners now and I'm not seeing my side of
things going down the drain for any English earl – even
though I might have married another gopher – or any
incompetent Scotsman with a chip on his shoulder. You've
got a history of running away from things, Rory, hon, even
to deserting me when things didn't work out your way. So
it's about time you started facing life head-on and
accepting your responsibilities.'

Lizzie had never written to him like that before. Was he
running away again? Well, what if he was! He had given
his all to Hamish's old steamship business, hauling it back
to a worthy enterprise, and look where it had got him! So,
if Lizzie and the rest of the world wanted to think badly of
him, that was up to them; he had only done his best even
if that best was not good enough in other people's eyes.

Then, shortly before war was declared in August, the
Admiralty requested permission to use Glengarth estate
from the security aspect of their shipping. Scapa Flow was
still not considered to be safe enough from the German
threat of sea invasion, so they were looking to disperse
their ships into secluded lochs. Rory agreed to Glengarth
being used by the Admiralty for the duration of the war,
and did what a great many others like him were now
doing. He turned his attention to the war effort.

Although he had gained a pilot's certificate for Mersey
and Clydeside navigation, had studied for his master's
certificate though never fully completing that course, and
was well equipped to continue as a 'land-lubber-turned-
sailor' in Benjamin Gammon's terms of endearment,
nevertheless promotion in pilotage for a young man such

as he was slow and laborious. However, he did not want to sit behind a desk all day long like Mr John of the Chanin-Beauly Line. While he was quite prepared to run the show Rory Roskillen's way, endless hours cooped up in an office was not to his liking. He wanted the freedom of the sea; but many of the old masters, captains of their own ships, resented a much younger man just because he held a certificate of competence, coming aboard to steer *their* ship into the confined navigational channels of their home waters. And while he was considered a 'bright boy' as far as his qualifications went, the facts that he was only twenty-four, had professional certificates to his name, possessed a hereditary Scottish title, and owned a steam-ship company, went in many ways against him.

Rory, always one to get impatient with the old die-hards and the untenable position in which he sometimes found himself, cast his eye elsewhere. So, even though in those early months of the war there was no call up, he offered his merchant-shipping expertise to the Royal Naval Reserve, Clyde Division. By the year 1914 the RNR had 30,000 reservists, and were recruiting men from the merchant branch for specialized training.

He was accepted by the RNR as an assistant signals officer, a very junior rank to start with, until his special-ized naval signals training had been completed. He under-went an intensive period of training in wireless telegraphy, flag and searchlight signals, the latter by Morse code, taking him back to his days at Darby's Nautical School in Liverpool when he had been studying for his Merseyside pilot's certificate.

He had accepted the new challenge as he had accepted all past challenges thrown at him, with gusto and complete dedication to what *he* wanted from life at that particular moment. Often the reckoning came later, but he never stopped to think about that. A year in the RNR, augmented by his previous seafaring knowledge, enabled him to qualify in Royal Naval signals far quicker than otherwise possible, after which he had orders to join the dreadnought fleet based at Scapa Flow as a junior signals officer with the rank of sub-lieutenant.

At the end of 1915 Rory wished he'd joined the
Merchant Fleet instead. At least it would have been far
more exciting dodging the German U-boats aboard an
armed cruiser, just as Gammon was doing. To date, the
life offered him in the British Grand Fleet had proved to
be extremely boring. Apart from a few minor skirmishes
in northern waters nothing terribly exciting appeared to be
going on at all.

The fleet was relegated to twiddling its naval thumbs at
Scapa Flow. The only action the super-dreadnoughts had
seen came under the headings of incessant repainting (and
it was surprising how many different shades of grey there
were), extended gunnery practice, or a brushing up of
Flag and Wireless Signals. 'What price boredom, hmmm?'
asked sub-lieutenant Rory Roskillen of himself. Lying in
his cramped bunk, he held in his hand Admiral Jellicoe's
A Note on Tactics, a revised course for the fleet, ordered
by Compass Pendant, Blue Pendant, or 9 Pendant, the
flags indicating either the amount of the alteration, or the
new course. It was a procedure Rory tried faithfully to
commit to memory.

Afterwards, he had decided to pen a long overdue letter
in answer to an earlier letter from Lizzie. She had
contacted him again from New York, informing him of
her decision to remain there until the war was over. She
gave the excuse that since the sinking of the *Lusitania*
earlier in the year, she was afraid to travel the Atlantic.
Reading between the lines Rory guessed that somewhere
nearer the truth was that Lizzie was already tired of her
English earl, hence her decision to remain in America.

Lizzie had gone on to ask him in her letter, 'What are
these Q-class, *KIL*-ships I keep hearing about?'

He had written back to her in the absence of anything
much else to do:

Some of our steamships have been converted for the Royal
Navy. They're being used for coastal-patrol work at the
moment. Gammon has written to tell me all about it. Apparently, camouflaged and fitted with smoke-boxes, they're
doing a grand job against enemy U-boats in throwing up

smoke-screens, allowing our boys time to 'get their asses out of it' – to use one of your endearing Americanisms, Lizzie! We are not allowed to place guns fore of the vessels classified as *armed* cruisers as opposed to *armoured*, because then we'd be in a position of aggression, not *defence*! Six-pounders mounted aft, means we fire them while we're *running-away*! Get it? That's a defensive position. Anything astern would make *us* the aggressor. Merchant ships are non-combatants, so meanwhile we're still losing tons of merchant shipping to the Boche.

Rory still could not make much sense of the orders himself!

It was while he was in the middle of answering Lizzie's letter that orders were received for 5th Battle Squadron to move to Rosyth Harbour. Thank God, were Rory Roskillen's own private thoughts as he put away pen and paper into his locker. Maybe we're going to see some action, after all!

However, this *could* be another false alarm to keep us on our toes, was his further thought on the way to the wireless room to supervise his watch. Five times before, they had been called out of harbour, only to find they were going on boring battle practice in the North Sea.

Early in 1916 the Squadron Flag Ship, *Barham*, of the 5th Battle Squadron was under the command of Rear-Admiral Hugh Evan-Thomas, a man everyone in the Squadron greatly admired. Evan-Thomas's flag-captain was Arthur Waller Craig.

On the 30th May, 5th Battle Squadron was in Rosyth Harbour when Room 40, the Admiralty's secret intelligence department, intercepted and decoded a special intelligence report, to the effect that the German High Seas Fleet were preparing for battle practice. They passed the report on to the Operations Division.

The operations officer asked where the directional stations placed German call sign DK.

'Wilhelmshaven, sir. Admiral von Scheer's base.'

'Thank you.' The operations officer asked no more questions, and passed the signal forward to the C-in-C, 'Places Flagship in Jade at 11:10 am GMT.'

The officer had been in too much of a hurry, and had passed the scrambled message to Admiral Jellicoe, Commander-in-Chief of the British Grand Fleet, without consulting Room 40 staff.

Room 40 staff had been aware of the German Naval codes for some time, as the codebook had fallen into the hands of the Russians, who had subsequently passed it to British intelligence. DK was the German Commander-in-Chief's harbour call sign. When he put to sea, he trans-ferred DK, his normal call sign, to the wireless transmission station at Wilhelmshaven. Room 40 had intelligence to the effect that this was done to cover the tracks of the High Seas Fleet, for they had done the same prior to the raids on Scarborough and Lowestoft.

Assuming that the German High Seas Fleet had not as yet left their base at Wilhelmshaven, Admiral Jellicoe, with no sense of haste, and without sending personally for Rear-Admiral Evan-Thomas of the Flagship *Barham* at Rosyth, to brief him on what was happening, sent a special signal to the Commander of the Battle Cruiser Fleet, Vice-Admiral, Sir David Beatty, to prepare for *possible* engagement with the enemy. The signal was to the effect that he wanted 5th Battle Squadron to be used only as a back-up force and not one in the forefront of any conflict with the enemy.

Hugh Evan-Thomas, with four super-dreadnought ships under his command, his own Flagship *Barham*, followed by *Valiant*, *Warspite* and *Malaya*, the most powerful and modern battleships on the seas, was understandably annoyed that the C-in-C considered them inferior to those of the German fleet. Admiral Jellicoe's comments via Vice-Admiral Sir David Beatty were less than courteous: 'I am reluctant to allow 5th B.S. to take the place of 3rd B.S. when they went north for practices at Scapa and only consent to agree to my urgent request on the strict under-standing and definite instruction that they are only to be used as a *Supporting Force* to avoid the possibility of their being engaged by a superior force when their lack of speed would prevent them from making good their retreat. Consequently, they are to be disposed five miles from anticipated position of sighting enemy.'

The Commander-in-Chief had said it all and Evan-Thomas's sigh of disappointment was a heartfelt one. A normally placid, kindly and tolerant man, he felt that any glory of a Nelson-dimension, would be gleaned by some other flamboyant character eager for blood, more in keeping with the Beatty image.

He issued orders to the effect that 5th Battle Squadron was 'to move east of the Long Forties, one hundred miles East of Aberdeen in place of 3rd Squadron.'

During his tour of duty Rory scanned the signals log. Admiralty had information that the German C-in-C's Flagship was still in the Jade River. Time message was logged, 11:10 am GMT. German call sign DK. Reconnaissance plane, *Engadine* unable to carry out air-recce, since Beatty wanted to conserve the few planes at his disposal until action was joined. Orders were to steam slowly, and conserve fuel, since there was no likelihood of encountering the enemy until two or three days out at sea.

They were to steer for Horns Reef.

Rory looked puzzled, and the chief telegraphist, among wireless signals personnel known as, 'SNORKILS', Super Nark Officer, Rosyth's Kill Squadron, said, 'I don't like it. Something funny going on here.'

'Do you consider Operations Division and Room 40 might have got the DK message between them wrong, sir?' Rory asked.

'Flag-Commander Egerton is on the bridge with the Admiral, right now, Roskillen. We obey instructions. Pass DK message on to the rest of 5th Squadron.'

'Yes sir!'

It was common knowledge that Room 40 staff, where the signals were deciphered by mostly civilians, were treated with scant regard by the Operations Division who, themselves, were obsessive about secrecy. Room 40 staff were expected to decode enemy wireless transmissions and have knowledge of where the German Fleet was stationed. Room 40 personnel were *not* supposed to interpret such information, or act on it. That was the job of the

big boys at Operations Division. There was little or no
liaison between the two departments.

According to the plan just received, if they were to
rendezvous with Admiral Jellicoe's main Battle Fleet far
enough north to cover the Northern Patrol against a
German effort to raise the blockade which had given rise
to so much ill-feeling between the British and Americans,
then Sir David Beatty's Battle Cruiser Fleet would have to
be sufficiently southward to intercept raiders. Such conditions could only be met if the distance between the two
British fleets was at least fifty miles.

Therefore, on signals coming in, to rendezvous to a
position in Lat. 56° 40′N., Long. 5°E., which was 260
miles from the Forth, made their position at 2 pm on the
31st May, 69 miles SSE of Admiral Jellicoe's Battle
Fleet.

Why on earth would the Admiral want such a wide
deployment area between the two fleets? Rory asked
himself in perplexity. And what was their cool, level-
headed Evan-Thomas, commanding 5th Squadron, going
to make of such an order?

At 1:51 pm on the 31st May the British and German
fleets were approaching each other almost at right angles –
and still not aware of each other's presence. The *Iron
Duke*, Admiral Jellicoe's ship, was fifteen and a half miles
short of her rendezvous with Vice-Admiral Sir David
Beatty's Battle Cruiser Squadron for the pre-arranged
time of 2 pm.

At sea, this meant almost one hour steaming behind
time.

But Admiral Jellicoe was unperturbed. The sea was
calm, visibility good, visible sunset time, the previous day,
logged at 8:20 pm GMT, which gave him a good few
daylight hours yet, of steaming time.

Confident that all was going to plan, and that there
would be no engagement with the enemy for at least
another twenty-four hours, he had already ordered the
destroyers to steam slowly in order to conserve fuel. The
C-in-C was not even dismayed when learning that the

seaplane carrier, *Campania*, his only means of air reconnaissance, was not with the fleet, owing to a series of
misconstrued signals. The *Campania* had been told to
follow the *Blanche*, the last light cruiser leaving the Forth
anchorage. But with forty miles needed to catch up with
the rest of the fleet, steaming at nineteen and a half knots,
Admiral Jellicoe, when learning that the *Campania* had
weighed anchor, ordered her captain to return to base
since the seaplane would have been no good to him after
dark.

The *Campania* in fact, was capable of twenty and a half
knots, and had been gaining on the Grand Fleet at over
three miles an hour, when the signal to return to the Forth
was received.

Then a message was sent to Sir David Beatty that, in
the event of the enemy fleet under the German Admiral
von Scheer and Vice-Admiral von Hipper, not being
sighted by 2 pm, Beatty was to close battle formation.

Sir David Beatty aboard the *Lion* sent a message to his
Battle Cruiser Commanders to alter course north by east.
It was sent at 2:15 pm. He also despatched a message to
5th Battle Squadron to look out for advance battle
cruisers of Admiral Jellicoe's fleet.

Aboard the *Barham*, signals were being received to the
effect that von Hipper and his German battleships had
been sighted fifty miles east.

At this time the two screens of the most advanced
cruisers were only sixteen miles apart. Contact would have
been made soon after, had not a Danish merchant ship
stopped midway between the two smoke screens, and
attracted attention by blowing steam.

The *Galatea*, flagship of the 1st Light Cruiser Squadron, was seventeen miles east of the *Lion*, and together
with the *Phaeton* closed up to the Danish ship when Rory,
static bursting his ear drums, intercepted the Morse signal,
'Enemy in sight ... destroyers ... others in the vicinity,
including submarines ... western ships of 2nd Scouting
Group ... *where the hell is Jellicoe!*' He scribbled down
the time, '2:20 sighting'.

Transmissions from other ships in the vicinity were

coming in fast and furious: 'Urgent ... two destroyers hostile, bearing ESE ... course unknown ... Time 2.28 pm.'

Messages were relayed at once to the bridge.

Beatty, in return, relayed an order to his own destroyer Commanders, 'Take up position as submarine screen when course is altered to SSE.'

This was a turn towards Horns Reef, so that his ships could get between the enemy and his base. Then at 2:39 the signal by flags was made to turn.

Wilfred Allan Egerton, the Barham's Flag-Commander said to Craig Waller, 'I don't think he's seen it, Captain.'

'... We ought to have made it by searchlight ... what's the Tiger doing? She's supposed to be repeating Beatty's signals to us,' came the Captain's reply.

In the W/T room a mass of conflicting messages arrived from all directions. Wireless telegraphy transmission had been ordered to be kept to a minimum, then contradicted: 'it is of great importance that all cruisers should plot the position of the enemy's ships as they are sighted or reported'. Then again: 'when the battlefleets are in sight of one another and reports of the enemy's movements are no longer necessary ...' And again: 'reports of movements, provided they are made in good time, may be of great value, and any ship in a position to see clearly what is occurring when it is probable that the Commander-in-Chief could not, should not fail to make a report.'

The use of searchlights during engagement of the enemy was prohibited for fear of giving away the Grand Fleet's position.

The rear ship Tiger was supposedly to blame for not repeating Beatty's flag signals. The Barham lay two points off the Tiger's bow, clear of the Lion's smoke, the wind coming from the west, so why didn't she forward the signals? were the comments of Evan-Thomas's officers aboard the Barham.

'They'll repeat it by searchlight now, won't they?' And even as one officer made the remark, others aboard the Barham realized that their own position would obscure any lamp signals, while the hazy conditions, the prevailing smoke from the battle cruisers as they steamed full ahead, and funnel gases would make it difficult to read the flags on that altered starboard bearing.

The 5th Battle Squadron's turn to starboard on the run to the north had increased the gap between the *Lion* and *Barham* by four and a half miles. The turn would have been made quicker had a Blue Pendant turn been asked for. A Blue Pendant meant that when the signal was hauled down, all ships addressed turned together to the course indicated.

No Blue Pendant signal was given.

Meanwhile, in trying to keep an eye out for Admiral Jellicoe's Grand Fleet, officers aboard the *Barham*, on account of the mix-up in the signalling arrangements, realized much later on that they had been looking in the wrong direction.

Craig Waller, the moment Beatty's first signal at 2:25 concerning the destroyers to take up positions had been received, had suggested to Evan-Thomas, to turn east at once.

Evan-Thomas refused, feeling that 5th Battle Squadron had been stationed five miles north as a link between the Battle Cruiser Fleet and the main fleet. And even though he himself was of Rear-Admiral rank, he had been schooled in the old traditions of the Navy and to go against the orders of the Vice-Admiral was unthinkable! 'My Admiral knows best; if he wants me to go anywhere else other than where he has stationed me, he will say so,' had been his defence in following Beatty's orders.

Then, at 3:30 pm, Sir David Beatty, aboard the *Lion* received the devastating news from Commodore Goodenough, aboard the *Southampton*, who was commanding the 1st Scouting Group of the 2nd Light Cruiser Squadron, that the enemy had been sighted in single line to the east, steering NW.

At fourteen miles apart, Beatty immediately altered course to the east. 'Hipper's bloody well supposed to be still in the Jade!' was his own defence as he rushed into the affray from a speed of twenty-three knots to twenty-five, thereby widening the gap further still between himself and the *Barham*.

At over six miles north-west of the battle cruisers, the *Barham* was unable to read the *Lion*'s flag signals.

The 5th Battle Squadron, so far behind on the run to the south, had not turned to starboard at the same time as the *Lion*. By the time the *Barham* received the searchlight signal from the *Lion*, which was immediately acted upon, the gap between the *Lion* and the *Barham* had widened to nine miles. Only the black hulls of 5th Battle Squadron were visible over the horizon, when Vice-Admiral Sir David Beatty came within what he thought was 18,000 yards of the German High Seas Fleet, which, in fact, was only within 15,000 yards of Vice-Admiral von Hipper's Scouting Forces.

Five Zeppelins had been sent up by the German Navy during the afternoon, examining the North Sea for the British Grand Fleet. Their intelligence reports were immediately sent to the German Admiralty, and thence to Admiral von Scheer and Vice-Admiral von Hipper aboard the *König* and the *Lützow* respectively.

At first, von Hipper thought that the battle cruisers on the horizon were part of the High Seas Fleet returning to base. When he received the wireless signal that British warships were closing at a mile a minute, von Hipper could hardly believe his eyes. There, silhouetted like sitting ducks against the setting sun, not 12,000 yards ahead of him, lay the British Light Battle Cruiser Squadron steaming as raggedly as a crocodile of schoolchildren, their flagship hauling round slowly, first ESE and then S.

'Are they playing musical ships, I wonder?' he asked his officers facetiously. 'It appears to me that the last ship doesn't know what the first one is doing!'

Minutes after the opening shot was fired from the *Lion*'s big guns, von Hipper ordered the *Lützow* to fire. The time was 3:48 pm on the 31st May.

The *Lion* altered course to SSE, and the *Lützow* followed, developing a parallel action.

The German range was far more accurate.

Within fifteen minutes the German Navy had made fourteen hits, as opposed to Beatty's forces striking only three with one miss-hit on a fixed range, while asking the searching question, 'Where the hell is Admiral Jellicoe and the rest of the Grand Fleet?'

And then a barrage of screaming shells through the smoke and mist of a northern afternoon, and with a sickening thump the *Lion* was hit on 'Q' turret.

In horror, British naval officers on the bridge of the *Barham* observed the armoured 'Q' turret of the *Lion* belching thick black smoke after a German shell burst into the centre of the ship. In moments the *Lion* was engulfed in fire.

'The *Lion*'s GONE!' cried Captain Donald of the Royal Naval Air Service, aboard the *Engadine*, seeing only the terrible smoke choking the *Lion*.

Half the roof turret had been blown into the air, the pieces crashing to the deck. Men in the turret's magazine, in the gunhouse and loading chamber, about to discharge the cages of cordite into the guns, were trapped. And when, all at once, something too terrible for ordinary comprehension becomes a reality for those taking part, there is a silence – a terrible, accusing stillness; a soundless darkness from which ordinary men emerge as the defiers of hell.

Major Harvey, Royal Marines, turret officer, mortally wounded aboard the *Lion*, managed to reach the voice-tube and give the handing-room crew instructions to close the magazine doors and flood the magazine. He died a few minutes later.

Inflammable material, contained for half an hour from igniting the rest of the ship by the fire-fighting apparatus brought into swift action, was hopelessly inadequate the moment the ship swung around, its course altered to 180° northward. Fanned by a head-on wind, within seconds flames reached as high as the mast-head.

'Bloody hell ... there goes, Beatty ...' Rory wasn't aware who had spoken aloud in the W/T room as the signals were received.

Hugh Evan-Thomas and his officers, on the bridge of

the *Barham*, observed the scene through spy-glasses.

'German destroyers, *Derfflinger* and *Seydlitz* engaging the *Queen Mary* in close action ... ranges of 14,000 to 15,800 ... closing ...' signals were relayed accordingly.

The fate of the *Mary* was interrupted within minutes with another message of destruction: the German Navy had wreaked another savage blow against Beatty's ships. Three shots fell on the upper deck of the *Indefatigable*. A terrible explosion followed, audible to the men on the *Barham*. Hauled out of line as she was sinking by the stern, another blast from the Germans struck her fore turret and she heeled over in a pall of black smoke twice the height of her masts.

Hugh Evan-Thomas's face twitched, a noticeable pallor to his lips. 'Full steam ahead. Move astern to join battle action formation.'

Atmospherics were interfering with wireless transmissions. Sub-lieutenant Rory Roskillen in the W/T room fought alongside the other telegraph officers trying to make sense of impossible signals interfered with by the high density of smoke and cordite in the air. The weather, too, had deteriorated, and a British reconnaissance plane, the only one out of four operating from the light cruiser, *Engadine*, was unable to keep both the enemy and the British Grand Fleet in sight, flying as she was at an altitude of 900 feet, due to low cloud. Her signals, too, were hard to monitor.

5th Battle Squadron's four super-dreadnoughts, moved in to take the place of the *Indefatigable*. Reputed to have the best gunners in the whole Battle Fleet, 5th Squadron gunners pin-pointed the enemy's gun flashes, and with rapid and accurate fire from the super-dreadnoughts' fifteen-inch guns, scored damaging hits to the *Moltke* and *Von der Tann*.

Cheers went up aboard the *Barham*.

Rory, battling against static, the noise, the conflicting reports being received in the W/T room, passed forward a signal that brought some light relief after the news of the sinking of the *Indefatigable*.

The *Southampton*, which had drawn alongside the

battered *Lion*, reported that the 'old man' had been seen on the open bridge, 'displaying a fierce and resolute character'.

A further rousting cheer greeted the news that the *Lion*, as well as the 'old man himself, thank God', had turned out to be Hipper-proof.

The *Lion* had been saved by Major Harvey's gallant action of closing magazine doors and flooding the magazines, thus preventing fire spreading to the charges stored in the magazine. Rory, remembering his own fire-fighting days on his trips with G. Smith and Company out of Queens Dock, Glasgow, to South Africa, knew the merits of such self-sacrificing action. But the *Ailsa Craig* had been a merchant ship, and, mercifully, he had never encountered battle-action then! This was an Armageddon alongside live ammunition, a baptism by fire. The *Lion* and everyone aboard her, had fire been allowed to get out of control, would certainly have been blown to pieces.

Rory, who had been paying the others no attention, looked up, and removing his headphones, said in disbelief: '*Queen Mary*, gone down with practically no survivors ... German ships are picking up those that can be found ...'

From the unprotected bridge of the *Lion*, Vice-Admiral Sir David Beatty, smoke-begrimed and more than a trifle *déshabillé*, watched the 1,000-foot-high plume of fire followed by thunderous explosions amidships. The splendid *Mary* broke in two, her stern high in the air, propellers still slowly revolving in some kind of fantastic death-dance.

Turning to his flag-captain, Sir David Beatty said with incredible composure, 'There seems to be something wrong with our bloody ships today.'

CHAPTER THIRTY-FOUR

Operations Room, Admiralty Headquarters, compounded its earlier mistake: 'All German submarines are being hurried from German ports to attack'. Signals giving position, course and speed were as of the *Lützow* at midnight. None of the following six signals outlining Admiral von Scheer's course or position were passed to Admiral Jellicoe.

Even before the warning got through, German torpedoes were being launched in rapid succession, score after score of them, to devastating effect despite their lumbering deployment.

The only thing German torpedoes had going for them was sheer weight of numbers, Rory maintained, basing this on Gammon's opinion from a time past. But unless more decisive action was taken from the British side, there would be even more British battleships lost, never mind the inaccuracy of German torpedoes and their lack of speed – even though they were consoling factors to the British. Rory, busy with sending signals to the bridge, kept track of 'submarine scores', which, in a time past, a time when he was a gentleman at Breedon Hall, he would have taken bets on, wagering his life against that of Cousin Humphrey. How far removed from his present existence it all seemed now. So, why was he thinking about Breedon Hall, his mother's home, in this crucial moment aboard a battleship in the middle of the high seas? Could this be the premonitions of a drowning man seeing his life pass before his eyes?

He brought his mind back to his work. After all, scoring power was what *really* mattered in the end. Anyone could read signs of a German torpedo bearing down; they came at one in typical German fashion, cumbersome, never giving up, but ploughing on like otters in a basinful of Lux flakes.

But – the big But for the Germans – because the torpedoes were losing momentum all the time, alternative action could be taken by the British well in advance of an attack. The Germans had been unable to conceal the firing wash of their torpedoes, as could the British. It had been easy for Evan-Thomas to turn and turn about as soon as he received crow's-watch guidance as to the direction of German torpedoes beyond the 100,000 yard range. With slowly decreasing impact thereafter, torpedoes aimed at the *Barham* had been unable to pin-point her, as she made her turns away, the rest of 5th Battle Squadron following.

'*Go west, Admiral, go west!*' was the general consensus among W/T personnel who had the situation summed up before those on the bridge – as soon as the signals were received, in fact. Such a cry in the dark from lesser mortals went unechoed, along with many more signals gone astray as sunset-time began to fall upon the two fleets locked in battle.

Then signals officers had been authorized to 'shutdown' on wireless activity; no more than that necessary, as when in port, so that the enemy would not be made aware of the British deployment of dreadnought destroyers.

Grand Fleet instructions were a contradiction in themselves: '*It is of the utmost importance that reports of sighting the enemy should reach the Admiral without delay. In order to ensure this, full use must be made of all the visual and W/T lines of communications which are available*' ... And in the next instant: '*W/T should be reserved for messages of the first importance to the Admiral, so that his line is not congested by messages of a secondary importance at a time when important messages are awaiting transmission ... The principle we work on is not to use more W/T than is necessary and not to have to send much more when you are at sea than when in harbour.*'

Sailors aboard Jellicoe's ships, steaming past the wrecks and the swimming survivors of Vice-Admiral Beatty's luckless light battle cruisers, began to cheer in the mistaken belief that these were the wrecks of the German High Seas Fleet. Jellicoe's Grand Fleet had not as yet sighted a single German battleship, but assumed the High Seas fleet must be very close since Beatty's battle cruisers appeared to have given the Germans a thorough good hiding.

Admiral Jellicoe wore an old blue Burberry, a tarnished gold-leaf admiral's cap and a white scarf around his throat. The steel strips on the heels of his shoes scraped the upper bridge of the *Iron Duke* as he stood looking intently at the magnetic compass. His aides were gathered around him, while the Fleet signal officer stood a little abaft.

'Hoist equal-speed SE,' said Admiral Jellicoe.

The signal officer cleared his throat, hesitant in clarifying such an important order where the Admiral was concerned: 'Would you make it a point to port, sir, so that they will know it is on the port-wing column?'

Admiral Jellicoe's weather-beaten face, lean and tanned, not twitching a muscle in the iron-control of his emotions, in clear and clipped tones replied: 'Very well. Hoist equal-speed pendant SE by E.'

The signal officer called over the boat-rail to the signal boatswain, 'Hoist equal-speed *Charlie London.*'

The signal *Charlie London*, SE by E, was repeated by wireless.

Two short blasts on the ship's siren, and the deployment to port was correctly effected.

The commanders of adjacent columns, watching out for signals from the *Iron Duke*, copied actions, two short blasts on ship's sirens, and the helm was put over. Visibility reduced to one and a half miles, the British Grand Fleet had to make the most of the few daylight hours remaining.

With practically an undamaged battle fleet, Admiral von Scheer made an extraordinary sixteen-point turn to starboard, an easterly course, heading for the centre of the arc formed by British battleships.

His leading battle squadron had taken the brunt of the British 5th Battle Squadron's unfailing shell hits; also he wanted to rescue the crew of the *Wiesbaden*, which lay damaged between the two firing lines, 'a burning wreck' according to the wireless message Admiral von Scheer transmitted to the Kaiser.

Because of the shut-down in British wireless telegraphy, the German wireless message was not picked up.

Admiral von Scheer realized that the High Seas fleet would have been enveloped by the rest of the Grand Fleet determined to engage him before dark. Then they would have prevented him from exercising his own initiative, finally cutting off his passage of return to the German Bight. He had been faced with the possibilities of a court-martial, the Kaiser's wrath, the scathing criticism of the German public; or, an alternative course of action that would bring into question British naval supremacy that had dominated all other sea-faring nations for five hundred years by dealing a devastating blow when least expected, thus putting an end to British maritime power once and for all . . .

Who could resist such a challenge? No German Admiral worth his salt could possibly turn his back and 'run-away' from a superior British fleet, 'superior' in warships, in numbers and in strategy – after all, they had the experiences of Trafalgar to fall back upon!

Oh, what glory for the Fatherland if he were to succeed!

In an action undertaken only once before, by Admiral Lord Nelson at Trafalgar, Admiral von Scheer made a T-stab right into the arch of the rainbow, to the heart of the British Grand Fleet.

The fact that actual, *adequate* knowledge as to the deployment of the German High Seas Fleet was missing, and that no *practical* torpedo-practice at Scapa Flow had been given to the Grand Fleet prior to Jutland, led to irrevocable mistakes being made. But post-mortems only ever come *afterwards*! Sub-lieutenant Rory Roskillen, still on W/T signals watch despite the clamp down on wireless telegraphy transmissions, chatted to his superior, Royal Signals Petty Officer Howard, on the subject of a coherent communication system.

'BATTLESHIPS, BATTLESHIPS, BATTLESHIPS' wireless call signs or flashing lights, as taught at RNR, Signals Branch, had they been sent out, would have prevented the chaos. Such call signs were not transmitted owing to orders emanating from a superior source, the Admiralty.

5th Squadron came under heavy attack during her turn to port. The *Warspite*, her helm jammed, made two wide circles which carried her within 10,000 yards of the enemy fleet. The *Warspite* sustained thirteen heavy hits, yet her commander maintained control of the ship and followed the *Barham* to within half a mile of the *Malaya*, when the helm again jammed.

Any minute now the Sadhu would appear before him, laughing his head off: *Your turn next, O child of Moloch* ... Rory didn't know why he should recall such a thing now, but suddenly, in that confined, claustrophobic space of the W/T room aboard the *Barham* he also remembered the sadistic beatings of old Boggy Shawmoss, his tutor, all those years ago: *Auguries of Innocence ... And some to misery are born* ... Let's face it, my laird, he told himself, you are not born to sit in a metal hole in the bowels of an iron monster spitting death and destruction all around while having to decipher dots and dashes spilling all sorts of conflicting signals in your ears – which even God Almighty is unable to make sense of. You are born to a laurel wreath around your head, not a set of twentieth-century headphones. You are born to be consort to the rich Lizzies of this world, to sip champagne and flirt with pretty women, to make the rest of the world work for you, not against you. You are born to sit in a plush chair in plush offices in the Broomielaw ... Oh, Scotland, Scotland the Brave! So why aren't you sitting at home, Rory Roskillen? After all, Glengarth is what you have craved ever since you were aware that it was Lindsay's inheritance ... Yes! He would probably be doing all those things even now had not the German Kaiser gone a little berserk over ruling the world:

'So, the good die young!'

'Are you speaking to me, Roskillen?'

'No, I'm speaking to God, Petty Officer.'

'Say one for me then.'

While the *Warspite* had been trying to regain course, she had drawn off enemy fire from the battle cruiser *Warrior* and saved it from destruction.

Rear-Admiral Arbuthnot of 1st Cruiser Squadron, aboard his flagship *Defence* sighted the enemy in the mist and ordered the *Defence* and *Warrior* to turn to starboard. In hot pursuit of the Germans, the *Defence* almost collided with the *Lion* as they passed within a hairsbreadth of each other, the *Defence* crossing the *Lion*'s bows. Vice-Admiral Beatty was forced to alter to port to avoid a collision and consequently fell out of the battle line.

Arbuthnot sighted the damaged German ship, *Wiesbaden*, between the two firing lines. Five thousand yards from the crippled *Wiesbaden*, he put the German warship out of action to stop her firing any more torpedoes. Then, to his horror, like a bad dream in which wild elephants stampeded him in a charge he was powerless to stop, the *Derfflinger* with four dreadnoughts in attendance, loomed out of the mist and bore down relentlessly upon his flagship. Within minutes the *Defence* was overwhelmed by a devastating blast of German big guns.

Utterly destroyed, in a hundred-foot-high plume of flame columning the evening sky, the *Defence* went with little dignity. She sank immediately beneath the waves. There were no survivors.

And on that same watery battlefield of mist and sea merging into nothingness, at twenty-five minutes to six o'clock, following an earlier hit an hour before, a German shell with a propellant, mainly of a compound of nitrocellulose and nitroglycerine, initiating a flashpoint far superior to that of British cordite charges, hit the *Barham*.

The shell burst amidships, putting out her wireless installations. Thick black acrid smoke belched through the W/T room, the explosion of such force that a pair of headphones became married to the short-wave transmitter.

Rory saw the man, his legs trapped in the steel doors

which had blown inwards, buckling at the bottom like corrugated cardboard at a crazy angle to leave a gap at the top to draw the fire. Through the gap, light from the corridor illuminated the darkness inside the wireless room. Bathed in the eerie green glow of a sea-grave, the wounded man was still alive, his legs nowhere.

When reality becomes too terrible for ordinary comprehension, there is a silence.

Until the screaming starts, and goes on and on and on ...

Fear is a totally irrational and negative emotion, sublieutenant Rory Roskillen told himself. Now what do I do? I am but a signals officer without any first-aid experience, so what do I do for someone hanging between his God and his legs?

A second explosion enveloped him in total darkness: he couldn't see a thing, not a damn thing. He could only hear men screaming, men cursing, men vainly trying to cut away the jammed doors behind which more men, injured men, were trapped, and men fighting to keep the fires from spreading to other parts of the ship, to save lives ... Rory began to sob.

Then he told himself to be calm, not to panic even though death was there, everywhere, an unwelcome visitor tramping over the bodies of men he knew, men with whom he had worked, lived, breathed, joked, slept, shared confidences, laughed, drank and prayed, and, faced with a common enemy, men who had become, above all, his *friends*!

What had he expected? What? He hadn't honestly expected to go to war and not get hurt or inflict injury, had he?

Go away, he said to his unwelcome visitor, the spectre of death.

'Keep your head down under the smoke. Breathe air and not fumes, and you might have a chance of living until they come for you.' He didn't know who had issued the order, yet orders were for troopers to obey, just as Nanny Delish had drummed into him as she boxed his ears all those years ago.

Why was the man who was practically dead still screaming his head off? Why couldn't the poor bastard feel nothing and thus relinquish his misery? Why couldn't he be like Rory Roskillen who couldn't feel a damn thing, nor see a damn thing and could therefore keep quiet – silent, as the waves passed over them all . . .

'Why am I feeling so calm all of a sudden? So totally in control of myself, the first time since Lindsay's death?'

He spoke! The man with no legs, actually spoke! He's not dead. Why isn't he dead?

When reality becomes too terrible for ordinary comprehension, there is a silence.

The *Invincible*, flagship of the 3rd Squadron, blew up, exactly in half, from the concentrated fire of four German battlecruisers and a German battleship. She took with her 1,026 men, leaving only six survivors.

Yet, despite all that, despite the appalling loss of lives, ships sunk, crippled, put out of action, despite the devastating power of German warships with iron casings far superior to that of the British, guns, torpedoes, everything, despite God on her side, Admiral Jellicoe had victory within his grasp, a total victory that would have been far more glorious than that of Trafalgar. But it all slipped away, with lives lost to no avail.

'How did it happen and why me? Isn't that what the Virgin Mary said? Keep crawling, sailor, and don't raise your head . . . smoke rises and you don't want to puncture your lungs with nitro . . . whatever . . . they put in bombs these days. You know, there's a funny little Cockney blighter running the gauntlet of torpedo attacks . . . convoys, guv, he says, is going to be the answer to them Huns ruining things for the merchant fleet. Can we hold out? Of course we can hold out, sailor. Am I in my right senses to say such a thing? Just blast the door open, if you can't hack through it. Never mind us, we're not going anywhere. Here sailor . . . hand me that fire-extinguisher. I'm in a better position than you to use it. I know all about fire-extinguishers . . . intravenous morphine? Never touch the stuff, SBA . . .'

When reality becomes too terrible for ordinary

comprehension, there is a silence.

'*I can't breathe ... oh, God, I can't breathe ... oh, God, don't touch anything, me least of all! The metal is burning ... red hot ... Jesus Christ, we're frying alive ... suffocating, bleeding to death ... that poor bastard pinned to the door must be slowly cooking without his legs ... rare, medium, well done ... You caught up with Lindsay, now it's my turn, I suppose, the last laugh is yours, Moloch!*'

'He's passed out, doc,' the SBA said.

'Thank God. At least the poor blighter's now out of his misery.'

The damaged *Warspite* was ordered to return to Rosyth, towed by the *Engadine*, until heavy seas made towing impossible. The *Engadine* rescued the crew of the *Warspite*, and with casualties from the *Barham*, steamed the one hundred and sixty miles full ahead to Rosyth Harbour. The German High Seas Fleet, ten miles closer to port than the *Engadine*, under cover of darkness and against very heavy odds, returned to anchorage in Wilhelmshaven, and stayed there for the rest of the war.

CHAPTER THIRTY-FIVE

Annie was crowded out by SBAs and QAs trying to read the same newspaper at once. It was dated Saturday, 3rd June, 1916.

'Blimey!' Sick Berth Attendant, Daniel Barnes, who was waiting to be sent to RN Training Hospital, Haslar, for his wardmaster's certificate, whistled through his teeth. 'The Kaiser'll be wearing his best bib and tucker after this fiasco. Got his spiked helmet all shined up as well, shouldn't wonder ... wouldn't want to be any of *our* admirals, today, not for love nor money!'

Casualties amounted to 6,784 officers and men, from the Grand Fleet, as opposed to 3,058 Germans; and 177 RN men had been picked up out of the water and taken prisoners by the Germans. No German had been taken prisoner. As far as battleships went, the paper stated, British losses were: two dreadnoughts (certain); one pre-dreadnought (certain); one battleship or battle cruiser (probable); one dreadnought (probable); four light cruisers (certain); one heavy ship or light cruiser (certain); nine destroyers (seven certain, two probable); and four submarines (one certain, three probable).

'They say it's only because the German ships were built with proper armour plating and superior stereo range-finders. Not like ours, all put together in a hurry!' another SBA ventured. 'Anyhows, I don't see how the Germans can say *they've* won. They went running back to Wilhelmshaven, with our Navy chasing after them all through the night.'

'Quite right, Coventry!' SBA Barnes hooked his finger into the back of his teeth to dislodge a piece of stringy bully-beef from the sandwich he'd just eaten.

'Well, nobody's *won*! Papers say so. They said we *could*

of won, since we were far superior to the Boche in Naval strategy. Inconclusive action, is what they call it.'

'Whatever they call it, still looks like we came off worse. What with all them ships and men lost. Germans lost only half of everything. *They* think they've won – von Scheer's been drinking champagne in the Jade.'

'How do you know?'

'Papers say so.'

'Look here, Ayres, and the rest of you dim-witted SBAs … QAs not included, ladies, as a mark of respect … Jutland proves nothing. It's tactics that matter. Any fleet that turns around and goes back to base before the fight is over, in *my* opinion, are the losers, *not* the winners! What do you think QA Gowrie?'

'I think, everyone, we should drink up and get back on duty, otherwise SNO Douglas will give us all a black mark.'

'Right you are, you're the boss, nurse.'

'Nursing *Officer*, please Barnes!' Annie eyed SBA Barnes sternly.

They left the staff-room to go back on duty, the two SBAs, Barnes and Ayres working with Annie on the morning shift. There had been precious little to do at Kingseat, nothing that really taxed one's nursing skills to any limit, as it was more of a long-term rehabilitation unit for RN staff. Annie had become so bored with her passive role that she had put her name down for a six-month course in obstetrics and gynaecology, followed by another six months in paediatrics – for which she would have to go to Edinburgh or back to Aberdeen. After all, half the intake in most RN hospitals comprised naval wives and children, so it would make a nice change.

When they reported back to Senior Nursing Officer Douglas after their mid-morning coffee-cum-lunch break, she informed them: 'There's a meeting of all ranks nursing staff being held in the conference room at two o'clock. You three have my permission to attend. I'll hold the fort. Nothing much is going on in the ward as it's Saturday. Doctors rounds, QA Gowrie, have been postponed until Tuesday afternoon: I think they've all gone to Jutland for the weekend to wrest the champagne from Admiral von Scheer's hand ... how the Germans call this *their* victory, I *don't* know! I mention it – doctors rounds, I mean – only because you're Duty Nursing Officer on Tuesday, Gowrie ... unless of course Matron has other ideas for you.'

'Wonder what this is all about?' SBA Barnes said on the way to the Conference Hall.

The Deputy Matron presided over the staff meeting. From the dais her voice boomed to the back of the hall, 'Come right in, nurses, don't be shy ... take your seats quickly. Any more of you? Well then, as you were the last one in, SBA Barnes, kindly shut the doors behind you and don't act like your name. Fire drill rule number one, nurse!'

She eyed him over her horn-rimmed glasses, the female Vice-Admiral. Amid the titters, SBA Barnes closed the hall doors.

'Well now, nurses,' Deputy Matron Grant began, looking very smart in her navy-blue QARNNS uniform, with scarlet cape and crisp white headdress. 'As you have all heard, over the last forty-eight hours a major sea-battle was fought not far off our shores. East coast ports have been on an 'alert standby' to receive damaged ships and wounded men, while our hospital ships have been shuttling too and fro with wounded Naval personnel for Rosyth, Dundee, Aberdeen and Scapa Flow. Needless to say, every pair of qualified hands is urgently required at our naval base hospitals. Now most of you who trained at Aberdeen will be going back there. Those of you who have come to us from Haslar and Chatham are asked to volunteer your services. And we all know what volunteering in the Navy means, don't we, nurses? It means that those who do not volunteer voluntarily, will be press-ganged into service.'

A ripple of titters drifted around the hall. Deputy Matron pushed her glasses back more firmly on the bridge of her nose before reading out a list of names of those nurses being transferred to RNH Aberdeen, immediately.

QA Gowrie's name was on the list, so, too, was that of SBA Barnes.

'Good show!' he nudged her in the ribs.

Annie did not like his familiarity – Barnes took too many things for granted just because he was a man in a man's world. 'I thought you were being sent to Haslar, Barnes.'

'Looks like I've just volunteered for RNH Aberdeen, QA Gowrie.'

She had to get in the last word. 'That's going to set you back a bit in your wardmaster's certificate, isn't it?'

'Not to worry. I prefer working among pretty faces, and most of them at Haslar are downright ugly. I did two years there – shortly before the Battle of Coronel. That must be ... let me see now ... about eighteen months back, serving with the hospital-ship *Phoenix* off the coast of Chile. A man of my experience, all that sick berth attendance, it's Royal *Albert and Victoria* Yacht duty next, you know, folks! Might even get made admiral yet.'

'Yeah, we know,' said SBA Ayres, punching Barnes in the shoulder as they messed about on the way back to the ward. 'How can we forget since you keep reminding us! Tea and aspirins for His Majesty after a royal broadside. So why are you still at Kingseat where nothing ever happens? Thought they'd at least detail you to serve on a ship at Jutland since you're so clever blowing down the flatus tubes ... begging your pardon, QA Gowrie.'

She ignored them both, and stepped ahead without encouraging their conversation, although she could hear them still gossiping behind her.

'Well, I've got my principles, Ayres.'

'Yeah, like what?'

'Like being QA Gowrie's right-hand man. Without my naval protection, she might rush off and marry the first surgeon-captain who asks her. Then look where we'd be on Ward 9, Burns Unit, Kingseat. All our fellows with stretched faces would go elsewhere if they knew our special nurse from *Ross-shire*, Scotland, had gone and got herself married. They'd die of broken hearts and so would I.'

Oh-oh, thought Annie to herself: SBA Barnes was really asking for it one of these days!

*

RN Auxiliary Hospital, Kingseat, five hundred miles above sea-level, seemed a million miles away from the spectre of an indomitable enemy seeking to disrupt a peaceful rural Scottish summer.

If it hadn't been for the naval nursing uniforms they were wearing, Annie would have thought that men out there had dreamt a war was on.

It was sweet to smell the countryside again, instead of wards awash with antiseptic and carbolic, and constant saluting; a world in which June flowers grew wild on the mountainsides and in the glens, where the birds sang, where life was taken for granted.

It was a way of life she, too, had taken for granted until it had gone beyond her reach. Annie was reminded so much of Glengarth. Even the milkmaids they passed smelled creamy and fresh and saucy as they drove the cattle up to the mountains for summer grazing, managing on the way to block the path of the open truck in which they were being jolted to pieces.

'Hello, darlin',' SBA Barnes said to a plump-cheeked, rosy-faced young lady wearing a gingham bonnet and summery pinafore dress. Her feet were bare. He leaned precariously out of the jolting truck taking them to Aberdeen fourteen miles away, 'How about you and me doing the light fantastic at the local barn-hop this evening?'

She giggled and slopped milk over the sides of the jug she was filling from a milk-churn balanced on the broad wooden step of the stile. The RN driver impatiently tooted the klaxon to get the girl to move her milk-cart to the side of the road instead of leaving it slap bang in the middle. Two youngsters, like Jack and Jill astride the stile, a loaf of bread under an arm each, waved. 'You going to blow up the Boche, mister?' asked the boy.

'No, son, we're going to pick up the pieces they left behind.'

'Like Mr Kitchener?'

'You could say that, son.'

'My granddadee says Mr Kitchener's ship got blown up yesterday by a mine. What's a mine, mister?'

'I wanna be a nurse,' the little girl said. 'Are they nurses, mister, with red crosses?' She pointed to the QAs, meek and mild in the back of the Naval truck, wishing they could get a move on to Aberdeen. 'They're pretty. I wanna go with them.'

'If you're good at darning socks, darlin', then come along by all means. Only bring big sister with you.'

The children giggled. 'Molly, Ma says be sure and take the bread round to Mrs Krankie ... wait for us ... we're coming!'

Dropping two fresh, home-baked loaves on the stile, they hopped across, almost knocking over the milk-churn. They jumped up to hang onto the tailgate of the truck for a free ride, scuffing the toes of already worn, buttoned boots on the rough surface of the road as it slowly began to move off again now that Molly had shifted her handcart to one side.

'Hey, you two come back ... Ma'll tan your hides ... hey mister, make them stop that.'

'Don't worry, Molly, they'll be back. So will I.' He blew her a kiss and the QAs, embarrassed by SBA Barnes and his bold behaviour which showed them up, were glad when Annie, the senior nurse there, and nearest to SBA Barnes and his antics said, 'Barnes, stop treading all over my feet and sit down will you! Don't encourage them to play silly games. Make them let go ... As soon as we pick up speed, they'll fall off and hurt themselves. Then we'll all be held responsible by the Admiralty!'

He reached into his pocket, took out two bars of chocolate and tossed them into the grassy verge. The two children let go of the tailgate. Giggling and laughing together, they fell onto the dusty road and, by the wayside, began to scrap over the chocolate.

Barnes sat down on the long narrow seat, pushing his SBA neighbour along to get himself more space. Folding his arms, he gazed up at the blue sky and the distant Grampians, whistling in a low key: 'If You were the Only Girl in the World'.

Annie, seated opposite, tried hard not to smile: he really was a dreadful fellow, even though he was quite the best SBA at Kingseat – and Barnes knew it!

Now she could smell the sea, hear the seagulls, feel the brush of the salty air on her face, reminding her of Glengarth ... no, she mustn't think about Glengarth. Glengarth was part of her past, a piece of her heart cut out and buried for ever up on Inchnadamph. She must think about other things ...

Annie began to think about what would be facing them at RNH Aberdeen. All those wounded men rescued after the Battle of Jutland. How many would there be? How badly injured?

Burns – first, second and third degree burns – shock, smoke-congested, perforated lungs, that sort of thing mostly; or so she had been informed by SBA Barnes who had encountered intense battleship action before. She was quite experienced in the specialized nursing of burns, and didn't feel too perturbed about it. It was the thought of the poor souls blown apart and still living with their gaping wounds, that filled her with dread.

At first, SNO Lorrimer and QA Gowrie did not hit it off at all well, simply because Annie got off to a bad start. She reported for duty on the RN Senior Officer's Orthopedic and Surgical Ward, abbreviated to OSI, the following morning. The evening before had been spent in settling in and getting briefed on what her duties would be. The layout of the hospital was of course familiar to her, although many of the nursing staff she had known during her year's training period in Aberdeen had either gone overseas or been transferred to other RN hospitals around the country. Lorrimer, therefore, was an unfamiliar face, and an English one at that. One who appeared to care little for the Scots. 'You're late, Gowrie,' she snapped, her lips tight as she regarded her watch. 'What's your excuse?'

Did she have one? Annie asked herself. She was five minutes late, but wouldn't have been, if she hadn't stopped to help a patient in the corridor sort out his crutches as he was in danger of toppling over them to break another leg.

Annie explained the reasons for her lateness, and was rudely interrupted, 'Speak up ... I don't understand your accent, nurse.'

'Then the misunderstanding is mutual, SNO Lorrimer,' she said, raising her voice.

'*Sister* Lorrimer, nurse! Oh, I know the Service recognizes certain modes of address above others, but I prefer to stick to what I'm used to. I am a civilian trained SRN, SCM, as well as QA, and therefore, on *my* ward you will be called Staff Nurse and I will be called Sister. SBAs will remain SBAs, since they are of the same standing as civilian-trained SENs who aren't as highly qualified as we SRNs ... now then, let's not waste any more time discussing rank. But tomorrow morning leave the nurses' quarters ten minutes earlier so that you can perform your good deeds out of ward-time.'

Annie smiled. 'Yes, Sister.'

Later in the day, during her two hours break between shifts, Annie encountered SBA Barnes with a very long face in the nurses' dining-room. 'Guess what?'

'What?' said Annie, setting down her tray at the table where the familiar faces of other nurses from Kingseat were gathered. This little contingent from 'home' all seemed equally as morbid as Barnes; not what Annie needed at all after a morning spent with Sister Lorrimer and a mournful bunch of Senior Officers suffering from the aftermath of Jutland.

'Now they tell us they *don't* want us. Typical Navy!'

'What *are* you talking about, Barnes?'

'We've got the push ... Kingseat nurses, I mean. First they want us, then they don't. I wish medical pundits at Admiralty would make up their minds. We're not needed here ... *they* say!'

'Nobody has told me that,' Annie replied, sipping a glass of milk and containing her amusement within the rim. Barnes always had been one of the theatrical sort. 'I wish they had. I'm stuck on OSI, with a Sister Lorrimer who has already started to treat me as though I want to put Mary Queen of Scots back on the throne of England.'

'Or the Kaiser,' said QA Dibby MacKay.

'Why don't they want us?' Annie wanted to know.

'Well, we don't know about you, Gowrie. You weren't invited to the Matron-in-Chief's little talk last night, were you?'

'No.'

'Then they obviously want to keep you here.'

'I thought that was the idea ... wounded sailors from Jutland ...'

'There *aren't* any,' SBA Barnes said, picking his teeth. 'Well, only about five hundred, that's all, spread around other RN hospitals. Rosyth got most. Six thousand got blown up and drowned, which didn't leave a lot to get sent home. Jeeze! Anyway, there's nothing much for us to do here, and so they want us to go to Gravelines instead.'

'Gravelines? Where's that?' Annie asked.

'France – between Dunkirk and Calais.' SBA Barnes pulled a face: 'All those Frenchies! Navy wants volunteers ... we know what *that* means! Go or else! They want us to lend a hand to the poor old hard-pressed Army in salvaging the poor sods from the Battle of the Somme ... 30,000 killed in one day! Jeeze. Makes Jutland look a bit like cat's puke in an ocean of vomit!'

'SBA Barnes! You are *disgusting*!' QA MacKay got up and took her meal-tray to another table. The other QAs joined her.

Annie, too, stood up. She had an important letter to write and wanted to do it during her brief time off. 'Well, Barnes, is it to be Gravelines or Haslar?'

'I'll choose France,' he said gloomily. 'I always wanted to join the French Foreign Legion.' He went back to picking his teeth by himself.

Annie never saw Sister Lorrimer leave her ward except to eat and sleep, both those undertakings done with frugality. She devoted her whole time and attention to the men in her care, her stamina and dedication being quite remarkable. She also possessed an aptitude for gaining extra supplies and little luxuries not usually seen in other ward kitchens: fresh fruit and vegetables, best beef steaks, chicken in aspic and once even, champagne, caviar and flowers for a certain dignified RN Officer assigned to her special care. He did not remain long on the ward, however, less than thirty-six hours before he and his splinted arm were whisked off elsewhere. Later on, Annie found out that he was a younger member of the Royal Family who had served at the Battle of Jutland. Perhaps he was now recuperating in the more gracious surroundings of Balmoral, she mused with a little smile to herself.

Annie's private opinion was that, had Lorrimer been at the War Office in place of some of the armchair Admirals and Generals with their maps and red-tape, there wouldn't have been half the chaos, for nobody really seemed to know what they were doing.

Each senior-ranking officer had his own cubicle and privacy. The cases OSI received were mainly fracture cases, so most of the RN Officers were not really desperately ill, merely incapacitated on traction or splinted. Sober, taciturn and sometimes insufferable in their demands, they were not much fun at all.

It was a different story on the other side of the corridor. The Senior Nursing Officer for OS2, which accommodated the junior-ranking RNs, was an Irish Sister by the name of O'Ginnity. There was no love lost between Lorrimer and O'Ginnity: they squabbled like two women (except when adversity drew them together) sharing the same kitchen, which indeed they did. Both Orthopedic-Surgical wards shared a communal kitchen, sluice and treatment room, though the senior and junior rank sitting-rooms were separate. When life on the opposite side of the coin got rather too boisterous, Sister Lorrimer (for O'Ginnity never would) clamped down on them by closing each cubicle door or drawing ward curtains, so that the cheerful *badinage* could not be heard by everyone else on the same floor, especially a complaining commander!

One afternoon Annie came on duty after a short break of two hours, and Sister Lorrimer gave her the 'mundane task' of checking temperatures and pulses which SBAs usually undertook. But SBA Chalmers, an old salt for fifty years or more, who was new to the life of a land lubber so that one forgot his age or that he was ever an Able Seaman, had reported sick with a stomach upset. Sister Lorrimer had given him a couple of hours off.

'I'm sorry, Staff Nurse,' she said, not usually of an apologetic disposition, 'TPR is an important little task I always like done. Q.I.D. Chalmers is very good with getting the mundane little tasks out of the way, even if he's not much good at the important jobs.'

Annie didn't mind in the least. The first signs of infection or internal bleeding could be detected by that routine check, so she did not think it to be anything but important. Besides, it was a change from the incessant dressing trolley, the surgical sterilization of instruments, medicines and injections. TPR time required little effort and even less backchat. A thermometer stuck in someone's mouth gave little chance for soulful reminiscences, although there was always the odd patient who could talk through the hind legs of a donkey.

Sister Lorrimer suddenly sat down at her desk and rubbed her hands over her face in a weary gesture that made Annie realize that even efficient Lorrimer could flounder in the disarray that sometimes overtook them all.

'Just look at the heaps of paperwork I'm expected to do in the middle of saving lives!' She flipped through the sheaves of paper on her desk, files, and requisition slips, treatment sheets and X-Ray notes – the array was endless. Lorrimer sighed in exasperation and took up her pen, her shoulders once more square beneath her cape. 'I really don't know what's happened during this war other than bureaucracy having gone mad. Far better they had spent their time drafting in the infantry to back up our gallant Grand Fleet Commanders caught between the Hun and the void, than ask me to draft out statistics on powdered egg and milk consumption per invalid!' Her feeble little jest held more than a grain of truth.

Before Annie started on the temperature round, she took Sister Lorrimer a cup of tea in her 'Judas-hole' as the nurses called it. Her office was another glass-partitioned cubby-hole at the end of the corridor, from which she could see what was happening down both sides of her ward.

Poor Sister Lorrimer, Annie thought to herself. She had never seen her morale so low. 'Thank you, Staff Nurse Gowrie,' she said, stirring the tea gratefully. 'By the way ... Sister O'Ginnity is also short-staffed today. She has no senior nurse with her until this evening. But it's no one's fault except her own. She really ought to work out her duty rosters better. When you've finished the TPR round, she'll be grateful for a little help as she had some new admissions this morning – transferred to us from Rosyth. Ask her what she wants of you. But don't stay more than an hour. O'Ginnity will keep you all night if she can get away with it.'

'Yes, Sister.'

Annie did the temperature round and then went across the corridor to Sister O'Ginnity's ward.

The wolf-whistles and cat-calls were to be expected: any new nurse, especially a QA, elicited such behaviour from O'Ginnity's 'rabble', who ought to be court-martialled according to Sister Lorrimer across the dividing line.

'I say ... it's Annie Gowrie come to give us a spirit rub! How's the weather on your side of the Grampians, nurse?'

'Down boy ... it's QA Gowrie to you ... ain't she sweet? Do you want me to turn over, nurse?'

Sister O'Ginnity stuck her head out of her office at the commotion. 'Oh, 'tis you, QA Gowrie! Right glad I am t' see you, gal. Take no notice o' them ... most of the ruffians are from the dockyards in any case. Now hush, all you brave men swinging t' lead! Lorrimer'll be after you. You've all seen Gowrie's face before and she's seen yours – and by that I mean the cheeky ones you sit upon ... I'm off for a cup o' strong, sweet tea, nurse, an' I deserve it. There's nothing to fret over while I'm gone. Most of these brutes can look after themselves. Ah, but I was forgettin' ... the one in the first cubicle came to us from Rosyth only this morning. Just mind him, that's all. He's a little fragile at t' moment and hasn't made much of a recovery since the Naval Surgeon at Rosyth cut bits off him. I'll see you in twenty minutes.' She took her cape and was gone.

Annie checked O'Ginnity's patients, making sure none was about to die on her, before going to attend the new patient. Chartboards were kept hanging on a hook outside each cubicle.

If the board itself had leapt up to knock her cold between the eyes, she couldn't have felt worse. Annie held the chartboard in her trembling hands. She felt sick and weak, and, with nowhere to escape to, looked around her in desperation. She couldn't leave the ward unattended, neither could she stay . . . SBA Barnes was coming down the corridor. 'QA Gowrie . . . I'm off. Came to say goodbye. Sister Lorrimer said you were taking care of O'Ginnity's ward for a bit . . . Hi there, Lieutenant Hibbert, no I'm not coming back to this ward, I'm going to France this evening . . . Right you are, sir, I'll tell the Jerrys . . . What's the matter . . . Annie?' SBA Barnes peered into her stricken face with concern. 'You ill or something?'

Normally she would have been dismayed at seeing him and would have remained aloof and distant. She grabbed hold of his sleeve displaying his SBA badge, hardly realizing what she was doing: 'Just . . . just nothing.' She took a deep breath and thrust the board into his hands. 'Just look after the ward for a minute . . . I can't. I must ask Lorrimer for a replacement . . .' Annie fled back to OS1.

Sister Lorrimer looked up in alarm when Annie burst unceremoniously into her office: 'For goodness sake, Staff Nurse! Whatever's wrong? Who's haemorrhaging and where is the fire?'

'I'm sorry . . .' Annie sat down on some files placed on the one and only chair behind the door, her breathing erratic.

'QA Gowrie! I shall report you to the Matron-in-Chief unless you pull yourself together. This is not the place to go to pieces, so kindly get up off that chair at once and resume your duties.'

'I can't.'

Lorrimer's brows quirked. She viewed Annie Gowrie

with ice-cold hauteur. 'You can't? Am I ... am I misunderstanding you yet again, nurse? Have you a pain?
Have you dysmenorrhea? Then take two aspirins and get
back to work.'

'I ... I want to be taken off this ward, please ... and ...
and the other one. We're always being asked to swop
around on the wards when we're short of staff ... it simply
isn't fair to double the nursing load like this.'

Sister Lorrimer's look was enough to freeze the German
High Command. Her eyes boring into Annie's soul, she
said, 'Are you questioning those in higher authority,
nurse?'

'No, Sister. I would, if I could ... go back to Sister
O'Ginnity's ward, but I can't.'

'*Get back to your work, Nurse!*'

'Please, Sister Lorrimer,' Annie beseeched. 'I can't.
Please transfer me ... anywhere ... even to ... to Gravelines. Anywhere, Etaples even ... but I can't stay here any
longer.'

'Indeed. And why not, pray?'

'That new patient ... in the side ward ... Sister
O'Ginnity's side ward ...' She realized she was not making
much sense, but Annie felt so wretched, she did not care if
they dismissed her immediately from the QARNNS.

'Nurse, you do realize, don't you, that this merits a
disciplinary action!'

'Yes, I know Sister Lorrimer. But Sub-lieutenant
Roskillen of the RNR signals corps is known to me
personally.'

The frosty silence was palpable. 'You know him. I see.'

Oh, God, Annie thought distractedly, her eyes seeking
everywhere but the look on Sister Lorrimer's face. How
could she expect the woman to understand! Annie buried
her face in her hands: *I know him, I know him ... and I
don't want him to die ... I don't want to be the one to have
to nurse him until he dies ...*

Annie heard Lorrimer let out her breath in a hiss of
derision. 'Well then, Staff Nurse Gowrie, since you didn't
run in here to tell me the Germans were at Westminster or
Edinburgh, I suggest you run out again and attend to poor

Sub-lieutenant Roskillen. I ignore your request for a transfer. I ignore your unprofessional conduct of the past few minutes. Your record was sent to me before you came to this ward and I know that you are a good nurse – a very good nurse. It would be a shame to lose you. That is why I refuse to relinquish you to Etaples or anywhere else Matron-in-Chief has been instructed to send our QA nurses. *Never* go to pieces like this again. You are part of a highly trained, qualified team, so your personal wishes are not important. What *is* important is your professional conduct in a moment of crisis. You, as well as I, know that a nurse *nurses*, independent of colour, creed, race, nationality or *rank*!'

Sister Lorrimer picked up a file and flicked it open. 'Since I, too, am covering for her, Sister O'Ginnity left this with me while she went for a few minutes well-earned respite. To bring us both up-to-date with the situation, these are the facts, nurse ... Sub-lieutenant Roskillen, Royal Naval Reserve, was severely wounded saving your freedom and mine! The flagship *Barham* on which he was serving, received several shell hits at the Battle of Jutland. The wireless room, where Sub-lieutenant Roskillen was on duty at the time, received a direct hit which killed several of his fellow officers. He himself was caught between steel doors, and even though his life was hanging by a thread, managed to keep up the morale of the other wounded men in several ways – not the least being that he himself took the fire-extinguisher in his own burned hands to aid the rescue team in cutting through inch-thick doors to rescue others who were wounded. He had to have one leg amputated on the spot. At Rosyth his other leg was pinned. After he has seen the specialists here, he will be sent to Kingseat for skin-grafts. So, nurse, I will not tolerate your selfish and unprofessional behaviour another second. You will get out there again, and you will dress his wounds in the same calm, professional manner as for any other sick, wounded or dying person brought to us.'

She turned back to her paperwork. 'And when Sister O'Ginnity is finished with you, clean the sluice. It's in a disgusting state.' She looked up then, her pale blue eyes as

hard as pebbles. 'Well, go on, Staff Nurse Gowrie, what
are you waiting for? You needn't worry about Sub-
lieutenant Roskillen recognizing you. Jutland also cost him
his eyesight.'

A terrible silence shut down on Annie.

She went back to Sister O'Ginnity's ward, all her
actions like those in a dream. SBA Barnes was still there,
hovering between bravado and uncertainty as he joked
with the men he had been nursing to date, while all the
time looking over his shoulder for Sister O'Ginnity or QA
Gowrie, hoping it would be the latter.

'Oh, Blimey, Annie ... sorry, QA Gowrie ... you
okay?'

She nodded.

A broad smile split his bland and boyish face. 'That's all
right then. You got me worried. Listen ... I hope you
don't mind me calling you Annie, as we've known each
other for a couple of years; and passing our exams
together must mean something ...' He waited for her to
smile, but she didn't. He cleared his throat awkwardly and
added, 'But now I'm going to France and getting out of
your hair for a bit, I wanted you to have this.'

He gave her a letter in the privacy of Sister O'Ginnity's
office.

Annie nodded and took it. 'Thank you, Daniel.'

SBA Barnes hovered a few more minutes, expectantly,
hoping she would open it and read it in front of him.
When she did not, but remained with a glazed, fixed look
about her, as though she were in deep shock, he left the
ward, a queer sort of feeling about her wringing his heart
because he didn't know whether she liked him or not. She
was a funny girl about that sort of thing and he never
knew which way to take her.

But she had called him Daniel for the first time!

CHAPTER THIRTY-SIX

Every night Annie prayed for him not to die. Every day when she passed his cubicle in the course of her duties she prayed that he would. She had even found an excuse to linger between one shift and another, just so that she could read his charts, his progress reports, trap an OS2 nurse into talking about the latest condition of Sublieutenant Rory Roskillen, until it became a standing joke. 'Hi, Annie, why don't you dress his wounds yourself today? O'Ginnity's wondering which ward you really belong to . . .'

Oh, no! To dress his wounds would be like turning the knife in her own wounds. Annie ran a mile from such a task even while she prayed for his recovery, watched over him from a distance, suffered with him.

And then one morning when she arrived on duty the cubicle curtains screening his private glass hell were drawn back – the first time in a week. The cubicle was empty, the bed stripped, an SBA already cleaning with carbolic soap the rubber-covered mattress, the locker, while clean linen was laid fresh and neat on the trolley ready for the bed to be made up for the next occupant.

Her feet anchored to the floor, Annie shut off her mind: corpses were part of her life. Rory Roskillen's removal from her life was just another hiccough in her destiny. Now there was nothing more to hold her to Glengarth, nothing!

The SBA lifted his head and grinned, mouthing something through the glass Annie couldn't understand. She was about to turn tail and run when she hesitated, beckoning him to the door. He opened it, stuck his head round and said cheekily, 'Checking up on me, eh, Staff? Didn't know you were attached to OS2 as well . . . sorry, sorry,

didn't mean to sound saucy ... please don't report me to
SNO O'Ginnity, please don't ... I done me carbolic best
'ginst germ warfare, Nurse, promise!' His eyes to the
ceiling, knee to the floor, hands together in prayer while
the wet carbolic sponge made drips everywhere, the SBA
beseeched her. But Annie was in no mood for SBA
Mandall's tom-foolery. SBAs seemed to think that making
jokes all the time was number-one priority in their Sick
Berth handbook.

'When?' she snapped, pointing to the empty cubicle.

'Last night ... whew! Five deaths ... five admissions.
What a night! Thank Gawd it's over. After this little lot is
made up ready for the next customer, I'm off to bed for a
few hours. Busy day ahead of you, QA Gowrie ... we're
shuffling and reshuffling everyone round again. Sending
the long-term ones to Kingseat to make room for those
shipped to us from Flanders. Talk is, they're launching a
big offensive in France shortly.'

Annie turned on her heel and Mandall became a bit
more sober.

'Sorry about SBA Barnes, Staff Nurse,' he said to her
swiftly retreating back. 'We all knew he had a bit of a
crush on you ... and I want to say I'm really sorry.'

Annie turned back to look at him. 'What are you
talking about SBA Mandall?'

'Gosh ... didn't you know? ... sorry, sorry ...'

'Please tell me what you're *trying* to tell me – and don't
bother to spare my feelings. SBA Barnes and I meant
nothing to each other.' Annie tried not to speak through
the grinding of her teeth, but her heart couldn't take much
more of this. And not only her heart but her whole self!
She knew that she would break down any minute, unless
God had a reason for all this misery.

'Dan copped it ... Flanders U-boat got the Sick Berth
Naval boat returning with RN wounded picked up off the
coast of Belgium. Dan was on escort duty ...'

Oh, God! She didn't want to know! She fled.

Without reporting sick, or even bothering to report at
all for morning duty despite having to pass the ward
office, Annie went back to her room in the nurses' quar-

ters, shared with three other QA nurses. Mercifully, at this time of the morning, the busiest time, the dormitory was empty.

Annie drew the curtains around her only little patch in the world, her bed, her locker, her clothes hook and her chair. She retrieved SBA Daniel Barnes's letter from her locker drawer where she had shoved it, unopened, a week ago. She threw herself down on her bed:

Dear Annie,

Hope you don't mind me calling you Annie, but I reckon we've known each other long enough to drop the QA SBA bit, haven't we? After all, we did the same exams and passed with the same flying colours. We ate the same ghastly meals, courtesy RN catering, in the same grisly mess room; walked the same corridors of power and nursed in the same wards at RN Auxillery Hospital, Kingseat.

I owe Kingseat a lot, Annie. That's where I met you. And even while we had to patch up all the ugly, mutilated, burned and destroyed men sent to us, we managed, didn't we? Between us – and Ayres, God bless his cotton socks – we got some good laughs out of it. Say yes, Annie, say yes, otherwise fighting this war doesn't mean a thing.

I've got a funny feeling about going to France – don't ask me why. This is a stupid war. Too much happening to register one minute, nothing the next. Silly me, forty years from now (post-Haslar fortieth time around!) when I'm Admiral on the Royal Yacht, I'll laugh about this and say, 'Dan boy, it was all in the mind. No such thing as premonitions.'

Which brings me to the point of this exercise. I don't know how you feel about me, but I feel a different man when I'm with you, Annie. I want you to know that you're the only girl for me. There's something special about you, QA Gowrie, and none of us SBA fellows knows what, except that we all feel good when you're around. So I'm getting my oar in first. When I get back to Kingseat (or RNH Aberdeen, whichever comes first) will you think about being SBA Barnes's own special lady?

Daniel

Only when the curtains around her bed were twitched back did Annie look up.

Sister Lorrimer, framed in floral cotton, Navy issue, regarded QA Gowrie rocking herself back and forth, a letter clutched theatrically to her heaving breast, her eyes as red as the Cross of Geneva. Lorrimer said in tight-lipped dismay, 'Staff Nurse Gowrie, this is *ludicrous*! I have been waiting over two hours for you to report on duty. I cannot run an efficient ward without your co-operation.'

Annie swallowed, and said nothing.

They said that Lorrimer had lost her fiancé on the first day of the war and that's why she was so bitter and twisted.

Annie didn't care. Not any more. There was too much sorrow and misery in one's own life to take notice of what happened in other people's lives. All she wanted to do now was resign from the Service or get dismissed from it so that she could go back to Jamie at Gairloch.

'Staff Nurse ...' Lorrimer sat down on the end of Annie's bed. 'Neither of us can go on like this. I need someone to back *me* up sometimes. That's what Staff Nurses are for, to provide the back-up system to a Ward Sister, to be her second-in-command, her fail-safe person. I'm not blaming you ... you're too good at what you do to apportion blame. In fact, the opposite is true, you care *too* much! I know what a trauma the last week has been to you, what with Sub-lieutenant Roskillen's admission to a ward right opposite your own. A man badly injured, a man known to you ... though I dare not pry into your personal life. But I sympathize, I want you to know that. This kind of situation is the great test of our strength as nurses.'

She took a deep breath and stood up. 'However, a good nursing sister also has to take into consideration the welfare of her nursing staff if a hospital is to function the way it should. I know that you are not happy working here ...'

'Oh, but I am, Sister Lor ...' Annie began.

She held up her hand. 'Let me finish, Nurse. Sometimes we are asked to perform tasks in the face of the enemy, tasks which would bring most people to their knees.

Sometimes the enemy is not always German. You are fighting something inside yourself, and you must resolve it by yourself, but not at *my* expense. I'm sorry to lose you. But Matron-in-Chief has had a little discussion with me and we both feel that your services are no longer required at RNH Aberdeen. You're being transferred back to Burns Unit, Kingseat. The RN bus leaves in three-quarters of an hour, nurse.'

Lorrimer brought the dividing curtains together carefully. 'Sub-lieutenant Roskillen ought to pull through after the effort I've been to in order to secure his own personal nurse. He was transferred to Kingseat last night when O'Ginnity needed room on OS2 for emergency admissions.'

So typical of any service, Annie thought to herself miserably. They only explain *after* the event!

Were there tears in Lorrimer's eyes?

Annie was never too sure.

She could only think about such things afterwards.

He, the reason why she had been transferred back to Kingseat – thanks to Lorrimer – did not speak unless it was absolutely necessary to ask for something he was unable to do for himself. In their separate roles they were strangers forced into a nurse-patient relationship, as asexual as that of mother and son.

He was the victim of war, unthinking, uncaring and far too shell-shocked to be aware of her, while she was yet another instrument of war's paradoxes, there merely to ease his suffering.

When she looked at him, mutilated like so many, those at sea, those on land, those in the air, for a few yards of vacant sea-water, mud, barbed wire, empty air, Annie wondered at it all – what the living and the dying and the suffering was all about.

Until she remembered Lorrimer in Aberdeen.

Annie hadn't been able to weep for Lindsay even while she had stood beside his catafalque, gazed unseeingly at his handsome body in the prime of life, graced in the splendour of his Highland regalia, at peace, serene and reposed for the last time in the great hall at Glengarth. The tears had all dried up on that day she had returned to Glengarth to stand beside him one last time, to be alone with him, just the two of them together in Glengarth's great hall ...

Pain, the hopelessness, the railing against fate, the beating of the breast, had been her broken-hearted protest when she had stood alone on the white sands of Rill and let the sands pour through her hands. But even then the tears, the real tears, had been missing.

The tears had only come with Daniel Barnes's death: why?

They said the war would last until 1920. They said it would be over by New Year 1917. They said all sorts of things nobody paid attention to any more. The saying of the moment, '*if you know a better 'ole, go to it*,' was on everyone's lips.

After Jutland had come the reckoning.

The Admiralty began to listen.

Representatives in both Houses began to listen.

Mr Winston Churchill at the Admiralty Office never listened to anyone. 'It would have been quite easy to divide the British Fleet with the 5th Battle Squadron leading the starboard division, and so take the enemy between two fires,' he said in criticism of Admiral Jellicoe.

'*Absurd!*' replied Admiral Jellicoe. 'Again I must remind Mr Churchill that this map, showing the position and Scheer's movements, was not in my possession at the time. I wish it had been ... Mr Churchill's excursions into the realms of naval tactics are, it is to be feared, not a great success.'

Flag signals and the lack of cohesive transmission of wireless messages were debated. The Blue Pendant turn was a matter of speculation for many a long month ahead.

'And isn't it fair to say that German seamen were issued with *suitable* protection in the event of any disaster, *at all times*, namely life-jackets to keep them upright in the water until rescued? At the Battle of Dogger Bank in January this year, for instance, German foresight and "material science" meant that when the *Blücher* was sunk, six hundred German sailors were picked up, while our sailors *drowned*!'

Cork lifebelts were then issued to British sailors, but only for special duties such as buoy jumpers. Inflatable waistcoats or life-jackets were issued only to the officers of the Royal Naval Air Service, who, in any case, were expected to buy their own life-saving equipment.

The verbal battle raged long after the last wreath had been shredded to pieces by North Sea waves.

The whole question of naval strategy, of armaments, material, chemical, medical and administrative science went on and on, overhauled time and time again, through the darkest years of the war.

One month after Sister Lorrimer had negotiated Staff Nurse Annie Gowrie's transfer to Kingseat so that she could be as near as possible to 'the man she knew', Annie came on duty one morning to find the curtains still drawn around Sub-lieutenant Roskillen's bed.

Curtains being a way of life on any ward, she wrenched them back. 'RNR Roskillen! *Why* are your bedside curtains still drawn when it's time for breakfast?'

'Are they nurse?' he replied, sounding bright enough. 'I'm sorry ... I couldn't tell. I'm still trying to locate the whisky bottle. Did the night nurse leave it on the floor?'

Flustered, Annie found the urinal and thrust it into his hand with the muttered excuse, 'No, *I'm* sorry ...' she closed the curtains again, and left him to his duty.

Outside the curtains her legs almost gave way and she had to take several deep breaths before she was able to totter down the rest of the ward on the morning, pre-breakfast round to check up on all her patients.

He was going to live, praise be!

'What are you looking so cheerful about this morning, Staff?' asked Captain Tethers of the Royal Naval Air Service, who was in the Burns Unit for facial skin grafting.

'It's a beautiful day, Captain!'

'It's raining, Staff Nurse.'

'But it's still a beautiful day!'

CHAPTER THIRTY-SEVEN

Senior Nursing Officer Douglas at Kingseat interrupted Annie's trend of thought while she tidied the treatment room. 'Gowrie, are you doing anything in particular?'

Annie hesitated, one always had to be doing something particular when a Ward Sister put such a question. 'Well, I was just . . .'

'Leave it. I have something more important for you to do. As nurses, we all know that a healthy mind makes a healthy body. I want you to take RNR Roskillen for a walk in the gardens. I want the fresh air to blow away the cobwebs of what's bothering him. He has been here much longer than any other officer wounded at Jutland. This is not good, nurse. They tell me you are someone who knew him before his war wounds. If that is the case, do something constructive about making him ready for discharge.' SNO Douglas turned on her heel and left Annie standing there with her mouth open. SBAs were usually the privileged ones to walk in the gardens with the male patients, so Douglas's order had taken Annie aback. However, she was not going to argue. Rory, after his initial re-entry into the world, had suddenly become morose and ill-tempered the moment skin-grafting treatment had been undertaken on the worst of his burns, mainly on his arms, hands and back; so he could no doubt do with a change of scenery, too, even though life for him was still black behind his eye bandages.

Half an hour later she was in the lift with him, the wondering sub-lieutenant wrapped in blankets in his wheelchair and protesting vociferously. 'What the hell is the Navy doing with me now? Where am I being taken?'

'For a walk in the garden.'

'Why?'

'Because QA-SNO Douglas ordered it.'

'Who's she, for God's sake?'

'England's answer to the Kaiser.'

Beneath his snowy bandages his fine lips gave a hint of a smile. 'What's your name?' he asked suddenly.

Annie hesitated. 'Nurse.'

Again, his lips twitched. 'Rank and serial number only, eh, Nurse?'

'That's right, RNR Roskillen.'

'You're Scottish – I can tell by the softness ... so tell me, Nurse, what does the garden look like? Are they keeping it in trim? Lawns mowed, hedges cut, weeds uprooted, roses dead-headed? Perhaps my seasons have become mixed up in the relentless pursuit of German warships ... and isn't it significant, Nurse, that the two most important things in a sailor's life – or his death – are separated by a simple vowel: warship and worship, two life support systems a sailor always falls back on for protection. Are the daffodils blooming as they do on the banks of the Breedon? Are the primroses shining like clusters of sunbeams beneath the hedgerows? And are the bluebells carpeting the woodland like reflections of heaven?'

He sounded bitter, lost and hopeless. Annie knew the feeling.

'RNR Roskillen,' Annie said. 'It's summer now.'

After a while he repeated her words: 'It's summer now ... and all the flowers dying.'

Annie gripped the handles of his wheelchair tighter still.

The sluice gates of the past suddenly opened by Sub-lieutenant Rory Roskillen, and feelings checked like the harnessed tides of a locked river suddenly came flooding back in torrential destruction to catch her unawares, to leave her drowning once more in the whirlpool of the two wars she had been fighting so hard, within and without.

Haunted, she stood again in the pine grove above Loch Garth, her grief over Lindsay's death so great she had been unable to separate reality from imagination, fact from fiction, truth from lies, as every day merged into one sorrow after another and grief swallowed her up.

And now again, how she wished, as never before, and

with all her heart, that Rory Roskillen had saved his brother from the crumbling cliff edge, and left her where she was; for then, this moment would not have arisen.

The mockery was turned inward upon herself, taking Rory with her.

Hero and heroine of ... of what? Or victims of Glengarth?

Gripping his wheelchair as though her life depended upon holding onto something, she heard his voice from a long way off. 'Come on, Nurse! Tell me what kind of flowers grow in a Grampian summer? Do we have Aberdeenshire edelweiss, gentian violets or even alpine roses? My mother loved flowers, especially English flowers. I'd have probably been a *mali* for her sake had she lived. Instead, I became a sailor for nobody's sake ...'

The self-pity was all there, pathetic to listen to.

Annie, crushed beyond words, crushed like the seashells of Rill, crushed like Rory Roskillen himself, desperately wanted to salvage something from the *mélange* of mishaps that had engulfed them all: 'Marsh marigolds, Rory, like sunbeams on Inchnadamph.' She wiped the back of her hand under her runny nose.

He gave a start.

And then he slumped forward in his chair, his shoulders sagging, his fingers plucking irritably, aggressively at his eye bandages. 'Get me the hell out of here! Take me back to the ward, Nurse!'

The following afternoon he rang his bell for attention and when SBA Ayres answered it, Rory said to him, 'Ayres ... not you. Send ... send the Scottish nurse to me.'

'QA Gowrie, you mean sir?'

'If that's her name,' Rory Roskillen growled.

'I think she's attending to Captain Tether's dressings at the moment, sir.'

'Well, when she's damn well finished with Tethers, tell her I want her.'

'Yes, sir.'

'Oh, and Ayres, draw the screens please. The light hurts my eyes.'

'But you've got eye-band ... oh, yes, sir, right away!' Ayres drew the screens.

Annie and Ayres were the only two on duty during the afternoon's slack period, so when her dressing round was finished she went to find out what their most difficult patient wanted of her.

'Nurse,' he began.

'RNR Roskillen, don't pretend you don't know who I am.' She held his hand even though he tried to untangle her clasp in his embarrassment. '*Rory!* Listen to me! You're not imagining it, it *is* me, Annie Gowrie from Rill.'

In a little while his fingers tightened around hers. His head thrown back against his pillows, he gave a grunt of disbelief. 'God in heaven! And I thought I was going out of my mind imagining such a thing.' He breathed harshly down his nose, 'What a bloody war! What a *bloody* laugh! What a bloody *fiasco*! Annie Gowrie gutting men in Kingseat, instead of fish in Wester-Ross ...'

'Shh ... Rory, calm down. The others will hear you ... I agree, it *is* a *bloody* fiasco! But it's not my fault. I didn't ask God to send me here at the *exact* moment you would be here. That's something we'll have to question him about later. All I know is, now that we *are* here together, we better make the most of it. A great many more out there never will – any more.' She thought about Daniel Barnes, gone to that watery grave Rory Roskillen had been saved from, and she was determined not to give up now.

Touching in its temerity, he gave a little smile. They were all learning to smile again, the art of rejoicing, even at the smallest thing that touched their beleaguered lives, a heart-warming step towards a healing.

Annie was glad to help him along.

'I don't know whether this is going to be a good or a bad thing for me, Annie Gowrie,' he said. 'I don't know whether I'm ever going to recover, what with you hovering in the background, bullying me to get better. I think I ought to ask to be transferred to another ward.'

'That's up to you. There are plenty of private rooms if you don't want the company of others. And if you stay here, we'll *all* be bullying you, SNO Douglas most of all.

She wants you to hurry up and get better and leave the bed free for someone else. As far as I'm concerned, RNR Roskillen, you're just another one of my patients, so don't expect any special treatment or privileges from me.'

'Aye aye, Cap'ain!' he touched his fingers to his snowy bandages in a naval salute.

A few days later he had a couple of visitors which seemed to cheer him up for as long as the visit lasted. 'Look at that, will you, Nurse,' said SNO Douglas as she and QA Gowrie took advantage of visiting time to catch up on paperwork and filing. They were able to see down the length of the ward through the office window. 'He hasn't so much of a death wish now, eh? We'll have to get Mr Gammon and Mr Ackker to visit Sub-lieutenant Roskillen more often.'

'Well now, guv,' Gammon was saying to Rory, 'an' that wasn't the end of the story, either. After the old man's ship received a direct 'it, Beatty goes off down to his cabin only ter find the bleedin' ship's cat 'as kittened in his best top 'at while the bombardment was at its 'ight.'

'Gamin, I don't know from where you pick up all this gossip ... you were never anywhere *near* the Battle of Jutland! It hurts to laugh, you fool! I'm still mighty sore all over, you know,' said Rory, laughing even when he thought he'd never laugh again.

'How did the skin graft go, Mr Rory, sir?' Ackker asked politely.

'Bloody painfully, Ackker. Left shoulder and back got the worst of it, but they say it's all healing nicely ... *they* say! What's Beatty calling his litter, Gamin?'

'Jutland, Jellicoe and Jade, shouldn't wonder – though I reckons, guv, the old man'd prefer ter ferget about that little lot. They're accusing 'im of "touching up" the evidence, covering 'is tracks, so ter speak. He says he never did a three-sixty degree turn, it was a 'S' turn. It don't make sense either way, guv, but he's sticking ter his story.'

'I agree, it doesn't make much sense ... mind you, by this time I wasn't too sure what was going on, either, Gamin, as I'd become a human doorstop by seven o'clock ... however,' Rory took a deep breath, memory mercifully blanked off for most of that horrendous experience, 'if his earlier turns were anything to go by, Beatty oughtn't to have worried about a thirty-two point turn looking silly on paper, because an 'S' turn a mile to starboard would only have presented his back to the enemy.'

'You mean he was running away from the Germans, Mr Rory, sir?' Ackker asked. 'Dirty rotten coward!'

'No Ackker, I don't think the old man was running away. He probably didn't *know* he was showing his tail-end to the Germans. Everything was chaotic, W/T, flag signals, which couldn't be read due to bad visibility, and then we were told to clamp down on W/T transmissions anyway. Aboard the *Barham* we didn't have much choice when our wireless installations were blown sky-high ... By the way, Gamin, how's the merchant shipping run these days?'

'Gawd-awful, guv. Losses get worse. Listen, Mr Rory, sir, when they promote you to the Admiralty, since they tell me you got yourself the VC ... fourteen for Jutland ain't bad, I suppose ...'

'You mean they're giving me fourteen VCs personally, Gamin?'

'Nar, guv, knock it orf! You knows what I mean ... guv, tell 'em about giving us convoys, will yer? It makes sense ter me, but them bods in 'igh places seem to 'ave got arses where most other people 'ave 'eads.'

'I agree, Gamin. But I don't think they'll have room for a blind man in the Admiralty.'

'You got a tongue, ain't yer, guv?'

'I think so, Gamin. Unless they cut that out too – but maybe Ackker here is a ventriloquist.'

'We're real proud of you, Mr Rory, sir, Gamin and me. Faith marlin' what you did for your fellow human beings was mighty heroic and saved a lot of human lives.'

'Who's been talking to you, Ackker?'

'Everyone, sir, saying what a brave man you were, employing that fire-extinguisher to good effect and tossing over the pain-killers and smoke-hoods to the others trapped inside a living inferno while they were trying to force the doors with metal tools and flame-cutters and your life was hanging by a thread . . .'

'Yes, well, Ackker, I wasn't in my right senses at the time. It was bloody hot . . . and while I'm flattered you consider me brave enough for the Admiralty I don't think they'll have me. I'm just a humble RNR man remember. Well now, there goes the bell. Time for you two to be off. Take care of yourselves dodging the Jerries . . . don't get yourselves torpedoed before I come back to Glasgow to sort out the mess everyone's got the business into while I've been away.'

'No 'ope of that, guv,' said Gammon tucking the chair he had been sitting on neatly into place at the foot of the bed. 'Ackker and me got nine lives.'

'Like Beatty's cat. I hope so.' Rory shook hands with them, feeling sad at their departure: they had given him a new lease on life, however short, these two old salts from the past. And now that his own career in RNR Signals appeared to be over, what was he going to do for the rest of the war? Indeed, the rest of his life! He didn't want to think about it.

'You reckon the Navy bus will take a couple of civvies like us back to Aberdeen, guv?'

'Why not? Just tell the driver your boss has won the Battle of Jutland single-handed and got himself the VC. That should do the trick.'

'Yeah, well, better be off now. That Sister is looking kind of funny at us. *Lady Leonora II*'s waiting for Ackker and me to get back afore nightfall. Jerry don't come out so much after dark. We got an important cargo of seashells ter take ter the London River.'

'Seashells?' Rory echoed.

'Yeah, guv, they're crushing 'em down an' using them in munitions now.'

'Jesus!'

After they'd gone Rory wanted a word with 'QA Gowrie.'

'When are you next off duty, Annie?'

She glanced at her nurse's watch. 'About half-an-hour ago.'

'Wonderful! Bring the wheelchair. Bring a pencil and

some paper. We're going to hold hands in the garden while I give you some dictation ... if they want to know at Admiralty the truth about charging the enemy haphazardly and recklessly, about 5th Battle Squadron having her rear-end shot to pieces, about Blue Pendants, thirty-two point turns and lack of proper communication, they can have *my* version! After all, I learned *my* tactics in old Peter Darby's School, Everton, and didn't get my pilot's certificate for nothing!'

'They might take back your medal,' Annie said, trying not to show how pleased she was at his change of heart and *this* thirty-two point turn for the better!

'They can bloody grind it down for munitions, for all I care. I need legs and eyes, not medals!' he growled.

'Your visitors obviously did you a world of good,' she said, taking his dressing-gown and one slipper from his locker, together with a blanket to wrap him in during his excursion outside; it wasn't *that* warm this afternoon.

'Gamin is a brick ... so is Ackker in his own funny way. Friends Annie! That's what friends are for ... now, get that pencil and paper. I hope you can write fast.'

'No fear about that! Scribbling down our nursing notes at high speed, verbatim, from Nursing Tutor, would get me a secretarial job any day – provided I can read back my own writing!' She put his dressing-gown round his shoulders while he manoeuvred himself awkwardly into the wheelchair she had brought up to his bed. 'Anyway, you'll soon be able to write your own notes – your own book even – as the eye specialist sent his report through today on your eye tests. The scar tissue is healing nicely, and as no damage was done to retina or brain, where the sighting mechanism is, there's no reason why full vision won't be restored to you in time. It's just the shell-blast that momentarily blinded you, so you're not going to be blind for ever. Isn't that good news?'

'Hmmm ... seeing is believing,' he grunted, flopping thankfully into the wheelchair. 'Anyway, why didn't the bloody eye-surgeon come and tell me this personally if he knows so much about it?'

'Because he's too busy at Rosyth. Besides *I'm* the

Nursing Officer in charge today, and, as such, am qualified to furnish you with the facts. The eye-surgeon will probably come and visit you tomorrow.'

'Let's hope so,' Rory said dryly.

'It's drizzling,' Captain Tethers RNAS said gloomily, stepping back into the ward from the verandah. He had bad facial scars from burns sustained when his plane had crashed at sea, straight into a pool of burning oil. Annie was only glad that Sub-lieutenant Rory Roskillen couldn't see the captain's face. 'Damn chilly, too, Roskillen.'

'Bring an umbrella, Annie,' Rory said.

The following afternoon SNO Douglas handed Annie two letters. 'They're for Roskillen ... read them for him. I'm going off-duty for half an hour. SBA Ayres and you can go to tea when probationer Phillips and I get back.'

Why is she doing this to me? Annie asked herself in despair as she took the letters to him, not really blaming anyone except herself for volunteering her services to all humanity, even to reading the letters of the blind!

'RNR Roskillen,' Annie said, whisking together the ward curtains around his bed, 'you have two letters awaiting reply. The sooner I read them to you, the quicker you can answer them ... via dictation!'

He gave a taut little grin, his mouth twisting wryly. 'I wish I could see what you look like in a nurse's uniform, fishergirl ...' And then he stopped and grew morose.

Annie looked at the stamps, 'One is from India and the other from Rutland.'

'Oh, read me Sula's letter first. I like to savour Kitty's letters, keeping them till last like the cherries in a fruit salad. I used to do that in my younger days, you know, Annie.'

Annie smiled to herself and drew up a chair beside his bed. His fingers stroked the back of her hand. 'Annie, tell me what you're doing here and *why* you're here. Tell me *everything.*'

'I'm here because I'm a good QARNN nurse who volunteered according to orders,' she said, steeling herself to face facts and start reliving life even when it hurt. 'After

... after Lindsay's death, and your leaving Glengarth, I had my baby. Then I went to do my training at RNH Aberdeen – which was the best choice I ever made. I qualified fully and then I was transferred to Kingseat to do a post-graduate course in the specialized nursing of burns and the rehabilitation of patients suffering from major disabilities. It's a very rewarding kind of nursing, seeing someone come back from ... from the verge of death. In March I was sent back to Aberdeen for a short spell and after Jutland, they again transferred me, back again to Kingseat ... no reason given. All I can say is that in the last week or two I've lived a lifetime.'

''Tis a small world, to be sure, Annie Gowrie. But worse things happen at sea ... or so they tell me.' He shifted his position in the bed. 'Your son, Annie, what have you named him?'

'Jamie.' She knew he would never ask her the all-important question. He was too much of a gentleman. 'Jamie is bonnie – oh, he's bonnie! Normal in every way. And speak! Why! He was speaking even in his cradle! And now he can string whole sentences together. Such a fine, strong, handsome, healthy boy is my wee Jamie – you'll have to see for yourself when you go home,' she told him proudly.

'Jamie,' he repeated. 'A grand name for a son ...' his chest heaved. 'You've made me an uncle, Annie Gowrie.'

He realized his mistake too late and became fidgety. 'Well, come on then, nurse, read me my letters since I'm as blind as a damned bat!'

Annie turned them over in her hand. One was what the nursing staff called a 'smudgy-letter', sealed with tears and painful to writer as well as recipient.

Better get it over with, Annie thought to herself, wondering what fresh heartache his sister in England had for him.

She read the one from India first, from his stepsister. It was cheerful, giving him news of her exotic Eastern life-style which read like a fairytale in contrast to their own lives.

Rory mumbled something under his breath, to which

Annie chose not to pay any attention.

She took up the letter with the smudged ink from his sister Kitty, posted from a place called Oakham.

My dearest Rory,

God willing this letter finds you recovering from your wounds. The Admiralty telegram, followed by your name in the naval casualty lists as 'injured in action' came as a shock to us all. Pray God you will soon be out of hospital and back with us.

As soon as you are fit and well Toby and I will meet the hospital train at Leicester. You will of course be recuperating with us in Oakham – although, if you want to, you can go to Breedon Hall which Charlotte and Rupert have turned into a convalescent home for officers. Dearest Rory, the correspondence we all have endeavoured to keep going throughout the years, despite the split in the family, will have relayed to you the sad occurrence of Uncle Austen's death following the news of the twins, Michael and Morden, dying at Passchendaele. I now must tell you about Humphrey. He was killed on June 5th at the battle for the Somme ...'

'*Stop!*' Rory blindly wrenched the letter from Annie's hand and tore it into shreds.

Struck with fear, because of what was happening to them as people, Annie stayed quite still by Rory's bedside until such time as the storm within him abated.

A blind man's tears must be the most harrowing experience ever: a reproach against humanity who had done this to him. She herself was bombarded by his grief.

'Annie? Annie ... are you there? Give me your hand ... What's it all for, Annie? Tell me, *tell me*! Lindsay was right ... we are of a cursed generation! You remember, Annie, that time we both went away to Glasgow, Lindsay and I? We took the boat, and when he was sailing it back into Loch Garth, he said something I'll always remember, *Moloch is insatiable!* I had no idea what he meant at the time, but now I do. Look at me, Annie, LOOK AT ME!'

'Rory, shhh! Oh, please ...' she held his head, smoothed the bandages, tried to take his mind off himself but knew, in the end, he had to talk it out, just as she had

had to let out the poison in her system after SBA Barnes's death, until the tears of a lifetime had all been used up.

'No don't ... *don't* look at me,' he said in the next breath. 'Close your eyes and think of Rory Roskillen as he used to be. I'm dead, Annie! I've passed through the fire and I'm sucked under the waves ... what more is wanted of me?'

'You must stop this, Rory ...'

'*NO!* Not when I hear the screams in my head, and in this infernal darkness behind my eyes there's a picture stuck for ever of white-hooded, mangled bodies, black and shrivelled, white turned black because they've melted away in agony. I'm one of the lucky ones, so they say! I live! A one-legged, blind and scarred man, I live! I'm one of the lucky ones because I'm *alive!*'

He began to tear off the bandages covering his eyes.

In the end he had to have an injection of laudanum to sedate him.

CHAPTER THIRTY-EIGHT

Rory certainly did have that death wish upon him now. The nursing staff were at a loss. He developed a high fever which in turn affected his lungs. His wounds and skin-grafts began to break down and he refused even to get up out of his bed for bed-making.

Sister Douglas had no option but to transfer him to the psychiatric wing of the hospital.

In desperation, the night before his transfer from the Burns Unit to the Psychiatric Unit, Annie had a good strict talking to him without caring who heard: 'Unless you pull yourself together, RNR Roskillen, there's going to be no hero's welcome for you at Glengarth! Only a madman's grave in a hospital cemetery, and that to me seems an utter waste of a good life. There's nothing wrong with you, Sub-lieutenant, except sheer bloody-minded-ness. You've made up your mind you've got nothing to live for, so you're taking the easy way out. I'm disgusted with you, a man of your standing! Men have fought and died at Jutland; they're dying by the thousands every day in France; and yet you're flinging it all back in the face of those white crosses lining *our* route to freedom! You owe them something, all those friends and cousins of yours who lost their lives for us, which means *you*! Stop feeling sorry for yourself, and pull yourself together. Get moving, get better, get out of here, and get home to face whatever life brings you – without a leg and without eyes if neces-sary. But we need this bed for a *real* man, not a moral coward and a self-pitying washout!'

From the other side of the screens came an enthusiastic show of hand-clapping. '*Well done*, Nurse! That's just what he needed!' It was Captain Tethers' voice, followed by others backing him up vociferously, '*Here here! Bravo!*'

Still there was no response from Rory Roskillen, so Annie let him have some more: 'Pay attention will you, and listen to this. I know you can still hear, even if you pretend you're deaf as well as blind. The eye-surgeon says there's no reason why you haven't regained your vision by now. Your bandages have been removed and the eyedrops will soon clear up any infection. When you want to see, you will, because all that is preventing you from doing so is your *mind*! It's called hysterical blindness, RNR Roskillen! Obstacle number one out of the way. Two, your shoulder and back took the grafting well and though it feels sore and your muscles weak, with physiotherapy you'll regain the proper use of those muscles. Your right leg fractures are mending well, if only you'll believe it. Problem three solved. As for the leg that's missing, they've made a brand new one for you that will be fitted as soon as you want to walk – on *both* legs! That to me solves all your problems. And if you're worried about your pretty face being scarred for life, don't be. You're not nearly as ugly as Captain Tethers, and he'll be the first to agree – won't you, Captain?'

'Thank *you*, Nurse!' came the retort from the other side of the curtains. 'And I thought I was the most handsome man in the ward! One just can't trust a woman, you know, Roskillen.'

'Come on, Roskillen,' another voice added his opinion. 'You were able to boost the morale of the men trapped with you in the *Barham*'s communications room, and you won *your* battle. The Admiralty don't give away Victoria Crosses for nothing.'

'There you are, Sub-lieutenant! You have everyone's vote. I can't face coming in here every day to see a man like you placing himself on a marble slab for no other reason than self-pity ... are you still listening to me?'

He pretended to be semi-comatose as well as oblivious to a lot more besides, so Annie shook his shoulder, her voice shrill with lack of sleep, worry, and an utter hopelessness of the situation.

'I've done this job long enough to know the difference between the living and the dead, and you're going to live.

Within the next month you're going to leave Kingseat and
get on that train to Achnasheen and whether you die on it
is your choice. We don't want to see you taking up a bed
any longer which someone not as selfish as you can do
with. SNO Douglas – who is not on duty this evening as
she has some time off – has given me her full permission
to bring you to your senses. She wants you to know that
you're not going to die because you have no eyesight, nor
for the reason that your leg was amputated, nor that your
body was badly burned, but you *will* die in a mental ward
if you continue to go on in this way.'

She had said her piece, and if that didn't work, nothing
would. Annie marched out of the ward and back to the
office.

SBA Ayres grinned. 'They ought to make you Matron-
in-Chief,' he said in admiration.

'First thing in the morning, SBA Ayres, prepare Sub-
lieutenant Roskillen to be transferred to his new ward.
The Psychiatrist and SNO Doyle between them might
be able to succeed where we have failed.'

The following morning, with Ayres pushing the wheelchair, Rory made the nurse stop by the ward office. Annie
was preparing the medicine trolley. 'Where's that bloody
Senior Nursing Officer? Why can't she speak for herself
instead of leaving everyone in the charge of a whippersnapper of a girl more accustomed to gutting fish than
holding her tongue?'

'If it is I you are addressing, RNR Roskillen, SNO
Douglas is not on duty till two o'clock this afternoon,
when this whippersnapper with more fish guts in her than
a certain gentleman I prefer not to name, goes off duty.
Enjoy your new ward. I believe it's bedlam.'

'You tell Douglas I'm taking this to a higher authority.
She has no right to transfer me to a Psychiatric Unit. Two
Naval doctors have to authorize such a procedure, not a
Nursing Officer.' He sounded breathless, and began to
cough from the exertion temper demanded.

'Two doctors *did* sign your transfer – they said you
needed psychiatric help ... SBA Ayres, just take a walk
around the ward for a moment. I have something else I

want to say to RNR Roskillen before he leaves us.'

SBA Ayres obligingly left them alone and Annie wheeled Rory's chair into the office and shut the door. 'Now then, Rory, please listen to me. Once upon a time in a different lifetime you asked me to marry you. I am now giving you my reply: *Yes!* Marry me please and take me away from this stinking hospital.'

He opened his mouth, but it was a bitter, ugly retort he made, 'Is that how they teach you to take care of your patients, Nurse Gowrie? To make a laughing stock of them?'

'Oh, Rory!' She almost laughed at how pathetic he sounded. 'I know you by now. In our own private world among the kelpies, hobgoblins and marsh marigolds on Inchnadamph, you told me you loved me. True love, the flawless diamond kind you talked about, doesn't change even though the world might – or were you lying to me then?'

'In those days, Annie Gowrie, I wasn't half a blind man.'

'*Ah!* But in those days I was half a blind woman, and there lies the truth!' Smiling to herself at the expression on his face, she turned his wheelchair around and opened the door: 'SBA Ayres, Sub-lieutenant Roskillen is ready now.'

Six weeks later SNO Doyle, a fat and jolly little nursing sister from Southern Ireland, sent for Annie during one of Annie's off-duty periods. She was the Sister-in-Charge of the Rehabilitation Unit, not the Psychiatric Unit they had threatened RNR Rory Roskillen with. But it had shaken him out of his apathy and he had responded well to SNO Doyle's methods of therapy, however non-Naval they were reputed to be!

'Holy Michael and all his angels!' SNO Doyle greeted Annie when she walked into her ward. ''Tis glad I am to see you, Gowrie! Merry hell that fine gentleman's been after leadin' me these past few days. Ever since they told him he could go home! Now look here, my fine laird – they tell me he is one, though he behaves like a navvy sometimes – see here, Roskillen, who's come ter see you!'

'How the hell can I see *who* it is? I'm as blind as a bat.'

'An' as ugly!' SNA Doyle retorted. 'Listen, Gowrie, there's nought the matter with his vision – he's just playing up again for sympathy. He knows just when there's a pretty face around he wants ter flirt with, don't yer, Roskillen?'

He sat on the edge of his bed dressed in his naval uniform while a poor harassed probationer struggled to get his artificial foot into a tight-fitting shoe. With two legs again, he was his old handsome self, especially with the dark glasses. His bright hair, regrown after its singeing, was worn in a different style. Not with a parting any more, but casually, so that it flopped over his forehead to conceal his scars which had become less than noticeable.

And they dared call women the vain ones! Annie smiled to herself.

He'd even grown a little moustache to give him a more distinguished air. Annie was glad to see him looking so fine and so well, though there was a lump in her throat because he reminded her so much of Lindsay.

Rory ignored everyone except the woman he wanted. 'Annie Gowrie ...' He put out his hand but SNO Doyle grasped it. 'To be sure, 'tis Annie Gowrie, Roskillen. Who else did yer think it was? Yer fine Queen Mary come ter kiss your sweet-talkin' lips?'

'Kiss my ... *Nurse!*' He let go her hand and barked at the unfortunate nurse on her knees before him trying vainly to tie his shoelaces as he balanced precariously on his artificial leg. 'What do you think you're playing at, woman? No blast it! I don't need crutches. Give me my walking stick and let me get out of here. I can't stand the smell of carbolic under my nose and this entire war has been full of damned carbolic virgins sacrificing themselves in the name of virtue while trying all sorts of ways to undermine a fellow's dignity. Now get out of here, all of you, I want to ask QA Gowrie to marry me.'

'Holy Mary! After all I've done fer the ingrate!' said SNO Doyle with a wink at Annie. 'But then, the wretched man's Scotch, and it's to be expected from the likes o' him. Armour-plated hip and leg-loose, blind as a bat with a tongue what's bin once in a bog and twice round the blarney stone, I'm thinking. Gowrie, you can *keep* him and a good riddance! Come along, Nurse Morris,' she said to the probationer still on her knees, 'let's leave him be. Let's you an' me find a brave Irishman and a Taffy what knows two good women when they sees one.'

She took her red-faced little nurse with her and left QA Gowrie to her saucy sub-lieutenant. Rory put out his hand again, 'Come here, Annie.'

'I'm right here, Rory.' She gave him her hand. 'You *can* see ... can't you?'

'Vaguely ... vision is improving.'

'What did I tell you?'

'Well, I won't be able to do without my white stick for a bit or drive a motor-car. But I'll still be able to read and transmit Morse signals which must be the next best thing to Braille ... Annie ...' he hesitated. 'Do I ... do I look very grotesque?'

She scoffed at his vanity. 'You look exceedingly good to me.'

'You're just saying that to be kind.'

'Yes, and I'm also saying it because it happens to be true.'

'Annie, I'm going back to Renfrew to really concentrate on the shipping side of the business. They *need* all the boats they can get at the moment, and so Clydeside is booming. Maybe, by the time the war ends and they return Glengarth to me, I'll be able to retire a rich man.'

Annie smiled. 'I'm so glad you've got something truly worthwhile to concentrate your energies on again, Rory.'

'My energies are concentrated on you ... come here. I love you, Annie Gowrie from Rill.' His arms came around her, holding her tightly. 'I always have done.'

'Rory, the ambulance is waiting ...'

'Let it wait. Will you marry me?'

'Not right now.' She pulled out of his embrace and turned away. 'Rory ... let's just ... let's just wait and see what happens.'

In a frozen tone of voice which sounded almost like Lindsay's in that moment, he said, 'I see. So you've changed your mind and don't want to commit yourself to an invalid, a scarred, ugly and useless old blind man for the rest of your life, is that it?'

'No, that's *not* it!' Annie said in exasperation as she turned back to face him. 'You know that's not the reason – and you're none of those things. I want you to go back to Glengarth or Glasgow, or wherever it is you are going now, to think about what you've asked me, and then ask me again when I come home.'

'Why?'

'Because ... you need time to think about it properly. This is not the right time or the right place.'

'What are you talking about? I love you. I'm asking you to marry me.'

'I'm ... I'm not of your class, Rory, and one day you might regret what you ask now, and be ashamed of me in the same way that Lindsay sometimes was. I couldn't bear that.'

'Christ almighty, Annie Gowrie, you do talk piffle! And I'm not Lindsay. When are you coming home?'

'I don't know ... that's why I can't say yes to anything right now. After the war's over, I suppose.'

He gave a stiff little smile and fingered his disguising glasses. 'Oh well, I suppose in the meantime I can always go and play bezique or tiddlywinks at Breedon Hall with all the other old has-beens like myself! Annie, don't you want to be mistress of Glen ... oh, forgive me, wrong job, I was forgetting. Don't you *want* to be my wife and live at Glengarth?'

'No, m'laird – and it's not the title bothering me, if that's what you're thinking. I'm tired of being a mistress, yes, but being a wife to you is going to make me another person altogether. I'm not sure if I'm ready for that just yet. I've got to be certain in my own mind I'm doing the right thing not only for our sakes but also Jamie's ... and talking of Jamie, please will you give him this letter. And this one, please, for Nurse Craig at Gairloch.' She took out two letters from her pocket and tucked them into his. 'Don't lose them. Craigie's contains money to feed and clothe my son.'

'Anything to do with money, I never lose ... any more. My aunt Ada at least taught me an unforgettable lesson. I'm now as thrifty as any Scotsman ... and Annie, please don't be afraid that I won't accept my brother's son as my own. Jamie will be *our* son, not just an adopted son or nephew.'

'Rory, there's so much to think about. Let's wait until I come home.'

'Annie Gowrie?'

'Yes, Sub-lieutenant Roskillen?'

'Do you love me?'

'With all my heart.'

'Then why are you still behaving like a stubborn wench?'

'I'm not being stubborn, Rory, I'm being practical for all our sakes.'

'Damn your practicality. I'm going to fight you all the way to the altar. Now kiss me.'

She did so, with pleasure. But he wouldn't release her and went on and on until he almost took her into the bed with him. Lightheaded and wanting to agree right there and then to everything he demanded of her, she pulled away at last with the breathless message, '*Bon voyage*, m'laird!'

'It doesn't seem right to leave you behind ... won't you apply for a discharge from the Service and come home with me?' he pleaded.

'Not yet, Rory. When the war's over.'

'Oh-oh, stubborn, *stubborn* wench!' He leant forward and kissed her on the nose, reaching his arms out for her once more, but she stepped smartly beyond his reach. 'You always were a heartache to me, Annie Gowrie, but one I'd dearly accept any day. I admire your sense of duty: you're not a woman, you're a hard-hearted, Regimental Sergeant-Major and a witch! But I love you, mermaid with the green eyes and coral-tipped toenails I'm dying to kiss one day. I'm *going* to marry you after what you've done to me. You can't just pick a fellow up and then drop him straight back, face first, in the muck. Not unless you want trouble from him ... come here, please, just one more time …' Someone tapped on the door of his private ward, and Rory, with a sigh of regret readjusted his dark glasses. 'Who the hell is it, now? Can't a fellow even propose in peace?'

A Sick Berth Attendant stuck his head around the door. 'I'm SBA Wilson, Staff Nurse Gowrie.' He shuffled in the doorway awkwardly. 'I'm looking for Sub-lieutenant Roskillen.'

'You've found him, SBA Wilson,' Rory said.

'Well, sir, there's a couple of gentlemen turned up to take you home in your own boat, sir.'

'Really? What are their names?' Rory asked.

'Mr Gammon and Mr Ackker, sir. They say they've got the *Lady Leonora* all shipshape and Bristol fashion to take you home.'

'Well, I know some damn silly things have been going on in this war, but a boat on dry land!'

'She's berthed in Aberdeen ready to sail the Moray Firth to collect some timber for the war effort, sir.'

'What else did they tell you, Wilson?' Rory tried to keep a straight face and Annie came to SBA Wilson's rescue.

'Thank you, Wilson, Sub-lieutenant Roskillen will be along in a moment.'

'By the way, Wilson,' Rory interrupted, his face quite serious, 'Do you know how many tin cans of petrol it takes to fill a tank in order to make it move out of the way of enemy fire?'

'No, sir.'

'Neither did the War Office, until someone suggested a depot at Calais and another one at Rouen. And do you know who that someone was?'

'No, sir.'

'Me, sir! It takes the Navy to sort out what the Army is doing. It ought to work better the other way around, too … now be a good chap and buzz off for two minutes more, will you? Tell Gammon and Ackker to wait for me in the quadrangle with a couple of anti-torpedo guns, will you?'

'Yes, sir.'

Rory turned back to Annie, his manner once more earnest. 'Annie, my darling, there's something I really want you to know: it's important. All my life I envied my brother because he stood to inherit Glengarth while I was made to feel the superfluous one ... my own dashed over-riding ego, immaturity and self-inflicted insecurity, I suppose. I never forgave my father for sending Lindsay home to Scotland and me to live with "Sassenach" relatives, though they were my own dear mother's relatives. Scotland was my home, and that's where I wanted to be, despite all other considerations. However ...' He cleared his throat, the words sticking. 'I'm glad about it as it turns out, because it has given me the best of both worlds. It has also made me realize that now I've got what I'd always wanted, I *don't want it any more*! The price has been too high, Annie. All I want is you – you and Jamie, my brother's son, to live life in a very simple and uncomplicated way, but with love and respect and contentment. Those are the things that matter most in life. Not inherited birthrights, titles, fame, fortune and glory which, in the end, count for nothing. You and me and Jamie sharing life together, that's what *is* important from now on.'

She touched his lips, fingering them lovingly, her empti-ness at long last assuaged by real promises like these, the reassurances she needed. 'And you are truly a gentleman, for it's not how *much* he has but how well bred he is.'

Rory gave a rueful little smile. 'So now that I've got all that off my chest, please will you pin my hard earned ribbons and medals over it to protect my heart's interests: after all, Annie Gowrie, England expects every man to look the part even if he doesn't always feel like it.'

Annie did so.

'Now kiss me Hardy or Kismet Hardy, but whichever it is, thank you, Annie Gowrie for giving me back my life.'

'Thank you, Rory Roskillen, for giving me back mine.'

The sunshine of her smile was enough to keep him going until he saw her again. He fumbled for his stick and Annie thrust it into his hand. Gammon and Ackker were waiting for him in the corridor.

Stiffly, he turned around and gave her a little wave, '*Au*

revoir, Annie. Come home soon. I'll be waiting for you and Jamie.'

Annie watched him walk away slowly but with assurance. Away from the war at sea and the battle he had always fought within himself for reasons only known to himself. Lindsay and Rory, strangers to themselves and to others, moulded by the fierce Scottish ancestry of their father and tempered by the English heritage of their mother: a formidable breed altogether those Roskillens of Ross-shire!

She heard the sound of bagpipes piping a pibroch through the great hall at Glengarth. She heard Lindsay whistling through the glen:

Bonnie Charlie's now aw'a,
Safely ower the friendly main.
Mony a heart will braek in t'wa,
Should he no come back again . . .

Annie closed her eyes and drew into herself all the sweet remembered scents of Glengarth, bracken and heather, pine trees, the dewy grass, rainwashed earth, the misty mountain, the salty sea, and she knew in her heart, somehow, some day, in the dark fens of the tangled woods the flowers would gleam once more.